SANDRA

hello, darkness

BROWN

POCKET STAR BOOKS
New York London Toronto Sydney

A Pocket Star Book published by
POCKET BOOKS, a division of Simon & Schuster, Inc.
1230 Avenue of the Americas, New York, NY 10020

Copyright © 2003 by Sandra Brown Management Ltd.

Originally published in hardcover in 2003 by Simon & Schuster, Inc.

ISBN: 0-7434-6675-6

Pocket Books First printing August 2004

10 9 8 7 6 5 4 3 2 1

POCKET STAR BOOKS and colophon are registered
trademarks of Simon & Schuster, Inc.

Cover design by Lisa Litwack
Front cover photo © Duncan McNicol/Getty Images

Manufactured in the United States of America

For information regarding special discounts for bulk purchases,
please contact Simon & Schuster Special Sales at 1-800-456-6798
or business@simonandschuster.com.

prologue

Up until six minutes to sign-off, it had been a routine shift.

"It's a steamy night in the hill country. Thank you for spending your time with me here on 101.3. I've enjoyed your company tonight, as I do each weeknight. This is your host for classic love songs, Paris Gibson.

"I'm going to leave you tonight with a trio of my favorites. I hope you're listening to them with someone you love. Hold each other close."

She depressed the button on the control board to turn off her microphone. The series of songs would play uninterrupted right up to 1:59:30. During the last thirty seconds of her program, she would thank her listening audience again, say good night, and sign off.

While "Yesterday" played, she closed her eyes and rolled her head around on her tense shoulders. Compared to an eight- or nine-hour workday, a four-hour radio show would seem like a snap. It wasn't. By sign-off, she was physically tired.

She worked the board alone, introducing the songs she had selected and logged in before the show. Audience requests necessitated adjustments to the log and careful attention to the countdown clock. She also manned the incoming telephone lines herself.

The mechanics of the job were second nature, but not

her delivery. She never allowed it to get routine or sloppy. Paris Gibson the person had worked diligently, with voice coaches and alone, to perfect the Paris Gibson "sound" for which she was well known.

She worked harder than even she realized to maintain that perfected inflection and pitch, because after 240 minutes on air, her neck and shoulder muscles burned with fatigue. That muscle burn was evidence of how well she had performed.

Midway through the Beatles classic, one of the telephone lines blinked red, indicating an incoming call. She was tempted not to answer, but, officially, there were almost six minutes left to her program, and she promised listeners that she would take calls until two A.M. It was too late to put this caller on the air, but she should at least acknowledge the call.

She depressed the blinking button. "This is Paris."

"Hello, Paris. This is Valentino."

She knew him by name. He called periodically, and his unusual name was easily remembered. His speaking voice was distinctive, too, barely above a whisper, which was probably either for effect or disguise.

She spoke into the microphone suspended above the board, which served as her telephone handset when not being used to broadcast. That kept her hands free to go about her business even while talking to a caller.

"How are you tonight, Valentino?"

"Not good."

"I'm sorry to hear that."

"Yes. You will be."

The Beatles gave way to Anne Murray's "Broken Hearted Me."

Paris glanced up at the log monitor and automatically registered that the second of the last three songs had begun. She wasn't sure she'd heard Valentino correctly. "I beg your pardon?"

"You will be sorry," he said.

The dramatic overtone was typical of Valentino. Whenever he called, he was either very high or very low, rarely on an emotional level somewhere in between. She never knew what to expect from him, and for that reason he was an interesting caller. But tonight he sounded sinister, and that was a first.

"I don't understand what you mean."

"I've done everything you advised me to do, Paris."

"I advised you? When?"

"Every time I've called. You always say—not just to me, but to everybody who calls—that we should respect the people we love."

"That's right. I think—"

"Well, respect gets you nowhere, and I don't care what you think anymore."

She wasn't a psychologist or a licensed counselor, only a radio personality. Beyond that, she had no credentials. Nevertheless, she took her role as late-night friend seriously.

When a listener had no one else to talk to, she was an anonymous sounding board. Her audience knew her only by voice, but they trusted her. She served as their confidante, adviser, and confessor.

They shared their joys, aired their grievances, and sometimes bared their souls. The calls she considered broadcast-worthy evoked sympathy from other listeners, prompted congratulations, and sometimes created heated controversy.

Frequently a caller simply needed to vent. She acted as a buffer. She was a convenient outlet for someone mad at the world. Seldom was she the target of the caller's anger, but obviously this was one of those times, and it was unsettling.

If Valentino was on the brink of an emotional breakdown, she couldn't heal what had led him to it, but she might be able to talk him a safe distance away from the edge and then urge him to seek professional help.

"Let's talk about this, Valentino. What's on your mind?"

"I respect girls. When I'm in a relationship, I place the girl on a pedestal and treat her like a princess. But that's never enough. Girls are never faithful. Every single one of them screws around on me. Then when she leaves me, I call you, and you say that it wasn't my fault."

"Valentino, I—"

"You tell me that I did nothing wrong, that I'm not to blame for her leaving. And you know what? You're absolutely right. I'm not to blame, Paris. *You* are. This time it's *your* fault."

Paris glanced over her shoulder, toward the soundproof door of the studio. It was closed, of course. The hallway beyond the wall of windows had never looked so dark, although the building was always dark during her after-hours program.

She wished Stan would happen by. Even Marvin would be a welcome sight. She wished for someone, anyone, to hear this call and help her get a read on it.

She considered disconnecting. No one knew where she lived or even what she looked like. It was stipulated in her contract with the radio station: She didn't make personal appearances. Nor was her likeness to appear in any promotional venues, including but not limited to all and any print advertising, television commercials, and billboards. Paris Gibson was a name and voice only, not a face.

But, in good conscience, she couldn't hang up on this man. If he had taken to heart something she'd said on air and things hadn't turned out well, his anger was understandable.

On the other hand, if a more rational person disagreed with something she had said, he simply would have blown it off. Valentino had vested in her more influence over his life than she deserved or desired.

"Explain how it's my fault, Valentino."

"You told her to break up with me."

"I never—"

"I heard you! She called you the night before last. I was listening to your program. She didn't give her name, but I recognized her voice. She told you our story. Then she said that I had become jealous and possessive.

"You told her that if she felt our relationship was constricting, she should do something about it. In other words, you advised her to dump me." He paused before adding, "And I'm going to make you sorry you gave her that advice."

Paris's mind was skittering. In all her years on the air, she'd never encountered anything like this. "Valentino, let's remain calm and discuss this, all right?"

"I'm calm, Paris. Very calm. And there's nothing to discuss. I've got her where no one will find her. She can't escape me."

With that statement, sinister turned downright scary. Surely he didn't mean literally what he'd just said.

But before she could speak her thought aloud, he added, "She's going to die in three days, Paris. I'm going to kill her, and her death will be on your conscience."

The last song in the series was playing. The clock on the computer monitor was ticking toward sign-off. She cut a quick glance at the Vox Pro to make certain that an electronic gremlin hadn't caused it to malfunction. But, no, the sophisticated machine was working as it should. The call was being recorded.

She wet her lips and took a nervous breath. "Valentino, this isn't funny."

"It isn't supposed to be."

"I know you don't actually intend—"

"I intend to do *exactly* what I said. I've earned at least seventy-two hours with her, don't you think? As nice as I've been to her? Isn't three days of her time and attention the least I deserve?"

"Valentino, please, listen—"

"I'm over listening to you. You're full of shit. You give rotten advice. I treat a girl with respect, then she goes out and spreads her legs for other men. And you tell her to dump me, like I'm the one who ruined the relationship, like I'm the one who cheated. Fair's fair. I'm going to fuck her till she bleeds, then I'm going to kill her. Seventy-two hours from now, Paris. Have a nice night."

chapter one

Dean Malloy eased himself off the bed. Groping in darkness, he located his underwear on the floor and took it with him into the bathroom. As quietly as he could, he closed the door before switching on the light.

Liz woke up anyway.

"Dean?"

He braced his arms on the edge of the basin and looked at his reflection in the mirror. "Be right out." His image gazed back at him, whether with despair or disgust, he couldn't quite tell. Reproach, at the very least.

He continued staring at himself for another few seconds before turning on the faucet and splashing cold water over his face. He used the toilet, pulled on his boxers, and opened the door.

Liz had turned on the nightstand lamp and was propped up on one elbow. Her pale hair was tangled. There was a smudge of mascara beneath her eye. But somehow she made deshabille look fetching. "Are you going to shower?"

He shook his head. "Not now."

"I'll wash your back."

"Thanks, but—"

"Your front?"

He shot her a smile. "I'll take a rain check."

His trousers were draped over the armchair. When he

reached for them, Liz flopped back against the heaped pillows. "You're leaving."

"Much as I'd like to stay, Liz."

"You haven't spent a full night in weeks."

"I don't like it any better than you do, but for the time being that's the way it's got to be."

"Good grief, Dean. He's sixteen."

"Right. Sixteen. If he were a baby, I'd know where he was at all times. I'd know what he was doing and who he was with. But Gavin is sixteen and licensed to drive. For a parent, that's a twenty-four-hour living nightmare."

"He probably won't even be there when you get home."

"He'd better be there," he muttered as he tucked in his shirttail. "He broke curfew last night, so I grounded him this morning. Restricted him to the house."

"For how long?"

"Until he cleans up his act."

"What if he doesn't?"

"Stay in the house?"

"Clean up his act."

That was a much weightier question. It required a more complicated answer, which he didn't have time for tonight. He pushed his feet into his shoes, then sat down on the edge of the bed and reached for her hand. "It's unfair that Gavin's behavior is dictating your future."

"*Our* future."

"Our future," he corrected softly. "It's unfair as hell. Because of him our plans have been put on indefinite hold, and that stinks."

She kissed the back of his hand as she looked up at him through her lashes. "I can't even persuade you to spend the night with me, and here I was hoping that by Christmas we'd be married."

"It could happen. The situation could improve sooner than we think."

She didn't share his optimism, and her frown said as much. "I've been patient, Dean. Haven't I?"

"You have."

"In the two years we've been together, I think I've been more than accommodating. I relocated here without a quibble. And even though it would have made more sense for us to live together, I agreed to lease this place."

She had a selective and incorrect memory. Their living together had never been an option. He wouldn't even have considered it as long as Gavin was living with him. Nor had there been any reason to quibble over her relocation to Austin. He had never suggested that she should. In fact, he would have preferred for her to remain in Houston.

Independently, Liz had made the decision to relocate when he did. When she sprang the surprise on him, he'd had to fake his happiness and conceal a vague irritation. She had imposed herself on him when the last thing he needed was an additional imposition.

But rather than opening a giant can of worms for discussion now, he conceded that she had been exceptionally patient with him and his present circumstances.

"I'm well aware of how much my situation has changed since we started dating. You didn't sign on to become involved with a single parent of a teenager. You've been more patient than I had any right to expect."

"Thank you," she said, mollified. "But my body doesn't know patience, Dean. Each month that passes means one less egg in the basket."

He smiled at the gentle reminder of her biological

clock. "I acknowledge the sacrifices you've made for me. And continue to make."

"I'm willing to make more." She stroked his cheek. "Because, Dean Malloy, the hell of it is, you're worth those sacrifices."

He knew she meant it, but her sincerity did nothing to elevate his mood, and instead only increased his despondency. "Be patient a little longer, Liz. Please? Gavin is being impossible, but there are reasons for his bad behavior. Give it a little more time. Hopefully, we'll soon find a comfort zone the three of us can live within."

She made a face. "'Comfort zone'? Keep using phrases like that and, next thing you know, you'll have your own daytime TV talk show."

He grinned, glad they could conclude the serious conversation on a lighter note. "Still headed to Chicago tomorrow?"

"For three days. Closed-door meetings with folk from Copenhagen. All male. Robust, blond Viking types. Jealous?"

"Pea green."

"Will you miss me?"

"What do you think?"

"How about I leave you with something to remember me by?"

She pushed the sheet away. Naked and all but purring, lying on the rumpled bedding on which they'd already made love, Elizabeth Douglas looked more like a pampered courtesan than a vice-president of marketing for an international luxury-hotel chain.

Her figure was voluptuous, and she actually liked it. Unlike most of her contemporaries, she didn't obsess over every calorie. She considered it a workout when she had to carry her own luggage, and she never denied herself dessert. On her the curves looked good. Actually, they looked damn great.

"Tempting," he sighed. "Very. But a kiss will have to do."

She kissed him deeply, sucking his tongue into her mouth in a manner that probably would have made the Viking types snarl with envy. He was the one to end the kiss. "I've really got to go, Liz," he whispered against her lips before pulling back. "Have a safe trip."

She pulled up the sheet to cover her nudity and pasted on a smile to cover her disappointment. "I'll call you when I get there."

"You'd better."

He left, trying to make it look as if he wasn't fleeing. The air outside settled over him like a damp blanket. It even seemed to have the texture of wet wool when he inhaled it. His shirt was sticking to his back by the time he'd made the short walk to his car. He started the motor and set the air conditioner on high. The radio came on automatically. Elvis's "Are You Lonesome Tonight?"

At this hour there was virtually no traffic on the streets. Dean slowed for a yellow light and came to a full stop as the song ended.

"It's a steamy night in the hill country. Thank you for spending your time with me here on 101.3."

The smoky female voice reverberated through the interior of the car. The sound waves pressed against his chest and belly. Her voice was perfectly modulated by eight speakers that had been strategically placed by German engineers. The superior sound environment made her seem closer than if she'd been sitting in the passenger seat beside him.

"I'm going to leave you tonight with a trio of my

favorites. I hope you're listening to them with someone you love. Hold each other close."

Dean gripped the steering wheel and rested his forehead on the back of his hands while the Fab Four yearned for yesterday.

As soon as Judge Baird Kemp retrieved his car from the Four Seasons Hotel parking valet and got in, he wrestled loose his necktie and shrugged off his jacket. "God, I'm glad that's over."

"You're the one who insisted we attend." Marian Kemp slipped off her Bruno Magli sling-backs and pulled off the diamond clip earrings, wincing as blood circulation was painfully restored to her numb earlobes. "But did you have to include us in the after party?"

"Well, it looked good for us to be among the last to leave. Very influential people were in that group."

Being a typical awards dinner, the event had run insufferably long. Following it, a cocktail party had been held in a hospitality suite, and the judge never passed up an opportunity to campaign for his reelection, even informally. For the remainder of their drive home, the Kemps discussed others who had been in attendance, or, as the judge derisively referred to them, "the good, the bad, and the ugly."

When they arrived home, he headed for his den, where Marian saw to it that the bar was kept well stocked with his favorite brands. "I'm going to have a nightcap. Should I pour two?"

"No thank you, dear. I'm going up."

"Cool the bedroom down. This heat is unbearable."

Marian climbed the curved staircase that had recently been featured in a home-design magazine. For the photo, she'd worn a designer ball gown and her canary-diamond necklace. The portrait had turned out quite well, if she did say so herself. The judge had been pleased with the accompanying article, which had praised her for making their home into the showplace it was.

The upstairs hallway was dark, but she was relieved to see light beneath the door of Janey's room. Even though it was summer vacation, the judge had imposed a curfew on their seventeen-year-old. Last night, she had flouted the curfew and hadn't come in until almost dawn. It was obvious that she'd been drinking, and, unless Marian was mistaken, the stench that clung to her clothing was that of marijuana. Worse, she'd driven herself home in that condition.

"I've bailed you out for the last time," the judge had bellowed. "If you get another DWI, you're on your own, young lady. I won't pull a single string. I'll let it go straight on your record."

Janey had replied with a bored, "So fucking what?"

The scene had grown so loud and vituperative that Marian feared the neighbors might overhear despite the acre of manicured greenbelt between their property and the next. The quarrel had ended with Janey stomping into her room and slamming the door, then locking it behind her. She hadn't spoken to either of them all day.

But apparently the judge's most recent threat had made an impression. Janey was at home, and by her standards, it was early. Marian paused outside Janey's door and raised her fist, about to knock. But through the door she could hear the voice of that woman deejay Janey listened to when she was in one of her mellow moods. She was a welcome change from the obnoxious deejays on the acid rock and rap stations.

Janey tended to throw a tantrum whenever she felt her

privacy was being violated. Her mother was disinclined to disturb this tenuous peace, so, without knocking, she lowered her hand and continued down the hallway to the master suite.

Toni Armstrong awoke with a start.

She lay unmoving, listening for a noise that might have awakened her. Had one of the children called out for her? Was Brad snoring?

No, the house was silent except for the low whir of the air-conditioning vents in the ceiling. A sound hadn't awakened her. Not even the soughing of her husband's breath. Because the pillow beside hers was undisturbed.

Toni got up and pulled on a lightweight robe. She glanced at the clock: 1:42. And Brad still hadn't come home.

Before going downstairs, she checked the children's rooms. Although the girls got tucked into their separate beds each night, they invariably wound up sleeping together in one. Only sixteen months apart, they were often mistaken for twins. They looked virtually identical now, their sturdy little bodies curled up together, tousled heads sharing the pillow. Toni pulled a sheet up over them, then took a moment to admire their innocent beauty before tiptoeing from the room.

Toy spaceships and action figures littered the floor of her son's bedroom. She carefully avoided stepping on them as she made her way to the bed. He slept on his stomach, legs splayed, one arm hanging down the side of the bed.

She took the opportunity to stroke his cheek. He'd reached the age where her demonstrations of affection made him grimace and squirm away. As the firstborn, he thought he had to act the little man.

But thinking of him becoming a man filled her with a desperation that was close to panic.

As she descended the staircase, several of the treads creaked, but Toni liked a house with the quirks and imperfections that gave it character. They had been lucky to acquire this house. It was in a good neighborhood with an elementary school nearby. The price had been reduced by owners anxious to sell. Parts of it had needed attention, but she had volunteered to make most of the repairs herself in order to fit the purchase into their budget.

Working on the house had kept her busy while Brad was getting settled into his new practice. She'd taken the time and effort to do necessary repairs before finishing with the cosmetic work. Her patience and diligence had paid off. The house wasn't only prettier in appearance, but sound from the inside out. Its flaws hadn't been glossed over with a fresh coat of paint without first being fixed.

Unfortunately, not everything was as easily fixable as houses.

As she had feared, all the rooms downstairs were dark and empty. In the kitchen, she turned on the radio to ward off the ominous pressure of the silence. She poured herself a glass of milk she didn't want and forced herself to sip it calmly.

Maybe she was doing her husband a disservice. He might very well be attending a seminar on taxes and financial planning. He had announced over dinner that he would be out for most of the evening.

"Remember, hon," he'd said when she expressed her surprise, "I told you about it earlier this week."

"No you didn't."

"I'm sorry. I thought I did. I intended to. Pass the

potato salad, please. It's great, by the way. What's that spice?"

"Dill. This is the first I've heard of a seminar tonight, Brad."

"The partners recommended it. What they learned at the last one saved them a bundle in taxes."

"Then maybe I should go, too. I could stand to learn more about all that."

"Good idea. We'll watch for the next one. You're required to enroll in advance."

He'd told her the time and location of the seminar, told her not to wait up for him because there was an informal discussion session following the formal presentation and he didn't know how long it would last. He had kissed her and the kids before he left. He walked to his car with a gait that was awfully jaunty for someone going to a seminar on taxes and financial planning.

Toni finished her glass of milk.

She called her husband's cell phone for the third time, and as with the previous two calls, got his voice mail. She didn't leave a message. She thought about calling the auditorium where the seminar had taken place, but that would be a waste of time. No one would be there at this hour.

After seeing Brad off tonight, she had cleaned up the dinner dishes and given the children their baths. Once they were in bed, she had tried to go into Brad's den, but discovered that the door to it was locked. To her shame, she'd torn through the house like a woman crazed, looking for a hairpin, a nail file, something with which she could pick the lock.

She had resorted to a screwdriver, probably damaging the lock irreparably, but not caring. To her chagrin, there had been nothing in the room to validate her frenzy or her suspicion. A newspaper ad for the seminar was lying on his desk. He'd made a notation about the seminar on his personal calendar. Obviously he had been planning to attend.

But he was also very good at creating plausible smoke screens.

She had sat down at the desk and stared into his blank computer screen. She even fingered the power button on the tower, tempted to turn it on and engage in some exploration that only thieves, spies, and suspicious wives would engage in.

She hadn't touched this computer since he had bought one exclusively for her. When she saw the labeled boxes he'd carried in and placed on the kitchen table, she had exclaimed, "You bought another computer?"

"It's time you had your own. Merry Christmas!"

"This is June."

"So I'm early. Or late." He shrugged in his disarming way. "Now that you have your own, when you want to exchange email with your folks, or do some Internet shopping, or whatever, you won't have to work around me."

"I use your computer during the day when you're at the clinic."

"That's my point. Now you can go online anytime."

And so can you.

Apparently he had read her thought because he'd said, "It's not what you're thinking, Toni." Here he had propped his hands on his hips, looking defensive. "I was browsing in the computer store this morning. I see this bright pink number that's small, compact, and can do just about everything, and I think, 'Feminine and efficient. Just like my darling wife.' So I bought it for you on impulse. I thought you'd be pleased. Obviously I was wrong."

"I am pleased," she said, instantly contrite. "It was a

very thoughtful gesture, Brad. Thank you." She looked askance at the boxes. "Did you say *pink?*"

Then they'd laughed. He'd enfolded her in a bear hug. He'd smelled like sunshine, soap, and wholesomeness. His body had felt comfortable, familiar, and good against hers. Her fears had been assuaged.

But only temporarily. Recently they had resurfaced.

She hadn't booted up his computer tonight. She'd been too afraid of what she might find. If a password had been required for access, her suspicions would have been confirmed, and she hadn't wanted that. God, no, she hadn't.

So she had done her best to restore the busted door-knob, then had gone to bed and eventually to sleep, in the hope that Brad would awaken her soon, brimming with knowledge about financial stratagems for families in their income bracket. It had been a desperate hope.

"I've certainly enjoyed your company tonight," the sexy voice on the radio was saying. "This is your host for classic love songs, Paris Gibson."

No seminar lasted until two o'clock in the morning. No therapy-group meeting lasted until the wee hours either. That had been Brad's excuse last week when he had stayed out most of the night.

His explanation had been that one of the men in his group was having a difficult time coping. "After the meeting, he asked me to go get a beer with him, said he needed an understanding shoulder to cry on. This dude has a *real* problem, Toni. Whew! You wouldn't believe some of the stuff he told me. I'm talking *sick*. Anyhow, I knew you would understand. You know what it's like."

She knew all too well. The lying. The denials. The time unaccounted for. Locked doors. She knew what it was like, all right. It was like this.

chapter two

This was creeping her out. Like, *really* creeping her out.

He'd been gone for a while now, and she didn't know when he would be coming back. She didn't like this scene and wanted to leave.

But her hands were tied. Literally. And so were her feet. The worst of it, though, was the metallic-tasting tape he had secured over her mouth.

Four—maybe five—times in the past several weeks, she had come here with him. On those occasions they had left drained of energy and feeling mighty good. The expression "screwed their brains out" sprang to mind.

But he had never suggested bondage or anything kinky. Well . . . nothing *too* kinky. This was a first and, frankly, she could do without it.

One of the things that had first attracted her to him was that he seemed sophisticated. He had been a definite standout in the migratory crowd comprised mostly of high school and college students looking for drink, dope, and casual sex. Sure, now and then you had your pathetic old geezer lurking in the bushes wagging his weenie at anybody unfortunate enough to glance his way. But this guy was nothing like that. He was way cool.

Apparently he had thought she was a standout, too.

She and her friend Melissa had become aware of him watching them with single-minded interest.

"He might be a cop," Melissa speculated. "You know, working undercover."

Melissa had been on a real downer that night because she had to leave for Europe the following day with her parents, and she couldn't imagine anything more miserable. She was trying like hell to get glassy-eyed stoned, but nothing had taken effect yet. Her outlook on everything had been sour.

"A cop driving that car? I don't think so. Besides, his shoes are too good to be a cop's."

It wasn't merely that he had looked at her. Guys always looked at her. It was the *manner* in which he had looked at her that had been such a major turn-on. He'd been leaning against the hood of his car, ankles crossed, arms casually folded over his midriff, perfectly still and, despite his intensity, seemingly relaxed.

He didn't gawk at her chest or legs—consistently the objects of gawking—but looked straight into her eyes. Like he knew her instantly. Not just recognized her, or knew her by name, but knew *her*, knew everything there was to know about her that was important.

"Do you think he's cute?"

"I guess," Melissa replied, self-pity making her indifferent.

"Well, I think he is." She drained her rum and Coke, sucking it through the straw in the provocative way she had perfected by practicing for hours in front of her mirror. Its suggestiveness drove guys crazy and she knew it, and that's why she did it.

"I'm going for it." She reached behind her to set the empty plastic cup on the picnic table where she and Melissa had been sitting, then came off it with the sinuous grace of a snake sliding off a rock. She shook back her hair and gave the hem of her tank top a tug while drawing a deep, chest-expanding breath. Like an Olympic athlete, she went through a preparatory routine before each big event.

So it had been she who had made the first move. Leaving Melissa, she had sauntered toward him. When she reached the car, she moved in beside him and leaned back against the hood as he was doing. "You have a bad habit."

Turning only his head, he smiled down at her. "Only one?"

"That I know of."

His grin widened. "Then you need to get to know me better."

With no more invitation than that—because, after all, that was the reason they were there—he took her arm and ushered her around to the passenger side of his car. In spite of the heat, his hand was cool and dry. He politely opened the door and helped her into the leather-upholstered seat. As they drove away, she shot Melissa a triumphant grin, but Melissa was rummaging through her pouch of "mood enhancers" and didn't see.

He drove carefully, with both hands on the wheel, eyes on the road. He wasn't gaping at her and he wasn't groping and that was certainly a switch. Ordinarily, the minute she got into a guy's car, he'd start grabbing at her, like he couldn't believe his good fortune, like she might vaporize if he didn't touch her, or change her mind if he didn't hurry up and get on with it.

But this guy seemed a bit detached, and she thought that was kinda cool. He was mature and confident. He didn't need to gape and grope to assure himself that he was about to get laid.

She asked his name.

Stopping for a traffic light, he turned to look at her. "Is it important?"

She raised her shoulders in an exaggerated shrug, the rehearsed one, the one that pushed her breasts up and squeezed them together better than any Wonderbra could have. "I guess not."

He left his eyes on her breasts for several seconds, then the light changed and he went back to driving. "What's my bad habit?"

"You stare."

He laughed. "If you consider that a bad habit, then you really need to get to know me better."

She had placed her hand on his thigh and in her sultriest voice said, "I look forward to it."

His place was a major letdown. It was an efficiency apartment in a guest hotel. A tacky red banner strung across the front of the two-story building advertised special monthly rates. It was in a seedy neighborhood that didn't live up to his car or clothes.

Noticing her disappointment, he'd said, "It's a dump, but it's all I could find when I first moved here. I'm looking for something else." Then he added quietly, "I'll understand if you want me to take you back."

"No." She wasn't about to let him think she was a stupid, prissy high school girl with no spirit of adventure. "Shabby chic is in."

The apartment's main room served as both living area and bedroom. The galley kitchen was barely shoulder width. The bathroom was even smaller than that.

In the main room was a bed and nightstand, a four-drawer bureau, an easy chair with a floor lamp beside it, and a folding table long enough to accommodate an elaborate computer setup. The furnishings were garage-sale quality, but everything was neat.

She went over to the table. The computer was already booted up. With only a few clicks of the mouse, she found what she anticipated finding. She smiled at him over her shoulder and said, "So you weren't out there tonight by accident."

"I was out there tonight looking for you."

"Specifically?"

He nodded.

She liked that. A lot.

The Formica bar separating the kitchen from the living area was used as shelving for photographic equipment. He had a 35-millimeter camera, several lenses, and various attachments including a portable tripod. It all looked intricate and expensive, out of place in the crummy apartment. She picked up the camera and looked at him through the viewfinder. "Are you a professional?"

"It's only a hobby. Would you like something to drink?"

"Sure."

He went into the kitchen and returned with two glasses of red wine. Cool. Wine showed that he had refined tastes and class. It didn't jibe with the apartment either, but she figured that his explanation for it was a lie. This probably wasn't his main residence, only his playground. Away from the wife.

Sipping her wine, she glanced around. "So where are your pictures?"

"I don't display them."

"How come?"

"They're for my private collection."

"'Private collection'?" Grinning at him slyly, she twirled a strand of hair around her finger. "I like the sound of that. Show me."

"I don't think I should."

"Why not?"

"They're . . . artistic."

He was looking at her in that straightforward way again, as though measuring her reaction. His stare caused her toes to tingle, her pulse to race, and that hadn't happened in a long time in the company of a guy. It was usually she who created tingles and racing hearts. It was rare and wonderful to be the one unsure of exactly what was about to take place. Exciting as shit.

Boldly she declared, "I want to see your private collection."

He hesitated for several seconds, then knelt down beside the bed and pulled a box from beneath it. He removed the top and took out a standard photo album bound in faux black leather. As he came to his feet, he hugged it close to his chest. "How old are you?"

The question was an affront because she prided herself on looking much older than she was. She hadn't been carded in years—but a glimpse of the butterfly tattoo on her right breast usually made a bouncer too stupid to ask for an ID. "What the hell difference does it make how old I am? I want to see the pictures. And anyway, I'm twenty-two."

Clearly he didn't believe her. He even tried unsuccessfully to hide his smile. Nevertheless, he set the album on the table and stepped away from it. Trying to appear nonchalant, she walked over to it and flipped open the cover.

The first photo was graphic and startling. From the angle at which the close-up had been taken, she assumed—correctly, she discovered later—that it was a self-portrait.

"Are you offended?" he asked.

"Of course not. Do you think I've never seen one

erect?" Her response wasn't nearly as blasé as she made it sound. She wondered if he could hear her pounding heartbeat.

She turned the page to the next shot and then to the next, until she had gone through the entire album. She studied each photograph, pretending to be as analytical as an art critic. Some were in color, some in black and white, but all except the first one were of naked young women provocatively posed. Anyone else might have considered them obscene, but she was too sophisticated to get uptight over exposed genitalia.

But by no stretch were they "artistic" studies of nudes. They were nasty pictures.

"Do you like them?" He was standing so close behind her now she could feel his breath in her hair.

"They're okay."

Reaching around her, he flipped back through several of the pages until he came to a particular shot. "This one's my favorite."

She didn't see anything that made this girl so special. Her nipples looked like mosquito bites against a flat, bony chest. You could count every rib and her hair had split ends. She had zits on her shoulders. A veil obscured her face, probably for good reason.

She closed the album, then turned to him and gave him her most seductive smile. Slowly she pulled her tank top over her head and dropped it to the floor. "You mean it's been your favorite up till now."

He caught his breath, then released it on a staggering exhalation. Moving slowly, he took her hand and placed it beneath her breast so that she was cupping it in her palm as though offering it to him.

He gave her the sweetest, most tender smile she'd ever seen. "You're perfect. I knew you would be."

Her ego soared. "We're wasting time." She unzipped her shorts and was about to remove them when he stopped her. "No, leave them there, low on your hips. Just like that." Quickly he reached for his camera. Apparently it was loaded with film and ready to fire, because he put his eye to the viewfinder.

"This is going to be great." He moved her closer to the floor lamp near the easy chair and adjusted the dingy shade, then backed away and looked through the camera again. "Lower the shorts just a little more. There. Right there."

He clicked off several shots in rapid succession. "Oh, lady, you're killing me." He lowered the camera and looked at her with pure delight. "You're a natural. You must've done this before."

"I've never posed professionally."

"Amazing," he said. "Now go sit on the edge of the bed."

He knelt on the floor in front of her and positioned her the way he wanted her. Legs. Hands. Head. Before he picked up the camera again, he kissed her inner thigh, sucking her skin against his teeth and leaving a mark.

For another hour, the picture taking continued along with the foreplay. By the time they actually did it, she was past ready. Afterward he refilled their wineglasses and lay beside her, stroking her gently all over and telling her how beautiful she was.

She had thought, *Now, here's a guy who knows how to treat a woman.*

When they finished their wine, he asked if he could take more pictures. "I want to capture your afterglow."

"So you'll have the before and after?"

He laughed and kissed her quickly and with affection. "Something like that."

He dressed her—yes, he had personally dressed her as she used to dress her dolls. He returned her to the park on the lake where they'd met and saw that she got safely into her car. As he closed the door, he kissed her lips softly. "I love you."

Whoa! That had taken her aback. A hundred guys had told her they loved her, but usually as they were fumbling to get a rubber on. More often than not these professions of love took place within the steamy interior of their cars or pickups.

But love had never been proclaimed softly, tenderly, and meaningfully. He'd even kissed the back of her hand before he let her go. She'd thought that was awfully sweet and gentlemanly.

They'd been together several times since that first night, and it was always good kicks. But soon, and predictably, he'd started whining. Where were you last night? Who were you with? I waited for hours, but you never showed up. When can I see you again?

His possessiveness took the fun out of being with him. Besides, the newness and novelty had begun to wear off. His photography didn't seem exotic anymore, just weird and often creepy. It was time to bring this to a halt.

Maybe he sensed that she'd decided to break it off tonight, because it had started off badly. They'd quarreled immediately after he picked her up. From there things had grown progressively worse.

He'd gone bizarre and scary on her with this bondage shit. Leaving her tied up for what was going on hours now. What if this dump caught on fire? What if there was a tornado or something?

She didn't like it. She wanted out of here. The sooner the better.

Before he left, he had at least turned on the radio and

tuned it to Paris Gibson's program. That provided her with some company. She didn't feel quite as abandoned as she would have felt in a total silence that accompanied the total darkness.

So she lay there listening to Paris Gibson's voice and wondering when the hell he was coming back and what other fun and games he had in mind.

chapter three

The red light on the control board went out. Valentino had hung up.

It was several seconds before Paris realized that the only sound she heard was that of her own heartbeat. The music had stopped. On the log monitor she saw a series of zeros where descending numbers should be counting down the time remaining on a song. How long had she been broadcasting dead air?

With twenty-three seconds left in her program, she depressed her microphone button. She tried to speak. Couldn't. Tried again.

"I hope you've enjoyed this evening of classic love songs. Please join me again tomorrow night. I'll be looking forward to it. Until then, this is Paris Gibson on FM 101.3. Good night."

By depressing two control buttons, she was off the air. Then she was off her tall swivel stool like a shot, yanking open the heavy studio door, racing down the dark hallway, and barreling into the engineering room.

Except for a box of take-out fried chicken on Stan's desk, the room was empty. She continued running down the hall, turning right at the first intersection of corridors and literally slamming into Marvin, who was dragging a dirty rag along an interior windowsill.

She gasped, "Have you seen Stan?"

"No." One thing you could say about Marvin—he was a man of few words. If he spoke at all, it was in monosyllables.

"Has he already left?"

This time, he didn't even give her a verbal reply, only a shrug.

Leaving the janitor, she ran to the men's rest room and pushed open the door. Stan was at the urinal. "Stan, come here."

Stunned by the interruption, he whipped his head around. "What—I'm sorta busy here, Paris."

"Hurry up. This is important."

She rushed back to the studio and wheeled her stool over to the Vox Pro. It recorded each incoming call for optional playback. There was also a mandatory recording made of everything that went out over the air. But that was another machine and another matter. Right now, she was interested only in the telephone call.

"What's going on?" Stan strolled in, looking at his wristwatch. "I've got plans."

"Listen to this."

"Remember, my shift ends when you sign off."

"Shut up, Stan, and listen."

He leaned against the edge of the control board. "Okay, but I really need to be leaving soon."

"Shh." Valentino had just identified himself. "This is a repeat caller."

Stan appeared more interested in the crease of his linen trousers. But when Valentino told her she would be very sorry, her coworker's eyebrows shot up. "What's that mean?"

"Listen."

He was quiet through the remainder of the recording. When it ended, Paris looked at him expectantly. He raised his narrow shoulders in a quick shrug. "He's a kook."

"That's it? That's your assessment? He's a kook?"

He snuffled. "What? You don't think he's *serious?*"

"I don't know." Turning, she punched the hot-line button on the board. That was the telephone line provided for the deejays' personal use.

"Who're you calling?" Stan asked. "The cops?"

"I think I should."

"Why? Nutcases call you all the time. Wasn't there one just last week who wanted you to be a pallbearer at his mother's funeral?"

"This is different. I talk to a lot of people every night. This one . . . I don't know," she added uneasily.

When her 911 call was answered, she identified herself and gave the operator a brief description of what had happened. "It's probably nothing. But I thought someone should hear this conversation."

"I listen to your program on my nights off, Ms. Gibson," the operator said. "You don't sound like the type to panic. There'll be a squad car there shortly."

Paris thanked her and hung up. "They're on their way."

Stan winced. "Do I have to hang around?"

"No, go on. I'll be fine. Marvin's still here."

"Actually he's not. He split. I saw him leaving on my way here from the men's room, where I was rudely interrupted midstream. A surprise like that, a guy could get hurt, you know."

She was in no mood for Stan tonight. "I doubt you'll suffer any damage." She waved him out. "Go on. Just lock the door behind you. I can let the police in."

Her nervousness must have conveyed itself and made him feel like a deserter. "No, I'll wait with you," he said glumly. "Go brew yourself some tea or something. You look rattled."

She *was* rattled. Tea sounded like a good idea. She headed for the employee kitchen, but never made it. An obnoxious buzzer sounded throughout the building, announcing that someone was at the main entrance.

Reversing her direction, she rushed toward the front of the building and was relieved to see two uniformed policemen on the other side of the glass door. Never mind that they appeared to be fresh out of the academy. One of them looked too young to shave. But they were all business and introduced themselves with stiff-lipped laconism.

"Thank you for coming so quickly."

"We'd been out this way and were headed back when we got the call," one explained. He and his partner were looking at her strangely, as most people did when they first met her. The sunglasses made them instantly curious.

Without acknowledging either her glasses or their curiosity, she led Officers Griggs and Carson through the labyrinth of dark corridors. "There's a recording of the call in the studio."

The unremarkable exterior of the building hadn't prepared them for the electronic sophistication of the studio. They gazed about them with curiosity and awe. She brought them back on track by introducing Stan. Their acknowledgments were clipped. No one shook hands. Paris used the mouse on the Vox Pro computer to play Valentino's recorded call.

No one spoke while they listened. Officer Griggs stared at the ceiling, Carson at the floor. When it ended, Griggs raised his head and cleared his throat, seemingly embarrassed by Valentino's crude language. "Do you get calls like this often, Ms. Gibson?"

"Weird and kooky sometimes. Heavy breathers and dirty propositions, but nothing like what you've just heard. Never anything threatening. Valentino has called before. He tells me about a wonderful new girlfriend, or a recent breakup that left him heartbroken. He's never said anything like this. Never anything even close to this."

"You think it's the same guy?"

They all turned to Stan, who had ventured the idea.

He continued, "Somebody else could have borrowed the name Valentino because they've heard him on your show and know that he's a regular caller."

"I guess it's possible," Paris said slowly. "I'm almost positive that Valentino's voice is disguised. It never sounds quite natural."

"That's not a common name either," Griggs said. "Do you think it's legit?"

"I have no way of knowing that. Sometimes a caller is reluctant to give even a first name, preferring to remain totally anonymous."

"Do you have a way of tracing calls?"

"Ordinary caller ID. One of our engineers added software to the Vox Pro that would give us a readout of the number, if it was available. Each call is also date and time stamped."

She brought up the information on the computer screen. There was no name, but a local telephone number, which Carson jotted down.

"This is a good start," he said.

"Maybe," Griggs said. "Considering what he called to say, why would he use a traceable number?"

Paris read between the lines. "You think it was a hoax?"

Neither of the policemen answered her directly. Carson said, "I'll call the number, see if anyone answers."

He used his cell phone, and after listening through numerous rings concluded that no one was going to pick up. "No voice mail either. Better call it in." He punched in digits, then while he was giving Valentino's number to whomever was on the other end, Griggs told her and Stan that the number would be traced.

"But my guess is that it was a guy using a name he'd heard on your program and just trying to get a reaction out of you."

"Like the sickos who make obscene phone calls," Stan said.

Griggs bobbed his cropped head. "Exactly like that. I bet we find a lonely drunk or a group of bored kids trying to have some fun by talking dirty, something like that."

"I hope you're right." Paris hugged herself and rubbed her arms for warmth. "I can't believe someone would do this as a joke, but I certainly prefer a joke to the alternative."

Carson disconnected. "They're on it. Shouldn't take long."

"You'll let me know what they find out?"

"Sure thing, Ms. Gibson."

Stan offered to follow her home, but it was a half-hearted offer and he seemed relieved when she declined. He bade them good night and left.

"How can we contact you when we know something?" Griggs asked as they wended their way through the building, toward the entrance.

She gave him her home telephone number, emphasizing that it was unlisted. "Of course, Ms. Gibson."

It surprised the two policemen that she was the one to

lock up the building for the night. "Are you here alone every night?" Carson asked as they walked her to her car.

"Except for Stan."

"What does he do and how long has he worked here?"

He doesn't do much of anything, she thought wryly. But she told them that he was an engineer. "He's on standby if anything should go wrong with the equipment. He's been here for a couple of years."

"Nobody else works the night shift?"

"Well, there's Marvin. He's been doing our janitorial service for several months."

"Last name?"

"I don't know. Why?"

"Never can tell about people," Griggs said. "Do you get along with these guys all right?"

She laughed. "Nobody gets along with Marvin, but he's not the type to make a scary phone call. He only speaks when spoken to, and then he more or less grunts."

"What about Stan?"

She felt disloyal talking about him behind his back. If she spoke candidly, it wouldn't be a flattering description, so she told them only what was relevant. "We get along fine. I'm sure neither of them had anything to do with that call."

Griggs smiled at her and closed his small notebook with a decisive snap. "Doesn't hurt to follow up."

Her home telephone was ringing when she let herself in. She rushed to answer. "Hello?"

"Ms. Gibson, it's Officer Griggs."

"Yes?"

"Did you get in okay?"

"Yes. I just disengaged my alarm. Have you learned anything?"

"That number belongs to a pay phone near the UT campus. A squad car was dispatched to check it out but nobody was around. The phone's outside a pharmacy that closed at ten. Place and parking lot were deserted."

In effect, they were back to where they had started. She had hoped they would trace the number to a sad and lonely individual like Griggs had described, a lost soul who had threatened her and an imaginary captive in a dire attempt to get attention.

Her initial misgivings returned. "So what now?"

"Well, there's not really anything to be done unless he calls again. I don't think he will, though. It was probably someone just trying to rile you. Tomorrow night, we'll have squad cars patrolling the area around that phone booth, watching for anyone lurking in the vicinity."

That wasn't satisfactory, but it was all she was going to get. She thanked him. He and his partner had done what was expected of them, but she wasn't ready to concede that Valentino's call was a prank and nothing to worry about. Even the origin of the call was worrisome. Wouldn't someone seeking attention leave obvious clues so that he could be traced and identified, chastened by the police, maybe even written up in the newspaper?

Valentino had used a public telephone so the call couldn't be traced. He didn't want to be identified.

That disturbing thought was uppermost in her mind as she made her way through the living area of her house, down the hallway, and into her bedroom. As always when she returned home from work, the rooms were dark and silent.

The houses neighboring hers were also dark and

hushed at this hour, but there was a difference. In those houses, the prayers of children had been heard before they were tucked in. Husbands and wives had kissed good night. Some had made love before settling beneath their blanket. They shared a bed, body heat, dreams. They shared their lives. Darkness was relieved by nightlights, small beacons of comfort that shone in rooms littered with toys and shoes, with the accoutrements of busy family life.

The nightlights in Paris's house only emphasized the sterile neatness of the rooms. Her movements were the only source of sound. She slept alone. That wouldn't have been her first choice, but that's the way it was, and she had come to accept it.

Tonight, however, the solitude was unnerving. And the cause was Valentino's call.

She'd had years of experience listening to voices, picking up nuances in speech, detecting underlying messages, separating truth from lies, and hearing more than what was said out loud. She was able to draw several conclusions about a person based strictly on his or her inflections. Calls had left her feeling happy, sad, reflective, annoyed, and, on occasion, downright angry.

None had left her feeling afraid. Until tonight.

chapter four

Her limbs were beginning to cramp from being held in one position for so long, and an itch on the sole of her foot was driving her nuts. Her face hurt and she could feel it swelling. She ached all over.

That son of a bitch, she thought, unable to curse him out loud because of the tape over her mouth.

Why had she ever thought he was so special? It wasn't like he took her to fabulous places and spent money on her. They'd never been anywhere together except this place, and it was a rathole.

She didn't know anything about him, not where he worked, not even his name. She'd never learned his name even by accident. It wasn't printed on anything in the apartment, no subscription magazines or mail, nothing. He remained nameless, and that should have been her first clue that he wasn't classy and intriguing, but just flat-out, freaking weird.

The second time they were together, he had defined the nature of their relationship. Laid down the ground rules, so to speak. He had opened the conversation while spreading baby oil over her, hoping to achieve a special effect in a series of photographs.

"Your friend . . . the one you were with the night we met."

"You mean Melissa?" she'd asked, feeling a stab of

jealousy. Was he wanting to invite Melissa to join them in a ménage à trois? "What about her?"

"Have you told her about us?"

"I haven't had a chance. Her folks made her go to France with them for vacation. I haven't seen or talked to her since the night I met you."

"Have you told anyone about me and what we do here?"

"Oh, sure. I announced it over breakfast to my parents." His poleaxed expression made her giggle. "No, silly! I haven't told anyone."

"That's good. Because this is so special, I like thinking that you and I are each other's best-kept secret."

"We are each other's secret. I don't even know your name."

"But you know me."

He stared deeply into her eyes, and she was reminded of her first impression of him, that he could see straight into her innermost being. He apparently had felt the instantaneous connection that she had. After all, he'd told her that first night that he loved her.

The secrecy was probably necessary because of a wife who knew nothing about his "hobby." She envisioned his missus as a missionary-position-only prude who would never understand, much less consent to, his need for variety and excitement. Pictures of Mrs. No-name masturbating? Get real. Never in a million. Probably not even a bare-boob shot.

That night his lovemaking had been especially ardent. He was focused, you might say, not just his camera. She lost count of the number of times they did it, but it was always different, so it never got boring. He couldn't get enough of her and told her so. It was a heady experience, being practically worshiped by a man so classy he could probably have any woman. She had thought she would never want it to end.

But that had been then.

Each time she saw him, his jealousy increased, until it began to irritate her and rob her of the pleasure of being with him. No matter how good the sex was, it wasn't worth the hassle he gave her about other men.

She had thought about standing him up tonight, but then changed her mind. He was going to take it hard whenever she told him she didn't want to see him anymore. She dreaded a scene, but better to put him out of his misery sooner rather than later.

He had been waiting for her at the appointed place. And, unlike the night they'd met, he didn't look at all cool and relaxed. He was agitated and edgy. The moment she joined him in his car, he started in on her. "You've been with somebody else, haven't you?"

She supposed she should be flattered that he was jealous, but she had a headache and was in no mood for the third degree. "Do you have a joint?" Having learned that she was fond of smoke, he always had some for her.

"In the glove compartment."

There were three in a Ziploc bag. She lit one and inhaled deeply. "Best thing for a headache." Sighing, she laid her head on the headrest and closed her eyes.

"Who was he?"

"Who was who?"

"Don't jerk me around."

His tone brought her head up.

"You've already been with someone tonight, haven't you?" His fingers were clenching the steering wheel. "Don't bother lying about it. I know you've just had sex with someone else. I can smell him on you."

At first she was surprised and a bit unnerved that he

knew. Had he been spying on her? But the uneasiness soon gave way to anger. Why was it any of his business who and when she screwed?

"Look, maybe getting together tonight isn't a good idea," she'd said. "I'm PMSing and I don't need any shit from anybody. Okay?"

His anger dissolved instantly. "I'm sorry I raised my voice. It's just . . . I thought . . ."

"What?"

"That we had something special here."

That's when she should have told him that she didn't want to see him again. Right then he'd given her an opportunity, but, damn it, she hadn't taken it. Instead she'd said, "I don't like you ragging me about where I go, what I do, and who I do it with. I get enough of that at home." She leaned back and pulled deeply on the joint. "Either chill or take me back to my car."

He chilled. He was subdued, even a little sullen, when they reached the apartment. "Want some wine?"

"Don't I always?"

She was already high from the weed. Might as well go all out and get really wasted. One mercy fuck, then she'd tell him they needed to cool it for a while—read *forever*—then she'd get the hell out of here and never come back.

His computer monitor was the only source of light in this room where the shades were always drawn. One of the more graphic photos of her was on his screen saver.

Seeing it, she said, "Tsk, tsk. That's definitely one of the 'afterglows,' isn't it? I'm such a naughty girl. Naughty but nice, right?" She winked at him as she accepted the glass of wine he brought from the kitchen.

She drank it like water, burped loudly and wetly, then extended the empty glass toward him in an impertinent request for a refill.

"You're acting like a slut." He calmly took the glass from her and set it on the nightstand. Then he slapped her. He slapped her so hard that tears came to her eyes even before the rocket of pain from her cheekbone reached her brain.

She cried out, but was too shocked to articulate a word.

He pushed her back onto the bed. She landed hard. The room seemed to tilt. She was more wasted than she'd thought. She struggled to get up. "Hey! I don't—"

"Oh, yes, you do."

He splayed his hand over her chest, holding her down while he wrestled with his belt and fly. Then he began tearing at her clothing. She swatted his hands, kicked at him, and called him every name in the book, but he wouldn't be stopped.

He pushed himself into her with such force that she screamed. He covered her mouth with his hand. "Shut up," he hissed, so close to her face she felt a shower of spit.

She bit into the flesh beneath his thumb. He yelped and withdrew his hand. "You bastard," she yelled. "Get off me."

To her astonishment, he began to laugh softly. "You fell for it. You thought I was serious."

She stopped struggling. "Huh?"

"I was just fulfilling your rape fantasy."

"You're crazy."

"Am I?" He thrust hard into her. "Can you honestly say you don't like it?"

"Damn right. I hate it. I hate you, you son of a bitch."

That caused him to smile, because in spite of what she said, she was responding. When it was over, each was exhausted and glistening with sweat.

He recovered first and went for his camera. "Stay just as you are," he said as he clicked off the first shot.

The flash seemed exceptionally bright. She was good and truly stoned.

"Don't move," he told her. "I have an idea."

Move? She was too lethargic to move. Her entire body throbbed, starting with her cheekbone—how was she going to explain a bad bruise?—and all the way down to her splayed thighs. Christ, she still had her sandals on. How funny was that? But she was too tired to trouble herself with taking them off. Besides, he had told her not to move.

Maybe she dozed for a minute or two. Next thing she knew he was back, bending over her, pulling her wrists together.

"What's that?" She roused herself and saw that he was using a necktie to bind her wrists together.

"A prop for a photograph. You've been a bad girl. You need to be punished." He climbed off the bed and picked up his camera and adjusted the focus.

That's when it began to get creepy and she felt the first twinges of apprehension. She had struggled to sit up. "Have I mentioned that I'm not into bondage?"

"This isn't bondage, this is punishment," he said absently as he moved to the lamp. He adjusted the shade, setting it first at one angle, then another, causing shadows to shift across her body.

Okay. Enough of this. She'd had it. After tonight, no more of him. Posing for him had been fun. It had been something different and, admittedly, it had been a kick to later look at the pictures of herself.

But he was getting too possessive and too . . . too out there.

"Look," she recalled saying sternly, "I really want you to untie my hands now."

Finally satisfied with the lighting, he began setting up the tripod.

Taking another tack, she softened her tone. "I'll do anything you want. You know I will. All you have to do is ask. Anything."

He still didn't seem to be listening. While he was distracted, she had inched toward the edge of the bed, calculating the distance to the door. But when she looked at it, something struck her as odd, and a cold dart of fear went through her when she realized that there was no doorknob on this side. Only a brass disk where the doorknob should have been.

That's when he had stopped tinkering with the camera. No doubt sensing her alarm, he had smiled down at her. "Where do you think you're going?"

"I want you to untie me."

"You moved and spoiled the lighting," he chided gently.

"Lighting, my ass, I'm *leaving*."

Her cheerleading days had paid off. She came off the bed with surprising strength and agility. But she didn't get far. He caught her by the hair and yanked her back, then shoved her down onto the bed.

"You can't keep me here," she'd cried.

"You just had to ruin it, didn't you?"

"Ruin what?"

"Us."

"There isn't any 'us,' you sick wacko."

"You had to cheat on me. Just like the others. Didn't you think I'd find out? I listen to Paris Gibson, too, you know. She put your call on the air. Thousands of people heard you telling her that you felt smothered by my possessiveness. You were going to take her advice and dump me, weren't you?"

"Oh, Jesus."

He'd stood over her, both fists clenched at his sides as though he were forcibly suppressing his rage. "You can't treat people like toilet paper and get away with it, you know."

And because he had become so freaking scary, she had wisely shut up.

He had taken a few more photos, then decided that her feet also needed to be tied. She had fought him as if her life depended on it, but he'd eventually slapped her so hard her ears rang. That was the last thing she heard.

When she came to, she was spread-eagled, her hands and feet tied to the bed frame beneath the box springs, her mouth taped shut. The apartment was empty. He was gone. She was alone, and no one knew where she was.

Over the passing hours, she had devised a dozen means of escape, but dismissed the ideas almost as soon as she conceived them. None was workable. She was helpless to do anything but wait for him to come back for more of his sick sex games.

Jesus, she thought, *what have I gotten myself into?*

"I hope you've enjoyed this evening of classic love songs. Please join me again tomorrow night. I'll be looking forward to it. Until then, this is Paris Gibson on FM 101.3. Good night."

Great. Now she didn't even have Paris to keep her company.

chapter five

Gavin Malloy was awfully drunk. The pleasant buzz from the cheap tequila wasn't quite so pleasant any longer. It was too hot to be drinking tequila shots. He should have stuck to beer. But he had needed something strong and nasty to drown his depression.

The hell of it was, he was still depressed.

The evening had been spoiled for him early on. His drinking had accomplished nothing except to make him light-headed, sweaty, and nauseous. Blearily he looked toward a clump of scraggly cedar trees and wondered if he could cover the distance over the rocky ground before he puked. Probably not.

Besides, he'd seen a couple disappear behind the trees a while ago. If they were still doing what they'd gone there to do, they wouldn't appreciate him hurling on them. Talk about coitus interruptus.

He chuckled at the thought.

"What're you laughing at?" his new friend asked, nudging him in the gut, which caused the tequila to slosh. The guy's name was Craig something. If he'd ever heard his last name, he'd forgotten it. Craig drove a Dodge Ram pickup, the biggest one made. Jet black. Fully loaded. It was one badass truck.

Gavin, Craig, and several others had been hanging out in the bed of the pickup for hours, waiting for something to happen. A group of girls had come by earlier, drunk some of their tequila, showed them just enough skin to get them excited, then wandered away with promises to return. So far they hadn't.

"What's funny?" Craig asked again.

"Nothing. Just thinking."

"'Bout what?"

What had he been thinking? He couldn't remember. Must not've been very important. "My old man," he said around a belch. Yeah, his old man had been in the back of his mind all night, bothering him like an itch he couldn't reach.

"What about him?"

"He's gonna shit 'cause I went out tonight. He grounded me."

"That sucks."

"You got grounded?" another guy jeered. "What are you, twelve?"

Gavin didn't know his name, only that he was an ass-hole with bad skin and worse breath who thought he was a lot cooler than he was.

Gavin had moved to Austin from Houston a week after the spring semester ended. Finding a new crowd during summer break hadn't been easy, but he had joined this group, who accepted him once they learned he was a guy who liked to party as much as they did.

"Awww, Gavin's scared of his daddy," the jerk taunted.

"I'm not scared of him. I just dread having my ass chewed again."

"Save yourself the hassle." This from the optimist who'd showed them earlier his inventory of condoms. "Wait till he goes to bed before you sneak out."

"I tried that already. He's a freaking bat. He's got like built-in radar or something."

This conversation was making the lousy evening lousier. Nothing could cheer him up tonight, not more tequila, not even the return of the girls, and chances were excellent that they weren't going to come back as promised. Why would they waste their time on losers like this bunch, like him?

He stood up, swaying dangerously. "I'd better split. If I'm lucky, he won't be home yet. He's with his girl-friend."

He waded through the others, then jumped off the tailgate. But he miscalculated the distance to the ground as well as the weakness in his knees and wound up face-down in the dirt.

His new buddies howled. Weak with laughter himself, he struggled to get upright. His T-shirt was so wet with sweat that when he tried to dust himself off, he left streaks of mud across the front of it.

"Tomorrow night," he told his friends as he staggered away. Where had he left his car?

"Don't forget tomorrow is your turn to bring the booze," Craig called.

"I'm broke."

"Steal it from your old man."

"I can't. He checks the bottles."

"Jesus, is he a cop in his spare time?"

"I'll see what I can do," Gavin mumbled as he turned in the general direction of where he'd parked.

"What if Miss Hotpants comes looking for you?" It was the asshole, calling to him in a singsong voice. His grin was ugly and goading. "What should we tell her? That you had to go home to your daddy?"

"Get fucked."

The obnoxious kid hooted. "Well, it's for sure you won't. Not tonight anyway."

One of the others muttered, "Shut up, dickhead."

"Yeah, give it a rest," the condom guy said.

"What? Wha'd I do?"

Craig spoke softly. "She dumped him."

"She did? When?"

Gavin moved out of earshot, which was just as well. He didn't want to hear any more.

He located his car. It wasn't that difficult to spot among all the others because it was a piece of shit. No badass pickup or sports car for him. Oh, no, nothing like that for Gavin Malloy. And you could forget a motorcycle. That wasn't going to happen as long as his old man was in charge, and probably not as long as he was drawing breath.

His car was a snore. It was a sensible, good-mileage means of transportation that would spoil the racy image of a Mormon soccer mom. And he was expected to be grateful for it.

He'd gotten a lecture when he expressed his low opinion of it. "A car isn't a toy, Gavin. Or a status symbol. This is a reliable first car. When you've proved that you're responsible enough to take care of it and use it safely, I'll consider an upgrade. Until then . . ." Blah-blah-blah.

The thing was an embarrassment. When the fall semester started at his new school, he would probably be laughed off campus for driving this heap. The dorkiest of the dorks wouldn't want to be seen with him.

In his present condition, he had no business driving anything and was just sober enough to realize it. He concentrated hard on keeping the center stripe in focus. But that only seemed to increase his dizziness.

He was still several blocks from home when he was forced to pull over, get out, and vomit. He spewed a torrent of tequila on some poor sucker's flower bed that formed a neat circle of color around the mailbox. Someone would have a disgusting surprise when they came out to get the mail tomorrow. To say nothing of the mailman.

Coordination shot, he climbed back into his car and drove the remainder of the way to the new house his dad had bought for them. It wasn't bad. In fact, Gavin kinda liked it. Especially the pool. But he didn't want his dad to know he liked it.

He was relieved to see that his old man's car wasn't in the driveway. But Gavin wouldn't put it past him to have laid a trap, so he slipped into the house through the back door and paused to listen. His dad would love to catch him sneaking in so he could ground him for longer, take away his cell phone, his computer, his car, and make his life even more miserable than it was.

That was his parents' main mission in life—to make *him* miserable.

Satisfied that the house was empty, he went to his room. His old man must still be with Liz. Screwing like rabbits, no doubt. They never did it here in his dad's bed. Did they think he was stupid, that he didn't know they were having sex when they spent the evening at her place?

It was easy to imagine Liz in bed. She had a hot body. But his old man? Rutting? No way. Gavin couldn't imagine anything more gross.

In his bedroom he turned on his computer even before he switched on the desk lamp. He couldn't fathom life without a computer. How had people survived before them? If his dad really wanted to punish him, that's the privilege he would revoke.

He checked for email. There was one from his mom, which he deleted without reading. Anything she had to say was salve for her conscience and he didn't want to hear it.

You'll come to realize that this is best for all of us.
You and your future are our main concerns, Gavin.
Once you have adjusted to the change . . .

Sure, Mom. Whatever you say, Mom. Bullshit, Mom.

He sat down at the desk and began composing an email letter. But not to his mother. His anger with her was mild compared to the animosity he felt for the recipient of this letter. Not that he planned on sending it. And because he didn't, he poured out all the anger that had been roiling inside him for days.

"What makes you think you're so hot anyway?" he wrote. "I've seen better. I've *had* better."

"Gavin?"

When the overhead light flashed on, he nearly jumped out of his skin. He quickly exited his email before his old man could read what was on his screen. He pivoted in his chair, hoping he didn't look guilty. "What?"

"I'm home."

"So?"

"You okay?"

"Why wouldn't I be? I'm not a kid."

"Did you eat some dinner?"

"Oh yeah," he said, smacking his lips. "Microwaved leftover pizza."

"You were invited to join Liz and me. You chose not to."

"Bet that broke your heart."

In the even, unruffled voice Gavin hated, his dad said, "If I hadn't wanted you to come along, I wouldn't have invited you." He came into the room. Gavin thought, *Oh, great.* "What've you been doing all evening?"

"Nothing. Surfing the net."

"What's that on your shirt?"

Perfect. He'd forgotten about the filth on his T-shirt. Dirt. Probably vomit, too. Ignoring the question, he turned back to face the computer. "I'm busy."

His dad took him by the shoulder and turned him around. "You went out. Your car isn't in the same place it was when I left and the hood is warm."

Gavin laughed. "You're checking the temperature of my car's engine? You need to get a life."

"And you need to get with the program." His father said this in a raised voice, which was rare. "You stink of vomit and you're drunk. Driving drunk, you could've killed somebody."

"Well, I didn't. So relax and leave me alone."

Dean stuck out his hand, palm up. "Give me your car keys."

Gavin glared at him. "If you think taking my keys will keep me cooped up in here, you're wrong."

Dean said nothing, just kept his hand extended. Gavin fished the keys from the pocket of his jeans and dropped them into his father's palm. "I hate the damn car anyway, so no big loss."

His dad pocketed the keys but didn't leave. He sat down on the edge of the unmade bed. "Now what?" Gavin groaned. "One of your famous lectures on how I'm pissing my life away?"

"Do you think I enjoy punishing you, Gavin?"

"Yeah, I think you do. I think you get off on being the big, bad father, having me to boss around. You enjoy telling me everything I'm doing wrong."

"That's ridiculous. Why do you say that?"

"Because you've never done anything wrong in your whole goddamn life. Mr. Perfect, that's you. It must be boring as shit to be so right all the time."

He was surprised to see his dad smile. "I'm far from right all the time and nowhere near perfect. Ask your mother. She'll tell you. But I know I'm right about one thing."

His dad paused and looked at him hard, probably hoping he would ask what that one thing was. He could wait till hell froze over. Finally he said, "It's right that you're living with me now. I'm glad you are. I want you here with me."

"Right. I'm sure you're just thrilled over the new living arrangements. You love having me around, cramping your style, getting in the way."

"In the way? Of what?"

"Of everything." The exclamation caused his voice to crack. He hoped his dad didn't mistake it for emotion, which it sure as hell wasn't. "I'm in the way of your life. Your new job. Liz."

"You're not in the way, Gavin. You're my family, my son. Liz and I wanted you with us tonight."

He scoffed. "For a cozy dinner? Just the three of us. Your new family. Then what? What was I supposed to do when you took her home? Wait in the car while you went inside for a quick blow job?"

He knew instantly that he'd gone too far. His dad wasn't one to fly off the handle when he got angry. He didn't lose his temper, rant and rave, stomp around, yell, or throw things. Instead, Mr. Self-control went very still. His lips narrowed and something funny happened to his eyes that made them seem to harden and sharpen and go right through you like steel picks.

But apparently there was a limit to his old man's restraint, and he'd just reached it.

Before he had even processed all this, his father was on his feet, and he was on the receiving end of a backhanded smack that caught him hard across the mouth and split his lip.

"You don't want to be treated like a kid? Fine. I'll treat you like an adult. That's what I would have done to any grown man who said something like that to me."

Gavin struggled to hold back tears. "I hate you."

"Well, too bad. You're stuck with me." He went out, soundly pulling the door shut behind him.

Gavin launched himself out of the chair. He stood in the center of his messy room, bristling with anger and frustration. But realizing he had nowhere to run, and no means of running if he had somewhere to go, he threw himself onto his bed.

He made swipes at the snot, tears, and blood that had mingled on his face. He felt like blubbering. He wanted to draw himself into the fetal position and cry like a baby. Because his life sucked. All of it. He hated everything and everybody. His dad. His mom. The city of Austin. Women. His stupid friends. His ugly car.

Most of all he hated himself.

chapter six

Without making it too obvious, Sergeant Robert Curtis was trying to see past the dark lenses of her sunglasses. Catching himself staring, he hastily held a chair for her. "Forgive my lack of manners, Ms. Gibson. I'll admit to being a little starstruck. Have a seat. Can I get you some coffee?"

"I'm fine, thanks. And I'm hardly a star."

"I beg to differ."

Curtis was a detective for the Austin Police Department's Central Investigative Bureau. He was fiftyish, compactly built, and neatly turned out, down to a polished pair of cowboy boots, the heels of which added a couple of inches to his stature. Although he was still no taller than she, he gave off an air of authority and confidence. A sport jacket was hanging on a coat tree, but his necktie was tightly knotted beneath a starched collar. His cuffs were monogrammed with his initials.

On the walls of the small enclosure were a detailed map of the state, another of Travis County, and a framed diploma. The built-in desk was nearly completely covered with paperwork and computer components, but somehow avoided looking messy.

Curtis sat down at his desk and smiled at her. "It's not every morning of the week I get visited by a radio personality. What can I do for you?"

"I'm not sure you can do anything."

Now that she was here, ensconced with a detective in his compact cubicle where he doubtless worked long hours, serving the public by snaring felons, she was second-guessing her decision to come.

Things that happened at two o'clock in the morning took on a different complexion in daylight. Suddenly, coming here seemed like a melodramatic and somewhat self-centered reaction to what probably amounted to a crank phone call.

"I called in a 911 last night," she began. "Actually early this morning. Two patrolmen, Griggs and Carson, responded. I have a case number for your reference." She gave him the number that Griggs had left with her.

"What kind of 911, Ms. Gibson?"

She gave him an account of what had happened. He listened attentively. His expression remained open and concerned. He didn't fidget as though she were wasting his time on something trivial. If he was faking his interest, he did it very well.

When she finished, she removed a cassette tape from her handbag and passed it to him. "I went to the station early this morning and made a copy of the call."

Insomnia had claimed her until dawn, when she finally surrendered to it. She got up, showered and dressed, and was back at the radio station by the time Charlie and Chad, the morning drive-time deejays, were reading the seven o'clock news headlines.

"I'll be happy to listen to your tape, Ms. Gibson," Curtis said. "But this department investigates homicide, rape, assault, robbery. Threatening phone calls . . ." He spread his hands wide. "Why'd you come to me?"

"I read your name in yesterday's newspaper," she admitted with chagrin. "Something about your testifying at a trial. I thought I'd get more personal attention if I asked to speak with a particular detective rather than just showing up without an appointment."

Now he looked chagrined. "You're probably right."

"And if my caller does what he threatens to do, it will fall to this department to investigate, won't it?"

Sobering instantly, Curtis left his chair and stepped outside the cubicle. He called across the room at large, asking if anybody had a cassette recorder handy. Within moments another plainclothes detective appeared with one. "Here you go."

He regarded Paris with patent curiosity as he handed the machine to Curtis, whose brusque, "Thanks, Joe," was as good as a dismissal. The other man withdrew.

Sergeant Curtis had been a random selection, but she was glad she'd come to him. He obviously had some clout and wasn't reluctant to use it.

He returned to his seat and inserted the tape into the recorder, saying in an undertone, "I see word has gotten around as to who you are."

Maybe, Paris thought. Or maybe the detective was simply wondering why she hadn't removed her sunglasses. This wasn't a particularly bright environment. In fact, it was a room without windows.

Curtis and the other detective probably assumed that she wore the sunglasses like a celebrity would, to conceal her identity in public or to add to her mystique as a media personality, that she wore them to shut others out. It would never occur to them that she wore the glasses to shut herself in.

"Let's see what Mr. . . . what was it? Valentino? . . . has to say for himself." Curtis pressed the Play button. *This is Paris. Hello, Paris. This is Valentino.*

When the tape ended, Curtis tugged thoughtfully on his lower lip, then asked, "Mind if I play it again?"

Without waiting for her consent, he rewound the tape

and restarted it. As he listened, he frowned with concentration and rolled his University of Texas class ring around his stubby finger.

At the end of the tape, she asked, "What do you think, Sergeant? Am I reading too much into a crank call?"

He asked a question of his own. "Did you try to call the number?"

"I was so stunned, I didn't think of calling back immediately, but I suppose I should have."

He dismissed her concern with a wave. "He probably wouldn't have answered anyway."

"He didn't when Carson called later. No voice mail either. Just an unanswered ring."

"The number on the caller ID, you say it was traced to a pay phone?"

"I'm sure the details are in the report, but Griggs told me that a patrol car in that area had been dispatched to check out the phone booth. But by that time—at least half an hour, maybe more—whoever placed the call was gone."

"Somebody could have seen him at the phone booth. Did the patrolmen ask around?"

"There was nobody to ask. According to Griggs, the area was deserted when the patrol car arrived." Curtis's questions were validating her concern, but that only increased her anxiety. "Do you think Valentino was telling the truth? Has he kidnapped a girl he plans to murder?"

Curtis made balloons of his ruddy cheeks before expelling a long breath. "I don't know, Ms. Gibson. But if he has, and if he sticks to his three-day deadline, we don't have time to sit around and talk about it. I don't want another kidnap-rape-murder case on my desk if I can possibly avoid it." He stood up and reached for his jacket.

"What can we do?"

"We start by trying to determine if he's for real or just a nut trying to win the attention of his favorite celebrity." By now he was ushering her through the maze of similar cubicles toward the set of double doors through which she'd entered the CIB.

"How do we make that determination?"

"We go to the authority on the subject."

Just as Dean was leaving the house, Liz called from the Houston airport. "You're already in Houston?"

"My flight from Austin was at six-thirty."

"Brutal."

"Tell me." After a short pause, she asked, "What happened with Gavin when you got home last night?"

"Your basic open warfare, both sides scoring hits and suffering casualties."

He balanced the cordless phone between chin and shoulder and poured himself a glass of orange juice. He'd lain awake for hours last night, and when he finally did fall asleep, he'd gone comatose. His alarm had been going off for half an hour before it awakened him. No time to brew coffee this morning.

"Well, at least he was home when you got there," Liz said. "He hadn't disobeyed."

Not wanting to recount his argument with Gavin, Dean harrumphed a nonverbal agreement. "What time is your first meeting in Chicago?"

"As soon as I arrive at the hotel. I hope O'Hare isn't too hairy and I can get through it quickly. What have you got on tap today?"

He outlined his day. She said she needed to run, that

she'd just wanted to say hi before her flight to Chicago. He told her he was glad that she'd caught him and wished her a safe flight. She said, "I love you." And he replied with, "Love you, too."

After disconnecting, Dean bowed his head, closed his eyes, and tapped his forehead—hard—with the telephone as though he were paying some kind of unorthodox self-flagellating penance.

Rather than getting his day off to the good start that Liz had obviously intended, her call put him out of sorts. Add the blasted heat and Austin's rush-hour traffic, and he was in a testy mood when he reached his office fifteen minutes late.

"Good morning, Ms. Lester. Any messages?"

Dean shared the secretary with several other people. She was competent. And friendly. His first day on the job, she had informed him that she was the divorced mother of two daughters and that it was okay for him to call her by her first name.

Unless his eyes were deceiving him, and he didn't think they were, since his arrival her necklines had gotten progressively lower and her hemlines higher. This gradual reduction of textiles could be in correlation with the rising summertime temperature, but he doubted it. Just to be safe, he had stuck to calling her Ms. Lester.

"Messages are on your desk. A fresh pot of coffee is brewing. Soon as it's ready, I'll bring you some."

Fetching him coffee wasn't in her job description, but this morning he was glad she'd volunteered. "Great, thanks."

He went into his office and closed the door, discouraging further conversation. He slung his jacket onto the wall rack, loosened his tie, and unbuttoned his collar button. He sat down at his desk and riffled through his messages, happy to see there were no urgent ones. He needed a few minutes to decompress.

He swiveled his desk chair around and adjusted the window blind so he could see out. The sunlight was glaring, but that wasn't why he dug his fingers into his eye sockets, then wearily dragged his hands down his face.

What was he going to do about Gavin? How many times could he ground him? How many more privileges could he revoke? How many more scenes like the one last night could they withstand? Arguments such as that inflicted damage that was often irreparable. Could any relationship survive constant onslaughts like that?

He sorely regretted smacking him. Not that Gavin hadn't deserved it for the insulting crack he'd made. Still, he shouldn't have struck him. He was the grown-up and he should have behaved as such. To lose his temper like that was juvenile. And dangerous. Loss of control could wreak havoc, and he knew that better than anyone.

Besides, he was determined to be a positive role model for Gavin. He didn't want to preach to him, but to set a good example. Last night, he had sent the wrong message on how to manage anger, and he was sorry for it.

He ran his fingers through his hair and wondered what was taking the coffee so freaking long.

Should he send Gavin back to his mother? "Not an option," he muttered out loud. No way. For a long list of reasons that included welshing on the agreement he and Pat had reached about their son, but the main one being that Dean Malloy deplored failure. At anything. He threw in the towel only when absolutely forced to.

Gavin had told him—more like *accused* him—of always being right. He'd said that it must be boring as shit to be so right all the time. *Hardly, Gavin,* he thought cynically. He didn't feel right about anything. Obviously he wasn't doing right by his son.

Or by Liz. Not by a long shot was he doing right by Liz. How long could he put off doing something about that?

"Dr. Malloy?"

Thinking that Ms. Lester was bringing the long-awaited, high-octane coffee, he kept his back to the door. "Just set it on the desk, please."

"There's someone here to see you." Dean swiveled his chair around. "Sergeant Curtis from CIB asked for a minute of your time," the secretary told him. "Is it all right if he comes in?"

"Certainly." He'd met the detective only once, but he'd seemed like a stand-up kind of guy. Dean knew that he was a hardworking and well-respected member of the Austin PD. He stood up as Curtis walked in. "Good morning, Sergeant Curtis."

"Just plain Curtis. That's what everybody calls me. Do you prefer Doctor or Lieutenant?"

"How about Dean?" They met in the center of the office and shook hands.

"Is this a bad time?" Curtis asked. "I apologize for barging in on you unannounced, but this might turn out to be important."

"No problem. Coffee is on the way."

"Make that coffee for three. I'm not alone." Curtis stepped back into the open doorway and motioned someone forward.

Despite her sunglasses, Paris feared that her expression was no less revealing than Dean's.

He appeared to be as dumbfounded as she'd been a few moments ago when she read his name on the office door she was about to enter, unaware, unprepared, unbolstered, and unable to stop the inevitable.

He gaped at her for several seconds before managing to articulate a startled, "Paris?"

Curtis divided a surprised look between them.

"Should I bring more cups, Dr. Malloy?"

That from the secretary.

Dean's gaze remained fixed on Paris as he replied, "Please, Ms. Lester."

The secretary withdrew, leaving Paris, Dean, and the detective standing frozen in an awkward tableau like actors who had forgotten their lines. Finally Curtis placed his hand beneath her elbow and nudged her forward. Unwillingly she went farther into the office, into Dean's space.

And like any space Dean had ever occupied, he dominated it. Not just physically, with his above-average height and broad shoulders, but with the strength of his personality. Immediately one sensed that this was a man of principle, unshakable conviction, and unwavering determination. He could be your staunchest ally or your most feared adversary.

Paris had experienced him as both.

Her throat had constricted, as though every blood vessel leading from her heart had converged there. The oxygen in the room seemed insufficient. She was breathing with difficulty while striving to appear perfectly composed.

Dean wasn't doing so well either. When it became obvious that shock had robbed him of manners, Curtis motioned Paris into the nearest chair. That snapped Dean out of his daze. "Uh, yeah, please, sit. Both of you."

As they were taking their seats, Curtis said, "I'm not a

detective for nothing. I gather you two know each other."

She relied on her voice to earn her living, but it had deserted her. She left it to Dean to do the talking.

"From Houston," he said. "Years ago. I was with the PD and Paris . . ."

He looked at her expectantly, leaving her no option but to take up the explanation. "I was a reporter for one of the television stations."

Curtis raised his pale eyebrows in surprise. "Television? I assumed you'd always been on radio."

She glanced at Dean, then shook her head. "I moved from TV to radio."

Curtis murmured an acknowledgment that said he understood the transition when clearly he didn't understand at all.

"Excuse me." Ms. Lester came in carrying a tray. As she set it on Dean's desk, she asked, "Cream and sugar, anyone?"

They all declined. She filled three mugs from a stainless-steel carafe, then asked Dean if there would be anything else. He shook his head and thanked her.

Curtis watched her leave. When he turned back around he remarked, "I'm impressed. They don't spring for personal assistants in CIB."

"What?" Dean looked at him with confusion, then at the empty doorway. "Oh, Ms. Lester. She's not my personal assistant. She just . . . She's just very efficient. Treats everybody over here like that."

"Over here" referred to the annex next door to the main building of police headquarters. It was accessible through a connecting parking garage, which was the route Paris and Curtis had taken. The detective didn't seem to buy Dean's explanation for the secretary's attention any more than Paris did, but he didn't comment on it further.

Paris wrapped both hands around the steaming mug of coffee, grateful for the warmth it provided. Dean took a gulp of his that probably blistered his tongue.

Curtis said, "I had no idea that I would be reuniting two long-lost friends."

"Paris didn't know about my transfer here," Dean said, watching her closely. "Or if she did—"

"I didn't. I assumed you were still in Houston."

"No."

"Hmm."

Curtis filled the ensuing gap in conversation. "Up until Dr. Malloy joined us, we used civilians and paid them a consulting fee. But for a long time, we'd been needing and wanting a psychologist on staff, a member of the department, someone with experience and training as a cop as well as a psychologist. Early this year, the funding was finally approved and we were lucky enough to lure Dr. Malloy here."

"How nice." She included both of them in her perfunctory smile.

After another short silence, Dean cleared his throat again and addressed the detective. "You mentioned a matter that could be important."

Curtis sought a more comfortable position in his chair. "Are you familiar with Ms. Gibson's radio program?"

"I listen to it every night."

Her head came up quickly and she looked at Dean with surprise. Their eyes connected for several seconds before he turned back to Curtis.

"Then you know she takes call-in requests and such," the detective said. Dean nodded. "Last night, she received a call that disturbed her. With cause." Curtis went on to explain the nature of Valentino's call, then concluded by saying, "I thought you might take a listen and give us your professional opinion."

"I'll be glad to. Let's hear it."

Curtis had brought the cassette player with him. He set it on the desk, rewound the tape, and after several false starts for which he apologized, her voice filled the taut silence: *This is Paris.*

By now she knew the dialogue word for word. As it played, she stared into her coffee mug, but in her peripheral vision she observed Dean. Individual parts of him. All of him. Surreptitiously she looked at his hands resting on the edge of his desk, fingers laced. He was slowly rubbing his thumbs together, and that, just that, caused a quiver deep in her belly.

Only once did she allow herself to look at his face. He'd been gazing into near space, but he must have felt her eyes on him because he focused on her sharply. His eyes still had the capability of making her feel like a butterfly pinned to a corkboard.

At one time, years ago, it had been thrilling to be looked at with that kind of intensity. Now it only made her remember things that should have been long forgotten. It resurrected sensations and emotions she had tried to bury and, until a few minutes ago, thought she had. She returned her gaze to her coffee mug.

When the tape ended, Dean asked if he could have a duplicate made.

"Of course," Curtis replied.

Dean ejected the tape and left the office only long enough to dispatch Ms. Lester on the errand. When he returned, Curtis said, "So you don't think this guy is just blowing smoke?"

"I want to listen to the recording several more times, but my first impression is that it's worrisome at the very least. Ever get a call like this before, Paris?"

She shook her head. "Listeners have reported UFOs, terrorist infiltration, asbestos in their attics. One night a woman called to tell me she had a snake in her bathtub and asked if I knew how to tell if it was poisonous. I get at least one proposal of marriage a week. I've had one offer of donor sperm. Hundreds of obscene propositions. But nothing like this. This . . . this *feels* different."

"Although he's called you before."

"A man identifying himself as Valentino calls periodically. I believe this is the same man, but I can't swear to it."

"Do you think he's someone you know?"

She hesitated before answering. "Honestly? I couldn't sleep last night for thinking about that. But I don't recognize the voice, and I believe I would."

"You would have an ear for voices," Dean said thoughtfully. "But it sounds to me as though he's trying to disguise his."

"To me, too."

"So it *could* be someone you know."

"I suppose. But I can't think of anyone who would play such a horrible prank."

"Have you recently made someone angry?"

"Not that I know of."

"Exchanged words?"

"I don't recall an incident like that."

"Have you said anything that would come across as an affront? To a coworker. Bank teller. Waiter. Grocery sacker. The guy who dries your windows at the car wash."

"No," she snapped. "I don't make a habit of provoking people."

Ignoring her annoyance, he pressed on. "Have you quarreled with a boyfriend? Ended a relationship? Broken someone's heart?"

She glared at him for several ponderous moments, then shook her head.

Serving as a tactful referee in a conflict he didn't understand, Curtis coughed behind his fist. "Couple of rookies, Griggs and Carson, handled this last night," he told Dean. "They were going to check out the radio station personnel first thing this morning. I'll follow up with them right now, see if they've learned anything. Excuse me."

Before she could protest—and how could she?—Curtis pulled his cell phone from the holster clipped to his belt and left the office.

Instead of warming her hands, the ceramic coffee mug had grown cold within them. She leaned forward and placed it on the edge of Dean's desk, giving the mug and the surface of the desk more focus than either warranted.

Unable to avoid it any longer, she looked at him. "I didn't plan this, Dean. When I came here this morning, I had no idea . . . I didn't know you were in Austin now."

"I could have told you at Jack's funeral. You wouldn't talk to me."

"No, I wouldn't."

"Why not?"

"It would have been inappropriate."

Leaning toward her, he said, softly but angrily, "After seven years?"

Jack had been the first to say that nobody could get to Dean the way she could. She seemed to be the only person on the planet with a knack for gouging a chink in his rigid self-control.

Still sounding angry, he said, "I thought the sunglasses

were only for the funeral. Have you still got—"

"I'm not going to talk about this, Dean. I'd leave if I could. If I'd known who Sergeant Curtis was bringing me to see—"

"You'd have turned tail and run. That's your MO, isn't it?"

Before she could form a reply, Curtis returned. "They're checking out the janitor, Marvin Patterson. Nothing solid so far. There appears to be some confusion that they're trying to sort through. Should have some info soon. Stan Crenshaw . . ." Here he paused and looked at Paris. "He's related to the station's owner?"

"He's Wilkins Crenshaw's nephew."

"A nepotistic hiring?"

"To be sure," she said candidly. "Stan does as little as possible and isn't very good at what little he does. His laziness is irritating and often inconvenient for those of us who work with him, but on a personal level we get along. Besides, it couldn't have been either him or Marvin, even if one of them would do such a thing. They were in the building when the call came in."

"Telephones being the high-tech gadgets they are these days, I've got the department's electronics wizard working on that angle. Officers are also talking to the people who work in the nearby pharmacy, seeing if they can pick up something there. Either an employee or a customer who's got a fixation on you. But . . ." He paused to tug on his ear. "We don't actually have the commission of a crime here. Just the threat of one."

"It's a serious threat."

"Right," the detective conceded thoughtfully. "Valentino said he heard the woman talking about him on your show. Do you remember a call like the one he describes?"

"Not off the top of my head. It must have been fairly recent, though, and it was a call that I played on the air. That narrows it down considerably. But I never would have told a caller to 'dump' someone."

"He could've been lying about that," Dean said. She and Curtis looked at him for clarification. "The call from the girlfriend could be an invention to justify—even to himself—what he plans to do to her."

It was a grim surmise. During their reflective silence, Ms. Lester returned with the original tape and the requested duplication. Dean played it again. "Something really bothers me," he said when it ended. "He refers to 'girls,' not women."

"Diminishing a female's status," Curtis remarked.

"In his estimation, it does. That gives us a clue into this guy's mind-set. His basic dislike and mistrust of women comes through loud and clear. If I had to profile him based on no more than this conversation, I'd categorize him as an anger-retaliator rapist."

Apparently Curtis was acquainted with the clinical term. "He's angry with women in general over real or perceived injustices."

"Yes. Possibly a result of sexual abuse, even incest. A dangerous motivation," Dean said. "Sex is his method of punishment. That usually translates to violent rape. If he wants to make his victim bleed, as he told Paris, then he'll have no qualms about killing her." His lips formed a grim line, which expressed the apprehension that all were feeling. "Another thing, the only other Valentino I ever heard of was Rudolph."

"The silent-film star," Paris said.

"Right. And his best-known film was *The Sheik*."

"In which he kidnaps and seduces, rather forcibly, a young woman." She knew the movie. She and Jack had seen it at a classic-film festival. "Do you think that's why he's using that name?"

"It could be a coincidence, but I'm not prepared to dismiss it as such." He thought about it only a second longer. "In fact, Curtis, I'm not prepared to dismiss any of this. My recommendation is that you take him at his word."

The detective agreed with a somber nod. "Unfortunately, I agree."

"I'd like to work with you on the case."

"I welcome your input. We'll take Valentino's threat seriously until it proves to be a hoax."

"Or proves to be real," Paris added softly.

chapter seven

Judge Kemp granted the defense attorney's request for a thirty-minute recess to consult with his client, hopefully to urge him to accept a plea bargain that would end the trial and free up the judge's afternoon.

He used the half hour to retire to chambers and clip hairs from his nostrils with a tiny pair of silver scissors. He used a mirror with a magnifying power of five times actual size. Nevertheless, it was a delicate procedure. The sudden ringing of his cell phone almost cost him a punctured septum.

A bit irritably, he answered his wife's call.

"Janey's not in her room," she stated without preamble. "She hasn't been there all night."

"You told me she was in when we got home."

"I thought she was because I could hear the radio through her door. It was still on this morning. I thought that was odd, because you know what a late riser she is, but I figured she was sleeping through it.

"I knocked on her door around ten. I wanted to take her to that new tearoom for lunch. That would be something we could do together. And it's a lovely little place, really. Bea and I were there last week and they have an exceptional gazpacho."

"Marian, I'm in recess."

Reigned in, she continued, "She didn't answer my

knock. At quarter to eleven, I decided to go in and wake her. Her room was empty and the bed hadn't been slept in. Her car isn't in the garage and none of the help has seen her."

"Maybe she got up early, made her bed, and left the house."

"And maybe the sky will fall this afternoon."

She was right. It was an absurd assumption. Janey had never made a bed in her life. Her refusal to do so was one of the reasons she'd been sent home from summer camp the one and only time they had ignored her protests and insisted she go.

"When did you last see her?"

"Yesterday afternoon," Marian replied. "She'd been lying out by the pool for hours. I persuaded her to come indoors. She's going to ruin her skin. She refuses to wear sunscreen. I've tried to tell her, but of course she won't listen. She says sunscreen is the stupidest thing she's ever heard of because it defeats the purpose.

"And, Baird, I really think you should say something to her about sunbathing topless. I realize it's her own back-yard, but there are always workmen around here doing one project or another, and I refuse to allow them a free peep show. It's bad enough she wears a thong, which, if you ask me, looks not only distasteful and unladylike, but terribly uncomfortable."

This time she stopped herself from going off on a tangent. "Anyway, yesterday I coaxed her to come inside during the hottest part of the day. I reminded her that we were going to the awards dinner and that she was restricted to the house. She flounced upstairs without speaking to me, slammed her door, and locked it. Apparently, she left last night sometime after we did, and she hasn't been home since."

He hadn't noticed that Janey's car was missing because he'd left his out front overnight, not parked in the garage. The next time he grounded Janey he would remember to confiscate her car keys. Not that that would stop her from sneaking out of the house and meeting up with those wild friends of hers, whose influence was doubtless the cause of her misbehavior.

"Did you call her cell phone?"

"I get her voice mail. I've left repeated messages."

"Have you checked with her friends?"

"Several of them, but none claims to have seen her last night. Of course, they could be lying to cover for her."

"What about that tart, that Melissa she's been spending so much time with?"

"She's in Europe with her parents."

His secretary knocked softly, then poked her head in and told him that everyone was back in the courtroom.

"Listen, Marian, I'm sure she's just punishing us for punishing her. She wants to give you a scare, and she's succeeding. She'll turn up. It's not as if this is the first time she's stayed out all night."

The last time Janey had failed to come home, she'd come close to being booked into the Travis County jail for public lewdness. She and a group of friends had availed themselves of a hotel's outdoor hot tub. Guests had complained of noise. When hotel security officers checked on the nature of the disturbance, they discovered a bubbling cauldron of young people in varying degrees of drunkenness and nakedness, engaging in all manner of sexual activity.

His daughter was among the drunkest. She was definitely the most naked, according to the Austin policeman who had personally fished her out of the water and separated her from the young man with whom she was coupled.

He had wrapped her in a blanket before transporting her home rather than to jail. He'd done it as a favor to the judge, not out of kindness toward the girl who had hurled invectives at him when he delivered her to her parents' doorstep.

The officer had been thanked with a hundred-dollar bill, which had tacitly bought his promise to exclude Janey's name from the incident report.

"Thank God the media didn't get wind of that story," Marian said now, reading the judge's mind. "Can you imagine the damage your reputation would have suffered?" She sniffed delicately and asked, "What are you going to do, Baird?" Thereby effectually dumping the problem into his lap.

"I'm in court all day. I haven't got time to deal with Janey."

"Well, you can't expect me to drive all over Austin looking for her. I'd feel like a dogcatcher. Besides, you're the one with the contacts."

As well as the hundred-dollar bills, he thought sourly. Over the last few years, he'd liberally doled out C-notes to ensure that his daughter's shenanigans remained a private matter.

"I'll see what I can do," he grumbled. "But when she does reappear—as I'm certain she will—don't forget to page me. I'll have my pager on vibrate if I'm in court. Punch in three threes. Then I'll know she's at home and won't waste anyone's time looking for her."

"Thank you, dear. I knew I could depend on you to handle this."

Curtis invited Dean to join him for lunch and he accepted, but not naively. He figured the detective was after background information on Paris. He could hardly blame Curtis for being curious, especially after the charged atmosphere they'd created in his office this morning.

He wouldn't give him anything, nothing that Curtis couldn't learn for himself by reading a published bio, but it would be interesting to watch the detective in action.

They were on their way down the steps in front of the building when Curtis was hailed from behind. The young uniformed cop who had called after him had just emerged from the glass doors. He offered a breathless apology.

"I hate to hold you up, Sergeant Curtis."

"We're only going to lunch. Do you know Dr. Malloy?"

"Only by reputation. I'm a little late welcoming you to the Austin PD. Eddie Griggs." He extended his hand. "A pleasure, sir."

"Thank you," Dean said as they shook hands. "You two take your time, I'll wait over here in the shade."

"I don't think Sergeant Curtis will mind you hearing this, seeing as how you're working with him on that Paris Gibson call. That's what this is about. Well, sorta. Indirectly."

"Let's all get in the shade," Curtis suggested.

They moved closer to the building to take advantage of the sliver of shadow it cast on the blazing sidewalk. Traffic whizzed past on nearby Interstate 35, but the rookie made himself heard.

"You issued a heads-up memo?" he said to Curtis. "About missing persons reports?"

"That's right."

"Well, sir . . . Judge Baird Kemp?"

"What about him?"

"He's got a daughter. High school age. Wild as a

March hare. Every now and then she gets a little too wild and crosses the line. She's real well known by cops on patrol after midnight."

He glanced around, checking to see if anyone entering or exiting the building was within hearing distance. "The judge is real generous to any officer who takes her home, keeps her out of jail and her name out of print."

"I get the picture," the detective said.

"So today," Griggs continued, "the judge called in a special request to some of his friends on the force. Seems that Janey—that's her name—didn't come home last night. Everyone's been asked to be on the lookout, and if she's spotted, the judge would be very appreciative to the officer who brought her home."

Dean hadn't yet met the judge, but he knew him by name. One of his first duties in Austin had been to try to talk a prisoner into helping the police apprehend his partner in crime, who, by comparison, was the more evil of the two and was still at large.

The prisoner had refused to cooperate. "I'm not giving them shit, man."

"Them," as opposed to "you," because Dean had placed himself on the prisoner's side, becoming his friend, sympathizer, and confidant. The good cop.

"My trial was rigged! Fuckin' rigged," the prisoner ranted. "You hear what I'm saying, man? That judge swayed the jury. Smug motherfucker."

His regard for his trial judge didn't differ from that of most convicted criminals. They rarely had a kind word for the robed individual who, with a final bang of the gavel, sealed their bleak futures.

Eventually Dean got information from the prisoner that resulted in his partner's arrest, but the man had maintained his low opinion of Judge Kemp, and, based on what Griggs had just told them, Dean thought it might have been justified.

Curtis said, "In this county alone, there could be a hundred teenagers who didn't come home last night, and whose current whereabouts are unknown to their parents. And that would be a conservative estimate."

Dean was thinking of his own teenager, who had alarmed his mother on more than one occasion by not returning home until well into the next day. "I agree. It's too soon to jump to conclusions about one unaccounted-for girl, especially if she makes a habit of staying out."

"Judge Kemp would shit a brick if his 'special request' became an all-points bulletin," Curtis remarked, his distaste showing. "All the same, thanks for telling us about this, Griggs. Good follow-up and good hustle. How come you came in so early today?"

"Putting in overtime, sir. Besides, I hoped I could, you know, help Paris Gibson. She was pretty shook up last night."

"I'm sure she will appreciate your diligence."

Curtis's statement was made tongue in cheek. Apparently, he'd noticed the same thing Dean had—the kid was smitten with Paris.

"Let's give Miss Janey Kemp a few more hours to sober up and find her way home before we link her to Ms. Gibson's caller," Curtis said.

"Yes, sir." The young policeman's manner was so militarily correct, Dean almost expected him to salute. "Have a good lunch, sir. Dr. Malloy."

Curtis continued down the sidewalk, but Dean hung back, sensing that Griggs still had something on his mind. If it concerned Paris, he wanted to know what it was. "Excuse me, Griggs? If something's nagging at you, we'd like to hear it."

It was clear the rookie didn't want to step on the toes of a detective with rank or an officer with an alphabet soup of degrees behind his name and a Dr. in front of it. All the same, he seemed relieved that Dean had invited him to speak his mind.

"It's just that this girl goes looking for trouble, sir." He lowered his voice to a confidential pitch. "One of our undercover narcs at the high school? He says she's great looking and knows it. A . . . a real babe. Says she's made moves on him that almost made him forget he was a badge." Griggs's ears had turned red. Even his scalp was blushing through his buzz haircut.

Hoping to relax the younger man, Dean quipped, "I hate when that happens. One of the reasons I never worked undercover."

Griggs grinned as though happy to learn that Dean was just a guy after all. "Yeah, well, what I'm saying is, she might've placed herself in a situation where something bad could happen."

"Flirted with danger and got more than she bargained for?" Curtis asked.

"Something like that, sir. From what I know of her, she does what she wants to, when she wants to, and doesn't account to anybody. Not even to her folks. Perfect candidate to be slipped some Rohypnol. If she crossed paths with this Valentino, and he's done what he claims, nobody would know it for a while. And that could be bad."

Curtis asked if anyone had looked for Janey Kemp in places where she was known to hang out.

"Yes, sir. That's what the judge wanted done. Covertly, of course. Couple of intelligence officers are on it as well as the regular patrolmen. But it's summer, so the Sex Club meets outdoors more nights than not, and the meet-

ing place changes every few nights to keep narcs and parents—"

"Sex Club?" Dean looked over at Curtis for an explanation, but the detective shrugged. Both looked back at
Griggs.

Nervous again, the young officer shifted his weight
from one polished shoe to the other. "You don't know
about the Sex Club?"

Paris arrived home exhausted. This was normally the
time of day she was getting up. Customarily she ate
breakfast when everyone else was having lunch. Today
she was off her schedule. If she didn't sleep a few hours
this afternoon, she would be a zombie by sign-off time
tonight.

But after her unexpected reunion with Dean, sleep
was unlikely.

She made herself a peanut butter sandwich she didn't
really want and sat at the kitchen table, a napkin in her
lap, pretending it was an actual meal. As she ate, she
sorted her mail.

When she came to the pale blue, letter-sized envelope
with the familiar logo in the upper-left-hand corner, she
stopped her methodic chewing. She washed down the
bite of sandwich with a whole glass of milk, as though
fortifying herself for the contents of the envelope.

The three-paragraph letter was from the director of
Meadowview Hospital. Politely but firmly, in language
that could not be misunderstood, he requested that she
retrieve the personal belongings of former patient the
late Mr. Jack Donner.

"Since you haven't responded to my numerous
attempts to reach you by telephone," the letter read, "I
can only assume that you never received those messages.

Therefore, let this letter serve to notify you that Mr. Donner's belongings will be removed from the facility if you do not collect them."

Her deadline to comply was tomorrow. Tomorrow. And he meant it. The date was underlined.

While Jack was a patient at Meadowview, Paris had been on a first-name basis with everyone on staff, from the director to the custodian. This read like a letter to a stranger. He'd reached the limit of his patience with her, no doubt because she had ignored his telephone messages.

She hadn't been back to the private nursing facility since the day Jack died inside room 203. In the six months since then, she hadn't had the wherewithal to return, not even to pick up his personal belongings. With very few exceptions, she'd gone to the hospital every day for seven years, but after leaving it that final day, she'd been unable to make herself return.

Her reluctance to do so wasn't entirely selfish. She didn't want to dishonor Jack by remembering him lying in that hospital bed, his limbs withering even though they were exercised every day by Meadowview's capable staff of physical therapists. He'd been no more self-sufficient than a baby, unable to speak anything except gibberish, unable to feed himself, unable to do anything except take up space and rely on dedicated health care professionals to tend to even his most personal needs.

That was the condition in which he'd lived—existed—the last seven years of his life. He deserved better than to be remembered like that.

She folded her arms on the table and laid her head on them. Closing her eyes, she envisioned Jack Donner as he'd been when she met him. Strong, handsome, vital, self-confident Jack . . .

*   *   *

"So you're the new one who's causing such a sensation."

He had spoken from behind her. When she faced him, her first impression was of the cockiness of his grin. Her assigned cubicle in the newsroom was barely large enough to turn around in. It was crammed with boxes that she was in the process of unpacking. Jack had pretended not to notice that he was contributing to the crowded conditions.

Coolly she repeated, " 'New *one.* ' "

"You're being talked about in the front offices. Don't force me to repeat what I've heard and risk a sexual harassment charge."

"I've just joined the news team, if that's what you mean."

"The 'award-winning' news team," he corrected, his grin stretching wider. "Don't you pay attention to our station's promos?"

"Are you in the promotions department?"

"No, I head the official host committee. In fact, I *am* the official host committee. It's my job to welcome all newcomers."

"Thank you. I consider myself welcomed. Now, if you'll—"

"Actually I'm in sales. Jack Donner." He stuck out his hand. They shook.

"Paris Gibson."

"Good name. Stage or yours for real?"

"Mine for real."

"You want to go to lunch?"

His audacity didn't give offense. Instead it made her laugh. "No. I'm busy." She raised her arms to indicate the boxes surrounding her. "It'll take me all afternoon to get this stuff organized. Besides, we just met."

"Oh, right." As he mulled over that dilemma, he gnawed on his lower lip in a manner he probably knew was cute and endearing. Then he brightened. "Dinner?"

She didn't go to dinner with him that night. Or the next three times he asked. In the ensuing weeks she worked her tail off, covering as many stories as the assignments editor would give her. She vied for as much airtime as she could get, knowing that exposure was the only way to build audience recognition of her name, voice, and face.

She was aiming for the evening anchor spot. It might take her a year or two to get there. She had a lot to learn and much to prove, but she saw no reason to set her sights on anything lower than the top. So she was way too busy getting herself established in the Houston television market to accept dates.

And Jack Donner was way too confident that she would ultimately submit to his charm. He was all-American-boy handsome. His personality was engaging, his humor infectious. Every woman in the building, from the college interns to the grandmother who ran the accounting department, had a crush on him. Surprisingly, men liked him, too. He'd held the top sales record for several consecutive years, and it was no secret that he was being groomed for management.

"Upper management," he confided in her. "I want to be GM and then, who knows? One day I might own my own station."

He certainly had the ambition and charisma to achieve whatever he set out to do, and getting a date with her was his primary short-term goal. Finally he wore her down and she accepted.

On their first date, he took her to a Chinese restaurant. The food was dreadful and the service even worse, but he kept her laughing throughout the meal by creating histories for each of the dour wait staff. The more rice wine he drank, the funnier the stories became.

When he opened his fortune cookie, he whistled. "Wow, listen to this." He pretended to read. "Congratulations. After months of trying to seduce a certain lady, tonight you get lucky."

Paris broke open her cookie and pulled out the fortune. "Mine says, 'Disregard previous fortune.'"

"You won't sleep with me?"

She laughed at his crestfallen expression. "No, Jack, I won't sleep with you."

"You're sure?"

"I'm sure."

But after four months of dating, she did. After six months, everyone at the TV station acknowledged them as a couple. By Christmas Jack had asked her to marry him, and by New Year's Day she had accepted.

In February it snowed. Houston, where snow was as infrequent as the Hale-Bopp comet, ground to a halt, which meant that the news teams worked overtime to cover all the weather-related stories, from school closings, to shelter for the homeless, to the myriad hazards of icy roadways. Paris worked for sixteen hours straight, going in and out of the weather, riding in a drafty news van, drinking lukewarm coffee, meeting deadlines.

When she finally got home, Jack was in her kitchen stirring a pot of homemade soup. "If I never loved you before," she said, lifting the lid on the pot and taking a deep whiff, "I do now."

"I'd cook for you every night if you'd move in with me."

"No."

"Why not?"

"We've been over this at least a thousand times, Jack," she said wearily as she pulled off soggy boots.

He knelt down to massage her frozen toes. "Let's go over it again. I keep forgetting your lame excuses. As you know, my dick is longer than my attention span. And aren't you glad?"

She withdrew her foot from between his warm hands. The massage felt entirely too good to be getting while they were having this oft-repeated argument.

"Until we're married, I'm maintaining my independence." Seeing that he was about to press his argument, she added, "And if you keep bugging me about it, I'll postpone the wedding for another six months."

"You're a hard woman, Paris Gibson soon-to-be Donner."

They ate their soup and finished the bottle of wine Jack had opened before her arrival. He didn't even suggest that he spend the night, and she was grateful for his sensitivity to her exhaustion.

As she bade him good night at her door, she noticed that the inch and a half of snow that had immobilized the city was already beginning to melt. All that ass-busting news coverage was made history by a few degrees on the thermometer.

"Thank God tomorrow is Saturday," she said with a sigh as she leaned against the doorjamb. "I'm going to sleep all day."

"Just wake up in time for tomorrow night."

"What's tomorrow night?"

"You're meeting my best man."

Recently he'd told her that his best friend from college was moving back to Houston after getting an advanced degree in something, from an out-of-state university somewhere that right now she couldn't remember. She knew only that Jack was very excited to have his friend returning to the area and couldn't wait to introduce them.

"How's he liking the Houston PD?" she asked around a wide yawn.

"Still too early to tell, he says, but he thinks he's going to like it. We're gonna try to scare up a game of basketball at the gym while you're snoozing the day away. We'll pick you up around seven tomorrow evening."

"I'll be ready." She was about to close the door when she called after him, "I'm sorry, Jack, what's his name again?"

"Dean. Dean Malloy."

Paris sat up, gasping.

She was in her own kitchen, but it took her a moment to orient herself. Revery had given way to dreaming. She'd been in a deep sleep. The angle of the sunlight coming through the window had changed. Her arms were tingling from the lack of circulation that lying on them had caused. Shaking them only heightened the prickling sensation. With a numb hand, she reached for the ringing telephone—the cause of her waking up so abruptly.

Out of habit, she said, "This is Paris."

chapter eight

"When was the last time you saw a dentist, Amy?"

"I don't remember. A few years maybe."

Dr. Brad Armstrong gave his patient a stern frown. "That's much too long between checkups."

"I'm scared of dentists."

"Then you haven't been to the right one." He winked at her. "Until now."

She giggled.

"You're lucky I've found only one cavity. It's small, but it needs to be filled."

"Will it hurt?"

"Hurt? I'll have you know that in this office, pain is a four-letter word." He patted her shoulder. "My job is to fix your tooth. Your job is to lie back and relax while I'm doing it."

"The Valium sure helps. I'm already getting sleepy."

"It doesn't take long."

His staff had cleared it with Amy's mother before giving her a low-dosage tranquilizer to relieve her anxiety and make the procedure less stressful for both patient and doctor. Her mother was coming back in a while to drive her home. In the meantime, he was free to look his fill as she drifted into la-la land.

According to her chart she was fifteen, but she was well formed. She had good legs. Her short skirt revealed smooth, tan thighs and muscled calves.

He loved summer. Summer meant skin. Already he dreaded the onset of fall and winter when women gave up sandals for boots, and bare legs for opaque tights. Skirts got longer, and shoulders bared in the summer by halters and narrow straps were covered with sweaters. The only good thing about sweaters was that sometimes they clung, and the suggestion of what was underneath could be wonderfully enticing.

His patient took a deep breath that shifted the paper bib to one side of her chest. He was tempted to lift it and look at her breasts. If she protested, he could always say he was returning the bib to its proper place, nothing more.

But he restrained himself. His nurse might come in, and, unlike his patient, she wasn't loopy on Valium.

He surveyed the girl's legs again. Relaxation had caused them to roll outward, leaving several inches of space between her knees. The stretchy fabric of her skirt fit like a second skin. It molded to the dip between her thighs and delineated the vee. Was she wearing panties? he wondered. The possibility that she wasn't inflamed him.

He also wondered if she was a virgin. Beyond the age of fourteen, few were. Statistically, the odds were good that she had been with a man. She would know what to expect from a man who was aroused. She wouldn't be that shocked if—

"Dr. Armstrong?" His assistant appeared, interrupting the daydream. "Is she ready for the deadening?"

He never let his patients even hear the word "shot."

He came off the low stool on which he'd been sitting, pretending to study the patient's X rays. "Yes. Go ahead. Let's give it ten minutes."

"I'll have everything ready."

He disposed of his latex gloves and went into his private office, closing the door behind him. His skin was feverish. His heartbeat was accelerated. If not for his lab coat, his assistant would have seen his erection. If not for her timely interruption, he might have made a dreadful mistake. And he couldn't afford to make another.

That last time, though—now, that had *not* been his fault.

That girl had been in his chair three times within two months, and with each visit she had become a little friendlier. Friendlier, hell, she'd flirted with him outright. She had known exactly what she was doing. The way she smiled up at him provocatively whenever she was reclined in his chair—hadn't that practically been an invitation to fondle her?

Then when he did, she had raised such a hue and cry it had brought his partners, all the hygienists, and most of the patients running down the hallway and into the treatment room where she stood screaming accusations at him.

If she had been the twenty-five-year-old she appeared to be, instead of the minor she was, those accusations would have been dismissed. As it was, they'd been believed, and he'd been invited to leave the practice. The following morning when he arrived at the office, his partners had met him at the door with a severance agreement that included a check amounting to three months' earnings. Under the circumstances, they considered that fair. Good-bye and good luck.

Sanctimonious pricks.

But the repercussions hadn't stopped there. The girl's parents, incensed that a normal, heterosexual male had responded to the inviting signals transmitted by their sexpot of a daughter, had filed charges of indecency with a child. As if she was a child. As if she hadn't asked for it. As if she hadn't liked having his hand slide between her thighs.

He was dragged into court like a criminal and, on the advice of his inept attorney, forced to apologize to the conniving little bitch. He'd pled guilty to the humiliating allegations in order to receive a "light sentence" of mandatory counseling and probation.

The judge's ruling was much lighter than Toni's, however. "This is the last time, Brad," she'd warned.

Since he had dodged incarceration, wouldn't you assume a celebration was in order? Oh, no. His wife had other plans, which included beating the subject of his "addiction" to death.

"I can't go through another ordeal like this," she told him. Then for hours she'd harped on his "destructive pattern of behavior."

Okay, there had been a few other incidents, like the one at the clinic where he'd first practiced. He had shown a dental hygienist some photographs. It was a joke, for godsake! How was he to know she was a Bible beater who probably thought babies should be born with fig leafs attached to their belly buttons. She had spread such vicious gossip about him, he'd left of his own accord. But Toni still held him responsible.

Finally she had concluded by saying, "Let me make this even clearer, Brad. I *won't* suffer through another ordeal like this. I won't allow our children to suffer through it. I love you," she declared tearfully. "I don't want to divorce you. I don't want to break up our home and family. But I will leave you if you don't get help and control your addiction."

Addiction. So what if he had a strong sex drive? Was that an *addiction?* She'd made him sound like a pervert.

He wasn't a complete fool, though. He knew he had to adapt to the world in which he lived. If society was going to be puritanical, then he must adjust to the accepted rules. He must walk the straight and narrow as defined by church and state, and they were in league on this issue. One misstep beyond their silly boundaries of so-called decency, and you were not only a sinner but an outlaw.

Even the mildest flirtation with another patient could cost him his career. It had taken him eight months to land this job in Austin, long after the severance check had been spent and the savings accounts depleted.

This clinic wasn't as prosperous as the previous one. His current partners weren't as specialized and renowned as his former associates. But the job paid the mortgage. And his family liked Austin, where no one knew the reason for their move here.

For weeks after that courtroom nightmare, Toni had flinched each time he touched her. She had continued sharing a bed with him, although he figured that pretense had been for the kids' benefit.

Eventually she had allowed him to hold her and kiss her, and then, after his group therapy leader had given him a gold star for the progress he'd made toward "healing," she had resumed having sex. She had seemed reasonably content . . . until a few nights ago when he'd been careless enough to stay out all night.

He'd devised a plausible story, and she might have continued believing it if he hadn't been so late getting home last night. The story about the tax seminar didn't fly. He had gone to the seminar and signed in, so there would be a record of his attendance. But he had never intended to stay and had left after the first boring hour.

He'd caught hell for it this morning. Toni shooed the

kids from the breakfast table and sent them upstairs to do chores. Then, without any warning, she demanded, "Where were you last night, Brad?"

No lead-in, just that angry, surprise attack that immediately pissed him off. "You know where I was."

"I was up until after two o'clock this morning and you weren't home yet. No tax seminar lasts that long."

"It didn't. It was over around eleven. I met a few guys there. We went out for a beer. Realized we were hungry. Ordered food."

"What guys?"

"I don't know. Guys. We exchanged first names. Joe, I think it was, is an executive at Motorola. Grant or Greg, something like that, owns three paint and body shops. The other one—"

"You're lying," she exclaimed.

"Well, thanks for giving me the benefit of the doubt."

"You haven't earned it, Brad. I tried to go into your office last night. The door was locked."

He stood up, pushing his chair away from the table so angrily it scraped loudly against the floor. "Big deal. The door was locked. I didn't lock it. One of the kids must have. But why were you going in there in the first place? To see what you could find to hold against me? To snoop? To spy?"

"Yes."

"At least you admit it." He expelled a long breath, as though taking time out to get a grip. "Toni, what's wrong with you lately? Every time I leave the house, you put me through a royal grilling."

"Because you're leaving the house more often and you stay away for long periods of time that you can't, or won't, account for."

"Account for? What, I'm not an adult? I'm not

allowed to come and go of my own free will? I have to check i with you if I decide to stop for a beer? When I need to take a piss, shall I call you first and ask permission?"

"It won't work, Brad," she'd said with maddening composure. "I'm not going to let you turn the tables and make me feel bad for asking why you were out until early this morning. Go to work. You're going to be late." That had been her exit line. She had stalked from the kitchen, her spine as straight as if she had a girder up her ass.

He'd let her go. He knew her. Once she reached that stage of righteous indignation, he could grovel for hours and nothing he said or did would appease her. She would stay frosty for days. Eventually she would thaw, but in the meantime . . .

Jesus! Was it any wonder that he wasn't eager to go home tonight? Who wanted to cozy up to a Popsicle? If he erred tonight, Toni was to blame, not him.

Thankfully he had discovered a new outlet for his "addiction." Sex in all its variations was his for the taking. Thinking about what was now available to him, he smiled.

Reaching beneath his lab coat, he stroked himself. He liked to stay semierect, so throughout the day he took sneak peeks at the photographs he kept locked in his credenza drawer, or, if he felt safe from intrusion, he visited favorite websites. Only a minute or two would do the trick. Some people drank coffee for a quick pick-me-up. He'd discovered something a hell of a lot more stimulating than caffeine.

It would be a long afternoon, but the anticipation alone was delicious.

Hurry, nightfall.

chapter nine

When Paris entered the room where they were waiting for her, Dean and the other two men stood up. They had convened in a small meeting room within the CIB that was ordinarily used to interview witnesses or question suspects. It was cramped quarters but confidentiality was assured.

Curtis pulled a chair from beneath the table for Paris. She nodded her thanks to him and sat down. She was still wearing sunglasses. Dean could barely detect her eyes behind the dark gray lenses. He hated to speculate as to why she never removed them.

"I hope it wasn't too inconvenient for you to come back downtown," Curtis said to her.

"I got here as quickly as I could."

In unison they all looked at the wall clock. It was coming up on two P.M. None needed to be reminded that twelve hours of Valentino's deadline had already expired.

The detective motioned to the third man in the room. "This is John Rondeau. John, Paris Gibson."

She leaned forward and extended her hand across the table. "Mr. Rondeau."

As they shook hands, he said, "A pleasure, Ms. Gibson. I'm a huge fan."

"I'm glad to hear that."

"I listen to you all the time. It's a real honor to meet you."

Dean drew a bead on the officer, whom he had met only minutes before Paris's arrival. Rondeau was young, trim, and good looking. A weight lifter, from the looks of his biceps. His face was lit up like a Christmas tree as he gazed at Paris. Plainly, like the rookie Griggs, Rondeau was instantly infatuated with her.

Dean suspected that Sergeant Curtis was, too. They'd gone to lunch at Stubb's. The Austin landmark, famous for its barbecue, beer, and live music, was only a few blocks from police headquarters. They'd walked.

During the lunch period there was no band playing in the amphitheater beneath the live oaks out back, but hungry state capitol personnel and downtown office workers lined up by the dozens to order cuts of smoked meat slathered with fiery sauce.

Opting to not wait for a table, he and Curtis had ordered chopped beef sandwiches and had taken them out onto the wood porch, where they stood in the shade to eat.

Dean had expected Curtis to ask him about Paris, but he'd thought the detective's approach would be subtle. Instead Curtis had dug into his sandwich, then asked him bluntly, "What's with you and Paris Gibson? Old flames?"

Maybe it was Curtis's candor that made him such a crackerjack investigator. He caught suspects off guard. Striving for nonchalance, Dean took a bite of his sandwich before answering. "More like water under the bridge."

"Lots of water, I'm guessing."

Dean continued chewing.

"You don't want to talk about it?" the detective probed.

Dean wiped his mouth with a paper napkin. "I don't want to talk about it."

Curtis nodded as though to say, Fair enough. "You married?"

"No. You?"

"Divorced. Going on four years."

"Kids?"

"One of each. They live with their mother."

"Has your wife remarried?"

Curtis took a drink of iced tea. "I don't want to talk about it."

They'd left it at that and moved the conversation back to the case, which actually wasn't a case yet, but which they feared would become one. But now Dean knew that Curtis was single, and the detective never let pass an opportunity to treat Paris to some show of chivalry.

Paris elicited that kind of attention from men. In all the time he'd known her, he'd never seen her play the coquette. She didn't simper. She didn't flirt or deliberately draw attention to herself or dress provocatively. It wasn't anything she *did*. It was something she *was*.

One glance at her and you wished you had a long time to study her. Her figure wasn't voluptuous like Liz's. In fact, hers was rather angular and boyish, and she was taller than average. Her hair, light brown streaked with several shades of blond, always looked slightly mussed, which was certainly sexy, he supposed. But that alone wasn't enough to rouse male interest.

Maybe it was her mouth. Women got painful collagen injections to achieve that pout. Paris had come by it genetically. Or was it her eyes? God knows they were pretty damn spectacular. Blue and fathomless, they invited you to dive in and splash around, see if you could ever plumb their depths. Not that you could tell anything about her eyes now, hidden as they were behind the sunglasses.

Young John Rondeau didn't seem to mind, though. He was practically transfixed.

"Have you learned something else since this morning?" she asked.

"Yes, but we don't know how significant it is." She had posed the question to Curtis, but by answering, Dean forced her to look at him, which she had studiously avoided doing since she entered the room. "We're here to discuss its validity."

Curtis chimed in, "Rondeau works in our computer crimes unit."

"I don't understand," Paris said. "How do computer crimes relate to what you requested of me?"

"We'll get to that," the detective replied. "I know it appears to have no relevance, and maybe it doesn't."

"On the other hand," Dean said, "it could all tie in together. That's what we're trying to determine. Are those the cassettes?" He gestured at the canvas tote she had carried in along with her handbag.

"Yes. The Vox Pro holds one thousand minutes of recorded material."

"So when a call comes in, it's automatically recorded?" Curtis asked. "That's how you screen calls, keep people from shouting obscenities to your audience?"

She smiled. "Some have tried. That's why each call is recorded. I then have the option of saving it and playing it on the air, or deleting it."

"How do you transfer the recordings onto cassette?" Dean asked.

"It isn't easy. As a favor to me, one of the engineers figured out a way. Periodically, he dumps—his term, not mine—the recordings off the Vox Pro computer onto cassettes for me."

"Why?"

She shrugged self-consciously. "Nostalgia, maybe. The more interesting conversations could also be useful if I ever put together a demo tape."

"Well, whatever your reasons for saving them, I'm glad you have them now," Curtis told her.

"I hope you understand that you lose quality in the duplication process," she said. "These tapes won't be as clear as the original."

"Doesn't matter," Dean said. "Quality might become an issue later if a voice print becomes necessary. But right now all we want to know is if the call Valentino referenced was real or a fabrication.

"That's why we asked to hear the calls you received during the past week. If there *was* such a call, and if hearing it on your program lighted Valentino's fuse, then we need to trace that call to the woman who placed it."

"If it's not too late," she murmured.

Judging by the expressions around the table, everyone in the room echoed her grim thought.

"Can you remember a call similar to the one Valentino described?" Curtis asked her.

"Possibly. I've been thinking about it since our conversation this morning. I got a call three nights ago. As I was driving here, I listened to it on the cassette player in my car. I marked the cassette and cued the call."

Dean found the marked cassette among the others in the bag, inserted it into the machine, and pressed Play.

This is Paris.

Hi, Paris.

What's on your mind tonight, caller?

Well, see, I met this guy a few weeks ago. And we really hit it off. I mean, it's been hot, hot, hot between us. (A giggle.) Sorta exotic.

That's probably all the detail we need on a family show.

(Another giggle from the caller.) But I like being with other guys, too. So now he's getting jealous all the time. Possessive, you know?

Do you want to take the relationship to another level?

You mean like do I love him? Hell, no. The whole thing has been about fun. That's it.

Perhaps not to him.

Then that's his problem. I just don't know what to do about him.

If you feel that the relationship is constricting, you probably shouldn't be in it. My advice is to make the break as quick and painless as possible. It would be cruel to string him along when your heart is no longer in it.

Okay, thanks.

"That's all," Paris said. "She hung up."

Dean switched off the recorder. For several moments there was a heavy silence, then everyone began talking at once. Curtis pointed to Paris, giving her the floor.

"I was just going to say that this call may have absolutely no connection to Valentino. It was a rather silly conversation. I only put her on the air because she was so animated. I gathered from her voice that she was young. My audience are mostly baby boomers. I've wanted to expand it to include the younger crowd, so when a call from someone obviously younger comes in, I generally use it."

"Did you get the phone number?"

"I checked the Vox Pro. The caller ID said 'unavailable.'"

"Did other listeners respond to your conversation with her?"

"You'll hear a few on the tape. Several offered interesting advice on how she should handle the breakup. Others I thanked for calling but didn't put them on the air and deleted their calls from the Vox Pro.

"I don't remember talking to anyone else this week about a breakup, even off the air. But I talk to dozens of

people every night. My memory isn't one hundred percent."

"Do you mind if we keep these tapes for a while?"
Curtis asked.

"They're yours. I had duplicates made."

"I think I'll have someone listen to all—how many
hours is it?"

"Several, I'm afraid. I went back three weeks. That's fifteen nights on the air, but of course I delete more calls than
I save."

"I'll have someone listen, see if there's a similar call
that's slipped your mind."

"Did Valentino call in response?" Dean asked.

"That night, you mean? No. He always identifies himself by name. Last night was the first time I'd heard from
him in a while. I'm definite on that."

Curtis stood up. "Thank you, Paris. We appreciate
your help. I hope coming back downtown wasn't too
much of an imposition."

"I'm as concerned as you are."

Apparently, he intended to escort her out, but she
remained seated. Curtis hesitated. "Is there something
else?"

Dean knew why Paris was reluctant to leave. Her
news-gathering instinct had kicked in. She wanted the
full story and didn't want to stop until she had it. "I'm
guessing she'd like to know what's going on," he said.

"I would, yes," she said with a nod.

Curtis hedged. "It's really a police matter."

"For you it is. But it's a personal matter to me,
Sergeant. Especially if Valentino turns out to be someone
I know. I feel responsible."

"You're not," Dean said, speaking more sharply than
he intended. Everyone looked toward him. "If he's for

real, he's a psychopath. He would be doing something like this whether or not he talks to you on the radio."

Curtis agreed. "He's right, Paris. If this guy is wound as tight as he sounds, he would've snapped sooner or later."

Rondeau said, "You're just providing him with a forum, Ms. Gibson."

"And because of that, you're our only link to him." Dean looked over at Curtis where he still stood beside her chair. "That's why I think she has a right to know the leads we're following."

Curtis frowned, but he resumed his seat. Then he looked directly at Paris and, with his characteristic bluntness, stated, "We might have a missing girl."

"'Might'?"

Dean watched her while she listened to Curtis's summary of what Griggs had told them about Judge Baird Kemp's daughter. He already knew the facts, so he was able to tune them out and concentrate on Paris, who was hanging on every word.

Obviously she had cultivated a sizable radio audience, but he wondered if she missed her TV news reporting. Like greasepaint for a stage actor, didn't it get into a person's blood?

She'd been a natural, earning the viewers' confidence with her solid and impartial reporting. She'd been smart enough to know that if she was too cutesy or glamorous they would regard her as an airhead who had probably slept her way into her job. Taken to the other extreme, she would've been thought of as a ball-breaking bitch with penis envy.

Paris had struck the perfect balance. She had been as aggressive a reporter as any of her male counterparts, but without any sacrifice to her femininity. She could've taken her career as far as she chose to take it.

If only.

Her soft exclamation brought him back into the present. "This girl hasn't been seen or heard from for almost twenty-four hours, and her parents are just now becoming worried?"

Dean said, "Hard to believe, isn't it? They haven't formally notified the police, so Janey's disappearance isn't official. But there've been no other missing persons reported. It's a long shot, but it's a coincidence that Curtis and I thought we should investigate."

She quickly connected the dots. "And if it turned out that this caller was the judge's daughter—"

"That's why we asked for the tapes," Dean said. "Did she give you her name?"

"Unfortunately, no. You heard the recording. And the name doesn't ring a bell. If I'd recently heard the name Janey, or Kemp, which is more unusual, I think I would remember. Besides, isn't this a stretch? It's an awfully broad coincidence on which to base an investigation."

"We thought so, too. Until we heard about this Internet club. The Sex Club."

"The *what?*"

Rondeau came to life. "That's where I come in." He glanced at Curtis as if asking permission to continue.

Curtis shrugged. "Go ahead. It's not as if she couldn't find out for herself."

Rondeau launched into his description. "The website has been online for a couple of years. Janey Kemp was one of the . . . founders, I guess you'd say. It started out as a message board where local teens could communicate, more or less anonymously. Using only their user names and email addresses.

"Over time the messages got more explicit, the subject matter racier, until the purpose of it has evolved into what it is now, which is, basically, an Internet personals column. They flirt via cyberspace."

"Flirt?" Dean scoffed. "The messages they exchange are more like foreplay."

The younger cop said, "I didn't want to offend Ms. Gibson."

"She's a grown-up and this isn't Sunday school." Dean looked at her directly. "The Sex Club's sole purpose is to solicit sex. Kids post messages advertising what they've done and what they're willing to do with the right partner. If they want more privacy with someone, they enter chat rooms and talk dirty to each other. Here's a sample." He opened a folder and removed the sheet he'd printed off the computer in Curtis's office.

She scanned it, registering her dismay. When she looked up, she said, "But these are kids."

"High school mostly," Rondeau told her. "They congregate at a designated spot each night. It's a huge swap meet."

Curtis said, "Part of the fun, it seems, is trying to match individuals with their user names, see if you can figure out who's who."

"And if a couple who've been chatting over the Internet find each other, they have sex," Dean said.

"Or not," Rondeau said, correcting him. "Sometimes they don't like what they see. The other person doesn't live up to expectations. Or someone better comes along in the meantime. No one's obligated to follow through."

"The computer crime guys discovered the website," Curtis said, "and since most of the users are minors, they brought it to the attention of the child abuse unit, which investigates sex offenses against children and child pornography, which falls under the auspices of the CIB." He folded his arms across his stocky torso. "It's a bleed-over investigation, meaning we can put a lot of people on it."

"That's the good news," Rondeau said. "The bad news is that stopping it is virtually impossible."

Paris was shaking her head with incredulity. "Let me make sure I understand. Girls like Janey Kemp go to a designated place and meet up with strangers whom they've teased, via the Internet, into believing they'll have sex."

"Right," Rondeau said.

"Are they insane? Don't they realize the risk they're taking? If they meet their chat room partner, who turns out to be less than a Brad Pitt, and say, 'No thanks,' they're placing themselves at the mercy of a man whom they've inflamed and who is . . . disappointed, to say the least."

"They're hardly at anyone's mercy, Ms. Gibson," the young cop said quietly. "We're not talking nuns here. These are party girls. They frequently charge the men for their favors."

"They ask for money?"

"Not ask. Demand," Rondeau told them. "And they get it. Plenty of it."

This information stunned them into silence. Eventually Curtis said, "What troubles us, Paris, beyond the obvious, is that anybody who applies for membership in this so-called club gets it. Getting a password and access to this website requires only a few clicks of a mouse. That means any sexual predator, any deviate, would know where to go to look for his next victim."

"What's more," Dean said, "his victim would probably go with him willingly. He'd have to put forth very little effort."

"This is alarming whether or not it has a connection to Valentino," she said.

"And we're fighting a losing battle," Rondeau said. "We bust up the kiddie porn rings. But for each one that's busted, dozens more spring up and thrive. We work with the feds, with Operation Blue Ridge Thunder, a nationwide information network that deals specifically with Internet crimes against children. That's more than we can handle. Teenagers consensually exchanging dirty email is a low priority."

Curtis said, "It's like writing tickets for jaywalking, while across town, gang members are shooting each other."

"What about Janey's parents?" Paris asked. "Have they been made aware of this?"

"They've had trouble with her," Curtis replied. "She has a history of misbehavior, but even they probably don't know about all her activities. We didn't want to alert them to a possible connection between her unknown whereabouts and Valentino's call until we had more to go on. We were hoping your audiotape would shed some light."

"It doesn't shed much, does it?" she said. "I'm sorry."

After a discreet knock, the door was opened and another detective poked his head in. "Sorry to interrupt, Curtis. I have a message for you."

He excused himself and left the room.

Paris consulted her wristwatch. "Unless I can be of further help, I should be going."

Rondeau nearly broke his neck getting out of his chair and helping her with hers. "What time do you have to be at the radio station, Ms. Gibson?"

"Around seven-thirty. And please call me Paris."

"Do you have to do a lot of preparation ahead of time?"

"I select the music myself and prepare my log—that's

the order in which songs are played. Another department, called 'Traffic,' has already logged the commercials.

"However, a lot of my programming occurs spontaneously. I never know what song someone from the audience is going to request. But I can insert that song into the log instantly, because we have a computerized library of music."

"Are you ever nervous when you go on the air?"

She laughed and shook her head, making the shaggy hairdo even shaggier and more attractive. "I've been doing it too long to get butterflies."

"Do you operate the equipment all by yourself?"

"If you're referring to the control board, yes. And I man my own telephone lines. I turned down having a producer. I like being a one-woman show."

"When you started, did you have to learn a lot of technical stuff?"

"Some, but, honestly, you probably know much more about the workings of a computer than I know about the physics of radio waves."

The implied compliment brought a silly grin to his face. "Does working alone ever get boring?"

"Not really, no. I like the music. And the callers keep me on my toes. Each broadcast is different."

"Don't you get lonely working alone every night?"

"Actually, I prefer it."

Before Rondeau asked her to father his children, Dean interceded. "I'll walk you out, Paris."

As he ushered her toward the door, she said, "I'd like to stay updated. Please ask Sergeant Curtis to call me when he knows something." Sergeant Curtis. Not him. The snub couldn't be more blatant, and it irritated the hell out of him. He was as much a cop as Sergeant Robert Curtis. *And* he outranked him.

He reached around her to grab the doorknob. But the door opened without his help and Curtis was on the other side of it. His complexion was several shades ruddier than usual. What was left of his pale hair seemed to be standing on end.

"Well, it's hit the fan," he announced. "Somehow a courthouse reporter learned that cops were looking for Janey Kemp. He confronted the judge about it as he was returning from lunch recess. His Honor is *not* happy."

"His daughter's life could be at risk and he's worried about media exposure?" Paris exclaimed.

Dean said, "My thought exactly. I don't give a shit if he's happy or not."

"Fine. You'll have an opportunity to tell him that to his face. We've been ordered by the chief to meet with Kemp and try to smooth his feathers. Right now."

chapter ten

Paris wheeled into the Kemps' circular driveway directly behind Sergeant Curtis's unmarked Taurus. She got out of her car at the same time he got out of his. Before he had a chance to speak, she said, "I'm coming with you."

"This is a police matter, Ms. Gibson."

If he was back to using her last name, he was irked. She held her ground. "I started this ball rolling when I came to see you this morning. If I never hear from Valentino again and the call last night turns out to be a hoax, then I owe you, the Austin police, and especially this family a profound apology. And if it isn't a hoax, then I am directly involved and so are they, which entitles me to speak with them."

The detective looked across at Dean as though seeking guidance on how to handle her when she took a stubborn stance. Dean said, "It's your call, Curtis. But she's good at talking to people. That's what she does."

Coming from a trained negotiator, that was quite a compliment. Curtis considered it for only a moment, then said grudgingly, "All right, but I don't know why you'd want to involve yourself in this any more than you already are."

"I didn't choose to be. Valentino involved me."

She and Dean followed him toward the door. For Dean's ears only she said, "Thanks for backing me up."

"Don't thank me yet." He nodded toward the wide front door, which was being opened as they made their way up the veranda steps. "Looks like he's been lying in wait."

Judge Baird Kemp was tall, distinguished looking, and handsome, except for his scowl, which he directed toward Curtis, whom he obviously knew by name. "I'm trying to keep a lid on this, Curtis, and what does the Austin PD do? Trot extra cops out to my house. What the hell is going on with you people? And who are they?"

To Curtis's credit, he kept his cool, although his face and neck flushed to a deeper hue. "Judge Kemp, Dr. Dean Malloy. He's the department's psychologist."

"Psychologist?" the judge sneered.

Dean didn't even bother extending the judge his hand, knowing it would be rebuffed.

"And this is Paris Gibson," Curtis said, motioning toward her.

If her name meant anything to the judge, he didn't show it. After giving her a cursory look, he glared at Curtis. "Are you the one who started the false rumor that my daughter is missing?"

"No, Judge, I didn't. You did. When you called one of the cops you've got on the take and told him to start looking for her."

A vein ticked in Kemp's forehead. "I told the chief that I demanded to know who was responsible for leaking that story, which has been grossly exaggerated. He sends me you, a shrink, and a—" He glanced at Paris. "Whatever. Why the hell are you here?"

"Baird, for godsake." A woman emerged from the house and upbraided him with a stern look. "Can we please do this inside where fewer people will have the opportunity of overhearing?" She gave their guests a collective once-over, which was just shy of hostile, then said stiffly, "Won't you come in?"

Again Paris and Dean followed Curtis. They were shown into an elaborately appointed living room that might have been a salon in Versailles. The decorator had padded her budget with an overload of brocades, gilt, beading, and tassels.

The judge marched over to a dainty liquor cart, poured himself a drink from a crystal decanter, and tossed it back as if it was a shot. Mrs. Kemp perched on the delicate arm of a divan as though she didn't intend to stay very long.

Curtis remained standing, looking as out of place as a fireplug in this room of froufrou. "Mrs. Kemp, have you heard from Janey?"

She glanced at her husband before answering. "No. But when she gets home, she'll be in serious trouble."

Paris couldn't help but think the girl could be in much more serious trouble now.

"She's a teenager, for christsake." The judge was still standing, too, glaring down at them as though about to sentence them to twenty years of hard labor. "Teenagers pull stunts like this all the time. Except when *my* daughter does it, it makes headlines."

"Don't you realize that negative publicity only makes a situation worse?"

For whom? Paris was dismayed that Mrs. Kemp's primary concern was publicity. Shouldn't she be more worried about the girl's absence rather than what would be said about it?

Curtis was still trying to be the diplomat. "Judge, I don't know who within the Austin PD spoke to that reporter. We'll probably never know. The culprit isn't going to come forward and admit it, and the reporter is going to protect his source. I suggest we move past that and—"

"Easy for you to say."

"Not at all easy." Dean spoke for the first time, and his tone was so imperative that all eyes turned to him. "I wish the three of us had come here, hat in hand, to beg your forgiveness for an error in judgment, a slip of the tongue, a false alarm. Unfortunately, we're here because your daughter could be in grave danger."

Mrs. Kemp moved off the arm of the divan and onto the seat cushion.

The judge rocked back on his heels. "What do you mean? How do you know?"

"Maybe I should tell you why I'm here," Paris said quietly.

The judge's eyes narrowed. "What was your name again? Are you that truancy officer who kept hassling us last year?"

"No." She reintroduced herself. "I have a radio program. It's on each weeknight from ten to two."

"Radio?"

"Oh!" Mrs. Kemp exclaimed. "Paris Gibson. Of course. Janey listens to you."

Paris exchanged glances with Dean and Curtis before turning back to the judge, who apparently was unfamiliar with her and her show. "Listeners call in and sometimes I put them on the air."

"Talk radio? A bunch of left-wing radicals spouting off about this, that, or the other."

He had to be the most unpleasant individual Paris had ever met. "No," she said evenly, "my show isn't talk radio." She was in the process of describing her format when he interrupted her.

"I get the picture. What about it?"

"Sometimes a listener calls to air a personal problem."

"With a total stranger?"

"I'm not a stranger to my listeners."

The judge raised a graying eyebrow. Apparently he wasn't used to people contradicting or correcting him. But Paris wasn't intimidated by someone she had already formed such a low opinion of.

Being flagrantly rude, he dismissed her and turned back to Curtis. "I still don't understand what a radio deejay has got to do with any of this."

"I think this will help explain." The detective set the portable tape recorder on a coffee table. "May I?"

"What is this?"

"Sit down, Baird," his wife snapped. Paris saw traces of apprehension in the other woman's eyes. Finally the severity of the situation was beginning to sink in. "What's on the recorder?" she asked Curtis.

"We want you to listen, see if you recognize your daughter's voice."

The judge looked down at Paris. "She called you? What for?"

She, along with the others, ignored him as the recording began.

Well, see, I met this guy a few weeks ago.

Paris noticed that Dean was watching Mrs. Kemp closely. Her reaction was immediate, but was it from recognizing the voice, or from the young woman's description of a short-lived but hot, hot, hot fling?

When it ended, Dean leaned toward Mrs. Kemp. "Is that Janey's voice?"

"It sounds like her. But she rarely talks to us with that much animation, so it's hard to tell."

"Judge?" Curtis asked.

"I can't tell for dead certain either. But what the hell difference does it make if it is her? We know she's got boyfriends. She flits from one to the other so fast we can't keep up. She's a popular girl. What's that got to do with anything?"

"We hope nothing," Curtis replied. "But it might tie in to another call that Paris received from a listener." While talking, he exchanged one cassette for another. Before he played the second tape, he said to Mrs. Kemp, "I apologize in advance, ma'am. Some of the language is rather crude."

They listened in silence. By the time Valentino wished Paris a nice night, the judge had his back to the room and was gazing out the front window. Mrs. Kemp was mashing a pale fist against her lips.

The judge came around slowly and looked at Paris. "When did you receive this call?"

"Just before sign-off last night. I called 911 immediately."

Curtis picked up from there and brought them up-to-date. "Janey's the only missing person who's been reported. If that's her talking to Paris earlier in the week, it could correlate."

"If I heard evidence that flimsy in my courtroom, I'd dismiss it."

"Maybe you would, Judge, but I won't," Curtis declared. "After the reporter confronted you, I understand you called off the unofficial search for your daughter. Well, sir, you should know that as we speak, patrolmen are intensifying their search and intelligence officers are tapping every resource."

The judge looked ready to implode. "Upon whose authority?"

"Mine," Dean said. "I made the recommendation and Sergeant Curtis acted on it."

Mrs. Kemp turned to him. "I'm sorry, we weren't formally introduced. I don't know who . . ." He introduced himself again and explained how he had become involved.

"Very possibly this will turn out to be a hoax, Mrs. Kemp. But until we know it is, we should take this caller seriously."

She stood up suddenly. "Would anyone like coffee?" Then before anyone could answer, she rushed from the room.

The judge muttered a string of curses. "Was that necessary?" he asked Dean.

Dean was barely restraining himself. Paris recognized the tension in his posture and the hardening of his jaw as he stood up and confronted the judge. "I hope to God you can file a formal complaint against me. I hope Janey comes waltzing in here and makes me look like a colossal fool. You'll then have the pleasure of calling me one, possibly even getting me fired.

"But in the meantime, your rudeness is unforgivable and your obstinance is stupid. We've been given a seventy-two-hour deadline, and so far you've wasted twenty minutes of it by being a jerk. I suggest we all set aside our egos and focus on finding your daughter."

The judge and Dean stared each other down. Neither submitted to the other in a silent contest of wills. Finally Curtis cleared his throat. "Uh, when was the last time you saw Janey, Judge?"

He actually seemed relieved to have an excuse to break eye contact with Dean. "Yesterday," he replied briskly. "At least Marian saw her then. In the afternoon. We got home late last night. Thought she was in her room. Didn't discover until this morning that her bed hadn't been slept in." He sat down and crossed one long leg over the other, but his insouciance appeared affected. "I'm sure she's with friends."

"I have a son about Janey's age," Dean told him. "He can be a challenge. There are times when you'd think we hated each other. Discounting the normal ups and downs of living with a teenager, would you say you're basically on good terms with Janey?"

The judge looked ready to tell Dean that his relationship with his daughter was none of his business. But he relented and said stiffly, "She's been difficult at times."

"Breaking curfew? Experimenting with alcohol? Going out with kids you'd rather she not associate with? I speak from experience, you understand."

By placing them on common ground, he was gradually breaking down the judge's barriers and Curtis seemed content to let him continue.

"All of the above," the judge admitted before turning to Paris. "Sergeant Curtis said this degenerate has called you before."

"A man using that name has, yes."

"Do you know anything about him?"

"No."

"You have no idea who he is?"

"Unfortunately, no."

"Do you intentionally provoke this kind of lewdness from your listeners?"

The implicating question took her aback. Before she could form a reply, Dean said, "Paris can't be held responsible for the actions of her listening audience."

"Thank you, Dean, but I can speak for myself." She met the judge's censorious stare head-on. "I don't care what you think of me or of my program, Judge Kemp. I don't need or desire your approval. I'm here only because I heard Valentino's message firsthand, and I share Dean—

Dr. Malloy's—concern. I respect his opinion both as a psychologist and a criminologist. Sergeant Curtis's investigative skills are unsurpassed. You'd be wise to give serious consideration to what they're telling you.

"As for my opinion, it's based on years of experience. I listen to people in every possible human condition. They talk to me through laughter and tears. They share their joy, sorrow, grief, heartache, exhilaration. Sometimes they lie. I usually can tell when they're lying, when they're faking an emotion in an attempt to impress me. They do that sometimes, thinking it will increase their chances of being put on the air."

She pointed toward the recorder. "He didn't even hint at being put on the air. That wasn't the reason he called. He called with a message for me, and I didn't get the sense that he was lying or faking it. I don't think it was a crank call. I think he has done, and is going to do, what he said.

"Insult me if it makes you feel better, but, regardless of anything you say, I'm going to do everything within my power to help the police get your daughter returned safely to you."

The taut silence that followed Paris's speech was relieved by the reappearance of Marian Kemp. It seemed she had timed it for just that purpose. "I decided on iced tea instead."

She was followed into the room by a uniformed maid carrying a silver tray. On it were tall glasses of iced tea garnished with lemon and fresh mint. Each glass rested on an embroidered linen coaster. A silver bowl of sugar cubes was accompanied by dainty sterling tongs.

Once they were served and the maid had withdrawn, Curtis awkwardly set his glass of tea on the coffee table. "There's another element to this that you should be made aware of," he told the Kemps. "Does your daughter have a computer?"

Marian replied, "She's on it all the time."

Judge and Marian Kemp listened in stony silence as Curtis told them about the Sex Club. When he finished, the judge demanded to know why his wife had been subjected to hearing about such filth.

"Because we need access to Janey's computer."

The judge erupted with vehement protests. He and Curtis launched into a heated argument over investigative procedure, privacy, and probable cause.

Finally Dean entered the fray. "Doesn't this girl's safety supersede points of law?" His shout silenced them, so he pressed his advantage. "We need a copy of everything on Janey's hard disk."

"I will not permit it," the judge said. "If such a thing as this Sex Club exists, my daughter has nothing to do with it."

"Soliciting to have sex with strangers," Marian Kemp sniffed. "Revolting."

"And speaking as a parent, terrifying," Dean said to her. "But I would rather be informed than ignorant, wouldn't you?"

Apparently not, he thought when neither the judge nor his wife answered. "We don't want to invade Janey's privacy, or yours. But her computer could yield clues to her whereabouts."

"Such as?" the judge asked.

"Friends and acquaintances you don't know. People who send her email."

"If you did discover anything incriminating, it would never be admissible in a court of law because it will have been illegally obtained."

"Then what have you got to worry about?"

The judge had laid that trap for himself and he realized it.

Dean continued, "If Janey has an email address book, which I'm sure she does, we could send out a blanket message to everyone on it, asking if they've seen her, and if they have, urge them to contact you."

"In effect announcing to the world that her mother and I can't keep track of our daughter."

Dean had no love for these people, but he didn't have the heart to state what was glaringly obvious: They wouldn't be here if the Kemps had kept better track of their daughter.

"Her friends will recognize her email address and open the letter," he said. "We'll sign the message from you, not the police, and promise that anyone coming forward with information can remain anonymous."

"Mrs. Kemp," Paris said gently, "an email would reach a lot of people much more efficiently than policemen canvasing Janey's hangouts. Besides, young people get nervous when cops approach even if they're doing absolutely nothing wrong. Janey's friends would be reluctant to talk to a policeman about her. They'd be much more likely to reply to an email."

It was a persuasive point lent even more potency by her mellow voice. Mrs. Kemp looked over at her husband, then back to Paris. "I'll show you to her room." The invitation seemed to include only Paris, who stood when Mrs. Kemp did and followed her out.

Without a word, the judge turned on his heel and stalked toward an adjacent room. From what Dean could see through the doorway before the judge slammed the door behind him, it appeared to be a library or study.

Curtis lightly slapped his thighs as he came to his feet. "That went well, don't you think?"

Dean grinned at the ironic remark, but he sure as hell didn't feel like smiling. "I guess His Honor is divesting himself of the whole ugly matter."

"I'll bet you my left nut he's in there on the phone giving the chief hell about the department's new shrink."

"I don't care. I meant everything I said, and I'd say it again."

"Yeah, well, occasionally I have to testify in his court. I have to play both ends against the middle. But I figure the next time I'm in the witness box, my testimony will be discredited." He ran his hand over his thinning hair. "I'm going outside to make a few calls, see if there's been any news that would make all of us sleep better tonight."

Dean followed him as far as the grand staircase. "I'll wait here for Paris."

"I thought you might."

He didn't have a suitable comeback for the detective's parting shot, so he let it pass. Sliding his hands into the pockets of his trousers, he took in the formal foyer. The floor was marble tile. Overhead was a lavish crystal chandelier that was reflected in the polished wood surfaces of twin consoles facing each other across the wide hall.

Above one of the tables hung an oil portrait of Marian Kemp. And on the opposite wall above the matching table was a painting by the same artist of a girl about seven years old. She was wearing a summer dress of white gauzy fabric. Her feet were bare. The artist had captured sunlight shining through pale blond curls. She looked angelic and achingly innocent.

Dean's cell phone vibrated inside his jacket pocket. He checked the LED and recognized Liz's cell number. He didn't answer, telling himself that now wasn't a good time. She had called twice before. Those hadn't been good times either.

Hearing footsteps in the deep carpeting of the staircase,

he looked up to see Paris and Marian Kemp descending. Paris subtly nodded at him. In her hand she was carrying a Zip disk, which she handed over as soon as she reached him. He slid it into his pocket. "Thank you, Mrs. Kemp."

Even though she had cooperated, she hadn't warmed to them. "I'll see you out."

She opened the front door, and when she saw the young woman standing in the driveway with Curtis, she exclaimed, "Melissa! I thought you were in Europe."

Upon hearing her name, the girl turned toward them. She was tall and lanky and was probably attractive underneath the makeup that had been applied with all the finesse of a brave preparing for the warpath.

"Hey, Mrs. K. I just got back."

"She's a friend of Janey's?" Dean asked Marian Kemp.

"Her best friend. Melissa Hatcher."

Behind Paris's car was a snazzy, late-model BMW convertible, but you would never guess by her clothing that this girl came from affluence. She was wearing a pair of denim cutoffs that left ragged strings trailing down her thighs. The waistband had also been cut off, leaving nothing but fringe to hold the shorts on her hipbones. Twin sapphires winked from her pierced navel. The neck and armholes of her T-shirt were oversized, making it no secret that she was wearing nothing beneath it.

Her striped knee socks looked unseasonably heavy, and the black boots laced to her ankles would have been more appropriate on a lumberjack or a mercenary who meant business. Incongruously, the large handbag hanging from her shoulder was a Gucci.

"Have you spoken to Janey since your return?" Marian Kemp asked.

"No," she replied, as though put out by the question.

"This guy here's been asking me all these questions. What's going on?"

"Janey didn't come home last night."

"So? She probably just crashed at somebody's place. You know." She shrugged, which slid her T-shirt off one shoulder. She sent a look Dean's way that was unmistakably flirtatious.

"Could you give us some names?"

She turned back to Curtis and eyed him up and down. "Names?"

"Of people Janey might've gone home with?"

"Are you heat?" The detective opened his sport jacket and showed her the ID clipped to his belt. "Oh shit. What's she done?"

"Nothing that we know of."

"She could be in danger, Melissa." Paris moved down the steps to join them.

The girl regarded her curiously. "Danger? What kind of danger? You a cop, too?"

"No, I work for a radio station. I'm Paris Gibson."

Melissa Hatcher's lips were painted a red so dark it was almost black. They fell open in astonishment. "Get out! You're fucking kidding, right?"

"No."

"Oh my God." Her delight was probably the most honest reaction the girl had shown in months. "How cool is this? I listen to your show. When I'm not listening to CDs. But sometimes, you know, you're just not in the mood for CDs. So that's when I turn on your program. Sometimes the music you play sucks, but you are totally bitchin', girl."

"Thank you."

"And I like your hair. Are those highlights?"

"Melissa, do you know if Janey has ever called me while I was on the air?"

"Oh, yeah. Coupla times. It's been a while, though. We called you on Janey's cell and talked to you but we didn't give our names and you didn't put us on the radio. Which was cool, 'cause we were wasted and you could probably tell."

Paris smiled at her. "Maybe next time."

"Has Janey called Paris recently?" Dean asked. Dark eyes lined in darker kohl slid over to him. Paris introduced him to the girl as Dr. Malloy. He stuck out his hand.

She seemed nonplused by the polite gesture, but she shook his hand. "What kind of doctor are you?"

"Shrink."

"Shrink? Jesus, what'd Janey do? OD or something?"

"We don't know. She hasn't been heard from in over twenty-four hours. Her parents are worried about her and so are we."

"We? You a cop, too?"

"Yes. I work for the police department."

"Hmm." Melissa shot them each a suspicious look, and Dean sensed her cautious withdrawal. They were losing her. Despite her being a Paris Gibson fan, her first loyalty would be to her friend. She'd be stingy with information about Janey.

"Like I said, I don't know anything about where Janey is or who she's called 'cause I just got back from France. I've been up for like thirty hours straight, so I'm gonna go home now and crash. When Janey shows up, tell her I'm back, will ya, Mrs. K.?"

Her Gucci bag slung a wide arc as she turned and sauntered toward her car. But just short of reaching it, she suddenly came back around, slapping her forehead with a hand weighed down by sparkling bangles and numerous rings.

"Holy shit, I just got it!" She pointed at Dean. "No wonder you're such a hottie. You're Gavin's dad."

chapter eleven

"Wake up, sleepyhead."

Janey opened her eyes. He was bending over her, his face close to hers, his breath ghosting over her face. He kissed her forehead. She moaned pitiably.

"Did you miss me?"

When she nodded, he laughed. He didn't believe her, and he would be wise not to. Because the first chance she got, she was going to kill the son of a bitch.

She tried to keep the malice she felt from showing in her eyes, having concluded that her best option was to appear submissive. The psycho wanted to play games, wanted her to beg, wanted to dominate her.

So, fine. She would be his contrite little plaything—until he turned his back on her, and then she was going to bash in his skull.

"What's this?" He noticed the stained bedsheet and tsked.

She'd peed herself. What did he expect? He had abandoned her here for God knows how long. She had held her bladder for as long as she could, but ultimately she'd had no choice except to wet the bed.

"You'll just have to change the sheets," he told her.

Okay, I'll remake the bed. Untie me and give me a fresh sheet and I'll strangle you with it.

He brushed aside a strand of her matted hair. "You

smell like piss and sweat, Janey. Have you been exerting yourself? Doing what, I wonder?" His gaze roved until it settled on the wall behind the bed. "Hmm. Scars in the paint. You've been rocking the bed so the headboard would knock against the wall, haven't you?"

Damn! She had hoped to annoy a neighbor who would eventually get so angry over the monotonous knocking that he'd come over and demand a stop to it. Then, when he was ignored, he would complain to the manager until the manager checked out the source of the noise.

She would be found and her father would be notified, and he would make certain this asshole never saw the light of day again. They'd lock him in a cell *beneath* the prison and give visitation rights to all the bull queers in the place.

Her daydream of rescue and vengeance died when he pulled the bed several feet away from the wall. "We can't have that, Janey." He bent down and kissed her forehead again. "Sorry to spoil your clever little plan, sweetheart."

She looked at him with a desperation that wasn't entirely feigned. She moaned imploringly.

"Do you need the toilet?"

She nodded.

"All right. But I need your promise that you won't try to get away. You would only get hurt, and I don't want to hurt you."

I promise, she said behind the awful tape.

He unbound her feet first. She had thought the instant they were free she would start kicking and fighting him, but, to her alarm, she discovered that her limbs were rubbery. Her legs were reluctant to move at all, and when they did, they did so sluggishly.

He untied her hands, then lifted her into his arms and carried her into the bathroom. He set her on her feet near the toilet, raised the lid, then gently lowered her onto the seat.

She reached for the tape across her mouth.

"You can remove it," he told her softly. "But if you scream, you'll regret it."

She believed him. It was painful to peel off the tape, but when she had done so, she sucked large drafts of air through her mouth. "I'd like a drink of water, please," she said, her voice a croak.

"Finish here first."

He made no move to leave. To her mortification tears came to her eyes. "Go out and close the door."

He frowned down at her impatiently. "Oh, please. This sudden modesty is absurd. Hurry up before I change my mind and make you wet yourself again."

When she was finished, she asked again for a drink of water.

"Certainly, Janey. As soon as you change your bed. You've left it so nasty. Dreadfully nasty."

She was dying of thirst, so she submissively exchanged the damp sheets for fresh ones. By the time she had completed the task to his satisfaction, she was exhausted and had broken out in a cold sweat.

He made her sit in the armchair, where he could watch her while he stepped into the kitchen and uncapped a plastic bottle of water. She'd hoped for a glass. She could have broken it and shoved a shard of glass into his throat. If she could've found the strength. She was abnormally weak even for someone who'd been lying in bed for hours. Had he drugged her last night? Was he doing so again now? Had he put something in her water?

Actually she didn't care. She was so thirsty, she drank the water greedily.

"Are you hungry?"

"Yes."

He made a pimiento cheese sandwich, then hand-fed it to her, pinching off small pieces one at a time and placing them in her mouth. She thought about biting his fingers, but that would still leave one of his hands free. She hadn't forgotten the slap that had made her vision blur and her ears ring. She didn't want to invite another.

Causing him even momentary pain would give her enormous satisfaction. She would love to sink her teeth into his flesh, draw blood. But in her present condition, it would be impossible to follow that up with a full-fledged attempt to overpower him. The satisfaction she would derive from it would be all too brief and would cost her dearly. Until she could achieve more than just getting him angry and retaliatory, she had best conserve her strength and try to devise a foolproof plan of escape.

When she'd finished the sandwich, he said, "I like you this way, Janey." He stroked her head and used his fingers to comb the tangles out of her hair. "Your submission is very arousing." He touched her nipples lightly. "It makes you so desirable."

He turned away from her only long enough to get his camera. The despised camera. It was the camera that had so intrigued her and made her think he was special. A special pervert, maybe. She hated the sight of that camera now and would like nothing better than to grind it into his face until both his facial bones and the camera had broken apart.

But she was too frightened to resist as he posed her for a series of obscene pictures.

"Get on the bed."

She considered begging, pleading, promising him money, swearing she'd never tell anyone about this, if only he would let her go. But maybe she would have more bargaining power if she did him one more time.

So she lay down on the bed and did exactly what he told her to do. When he was finished, she didn't even have the energy to raise her head. He had drugged her. She was sure of it now.

She watched in dread as he opened the nightstand drawer and removed a roll of duct tape. "No," she whimpered. "Please."

"I hate having to do this, Janey, but you're a whore. Your love isn't pure. You're dishonest. You can't be trusted even to remain quiet."

"I will. I swear."

That was all he allowed her to say before clamping a strip of tape over her mouth. This time he also used the tape to secure her wrists and ankles to the bed frame, winding it so tightly there was absolutely no give.

He showered before he dressed. Standing beside the bed, he calmly threaded his belt through the loops of his trousers. "Are you crying, Janey? Why? You used to be the ultimate party girl."

He stuffed the soiled bed linens into a laundry bag and picked up his keys. He was almost to the door when he snapped his fingers and turned back. "I almost forgot. I have a surprise for you."

He took an audiocassette from the pocket of his jacket and placed it in the player that was built into his sound system. "I recorded this last night. I think you'll find it interesting." He pressed the Play button, then blew her a kiss and left. He locked the door from the outside.

There were thirty seconds of silence on the tape, then a ringing telephone. It rang several times before Janey heard a familiar voice say, "This is Paris."

"Hello, Paris. This is Valentino."

His name is Valentino?

That was her first thought, because she instantly recognized his voice. It wasn't his normal speaking voice, but the other one, the one he sometimes used when they were in bed. She had thought it was amusing, the way he could lower the pitch of his natural voice, make it whispery, make it sound as though it went with doing something naughty—as it usually had.

Now, hearing that voice in stereo only gave her chills.

Listening as he told Paris Gibson their story from his perspective, Janey breathed rapidly through her nose, watching the machine in fascination, listening to the recording with an anxiety that soon escalated into terror. When he told Paris Gibson his plans for her, she began screaming into the hollow chamber of her taped mouth.

But of course no one could hear her.

Toni Armstrong arrived at her husband's dental office just before closing. One of the other dentists in the practice paused on his way out to speak with her. He apologized for not yet having had her and Brad over for dinner. They exchanged promises to get a date on the calendar soon.

Seemingly Brad had no trouble keeping up appearances. She would do the same for as long as she could.

When she walked into the office, the receptionist was surprised to see her. "I got a baby-sitter and thought I'd treat Brad to an unscheduled dinner out," she explained.

"Oh, golly, Mrs. Armstrong, Dr. Armstrong left a couple of hours ago."

At least to the other woman, her dismay would look like disappointment. "Oh, well, so much for my surprise evening. Did he tell you where he was going?"

"No, but I'm sure he has his cell phone."

"I'll give him a call. Will I be keeping you if I use his office?"

"Not at all. Take your time. I've got some filing to do before I leave."

Since Brad was the newest partner, his was the smallest office, but Toni had done her best to make it attractive. Degrees and diplomas in matching frames formed an attractive arrangement on the wall. Family photographs were tucked among the dental health books on the shelves behind his desk. His desktop was neat.

She hoped the setting was as benign as it appeared.

Sitting down in his desk chair, she commenced her search. All his drawers were locked, but she had anticipated that and had come prepared. A bent bobby pin opened them with minimum effort.

Truthfully, she *had* secured a baby-sitter for tonight. She had taken care with her hair and makeup and had dressed up in the hope of surprising Brad with an evening out—to make amends for this morning.

Throughout the day, their quarrel had haunted her. Brad had left the house angry. She had been hurt as well as angry. Housecleaning, menu planning, and the myriad other chores that filled her days had kept her busy. But nothing could take her mind off their argument and the possibility, however slight, that she might have been wrong.

What if Brad hadn't been lying about where he'd been last night?

Maybe she had gone looking for trouble where none existed. If he had been telling her the truth, how frustrating it must have been for him to try to make himself believed, knowing that she would think the worst.

Chances were slim that he had attended a seminar and gone for a beer afterward, but in order to hold her family together, she was desperate enough to act on that chance.

So this afternoon, she had hoped to intercept him at the office with a pleasant surprise, an olive branch of a dinner reservation at an Italian restaurant he'd been wanting to try. By spending an evening alone with him, away from the house and kids, with a bottle of wine and lovemaking later on, she had hoped to win his forgiveness for misjudging him and be able to put the ugly episode behind them.

But he wasn't where he was supposed to be. He had left work early without an explanation and without informing anyone of his destination. It was a familiar pattern, a recognizable signal, that made her heartsick and justified her picking the locks on her husband's desk drawers.

A few moments later, her suspicion was validated. Inside the lower drawer of his credenza was a treasure trove of pornography.

The printed material ranged from relatively mild to extremely graphic. Some of the crudest pictures, both in subject matter and composition, surely had been taken by amateur photographers.

Brad was an addict. Like all addicts, he was susceptible to bingeing. And it was during a binge that an addict was capable of doing something he or she wouldn't ordinarily do, like sexually harassing a coworker or fondling a patient who was a minor.

And God only knew what else.

chapter twelve

There was a wet swimsuit on the utility room floor when Dean passed through it on his way into the house. He found Gavin semi-reclined on the sofa in the den. He was desultorily punching the TV remote, changing stations every ten seconds. He was wearing only a towel around his waist and his hair was wet.

"Hi, Gavin."

"Hi."

"Have you been in the pool?"

Without taking his eyes off the television screen, he replied, "No. I just like to sit around in a towel."

"When you take the wet towel to the utility room, you can also pick up the swimsuit you left on the floor."

Gavin punched through another few stations.

Dean said, "Shower, then we'll go eat."

"I'm not hungry."

"Shower, then we'll go eat," he repeated.

"And if I don't, are you going to hit me again?"

The look Dean shot him apparently conveyed his shrinking patience. Gavin threw down the remote and stalked from the room. Just before moving through the door, he whipped off the towel, baring his ass to Dean, literally as well as figuratively. In spite of himself, Dean gave Gavin two points for the symbolic gesture.

Without asking Gavin's preference, he drove to

a chain restaurant that was one of their staples. Gavin sulked, responding in monosyllables to Dean's attempts at conversation.

When their order arrived, Dean asked him if his burger was cooked the way he liked it.

"It's fine."

"I apologize for not having more dinners at home."

"Doesn't matter. Your cooking sucks."

Dean smiled. "I can't argue that. You probably miss your mom's homemade pasta sauce and pot roast."

"Yeah, I guess."

"But all you ever seem to want is burgers or pizza anyway."

Immediately on the defensive, Gavin said, "Something wrong with that?"

"No. I had the same diet when I was your age."

Gavin snorted as though to say he didn't realize they had burgers and pizza that far back in ancient history.

Dean tried again. "I saw an old friend today. Do you remember Paris Gibson?"

Gavin looked at him scornfully. "Do you think I'm retarded?"

"It was a long time ago and you were just a boy. I wasn't sure you would remember her."

"'Course I do. Her and Jack. They were gonna get married, but he got killed."

"He didn't get killed. He survived the accident. He didn't die until a few months ago."

"Huh. She's on the radio here now."

Dean was surprised. "So you knew that?"

"Everybody knows that. She's popular."

"Yeah, I understand she has quite a following. She told me today she's trying to cultivate a younger audience. Do you ever listen to her program?"

"I have. Not every night. Sometimes." Gavin dipped a french fry into a glob of ketchup. "Did you call her up, or what?"

"Uh, no. She had a crank call last night from a listener."

"Seriously?"

"Hmm," Dean said around a bite of his grilled chicken. "She reported it to the police. I was consulted. She and the detective wanted my take on it."

"Detective? Was it that bad?"

"Pretty bad."

He signaled the waitress and asked her to bring Gavin another Coke. For someone who wasn't hungry, he had wolfed down his cheeseburger in record time. "And bring us an order of queso and chips, too, please." Gavin would never ask for more, but Dean knew he was probably still hungry.

"I also saw a friend of yours today," he remarked casually.

"I don't have any friends here. All my friends are in Houston. Where I used to live. In my own house. Until my mother married that jerk."

Here we go, Dean thought. "She had been single for a long time, Gavin."

"Yeah, 'cause you divorced her."

"Funny. Last night you said she divorced me. Actually, you're right on both accounts. We agreed to divorce because we knew it would be best."

"Whatever," Gavin said with a bored sigh and turned his head to gaze out the window.

"Don't you think your mother has a right to be happy?"

"Who could be happy with him?"

Dean wasn't overly impressed with Pat's choice either.

Her husband was rather bland, so lackluster that one had to work at having a conversation with him. But he seemed besotted with Pat and she with him.

"So what if he doesn't have a dynamic personality, can't you just be glad that your mother has found someone she cares about, who also cares for her?"

"I'm glad, I'm glad. I'm ecstatic, okay? Can we drop it now?"

Dean could have reminded him that he'd been the one to bring up the topic, but he let it pass. The waitress came with their additional order.

"Anything else?"

She had addressed Gavin, not him, and for the first time, Dean tried to see his son through a young woman's eyes. Parental bliss notwithstanding, Gavin was a good-looking kid. His brown hair had the wavy texture of his mother's and he must secretly like it because—thank God—he hadn't had it sculpted into a bizarre style or had it dyed a color that glowed in the dark.

His eyes were whiskey colored and slightly brooding. You couldn't tell it now when he was slouching, but he was already over six feet tall, and had the strong, lean build and supple grace of a natural athlete.

Dean smiled at the waitress. "We're fine now, thanks." As she moved away, he said, "She's cute."

Gavin glanced at her indifferently. "She's okay."

"Cuter than the young woman I met today." Regarding Gavin closely, he said, "Melissa Hatcher."

Unmistakably, the name registered. Dean was sure of it. But Gavin played dumb. "Who?"

"She said she knew you."

"She doesn't."

"Then why would she say she did?"

"How should I know? She got the name wrong, or

mixed me up with someone else." He was fiddling with the drinking straw in his glass of Coke, avoiding eye contact.

"I introduced myself to her and after we had talked for a while, she said, 'You're Gavin's dad.' She knew you."

"Maybe she'd been warned off me 'cause you're a cop."

"You mean, who wants to be friends with a cop's kid?"

He looked at Dean resentfully. "Something like that."

"Janey Kemp?"

This time Gavin couldn't as easily hide his reaction. His expression became guarded instantly. "Who?"

"Janey Kemp. From what I've heard about her, she wouldn't want to be friends with a cop's kid. Do you know her?"

"I've heard of her."

"What have you heard?"

Gavin scooped up a bite of queso and through a mouthful said, "You know. Stuff."

"Like what? That she's wild? Easy?"

"It's been said."

"Have you ever met her?"

"I may've bumped into her a couple of times."

"Where?"

"Jeez, what is this? The Spanish Inquisition?"

"No, I'm saving the thumbscrews for later. Right now I'm just curious to know where you've bumped into Janey Kemp and her friend Melissa. It must have been enough times that my name meant something to her. Even before that, she recognized me because you and I favor each other."

Gavin squirmed in his seat, shrugged his shoulders.

"They hang out with all those rich, snooty kids. I've seen them around, is all. At the movies. The mall. You know."

"The lake?"

"Which one? Town or Travis?"

"You tell me."

"I've seen 'em a few times, okay? I don't remember where."

Dean laughed. "Gavin, don't bullshit me. If I were your age, and I had met Melissa Hatcher, and she was dressed anything like she was today, I would remember it in minute detail." He pushed his plate aside and leaned forward. "Tell me what you know about the Sex Club."

Gavin kept his expression blank, but again his eyes gave him away. "The what?"

"Last night, when you disobeyed and went out, did you go to Lake Travis?"

"Maybe I did. So what?"

"I know that kids congregate in specified spots around the lake. Did you see Janey Kemp among the crowd last night? And before you give me some bullshit answer, you should know that she's been missing for over twenty-four hours."

"Missing?"

"She didn't come home after going out last night. No one's heard from her. Late this afternoon, just before I left headquarters, patrol officers discovered her car. It was parked near a lakeside picnic area in a clump of cedar trees. No sign of Janey. Apparently she met someone last night and left with that person. Did you see her? Was she with someone?"

Gavin lowered his eyes to his ravaged plate and stared at it for several moments. "I didn't see her."

"Gavin," he said, lowering his voice, "I know the ironclad rule against ratting on your friends. The same rule applied when I was growing up. But this isn't a matter of loyalty or betrayal. It's much more serious.

"Please don't try to protect Janey or anyone else by holding back information. Drinking, drugs, whatever else was going on last night, I'm not interested in right now. If Janey left with the wrong guy, her life could be in jeopardy. With that in mind, are you absolutely certain you didn't see her?"

"Yes! God!" He glanced around, realizing he'd drawn attention to himself from people at nearby tables. He slumped in the booth and mumbled to his lap, "Why're you picking on me?"

"I'm not picking on you."

"You're being a cop."

Dean took a deep breath. "Okay, maybe. I'm coming to you as a source of information. Tell me what you know about the Sex Club."

"I don't know what you're talking about. I gotta pee." He slid to the end of the booth and was about to leave, but Dean ordered him to stay where he was.

"You've been potty trained since you were three. You can hold it for a few more minutes. What do you know about the Sex Club?"

Gavin rocked back and forth, staring angrily through the window, his expression hostile. Dean thought he would refuse to answer him, but eventually he said, "Okay, I've overheard guys talking about this website where they swap email with chicks. That's all."

"Not quite all, Gavin."

"Well, that's all I know about it. I didn't go to school with these kids, remember? I got ripped up by the roots and transplanted here, so they're not—"

"You've been hanging out with a group of kids almost since the day we moved here. Your 'Oh woe is me, I had to leave my friends' refrain is getting a little tired. You need to think of something else to bitch about.

"In the meantime, this girl may be fighting for her life, and I'm not exaggerating. So stop sulking and feeling sorry for yourself and give me a straight answer. What do you know about this Internet club and Janey Kemp's participation in it?"

Gavin held out for several more moments, then, as though resigned, laid his head against the back of the booth. "Janey meets up with guys she's met over the Internet, and they have sex. She'll do anything. Her and that Melissa."

"So you do know them."

"I know who they are. Lots more girls are in the club. I don't know all their names. They come from schools all over the city. There's this message board and the members talk about what they do."

"Have you joined this club, Gavin?"

He sat up. "No! You have to know how to get in, and I haven't asked 'cause I'd feel like a dork for not knowing already."

"It's not that much of a secret. The department's computer crime unit is on to it."

The boy laughed. "Yeah? What are they gonna do about it? They can't stop it, and everybody knows that."

"Soliciting sex is a crime."

"You would know," he muttered resentfully. "You're the cop."

He parked in a grove of live oak trees where others had left their cars. He had a Styrofoam chest of beer and wine coolers in the trunk. He selected a beer and carried it with him as he strolled toward the lakeshore and the wood-plank fishing pier that extended thirty yards out over the water.

This was tonight's meeting place.

He had come to check things out.

He had dressed to blend into the crowd. The baggy shorts and T-shirt were Gap issue, exactly like the younger people wore. Nevertheless, he kept the bill of his baseball cap pulled down low so it would shadow his face.

Some of the people here tonight were familiar. He'd seen them before at similar gatherings, or in the clubs on Sixth Street and around the university campus. Others were new to him. There were always fresh new faces.

Name your pleasure—drink, drugs, sex—it was available. And tonight you could even indulge in gambling. On the beach, a girl wearing only bikini trunks and a straw cowboy hat was on her knees fellating a guy. Bets were being placed on how long the guy could hold out before climaxing.

He joined the ring of cheering onlookers that had formed around the couple and wagered five bucks. One had to admire the guy's self-control because the girl had know-how. He lost his bet.

Unhurried, he strolled along the pier. He didn't invite attention, but ordinarily he didn't have to, and tonight proved to be no different. He was soon approached by two girls who were acting so lovey-dovey that right away he knew they were on Ecstasy.

They hugged him, stroked him, kissed him on the mouth, told him he was gorgeous, the moon was awesome, the night air was divine, and life was beautiful.

They asked him to hold their clothes while they went skinny-dipping. He watched from the pier as they cavorted like water nymphs, occasionally pausing to wave and throw kisses up to him.

When they came out of the water and dressed—well,

partially—he took them to his car and gave them each a beer.

One of the girls fixed her glassy eyes on him. "Do you like to party?"

"I'm here, aren't I?" Clever answer. Noncommittal. Affirmation was only implied.

She fondled him through his shorts and giggled. "I believe you do."

"We *love* to party," the other drawled.

They did, too. Over the course of the next hour, in the backseat of his car, they showed him just how much the party girls they were. When he finally told them he must go, they were reluctant to say good-bye. They kissed and caressed him and begged him to stay for more fun and games.

He finally disentangled himself and made his departure. As he was steering his car through the makeshift parking lot toward the main road, he noticed a couple of guys looking at him with blatant envy. They must have seen him getting out of his backseat with the two babes, extricating himself from their clinging limbs and drug-induced affections.

Did these losers wish they were as lucky in love as he was? You bet your ass they did.

But he also marked a guy he recognized as an undercover narcotics officer. The cop was thirty, but didn't look a day over eighteen. He was transacting with a known drug dealer through the open window of a car.

What's the difference in the narc buying drugs and what I'm doing? John Rondeau asked himself.

Not a damn thing. To effectively fight a crime, you had to understand the nature and mechanics of it. Ever since his unit had discovered the Sex Club, he had appointed himself to do some research. After hours and on-site, of course.

His ambition was to get promoted to CIB, which was the pulse of the department. That's where all the exciting police work was done, and that's where he wanted to be.

Toward that promotion, he could really distinguish himself with this Kemp case. It had elements that received notice, namely, a celebrity, sex, and minors. Put them together and you had yourself a humdinger of an investigation.

To the computer crime unit, the Sex Club was old hat. They'd known about it for months and, realizing the futility of trying to shut it down, had more or less forgotten about it.

But the messages left on the discussion boards continued to blow Rondeau's mind. He'd made it his duty to check out the situation, see if the members really did what they boasted or simply exchanged their wildest fantasies via email. He had discovered that most of the claims were not exaggerations.

And it was a good thing he had done the research. If he hadn't had hands-on knowledge, he wouldn't have been able to answer intelligently and thoroughly all the questions put to him by Curtis, Malloy, and Paris Gibson this morning. So it really was for the benefit of the PD that he'd been putting in this unpaid overtime, wasn't it?

However, more investigative work was required. It was all about his getting a promotion to CIB. It was his job, his sworn duty. He was working undercover, that's all.

Not surprisingly, Brad Armstrong wasn't at home when Toni returned from his dental office. She explained to the startled baby-sitter that she didn't feel well and that she and Dr. Armstrong had canceled their plans for an evening out. She paid her for five hours.

Three times she had called Brad's cell phone. Three times she'd left voice-mail messages to which he hadn't responded. She fixed the children hot dogs for dinner. After they'd eaten, she played a game of Chutes and Ladders with the girls while her son watched a *Star Trek* rerun.

They were trooping upstairs to take their baths when Brad came in with chocolate bars and bear hugs. For Toni there was a bouquet of yellow roses, which he sheepishly presented to her. "Can we be friends again? Please?"

Unable to look at the insincere apology in his eyes, she lowered her head. He took that as acquiescence and kissed her quickly on the cheek. "Have you eaten?"

"I was waiting for you."

"Perfect. I'll put the kids to bed. You get something on the table. I'm famished."

What she had on the table when he returned to the kitchen wasn't what he expected. The unappetizing display stopped him dead in his tracks. "Where'd you get all that?" he demanded angrily. "Never mind. I know where you got it."

"That's right. I found it this afternoon when I went to your office. Where you were conspicuously absent, Brad. You didn't tell anyone where you were going, and you haven't answered your cell phone for hours. So don't put *me* on the defensive. I refuse to apologize for violating your privacy when this is what your privacy is protecting."

As soon as he was confronted with the evidence of his sickness, the fight went out of him. It was a physical diminishing, a deflation both of spirit and body. He pulled out a chair and sat down at the table, his shoulders slumping, his hands falling listlessly into his lap.

Toni took a plastic trash bag from the pantry and scooped the collection of sordid photographs and magazines into it. Then she closed it with a twist tie and carried it to the garage.

"I'll take it to a Dumpster in the morning," she told him when she came back in. "I would hate for the bag to come open accidentally and our neighbors, or even the garbage collectors, to see what's inside."

"Toni, I'm . . . There's really no defense I can offer, is there?"

"Not this time."

"Are you going to leave me?" He reached for her hand and clasped it damply. "Please don't. I love you. I love the kids. Please don't destroy our family."

"I'm not destroying anything, Brad," she said, pulling her hand free. "You are."

"I can't help myself."

"Which is all the more reason for me to leave and take the children. What if one of them had found those pictures?"

"I'm careful about that."

"You're careful to conceal it the way a drug addict hides his stash or the alcoholic keeps a hidden bottle in case of an emergency."

"Oh, come on," he cried.

His contrition was gradually dissipating. Hostile defensiveness was setting in. Next would come an air of superiority. They'd played this scene many times before. His transition from penitent to martyr was virtually scripted and Toni knew to anticipate each phase of it.

He said, "Comparing a harmless hobby to drug addiction is ridiculous and you know it."

"Harmless? Some of those pictures are of underage girls. They're exploited by corrupt and depraved people for your entertainment. And how can you call it harmless when it affects your career, our family life, our marriage?"

"Marriage?" he sneered. "I don't have a wife anymore, I've got a jailer."

"If you continue, you may well wind up in jail, Brad. Is that what you want?"

He rolled his eyes. "I'm not going to jail."

"You could, unless you admit to yourself and to others that you're a sex addict and get the help you need to combat it."

"Sex addict." He snuffled a laugh. "Do you hear how absurd that sounds, Toni?"

"Dr. Morgan doesn't think it sounds absurd."

"Jesus. You called him?"

"No, he called me. You haven't been to the therapy group in three weeks."

"Because it's a waste of time. All those guys talk about is whacking off. Now, I ask you, is that a productive way to spend an evening?"

"It's court mandated that you attend the meetings."

"I guess you're going to tattle to my probation officer. Tell him I've been a bad boy. I haven't been going to therapy with the other pervs."

"I don't have to tell him. Dr. Morgan already did."

"Dr. Morgan is the worst sicko in the group!" he exclaimed. "He's a recovering 'addict' himself. Did you know that?"

She continued unflappably. "Dr. Morgan is required to report more than two consecutive absences to your probation officer. You have an appointment with him tomorrow morning at ten o'clock. It's compulsory."

"I guess it doesn't matter if I cancel patient appointments and get my partners pissed at me."

"That's a consequence you'll have to pay."

"Along with sleeping on the sofa, I suppose."

"I would prefer that you did."

His eyes narrowed into a glare. "I bet you would. Since you obviously don't like anything we do in bed."

"That's not fair."

"Fair? I'll tell you what's not fair. It's having a wife who'd rather snoop than fuck. When was the last time we did? Do you even remember? No, I doubt you do. How can you think of sex when you're so busy spying?"

He came to his feet and advanced on her. He curved his hand around the back of her neck and gave it a squeeze that was too hard to be mistaken for affection.

"Maybe if you put out more often, I wouldn't have to resort to looking at my dirty pictures."

He yanked her forward. She turned her head to avoid his kiss and tried to push him aside. But he backed her against the counter and pinned her there. Shocked, she cried out, "Stop it, Brad. This isn't funny."

Her anger only seemed to excite him. His face suffused with color as he ground his lower body against hers. "Feel that, Toni? Feel good?"

"Leave me alone!"

She pushed him hard enough to send him reeling backward and crashing into the table. Covering her mouth with her hand, she tried to stifle her sobs. She was equally outraged and frightened. She'd never seen him this way. Her husband had become a stranger.

He regained his footing and collected himself, then snatched up his jacket and keys. The house shook with the impact of the slamming door. Toni staggered to the nearest chair and sank onto it. For several minutes she wept softly, not wanting the children to hear.

Her life was falling apart and she was incapable of

doing anything about it. Even now she loved Brad. He refused to get help to rid himself of this illness. Why was he intent on destroying the love they'd once had? Why would he willfully choose his "harmless hobby" over her, over his children? Weren't they worth more to him than his—

In a heartbeat, she was out the door to the garage. The trash bag in which she had placed the pornography was gone.

Brad had taken his first love with him.

chapter thirteen

Paris had an office at the radio station, which she worked in when she wasn't on the air. Although "office" was an aggrandizing word for the small room. It couldn't claim a single redeeming feature, not even a window. Decades ago the plaster walls had been painted an ugly manila color. The acoustic ceiling tiles sagged and bore generations of water stains. Her desk was made of ugly gray Formica, chunks of which had been gouged out, probably by a previous occupant who was hopelessly depressed over his surroundings.

Nothing in the office belonged to her. There were no framed diplomas on the walls, or posters of vacation destinations fondly remembered, no candid snapshots of grinning friends, or posed family portraits. The room was barren of anything personal, and that was intentional. Pictures and such invited questions.

Who's that?

That's Jack.

Who's Jack? Your husband?

No, we were engaged, but we didn't get married.

Why? Where's Jack now? Is he the reason you wear sunglasses all the time? Is he the reason you work alone? Live alone? Are alone?

Even the friendly prying of coworkers could bring on severe heartache, so she tried to prevent it by keeping her relationships with them strictly professional and her office space devoid of any hints about her life.

The office wasn't without clutter, however. The unsightly surface of her desk was covered by mail. Bags of it were dumped onto it daily—fan letters, ratings charts, inner-office memos, and the endless reams of material sent to her by record companies promoting their newest releases. Since there was no space for even a file cabinet in the room, she sorted and tossed as efficiently as possible, but it was an unending task.

She had attacked the pile of correspondence after making her music selections for that night's show and entering them into the program log. She'd been at it for an hour when Stan materialized in the open doorway. His expression was petulant. "Thanks a lot, Paris."

"For what?"

He came in and closed the door. "Guess who came to see me today?"

"I hate guessing games."

"Two of Austin's finest."

She laid aside her letter opener and looked up at him. "Policemen?"

"And I have you to thank for it."

"They came to your house?" She had thought that either Carson or the eager Griggs would have called Stan only to ask follow-up questions.

He moved aside a stack of envelopes and sat down on a corner of the desk. "They interrogated me and jotted down my answers in little black notebooks. Very gestapoesque."

"Stop dramatizing, Stan."

Because of her return trip to the police station, followed by the upsetting visit with the Kemps, she'd had no time to sleep. Before she could rest, she had to do a four-hour radio program and do it as though nothing was wrong. It was a daunting prospect.

Dealing with Stan's wounded pride wasn't the best use of her limited stamina or the time remaining before the evening deejay turned the broadcast studio over to her.

"This morning, I reported Valentino's call to a detective," she explained. "As it turns out, a young woman from this area is unaccounted for. The police are investigating to see if there's a connection between her disappearance and Valentino's call. They're conducting routine background checks on everyone who's involved, even remotely. So don't take offense. They didn't single you out. Marvin is also on their list of people to talk to."

"Oh, great. I rank right up there with a *janitor*. I feel much better now."

For once she felt his sarcasm was warranted. "I'm sorry. Truly. The police are being thorough because they're as convinced as I am that this was no crank call. I hope we're all overreacting and it turns out to be nothing. But if our hunches are right, a girl's life is at stake. Nevertheless, I regret that you were dragged into this by happenstance."

He was mollified, but only slightly. Stan's first consideration was always Stan. "The police also talked to our general manager. Of course, he immediately called Uncle Wilkins, who in turn called the chief of police and, from what I understand, gave him an earful."

"Then I'm sure you've been cleared of all suspicion."

"I was actually under suspicion?" he exclaimed.

"Figure of speech. Forget it. Go out and buy a new gadget. There's bound to be one on the market you don't have yet. Treat yourself. You'll feel better."

"It's not that easy, Paris. My uncle was even more incensed than I was. He's been talking to the GM off and on all afternoon, wanting to know 'what the hell is going on.' I paraphrase, of course. You can count on being summoned into the inner sanctum yourself."

"I already have been."

The station's general manager had called her on her cell phone as she was leaving the Kemp estate. He had asked for a meeting, but he'd put it in the form of a mandate, not a request. She'd received a dressing-down for not telling him about Valentino's call before notifying the police. His primary concern was the station's reputation.

"I played him the recording of the call," she told Stan. "It disturbed him, as it's disturbed everyone who's heard it. He spoke with Sergeant Curtis, the detective who's heading the investigation."

The GM had talked to Curtis via speakerphone, making Paris privy to their conversation. He had agreed that Paris and everyone at 101.3 should cooperate with the police to the fullest extent, but stipulated that if Janey Kemp's disappearance became a big news story, he wanted the radio station's involvement to be minimized.

Curtis's response had been, "Frankly, sir, I'm more worried about this girl's life than I am your radio station's call letters showing up in the press."

Before she left the GM's office, he had peevishly reminded her that her precious anonymity might soon be blown. She had already thought of that, and hoped it didn't come to pass. For years she had safeguarded her privacy with the fanaticism of a miser protecting his stockpile of gold. She never again wanted to be the pivotal figure in a sensational news story.

But she agreed with Curtis—rescuing Valentino's victim superseded everything else. By comparison, the impact it would have on her life was trivial.

To further pacify Stan, she said, "Rest assured that I received a proper scolding for jumping the chain of command. You weren't the only one who had his hands slapped today. Now, can I please get back to work?"

"It was a wristwatch with a built-in GPS."

"What was?"

"The gadget I bought myself today."

She laughed as he blew her an air kiss and headed for the door. Over his shoulder he said, "Oh, by the way, Marvin called in sick."

"Sick?"

"Switchboard left a message on my voice mail," he called back. "That's all it said."

To her knowledge Marvin had never called in sick before, making her curious about the nature of his sudden illness. She left the mail sorting for another time and headed toward the small employee kitchen at the back of the building.

At this time of night, the building was hushed and dimly lighted. Other station personnel were long gone, their offices dark. Paris was accustomed to the silence, the darkness, and the pervasive odors of dust scorched by electronic equipment, burned coffee, and carpet that had absorbed decades of tobacco smoke before smoking was outlawed in the workplace.

FM 101.3 was owned and operated by the Wilkins media conglomerate, which included five newspapers, three network-affiliated television stations, a cable company, and seven radio stations. The corporate offices occupied the top three floors of an Atlanta skyscraper that was upscale and sleek, with glass pods for elevators and a two-story waterfall in the sterile granite lobby.

This facility, rescued from a bankrupt previous owner, was as far from upscale and sleek as a woolly mammoth.

There was no waterfall in the lobby, only a water cooler that gurgled and occasionally leaked.

The unattractive, single-story brick structure was situated on a hill on the outskirts of Austin, several miles from the state capitol dome. The building hailed from the early fifties and looked it. It had passed through the hands of twenty-two penny-pinching owners.

Rundown and tacky, it was virtually overlooked by the corporate suits—except when they reviewed the ratings charts. Appearance wise, FM 101.3 was an unsightly wart on the glossy corporate image. But it was healthfully in the black, a reliable producer of revenue.

Despite the building's shortcomings, Paris liked it. It had soul. It bore up well despite its scars.

After the dark hallways, the flickering fluorescent light in the kitchen seemed excessively bright. It took several seconds for her eyes to adjust to the glare even behind her tinted lenses. She took a tea bag from her personal stock in the cabinet and put it in a cup of water she heated in the vintage microwave. The water had barely begun to color when she heard voices.

Looking into the hallway, she was stunned to see Dean trailing several steps behind Stan, who was saying to him, "She didn't tell me she was expecting a visitor."

"She isn't expecting me."

Spotting her, Stan said, "He was tapping on the front door. I didn't let him in until he showed me his cop's badge."

Trying to hide her consternation from her coworker, she said, "Dr. Malloy works with the Austin PD. He was consulted for a psychological assessment of Valentino's tape."

"So he said." Stan looked Dean up and down. "Two for the price of one. A cop and a shrink."

"Something like that," he replied, smiling tightly.

Stan looked from one to the other, but when neither spoke, he must have realized that his company was no longer wanted. He said to Paris, "If you need me, I'll be in the engineering room."

Dean watched as Stan retreated down the hallway. When he was out of earshot, he turned back to Paris. "That's Crenshaw? The owner's nephew? Is he gay?"

"I have no idea. What are you doing here, Dean?"

He stepped into the kitchen, immediately reducing its already limited floor space. "Someone should be here with you during your shift."

"Stan's with me."

"You would trust him with your life?"

She smiled wanly. "You have a point."

"Until we know more about this character calling himself Valentino, you should have police protection."

"Curtis offered to send out Griggs and Carson. I said no."

"I've met Griggs. He seems to be on his toes and a real Boy Scout, but neither he nor . . ."

"Carson."

" . . . has hostage-negotiation training. I should be here if Valentino calls again. If I sense that he's close to losing it, I could talk to him, hopefully persuade him to identify his captive and tell us where he's keeping her."

That being his field of expertise, it was a plausible excuse for his being there. Nevertheless, she questioned his motive. "He may not call. You will have wasted your whole evening."

"It wouldn't be wasted, Paris. I'm also here because I wanted to see you."

"You've seen me."

"Alone."

She set the mug of tea on the stained counter, turning her back to him. "Dean, please don't do this."

He moved up close behind her, and she held her breath, fearing he would touch her. She was unsure as to what her reaction would be if he did, so she didn't want to be tested.

"Nothing has changed, Paris."

She gave a rueful laugh. "Everything has changed."

"When you walked into my office this morning, it came back. All of it. I got slam-dunked just like I did the first time I saw you. Remember? It was the night after the snow."

Houston's snowfall had been reduced to a cold rain that gusted inside when she opened her front door to admit Jack and Dean.

She waved them inside hastily so she could close the door. Jack's introduction got lost in the flurry of their shedding damp overcoats and trying to close stubborn umbrellas that were dripping on her entry floor.

Once she had hung their coats on the coat tree and propped their umbrellas in the corner, she turned and smiled up at her fiancé's best friend. "Let's start over. Hello, Dean. I'm Paris. It's a pleasure to meet you."

"The same goes for me."

His handshake was firm, his smile warm and friendly. He was a couple inches taller than Jack, she noticed. His brown hair was showing signs of premature gray at his temples. He wasn't classically handsome like Jack, but ruggedly so. Jack had told her that Dean had to beat women off with a stick. She could see why. The asymmetric features of his face were arresting. They were counterbalanced by his eyes, which were pale gray and outlined by dark, spiky lashes. An absorbing combination.

He said, "I thought Jack was lying."

"Jack lie? Never!"

"When I asked him what you looked like, he said you would take my breath away. I thought he was exaggerating."

"He does tend to do that."

"He didn't this time."

From across the room, Jack grinned at them. "While you two are discussing my character flaws, I'm going to fix a round of drinks."

They enjoyed a convivial dinner at Jack's favorite steak house. After the meal they migrated to the adjacent bar, where they sat in front of the fireplace and sipped after-dinner coffees. The men regaled her with stories about their college days. Of course, Jack dominated the conversation, but Dean seemed willing to yield him center stage. Jack was a talented, witty storyteller.

Dean was an excellent listener. He asked her about her work, and while she was describing a normal workday, he never broke eye contact. He gave her the attention he would give an oracle divulging the future of mankind. He hung on every word and asked pertinent questions. That was Dean's special gift—making the other person feel as if they had become the center of his universe.

Jack's enjoyment of the evening included imbibing too much brandy. He was sleeping in the backseat when Dean pulled his car to a stop in front of her town house.

"I think we've lost him," he remarked.

She looked back at her fiancé, who was snoring softly through his open mouth. "I think you're right. Will you see him home safely and into bed?"

"As long as I don't have to kiss him good night."

She laughed. "I had heard so much about you from

Jack, I already considered you my friend, too. Promise me that you'll join us for another evening soon."

"That's a promise."

"Good." She reached for the door handle.

"Wait. I'll see you in."

Despite her protests, he got out and came around with an umbrella as she alighted from the passenger seat. He walked with her to the front door. He even took her key from her, unlocked the door with his free hand, and waited until she had disengaged the alarm system.

"Thank you for seeing me in."

"You're welcome. What's the date?" he added.

"The date?"

"Of the wedding. I need to put it on my calendar. The best man's gotta be there, you know."

"I haven't set the date yet. Sometime in September or October."

"That long? Jack gave me the impression it would be sooner."

"It would be if he had his way, but I want to use fall colors."

"Yeah, that'd be nice. Church wedding?"

"Presbyterian."

"And the reception?"

"Probably a country club."

"A lot of planning."

"Yes, a lot."

"Hmm."

He seemed not to notice that rainwater dripped off the metal tips of the umbrella frame and splashed onto his shoes. She didn't notice that rain was being blown inside and onto her floor. Even that first night, the look they shared was perhaps several moments too long.

Dean had been the one to eventually break the stare, saying huskily, "Good night, Paris."

"Good night."

Often when future spouses are introduced to long-standing best friends, they despise one another on sight, making it awkward for the one in the middle who loves them both. She had liked Dean from the start.

She hadn't known any better than to consider that a good omen.

Now Dean reached for her hand and turned her around to face him. He looked at her with the same disturbing penetration as he had the night they'd met, and it had the same magnetic effect. She felt her will dissolving and knew that if she didn't fight it immediately, she would be lost.

"Dean, I beg you. Leave this alone."

She tried to step around him, but he blocked her path. "Our circumstances may have changed, Paris, but not what counts."

"What counts is what always has counted. Jack."

"He went through hell," he said. "I know that."

"You couldn't possibly know the hell his life was after that night."

He lowered his face to bring it closer to hers. "That's right, I don't. Because you made it clear I was not to come and see him. Ever."

"Because he wouldn't have wanted you—especially you—to see him that way," she said, her voice cracking. "But take my word for it, his was a living death for seven years before his heart made it official and stopped beating."

"I regret what happened to him as much as you do," he whispered urgently. "Don't you know that? Do you think I could blithely forget? Jesus, Paris, do you think I'm that callous? I've had to live with what happened, just as you have."

He expelled a long breath and pushed his fingers through his hair. He gazed at a spot above her head for a moment before his eyes moved back to her. "But at the risk of making you angry, I have to say this. What happened to Jack was his fault. Not yours, not mine. His."

"The accident wouldn't have happened if—"

"But it *did*. And we can't go back and undo it."

"Guilt management 101, Dr. Malloy?"

"Okay. Yeah. Simply put, I'm not going to let regret eat me alive. I've let it go."

"How nice for you."

"So your method of guilt management is better? Emotionally healthier? You think it preferable to dig a hole and hide in it?" He gave the untidy kitchen a scornful glance. "Look at this place. It's a dark, dirty, dreary rathole."

"I like it."

"Because it's no better than you think you deserve."

When he moved a step closer, her reaction was to hug her elbows tighter as a means of self-defense against his nearness. It was also a defense against the truth of what he was saying. She knew he was right, which only made her more determined not to listen.

"Paris, God knows you're good at what you do here. Your listening audience loves you. But you could've written your own ticket in TV news."

"What do you know about it?"

"I know I'm right. Furthermore, *you* know I'm right."

Unable to look into his persuasive eyes, she lowered her head and stared at the sliver of linoleum flooring between his shoes and hers. She curbed the impulse to grab his lapels and plead with him either to drop the subject or to convince her that she had paid her penance. "I did what I had to do," she said softly.

"Because you felt it was your duty?"

"It was."

"'Was,'" he repeated with a soft emphasis. "What duty do you owe Jack now that he's dead?" He took her by the shoulders. It was the first time in seven years that they had touched. A tide of heat surged through her and she struggled against the compulsion to lean into him and press her body to his.

Instead she said, "Dean, please, don't. I had to make some hard choices, but I made them. As you said, it's done. In any case, I won't argue with you about this."

"I don't want to argue either."

"Or talk about it," she added.

"Then we won't."

"I don't even want to think about it."

"I'll never stop thinking about it."

The timbre of his voice lowered. His fingers closed more tightly around her shoulders. Barely but noticeably he came closer, close enough for their clothing to touch and for her to feel his breath on her hair.

The subject had shifted from Jack's death to a topic that was even more unsettling and better avoided. She dared to raise her head and meet his gaze.

"Why do you hide in the dark, Paris?"

"I don't."

"Don't you? I could barely find my way down that hallway."

"You get used to it."

"'Hello, darkness, my old friend.'"

"You're quoting Simon and Garfunkel?"

"Is that your theme song these days?"

"Maybe you should have been the deejay." She smiled, hoping to lighten the tone of the conversation, but he wouldn't be deterred.

His eyes moved over her face. "You're beautiful, but no one in your listening audience knows what you look like."

"It isn't necessary. Radio is an aural medium."

"But normally radio personalities promote themselves. You have no identity beyond your voice."

"Which is all the identity I need. I don't want to focus attention on myself."

"Really? Then maybe you should dispense with the sunglasses."

"She can't. Her eyes are sensitive to light."

Neither realized that Stan was there until he spoke. As they turned toward him, Dean dropped his hands from her shoulders.

Stan eyed him mistrustfully, but his message was for Paris. "It's five to ten. Harry's going into the news update and final commercial break. You're up."

chapter fourteen

"Hey, Gav!"

Gavin glanced over his shoulder, saw who had hailed him, then waited for Melissa Hatcher to catch up with him. When she got close enough to read his expression, her smile dissolved.

Foregoing any greeting, he said, "Way to go, Melissa. Were you trying to ruin my life, or were you just too stupid to not keep your mouth shut?"

"You're pissed?"

"You bet your ass I'm pissed."

"What for? What'd I do?"

"You told my dad we knew each other."

"So, what's the big deal?"

"The big deal is that we're having a burger at Chili's tonight and he starts in on the Sex Club."

She propped her hand on her hip. "Oh, like I'd tell your dad about the Sex Club. Duh!"

"Well, he heard about it from somebody."

"Probably that other cop. The short, bald one." She puffed on a lighted joint, then offered it to him. "Here. You look in need of some major chilling out."

He pushed the marijuana aside. "What do you know about Janey?"

"She's in deep shit. With her folks. The cops. Everybody." Spotting a group of acquaintances beyond Gavin's shoulder, she waved, calling out, "Hey, y'all, I'm back from France, and have I got stories!"

Gavin sidestepped, blocking her view of the others and forcing her to look at him. "Is Janey really missing?"

"I guess. I mean, that's what your dad told me. By the way, he's hot. Does he have a girlfriend?"

The dope alone couldn't be blamed for her being a mental zero. She hadn't started out with enough gray matter to brag about. "Melissa, what do you know about Janey?"

"Nothing."

"You're her best friend," he argued.

"I've been out of the frigging country," she said crossly. "I haven't seen Her Highness in weeks. All right?" She took another hit of weed. "Look, I've got people waiting for me. Chill, why don't you."

She left him to join a group who had attached a garden hose to a keg of beer and were taking turns guzzling from it. A lot was lost on the ground, but no one seemed to notice or care. There was always more where that came from.

Gavin joined his friends, who were once again congregated in and around Craig's pickup. He surrendered the unopened bottle of Maker's Mark he'd stolen from his dad's liquor cabinet. As busy as his old man was tracking down Janey Kemp, it might be several days before he noticed he was short a bottle of bourbon.

Craig went to work on the red wax seal with his pocketknife. "Did you catch hell last night?"

"And then some." Gavin put his back against the rear fender while his eyes scoured the crowd in search of a familiar face and form.

"You were so wasted."

"Hurled on the way home."

"Oh, man."

"I shit you not." He recounted the incident at the mailbox. "I'm talking projectile vomiting."

Their laughter was interrupted when another of the boys brought up Janey's name. "Y'all hear about her disappearance?"

"It was on the local news," another said. "My mom asked if I knew her."

"Bet you didn't tell her how well you know her."

"Yeah, bet you didn't tell your mom that you know Janey in the biblical sense."

"What do you know about anything biblical?"

"My cousin's a preacher."

"So what happened to you?"

"He tried to save me. It didn't take. Pass the bottle."

The others continued to swap insults along with swigs of the whiskey. Craig climbed out of the truck and came to stand beside Gavin. "What's with you tonight?"

"Nothing."

"Just bummed, huh?" Craig gave him an opportunity to explain his mood, but then gave up with a shrug and joined Gavin's perusal of the crowd. Suddenly, in an excited whisper, he said, "Hey, see that guy over there?"

Gavin looked in the direction Craig indicated and saw a man climbing from the backseat of a car, rearranging his clothes and pulling on a baseball cap. Two girls got out behind him. They were lookers. Barbie-doll types, blond and chesty, although their bony sternums suggested implants.

"Their tits are fake," Gavin remarked.

"Who cares?"

Obviously not Craig, who continued to ogle. "Wonder if the girls know he's a badge?"

Gavin reacted with a start. "A cop? No way."

"I've heard it rumored."

As they watched, the trio engaged in a group hug. Then the man shooed away each girl, but not before giving her an affectionate smack on the butt and a promise to see her again soon.

The girls ambled away, unfortunately in the opposite direction from Craig and Gavin. The man got back into his car, this time in the driver's seat, and as he maneuvered it around Craig's Ram, he and Gavin made eye contact.

"Smug SOB," Craig muttered.

"You're *sure* he's a cop?"

"Ninety-nine point nine percent."

"Then what's he doing here?"

"Same thing we are, and tonight he scored big."

"Yeah, times two."

"Lucky prick." They watched until the taillights disappeared, then Craig said, "I saw you talking to Melissa."

"That's what she's good at. Talking." He told Craig about his dad's chance meeting with her at the Kemp house. "He knows about the Sex Club."

"Don't worry about it," Craig said with a disdainful sniff. "What are they gonna do, seize all the computers?"

"Exactly what I asked my old man. They're pissing in the wind."

Gavin was talking tougher than he felt. Worry gnawed at him like a hunger pain. That's why he had defied his dad once again by leaving the house tonight. He was going to be in trouble anyway, so what the hell? It was a matter of degree.

Weeks ago, planning for an emergency like this, he'd had a spare car key made. As soon as his dad had dropped him off at home and left for the radio station, he was outta there, too. But he didn't feel as cavalier as his defiance implied. He was sick with apprehension over what the next few days might yield.

"Where do you think she is?"

Craig's question broke into his thoughts as though he'd been reading them. "Who, Janey? How the hell should I know?"

"Well, I thought you might."

"Why?"

Craig looked at him with annoyance. "Seeing as how you were with her last night."

As the last few bars of "I'll Never Love This Way Again" faded into silence, Paris spoke into her microphone. "That was Dionne Warwick. I hope you have someone in your life who can look inside your fantasies and make each one come true."

The studio felt claustrophobic tonight and Dean was the reason why. He'd sat for the last three hours and sixteen minutes on a tall, swivel stool identical to hers, far enough away to give her freedom of movement and access to all the controls, but close enough for her to be constantly aware of him. He sat motionlessly and for the most part silently, but his eyes followed her every move.

She felt them especially now when she mentioned fulfilling fantasies. "It's a toasty eighty-two degrees at one-sixteen, but I'll be playing cool classics until two o'clock here on 101.3. Let me know what's on your mind tonight. Call me.

"I've had a request from Marge and Jim, who are celebrating their thirtieth wedding anniversary. This was their wedding song. It's from the Carpenters. Happy anniversary, Marge and Jim."

As "Close to You" began to play, she punched the

button to turn off her mike, then glanced across at Dean as she depressed one of the blinking telephone lines. "This is Paris."

"Hi, Paris. My name's Roger."

Throughout the program, each time she had answered one of the phone lines, she and Dean had feared, and yet hoped, that Valentino would be the caller. He'd brought a portable cassette recorder with him. It was loaded and ready to record.

His shoulders relaxed along with hers as she said, "Hello, Roger."

"Can you please play a song for me?"

"What's the occasion?"

"Nothing. I just like the song."

"That's occasion enough. What song would you like to hear?"

Facilely she inserted the requested number into the log, substituting it for one already on deck. Then digging her fists into her lower back, she stood up and stretched.

"Tired?" Dean asked.

"I got virtually no sleep last night and never caught a nap today. You must be tired, too. You're not accustomed to these hours."

"More accustomed than you think. I rarely sleep through a whole night anymore. I doze while listening for Gavin to come in."

"Is he with you for the summer?"

"No, more or less permanently."

She registered her surprise. "Nothing's happened to Pat?"

"No, no, she's good," he said in quick response to her concern. "Doing great, in fact. She finally remarried. He's a nice guy in everyone's opinion except Gavin's."

Paris had met Dean's ex-wife at one of Gavin's Little

League games, and she and Jack had once been invited to her house for Gavin's birthday dinner. She remembered her as a petite and pretty woman, but rather serious and structured.

Without her having to ask, Jack had confided to her that Dean had married straight out of college. The union had lasted less than a year. "Really only long enough for them to get Gavin home from the hospital. They were unsuited and knew it and agreed it would be best, even for the kid, if they cut their losses and made a clean break when they did."

Although Gavin had lived with Pat, Dean saw him several times a week and had been actively involved in all phases of his life. He joined Pat at teacher conferences, coached T-ball and soccer teams, participated in and contributed to every aspect of Gavin's development. Following a divorce, a child's upbringing was most often abdicated to the custodial parent. Paris had admired Dean for taking his responsibilities as a father so seriously.

"He and his stepfather weren't getting along?" she asked.

"Gavin's fault. He had moved beyond misbehaving to being downright impossible. Pat and I agreed that he should live with me for a while." He described their tenuous coexistence. "The hell of it is, Paris, I was looking forward to having him with me. I want this arrangement to work."

"I'm sure it will, given time. Gavin is a sweet kid."

He laughed. "Lately, I would beg to differ. But I hope that sweet kid you remember is still in there somewhere behind all that hostility and surliness."

At half past the hour she read a few headlines of news off the information monitor. Following that came several minutes of commercials, during which she took calls. One caller asked her for a date. She graciously declined.

"Maybe you should have accepted," Dean teased. "He sounded desperate."

"Desperately drunk," she said, returning his smile as she deleted the call from the Vox Pro.

The next call came from a giddy couple who'd just become engaged. "He asked me to open a bottle of wine and then handed me a glass with the ring in it." Even her squeal couldn't disguise a charming British accent. "My friends in London won't believe it! We faithfully watched *Dallas* when we were girls and dreamed of someday meeting a handsome Texan."

Laughing because of the young woman's obvious delight, Paris asked what song they wanted her to play.

"'She's Got a Way.' He says Billy Joel could've written it about me."

"And I'm sure he's right. Is it okay if I share our conversation with the listening audience?"

"Fantastic!"

She jotted down their names and answered a few more calls. After the sequence of commercials, she replayed the conversation with the engaged couple and followed it with their requested song, then "Precious & Few," which segued into "The Rose."

Operating the board was second nature to her, so she was able to do all this while continuing her conversation with Dean about Gavin. "What did he say when you told him about meeting Melissa Hatcher?"

"He pretended not to know her."

Paris looked at him inquisitively and he read her thought.

"Yeah, that bothers me, too. Why didn't he want to admit that he knew her? He didn't admit to knowing Janey Kemp either, until I pressed him on it."

"How well does he know her?"

"Not very. At least that's what he told me, but these days I don't always get the truth."

"Not like the time he bent the wheel on his bicycle."

"You remember that?"

"Jack and I had come over to your house for a cook-out. Gavin was staying with you that weekend. He'd been riding bikes with neighborhood kids, but came home pushing his. The spokes of his front wheel were bent almost in half. You asked if he'd been popping wheelies and when he confessed, you sent him to his room for the rest of the evening."

"Which might have been punishment enough because he loved being around you and Jack. But I also made him do chores to earn enough money to replace the wheel."

"Tough but good parenting, Dean."

"You think?"

"I do. You made your point about the value of property, but it wasn't the damage to the bike that upset you."

He smiled ruefully. "I'd told him a thousand times not to pop wheelies or jump curbs because it was dangerous. I didn't want him to become an organ donor."

"Right. He could just as easily have busted his head or broken his neck. You were upset over what could have happened, and that's why you were angry."

"I guess I should have explained that to him."

"He knew," she said softly.

He looked across at her and the connection was more than just visual. It lasted through the remainder of the Bette Midler song. As it wound down, Paris turned back to the control board and engaged her mike.

"Don't forget to join Charlie and Chad tomorrow morning. They'll keep you company as you drive to work. In the meantime, this is Paris Gibson with a romantic lineup of classic love songs. The phone lines will be open right up till two o'clock. Call me."

When the next series of songs began, she glanced up at the log monitor. "Only nine minutes left in the program."

"Isn't this about the time he called last night? Right before sign-off?" When she nodded, he said, "Will you be able to talk to him uninterrupted if he does call?"

She pointed to the countdown clock on the screen. "That's the amount of time remaining for everything that's logged to play. Two more selections follow this one."

He calibrated. "So after the last song ends, you'll have barely enough time to say good night and sign off."

"Right."

He glanced at the phone lines on the control board. Three were blinking. "If it's not Valentino, don't engage the caller in a lengthy conversation. Keep the lines open. And if it is him, remember to ask to speak to Janey."

She took a deep breath, checked to see that Dean's finger was on the Record button of the portable machine, then answered one of the phone lines. Rachel wanted to request a song for her husband, Pete, "It Might Be You."

"Ah, Stephen Bishop."

"It was the first song we danced to at our wedding reception."

"It's such a good choice, it deserves a prime spot." Paris promised to play it the following night in the first half hour of her program.

"Awesome. Thanks."

Paris glanced again at Dean before depressing another of the blinking buttons. "This is Paris."

"Hello, Paris."

Her blood ran cold at the sound of his voice. Frantically she cut her eyes to Dean, who started the portable recorder. The Vox Pro screen registered a phone number, which he scribbled down. He stared into the screen as though willing it to give up not just the telephone number but also the image and identity of the caller.

"Hello, Valentino."

"How was your day? Busy?"

"I managed."

"Come now, Paris. Share. What did you do today to keep yourself occupied? Did you think of me at all? Or did you write me off as a crank? Did you talk to the police?"

"Why would I? Unless you let me speak to the girl, I have no reason to believe that she exists and that what you told me last night is true."

"Stop playing silly games, Paris. Of course she exists. Why would I make such a claim if it weren't true?"

"To get my attention."

He laughed. "Well, did it? Will you pay attention this time?"

"This time?"

"You ignored me when I warned you before, and look what happened."

She looked at Dean and shook her head with misapprehension. "What are you talking about, Valentino?"

"Wouldn't you like to know?" he taunted. "Ask me nicely and I may give you a few hints. But you have to ask me *very* nicely. Now, that's an exciting thought." He inhaled deeply, loudly, so she could hear it. "Your voice alone is enough to arouse me. I think about us together, you know. Someday soon, Paris."

She shuddered with repugnance but continued in a bland tone. "I don't believe you have a girl with you. You're all talk and this is a hoax."

Dean nodded approval.

"More games, Paris? I advise against them. You've already squandered twenty-four of your seventy-two hours. The next forty-eight are going to be much more fun for me than for you. As for my captive, she's a little tired, and all her whining and pleading is beginning to grate on my nerves. But she's still a hot fuck, and I'm due."

The line went dead.

"It's not the same number he called from last night," Dean said as he reached for his cell. "Did you notice anything different tonight, Paris? Any change in his inflection or tone from last night?"

Dean was a policeman, she wasn't. Revolted by the call, she was finding it harder to launch into the mode of crime solver. "No," she replied hoarsely. "He sounded the same."

"To me, too, but I thought you might've picked up— Hey, Curtis, he just called," he said into his cell phone. "Different number. Ready?"

As he reeled it off to the detective, Stan pushed open the soundproof door. "Uh, Paris, we've got dead air."

She hadn't realized the music had stopped. Quickly she signaled for quiet and engaged her mike. "Be safe, be happy, love someone. This is Paris Gibson wishing you a good night." She punched a few buttons, then announced, "We're off."

"The creep called again?" Stan asked.

Dean had turned his back to them while he continued his telephone conversation with Curtis.

To Stan she said, "Leave a note for the morning engineers. Ask them to dump the last call on the Vox Pro onto a cassette and make several copies. They'll be better than the one Dean's portable made."

He looked affronted. "I know how to transfer it to cassette, Paris. I could do it right now."

She hesitated, uncertain of his skill. But he looked so crestfallen, she added, "Thanks, Stan, that would be a help."

Dean ended his call, then turned around and grabbed his jacket off the back of the stool and picked up the portable recorder, all in one fluid motion. "The number belongs to another pay phone. Units are already rolling."

"I'm going, too," Paris said.

"Damn straight you are. No way would I leave you alone now."

He pulled open the door. As they rushed out, she called back to Stan. "Could you drop those cassettes off at my house?"

Dean pushed her through the door before Stan had time to answer.

chapter fifteen

Melissa Hatcher was jealous of Janey Kemp for all the reasons that customarily inspire jealousy. Janey was wealthier, prettier, smarter, more popular, and more desired. However, there was one attribute Melissa had that Janey did not: shrewdness.

Had Melissa made Janey her rival, she automatically would have fallen into a distant second place in a two-woman contest. Instead, she had been cunning enough to make Janey her best friend.

But on her first night back from France, when she should have been the center of attention, all anyone wanted to talk about was Janey and her mysterious disappearance. Melissa was miffed. She had tales of the nude beaches on the Côte d'Azur, of the wine she'd drunk and the drugs she'd done. How she'd come to obtain a nipple ring in St. Tropez was a story that would hold an audience captive for half an hour.

But no one was interested in her recent adventures abroad. Janey was the name on everyone's lips, the topic of every conversation.

Melissa didn't believe any of the wild speculations being circulated about her friend's whereabouts. They ranged from her eloping with the Dallas Cowboys rookie quarterback whom she'd met in a club on Sixth Street, to having been kidnapped for ransom that her old man refused to pay, to being snatched by a pervert and made his sex slave.

My ass, Melissa thought resentfully.

If Janey was honeymooning with one of the Dallas Cowboys, she would've made sure that everybody knew about it. Melissa wouldn't put it past the judge to refuse to pay a ransom to kidnappers, but he would do so in front of lights and cameras and use it to campaign for his reelection. And if anybody was being made a sex slave, it was probably the guy who was shacked up with Janey.

Janey was getting stoned. She was getting balled. End of story. When she felt good and ready, she would reappear and gloat over the stir she'd created. She would milk it for all it was worth. That was Janey. She thrived on shocking and agitating people.

How like her so-called best friend, Melissa thought, to steal the limelight on her first night back from Europe. The evening had turned into a real drag, and she was in a sour mood. Having heard enough about Janey to last a lifetime, Melissa decided to go home and submit to jet lag.

But when she spotted the older guy, she changed her mind.

She had seen him before. Her memory wasn't 100 percent reliable, but she was almost positive that Janey had been with him at least once. As galling as it was to admit, he probably would choose Janey over her if Janey was here. Which she wasn't.

So Melissa sauntered over to where he stood leaning against the driver's door of his car, observing. "You going or coming?"

He looked her up and down, then formed a slow grin. "Right now, neither."

She slapped his arm playfully. "I think you took my meaning wrong."

"You didn't intend the double entendre?"

She wasn't sure what that was, so she shrugged and gave him her most beguiling smile. "Maybe."

He was nice looking. Around thirty-five, she'd guess. A little old and geeky, but so what? At least he would be impressed by her travels.

"I just got back from France."

"How was it?"

"Frenchy."

He smiled in appreciation of her wit.

"It was a total blast. I didn't know what the hell they were saying, but I liked listening to them talk. I saw this guy drinking wine with breakfast. Parents give it to their kids, can you believe that? And people sunbathe nude on public beaches."

"Did you?"

She grinned slyly. "What do you think?"

He reached out and brushed her arm. "Mosquito."

"They're vicious tonight. Maybe we should get in your car."

He ushered her to the passenger door and opened it for her, then went around and got in on the driver's side. He started the motor and turned on the air conditioner.

"Hmm, this is much better," she said, wiggling against the cool leather upholstery. "Nice car," she said, taking in the interior. Glancing into the backseat, she asked, "What's that?"

"A plastic trash bag."

"Duh! I know that. What's in it?"

"Want to see?" He reached between the seats and picked up the bag, then set it in her lap.

"It's not dirty laundry, is it?" she asked, and he laughed.

Melissa undid the twist tie and peered inside, then

took out a magazine. The title and cover couldn't have been more explicit, but she feigned nonchalance. "In France, you can buy fetish mags like this on every street corner. Nobody thinks anything about it. Can I look?"

"Be my guest."

By the time she'd gone through the magazine, his fingers were strumming the inside of her thigh. He lowered his head to nuzzle her breast. "What's this?"

"My souvenir from France." She raised her top and proudly showed him her nipple ring. "I met this guy on the beach who knew this dentist who does body piercing on the side."

He began to laugh.

"What's funny?"

He flicked the silver ring with the tip of his finger. "Inside joke."

There were seven calls from Liz on Dean's home telephone voice mail. He listened to all seven.

"I can't imagine why you haven't called me," the last message began. "I've gone beyond angry, Dean. I'm scared. Has something happened to you or Gavin? If you get this message, please call. If I don't hear from you within an hour, I'm going to start calling the Austin hospitals."

The message had been left at 3:20 A.M. There was a similar one on his cell phone voice mail. The last thing he wanted was to talk to Liz. No, the last thing he wanted was to have her start calling the hospitals.

He dialed her cell phone, which she answered on the first ring. "I'm okay," he said immediately. "No one's in the hospital, and you have every right to be mad as hell. Let fly."

"Dean, what is going on?"

He slumped into a chair at his kitchen table and plowed his fingers through his hair. "Work. We've got a crisis situation."

"I haven't heard any news about—"

"Not a national crisis. Not a plane crash, standoff, mass murder, nothing like that. But it's a tricky case. I got involved early this morning . . . yesterday morning, rather. I was consulted as soon as I got to my office, and I've been on it all day. I just got home and I'm beat. None of which is an excuse for not returning your calls."

"What kind of case?"

"Missing girl. Egotistical suspect. He's called and told us what he plans to do to her unless we can locate her before his deadline." He didn't have the energy to tell her more than that. Besides, the details would have included Paris. Liz didn't know about Paris, and this wasn't the time to try to explain a situation of that complexity.

"I'm sorry you had such a hellish day."

"Jesus, Liz, I'm the one who's sorry."

He had much to be sorry for. Sorry for pretending to return her love, and pretending so well that she believed he did. Sorry for not telling her to remain in Houston as she should have done. Sorry for wishing that her trip to Chicago would last longer than a few days.

Lamely he asked, "How did the meetings with the Swedes go?"

"Danes. They accepted my proposal."

"Good. Not surprising, though."

"How's Gavin?"

"He's all right."

"No more arguments?"

"We've avoided bloodshed."

"You sound exhausted. So I'm going to hang up and let you get some rest."

"Again, about today—"

"It doesn't matter, Dean."

"The hell it doesn't. I caused you a lot of unnecessary worry. It matters."

He was angry with her for not being angrier with him. It would have eased his conscience if she'd been royally pissed off. He didn't want her to be understanding. He didn't want to be let off the hook gently. He wanted her to be mad as hell.

But a full-fledged fight would have required energy he didn't have, so he let it drop with a feeble, "Well, anyway, I apologize."

"Accepted. Now go to bed. We'll talk tomorrow."

"I promise. Good night."

"Good night."

He took a long drink straight from the bottle of water in the fridge, then moved through the dark house, toward the bedrooms. There was no light beneath Gavin's door, not even the glow of his computer monitor. He paused to look in.

Gavin was asleep. Wearing only his underwear, he was lying on his back, long limbs flung wide, covers kicked away. He was almost as long as the bed. He was breathing through his mouth, as he'd done since he was a baby. He looked very young and innocent. At sixteen, he was on the borderline between boy and man. But asleep, he seemed much more like a child than a grown-up.

Dean realized, as he stood looking down at his son, that the painful twinge he felt deep inside his chest was love. He hadn't loved Gavin's mother, nor she him, really. But both had loved Gavin. From the day they knew he'd been conceived, they had channeled the love they should have had for each other into the person they had created.

Obviously they had failed to communicate the depth of that love to Gavin. He still didn't believe that correction was for his protection and that discipline wasn't a pleasant pastime for them, but a demonstration of how important he was to them.

Damn it, Dean had wanted to be a good parent. He'd wanted to get it right. He hadn't wanted his son to doubt for one moment of his life that he was loved. But somewhere along the way he must have tripped up, done something wrong, omitted doing something he should have. Now his son held him in contempt and made no secret of it.

Feeling the weight of his failure, Dean backed away from Gavin's bed and quietly closed the door behind him.

The master bedroom was a large room with a high cove ceiling, wide windows, and a fireplace. It deserved better decorating than what he'd done, which amounted to nothing more than basic furnishings and a bedspread. When he'd moved in, he'd told Liz he was saving the decorating for her to do after they married. But he'd been lying to her as well as to himself. He'd never even invited her to spend the night in this bed.

He plugged his cell phone battery charger into a wall socket in the bathroom so it would be handy in case of a call, then stripped and got into the shower and let the hot water pound into him while he mentally reviewed everything that had taken place after Valentino's call.

The race to the pay telephone had been a wasted effort for all concerned—for the cops in the three squad cars who had converged on it, for Sergeant Robert Curtis, who had arrived as neatly dressed as he was during daylight hours, and for Paris and him.

They had arrived shortly after it was confirmed that

Valentino was no longer anywhere in the vicinity of the pay phone from which his call had originated. The Wal-Mart store had been closed for hours. The parking lot was a vast desert of concrete. There were no witnesses except for a stray cat who had helped himself to the remnants of a hot dog someone had tossed toward a trash bin, but missed.

"And the cat's not talking," Curtis said wryly as he summed up the situation for them.

He and Paris had joined the detective in his car to conduct a postmortem on the aborted effort to catch Valentino. Paris climbed in the back. He sat in the passenger seat. "I made a cassette recording as the call came in," he told Curtis.

"Let's hear it."

He played the tape once, then rewound it and they listened to it a second time. When it ended, Curtis remarked, "He doesn't seem to know we're after him."

"Which could work in our favor," Dean said.

"Only until tomorrow when it shows up in the newspaper." Curtis turned to Paris. "What does he mean when he says you didn't heed him the last time?"

"Just as I told him, I have no idea."

"You don't recall a previous warning?"

"If I had ever received a call like this, I would have reported it to the police."

"Which is what she did last night." Dean didn't like the way the detective was looking at Paris. "What are you getting at?"

"Nothing. Just thinking."

"Then do us the courtesy of thinking out loud."

Curtis turned to him and seemed ready to take issue with his tone of voice, then must have remembered that Dean outranked him. "I was just thinking about Paris."

"Specifically?"

"How she's gone out of her way to remain anonymous. Which, frankly, I don't get," he said, turning back to her. "Other people in your field are extroverts. Publicity hounds. Their pictures are on billboards. They make personal appearances, stuff like that."

"I'm not like the wild and crazy drive-time jocks. My program isn't hyper like theirs. The music is different, and so am I. I'm the disembodied voice in the dark. I'm the sounding board when no one else will listen. If my listeners knew what I looked like, it would compromise the confidentiality I share with them. It's often easier for people to talk to a stranger than to a trusted friend."

"It's certainly easier for Valentino," he remarked. "If he *is* a stranger to you."

"He may be now, but he doesn't want to remain a stranger," Dean said. Paris and Curtis were sharp enough to know he was referring to Valentino's suggestion that he and Paris would soon be lovers.

Curtis, however, was still following his original train of thought. "You know," he said, "some of those phone sex people are very ordinary looking. Fat, ugly, a far cry from what their voices suggest about them."

Dean knew this wasn't a random observation. "Okay, you've tossed out the bait. I'll bite."

"Instead of lounging on a bed of satin sheets in skimpy lingerie, like they want their callers to fantasize, they're actually in sweats and sneakers, working out of their untidy kitchens. It's all about imagination." He turned to address Paris. "Folks hear your voice and conjure up a mental image of you. I did it myself."

"And?"

"I wasn't even close. I envisioned you dark haired and dark eyed. A fortune-teller type."

"I'm sorry to disappoint."

"I didn't say you disappointed me. You're just not as exotic looking as your voice indicates." He shifted more comfortably in his seat so he wouldn't have to crane his neck to talk to her. "All this is to say that some people may have formed an unwholesome image of you. Valentino appears to be one of those people."

"Paris can't be responsible for a listener's imagination," Dean said. "Especially if he suffers from mental, emotional, or sexual problems."

"Yeah, you said that before." More or less dismissing Dean's comment as irrelevant, the detective continued to address Paris. "Is there a personal reason you want to remain anonymous?"

"Absolutely. To protect my privacy. When you're a television personality, you're always in the public eye, even when you're not on the air. I didn't like that aspect of my work. My life was an open book. Everything I said or did was subject to criticism, or speculation, or judgment from people who didn't know anything about me.

"Radio enables me to stay in the business but out of the spotlight. It allows me to go anywhere without being recognized and scrutinized and to keep my private life just that."

Curtis's harrumph implied that he knew he wasn't hearing the whole story but was willing to let it go for now. "How long did you say you keep the recordings of your phone calls?"

"Indefinitely."

He grimaced. "That's a lot of phone calls."

"But remember, I only save the ones that I feel are worth saving."

"Even at that, we're talking what? Hundreds?" She nodded. He said, "We'd use up a chunk of our remaining

forty-eight hours listening to all those calls, trying to find
the one Valentino referred to tonight. But if we go in by
the back door—"

"By looking at cold cases," Dean said, seeing suddenly where Curtis was headed.

"Right. I called a friend over there." The cold-case
unit worked out of a separate building a few miles from
headquarters. "He promised to check, see if any of their
cases have a similarity to Janey Kemp's."

"And if so, we can check to see if Paris received a call
from Valentino around that time."

"Don't get too excited," she cautioned them. "I might
not have saved that call. Besides, how could I have dismissed a warning of murder?"

"I doubt he was so blatant the first time," Dean told
her. "It's symptomatic of serial rapists to get progressively
bolder. They start out cautiously and get more daring with
each offense until they're practically courting capture."

Curtis agreed. "That's been my experience."

"Some actually want to get caught," Dean said.
"They're begging to be stopped."

"Somehow I don't think Valentino fits into that cate-
gory," she said. "He sounds very self-assured. Arrogant."

Dean looked across at Curtis and could tell that the
veteran detective agreed with her. Unfortunately, so did
Dean.

"On the other hand," he said, "he could be manipulating us. Maybe you don't remember any such call because
there wasn't one. Valentino could be trying to distract us
with a red herring."

"Could be," Curtis said. "I get the distinct feeling he's
laughing up his sleeve." He asked Paris, "What do you
know about Marvin Patterson?"

"Until yesterday, only his first name."

"Why?" Dean asked the dectective.

"He's split," Curtis said. "Officers called his place to see if he was at home, told him they were on their way to talk to him. By the time they arrived, Marvin Patterson was gone. Vacated in a hurry. Dirty breakfast dishes in the sink and his coffeepot still warm. That's how fast he cleared out."

Paris asked, "What's he got to hide?"

"We're investigating that now," Curtis replied. "The Social Security number he put on his job application at the radio station was traced to a ninety-year-old black woman who died in a rest home several months ago."

"Marvin Patterson was an alias?" Dean asked.

"I'll let you know when we know."

Paris said, "Marvin, or whatever his name is, may have something to hide, but I don't believe he could possibly be Valentino. He uses that creepy whisper, but he's articulate. If Marvin speaks at all, it's a mumble."

Dean asked her what Marvin looked like. "How old is he?"

"Thirtyish. I've never really paid much attention to his looks, but I would describe him as nice looking."

Curtis said, "Let's wait and see what turns up."

"Has anything useful been found on Janey's computer?" Dean asked.

"Smut. Lots of it. Written by other kids."

"Or predators."

Curtis conceded Dean's point. "Wherever it originated it's raw stuff, especially coming from high school kids. Rondeau printed out her email address book and is in the process of tracing the users."

After that, they'd parted company. Paris's protests against having police protection were overruled. Curtis had already dispatched Griggs and Carson to her house.

"They're both starstruck. If they were guarding the president, they couldn't be taking it more seriously. They'll be parked at your curb all night."

Dean drove her home. "What about my car?" she asked when he refused to return her to the radio station so she could pick it up.

"Ask one of your admirers to retrieve it in the morning."

She directed him to her house. It was located in a wooded, hilly area on the outskirts of downtown. The limestone house was tucked into a grove of sprawling live oaks and garnished with well-maintained landscaping. A curved walkway lined with white caladiums led up to a deep porch. Twin brass light fixtures glowed a welcome from either side of a glossy-black front door.

Incongruous with the coziness of the property was the patrol car parked at the curb. The two young policemen practically leaped from it when Dean and Paris pulled up behind them.

Dean waved back the ever-ready Griggs. "I'll see her in."

He'd insisted on going inside with her, and even though her alarm control panel hadn't registered a disturbance since she set it, he went through every room of the house, looking inside closets, behind shower doors, and even beneath the bed.

"Valentino doesn't strike me as the type who would hide under a bed," she said.

"A rapist often hides in his victim's house, waiting for her to return home. That's part of the thrill."

"Are you trying to frighten me?"

"Definitely. I want you good and scared, Paris. This guy wants to punish women, remember? He's angry with Janey—at least we're still presuming it's Janey—for cheating on him. He's angry with you for taking her side."

"I didn't even know there were sides to be taken."

"Well, that's his skewed perception of it and perception is—"

"Truth. I know."

"The suggestion that you and he would soon be together as lovers actually meant that you would be his next victim. He doesn't differentiate between the two."

She pulled her lower lip through her teeth. "When he's finished with Janey, he'll come after me."

"Not if I can help it." He went to her then and placed his hands on her shoulders. "But until we have him in custody, be afraid of him."

She smiled wanly. "I'm not actually afraid. But I'm not stupid either. I'll be careful."

When she'd tried to move away, he hadn't let her go. "This is the first time in our friendship that we've been in a bedroom together."

"Friendship?"

"Weren't we friends?"

She hesitated for several beats before saying quietly, "Yes. We were friends."

"Good friends."

That's when he had reached up and removed her sunglasses, tossed them into a nearby chair, then anxiously searched her eyes. They were as beautiful as he remembered. Deeply blue, intelligent, expressive. They gazed back at him steadily and with seeming clarity.

He exhaled a deep sigh of relief. "I was afraid that you'd lost sight in one eye, or suffered a serious injury, and that was the reason for the sunglasses."

"No permanent damage was done," she said huskily. "I wasn't even left with noticeable scars. But my eyes are still very sensitive to bright light."

Without breaking their eye contact, he leaned forward

to reach behind her for the wall switch. He flicked it down and the room went dark. He remained inclined forward, so they were touching from chest to knees, and when she didn't move away, he slid his hands around her neck and up into her hair. He tilted her face up as he lowered his.

"Dean, don't."

But the words were no more than an uneven sigh against his lips as he settled them upon hers. They parted simultaneously, and when their tongues touched, her groan echoed the hunger behind his own. He backed her against the wall, wanting to feel her and taste her. Wanting.

He curved his arm around her waist and drew her lower body up against his, increasing the pressure where already the pressure was intense. She broke off the kiss and moaned his name.

He brushed his lips across her eyes, her cheekbones, whispering, "We've waited long enough for this, Paris. Haven't we?"

Then he returned to her mouth and kissed her even more passionately than before. He worked his hand between their bodies and covered her breast. Her nipple was erect even before his thumb found it. He felt her hands tensing on the muscles of his back, felt the upward and forward angling of her hips.

He remembered muttering something unintelligible, even to himself, as he lowered his head, his mouth blindly seeking her breast.

"Ms. Gibson? Dr. Malloy?"

Dean jerked as though he'd been shot. Paris froze, then squeezed out from between him and the wall.

He saw red. "That goddamned rookie. I'm gonna kill him."

And at that moment he had meant it. He might have stormed down the hallway and throttled Griggs with his bare hands—as he'd wanted to do—if Paris hadn't grabbed his arm and held him back. She stepped around him and, straightening her hair and clothing as she went, made her way through the house and into the living room.

Griggs was standing on the threshold of the front door. "You left the front door standing open," he said to Dean, who was only half a step behind Paris. "Everything all right?"

"Everything is fine," Paris told him. "Dr. Malloy was kind enough to check my house."

Griggs was staring at her strangely. Either he had noticed that her color was high and her lips were swollen, or he was surprised by her breathlessness, or he was shocked to see her without her sunglasses, or a combination of all of that.

At that moment Dean was incapable of diplomacy and stated bluntly, "You can leave now." He had never liked cops who pulled rank, but this was one time he did and didn't feel bad about it.

Paris was more gracious. "Dr. Malloy will be leaving momentarily. We both appreciate your diligence."

"Uh, some guy . . . Stan? Dropped these off for you." He extended several cassettes.

"Oh, right. Thank you."

"Just leave them there on the table."

Griggs did as Dean ordered. He took another apprehensive glance in his direction, then scuttled out, pulling the door closed behind him.

Dean reached for Paris again, but she avoided his touch. "That shouldn't have happened."

"The interruption? Or the kiss?"

She shot him a baleful look. "It was more than just a kiss, Dean."

"You said it, not me."

She wrapped her arms around her middle. "Don't read anything into it. It won't be repeated."

He looked at her for several moments, taking in her tense expression, her taut posture, and said quietly, "Don't do this, Paris."

"What? Come to my senses?"

"Don't withdraw. Close up. Shut me out. Punish me. Punish yourself."

"You need to go. They're waiting for you to leave."

"I don't care. I've waited for seven years."

"For what?" she asked angrily. "What were you waiting for, Dean? For Jack to die?"

The words hurt, as she'd known they would. She'd said them deliberately to hurt and provoke him, but he'd be damned before he allowed himself to become either. Tamping down his own anger and keeping his voice calm, he said, "I've waited for a chance to get even this close to you."

"And then what did you expect to happen? Did you expect me to fall into your arms? To forget everything that happened and—"

When she broke off, he raised his brow inquisitively. "And what, Paris? And love me? Is that what you were going to say? Is that what you're so goddamn afraid of? That we might actually have loved each other then and still do?"

She had refused to answer him. Instead she'd marched to her front door and pulled it open.

With watchdogs at the curb, he'd had no choice but to leave.

By now the water in his shower had grown cold, but his body was still feverish with a burning desire to know—if he had been able to wring it out of her—what her answer to his question would have been.

chapter sixteen

Janey had abandoned her plans for retribution and was focusing strictly on survival.

Her attempts to escape from this room seemed as remote as her memories of childhood birthday parties. She'd seen photographs taken at those parties, but felt no connection with the little girl wearing the silver paper tiara and blowing out candles on a bakery-made cake. Likewise, her memories of trying to escape from her captor, of plotting his punishment, seemed to be vague recollections of someone else. Such courageous strategizing was unimaginable to her now.

She was so weak that even had her arms and legs not been restrained, she couldn't have moved. He hadn't given her food or water the last two times he'd been there. She could live with the hunger but her throat was raw from thirst. She had implored him with her eyes, but her silent pleas were ignored.

He was cheerful and talkative, blasé even. He tilted his head to one side and regarded her with renewed interest. "I wonder if you're missed, Janey. You've treated so many people badly, you know. Especially men. Your special talent, certainly your hobby, has been to get men to desire you and then to humiliate them with a public rejection.

"I'd been watching you for a long time before you

approached me that first night. You didn't know that? I had. I figured out your email name: pussinboots. Right? Very clever. Especially since you enjoy wearing western boots. Your favorites are the red ones, aren't they? You even wore them here one night. Wait! Hold on."

He rummaged around the room until he found the photo album he was seeking. "Yes, here you are in your boots. Only your boots, in fact," he added with a sly grin.

When he turned the photograph toward her, she averted her head and closed her eyes. Which made him angry. "Seriously, do you think anybody is really sorry that you're missing?"

He'd left shortly after that. She had been relieved to see him go but terrified that he would never return. In spite of the tape across her mouth, she sobbed noisily. Or maybe her weeping only sounded loud to her own ears. When she choked, she panicked, wondering if a person could drown in tears.

Get a grip, Janey!

She could do this. She could survive him. She could hold out until rescue came, and it would come soon. Her parents would be turning Austin upside down looking for her. Her daddy was rich. He would hire private investigators, bring in the FBI, the army, whatever it took to find her.

She'd hated some of the die-hard cops on the Austin PD force, the ones who gave her a hard time about driving drunk, and disorderly conduct, and the illegal substances often in her possession. If she hadn't been Judge Kemp's daughter, the cops who went by the book would have busted her too many times to count.

But she had also balled a few of Austin's finest, the younger, good-looking officers who had a more liberal outlook than the veterans, like the narcotics officer who worked undercover at her high school. He'd been a challenge to seduce, and when he'd finally surrendered, a letdown.

Nevertheless, she wasn't entirely without friends in the police department. They would be searching, too.

And her tormentor had called Paris Gibson. Why he had, Janey couldn't imagine and didn't care. He was obviously proud of that call, because he had recorded it just so he could play it for her. Had he wanted her to know that he was on a first-name basis with a well-known radio personality? The egotistical idiot. Didn't he know that Paris was on a first-name basis with anybody who called her?

Whatever. The important thing was that he had involved her. She could pull a lot of strings. No one was going to ignore Paris Gibson.

But Janey's burst of optimism quickly fizzled. Time was running out. Her captor had told Paris that he was going to kill her within seventy-two hours. But when had he made that call? How much of that time had already expired? She'd lost all track of the days and rarely even knew if it was daylight or dark. What if she was in hour seventy-one of the seventy-two?

Even if he didn't murder her, she could die of neglect. What if he simply never came back? How long could she survive without food and water? Or what if—and this was her greatest fear—what if he was right and nobody gave a damn that she was gone?

He hadn't enjoyed the comfort of his own bed last night, but Dr. Brad Armstrong was feeling sprightly when he arrived at the dental clinic a half hour before his first appointment.

He'd had a busy night and had snatched no more than a couple hours of sleep. But sleep wasn't the only way one could get energized. A girl with a silver ring through her nipple—now, that could get a man supercharged.

He was chuckling to himself as he entered the building and greeted the receptionist.

"Good morning, Doctor. I assume Mrs. Armstrong located you last evening. She was so disappointed that her surprise date was spoiled."

"We had a quiet dinner together after the kids went to bed, so it worked out okay. Any messages for me?"

"A Mr. Hathaway has called twice, but he didn't leave a message either time. He only asked that you return his call. Shall I get him on the line for you?"

Mr. Hathaway was his probation officer. On his best day, Hathaway was a humorless tight ass who loved peering at people over the top of his granny glasses. His idea of intimidation, Brad supposed. "No thanks, I'll try him later. No other messages?"

"That's it."

Toni must really be upset this time. Ordinarily she would have tried to reach him by now if only to assure herself that he hadn't had a head-on with an eighteen-wheeler, suffered a heart attack, or been mugged and murdered. It was always she who took the initial steps toward making up. Isn't that what a loving, supportive wife was supposed to do when her husband stormed from the house after a quarrel?

So he really couldn't be blamed for anything he'd done last night, could he? He'd broken vows, but his backsliding was more Toni's fault than his. She hadn't even tried to be compassionate and understanding. Instead she had scolded him.

He had a collection of erotic magazines and pictures.

Big deal. Some might call the material pornographic, but so what? And maybe his collection was more extensive than the next guy's. Was that grounds for making it into a federal case?

After last night, her next accusation would be that he had played too rough. He could hear her now. *Where is that aggression coming from, Brad? I don't know you anymore.* Toni had many fine qualities, but she lacked a spirit of adventure. Anything novel or experimental frightened her. He'd seen the fear in her eyes last night.

She should take lessons from that girl he'd met at the lake. Melissa, her name was. That's what she'd told him anyway. He certainly hadn't given her his name, but he didn't remember her asking. To an adventurous girl like her, names were unimportant.

He'd seen this one around a lot, with many different partners, so, not surprisingly, she hadn't been shocked by his graphic pictures. In fact, she had demonstrated a sincere appreciation for them. They had really steamed her up. She'd been all over him. That girl was something else, her and her nipple ring. Toni would probably have him committed if he suggested a body piercing. But, damn, what a turn-on.

He settled into his desk chair and booted up his computer. Other people in the office had been curious as to why he'd placed his monitor with the back of it facing out into the room rather than up against a wall so all the cables wouldn't show. He'd contrived an explanation, but the real reason was that it was nobody's business but his what was on his monitor.

He visited his favorite websites, but was disappointed that the material hadn't been updated since yesterday morning. Even so, he scanned them all, looking specifically for women with nipple rings. He didn't find any.

He would do some research later, surf the Internet until he located some new, exotic websites. Maybe a Sex Club member had discovered some interesting ones that he didn't yet know about. Leave it to kids to be at the forefront of discovery.

He entered his password and went into the site. He went straight to the message board and was about to type in an inquiry when someone knocked on his office door, then immediately pushed it open.

"Dr. Armstrong?"

"What?" he said brusquely.

"Sorry," an assistant said. "I didn't mean to disturb you. Your first patient has been prepped."

He forced himself to smile. "Thank you. I'll be there as soon as I finish this email to my mom."

She ducked out. He glanced at the clock. He'd been in the office for over a half hour, but it had seemed like five minutes. "Time flies . . . ," he chuckled to himself. Some men read the stock-market report over their morning coffee, some the sports page. He had another interest. Was that a crime?

He returned to his home page and, just to be on the safe side, engaged the service that deleted all his Internet connections so they couldn't be traced.

He'd treated three patients before he was able to take a break. A newspaper had been left at the coffee bar. He carried it, a doughnut, and a cup of coffee into his office with him. He sipped the coffee, took a bite from the doughnut, and flipped up the front page of the newspaper . . . nearly choking when he saw her picture.

It was a serious portrait, probably last year's school photo. Laughably ironic, she looked demure. She seemed to be staring straight at him in a way that made him want to look away. He couldn't.

Accompanying the picture was a story about her: county judge's daughter—Jesus; high school senior; previous malfeasances; a three-day suspension from school last semester; her mysterious disappearance.

The reporter went into detail about her membership in an Internet club, the purpose of which was to solicit sex partners. It was all there in black and white. The writer described how it worked, the chat rooms, the sexually explicit messages left on the website, the secret gatherings—which were no secret to the members—and the licentious acts that ensued at these meeting places. Anyone with whom Janey had had contact was being pursued and questioned by the police. A reference was made that hinted at a possible connection to Paris Gibson's radio program.

Brad placed his elbows on his desk and clasped his head between his hands.

Sergeant Robert Curtis, who has organized a team of investigators, wouldn't comment on Ms. Kemp's alleged connection to the Sex Club, although Officer John Rondeau of the Computer Crimes Division said that such a connection had not been ruled out.

"We're still exploring that," Rondeau said.

The officers declined to comment when asked about the possibility of foul play.

The write-up also said that Austin PD personnel had refused to comment when asked why a homicide detective was overseeing a missing persons case. The more loquacious Rondeau did tell the reporter, "At this point in time, we've had absolutely no indication of foul play and are assuming that Ms. Kemp is a runaway." Good answer, but it didn't address the question.

There was one quote from Judge Kemp. "Like all teenagers, Janey can be inconsiderate and irresponsible when it comes to notifying us of her plans. Mrs. Kemp and I are confident that she'll soon return. It's much too soon for alarming speculation."

Brad actually jumped when his phone rang. With a shaking hand, he reached for the intercom button. "Yes?"

"Your wife is on line two, Dr. Armstrong. And your next patient has arrived."

"Thanks. Give me five minutes."

He wiped the sweat off his upper lip and took several deep breaths before lifting the telephone receiver. It was time to play meek.

"Hi, hon. Look, before you say anything, I just want you to know how sorry I am about last night. I love you. I hate myself for saying the things I did. That trash bag of stuff? History. I threw it away. All of it. As for the . . . the other . . . I don't know what came over me. I'm—"

"You missed your appointment."

"Huh?"

"Your ten o'clock appointment with Mr. Hathaway. He called here because he's been unable to reach you at your office."

"Christ. I forgot about it." The truth was, he had. He'd come into his office, killed a half hour on the Internet, seen three patients, read the front-page story.

"How could something that important slip your mind, Brad?"

"I had patients," he replied testily. "They're pretty damn important, too. Remember our mortgage? Car payment? Grocery bill? I have a job."

"Which won't matter if you get sent to prison."

He glanced down at the picture of Janey Kemp. "I'm not going to prison, not for missing one appointment with my probation officer."

"He's being lenient. He rescheduled you for one-thirty this afternoon."

She was back on her high horse, talking to him like he was no older than their son. He was a grown-up, by God. "Apparently I'm not getting through to you, Toni. I've got work."

"And an addiction," she snapped.

Jesus, she was cutting him no slack whatsoever. "I told you I got rid of the magazines. I tossed the bunch of them in a Dumpster. Okay? Happy now?"

Rather than sounding happy, her laugh sounded terribly sad. "Okay, Brad, whatever. But you're not fooling anybody. Not Hathaway, and certainly not me. If you don't keep this appointment, he'll have to report it, and you'll have to face the consequences."

She hung up on him.

"And the horse you rode in on, sweetheart!" he shouted to the telephone receiver as he slammed it down. He sent his chair rolling back on its casters as he shot to his feet. Placing one hand on his hip and rubbing the back of his neck with the other, he began to pace.

Any other time, he would be really pissed off at Toni for taking such a high-handed tone with him. And he was pissed off. Matter of fact, he was mad as hell. But Toni would keep. Today he needed to focus on a much more serious problem.

When you lined it all up, things didn't look so good for him. He was a convicted sex offender. The charge had been a complete falsehood and the trial a farce. Nevertheless, it was there on his personal record.

Last night he'd had sex with a young woman. God help him if she was under seventeen. Never mind that she was as experienced as a ten-dollar whore—ten dollar, hell. For round two he'd given her a fifty-dollar "gratuity." Despite her experience, if she was a minor, he'd committed a crime. And his wife, who had the ear of his group therapist and his probation officer, was probably already yapping to them about his recent violent tendencies.

But what really had him concerned, what was causing his bowels to spasm, was that he couldn't remember if he'd ever seen Melissa in the company of Janey Kemp.

chapter seventeen

Sergeant Curtis called Paris while she was spreading a piece of toast with peanut butter. "I mentioned cold cases last night?"

"There's one that's similar?"

"Maddie Robinson. Her body was discovered three weeks after her roommate reported her missing. A cattleman found it in a shallow grave in one of his pastures. Middle of nowhere. Cause of death, strangulation with a ligature of some kind. Decomposition was advanced. Scavengers and the elements had done significant damage."

Paris set aside her breakfast.

Curtis continued, "But the coroner was able to determine that the body had been washed with an astringent agent." There was a significant pause before he added, "Inside and out."

"So even if it had been found sooner—"

"The perp had made damn sure any DNA evidence would be compromised to the point of making it negligible. Also no sign of either shoe prints or tire tracks. Probably weather eroded. No clues on clothing because there was none."

Paris felt heartsick for the victim who had suffered such a horrible and ignominious death. She asked Curtis what he knew about her.

"Nineteen. Attractive but not a stunning beauty. She was a student. Her roommate admitted that they weren't exactly nuns. Partied a lot. They went out nearly every night. Here's where it gets really interesting. According to her, Maddie had been seeing someone she referred to as 'special.'"

"In what way?"

"She didn't know. Maddie was vague about what set this guy apart. The girls had been friends since junior high school. Usually confided everything. But Maddie wouldn't tell her anything about this mystery guy except that he was cool and wonderful and special."

"The roommate never saw him?"

"Didn't come to their apartment. Maddie would meet him. The roommate didn't know where. He never even called their apartment phone, only Maddie's cell. The roommate's theory was that he was married, and that was the reason for the secrecy. For all their exploits, she and Maddie had drawn the line at sleeping with married men. Not for moral reasons, but because there was no future in it, she said.

"One day Maddie was in love, the next she announced that she was breaking off the relationship. She told her roommate that he was getting too possessive, which irritated her since he never took her on a real date. The only place they ever went was to his apartment—which she described as dreary—where they'd have sex. She hinted that it had become bizarre, even for her, and she enjoyed novelty. The roommate pressed her for details, but she refused to talk about it. All she'd say was that the affair was over.

"To cheer her up, the roommate prescribed getting laid by someone else. Maddie took her advice. They went out, drank a lot, and Maddie brought a guy home with her. He was later cleared as a suspect.

"Maddie Robinson was last seen on the shore of Lake Travis, where a large group of young people were celebrating the start of summer break. She and the roommate got separated. The roommate went home alone, assuming that Maddie had found a partner for the night. This was nothing unusual. But when Maddie hadn't come home twenty-four hours later, she notified the police.

"I wasn't assigned the case, so it didn't spring immediately to my mind. The trail got cold for the CIB detectives who were investigating, and the case got turned over to the other unit." Summary complete, he took a deep breath.

"So this happened roughly around the time spring semester ended?"

"Late last May. The body was found June twentieth. Do you have recorded calls from that far back?"

"In my files. Shall I bring you duplicates?"

"ASAP. Please."

"Stan?"

He jumped when Paris walked into her office and caught him seated behind her desk. He recovered quickly and greeted her with a glum, "Hey."

She tossed her handbag onto the pile of printed material on her desk. "You're in my seat."

Before coming into her office, she had gone to the storage room and retrieved several CDs containing recorded call-ins that she'd had transferred off the Vox Pro. She'd left them with an engineer and asked him to duplicate their contents onto audiocassettes.

"Cassettes? That's working backward, isn't it?" he'd grumbled.

Without wanting to explain that the CIB was still working with audiocassettes, she simply said, "Thanks," and left before he had an opportunity to refuse her odd request.

"What are you doing in my office?" she asked Stan now as she replaced him in her chair. As he'd done the night before, he cleared a corner of her desk and perched there, uninvited.

"Because I don't rate an office, and this was the most private place to wait."

"For what?"

"My uncle Wilkins. He's in a conference with the GM."

"About what?"

"Me."

"Why, what'd you do?"

He took exception. "How come everybody automatically assumes that I screwed up?"

"Did you?"

"No!"

"Then why is your uncle Wilkins having a conference about you with our GM?"

"Because of that goddamn phone call."

"Valentino's phone call?"

"It churned up some stuff. My uncle flew out here in the company jet early this morning, called and woke me up, ordered me to meet him here, and he meant immediately. So I break my neck to get here, and he's already behind closed doors. I haven't even seen him yet."

"What 'stuff'?"

Rather than answer her question, he asked one of his own. "Do I do a good job around here, Paris?"

She shook her head with amusement and dismay. "Stan, you don't do any job around here."

"I'm here every single weeknight until two o'clock in the freaking morning."

"You're here in body. You occupy space. But you don't do any work."

"Because nothing ever goes wrong with any of the machines."

"If it did, would you know how to correct it?"

"Maybe. I'm good with gadgets," he said petulantly.

"'Gadgets' isn't exactly the word I would use to describe millions of dollars' worth of electronics. Do you even understand radio technology, Stan?"

"Do *you*?"

"I don't have the title of engineer."

He was a spoiled brat, prone to whining. On any given night she felt like throttling him for his incompetence and casual approach to his job. Ineptitude was forgivable, but indifference wasn't. Not in her book, anyway.

Every time she spoke into her microphone, she was aware that hundreds of thousands of people were listening to her. She was touching them with her voice, in their cars and where they lived. She became a partner in whatever they were doing at the time.

To her the listening audience wasn't just a six-digit number on which to base an advertising rate. Each number represented an individual who was giving her his time and to whom she owed the best programming she could provide.

Stan had never considered the human factor of their audience. Or if he had, it hadn't been translated into work. He'd never shown any initiative. He put in his time, counting the minutes until sign-off, and then rushed out to do whatever it was that he did.

But in spite of all that, she couldn't help but feel sorry for him. He wasn't here by choice. His future had been dictated the second he was born into the Crenshaw family. His uncle was a childless bachelor. Stan was an only child. When his father died, he became the heir apparent to the media empire, like it or not.

No one in the corporation seemed willing to accept or admit that he was uninterested and ill-equipped to assume control when his uncle Wilkins stepped down, which probably wouldn't be until he was pronounced dead.

"I'm learning the business from the bottom up," he told Paris sulkily. "I need to know a little about every aspect of it so I'll be ready when it's time for me to take over. At least that's what Uncle Wilkins thinks."

"What stuff did Valentino's call churn up?"

His mouth twisted into a scornful frown. "It's nothing."

"It was enough to get your uncle Wilkins in a spin."

He heaved a huge sigh. "Before I was assigned—read 'banished'—to this swell radio station, I was working at our TV station in Jacksonville, Florida. Compared to this dump, it was paradise. I had a fling with one of the female employees."

"Then you're not gay?"

He reacted as if he'd been jabbed in the spine with a hot poker. "Gay? Who says I'm gay?"

"There's been speculation."

"Gay? Jesus! I hate these stupid rednecks around here. If you don't drive a dual-axle pickup, drink Bud from a bottle, and dress like the Sundance Kid, you're queer."

"What about the woman in Florida?"

He picked up a paper clip and began reshaping it. "We got carried away in the office. Next thing I know, she's crying sexual harassment."

"Which was untrue?"

"Yes, Paris, it was untrue," he said, enunciating each word. "The charge was as bogus as her thirty-six-C cups.

I didn't coerce her into having sex with me. In fact, she was on top."

"More information than I needed, Stan."

"Anyhow, she filed suit. Uncle Wilkins settled out of court, but it cost him a bundle. He got pissed at *me*, not her. Can you believe that? Said, 'How stupid do you have to be to take your dick out at work?' I asked him if he'd ever heard of Bill Clinton. A remark he didn't appreciate, especially since all our newspapers had endorsed him for president.

"Anyway, that's why I'm here, serving time." He tossed the now-misshapen paper clip into the wastebasket. It made a soft ping when it struck the metal bottom. "And that's why he hopped the company jet and flew here this morning."

Paris could guess the rest. "After you told him about being questioned by the police, Wilkins thought he should come to Austin and make certain this unfortunate episode in Florida didn't rear its ugly head."

"He called it damage control."

"Spoken like a true corporate godfather."

She now had the picture. Stan had been foisted onto 101.3 as punishment for mixing business with pleasure. Uncle Wilkins had omitted telling management about the incident with the company employee, but felt he should explain it now before the Austin PD uncovered it and suspicion was cast on his nephew.

"Was that the only incident, Stan?"

His eyes narrowed as he looked down at her from his lofty angle. "What do you mean?"

"The question was simple enough. Yes or no?"

The starch went out of him then. "That was the only time, and, believe me, I learned my lesson. I'll never touch another employee."

"As an owner, that could make you vulnerable to litigation."

"I wish somebody had warned me about that before I went to Jacksonville."

Paris passed up telling him he shouldn't have had to be warned. That was a policy he should have adopted without being told. She also refrained from calling him a creep for doing it under any circumstances.

He looked across at her with a wounded expression. "Everybody thinks I'm gay?"

How like Stan to prioritize the least important point. "You dress too well."

The electrician who'd duplicated the recordings stepped in to tell her that the cassettes were ready and that he'd left them for her at the lobby desk.

"More cassettes?" Stan said.

"This may not be the first time Valentino heralded a murder by calling me."

"What happened last night after you and Malloy raced out of here? I gather you didn't catch Valentino."

"No, unfortunately." She told him about the pay phone at the Wal-Mart store. "Patrol cars were there within minutes, but no one was around."

"I heard about the missing girl on the news this morning. Front page of the paper, too."

She nodded, recalling the quote from Judge Kemp. Janey's parents were holding fast to their belief that her absence was by choice, which, to Paris's mind, was a monumental mistake. On the other hand, she hoped they were right.

She stood up and gathered her handbag, preparing to leave. "I'll see you tonight, Stan."

"Who's Dean Malloy?"

The question came from out of the blue and caught

her off guard. "I told you. Staff psychologist for the APD."

"Who moonlights as a bodyguard?" He gave her a sardonic look. "When I dropped off those cassettes at your house last night, the cop told me that Malloy was inside with you."

"I'm missing your point."

"Deliberately, I think. Who is Malloy to *you*, Paris?"

If she didn't tell him, he might go digging on his own and learn more than she preferred him to know. "He and I knew each other in Houston years ago."

"Mmm-hmm. I'm guessing you knew each other pretty well."

"Not pretty well, Stan, *very* well. He was Jack's best friend."

Closing the conversation with that, she stepped around him and moved toward the door. But at the threshold, she paused and turned back. "What do you know about Marvin?"

"Only that he's a jerk."

"Is he into computers, the Internet?"

He snuffled. "Like I would know. I haven't exchanged more than a few grunts with him. Why the sudden interest?"

She hesitated, not knowing if Marvin's apparent flight was information that Curtis would want to be shared. "No reason. See you tonight."

Paris and Sergeant Curtis sequestered themselves in a small interrogation room and sat across from each other at a scarred table. On it were the portable recorder he had used the day before and the cassette tapes she had brought from the radio station.

They began their search for Valentino's calls by listening to tapes recorded up to a week before Maddie Robinson's disappearance. Yesterday she and Dean had agreed that Valentino was altering his voice. The affectation made it distinctive and instantly recognizable, thereby allowing her to fast-forward past voices obviously not his.

Curtis left briefly to get them fresh coffees. When he returned, Paris told him excitedly, "I think I've found it. We don't have a date-and-time stamp like we would on the Vox Pro, but it's on a cassette of recordings made about that time. He was especially morose that night, but I aired this call anyway. His statements provoked follow-up calls that kept my phone lines busy for hours."

Curtis resumed his seat. "You made him a celebrity for the evening."

"Unwittingly, I assure you. Ready?" She started the tape.

Women are unfaithful, Paris. Why is that? You're a woman. When you've got a man practically eating out of your hand, why would you want another? Isn't quality better than quantity?

I'm sorry you're unhappy tonight, Valentino.

I'm not unhappy, I'm angry.

Not every woman is unfaithful.

That's been my experience.

You just haven't found the right woman yet. Would you like to hear a special song tonight?

Like what?

Barbra Streisand sings a wonderful rendition of "Cry Me a River." It's a cliché, but what goes around comes around.

Play the song, Paris. But even if she gets dumped the way she dumped me, it won't be the retribution she should receive.

Paris stopped the cassette and looked across at Curtis, who was thoughtfully twirling his ring around his finger again. He said, "I guess the retribution he felt she deserved was to choke her to death and bury her body in a goddamn cow pasture. Excuse my French."

Paris lowered her head into her hands and massaged her temples. "I never would have gathered from what he said that he was plotting to kill her."

"Hey, don't beat yourself up over this. You're not a mind reader."

"I didn't detect a real threat in what he said."

"No one would have. And anyway, we're still guessing. Valentino may have no connection whatsoever to Maddie Robinson."

She lowered her hands and looked at him. "But you think they're connected, don't you?"

Before he could answer, John Rondeau pushed open the door. He smiled brightly at Paris. "Good morning."

"Hi, John."

He seemed pleased that she remembered his name. "Making progress?"

"We think so."

"So am I." He looked at Curtis. "Can I see you outside for a minute?"

Curtis got up. "Back in a sec."

"I'll see if I can find any other calls from Valentino."

The detective left with the younger man and was gone much longer than a sec. By the time he returned, she had scored again. "This call is on the same cassette, which means they couldn't have come in more than a few days apart.

"He's a totally different Valentino. Very upbeat. He claims that the unfaithful lover is 'out of his life' and he stresses the word 'forever.' You'll hear on the tape the difference in his mood." Sensing that Curtis was only half-listening and seemed distracted, she paused to ask, "Is something wrong?"

"Maybe. I hate to think this might be bad, but . . ." He ran his hand around the back of his thick neck as though it had suddenly begun to ache. "I suppose you know that Malloy has a son."

"Gavin."

"You know him?"

"I knew him as a little boy. I haven't seen him since he was ten." Curtis's anxiety was evident. She felt a stab of fear for Dean. "Why, Sergeant? What about Gavin? What's happened?"

chapter eighteen

"Gavin?"

"Yeah?"

Dean pushed open his son's bedroom door and went in. "Boot up your computer."

"Huh?"

"You heard me."

Gavin was lying on his bed watching ESPN. He should have something more constructive to do than watch a replay of a soccer game between two European teams. Why wasn't he up and dressed, doing something rather than lazing in bed?

Because I haven't made him, Dean thought.

He had a lazy son because he'd been a lazy parent. Trying to make Gavin get off his butt hadn't been worth the quarrels that invariably followed. Lately, to avoid a hassle, he'd let a lot of things go. He shouldn't have. He wasn't trying to win a popularity contest with Gavin. He wasn't his buddy, his pastor, or his therapist. He was his father. It was past time for him to start exercising stricter parental authority.

He snatched the remote control from Gavin's hand and switched off the television set. "Boot up your computer," he repeated.

Gavin sat up. "What for?"

"I think you know."

"No I don't."

The disrespectful tone and insolent expression stoked Dean's temper. He felt it smoldering like a nugget of coal inside his chest. But he wouldn't yield to it. He would not.

He said tightly, "We can go straight to the police station, where they're waiting to interrogate you about Janey Kemp's disappearance, or you can boot up your goddamn computer so at least I'll know what we're up against when I get you down there. Either way, your days of jerking me around are over."

He had stayed home this morning to organize and type his notes on a suspect he had interviewed several days ago. The detective overseeing that case was growing impatient with the delay.

He knew that if he went to his office, he couldn't have concentrated on anything except Paris and the case in which she was involved. He couldn't have kept himself out of the CIB, where he knew she and Curtis would be listening to her tapes.

So he'd called Ms. Lester, told her he would be working at home, and forced himself to tackle the overdue report. He had just finished it when Robert Curtis called and gave him what could be life-altering news.

"The police want to question me?" Gavin asked. "How come?"

Dean had been clinging to a thread of hope that John Rondeau had made a grave error, but Gavin's worried expression was a dead giveaway that the information was correct.

"You lied to me, Gavin. You're an active member of the Sex Club. You've exchanged numerous email letters with Janey Kemp, and, based on what you two wrote back and forth, you know her a hell of a lot better than you led me to believe. Do you dispute any of this?"

Gavin was now seated on the edge of his mattress, his head hanging between hunched shoulders. "No."

"When was the last time you saw her?"

"The night she disappeared."

"What time?"

"Early. Eight or so. It was still light."

"Where?"

"At the lake. She's always there."

"Had you arranged to meet her there that night?"

"No. She'd been giving me the leper treatment for the last few weeks."

"Why?"

"She's like that. Gets you to like her and then, you know, you're history. I heard she's been seeing this other guy."

"What's his name?"

"Don't know. Nobody does. Rumor is he's older."

"How old?"

"I don't know," Gavin whined, becoming impatient with all the questions. "Thirty-something, maybe."

"So what happened the other night?"

"I went up to her and we started talking."

"You were mad at her." Gavin looked up at him, silently asking how he knew that. "In your last email to her, you called her a bitch. And worse."

Gavin swallowed hard and dropped his head again. "I didn't mean anything by it."

"Well, that's not how the police are going to see it. Especially since she's been missing since that night."

"I don't know what happened to her. Swear to God I don't. Don't you believe me?"

Dean desperately wanted to, but he resisted the urge to go easy on him. Now wasn't the time to turn soft. Gavin needed him to be tough, not Mr. Nice Guy. "We'll get to the part about believing you later. Boot up your computer. I need to see how bad it is."

Reluctantly Gavin moved to his desk. Dean noticed that he typed in a user name and a password to get in, which would've been unnecessary if he had nothing to hide.

The home page of the Sex Club had been designed by amateurs. It was the cyberspace-age version of rest room wall graffiti. Dean motioned Gavin aside. He sat down in the desk chair and reached for the mouse.

"Dad," Gavin groaned.

But Dean ignored him and went straight to the message board. Curtis had given him the names Gavin and Janey had used: blade and pussinboots, respectively. For ten minutes, he scrolled through the messages, stopping to read the ones written by his son and the judge's daughter. It was difficult reading.

The last message Gavin had emailed her was crude, insulting, and, now, incriminating. Sick at heart, Dean closed the website and turned off the computer. For several moments he stared into the blank monitor screen, trying to link the writer of what he'd just read with the little boy he had taught to use a baseball glove, the kid with the gap-toothed smile and sprinkling of freckles across his nose, the youngster whose biggest problem used to be foot odor.

Dean couldn't afford the time to indulge in his personal despair now. He must save it for later. More imperative was clearing his son of all suspicion.

"This is one time you had better come clean with me, Gavin. I want to help you, and I will. But if you lie to me, I'll be hamstrung and unable to help you. So no matter how bad it is, is there anything else I should know?"

"Like what?"

"Anything about Janey and you. Did you actually ever have sex with her?" He nodded toward the computer. "Or was this only talk?"

Gavin looked away. "We did it once."

"When?"

"Month ago, six weeks," he said, raising his shoulders. "Not long after I met her. But we'd already been exchanging emails. I was the new kid in town. I think that's the only reason she was interested in me."

"Where did this take place?"

"A whole bunch of us met at some park. I can't remember the name of it. She and I broke away from the group, got in my car." Resentfully, he added, "Didn't you ever do it in the backseat of a car?"

He was trying to pick a fight. The transference of guilt was a classic distraction tactic that Dean recognized and refused to buy in to. "Did you use a rubber?"

"Of course."

"You're sure?"

"I'm sure. Jeez."

"And you were with her only that one time?"

Gavin rolled his shoulders, pushed back a hank of hair that had fallen over his forehead, looked everywhere except at Dean.

"Gavin?"

He sighed theatrically. "Okay, one other time. She went down on me."

"Same questions."

"Where did it happen? Behind some club on Sixth Street."

"In public?"

"Yeah, sorta, I guess. I mean, we were out in the open, but nobody else was around."

He had a flash image of himself calling Pat and telling

her that her baby boy was in jail for public lewdness. *Where were you, Dean?* she would have asked. Where *had* he been while his son was composing smutty letters and getting blow jobs in alleyways?

The self-accusations had to be shelved until later, too. "Those two times? That's it?"

"Yeah, she cooled it, dumped me."

"But you weren't ready to be dumped."

Gavin looked at him as if he was crazy. "Hell, no. She's hot."

"To say the least," Dean said in an undertone. "If there's anything else, you'd better tell me. I don't want any more ugly surprises, something the cops have discovered that you haven't told me."

Gavin wrestled with indecision for at least half a minute before he said, "She, uh . . ." He opened a desk drawer, removed a paperback copy of *The Lord of the Rings,* and took out a photograph that had been secreted between the pages. "She gave me this the other night."

Dean reached for the photograph. He didn't know which astonished him more, the girl's graphic pose or her shameless smile. He slipped the picture into his shirt pocket. "Get showered and dressed."

"Dad—"

"Hurry. I've been instructed to have you there by noon. A lawyer is meeting us there."

Finally, the gravity of his predicament seemed to have penetrated layers of adolescent insolence. "I don't need a lawyer."

"I'm afraid you do, Gavin."

"I didn't do anything to Janey. Don't you believe me, Dad?"

His sullenness had dissolved. He looked young and scared, and Dean experienced that same twinge in his heart that he had felt the night before when he watched him sleep.

He wanted to embrace him and assure him that everything would be all right. But he couldn't promise that because he didn't know it to be true. He wanted to tell him that he believed him implicitly, but, unfortunately, he didn't. Gavin had betrayed his trust too many times.

He wanted to tell him he loved him, but he didn't say that either. He was afraid that Gavin would rebuke him for it being too little too late.

Paris had been pacing the hallway for more than an hour, waiting. Nevertheless, she reacted with a start when Dean emerged through the double doors of the CIB, where he, Gavin, and an attorney had met with Curtis and Rondeau in an interrogation room.

He looked surprised to see her. "I didn't know you were here."

"I couldn't leave until I knew that Gavin was all right."

"So you know?"

"I was with Curtis listening to the tapes when . . ." She stopped, unsure of what she should say.

"When my son became a suspect?"

"As far as we know, no crime has been committed and Janey is with a friend."

"Sure. That's why Curtis is putting Gavin through the wringer."

She pushed him toward a bench and made him sit down. It was an ugly, sad-looking piece, a cheap metal frame supporting a blue vinyl cushion with the stuffing poking up through numerous cracks. Probably it had been mindlessly picked at by the restless hands of witnesses, suspects, and victims who had occupied this same bench while despairing over their fate or that of someone they loved. They wouldn't have been in this place unless their lives had been upended, perhaps permanently.

"How is Gavin handling it?" she asked softly.

"He's subdued. Not giving off any attitude, thank God. I think it's finally sunk in that he's in deep shit."

"Only because he exchanged sexually explicit emails with Janey. So did a lot of others."

"Yeah, but Gavin has demonstrated a real creative flare," he said with a bitter laugh. "Did they show you any of the stuff he'd written?"

"No. But even if I'd read it, it wouldn't have changed my opinion of him. He was a terrific little boy, and he'll be a fine young man."

"Two days ago I thought breaking curfew was a major offense. Now . . . this. Jesus." Sighing, he propped his elbows on his knees and covered his face with his hands.

Paris placed her hand on his shoulder. It was instinctive. He needed to be touched, and she needed to touch him. "Have you called Pat?"

"No. Why upset her if it turns out to be nothing except some dirty emails?"

"Which I'm sure is exactly what it'll turn out to be."

"I hope. Twice he talked us through his actions that night. The accounts didn't vary."

"Then he's probably telling the truth."

"Or his lie has been well rehearsed."

Staring straight ahead, toward the open staircase across the hall, he tapped his clasped fingers against his lips. "I talk to liars every day, Paris. Most people lie to one degree or another. Some don't even realize they're lying. They've said or believed something for so long that it becomes their truth. It's my job to filter out their bull-shit until I get to the real truth."

When he paused, Paris remained silent, giving him an opportunity to organize his thoughts. The warmth of his skin radiated up through his shirt and into her palm where it still rested on his shoulder.

"Gavin admits to driving home drunk," he said. "He admits to stopping along the way to barf in someone's yard and to disobeying me by leaving the house in the first place.

"He owns up to liking Janey, or at least liking what they did together. He says he talked to her that night and tried to persuade her to go somewhere with him. She shot him down cold.

"He got mad, said things, some of which I can't believe came out of my son's mouth. He confesses to being furious when he left her, but he insists that he did. He says he joined a group of guys and remained with them, drinking tequila, until he left for home. He didn't see Janey again."

Turning his head, he locked gazes with her. "I believe him, Paris."

"Good."

"Am I being naive? Is that wishful thinking?"

"No. I think you believe him because he's telling the truth." She gave his shoulder a light squeeze of reassurance. "Is there anything I can do?"

"Have dinner with us tonight. Gavin and me."

Not expecting that, she quickly removed her hand from his shoulder and looked away. "I work at night, remember?"

"There's plenty of time to have dinner before you go to the station. We'll start early."

She shook her head. "I have something to do this

afternoon that can't be postponed. Besides, I don't think
it's a good idea."

"Because of what happened last night?"

"No."

"Yes."

Vexed by his perception, she said, "Okay, yes."

"Because you know that if we're together it's going to
happen again."

"No it won't."

"It will, Paris. You know it will. Furthermore, you
want it to just as much as I do."

"I—"

"Dean?"

Upon hearing his name, they sprang apart. A woman
had just alighted from one of the elevators and was coming toward them. There was only one word to describe
her: stunning.

Her tailored suit emphasized her curvy figure rather
than detracted from it. Excellent legs were shown off by
a fashionably short skirt and high heels. Lip gloss and
mascara were her only makeup, and no more than that
was needed. She wore no jewelry other than discreet diamond studs in her ears, a slender gold chain at her
throat, and a wristwatch. Her pale, shoulder-length hair
was parted down the middle, the style loose, classic, and
uncomplicated. A California girl in a power suit.

Dean shot to his feet. "Liz."

She graced him with a dazzling smile. "Everything
went so well in Chicago, I wrapped things up a day early.
Made all my flight connections and thought I would surprise you with a late lunch. Ms. Lester told me I could
find you here, and apparently I did pull off a surprise."

She hugged him, kissed him on the mouth, then turned
and gave Paris an open and friendly smile. "Hello."

Dean made a terse introduction. "Liz Douglas, Paris Gibson."

Paris didn't remember coming to her feet, but she found herself standing face-to-face with Liz Douglas, whose handshake was firm, like a woman accustomed to conducting business primarily with men. "How do you do?" Paris said weakly.

"A pleasure to meet you. Are you a policewoman? Do you work with Dean?" She was trying to see past Paris's tinted lenses and probably had assumed she was an undercover officer.

"No, I work in radio."

"Really? Are you on the air?"

"Late night."

"I'm sorry, I don't—"

"No need to apologize," Paris told her. "My program comes on when most people are already in bed."

After a brief but awkward lapse in conversation, Dean said, "Paris and I knew each other in Houston. Years ago."

"Ah," Liz Douglas said, as though that was an explanation that clarified everything.

"You'll have to excuse me. I'm late for an appointment." Paris turned to Dean. "Everything will be fine. I know it will. Please tell Gavin hello for me. Ms. Douglas, nice to meet you." She walked quickly away, toward the elevators.

Dean called her name, but she pretended not to hear and kept walking. As she disappeared around the corner, she heard Liz Douglas say, "I get the distinct impression I interrupted something. Is she in some sort of trouble?"

"Actually, I am," he replied. "Gavin and I."

"My God, what's happened?"

By then an elevator had arrived. Paris stepped into it and was grateful to find herself the sole passenger. She leaned against the back wall as the doors slid closed. She didn't hear any more of Dean's conversation with Liz. But she didn't need to. The familiarity with which they'd kissed said a lot.

He would no longer need her hand on his shoulder. He had Liz to console him now.

Gavin knew that if he lived to be a hundred, this would go down as the worst day of his life.

For this visit to the police station, he had dressed in his nicest clothes, and his dad hadn't even had to tell him to. They were probably ruined now because for the past hour and a half he'd been leaking sweat from every pore. The BO would never come out.

On TV and in movies, suspects under interrogation made themselves look guilty with their body language. So he tried not to fidget in the uncomfortable chair, but sat up straight. He didn't let his eyes dart about the room, but looked directly at Sergeant Curtis. When asked a question, he didn't elaborate, but spoke truthfully and concisely, although the subject matter was embarrassing.

He took his dad's advice—now was not the time to withhold information. Not that he was trying to cover up anything. They already knew about the emails, the Sex Club, all that. He didn't know Janey Kemp's whereabouts or what had happened to her. He was as clueless about her fate as they were.

Yes, he'd had sex with her. But so had every guy he'd met since coming to Austin, with the exception of his dad and the men in this room.

All but one. And more than Curtis's persistent questions, it was that one who was making him sweat. He'd been introduced as John Rondeau.

The instant Rondeau walked into the room Gavin recognized him. After all, he'd seen him just last night with two busty babes, climbing from the backseat of a car. And it sure as hell hadn't been a prayer group.

There was no mistaking that the young cop had recognized him, too. When he saw Gavin, his eyes had widened slightly but returned to normal in a nanosecond. Then he had clapped a warning stare on Gavin that made his scrotum shrink and snuffed any comment he might have made about having seen this guy before.

The others, including his dad, probably took Rondeau's stare as stern disapproval of the emails he had swapped with Janey. But Gavin knew better. Gavin knew Rondeau was threatening him with severe consequences if he betrayed his extracurricular activities to his superiors.

Gavin felt even more afraid when Curtis asked his dad to leave the room. Lately, his old man had been a real hard-ass, constantly riding him about one thing or another. It had gotten to where Gavin dreaded the sight of him, knowing he was about to receive a lecture on something. But he was glad to have his dad on his side today. And no matter how bad the situation became, Gavin knew he wouldn't abandon him.

He remembered once when they'd gone to the Gulf Coast for a long weekend. His dad had cautioned him about swimming out too far. "The waves are stronger and higher than they look from the beach. There's also a strong undertow. Be careful."

But he'd wanted to impress his dad with what a good swimmer and body surfer he was. Next thing he knew, he couldn't touch bottom and the waves just wouldn't let up. He panicked and floundered. He went under, knowing he was doomed to a death by drowning.

Then a strong arm closed around his chest and hauled him to the surface. "It's okay, son, I've got you."

He sputtered and struggled, still trying to find a footing.

"Relax against me, Gavin. I won't let you go. I promise."

His dad towed him all the way back to shore. He didn't bawl him out when they got there either. He didn't say, "Stupid kid, didn't I tell you? When are you going to listen and learn?"

He'd just looked real worried while he thumped him on the back until he'd coughed up all the seawater he'd swallowed. Then he had wrapped him in a beach towel and hugged him tight against his side for a long time. Not saying anything. Just staring out across the water, holding him close.

When the weekend was over and his mom had asked if everything had gone okay, his dad had winked at him while telling her that everything had been fine. "We had a great time." He never did tell her that Gavin would've been a goner if he hadn't saved him.

Gavin trusted him to be there to grab him if he sank today, too. His dad was like that. A good person to have around during a crisis.

That's why it had stressed him when the detective asked his dad to wait outside while they talked to Gavin alone. "I'll leave, but only if the lawyer stays," his dad had stipulated.

Curtis had agreed. Before he left, his dad had looked at him and said, "I'll be right outside, son," and Gavin was confident that he would be.

After he left, Curtis had looked at him so hard, he'd

begun to squirm in his seat despite his determination not to. He was beginning to wonder if the detective had gone mute by the time he said, "I know it's hard to talk about certain things in front of your dad. Girls and sex. Stuff like that."

"Yes, sir."

"Now that your father isn't here, I'd like to ask you some questions of a more personal nature."

More personal than they'd already been? You gotta be kidding me. That's what he'd thought, but he'd said, "Okay."

But the questions were basically the same ones his dad had asked him before they left the house. He responded to Curtis just as candidly. He told him about the times he and Janey had had sex.

"You didn't engage in any sexual activity with her that last night you saw her?"

"No, sir."

"Did you see her having sex with anyone else?"

What, did they think he'd watch? Did they really think he was that sick? "I wouldn't have gone up to her and started talking if she'd been with another guy."

"Did you touch her?"

"No, sir. I tried to take her hand once, but she pulled it back. She told me I was needy, and that my neediness had gotten to be a real pain."

"That's when you called her a bitch and so forth?"

"Yes, sir."

"What was she wearing?"

Wearing? He couldn't remember. When he called up an image of her, he saw only her face, the sultry eyes, the smile that was both inviting and cruel. "I don't remember."

Curtis looked over at Rondeau. "Can you think of anything else?"

"Where'd you get the picture of her?"

Gavin dreaded looking directly at him, but he did. "She gave it to me."

"When?"

"That night. She said, 'Get over it, Gavin.' Then she gave me the picture. A 'souvenir,' she called it. When I got to missing her, I could use it, you know, to get off."

"Did she tell you who took the picture?"

"Some guy she's been seeing."

"Did she say his name?"

"No."

"Did you ask?"

"No."

Curtis waited to see if Rondeau had anything else he wanted to ask, but when he sat back, satisfied, Curtis stood up. "That's it for now, Gavin. Unless you can think of anything else."

"No, sir."

"If you do, notify me or tell your father immediately."

"I will, sir. I hope she's found soon."

"So do we. Thank you for your cooperation."

As promised, his dad was waiting outside the CIB, but Gavin was surprised to see that Liz was with him. Immediately she rushed toward him. She asked if he was all right and smothered him in a hug.

"I've gotta go to the bathroom," he mumbled and moved away before anyone could stop him.

No one was at the urinals. He slipped into one of the stalls and checked for feet beneath the partitions. When he was sure he was alone, he bent over the toilet and vomited. He hadn't had much to eat today, just some cereal for breakfast, so mostly he spewed bile and then had the dry heaves until the blood vessels in his neck seemed on the verge of bursting. The spasms were so violent, they made his torso sore.

Fear had caused him to vomit once before. When he was fourteen, he had sneaked his mother's car out. She was on a date with the man she'd ultimately married. Since she had abandoned him to go to dinner with that loser, Gavin had felt it served her right if he drove her car illegally.

He'd gone only as far as the nearest McDonald's, where he'd scarfed down a Big Mac. On his way home, only a block from his house, a neighbor's new golden retriever darted right into the path of his car. The puppy had been the talk of the neighborhood. He was cute and friendly, and when Gavin had gone down to meet him a few days earlier, he had licked his face enthusiastically.

He had braked in time to prevent a tragedy, but he had come close enough to killing the puppy that as soon as he got home, he'd thrown up his ill-gotten meal. His mom never knew that he'd taken the car out, and the puppy had grown into a dog that still thrived. Beyond a guilty conscience, he hadn't had to face any consequences.

He hadn't been as fortunate this time.

He flushed the toilet twice before leaving the stall. At the sink he splashed double handfuls of cold water over his face, rinsed his mouth out several times, then bathed his face some more before turning off the faucet and straightening up.

Before he could even register that Rondeau was there, the cop had one hand on the back of his head and the other in an iron grip around his wrist and was pushing his hand up between his shoulder blades.

chapter nineteen

Rondeau shoved Gavin's face against the mirror. It struck with such impact, Gavin was surprised the glass didn't crack. He wasn't sure about his cheekbone. The pain brought unmanly tears to his eyes. His arm felt like it was being wrenched from his shoulder socket. Gasping, he said, "Let go of me, asshole."

Rondeau hissed directly into his ear, "You and I have a secret, don't we?"

"I know your secret, Officer Rondeau." His lips were smushed against the mirror, but he could make himself understood. "While you're off duty from the police department, you fuck high school girls."

Rondeau rammed his hand up higher between Gavin's shoulder blades, and in spite of Gavin's determination not to show any fear, he cried out. "Now let me tell you your secret, Gavin," he whispered.

"I don't have a secret."

"Sure you do. You'd had your fill of that little bitch's games. You figured it was time she was taught a lesson. So you arranged to meet her. She got abusive and you got mad."

"You're crazy."

"You were so enraged, so humiliated, you lost it, Gavin. In the state of mind you were in, I can't hazard to think what you did to her."

"I didn't do anything."

"Of course you did, Gavin," he said smoothly. "You had the perfect motive. She dumps you, then makes you a laughingstock. She ridiculed you on the message board, for everybody to read. A 'dickless dud.' Isn't that how she referred to you? You couldn't have that. You had to shut her up. Forever."

Rondeau's salesmanship made the scenario sound plausible. Gavin panicked at the thought of how many other policemen, including Sergeant Curtis, Rondeau could convince.

"Okay, she was making fun of me, and I was mad at her," he said. "But the other is crap. I was with friends that night. They'll vouch for me."

"A bunch of rednecks and jocks stoned on tequila and grass?" Rondeau scoffed. "You think anything they testify to will hold up in court?"

"Court?"

"I hope you've got another alibi lined up, Gavin. Something stronger than the testimony of those losers you hang out with."

"I don't need an alibi because I didn't do anything to Janey except talk to her."

"You didn't hit her on the head with a tire iron and roll her body into the lake?"

"Jesus! No!"

"You're not shitting bricks every waking moment, wondering when her body will be discovered? I'll bet I can find somebody who will testify to seeing you and Janey in a struggle."

"They'd be lying. I didn't do anything."

Rondeau stepped even closer, mashing Gavin's thighs against the sink. "Whether you did or not, I really don't care, Gavin. They can let you go, or they can send you away for the rest of your life, it makes no difference to me. But if you rat me out, I'll make sure you look guilty as shit. I'll lead them to believe—"

"What the hell is going on?"

Gavin felt the rush of air immediately after hearing his dad's booming exclamation from the doorway. He yanked Rondeau away from him and slammed him against the tile wall, then used his hand like a staple against Rondeau's neck to hold him there.

"What the hell do you think you're doing?" His voice reverberated off every hard surface of the room. "Gavin, are you all right?"

His cheek was throbbing and his shoulder hurt like hell, but he wasn't going to complain in front of Rondeau. "I'm okay."

His dad looked him over, as though to reassure himself that he wasn't seriously hurt, then turned back to Rondeau. "You'd better make this good."

"I'm sorry, Dr. Malloy. I've been reading that stuff your son wrote. It just . . . It's disgusting, some of it. I've got a mom, a sister. Women shouldn't be talked about like that. When I came in here to take a leak, I saw him and just blew my cool, I guess."

Gavin wouldn't have wanted to be in Rondeau's shoes. His dad was practically breathing fire into his face and his hand hadn't relaxed its pressure on his throat. Rondeau's face was turning red, but he stood stock-still, as though afraid that if he moved, he could set off an eruption of wrath that he would be powerless to combat.

Finally, Dean lowered his hand, but his eyes were just as effective at keeping Rondeau nailed to the wall. His voice was quiet and controlled, but menacing. "If you ever touch my kid again, I'll wring your fucking neck. Do you understand me?"

"Sir, I—"

"Do you understand me?"

Rondeau swallowed, nodded, then said, "Yes, sir."

Despite his meekness, it was several moments before Dean released him from his stare and stepped back. He extended his arm toward Gavin. "Let's go, son."

Gavin glanced at Rondeau as he walked past him. The young cop might have convinced his dad that he'd experienced an uncontrollable surge of righteous indignation for which he was truly sorry.

But Gavin wasn't fooled. Rather than creating more trouble for himself, he would keep Rondeau's dirty little secret. What did he care if the cop led a double life that included screwing underage girls? The girls hadn't seemed to mind.

Once they'd left the rest room, Gavin took a glimpse at his dad. His jaw was clenched and he looked ready to make good on his threat to wring Rondeau's neck. He was glad that he wasn't on the receiving end of that simmering anger.

He figured that his cheekbone would soon be sporting a bruise, and possibly it was already beginning to discolor because the moment Liz saw them, she knew something had happened.

"What's wrong?"

"Nothing, Liz," Dean told her. "Everything's fine, but I have to skip lunch. Sergeant Curtis has paged me."

Apparently, while he was in the john heaving up his guts, his dad had filled her in on what was going on.

"There's somebody he wants me to talk to. I'm sorry you cut your trip short only to rush back to this mess."

"If it's your mess, it's my mess," she said.

"Thanks. I'll call you at home tonight."

"I'll be glad to wait until you're free."

Dean shook his head. "I have no idea how long I'll be. This could take the rest of the afternoon."

"Oh, I see, well . . ." She looked so disappointed Gavin felt sorry for her. "You're too valuable around here for your own good. Would you like me to drive Gavin home?"

Inwardly Gavin groaned, *Please no.* Liz was okay. She was certainly great to look at. But she tried too hard to make him like her. Often her efforts were so transparent that he resented them. He wasn't a little kid who could be won over with bright chatter and excessive interest in him.

"I appreciate the offer, Liz, but I'm going to send Gavin home in my car."

Gavin whipped his head toward his dad, thinking he must not have heard him correctly. But no, he was passing him his car keys. Two nights ago, he had made Gavin surrender the keys to his rattle-trap. Now he was entrusting him with his expensive import.

This demonstration of his trust meant more than when he had threatened Rondeau with death. Protecting your kid was required, but trusting him was a choice, and his dad had chosen to trust him when he had given him no reason to. If fact, he'd given him every reason not to.

It was something he needed to think about and analyze. But later, when he was alone.

"I'll call you when I'm ready to leave, Gavin. You can come back and get me. Does that sound like a plan?"

His throat was awfully tight, but he managed to squeak out, "Sure, Dad. I'll be waiting."

Even though her present situation was chaotic, Paris didn't use it as another excuse to postpone the necessary trip out to Meadowview.

And perhaps after kissing Dean last night, guilt also

had motivated her to call the director of the perpetual care facility and tell him that she would be there at three o'clock.

When she arrived promptly, he was in the atrium entrance to greet her. As they shook hands, he looked abashed and apologized for the tone of the letter she had received the day before.

"In hindsight I wish my wording hadn't been quite so—"

"No apology necessary," she told him. "Your letter prompted me to do something I've needed to do for months."

"I hope you don't think I'm insensitive to your grief," he said as he led her down the hushed corridor.

"Not at all."

Jack's personal effects had been placed in a storage room. After unlocking the door, the director pointed to three sealed boxes stacked on a metal shelving unit. They weren't large and didn't contain much. Paris could easily have carried them all to her car, but he insisted on helping her.

"I'm sorry for any inconvenience my delay has caused you and the staff," she said as they placed the boxes in the trunk of her car.

"I understand why you'd want to stay away. The hospital couldn't hold good memories for you."

"No, but I never had to worry about the treatment Jack received here. Thank you."

"Your generous donation was thanks enough."

After settling Jack's outstanding medical bills, she had donated the remainder of his estate to the facility, including the sizable life insurance policy he had obtained when they became engaged. She was the beneficiary, but she could never have kept the money.

She and the director had parted company in Meadowview's parking lot, under a broiling sun, knowing it was doubtful they would ever see each other again.

Now the three boxes sat on Paris's kitchen table. There would never be a good time to open them, and she would rather have it over and done with than continue to dread it. Using a paring knife, she slit the packing tape on all three boxes.

In the first were pajamas. Four pair, neatly folded. She'd bought them for him when he was first admitted to Meadowview. They were soft now from being laundered countless times, but they still had the cloying, antiseptic smell she associated with the hallways of the hospital. She closed the box.

The second contained mostly papers, those notarized, triplicate documents from insurance companies, county courthouses, hospitals, medical and law offices, which reduced Jack Donner to a Social Security number, a statistic, a client, an entry for an accountant to tabulate.

As executor of his will, she'd had to deal with all the legalities inherent in a person's demise. All the wherefores and hereins were past tense now, the documents obsolete. She had no need or desire to read them again.

Only the third box remained. It was the smallest of the three. Even before opening it, she knew the contents would be the most upsetting because the articles inside were Jack's personal possessions. His wristwatch. Wallet. A few favorite books, which she had read aloud to him during her daily visits to Meadowview. A framed photograph of his parents, who were already deceased when Paris met him. She had thought it a blessing that they hadn't lived to see their only child so reduced.

Shortly after moving him to Meadowview, she had emptied his house. His clothes she had given to a charity.

Then, steeling herself, she had sold his furniture, his car, snow skis, bass-fishing boat, tennis racquets, guitar, eventually the house itself, to pay the astronomical medical bills that the insurance didn't cover.

So this was all that Jack Donner had owned when he died. He'd been left with nothing, not even his dignity.

His wallet was soft from wear. His credit cards, long expired, were still in their slots. Behind a plastic shield, her own face smiled up at her. Noticing a sliver of paper behind the photo, she pinched it out. It was a newspaper clipping that Jack had folded several times so it would fit behind her picture.

She unfolded it and saw another picture of herself. Only this one wasn't a flattering studio portrait. This one had been snapped by a photojournalist. He had captured her looking tired, bedraggled, and disillusioned as she stood gazing into the distance, her microphone held forgotten at her side. The headline read, "Career-making Coverage."

Tears blurring her eyes, she rubbed the edges of the clipping between her fingers. Jack had been proud of the job she'd done, proud enough to save the newspaper article about it. At any point in time afterward, had he realized the cruel irony of his pride in her work on that particular story?

Funny, that a total stranger to them, someone they never even met, would have such a catalytic impact on their lives. His name was Albert Dorrie. He changed Jack's and her destiny the day he decided to hold his family hostage.

It had been an uneventful Tuesday until the story broke just before lunchtime. When those in the newsroom heard that a woman and her three children were being held at gunpoint in their home, they were galvanized into action.

A cameraman was assigned to go to the scene. As he hastily gathered his equipment, the assignments editor ran a quick inventory of his available reporters. "Who's free?" he barked.

"I am." Paris remembered raising her hand like a schoolgirl who knew the correct answer.

"You've got to record the voice-over for that colon cancer prevention story."

"Recorded and already with the editor."

The veteran newsman rolled his cigarette, which was never lighted inside the building, from one side of his nicotine-stained lips to the other while contemplating her with a scowl. "Okay, Gibson, you get on it. I'll send Marshall to take over for you when he finishes at the courthouse. In the meantime, try not to fuck up too bad. Go!"

She piled into the news van with the video cameraman. She was hyper, anxious, excited to be covering her first late-breaking story. The video photographer facilely navigated Houston freeway traffic while humming Springsteen.

"How can you be so calm?"

"Because tomorrow there'll be some other nutcase, doing something equally psychotic. The stories are the same. Only the names change."

To some extent, he was right, but she figured his mellow mood was largely due to the joint he was smoking.

Barricades had been placed at the end of a street in a middle-class neighborhood. Paris leaped from the van and ran to join the other reporters who were clustered around the SWAT officer currently acting as spokesperson for the Houston PD.

"The children range in age from four to seven," Paris

heard him say as she wedged herself into the mass. "Mr. and Mrs. Dorrie have been divorced for several months. She recently won a child custody dispute. That's all we know at this time."

"Was Mr. Dorrie upset over the custody ruling?" one reporter shouted.

"One would assume, but that's only speculation."

"Have you talked to Mr. Dorrie?"

"He hasn't responded to our attempts."

Paris's cameraman had caught up with her. Reaching through the crowd, he passed her a microphone that was connected to his camera.

"Then how do you know he's in there, holding his family at gunpoint?" another reporter asked.

"Mrs. Dorrie called in a 911 and was able to convey that message before she was disconnected, we believe by Mr. Dorrie."

"Did she say what kind of firearm he has?"

"No."

Paris asked, "Do you know what Mr. Dorrie hopes to gain by this?"

The SWAT officer said, "At this time, all I know for certain is that we have a very serious situation on our hands. Thank you."

With that, he concluded the briefing. Paris turned to the cameraman. "Did you get my question on tape?"

"Yep. And his answer."

"Such as it was."

"The newsroom called. They're gonna come to you live in three minutes. Can you think of something to say?"

"You focus the camera, I'll think of something to say."

She staked out an advantageous spot from which to

do her live cut-ins. The Dorrie house could be seen in the background at the far end of a narrow, tree-lined street, which on any other afternoon would probably have been serene.

Now it was thronged with emergency vehicles, police units, news vans, and people who had come to gawk. Paris asked one of the Dorries' neighbors if she would talk to her on camera about the family, and the woman happily consented.

"I always thought he was a nice man," the woman said. "Never woulda thought he'd snap like this. You just never know about people. Most are crazy, I guess."

An hour into the standoff, Paris spotted Dean Malloy arriving in an unmarked car. He seemed impervious to onlookers and walked with confident determination as uniformed officers escorted him past the gaggle of reporters and toward the SWAT van that was parked midway between the barricade and the house. Paris watched him enter the van, then called her assignments editor and reported this update.

"Will you shut the hell up!" he shouted to the voices in the background. "Can't hear myself think." Then to Paris, "Who is he again?"

She repeated Dean's name. "He's a doctor of psychology and criminology, on staff with HPD."

"And you know him?"

"Personally. He's trained to negotiate with hostage takers. He wouldn't be here if they didn't think they needed him."

She went live with this breakthrough, scooping all the other stations.

By hour three of the standoff, everyone was growing a little bored and perversely wishing that something would happen.

Paris got a lucky break when she noticed a small woman standing at the edge of the crowd of spectators. She was being supported by a man at her side while she wept copiously but silently.

Leaving her microphone and cameraman behind, Paris approached the couple and introduced herself. Initially the man was antagonistic and told her bluntly to get lost, but the woman finally identified herself as Mrs. Dorrie's sister. At first she was reluctant to talk, but Paris eventually learned the stormy history of the Dorrie marriage.

"This background information could be very useful to the police," she told the woman gently. "Would you be willing to talk to one of them?"

The woman was wary and frightened. Her husband remained hostile.

"The individual I have in mind is not an ordinary policeman," she told them. "He's not a SWAT officer. His sole purpose in being here is to see that your sister and her children come out of this situation unharmed. You can trust him. I give you my word."

Minutes later, Paris was trying to coax a uniformed policeman to carry a note to the SWAT van and hand-deliver it to Dean. "He knows me. We're friends."

"I don't care if you're his sister. Malloy's busy and doesn't want to talk to a reporter."

She signaled her cameraman forward. "Are you rolling tape?"

"I am now," he said, swinging his camera up to his shoulder and looking into the eyepiece.

"Be sure to get a close-up of this officer's face." She cleared her throat and began speaking into the microphone. "Today Officer Antonio Garza of the Houston Police Department impeded efforts to rescue a family being held hostage by an armed gunman. Officer Garza declined to convey an important message to—"

"The hell you doing, lady?"

"I'm putting you on TV as the cop who screwed up a hostage rescue."

"Give me the friggin' note," he said, snatching it from her hand.

It was a long, agonizing quarter of an hour before Dean stepped from the van and walked toward the barricade. He batted aside microphones thrust at him as he scanned the faces in the crowd. When he saw Paris waving at him from outside her station's news van, he made a beeline toward her.

"Hello, Dean."

"Paris."

"I wouldn't ever take advantage of our friendship. I hope you know that."

"I do."

"I wouldn't have drawn you away if I didn't think this was vitally important."

"So your note indicated. What have you got?"

"Let's get inside."

They scrambled into the back of the van, where she had persuaded Mrs. Dorrie's sister and brother-in-law to wait. She made introductions. Space was limited even though the cameraman had remained outside. Paris didn't want to spook them with the camera and lights.

Dean hunkered down in front of the distraught woman and spoke quietly and calmly. "First of all, I want you to know that I'm going to do everything within my power to keep your sister and her family from getting hurt."

"That's what Paris said. She gave us her word that we could trust you."

Dean cast a quick glance at Paris.

"But I'm afraid the policemen will storm the house," the woman said, her voice breaking emotionally. "If they do, Albert will kill her and the children. I know he will."

Dean asked, "Has he threatened their lives before?"

"Many times. My sister always said he would wind up killing her."

He listened patiently to what she had to impart, interrupting only when he needed a point clarified, gently prodding her when she faltered. The van grew warm and stank of marijuana. Dean seemed unaware of the uncomfortable surroundings, of the sweat that beaded his forehead. His eyes never wavered from the sobbing woman's face.

He asked pertinent questions and must have committed her answers to memory because he wrote nothing down. When she had told him everything she knew that could be relevant, he thanked her, reassured her that he was going to bring her sister and the children out safely, then asked her if she would stay close by in case he needed to speak to her again. She and her husband agreed.

As they emerged from the stuffy van, Paris passed Dean a bottle of water. Absently he drank from it as they walked toward the barricade. A deep worry line had formed between his eyebrows.

Finally she ventured to ask if the interview had been helpful.

"Absolutely. But before it can help, I've got to get Dorrie to talk to me."

"You have his cell number now."

"Thanks to you."

"I'm glad I could help."

Garza and other uniformed policemen held back the crowd of reporters calling questions to Dean as he stepped through the barricade. He started to walk away, but paused long enough to turn back and say, "You did good, Paris."

"So did you."

She remained where she was, watching him until he disappeared into the SWAT van, then called her assignments editor and told him what had happened.

"Good work. Helps to have friends in high places. Since you've got a rapport with the head kahuna, stay put, see it through to the end."

"What about Marshall?"

"I've made it your baby, Paris. Don't disappoint me."

An hour later, she learned along with all the other media that Malloy was finally in conversation with Dorrie. He had persuaded the man to let him speak to Mrs. Dorrie, who had tearfully told him that she and the children were still alive, physically unharmed but terribly frightened.

Paris went live with that report at the top of the five o'clock news. She repeated it at six o'clock because there'd been no further developments and, at the conclusion of the newscast, did a general recap of the events that had taken place throughout the long day. She also fielded extemporaneous questions from the anchors.

Jack arrived at seven with burgers and fries for her and her cameraman. "Who's been smoking weed?" he asked.

"She has," the cameraman replied as he popped a french fry into his mouth. "Can't get her off the stuff."

But when he finished his meal and stepped from the van, he hesitated. "Jack, about the . . . uh . . ."

Jack smiled guilelessly. "I don't know what you're talking about."

The cameraman was visibly relieved. "Thanks, man."

When they were alone, Paris shot Jack a look of vexation. "A fine manager you'll make."

"A good manager instills loyalty." His easy grin turned to an expression of concern as he reached out and stroked her cheek. "You look exhausted."

"My blusher wore off hours ago." Recalling Dean's disregard for his personal discomfort, she added, "How I look on camera doesn't seem very important in light of what I'm reporting."

"You've done a fantastic job."

"Thanks."

"No, I mean it. The station is all abuzz."

That morning, when she'd left in the news van, she had approached the story as an opportunity to strut her stuff, win some attention, create the buzz Jack had mentioned.

Over the course of the day, that had changed. The turning point had been Dean's conversation with Mrs. Dorrie's sister. It had opened her eyes to the grim reality of the story, given names to the people involved, made it a human tragedy rather than a vehicle to propel her career forward. It seemed distasteful to benefit from the misfortune of others.

"Have you seen Dean any more?" Jack asked, breaking into her thoughts.

"Only once. He came out midafternoon to ask Mrs. Dorrie's sister about the children's favorite foods, toys, games, pets. He wanted to personalize his conversations with Mr. Dorrie."

Jack frowned thoughtfully. "It'll be personalized for Dean if this goes south."

"All he can do is his best."

"I know that. You know that. Everybody knows that except Dean. Mark my words, Paris. If five people don't walk out of that house, he'll beat himself up over it."

Jack hung around for another hour, then left with her

promise to call him if the situation changed. It didn't. Not for hours. She was sitting in the passenger seat of the van, organizing her notes and trying to find a new angle to the story, when Dean tapped on the windshield.

"Has something happened?" she asked.

"No, nothing. Sorry if I alarmed you," he said, coming to stand beside the open window. "I just had to get out of that van for a while, get some fresh air, stretch my legs."

"Jack said to tell you to hang in there."

"He came around?"

"To bring us burgers. Have you had anything to eat?"

"A sandwich. But I could stand a drink of water."

She passed him a bottle. "I've been drinking from it."

"Like I care." He took a long swallow, recapped it, and handed it back to her. "I have a favor to ask. Would you call Gavin? Whenever I'm involved in something like this, he gets scared." He gave her a fleeting smile. "Too many cop shows on TV. Anyhow, tell him you've talked to me and assure him that I'm okay."

Reading the question in her eyes, he added, "I've already spoken to him. So has Pat. But you know how kids are. He'll come nearer to believing it if it comes from someone not his parent."

"I'll be happy to. Anything else?"

"That's it."

"Easy enough."

His necktie had been loosened and his shirtsleeves were rolled back to his elbows. He propped his forearms in the open window, but turned his head in the direction of the house. He stared at it for a long while before he said softly, "He may kill them, Paris."

She didn't say anything, knowing that she wasn't expected to. He was confiding his worst fear to her, and she was glad he felt comfortable enough with her to do that. She only wished she could think of a reassurance that didn't sound banal.

"I don't know how a man could shoot his own children, but that's what he says he's going to do." Lowering his head to his clasped hands, he rubbed his thumb across his furrowed brow. "Last time I talked to him, I could hear one of the little girls crying in the background. 'Please, Daddy. Please don't shoot us.' If he decides to pull that trigger, there's not a goddamn thing I can say or do to stop him."

"If it weren't for you, he probably would have pulled the trigger already. You're doing the best you can." Then, without any forethought, she touched his hair.

He raised his head immediately and looked at her, possibly wondering how she knew that he was doing his best, or needing to hear that he was. Or maybe just to verify that she had touched him.

"Word filters back to us, you know," she said in a voice barely above a whisper. "From other cops. They all think you're incredible."

In a voice equally low, he asked, "What do you think?"

"I think you're pretty incredible, too."

She would have smiled, as one friend to another, but a smile seemed inappropriate for a multitude of reasons. The situation, for one. The tightness that had seized her chest until she could barely breathe, for another. But especially because of the intensity of feeling with which Dean was looking at her.

As on the night they met, the stare stretched into more than just an exchange between friends. Only this time it lasted even longer and the gravitational pull between them was much stronger.

She would have lowered her hand, which was still raised, an exposed culprit that had acted of its own volition. But lowering it would only have made its transgression more noticeable and lent it the meaning she didn't dare acknowledge.

Later she wondered if they'd have kissed if his pager hadn't beeped.

But it did and broke the spell. He checked the LED. "Dorrie's asking to talk to me." Without another word, he sprinted to the van.

It was midnight before he finally negotiated the release of the children. Dorrie was afraid that SWAT officers were going to rush the house. Dean assured him that he wouldn't allow that to happen if he would let the kids leave. Dorrie agreed on the condition that Dean come as far as the porch and carry them away from the house himself. Of course, Paris didn't know the terms of this negotiation until the crisis was over.

She was talking to Mrs. Dorrie's sister when the cameraman came jogging over to them and said, "Yo, Paris, Malloy is walking up to the house."

With her heart in her throat, she watched as Dean stood, his hands raised high into the air, at the edge of the porch. No one could hear what he and Dorrie said to one another through the door, but he remained in that vulnerable position for what seemed to her an eternity.

Eventually the door was opened from inside the house and a little boy slipped through, followed by an older girl carrying a smaller child. All were crying and shading their eyes against the bright lights aimed at the house.

Dean placed his arms around their waists and, carrying them against his body, delivered them to the Child Protection Services caseworkers who were standing by to receive them.

One of Dorrie's bargaining points, Paris learned later, was that the children were not to be handed over to his sister-in-law, who'd always hated him and had tried to turn his wife against him.

When Paris did a stand-up reporting the children's release, her voice was hoarse with fatigue and her appearance ragged, but a spirit of optimism had rejuvenated everyone at the site.

She concluded her stand-up by remarking on that mood shift. "For hours it seemed as though this standoff might have a tragic ending. But police personnel are now hopeful that the release of the children unharmed signifies a breakthrough."

Her last word was punctuated by two loud gunshots. The noise silenced Paris and other reporters doing similar stand-ups. In fact, she had never experienced a silence that sudden and that profound.

It was shattered by the third and final shot.

Paris stared at the clipping one last time, then refolded it exactly as Jack had done and replaced it behind her photograph in his wallet. She returned the wallet to the box, sick with the knowledge that if Jack had ever connected the night of the standoff to what transpired afterward, he might not have saved the clipping, but would have ripped it to shreds.

chapter twenty

She was a small woman. The hands twisting the damp tissue could have belonged to a child. Her legs were crossed at the ankles and tucked beneath the chair. She was as jittery as a piano student at a recital, awaiting her turn to play.

Curtis introduced them. "Mrs. Toni Armstrong, this is Dr. Dean Malloy."

"How do you do, Mrs. Armstrong?"

Curtis was being as gallant with her as he had been with Paris. "Can I get you something to drink?"

"No thank you. How long do you think this will take? I've got to pick up my children at four."

"I'll have you out of here well before then."

Prior to this meeting, Dean had been briefed for all of thirty seconds, the time it had taken him to walk to Curtis's cubicle after seeing Gavin and Liz off. He didn't have a clue as to why he'd been summoned to sit in on this interview. He remained standing, propping himself against the wall, for now a silent observer.

Mrs. Armstrong wasn't the shrinking violet her dainty appearance implied. It must have appeared to her that she was being ganged up on, because she put a stop to the pleasantries and cut to the chase.

"Mr. Hathaway said you had asked to see me, Sergeant Curtis, so I'm here. But no one has explained why you wanted to talk to me. Should I call my lawyer? Is my husband in some kind of trouble that I don't know about?"

"If he is, we don't know about it either, Mrs. Armstrong," Curtis replied smoothly. "But he has violated the terms of his probation, correct?"

"That's right."

"And Hathaway says you've recently noticed other troubling behavior."

She lowered her head. "Yes."

Curtis nodded sympathetically. "Hathaway called one of the SOAR officers, who then brought your husband to my attention."

Dean was beginning to see where this was going. SOAR—Sex Offender Apprehension and Registration—was under the auspices of the CIB. The detectives who specialized in sex offenses would know about Curtis's investigation. Too often those crimes and homicide overlapped.

"Could you please fill me in on the background?" Dean asked.

"Eighteen months ago Bradley Armstrong was convicted of molesting a minor and sentenced to five years' probation, mandatory group therapy, and so forth. Lately he's been skipping meetings.

"His probation officer scheduled two appointments with him today. He didn't show. Mrs. Armstrong notified his attorney, who went to his office—he's a dentist—to urge him to comply, get his act together. He'd split, although he had appointments with patients scheduled for this afternoon. Nobody knows where he is. He isn't answering his cell phone."

Toni Armstrong said, "I'm glad Hathaway called you. I'd rather Brad be arrested for violating his probation than . . . than for something else."

"Like what?" Dean asked.

"I'm afraid he's on the brink of committing another offense. He's doing everything he's not supposed to do."

Curtis, sensing that a rapport had been established, offered Dean his desk chair. Once he was seated, he said, "I know it's difficult for you to talk about this, Mrs. Armstrong. We're not trying to make the situation harder on you. In fact, we'd like to help."

She sniffed, nodding. "Brad is collecting pornography again. I found it in his office. I can't crack his computer because he's constantly changing the password to keep me out, but I know what I would find. It came out during his trial that he had bookmarked dozens of websites. And I'm not talking about artistic or elegant erotica. Brad goes for the very hard-core stuff, especially if the girls are in their teens.

"But that's not the worst of it. I haven't even told his probation officer all of it." She smiled at Dean wanly. "I'm not sure why I'm telling you. Except that I want Brad stopped before he gets into real trouble."

"What didn't you tell Mr. Hathaway?"

In fits and starts, she told them about her husband's frequent absences from his office and home, his lies, and his justifications for his actions. "All of which I know are signs that he's losing control over his impulses."

Dean agreed with her. These were classic bad signs. "Has he become defensive when you try to talk to him about it? Overly sensitive and angry? Does he accuse you of being suspicious, of not trusting him?"

"He turns every argument away from himself and tries to throw the blame on me for being unsupportive."

"Has he become violent?"

She related what had taken place in their kitchen last night.

When she finished, Dean asked quietly, "You haven't seen him since he stormed out?"

"No, but we spoke by phone this morning. He apologized, said he didn't know what had come over him."

"Has he ever been rough with you before?"

"Not even playfully rough. I've never seen him like that before."

Another bad sign, Dean thought.

She must have read the concern in his expression. Her eyes bounced between him and Curtis. "I still haven't been told why I'm here."

"Mrs. Armstrong," Curtis said, "does your husband ever listen to late-night radio?"

"Sometimes," she replied hesitantly.

"Has he ever disappeared before?"

"Once. Just after his patient's parents charged him with molesting their daughter. He was missing for three days before he was found and arrested."

"Where was he found?"

"In a motel. One of those residence places. He said he went into hiding because he was afraid no one would believe his side of the story."

"Did you?" Dean asked.

"Believe him?" Sorrowfully she shook her head. "That wasn't the first time a patient or coworker had complained about inappropriate behavior or touching. Different dental practices, different cities, even. But the same complaint.

"Brad's behavior leading up to that incident was similar to what it has been recently. Only this time, it's more pronounced. He's not trying so hard to hide it. He's more defiant, and that's making him reckless. That's why it was so easy to follow him."

"You followed him?"

Simultaneously with Dean's question, Curtis asked when this had taken place.

"One night last week." She rubbed her forehead as though ashamed of the admission. "I can't remember exactly. Brad had called from his office and said he wouldn't be coming home until late. He made up an excuse, but I saw through it. I asked a neighbor to watch my children.

"I got to his office before he left, so I was able to trail him from there. He went to an adult book and video store and stayed for almost two hours. Then he drove out to Lake Travis."

"Where specifically?"

"I don't know. I would never have found the area if I hadn't been following him. It wasn't a developed area. No homes or commercial buildings around. That's why I was surprised to see so many people there. Mostly young people. Teenagers."

"What did he do there?"

"For the longest time, nothing. He just sat in his car, watching. There was a lot of drinking, messing around, pairing off. Eventually Brad got out and approached a girl." She lowered her head. "They talked for a while, then she got into the car with him. That's when I left."

"You didn't confront him?"

"No," she said, smiling ruefully. "I was the one who felt dirty. I just wanted to get away from there, go home and take a long shower. Which is what I did."

In deference to her embarrassment, neither Dean nor Curtis said anything for a moment. Finally Curtis asked, "Could you identify the young woman you saw with him?"

She thought about it for a moment, then shook her head. "I don't think so. All that registered with me was that she was probably still in high school. It was dark, so I never got a good look at her face."

"Blond or dark hair? Tall, petite?"

"Blond, I think. Taller than me but shorter than Brad. He's five-ten."

"Could this be her?" Curtis reached for the picture of Janey Kemp that had run in the newspaper and held it out to her.

She looked at it and then at them individually. "Now I know why you wanted to see me," she said, her eyes filling with fear. "I read about this girl. A judge's daughter who's missing. That's it, isn't it? That's why I'm here."

Rather than answer her, Curtis said, "Did you ever tell your husband what you'd seen, that you had him cold?"

"No. I pretended to be asleep when he came in that night. The next morning, he was cheerful and affectionate. Teasing the kids, making plans with them for the weekend. Being the perfect husband and daddy."

She was contemplative for a moment. Dean sensed that Curtis was about to break into her thoughts with another question, but he subtly motioned for him to hold off.

Eventually Toni Armstrong raised her head and spoke directly to Dean. "Sometimes I think Brad actually believes his lies. It's as if he's living in a fantasy world where there are no consequences for his actions. He can do as he pleases without fear of getting caught or paying a penalty."

That was the most disturbing thing she'd told them. Dean doubted that she realized that, but Curtis did. When Dean glanced over at him, the detective was frowning thoughtfully.

He knew, as Dean did, that the profiles of serial killers

and sexual predators typically included an elaborate fantasy life, one that was so compelling and so real to them that they acted it out. They often believed themselves to be above the laws of a society that had grievously wronged them, and answered only to a god who understood, and even sanctioned, their perversity.

Curtis cleared his throat. "I appreciate your time, Mrs. Armstrong. Since the subject matter is so upsetting, I especially appreciate your candor."

But she wasn't going to be whisked away that easily. "I've told you some awful truths about my husband, but he could not be involved in the disappearance of this young woman."

"We have no reason to believe that he is. None. As I said, we're following numerous leads." Curtis paused, then added, "With assistance from you, we could eliminate him as a suspect."

"How could I help?"

"By letting our experts try to crack his computer. Get into his files, see what they find. This girl was heavily into a website where sexually explicit messages are posted. She made a lot of contacts that way. If she and your husband never corresponded, then chances are slim that he knew her."

She thought about it, then said, "I won't agree to that until I've consulted Brad's attorney."

Curtis accepted the condition but didn't look happy about it.

Dean's opinion of Mrs. Armstrong went up another notch. She was no pushover. This toughness probably hadn't been in her nature before the difficulties brought on by her husband's addiction. She'd had to acquire it in order to hold on to her sanity and survive.

Curtis waited as she got out of the chair and walked

her out of the cubicle. "Thank you for obliging us, Mrs. Armstrong. I hope your husband is located soon and that he gets the help he needs."

"He could not be the man you're looking for."

"Probably not. Besides, we're not sure that Janey Kemp has met with foul play. But, as you've no doubt learned, all prior offenders come under suspicion any time a sex offense is alleged. Your husband picked a bad time to miss an appointment with his probation officer, that's all."

That wasn't all, and she was smart enough to realize it. But she was also too polite to call Curtis a liar to his face. Instead, she told them good-bye.

"Nice lady," Curtis remarked once she was out of earshot.

"Intelligent, too." Curtis looked at Dean for elaboration. "Her husband is on a downward spiral, and she knows it. She also recognized your bullshit for what it was. In spite of what you told her, you obviously think there could be a connection between Armstrong's disappearance and Janey's."

"Can't rule it out." Curtis eased himself into his desk chair and indicated the other one to Dean. He took a Baby Ruth from a glass canister on his desk and offered one to Dean.

"No thanks."

As he unwrapped the candy bar, Curtis said, "Armstrong's own wife saw him solicit a minor for sex. He went to that remote place on the lake for that specific purpose. And how did he know to go there? Only one way."

"The Sex Club," Dean said.

"Exactly. He probably uses the message board like a menu. Whets his appetite by reading what's posted there, then goes out looking for the girl who posted it. And the girl Toni Armstrong saw him with matches Janey Kemp's general description."

"*Very* general," Dean said. "She described half the high school girls in and around Austin."

"All the same, it's a coincidence that cuts very close. You agree?"

Dean raked back his hair. "Yeah, yeah, I agree."

He had felt empathy for Toni Armstrong. He identified with hoping to God you were right to believe in the innocence of a loved one in whom you had little trust.

"If she doesn't volunteer his computer soon, I'm going to request a court order," Curtis told him. "Rondeau may be able to track Armstrong through Janey's email address book, but it'll take longer. In the meantime, I've put everyone on alert that I want to talk to Dr. Armstrong as soon as he surfaces. We've already put out an APB on his car."

"Speaking of which, any lab results back from Janey's car?"

Curtis grimaced. "Evidence overkill. They collected trace evidence of every fiber, either natural or manufactured, known to man. Carpet, clothing, paper. Every frigging thing. It'll take weeks to sort it all out."

"Fingerprints other than Janey's?"

"Only several dozen. They're searching for matches. Maybe we'll get lucky and one of them will be Brad Armstrong's. They also collected traces of soil, food, plants, and controlled substances. You name it, we found it, and we can readily identify it. But if we'd collected evidence from a KOA campground, it couldn't be more scattershot.

"The girl practically lived in her car. According to her friends, even her own parents, she entertained in it extensively. She ate, drank, slept, and screwed in it. The only thing we've matched with certainty is a human hair, and it matches one we took from her hairbrush in her bathroom at home. Oh, and a speck of dried fecal matter. Identified as canine, which makes sense because we also collected several dog hairs that match those of the family pet."

"I don't remember seeing or hearing a dog."

"Stays in the laundry room. The judge is allergic." Curtis finished his candy bar, wadded up the wrapper, and tossed it into the trash can. "That's it so far."

"Nothing was found that sheds light on what happened to her," Dean remarked.

"No sign of a struggle, like ripped clothing or scuff marks on the interior surfaces. Only one hair, not like a clump that had been pulled out. No broken fingernails that would indicate resistance. No blood. The gas tank was half full, so she hadn't run out. No malfunction of the motor. Sufficient air in all the tires. It appears she left the car under her own power and locked it behind her."

"Intending to come back," Dean added thoughtfully. "What about other tire tracks in the area?"

"You know how many people have signed on to the Sex Club website at one time or another? Several hundred. I think every last one of them was congregated there that night. Say two or three rode together, you've still got a hundred vehicles. We've made a few imprints and are running down the makes and models, but it's going to take days, if not weeks, which we don't have.

"And matching DNA samples, even once we've isolated them, takes time. A lot of time. It sure as hell can't happen in"—he consulted his wall clock—"less than thirty-six hours."

"What about the photograph she gave Gavin? Any leads from that?"

"Taken with a film camera, not digital. The film wasn't developed at your corner one-hour photo."

"Our guy has his own darkroom?"

"Or uses someone else's. I've got several people working that angle, trying to track down suppliers of photographic paper and chemicals, but again—"

"Time."

"Right. And our amateur shutterbug may not buy his products over the counter. He could get them by mail order or buy them online." His thinning crew cut certainly didn't need smoothing, but he ran his hand over it as though it did. "Something else to toss into the gumbo, remember Marvin the janitor?"

"What about him?"

"Aka Morris Green, Marty Benton, and Mark Wright. Along with Marvin Patterson, those are the aliases we know of."

"What's his story?"

"Real name Lancy Ray Fisher. In and out of JV court numerous times on petty charges. At age eighteen he did time in Huntsville for grand-theft auto. Got the sentence reduced by ratting out a cell mate who had boasted to Lancy Ray about a murder. But once free, assorted felonies followed, for which he served minimum sentences, usually by plea bargaining. Best known for bad checks and credit card theft."

"Where is he?"

"Don't know. We're still looking and so is his parole officer. He dove underground when we called ahead. Griggs and Carson got an ass chewing for that. Anyhow, Marvin's avoidance of us leads me to believe that violating parole isn't his only crime and that cleaning the toilets at the radio station isn't his sole source of income."

"Or that he's got something worse to hide," Dean said.

"We got a warrant and searched his place. No computer."

"He could've taken it with him."

"Could've, but he left behind other goodies."

"Like?"

Curtis ran down a list of electronics that would be hard to come by on an average janitor's salary. "Mostly sound equipment. Fancy stuff. We also carried out boxes of crap we're still sorting through. But here's where it gets really interesting. One of those felonies I mentioned? Sexual assault. His DNA is on record."

"If you could match him to trace evidence found in Janey's car—"

"If I had the time to match it, you mean."

Dean shared the detective's frustration. It was an upside-down case. They had good leads, but no crime and no victim. They were looking for an abductor without knowing for certain that Janey Kemp had been abducted. They were working under the assumption that she was being held against her will, that her life was in peril, but for all they knew—

A fresh thought struck Dean. "What if . . ."

Curtis looked at him, prompting him to continue. "Say it. I'm open to any ideas at this point."

"Is it possible that Janey herself is behind this?"

"For attention?"

"Or fun. Could she have put a male friend up to calling Paris just for kicks, just to see how far it would go and what would happen?"

"It's not that far-fetched an idea. But it's not original either. I went over to the courthouse this morning to talk to the judge and—"

"He's carrying on business as usual?"

"Right down to the black robe," Curtis said with dislike. "He clings to the notion that Janey is doing this to spite him and his wife. Come the election in November, the judge doesn't need any adverse publicity. Clean family image and all that. He thinks Janey is trying to scotch his chances to keep his seat on the bench."

"Damn."

"What?"

"I'm thinking like Judge Kemp now?"

Curtis chuckled. "And you could both be right."

They mulled it over for several seconds before Dean said, "I don't think so, Curtis. Valentino convinced me. Either Janey's anonymous prankster friend knows enough psychology to pass for the real thing, or he is."

"I have to think he is."

"Janey kept an appointment with this guy. They met in a designated place. She secured her car and rode away with him."

"It would appear," Curtis said.

"Which is consistent with Gavin's story."

The detective stared thoughtfully at the toe of his polished boot. "Gavin could've taken her somewhere in his car so they'd have privacy to thrash things out."

"And instead, Gavin thrashed her? Is that what you're thinking?"

Curtis looked up and shrugged as though to say, *Maybe.*

"After talking briefly to Janey, Gavin joined his friends. He gave you a list of names and numbers. Have you checked with them?"

"Working on it."

The detective's noncommittal answer irritated Dean even more. "Do you think he could disguise his voice enough to sound like Valentino? Don't you think I'd be able to identify my own son's voice?"

"Would you want to identify it?"

Dean could withstand criticism. Sometimes his analysis of a suspect, a potential witness, or a cop in trouble wasn't received well and made him unpopular with fellow officers. It was an accepted hazard of his job.

But this was the first time his integrity had come into question. Ever. And it made him madder than hell. "Are you accusing me of obstructing justice? You think I'm withholding evidence? Do you want a strand of Gavin's hair?"

"I may later."

"Any time. Let me know."

"I meant no offense. The thing is, you hold back a lot, Doctor."

"For instance?"

"You and Paris Gibson. There's more there than you let on."

"Because it's none of your goddamn business."

"The hell it's not," Curtis said, his ire rising to match Dean's. "This whole thing started with her." He leaned forward and lowered his voice so that anyone beyond the cubicle couldn't overhear. "You two were a dynamic duo during a standoff situation down in Houston. Made all the papers, TV news."

"People died."

"Yeah, I heard that. Tore you up pretty bad. You took some time off to get your head on straight."

Dean fumed in silence.

"Not long after that, Paris's fiancé, your best friend—something else you failed to mention—becomes incapacitated. She quits TV news and devotes herself to taking care of him, and you—"

"I know the history. Where'd you get your information?"

"I have friends in the HPD. I asked," he replied without apology.

"Why?"

"Because it occurred to me that maybe this Valentino business stems from all that."

"It doesn't."

"You're sure? Valentino's hang-up seems to be unfaithful women. Do you think an attractive and vital woman like Paris remained faithful to Jack Donner for the whole seven years she cared for him?"

"I don't know. I lost contact with her and Jack after they left Houston."

"Entirely?"

"She wanted it that way."

"I don't get it. You were going to be best man at their wedding."

"Your Houston source was very thorough."

"He didn't tell me anything that wasn't in print. Why did Paris ask you to stay away?"

"She didn't ask, she insisted. She was abiding by what she thought Jack would want. We'd been athletes together in college. Buddies, and all the physical rowdiness that implies. He wouldn't have wanted me to see him so debilitated."

Curtis nodded as though it was a valid answer, but maybe not a complete one. "And something else that strikes me as curious," he said. "The sunglasses."

"Her eyes are sensitive to light."

"But she wears them in darkness, too. She had them on last night when you arrived at the Wal-Mart store. It was the middle of the night and there wasn't even a full moon." Curtis fixed an incisive look on him. "It's almost like she's ashamed of something, isn't it?"

chapter twenty-one

Stan would rather have had an appointment with a proctologist than with his uncle Wilkins. Either way, he was going to get his ass reamed, but at least a proctologist would wear gloves and try to be gentle.

Their meeting place, the lobby bar of the Driskill Hotel, was in Stan's favor. Since Wilkins planned to fly back to Atlanta that evening, he hadn't booked a suite. *Thank God*, thought Stan as he entered the downtown landmark. It was unlikely that his uncle would flay and fillet him in a public arena. Wilkins hated scenes.

The hotel lobby was as tranquil as a harem during afternoon-nap time. The stained-glass ceiling provided subdued illumination. One tended to walk as quietly as possible across the marble mosaic floors. Nor did one wish to disturb a single glossy frond as one passed a potted palm. Sofas and chairs invited one to languish on the deep cushions and enjoy the flute solo filtering through invisible speakers.

But at the center of this oasis of cool serenity squatted a poisonous toad.

Wilkins Crenshaw was well under six feet tall, and Stan suspected he wore elevator lifts in his shoes. His gray hair had a yellowish tint and was so sparse that it barely concealed the age spots on his waxy scalp. His nose was overly wide, which matched fleshy lips, the lower one curling downward. He bore a resemblance to an amphibian of the ugliest genus.

Stan figured his uncle's appearance was the main reason he had stayed a bachelor. The only appeal Wilkins might hold for the opposite sex would be his money, which was the second reason he was still single. He was too stingy to share even a small slice of his financial pie with a spouse.

Stan also guessed that his uncle had been a nerdy outcast in the military academy to which he and his father had been sent by his grandfather. From there the brothers had been given no option other than attending the Citadel. Upon graduation each had served a stint in the air force. Then, having earned the appropriate degrees and done their patriotic duty, they had been allowed to join the family business.

At some point during these passages into manhood, the nerdy Wilkins had turned mean. He had learned to fight back, but his weapon of choice was brainpower, not brawn. He didn't use his fists, but he had a remarkable talent for instilling fear. He fought dirty and took no prisoners.

He didn't stand when Stan joined him at the small round cocktail table. He didn't even greet him. When the pretty young waitress approached, he said to her, "Bring him a club soda."

Stan despised club soda, but he didn't change the order. He would do his best to make this meeting as painless as possible. Smiling pleasantly, he began with flattery. "You're looking well, Uncle."

"Is that a silk shirt?"

"Uh, yes."

It was a family trait to dress well. As though to compensate for his physical shortcomings, Wilkins was always immaculately garbed and groomed. His shirts and suits were tailor-made, mercilessly starched and steamed. A wrinkle or loose thread didn't stand a chance.

"Do you go out of your way to dress like a queer? Or do you just come by that faggoty look naturally?"

Stan said nothing, only nodded his thanks to the waitress when she delivered his club soda.

"You must've inherited that flamboyant style of dress from your mother. She liked ruffles and such. The more the better."

Stan didn't dispute him, even though his shirt wasn't in the least flamboyant, not in style or color. And he seriously doubted his mother had ever worn a ruffle in her life. She'd never looked anything except perfectly correct. She'd had excellent taste and in his opinion remained the most beautiful woman he had ever seen.

But arguing any of this would be pointless, so he changed the subject. "Did your meeting with the GM go well?"

"The place is still making money."

Then why, Stan wondered, was he scowling? "The latest ratings were very strong," he remarked. "Up several points over the previous period."

He'd done his homework so he could impress his uncle with this quote. He only hoped Wilkins didn't quiz him by asking the dates of the last ratings period or to explain what a point was.

His uncle gave a noncommittal grunt. "That's why this business with Paris Gibson is so upsetting."

"Yes, sir."

"We can't have our radio station involved."

"It's not exactly *involved*, Uncle. Only peripherally."

"Even to a minor extent, I don't want us connected to

something as unsavory as a teenage girl's disappearance."

"Absolutely not, sir."

"That's why I'm going to tear your fucking head off and piss down the hole if you had anything at all to do with making those phone calls."

Uncle Wilkins had learned something besides meanness from his days in the military. He'd learned to express himself in language that could not be misinterpreted. The crudeness of his statement was topped only by its effectiveness.

Stan quailed. "Why would it even cross your mind that I could—"

"Because you're a fuckup. You have been since your mother expelled you. From the moment you drew breath, she knew you were a mewling little turd. I think that's why, when she got sick, she just lay down and died."

"She had pancreatic cancer."

"Which gave her a good excuse to finally rid herself of you. Your father also knew you weren't worth spit. He didn't want to be burdened with you. That's why he sucked so hard on his pistol, it blew the back of his head off."

Stan's throat closed. He couldn't speak.

Wilkins was relentless. "Your father was weak to begin with and your mother made him weaker. He felt it was his duty to remain married to her even though it was her personal goal to fuck every man she met."

Cruelty was his uncle's lifeblood. Having experienced it for thirty-two years, Stan realized he should be used to it. He wasn't. He glared at Wilkins with unmitigated hatred. "Father had affairs, too. Constantly."

"More than any of us know, I'm sure. He poked every

woman he could in order to convince himself that he still could. Your mother didn't permit him in her bed. He seemed to be the only man she had an aversion to."

"Besides you."

Wilkins closed his hand so tightly around his glass of bourbon that Stan wondered why the crystal didn't break. He had scored a direct hit and it felt good. He knew exactly where his uncle's disdain for his mother was coming from. Countless times, Stan had heard her laugh lightly and say, "Wilkins, you're such a disagreeable toad."

Coming from his mother, who adored men, that was a colossal put-down. Moreover, she had never shown any fear of Wilkins, and that would be the ultimate insult. He thrived on making people afraid of him. With her, he had failed utterly. Stan delighted in reminding him of it.

A slurp of bourbon restored him. He said, "Considering your dysfunctional parents, it's little wonder you have problems with sex."

"I don't."

"All evidence being to the contrary."

Stan's face turned hot. "If you're talking about that woman in Florida—"

"Who you tried to hump over her fax machine."

"That's her version," Stan said. "It wasn't like that. She was all over me until she got cold feet, afraid someone was going to walk in."

"That's not the only time I've had to bail you out because you couldn't keep your pants zipped. Just like your father. If you had half the aptitude for business that you do for fornicating, there would be more money in the till for all of us."

That, Stan suspected, was the crux of Uncle Wilkins's animosity. He couldn't touch the sizable trust fund Stan's parents had set up for him, which included not only what he had inherited upon their deaths, but a large share of the corporation's earnings ad infinitum. The terms were irrevocable and irrefutable. Even Wilkins with all his power and influence couldn't invalidate his trust and steal his fortune.

"That time at the country club swimming pool, what were you trying to prove when you exposed yourself to those girls? That you could get it up?"

"We were eleven years old. They were curious. They begged me to see it."

"I guess that's why they went screaming to their parents. I had to shell out a few grand to keep the incident under wraps and to keep you from being permanently banned from the club. You got expelled from prep school for whacking off in the shower."

"Everybody whacked off in the shower."

"But only you got caught, which indicates an absence of self-control."

"Do you intend to parade all my adolescent indiscretions past me? Because if you do, I'm going to order a drink."

"We haven't got time for me to parade all your indiscretions past you. Not during this meeting." He checked his wristwatch. "I'll be leaving shortly. I told the pilot I wanted wheels up at six."

May you crash and burn, Stan thought.

"What I want from you," Wilkins said, "is a denial that you've been making dirty phone calls to that woman deejay."

"Why would I do that?"

"Because you're a sick little fucker. It cost me a fortune for your shrink to tell me what I already knew. Your parents created a mess—you. And left me with the job of cleaning it up. I'm just glad that—so far at least—all your 'indiscretions' have been with women."

"Stop it," Stan hissed.

He wished he had the nerve to leap across the table, take hold of his uncle's short, fat neck, and squeeze until his bulging frog eyes popped from their sockets and his tongue protruded from his fat lips. He would love to see him dead. Grotesquely, painfully dead.

"I didn't make those phone calls," he said. "How could I? I was in the building with Paris when those calls came through from public telephones miles away from the station."

"I've checked it out. It's possible to reroute calls, make it look like they're coming from one phone when they actually originate on another. Usually a disposable cell phone, one that's been stolen perhaps. Makes the calls virtually untraceable."

Stan was flabbergasted. "You checked out how it could be done, even before you asked me if I'd been doing it?"

"I haven't gotten to where I am by being stupid and careless like you. I didn't want one of your so-called indiscretions blowing up in my face. I don't want to be left looking like a schmuck for trusting you to keep your dick where it belongs. As it is, I've got to answer to the board of directors for paying you a salary when it's a challenge for you to replace a lightbulb."

Wilkins fixed him with an unwavering stare and held it until Stan said, "I didn't rig any phone calls."

"The only thing you're good at is tinkering with gadgets."

"I didn't rig any phone calls," he repeated.

Wilkins eyed him shrewdly as he took another drink from his glass. "This Paris. Do you like her?"

Stan kept his expression impassive. "Yes, she's okay."

His uncle's stare turned harder, meaner, and, as usual, Stan yielded to it. He always did, eventually. And he hated himself for it. He *was* a mewling little turd.

He fiddled with the soggy cocktail napkin beneath his untouched club soda. "If you're asking me if I've ever entertained sexual thoughts about her, then yes. On occasion. She's attractive and has that whiskey voice, and we spend hours alone together every night."

"Have you tried with her?"

He shook his head. "She made it plain she's not interested."

"So you did try and she turned you down."

"No, I never tried. She lives like a nun."

"Why?"

"She was engaged to this guy," he said in a tone that conveyed his exasperation over the uselessness of this conversation. "He was in a private hospital up near Georgetown, north of here. Very exclusive. Anyhow, Paris went to see him every day. People around the station told me she did this for years. He died not too long ago. She took it hard and still isn't over it. Besides, she's not the type who could, you know . . ."

"No, I don't know. Not the type who could what?"

"Who could be seduced."

Wilkins stared at him for an interminable length of time, then peeled enough bills from his money clip to cover their tab. He placed them beneath his empty glass as he stood up. Reaching for his briefcase, he looked down his wide, unsightly nose at Stan.

"'Seduce' is a word that means you have to persuade a woman to have sex with you. Not at all confidence inspiring, Stanley."

As his uncle moved away, Stan said under his

breath, "Well, at least I'm not so butt ugly I have to pay for it."

Stan learned one thing from the meeting. There was nothing wrong with his uncle's hearing.

The mobile home was no longer mobile. In fact, it had been in place for so many years that one corner of it listed. In front, a cyclone fence enclosed a small yard where nothing grew except Johnsongrass and sticker patches. The only nod toward landscaping were two cracked clay pots from which sprouted faded plastic marigolds.

A neighbor kid had kicked a soccer ball over the fence and into the yard but had never bothered to retrieve it. It had long since deflated. A two-legged charcoal grill that had been bought at a garage sale years before had been propped against the exterior wall of the house. The bottom of it was completely rusted out. The television antenna on the roof was bent almost to a right angle.

It was derelict, but it was home.

Home to three neglected and foul-tempered cats who'd never been housebroken, and a slattern who was addicted to coffee and Winstons, which she continually puffed in spite of the wheeled oxygen tank to which she was connected by a cannula.

She was wheezing heavily when the door to the mobile home creaked open, causing a wedge of sunlight to cut across the picture on her television screen. "Mama?"

"Shut the goddamn door. I can't see my TV with that light shining on it, and my story's on."

"You and your stories." Lancy Ray Fisher, aka Marvin Patterson, came in and shut the door behind him. The room was plunged into foggy darkness. The black-

and-white picture on the television set improved, but only slightly.

He went straight to the refrigerator and looked inside. "There's nothing in here to eat."

"This ain't the Luby's Cafeteria and nobody invited you."

He scrounged around until he came up with a slice of bologna. On top of the fridge there was a loaf of white bread. He pushed aside one of the cats so he could get to it, then folded the bologna into a stale slice. It would have to do.

His mother said nothing else until the soap opera went into a commercial break. "What're you up to, Lancy?"

"What makes you think I'm up to something?"

She snorted and lit a cigarette.

"You're going to blow yourself up one of these days, smoking around that oxygen tank. I only hope I'm not here when you do."

"Make me one of them sam'iches." He did and as he passed it to her, she said, "You only come around when you're in trouble. What'd you do this time?"

"Nothing. The landlord is repainting my apartment. I need a place to stay for the next few days."

"I thought you were hot and heavy with some new girlfriend. How come you ain't staying with her?"

"We broke up."

"Figures. She find out you're a con?"

"I'm not a con anymore. I'm an upstanding citizen."

"And I'm the queen of Sheba," she wheezed.

"I've cleaned up my act, Mama. Can't you tell?"

He held his arms out to his sides. She looked him up and down. "What I see is new clothes, but the man underneath 'em ain't changed."

"Yes I have."

"You still making them nasty movies?"

"Videos, Mama. Two. That was years ago, and I only did it as a favor to a friend."

A friend who had paid him in cocaine. For as much as he could snort, all he had to do was get naked and screw. But then Lancy had started screwing one of the "actresses" off the set as well as on, and the jealous director began complaining about the size of his "package." In a medium where size mattered, Lancy just wasn't making the grade. "Nothing personal, you understand."

But of course Lancy had taken it personally. They'd had a parting of the ways, but not before Lancy made the director bleed and beg that his own package be left intact.

That had been a long time ago. He didn't do hard drugs now. He didn't play in dirty videos. He had improved every aspect of himself.

But apparently his mother didn't think so. "You're just like your daddy," she said as she noisily chewed her sandwich. "He was a shifty bastard, and you got the same sneaky look about you. You don't even talk natural. Where'd you learn to talk so fancy all of a sudden?"

"I'm working at the radio station. I listen to people on the radio. I've picked up speech patterns from them. I've been practicing."

"Speech patterns, my ass. Wouldn't trust you as far as I could throw you."

She went back to watching her soap. Lancy moved down the narrow hallway, stepping around piles of cat shit, and squeezed into the tiny room in which he slept when he was between incarcerations or employment, or at times like this when he needed to disappear for a few days. This was his last resort.

He knew his mother searched the room each time he left, so when he pried up the loose vinyl tile beneath the twin bed, he did so with the fear of what he would find. Or, more to the point, not find.

But the cash, mostly hundred-dollar bills, was there in the small metal box where he'd stashed it. Half of it rightfully belonged to a former partner, who'd been convicted of another crime and was now serving a prison sentence. When he got out, he would come looking for Marty Benton and his share of the loot. But Lancy would worry about that when and if the time ever came.

The amount had shrunk considerably from what it was originally. He'd used a sizable portion of it to buy his car and new threads. He'd rented an apartment . . . well, two, actually. He had invested in the computer that was now inside the trunk of his car.

His mother would rag him about throwing away good money on a foolish contraption like a computer when she was still watching her stories in black and white. She didn't understand that in order to succeed at any endeavor, legal or ill, a person had to be computer savvy. Lancy had trained himself to be. To avoid the old bitch's harping, he would take his laptop inside and access the Internet through his cell phone only when she was asleep.

He counted his cash, stuffed several of the bills into his pocket, then returned the rest to their hiding place under the floor. This was his emergency fund, and he hated like hell having to tap into it now. Although this definitely qualified as an emergency.

Shortly after being released from his last incarceration, he'd landed a good job, but had been too stupid to appreciate it. One of the dumbest things he'd ever done was steal from the company. Not that he had thought of it as stealing, but his boss sure as hell had.

If he'd asked to purchase the cast-off equipment for a nominal amount, the boss probably would have told him to take what he wanted, that he was welcome to it. But he hadn't asked. He had reverted to his old ways. Catch as catch can. Get it while the gettin's good. One evening before leaving work, he had helped himself to the obsolete equipment, thinking no one would miss it.

But somebody had. He, being the only ex-con on the payroll, was the first person the boss suspected. When accused, he confessed and asked for a second chance. No dice. He was fired and had escaped criminal charges only because he returned everything he'd taken.

The experience had taught him several lessons, primarily never to tell the truth on a job application. So when Marvin Patterson applied for the job at the radio station, he checked the No box to the questions about arrests and convictions.

Lousy as it was to mop up after other people, that job had been a boon. When he got it, he felt that fate, or his fairy godmother, or some power beyond himself had compelled him to steal that stuff. If he hadn't been fired from that first job, he wouldn't have had the way cleared for him to work at 101.3.

Not only had the janitorial job been gainful employment that kept his parole officer pacified, it had kept Lancy from having to deplete his stash. And, most important, it had allowed him to be near Paris Gibson every night.

Unfortunately, there was no returning to that job now. Nor could he go back to his apartment, write a check on Marvin Patterson's bank account, or use an ATM to withdraw from it, all of which were surefire ways of letting yourself be found when you didn't want to be.

The minute those cops called telling him to stay put,

that they were on their way over to talk to him about harassing Paris Gibson with a dirty phone call, he knew his goose was cooked. Just like that, he'd become an ex-con again and had acted accordingly. He'd grabbed his cell phone, his computer setup, some clothing, and cleared out.

His first stop had been his second residence, a dump of a place that he kept leased under an assumed name. What might seem like an unnecessary luxury had proved itself to come in handy.

But as he approached the parking lot, he spotted a police car at the IHOP across the street. He had driven past without pulling in. He told himself it was probably just a coincidence, that if the cops were lying in wait for him to show up there, they wouldn't be in marked cars. But he was taking no chances.

He had destroyed Marvin Patterson's fake IDs. Hello, Frank Shaw.

He'd swapped the license plates on his car, too, switching them for some he had stolen months ago.

No matter what anybody said about reform and rehabilitation, no cop, or judge, or decent, law-abiding citizen was going to extend to an ex-con the benefit of the doubt. You could swear on the Good Book that you were a changed man. You could beg for an opportunity to prove yourself. You could promise to become a contributing member of the community. It didn't matter. Nobody gave a con a second chance. Not the law, or society, or women.

Especially women. They'd do all manner of sex with you but got squeamish when it came to a criminal record. There they got finicky. There they drew the line. Did that make sense?

Not to Lancy. But whether or not it was reasonable,

that was the rule. Since he didn't conform to the rule, he had tried changing himself into a man who did. He dressed better, talked better, treated women like a gentleman would.

So far, the transformation hadn't met with stunning success. He'd had a few promising prospects, but eventually they'd gone the way of his other relationships. It was like there was a stain on him that could be seen only by women.

He just couldn't make them like and respect him. Starting with his own mother.

chapter twenty-two

"We know this is last minute, but we're hoping you'll go to dinner with us."

Paris looked from Dean to Gavin. In seven years, he had grown tall, lean, and handsome. His hair had darkened slightly and the bone structure of his face was more defined, but she would have recognized him even on sight.

"This is a cliché," she said, "and you'll hate me for saying it, but I can't believe you're so grown up." She clasped one of his hands between hers. "It's so good to see you again, Gavin."

With a mix of embarrassment and shyness, he said, "It's good to see you, too, Ms. Gibson."

"When you were nine, Ms. Gibson was appropriate. Coming from you now it makes me sound ancient. I'm Paris from now on, okay?"

"Okay."

"How about dinner?" Dean asked.

"I've already got something started."

He raised his eyebrows expectantly, putting her on the spot and giving her little choice except to say, "There's plenty if you and Gavin don't mind eating in."

"It will be a welcome change." Dean nudged Gavin across her threshold. "What are we having?"

"You weaseled an invitation out of me and now you're choosy?"

"Anything but liver or rutabagas."

"Angel-hair pasta with pork tenderloin and veggies. No rutabagas."

"My mouth is already watering. What can we do to help?"

"Uh." Suddenly she felt at a loss. It had been so long since she had entertained, she'd forgotten how. "We could all have something to drink."

"Sounds good."

"I have a bottle of wine . . ." She gestured toward the back of the house.

Dean said, "Lead the way."

In the kitchen, she assigned him the job of opening the Chardonnay, while she poured a Coke over ice for Gavin. Dean made himself right at home. She and Gavin were more awkward with the situation. "There's a CD player in the living room," she said to him. "But I'm not sure I have any music you'll like."

"I'll like it. I listen to your show sometimes."

Pleased to know that, she told him where to find her CD player. He left the kitchen for the living room. As soon as he was out of earshot, she said to Dean, "Am I to acknowledge the bruise on his face or not?"

"Not."

It had been impossible not to notice the dark bruise and slight swelling beneath Gavin's right eye. Naturally she'd wondered how he had come to have such a painful-looking injury. But Dean seemed angry and upset about it, so she changed the subject by asking how Gavin's meeting with Curtis had gone.

"Curtis said Gavin stuck to his original story, telling him nothing that he hadn't told me. He and Janey argued, then he joined a group of friends. Never saw her again."

"Does Curtis believe him?"

"Noncommittal. He didn't detain Gavin, which I take as a positive sign. Also, Valentino has a mature voice. I don't think Gavin could pull that off, even if he tried. And where would Gavin be holding a girl hostage? He doesn't have access to a place. He would have had to kill her that night and—Jesus, listen to me." He braced his hands on the edge of the counter and stared into the bottle of wine.

"Gavin had nothing to do with Janey's disappearance. I just know that, Dean."

"I don't think he did either. But I also never would have guessed he was doing the other stuff. It's been disconcerting, to say the least, to discover that my son has been leading a secret life."

"To some extent, don't all teenagers?"

"I suppose, but I've made it easy for him. I wanted him to like living with me, so I've soft-pedaled the discipline. It didn't seem like I was going easy on him, but I suppose I haven't been as diligent or consistent as I should have been. Gavin took advantage of that."

Turning his head to address her, he added, "With all my psychological training, shouldn't I have realized that I was being conned?"

Just then Gavin called from the living room, "Is Rod Stewart okay?"

"Great," Paris called back. Then to Dean, she said, "Cut yourself some slack. It's a child's duty to try and bamboozle his parents. As for discipline, techniques from a textbook don't always translate to real life."

"But how can it be this hard to get right?"

She laughed softly. "If it were easy, if one system worked for every child, a lot of so-called experts would be out of work. What would they discuss on afternoon talk shows? Think of the chaos, to say nothing of the economic crisis, that well-behaved and obedient children would create."

After winning a smile from him, she dropped the joking. "I'm not making light of your concern, Dean. In fact, it's admirable. Gavin may have gotten off track, but he'll turn out all right."

He poured wine into the two stemmed glasses she had set out and handed one to her. "We can hope." He clinked their glasses.

She looked at him over the rim of hers as she took a sip. "He comes by it naturally, you know."

"What's that?"

"Gavin isn't the only master manipulator in the Malloy family."

"Oh?"

"Very crafty of you, showing up here with him in tow after I had already declined a dinner invitation."

"It worked, didn't it?"

"As a psychologist, how would you classify a man who uses his child to get a dinner invitation out of a woman?"

"Pathetic."

"How about two-timing?"

Dean's smile faltered. "You're referring to Liz."

"Did you tell her about your dinner plans for tonight?"

"I told her I needed to spend time with Gavin."

"But you didn't mention me."

"No."

"She seemed to have a rightful claim to your evenings."

"She has had, yes."

"Exclusive claim?"

"Yes."

"For how long?"

"Couple of years."

That came as an unpleasant shock. "Wow. When I knew you in Houston, your affairs lasted no more than a couple of weeks."

"Because the woman I wanted was taken."

"We're not talking about that, Dean."

"The hell we're not."

"We're talking about you and Liz. A two-year relationship implies—"

"Not what you're thinking."

"What is *Liz* thinking?"

"Dad?" From the open doorway, Gavin hesitantly interrupted them. He was extending a cell phone to Dean. "It's ringing."

"Thanks." He reached for the phone and read the incoming number on the LED. "Gavin, help Paris."

He left the kitchen before answering the phone, causing Paris to wonder if the call had been from Liz.

"What would you like me to do?" Gavin offered.

"Set the table?"

"Okay, sure. My mom made me do it all the time."

She smiled at him. "I remember whenever Jack and I went to your dad's house for dinner and you were there, that was your chore."

"Speaking of, I, uh, haven't had a chance to tell you. I'm sorry about him, you know, dying."

"Thank you, Gavin."

"I liked him. He was cool."

"Yes he was. Now," she said briskly, "do you think we should use the dining room, or eat here in the kitchen?"

"Kitchen's okay with me."

"Good." She showed him where the napkins, dishes, and cutlery were kept and he began setting the table while she sautéed the vegetables and strips of pork. "Are you looking forward to school this year?"

"Yeah. Well, I mean, I guess. It'll be tough, not knowing anybody."

"I can relate. My dad was career army." She filled a pot with water to boil the pasta. "We moved all over the map. I went to three different elementary schools and two junior highs. Luckily he retired, so I got to attend only one high school. But I remember how hard it was to be the new kid."

"It sucks."

"You'll adjust in no time. I remember when you had to switch Little League teams, midseason. You went from being a Pirate to a—"

"Cougar. You remember that?"

"Very well. Your coach had to quit."

"His job transferred him to Ohio or someplace."

"So all the boys on his team were divided up among the others. You weren't at all happy about it, but it turned out to be the best thing that could've happened. The Cougars needed a good shortstop, and you filled that position. The team went on to be district champs."

"Just city," he said modestly.

"Well, to hear your dad talk, it was the World Series. For weeks all Jack and I heard from him was 'Gavin did this, Gavin did that. You should've seen Gavin last night.' Drove us nuts. He was so proud of you."

"I made an error in one of the playoff games. The other team got a run because of it."

"I was at that game."

"That's why it sucked so bad. Dad had invited y'all to come watch me. I'm sure he could've killed me, then died of embarrassment."

She turned away from the range and looked at him. "Dean was most proud of you then, Gavin."

"He was proud of me for screwing up?"

"Hmm. In the next inning, you hit a double that batted a runner in."

"I guess that made up for it."

"Well, yes, to the fans and your teammates. But when Jack thumped your dad on the back and told him that you had redeemed yourself, Dean said you had redeemed yourself by getting right back into the game. He was more proud of the way you handled the mistake than he was of your hitting a double."

Turning back to the stove, she put the angel-hair pasta into the boiling water. When she turned back around, Gavin was still frowning skeptically. She nodded. "Truly."

And when she said that, she experienced a moment of realization. *Listen to yourself,* she thought. After making a mistake, Gavin had gotten right back into the game. He hadn't slunk into the dugout and spent the remaining innings on the bench, grinding his cleats into the dirt while beating himself up over his error.

Last night Dean had said he hadn't let his guilt and regret eat him alive. He had let it go.

Maybe there was a lesson to be learned from these Malloy men.

Dean returned to the kitchen, interrupting her disquieting thoughts. "That was Curtis." He glanced at Gavin as if reluctant to talk about the case in front of him, but he continued without asking Gavin to excuse himself. "The case has gone stale on him."

"What's happening?"

"He's got intelligence officers trying to run down Lancy Fisher."

"Who?"

"You know him as Marvin Patterson." He gave them a brief summary of Marvin's colorful criminal career. "He's wanted for questioning. And so is a Bradley Armstrong, a convicted sex offender who has violated his probation and flown the coop. He's got men checking into the telephone angle to see if it can be figured out how Valentino is rerouting calls. And Rondeau . . ."

He paused to glance at Gavin, who ducked his head.

"He's still working the computer side of this thing. They didn't find a computer in Marvin's place, but they found discs and CDs, so more than likely he took a computer with him. All this to say that Curtis is stuck in neutral. Since nothing new has turned up, I suggested to him that we see if we can provoke Valentino."

"Into doing what?"

"Poking his head out."

"How?"

"Through you."

"Me? On the air?"

"That's the idea. If you sing Janey's praises, make her out as a victim, maybe he'll call you to justify himself. He may talk longer and inadvertently give us a clue to his location or identity.

"The point is to keep the emphasis on Janey," he continued. "Personalize her. Repeat her name frequently. Make him think of her as an individual, not just his captive."

She looked at him doubtfully. "Do you think that tactic will work with Valentino?"

"Not entirely, no. But it'll also offend his ego if this is all about her instead of him. He wants to be the star, the one everybody's talking about. So by making her the focus, he may not be able to resist coming out to say, 'Hey, look at me.'"

Paris glanced at the clock.

Dean spoke her thought out loud. "Right. We've got just over twenty-four hours to stop him from doing what he threatened. Tonight could be the last chance we'll get to change his mind. He shouldn't be nudged into doing something extreme, which could have tragic results. But possibly you could persuade him to release her."

"That's not an easy assignment, Dean. There's a fine line between goading and persuading."

He nodded somberly. "I almost regret coming up with the idea because of that."

"What does Curtis think?"

"He jumped on the idea. Gung ho on it. But I reigned him in, told him it wasn't going to happen unless you were one hundred percent comfortable with it."

He came to stand closer to her. "Before you make a decision, there's something else to think about, and it's no small consideration. In fact, it's a major one. Valentino started out angry with you. He's doing this to punish you as well as the woman who wronged him. If you begin pressuring him, on any level and in any manner, he's likely to get angrier and you'll be the target. He's already made one veiled threat."

"Are you trying to talk me out of it?"

"Sounds like that, doesn't it?" he said with a wry smile. "Don't give a thought to disappointing Curtis or me. Taking risks is part of our job, but you didn't sign up for it. This has got to be your call, Paris. You say nix it, it's nixed. Think about it. You can give me your answer after dinner."

"I don't have to think about it. I'll do or say whatever is needed to get that girl home safely. But I'll need your guidance."

He reached for her hand and gave it a firm, quick squeeze. "I'll be right there with you, coaching you on what to say. I'd be there with you anyway."

Aware of Gavin watching them with interest, she turned away from Dean, announcing, "The pasta's ready."

"Hello? Brad, is that you? If so, please talk to me."

He hadn't planned what he would say when his home phone was answered, but he had been compelled to call if only to assure himself that his family was still there. As soon as he heard one of their sweet voices, he figured he'd think of something appropriate.

But upon hearing the tremor in his wife's plea, Brad Armstrong couldn't say anything. Her evident distress undid him. His throat seized up and he couldn't speak. He clenched the phone in his sweaty hand and considered hanging up.

"Brad, say something. Please. I know you're there."

He expelled a breath that was half sob, half sigh. "Toni."

"Where are you?"

Where was he? He was in hell. This shabby room had none of the amenities of the lovely home she had made for him and the kids. There was no sunlight in this room, no good smells. Here the blinds were tightly drawn, blocking out all light except for what came from one feeble bulb in the lamp. The room stank, mostly of his own despair.

But his surroundings weren't the worst of it. The real hell was his state of mind.

"You must come home, Brad. The police are looking for you."

"Oh, God." He had feared it, but having his fear realized made his stomach roil.

"I went to the police station this afternoon."

"You did what?" he asked, his voice breaking. "Toni, why did you do that?"

"Mr. Hathaway had to report you to SOAR." She explained how she had wound up in the office of a detective, but he was so distraught he caught only a portion of what she said.

"You talked about your own husband to the police?"

"In an effort to help you."

"Help me? By sending me to prison? Is that what you want for me and our children?"

"Is that what *you* want for them?" she countered. "You're the one who's destroying our family, Brad. Not me."

"You're getting back at me for last night, aren't you? That's what this is about. You're still angry."

"I wasn't angry."

"Then what do you call it?"

"Frightened."

"Frightened?" he snorted. "Because I wanted to make love? From now on, should I alert you in advance that I want to have sex?"

"It wasn't about sex, and it certainly wasn't lovemaking, Brad. It was aggression."

He rubbed his forehead, and his fingers came away wet with sweat. "You don't even try to understand me, Toni. You never have."

"This isn't about me and my shortcomings as a wife and human being. It's about you and your addiction."

"All right, all right, you've made your point. I'll go back to group therapy. Okay? Call the police and tell them you made a mistake. Tell them we had an argument and this was your way of getting back at me. I'll talk to Hathaway. If I suck up to him, he'll be lenient."

"It's too late for apologies and promises, Brad."

The finality and conviction with which she spoke alarmed him to an even greater extent.

"You've already been given more chances than you deserve," she continued. "Besides, it's no longer in my hands or Mr. Hathaway's. It's a police matter now, and I have no choice but to cooperate with them."

"By doing what?"

"Giving them access to your computer."

"Oh, Jesus. Oh, Christ. You do have a choice, Toni. Don't you see that you're going to ruin me? Please, honey, please don't do this."

"If I don't give them permission to get into it, they'll get a court order or a search warrant, whatever is required. It's really not up to me."

"You could . . . Listen, I could tell you how to clear it so they couldn't find anything. Please, Toni? It's not hard. A few clicks of the mouse, that's it. It's not like I'm asking you to rob a bank or something. Will you do that for me, honey? Please. I'm begging you."

She said nothing for a time, and he held his breath hopefully. But tonight his wife was springing one ugly surprise after another on him.

"One night last week I followed you out to Lake Travis, Brad."

Blood rushed to his head as his penitence turned to rage. "You were spying on me. I knew it. You admit it."

"I saw you with a high school girl. You and she got into your car. I can only presume that you had sex with her."

"You're goddamn right I did!" he shouted. "Because my wife cringes every time I touch her. Who could blame me for getting laid where and when I can?"

"Have you ever been with that girl who's missing? The judge's daughter. Janey Kemp?"

His breathing sounded abnormally rapid to his own ears, and he wondered if it sounded that way to Toni—or to anyone else who might be listening in. That possibility struck terror in him. Why was she asking him about Janey Kemp?

"Do the cops have the house phone tapped?"

"What? No. Of course not."

"While you were making chummy with the cops, did you set me up to get caught? Are they eavesdropping on this conversation? Is this call being traced?"

"Brad, you're talking crazy."

"Wrong, I'm not talking at all."

He disconnected, then dropped the cell phone as though it had painfully stung his hand. He began to pace the stuffy, claustrophobic room. They knew about him and Janey. They had found out, just as he had feared they would.

That . . . that Curtis. Sergeant Curtis. Is that who Toni said she had talked to this afternoon? Wasn't he in charge of investigating Janey's disappearance?

He'd been afraid of this. As soon as he saw her picture on the front page of this morning's paper, he had known it was only a matter of time before the police would be looking for him. Someone would have seen him with Janey and reported it.

Now he would have to be very careful about where he went. If he was spotted, he could be arrested. That couldn't happen. That *could not* happen. In jail, other prisoners did terrible things to men like him. He'd heard stories. His own lawyer had told him about the horrors that awaited a sex offender in prison.

God, he was in a fix. And he had Janey Kemp to thank for it, the teasing little slut. Everyone was against him. Janey. His wife, the raging nag. Hathaway, too, who wouldn't know what to do with a boner if he ever got one, which was unlikely. The parole officer was jealous of Brad's success with women. Out of spite, he would happily hand him over in handcuffs to be taken straight to prison.

But Brad's rage was short-lived. His fear returned, overwhelming him. Sweating profusely, gnawing his inner cheek, he paced the room aimlessly. This business with Janey could spell real trouble for him.

He should've stayed away from her. He saw that clearly now. He had known her by reputation even before she approached him the first time. He had read the messages posted about her on the Sex Club website, knew she was as sexually adventurous as he. He also knew she was a spoiled, rich brat who treated former lovers like dirt and poked fun at them on the Internet message board.

But he had been flattered that one of the most desired girls in the Sex Club had come on to him. What was he supposed to do, turn her down? What man could? Even knowing that he might be dooming himself, he hadn't been able to resist her allure. It was worth the danger that being with her posed.

Indulging his fantasies came with accepted risks. He knew he was courting disaster each time he picked up a high school girl, or fondled a patient, or jerked off in a video store, but the risk of getting caught contributed to the thrill.

He constantly challenged himself to see how much he could get away with. Paradoxically, his desire fed on gratification. The farther his escapades took him, the deeper he wanted to explore. Novelty was fleeting. There was always another boundary to cross, one more step to take.

But as he agonized in his private hell, he realized that he might have carried *this* fantasy one step too far.

chapter twenty-three

"**B**oo!"

Paris, who had just stepped into the dark hallway from the snack room, reacted by sloshing hot tea over her hand. "Damn it, Stan! That wasn't funny."

"I'm sorry. Jeez. I wasn't really trying to scare you." He rushed into the tiny kitchen and tore several paper towels off the roll. "Need butter? Salve? The emergency room?"

She blotted the tea off her hand. "Thanks, but no."

"I can't see your eyes, but I get the impression you're glaring."

"That was a silly thing to do."

"Why're you so jumpy?"

"Why're you so juvenile?"

"I said I was sorry. I'm just feeling exuberant tonight."

"What's the occasion?"

"Uncle Wilkins is winging his way back to Atlanta. Anytime there are several states between us, it's cause for celebration."

"Congratulations. But, just for the record, I don't like being scared. I never think it's funny." Stan fell into step behind her as she made her way back to the studio. Once they were in the light, she saw the bruise. "Ouch, Stan, what happened to your face?"

Gingerly he touched the spot at the side of his mouth. "Uncle smacked me."

"You're joking, right?"

"No."

"He struck you?" she exclaimed, then listened with dismay as he told her about their meeting in the lobby of the Driskill.

At the end of his account, he shrugged indifferently. "What I said pissed him off. It's not the first time. No big deal."

Paris disagreed, but Stan's relationship with his uncle was none of her business. "All around me, men are getting punched today," she muttered, thinking of Gavin's unexplained bruise. She sat down on her stool and glanced at the log monitor to see that she still had over five minutes of music on deck.

Without being invited to, Stan took the other stool. "Are you spooked by this Valentino business?"

"Wouldn't you be?"

"Uncle Wilkins asked if I was your mystery caller."

She cut a glance toward him as she stirred a packet of sweetener into her tea. "You're not, are you?"

"As if," he replied. "Although I am sexually maladjusted. At least according to Uncle Wilkins."

"Why would he think so?"

"Bad genes. Mother was a slut. Father was a lecher. Uncle hires hookers he thinks no one knows about. I suppose he thinks the apple didn't fall too far from the tree. But aside from being a sexual deviate, he thinks I'm a royal fuckup."

"He told you that?"

"In so many words."

"You're a grown man. Why do you take that crap from him? You certainly don't have to stand for his slapping you."

Stan looked at her as though she was deranged. "How do you suggest I stop it?"

He had a knack for making her want to throttle him one minute and pat him consolingly the next. A lot of juicy gossip had been circulated when Stan's father committed suicide. If there was any basis to it whatsoever, the Crenshaw family was indeed dysfunctional on many levels. It wasn't surprising that Stan had psychological issues that needed sorting out.

As the last of the songs wound down, she signaled him to be quiet and engaged her mike.

"That was Neil Diamond. Before that Juice Newton was singing about 'The Sweetest Thing.' I hope you were listening, Troy. That song was a request for you from Cindy. I'll be taking other requests until two o'clock. Or, if you have something on your mind, I invite you to share it with me and my listeners. Please call."

From that she went directly into two minutes of commercials.

"Do you think he'll call tonight?" Stan asked after she'd turned off her mike.

"I assume you mean Valentino. I don't know. It wouldn't surprise me."

"No clues as to who he is?"

"The police are investigating several possibilities, but they have little to go on. Sergeant Curtis is hoping he'll call tonight, maybe say something that would give them fresh leads." She looked at the blinking telephone lines on the control board. "I know another call from him could be valuable, but it gives me the creeps to talk to him."

"Now I really feel bad about scaring you. I was teasing."

"I'll survive."

"Holler if you need me." He headed for the door.

"Oh, Stan, Dr. Malloy will be arriving shortly. Would you please keep an eye on the front door and let him in?"

Stan did an about-face and returned to the stool. "What's with you and the studly shrink?"

Paris shushed him and answered one of the phone lines. "This is Paris."

The male caller requested a Garth Brooks song from the sound track of the movie *Hope Floats*. "For Jeannie."

"Jeannie sounds like a lucky girl."

"It's on account of you that we're together."

"Me?"

"Jeannie was offered this job out in Odessa. Neither of us had told the other how we felt. You advised her not to leave before telling me her feelings. She did, and I told her I felt the same, so she stayed at her job here and we're getting married next year."

"I'm glad it worked out so well."

"Yeah, me, too. Thanks, Paris."

She inserted "To Make You Feel My Love" into the program log and answered another line. The caller requested that she send a happy birthday wish to Alma. "Ninety? My goodness! Does she have a favorite song?"

It was a Cole Porter tune, but within seconds Paris had located it in the computerized music library and programmed it to play behind the Brooks ballad.

After taking care of that business, she looked over at Stan. "Are you still here?"

"Yes, and my question stands. And don't tell me you and Malloy are old friends from Houston."

"That's exactly what we are."

"How'd you meet?"

"Through Jack. Their friendship outlasted college."

"But it didn't outlast you." She whipped her head toward him. "Ah, just a wild guess, but a correct one, I see."

"Get lost, Stan."

"I take it that this is a sensitive subject."

Exasperated, and knowing that he would bug her about this until she was forthcoming, she asked, "What do you want to know?"

"If Malloy was such a good friend of yours and Jack's, I want to know why I never heard of him until last night."

"We drifted apart when I moved Jack here."

"Why did you move Jack here?"

"Because Meadowview was the best health care facility for his particular needs. Jack was unable to maintain a friendship. I was busy overseeing his care and establishing myself in this job. Dean had his own busy life in Houston, including a young son. It happens, Stan. Circumstances affect friendships. Haven't you lost touch with some of your friends in Atlanta?"

Undeterred, he said, "Jack was the reason you gave up a career in TV news and came to work at this dump?"

"Around the time of his accident, I made a career change. Okay? Satisfied? Therein lies the whole story."

"I don't think so," he said, his eyes narrowing on her. "It sounds logical, even plausible, but it's too pat. I think you're leaving out the shadings."

"Shadings?"

"The nuances that make for a really good story."

"I'm busy, Stan."

"Besides, nothing you've told me explains the electricity that was arcing between you and Malloy last night. It nearly singed my eyebrows. Come on, Paris, give," he wheedled. "I won't be shocked. You've glimpsed the ugly underbelly of my family and nothing could be more scandalous. What happened with the three of you?"

"I've told you. If you don't believe me, that's your

problem. If you want shadings, invent your own. I really don't care as long as it keeps you occupied. In the meantime, can't you find something productive to do?"

She returned her attention to the board, the phone lines, the log monitor, and the studio information monitor, where a new weather report had been submitted by a local meteorologist.

Stan sighed with resignation and moved toward the door once again. Speaking over her shoulder, Paris called to him, "Don't touch anything breakable."

But as soon as he walked out, her flippancy dissolved. She tossed her tea, which was now tepid and bitter, into the trash can. She wanted to choke Stan for resurrecting disturbing memories.

But she couldn't dwell on them. She had her job to do. Engaging her mike, she said, "Once again, happy birthday to Alma. Her request took us back several generations, but every love song is a classic here on FM 101.3. This is Paris Gibson, your host until two o'clock tomorrow morning. I hope you'll stay with me. I enjoy your company. I also enjoy playing your requested songs. Call me."

She and Dean had agreed that she wouldn't address any remarks to Valentino or mention Janey until he arrived. They'd left her house at the same time, but he was going to drive Gavin home before coming to the station.

Dinner had gone well. By tacit agreement, they didn't talk about the case in which they had all become involved. Instead their conversation touched on movies, music, and sports. They laughed over shared memories.

As they were leaving, Gavin thanked her politely for the dinner. "Dad's a lousy cook."

"I'm no Emeril either."

"You come closer than he does."

She could tell that Dean was pleased by how well she and Gavin had gotten along and how relaxed their dinner together had been. She had felt very mellow herself, and she had drunk only a half glass of Chardonnay—her limit on a worknight. Her enjoyment was lessened only by knowing that she'd kept them away from Liz Douglas for the evening.

During the next series of commercials, she cleared the phone lines. Each time she depressed a blinking button, she did so with dread, which made her angry with Valentino. He had made her afraid to do the work that had been her salvation. This job had kept her grounded during the seven years she had overseen Jack's health care. She'd been able to endure those interminable days spent at the hospital only by knowing that she could escape to the radio station that night.

She received a call from a young woman named Joan, whose personality was so bubbly Paris decided to put her on the air. "You say you're a Seal fan."

"I saw him once in a restaurant in L.A. He looked super cool. Could you play 'Kiss From a Rose'?"

Moving by rote, she slipped the request behind three songs already on the log.

What was keeping Dean? she wondered. He was putting up a good front, but she could tell he was deeply worried about Gavin's connection to Janey Kemp. Any parent who loved his child would be concerned, but Dean would blame himself for Gavin's misconduct and look upon it as a failure on his part.

Just as he had assumed blame when Albert Dorrie's standoff with Houston police resulted in tragedy.

There it was again. Another reminder. No matter how hard she tried to avoid it, her mind kept going back to that. To that night.

*   *   *

Dean showed up at her condo eighteen hours after Mr. Dorrie had made orphans of his three children by killing first his estranged wife and then himself.

He arrived unannounced and apologetic. "I'm sorry, Paris. I probably shouldn't have come over without calling first," he said as soon as she opened the door.

He looked as if he hadn't even sat down during the last eighteen hours, much less slept. His eyes had sunk into the dark circles surrounding them. His chin was shadowed with stubble.

Paris had rested very little herself. Most of the day had been spent in the TV newsroom, where she had edited together an overall perspective of the incident for the evening newscasts.

Tragically the story wasn't that unusual. Similar incidents happened routinely in other cities. It had even happened in Houston before. But it had never happened to *her*. She had never witnessed something like that up close and personal. Being on the scene and living through it was far different from reading about it in the newspaper or listening with half an ear to television news reports while preoccupied and doing something else.

Even her jaded cameraman had been affected. His ho-hum attitude was replaced by dejection when the news van followed the ambulance bearing the two bodies to the county morgue.

But no one who had experienced it took the calamity to heart the way Dean did. His despair was etched deeply into his face as Paris motioned him inside. "Can I get you something? A drink?"

"Thanks." He sat down heavily on the edge of her sofa while she poured each of them a shot of bourbon. She handed him a highball glass and sat down beside him. "Am I keeping you from something?" he asked dully.

"No." She motioned down at her white terry-cloth spa robe. Her face was scrubbed clean; she'd let her hair dry naturally after a long soak in the tub. He usually didn't see her like this, but she wasn't concerned about her appearance. Things that had seemed important twenty-four hours ago had paled into insignificance.

"I don't know why I came," he said. "I didn't want to be out, with people. But I didn't want to be alone either."

"I feel the same."

She had begged off spending the evening with Jack. He'd been desperate to cheer her up and help take her mind off what she'd been through. But she wasn't yet ready to be cheered up. She wanted time to reflect. Furthermore, she was exhausted. Going to a movie or even to dinner seemed as remote as flying to the moon. Even making small talk with Jack would have required energy she didn't have.

Talking didn't seem to be the purpose of Dean's visit. After those few opening statements, he sat staring into near space, taking periodic sips from his highball glass. He didn't fill the silence with pointless conversation. Each knew how rotten the other felt about the way the standoff had ended. She guessed that, like her, he derived comfort just from being near someone who had shared the tragedy.

It took him half an hour to finish his whiskey. He set the empty glass on the coffee table, stared at it for several seconds, then said, "I should go."

But she couldn't let him leave without offering some consolation. "You did everything you could, Dean."

"That's what everybody tells me."

"Because it's true. You did your best."

"It wasn't good enough, though, was it? Two people died."

"But three lived. If not for you, he probably would have killed the children, too."

He nodded, but without conviction. She stood up when he did and followed him to the door, where he turned to face her. "Thanks for the drink."

"You're welcome."

Several seconds ticked by before he said, "I caught your story on the six o'clock news."

"You did?"

"It was good."

"Trite."

"No, really. It was good."

"Thank you."

"You're welcome."

Holding her with a stare, his eyes seemed to implore her in a way that she knew her own must mirror. Emotions that she couldn't deny, but had held in rigid check for months, erupted inside her. By the time Dean reached for her, she was already opening her lips to receive his kiss.

Later, when she relived it and was able to be brutally honest with herself, she realized that she had wanted him to kiss her, and that if he hadn't initiated it, she would have.

She had to touch him or die. The need for him was that essential.

Dean must have felt the same. His mouth mated with hers possessively and hungrily. Pretense and politeness were shattered. The constraints of conscience snapped. Tension that had been building for months was given vent.

She threaded her fingers up through his hair. He

unknotted the tie belt of her robe and when he slid his hands inside, she didn't protest but rose up on tiptoes to bring their bodies flush against each other. They fit. And the perfection of it brought a temporary end to the kissing and they just held each other, tightly.

Paris's mind spun with sensual overload. The cold metal of his belt buckle against her belly. The texture of his trousers against her bare thighs. The fine cotton of his shirt against her breasts. His body heat seeping into her skin.

Then his lips sought hers again. As they kissed, his hand moved to her breast. His thumb brushed her distended nipple, then he bent his head to take it into his mouth, sucking it with urgency. Gasping his name, she clutched his head against her.

As he lowered her to the floor, she undid the buttons on his shirt and pushed it off his shoulders, but that's as far as it got before he was kissing her again. Between her thighs she felt him grappling with his belt and zipper.

The tip of his penis nuzzled her pubic hair, probed, and then was inside her.

His fullness stretched and filled her. He settled his weight onto her and she absorbed it gladly, squeezing his hips between her thighs. The pressure was incredibly sweet. The sounds that rose up from her chest were a joyous mix of laughter and weeping.

He kissed away the tears that leaked from the corners of her eyes, then clasped her head between his strong hands and laid his forehead against hers, rolling it gently back and forth as they exchanged the air they breathed and the ultimate intimacy.

"God help me, Paris," he said raspily, "I just had to be inside you."

She slid her hands beneath his clothing and pressed his buttocks with her palms, drawing him even deeper into her. He hissed a swift intake of air and began to move. With each smooth thrust, the intensity of the pleasure increased. And so did the meaningfulness. Cradling her chin in one hand, he tilted her face up for a kiss.

He was still kissing her when she came, so that her soft cries were released into his mouth. Within seconds he followed her. And still, they clung to each other.

Their separation was gradual and reluctant. As the physical ecstasy began to recede, the moral significance of what they had done encroached. She tried to stave it off. She wanted to rail at the unfairness of it. But it was inexorable.

"Oh, Lord," she moaned, and, turning onto her side, faced away from him.

"I know." He placed his arm across her waist and drew her back against his chest. He kissed her neck lightly and brushed strands of hair off her damp cheeks.

But his hand froze in the act when her telephone rang.

Earlier she had set her answering machine to pick up, so she could monitor calls. Now Jack's voice blared from the speaker, making him a third presence in the room.

"Hi, babe. Just calling to check on you, see how you're faring. If you're asleep, never mind calling me back. But if you're up and want to talk, you know I'm willing to listen. I'm worried about you. Dean, too. I've been calling him all evening, but he's not answering any of his phones. You know how he is. He'll be thinking it was his fault that the standoff turned out the way it did. I'm sure he could use a friend tonight, so I'll keep trying to reach him. Anyway, love you. Rest well. 'Bye."

For the longest time, neither of them moved. Then Paris disentangled herself from Dean and crawled as far as the coffee table, where she pressed her head against the wood, hard enough to hurt.

"Paris—"

"Just go, Dean."

"I feel as badly as you do."

She looked at him over her shoulder. It was bare; she had dragged her robe along behind her like a bridal train. Frantically she tugged up the sleeve to cover the exposed slope of her breast. "You couldn't possibly feel as badly as I do. Please leave."

"I feel bad for Jack, yes. But I'm damned if I regret making love to you. It was destined to happen, Paris. I knew it the minute I met you, and so did you."

"No, no I didn't."

"You're lying," he said quietly.

She snuffled a laugh. "A minor offense compared to fucking my fiancé's best man."

"You know that's not what this was. It would be much easier for us if that's all it was."

That was true. Behind the shame, her heart was breaking from the despair of knowing that it would never happen again. Perhaps she could have forgiven herself a simple tumble, a hormonal rush, a temporary fall from grace. But it had been far too meaningful to dismiss and forgive.

"Just leave, Dean," she sobbed. "Please. Go."

She laid her head on the table again and closed her eyes. Scalding tears rolled down her cheeks as she listened to the rustle of his clothing, the jangle of his belt buckle, the rasp of his zipper, and his muffled footfalls on the carpet as he walked to the door. She endured a purgatorial silence until she heard the door open, then close quietly behind him.

"Paris?"

With a start, she looked behind her, toward the studio

door. Dean was standing there, as though he had materialized from out of her memory.

She'd been so lost in thought, it took several seconds for her to process that this was the here and now, not an extension of her reverie. She swallowed thickly and motioned him in. "It's okay. My mike's not on."

"Crenshaw said I could come in if I didn't make any noise."

He sat on the stool beside hers, and for one insane moment, she felt like throwing herself at him, taking up where they had left off in her recollection. His scruff that night had left whisker burns on her skin. Within a few days they had faded. But the sensual imprints made on her mind had never gone away. Last night's kiss had revealed how vivid and accurate they were.

"Nothing yet from Valentino?"

She shook her head to answer him, but also to clear it of the persistent sensual tweaks. "Did you get Gavin home all right?"

"With orders that he's not to leave, and I don't think he'll disobey me tonight. It shook him up to be questioned at the police station today. He was certainly on his best behavior tonight. Of course, he was trying to impress you."

"Well, he succeeded because I was impressed. He's great, Dean."

He nodded thoughtfully. "Yeah."

She watched him for a moment, noticing the worry line that had formed between his eyebrows. "But?"

He brought her into focus. "But he's lying to me."

chapter twenty-four

Sergeant Robert Curtis was working overtime. He was ensconced in his cubicle inside the CIB, where only one other detective was burning the midnight oil, on a robbery case.

The radio on Curtis's desk was tuned to FM 101.3. He was listening to Paris Gibson's voice while reading the information he'd gleaned about her suspended television career and departure from Houston. His friends in the HPD had been thorough, faxing him everything that had ever been printed about Paris, Jack Donner, and Dean Malloy. It was interesting stuff.

The search of Lancy Ray Fisher's, aka Marvin Patterson, apartment had yielded some surprises, too, specifically, a box of cassette tapes, all of Paris Gibson's radio program.

Now, why, the detective asked himself, would a con cum janitor have such a burning interest in Paris that he would collect recordings of past programs when he could listen to her live every night?

Lancy's mother hadn't provided any insight.

An intelligence officer, having weeded through miles of red tape and reams of records, had located her. Currently she lived in a mobile-home park in San Marcos, a town south of Austin.

Curtis himself had made the thirty-minute drive there. He could have dispatched another detective to conduct the interview, but he'd wanted to hear firsthand why Mrs. Fisher's son, Lancy, living under the alias Marvin Patterson, was seemingly obsessed with Paris Gibson.

The interior of Mrs. Fisher's domicile was even worse than the exterior portended, and she was as untidy and inhospitable as her home. When Curtis showed her his ID, she was at first suspicious, then belligerent, and, finally, abusive.

"Why don't you take your sorry ass outta here? I got nothing to say to no goddamn cop."

"Has Lancy been to see you recently?"

"No."

Curtis knew she was lying, but he got the impression that there was no love lost between mother and son and that she would welcome a chance to air her complaints. Rather than challenge the truthfulness of her reply, he remained quiet and tried to pick the cat hair off his trousers while she sucked on a cigarette and he waited until she decided to unload.

"Lancy's been a thorn in my side since he was born," she began. "The less he comes around me, the better I like it. He lives his life and I live mine. Besides, he's gone and got uppity."

"Uppity?"

"His clothes and such. Drives a new car. Thinks he's better'n me."

Which wouldn't be saying much, Curtis thought. "What make and model is his car?"

She snorted. "I can't tell one Jap car from another."

"Did you know he was working at a radio station?"

"Sweeping up is what he told me. He had to take that job after getting fired from his other one on account of stealing. That was a good job and he went and blowed it. He's dumb as well as no'count."

"Did you know he used an assumed name?"

"Wouldn't surprise me what that boy did. Not after he was a cokehead and all." Leaning forward, she wheezed in an undertone, "You know, that's why he did them dirty movies. To get dope."

"Dirty movies?"

"My neighbor lady? Two rows over? She come running over here one night not long ago, says she's seen my boy, Lancy, wagging his thing in some nasty movie she rented at the video place. I called her a fuckin' liar, but she said, 'Come see for your ownself.'"

She sat up straighter, striking the righteous pose of a recent convert with only contempt for the unshriven. "Sure enough, there he was, nekkid as a jaybird, doing such as I ain't never saw did before. I's embarrassed to death."

Curtis feigned sympathy for a mother whose son had gone astray. "Does he still work in the, uh, film industry?"

"Naw. Don't do drugs no more either. Leastways he says he don't. It was a long time ago. He was just a kid. But still." She lit another cigarette. Curtis would leave there feeling and smelling like he had smoked three packs himself.

"What name did he use when he made the movies?"

"Don't remember."

"What were the titles of the movies he was in?"

"Don't remember and don't want to know. Guess you could ask my neighbor. And how come an old lady like her is watching trash like that anyway? She ought to be ashamed of herself."

"Does Lancy have a lot of girlfriends?"

"You don't listen too good, do you? He don't tell me *nuthin'*. How would I know anything about girlfriends?"

"Has he ever mentioned Paris Gibson?"

"Who? That a boy or a girl?" Her puzzled reaction was too genuine to have been faked.

"Doesn't matter." He stood up. "You know, Mrs. Fisher, that aiding and abetting is a felony."

"I ain't aided or abetted nobody. I done told you Lancy ain't been here."

"Then you won't mind if I look around."

"You got a warrant?"

"No."

She blew a gust of smoke up at him. "Oh, what the hell. Go ahead."

It wasn't a large place, so except for having to avoid hissing cats and their droppings, his walk through it didn't take long. Nor did it take him long to determine that someone had slept in the spare bedroom. The narrow bed had been left unmade and there was a pair of socks on the floor beside it. When he knelt down to pick up one of the socks, he noticed the loose floor tile beneath the bed. It came right up with a little nudge of his pocketknife.

Replacing what he found there exactly as he'd found it, he rejoined Mrs. Fisher in what passed for the living room. He asked who the socks belonged to.

"Lancy must've left them last time he was here. Long time ago. He never did pick up after hisself."

Another lie, but he'd be wasting his time to dispute it. She would continue lying. "Do you know if Lancy has a computer?"

"He thinks I don't know about it, but I do."

"What about a cassette recorder?"

"Don't know about that, but all them modern contraptions are a waste of good money, if you ask me."

"I'm going to leave you my card, Mrs. Fisher. If Lancy comes here, will you call me?"

"What's he done?"

"Avoided questioning."

"'Bout what? Can't be anything good."

"I'd just like to talk to him. If you hear from him, you'd be doing him a favor to notify me."

She took his business card and laid it on the cluttered TV tray beside her reclining chair. He didn't quite catch what she muttered around the cigarette dangling from her lips, but it didn't sound like a promise to do as he asked.

He was anxious to get into the fresh air and away from the potential of being blown to smithereens when her oxygen tank exploded, but at the door he paused to ask one further question. "You said that Lancy got fired from a good job for stealing."

"That's what I said."

"Where was he working?"

"The telephone company."

As soon as he got into his car, Curtis contacted the San Marcos PD, explained the situation, and asked them to keep surveillance on Mrs. Fisher's mobile home. He then got another detective in his own unit busy running down Lancy Ray Fisher's employment record at the telephone company.

Traffic on northbound Interstate 35 was reduced to a crawl because of road work, so by the time he reached headquarters, the information he'd sought was already available. Fisher's employment records at Southwestern Bell were in his real name. He'd been an excellent employee until he'd gotten caught stealing equipment.

"High-tech stuff at the time," the detective reported. "More or less obsolete now because the technology changes so quickly."

"But still useable?"

"According to the expert, yeah."

Armed with that information, Curtis bumped Lancy Ray Fisher up to the viable suspect list and turned his attention to the materials he'd been faxed from Houston.

Included were copies of newspaper articles, transcriptions of TV news coverage, and materials printed off the Internet. They told a tragic story and filled in some of the gaps that Malloy had been averse to filling.

For instance, Curtis now understood why Paris Gibson wore sunglasses. She had suffered an injury to her eyes in the same auto accident that had robbed Jack Donner of his life—except for a beating heart and minimal brain function.

Paris had been riding on the passenger side of the front seat, with her seat belt buckled. When the car struck the bridge abutment at a high rate of speed, air bags deployed. But they weren't any help against flying glass from the windshield, which was supposed to have been shatterproof, but wasn't, especially not when the 185-pound driver of the vehicle was catapulted through it.

Jack Donner was not wearing his seat belt. The air bag retarded his ejection from the car, but didn't prevent it. He sustained severe head trauma. The damage was irreparable and extensive. He was rendered physically helpless for the remainder of his life.

His mental capacity was limited to reacting to visual, tactile, and auditory stimulation. The responses were feeble, on the level of a newborn, but enough to prevent him from being classified as brain dead. No one could pull the plug.

Reportedly, his friend Dr. Dean Malloy of the HPD had been first on the scene. He had been following Mr. Donner in his own car, had witnessed the accident, and had made the 911 call from his cell phone. By all accounts, he was a caring and self-sacrificial friend, who for days following the accident kept vigil outside Ms. Gibson's hospital room and Mr. Donner's ICU.

The last follow-up story on Jack Donner's tragic fate reported that Paris Gibson had recovered from her minor injuries and, having resigned from her position at the TV station, was moving Donner to a private nursing facility.

She was quoted as thanking all her friends, associates, and fans who had sent flowers and cards wishing her and her fiancé well. She would miss her job and all the wonderful people in Houston, but her life had taken an unexpected turn, and now she must follow a new path.

There was no mention of Dean Malloy in the final story, an omission that practically screamed at Curtis. When one disappears from the radar screen of a strong and lasting friendship, there's got to be a good reason.

No deep, dark mystery there. He'd seen the way Malloy looked at Paris Gibson and vice versa. With I-want-to-see-you-naked lust. But it was also the care they took *not* to look at each other that gave away a yearning that went deeper than just the physical. It was the avoidance that incriminated them. If this was visible to him after having known them for only two days, it must have been glaringly obvious to Jack Donner.

Conclusion: In a love affair, three was one too many.

As he listened to Paris's program, his anger mounted.

She made no mention of him, of Valentino.

But she talked endlessly about Janey Kemp. She went on about how badly her parents wanted her to be returned to them unharmed. Told about her friends, who were worried for her safety. Extolled her virtues.

What a farce! Janey had told him how much she

despised her parents, and the feeling was mutual. Friends? She made conquests, not friends. As for virtues, she was without them.

But to hear Paris tell it, Janey Kemp was a saint. A beautiful, charming, friendly, kind American ideal.

"If you could only see her now, Paris," he said in a whispered chuckle.

Janey disgusted him so much now that he had stayed with her only briefly today. She didn't look beautiful and enticing anymore. Her hair, once bouncy and silky, had looked like old rope coiled about her head. Her complexion was sallow. The eyes that could be sultry or scornful at will were now dull and lifeless. Barely acknowledging his presence in the room, she had stared vacantly and unblinkingly, even when he snapped his fingers an inch from her nose.

She seemed half dead and looked even worse. A shower would improve things, but he just couldn't be bothered with carrying her into the bathroom to wash her.

He couldn't be bothered with much of anything except dealing with this jam he'd gotten himself into. Time was running out for him to arrive at a workable solution. He had extended to Paris a seventy-two-hour deadline, and if he had any character at all, any sense of pride, he really should stick to that timetable.

Janey had become more of a liability than he had anticipated. There also remained the question of what to do about Paris.

He really hadn't looked beyond bringing Janey here and using her the way she begged to be used. She was a whore who advertised her willingness to try anything. He had called her bluff, that's all. Her boasts hadn't been empty ones either. She'd proved herself to be a gourmand of debasement.

He hadn't seriously planned on this ending with her demise, any more than he had planned to kill Maddie Robinson. That's just the way his relationship with Maddie had evolved. She'd said, "I don't want to see you anymore," and he had made certain that she wouldn't. Ever. When you looked at it that way, she had decided her fate, not him.

As for Paris, he hadn't thought much beyond placing that first call and telling her that he had taken action against the woman who had wronged him. He had wanted to frighten her, rattle her, and hopefully make her aware of her intolerable smugness. Who was she to dispense advice on love and life, sex and relationships?

What he hadn't anticipated was that his phone call to her would launch a police investigation and become the media event that it had. Who would have thought everyone would get so uptight over Janey, when she was getting exactly what she had asked for?

No, it had grown into something much larger than he had bargained for. He felt himself losing control of the situation. To survive, he must get back that control. But where to start?

One way would be to release Janey.

Yes, he could do that. He could dump her near her parents' house. She didn't know his name. He could clear out this room so that if she ever brought the cops to the "scene of the crime," he would be long gone. He would have to stop going to the meeting places of the Sex Club or risk being seen by her, but finding action was never a problem. The Sex Club was only one resource.

It wasn't a perfect plan, but probably the best course of action left to him. He would call Paris tonight at the appointed time and tell her that he'd only wanted to toy with her, make her realize that she shouldn't play with people's emotions and hand out glib advice. *I never dreamed you would take me seriously, Paris. Can't you take a joke? No hard feelings, okay?*

Yes, that was definitely a workable plan.

" . . . here on FM 101.3," he heard Paris say, interrupting his thoughts. "Stay with me until two A.M. I just got a call from Janey's best friend, Melissa."

Melissa.

"Melissa, would you like to say something to the listening audience?" Paris asked.

"Yeah, I just, you know, want Janey back safe," she said. "Janey, if you can hear this and you're okay, come home. Nobody's gonna be mad. And if someone out there is holding my friend against her will, then I have to tell you that's totally uncool. Let her go. Please. We just want Janey back. So . . . I guess that's it."

"Thank you, Melissa."

Wait, was he supposed to be the *villain* of this piece? He hadn't done anything to Janey Kemp that she hadn't wanted done. And Paris wasn't the snow princess she wanted everyone to believe either. She was no better than anyone else.

He dialed a number he knew by heart, knowing that this call couldn't be traced to his cell. He'd made certain of that.

"This is Paris."

"The topic tonight is Dean Malloy."

"Valentino? Let me speak to Janey."

"Janey is in no mood to talk," he said, "and neither am I."

"Janey's parents wanted me to ask you—"

"Shut up and listen to me. If you and your boyfriend don't move quickly, you'll have *two* deaths on your consciences. Janey's. And Jack Donner's."

*   *   *

"I'd feel better if you stayed at my house until this is over. I've got an extra bedroom. Nothing fancy, but you'd be comfortable. And safe."

Dean had insisted on following her home and seeing her inside. As before, Valentino's call had been routed through a deserted pay phone, which provided no leads. The police were now convinced that he never went near those pay phones.

This call had been most disconcerting because he had sounded even angrier and edgier than before. He had alluded again to Janey's death. And of course the reference to Dean and Jack had been an alarming new element. Either Valentino was excellent at guessing, or he knew with certainty that Jack's death implicated her and Dean to some extent.

"Thanks for the offer, but I'll be safe here." She went through her front door ahead of him. Once inside, he switched on a table lamp. She immediately turned it off. "I feel like a goldfish with the lights on. They can see in."

Dean glanced at the squad car parked at her curb. "Griggs has a replacement, I see."

"His night off. Curtis told me the personnel would be different but that this team of officers was just as vigilant." As Dean closed the door, she asked, "What about Gavin?" Valentino had spoken about Dean with such disdain, they were concerned not only for his and Paris's safety, but for Gavin's as well.

"Taken care of. Curtis dispatched a squad car to my house. I called Gavin and told him to expect it."

"Liz?"

"I didn't think officers were necessary, but I called and gave her a heads-up. Told her to be sure her alarm was set and to call me if anything unusual happened."

"Maybe she's the one who should be staying in your spare bedroom."

Rather than picking up the gauntlet, he said, "That's another conversation, Paris."

She turned and headed for the kitchen. He followed. It was two-thirty in the morning, but they were too troubled to sleep. "I'm going to have some hot chocolate," she said. "Want some?"

"It's eighty degrees outside."

She gave him a take-it-or-leave-it look.

"Juice?" he asked.

While her water was heating in the microwave, she poured him a glass of orange juice and took a package of cookies from the pantry. "What do you think he's lying about?"

"Valentino?"

"Gavin. Earlier tonight, you told me you thought he was lying to you. We got busy with all the calls coming in and never got around to finishing the conversation."

He stared into his glass of juice for a moment, then said, "That's the hell of it. I don't know what he's lying *about,* I just know that he is."

After stirring a packet of instant cocoa mix into her cup of hot water, she motioned for him to bring the cookies and follow her into the living room. She took one corner of the sofa, he the other. The package of cookies was placed on the cushion between them. The lamp stayed dark, but the glow from the porch lights came through the front windows, so they could see well enough. She removed her sunglasses.

"Do you think he's lying about his activities that night?" she asked.

"By omission, maybe. I'm afraid that there was more to his meeting with Janey than he wants to share."

"Like that they had sex?"

"Possibly, and he doesn't want anybody to know."

"Because that would make his story of leaving her to join friends less credible."

"Right." Dean munched a cookie. "But realistically, how could he be Valentino? It doesn't sound like him. He doesn't know about us." He looked over at her. "That part, anyway. He doesn't have the technical skills to reroute telephone calls."

"I asked Stan about how that technology works."

"How would he know?"

"He likes gadgets, expensive toys. Don't give me that look," she said when his eyebrow formed an inquisitive arch. "He's not Valentino. He hasn't got the balls."

"What do you know about his balls?"

"Please," she groaned. "Do you want to hear this or not?"

He gave a noncommittal harrumph as he reached for another cookie.

She continued, "Stan said it wouldn't be hard to do. Anyone with access to some equipment could probably learn how to do it over the Internet."

"What about somebody who had worked for the phone company?"

"It would probably be a snap. Why?"

"Before becoming a janitor, Marvin Patterson was an installer for Southwestern Bell."

Dean had followed her home from the radio station in his own car. During the drive, he'd had a lengthy cell phone conversation with Curtis. He recounted for her now everything that the detective had learned about Lancy Fisher.

"He had a collection of audiotapes? Of my show? What could that mean?"

"We don't know," Dean replied. "That's why Curtis has intelligence guys out tapping all their informers, trying to find the shy Mr. Fisher. We've got plenty of questions for him, number one being why the preoccupation with you."

"Which comes as a shock. He never showed the least bit of interest in me. Kept his head down and rarely spoke."

"Strange behavior for a former actor."

"Actor? Marvin?"

"He appeared—all of him—in a couple of porno videos."

"What!" she exclaimed. "Are you sure we're talking about the same man?"

He told her what Curtis had learned from Lancy Fisher's mother. "None of which explains why he taped your show every night. Or so it seems. He had ninety-two cassettes in all. Not very good quality, Curtis said. Probably recorded directly off the radio. Hours of love songs and Paris Gibson's sexy voice. It could be that Marvin just jerked off while listening to you. But that's a lot of jerking off."

"Spare me that image, please."

"Did he ever—"

"Nothing, Dean. He never mumbled more than a few words to me. Never even looked me in the eye that I can recall."

"Then as far as this case goes, he may be as innocent as the driven snow. He may have disappeared only because he's an ex-con and as such has a natural aversion to police interrogations even if he's got nothing to hide."

He paused and watched her closely for several moments, long enough for her to ask, "What?"

"Curtis has become a regular Sherlock Holmes into our past."

She blew on her hot cocoa, but she'd suddenly lost her appetite for it. "What's the good news?"

"There isn't any. He told me straight out that he knew the facts behind your leaving Houston. The accident. Jack's head injury. Your resignation from TV. And so forth."

"That's all?"

"Well, he stopped with that, but the silence that followed was teeming with curiosity and insinuation."

"Let him insinuate all he wants."

"I did."

She set her cup on the coffee table, then with a heavy sigh laid her head against the sofa cushion. "I'm not surprised by his curiosity. He's a detective, after all. And he didn't even have to dig very deep. Just scratch the surface and there's my life for all to see."

"I'm sorry."

She smiled faintly. "Doesn't matter. Other aspects of this are more important. Namely, Gavin." Leaving her head against the cushion, she turned it to look at Dean. "What happened to his face today?"

"I didn't hit him, if that's what you're getting at."

Affronted by his tone and the statement itself, she shot bolt upright. "That's not at all what I was 'getting at.'" Retrieving her mug of cocoa, she angrily stalked from the room, saying as she went, "Lock the door on your way out."

chapter twenty-five

With jerky, angry motions, Paris rinsed out her cocoa mug, then switched off the light above the kitchen sink. When she turned, Dean was standing in the open doorway, silhouetted against the faint light coming from the living room.

"I'm sorry I snapped at you."

"That's not what made me mad," she said. "It's that you would think that *I* would think that you had hit Gavin."

"But I did, Paris."

The admission stunned her into silence.

"Not today," he continued. "Several days ago. He provoked me, I lost my temper and backhanded him across the mouth."

Her anger evaporated as quickly as it had formed. "Oh. Then I struck a nerve, didn't I?" After a beat, she added softly, "I know what happened that time at Tech."

He looked at her sharply. "Jack told you?"

"He told me enough. But only after I'd commented on your rigid self-control."

He slumped against the doorjamb and closed his eyes. "Well, my self-control failed me the other night with Gavin, and again today with Rondeau."

"Rondeau?"

He told her about the scene he'd interrupted when he

went into the men's room. "He had Gavin's face shoved up against the mirror. That's what caused the bruise on his cheek. I wanted to kill the guy."

"I would have wanted to myself. Why would he do such a thing?"

"He said he had a mother and a sister, and the obscene messages that Gavin had left on the website offended him so much that when he saw him, he lost it. A sorry excuse that stank of bullshit."

"Does Curtis know about this?"

"I didn't tell him, and I can't see Rondeau confessing."

"You're going to let the matter drop?"

"No. Hell no. But I'll deal with Rondeau in my own way and without any interference from Curtis." He laughed without humor. "Going back to our detective friend, he's a dogged cuss. He's not going to give up until he knows everything about our 'cozy little trio,' as he put it."

"Meaning you, me, and Jack."

"He's not dense, Paris. He knows there's more to the story than what was reported in the media, and much, much more that we're not telling him."

"It's none of his business."

"He thinks it is. He thinks Valentino may harken back to that."

She tried to turn away, but he reached for her and turned her back around. "We've got to talk about this, Paris. We didn't address it when we should have, seven years ago. If we had, Jack might not have gotten drunk that night. We should have gone to him, sat him down, and told him—"

"That we had betrayed him."

"That we had fallen in love, that neither of us had set

out to, but it had happened, and that's just the way it was."

"So sorry, Jack. Rotten luck. See ya 'round."

"It wouldn't have been like that, Paris."

"No, it would have been worse."

"Worse than what, for godsake? Worse than how it ended?"

He took a deep breath and continued in a quieter, more reasonable tone of voice. "Jack was smarter than you gave him credit for. And a lot more perceptive. He could tell we were avoiding each other. Didn't you know he would want to learn the cause of it?"

Of course, he was right. She had sold Jack short by thinking that if she pretended nothing had changed, he would never learn that everything had. His fiancée and his best friend had made love. Their relationships—hers with Jack, his with Dean, hers with Dean—had been irrevocably altered. They couldn't revert to the way things had been. She'd been naive to think they could.

"I thought . . . thought . . ." She lowered her head and massaged her temple. "I don't remember what I thought, Dean. I just couldn't go to him and say, 'Remember the night after the standoff, and I told you that I wanted to be alone? Well, Dean came over to my place and we had sex on the living room rug.'"

Instead she'd taken a more subtle approach and declined each time Jack tried to get the two of them together. Her excuses became increasingly lame. "Eventually Jack demanded to know why I didn't like you anymore."

"I had a similar conversation with him," Dean said. "He asked me if you and I had crossed swords during the standoff. Had the crisis brought out the cop in me and the reporter in you, and never the twain shall meet. I told him he was way off base, that we liked and respected each other a lot. So he put it to the test with that surprise dinner."

Yes, that fateful dinner, she thought. Jack had arranged for them to meet at one of their favorite restaurants. She and Dean had arrived independently, not expecting to see the other there.

Being face-to-face for the first time since that night was as awkward for them as she had feared it would be. Making eye contact was difficult, but she couldn't keep herself from looking at him, and each time she did, she caught him stealing a glance at her. Yet their conversation had been stilted and formal.

"That dinner was an endurance test for me," Dean said. "You had rebuffed all my attempts to talk to you."

"It had to be a clean break, Dean. I didn't trust myself even to talk to you on the phone."

"Jesus, Paris, I was dying on the inside. I needed to know what you were thinking. If you were all right. If you were pregnant."

"Pregnant?"

"We hadn't used anything."

"I was on the pill."

"But I didn't know that." He smiled with chagrin. "Selfishly, I hoped you had conceived."

She couldn't admit to him even now that she'd clung to the same vain hope and was disappointed when she'd gotten her next period. A baby would have forced her to tell Jack the truth. It would have been her and Dean's justification for having to hurt him. But it hadn't happened.

"I went through hell agonizing over the state you were in when I left you that night," he was saying. "And suddenly there you were, sitting three feet across the dinner table from me, and I still couldn't ask or say anything I wanted to.

"And that wasn't all. Deceiving Jack was killing me," he continued. "Every time he told another joke, or threw his arm around me and called me his good buddy, I felt like Judas."

"He was trying his best to make it a fun evening. Ever the social chairman."

Jack had seemed determined to ignore the awkwardness between them. He had drunk too much, talked too loud, laughed too hard. But during dessert, he finally gave up and demanded to know what was going on.

"Look, I've had it with you two, okay?" he'd said. "I want to know, and I want to know now. What happened to make you so uncomfortable around each other? I'm guessing that either (a) you had a tiff during that standoff, or (b) you've been seeing each other behind my back. So tell me what the squabble was about, or fess up."

Thinking he'd made a clever joke, he folded his arms on the table and grinned at them in turn.

But Dean didn't respond to Jack's grin, and she'd felt as if her face would crack if she attempted a smile. Their silence spoke volumes. Even so, it was several moments before realization struck Jack, and when it did, it was a painful thing to watch. His grin collapsed. He looked first at her, almost quizzically. Then he looked at Dean as though willing him to laugh and say something like "Don't be ridiculous."

But when neither of them said anything, he realized that out of his jest had emerged the truth. "Son of a bitch," he said. He surged to his feet and sneered at Dean, "Dinner's on you, friend."

Apparently Dean had been following her thoughts because he said, "I'll never forget the look on his face when he put it together."

"Nor will I."

"In my haste to follow him out and try to stop him from getting behind the wheel of his car, I knocked over my chair. By the time I got it upright, the two of you had disappeared."

"I don't remember running through the restaurant after him," she said. "But I vividly remember catching up with him in the parking lot. He yelled at me, told me to leave him alone."

"But you didn't."

"No, I begged him to let me explain. He only glared at me and said, 'Did you fuck him?'"

Dean dragged his hand down his face, but the gesture did little to rub the regret from his features. "From all the way across the parking lot, I heard him say that. I heard you telling him that he shouldn't drive, that he was too drunk and too angry."

Heedless of her pleas, Jack had gotten into his car. She'd run around to the passenger side and luckily had found it unlocked. "I got in. Jack ordered me out. But I refused and instead buckled my seat belt. He cranked the motor and floored the accelerator."

They were silent for a time, lost in the recollections of that horrible night. Dean was the first to speak.

"He had every right to be furious with us for sleeping together. If our roles had been reversed, I . . . God, I don't know what I would have done. Torn him limb from limb probably. He was hurt and angry, and if he'd wanted to kill himself over it, there's really nothing we could have done to stop him, that night or on any future night. We wronged him, Paris. We'll live with that for the rest of our lives. But he wronged you when he drove off with you in that car."

He placed his hands on either side of her neck and caressed it with his fingertips. "That's what I blame him for. He could have killed you."

"I don't think it was his intention to kill anybody."

"Are you sure?" he asked gently. "What did you say to each other during those two minutes between the restaurant parking lot and that freeway overpass?"

"I told him I was sorry that we had hurt him. I told him that we both loved him, that it had been an isolated incident, a physical release after a traumatic experience, that if he could forgive us, it would never, ever happen again."

"Did he believe you?"

A tear slid unchecked down her cheek and she said huskily, "No."

"Did *you* believe you?"

She closed her eyes, squeezing out fresh tears. Slowly she moved her head from side to side.

Inhaling deeply, Dean drew her to his chest and stroked her hair.

"Maybe I should have said more," she said.

"Lied to him?"

"It might have saved him. He was enraged. Beyond reason. I tried to get him to pull over and let me drive, but he speeded up instead. He lost control of the car. He didn't drive into that abutment on purpose."

"Yes he did, Paris."

"No," she said miserably, not wanting to believe it.

"If a driver loses control, he reflexively stomps on the brake. I was right behind you. His brake lights never came on." He tilted her head back, forcing her to look at him. "Jack loved you, I don't doubt that. He loved you enough to want you as his wife. He loved you enough to fly into a jealous rage when he found out that you'd been with me.

"But," he said with emphasis, "if he had loved you the way he should have, unselfishly and unconditionally, he never could have considered taking you out along with him. As pitiful as his last years were, I never forgave him for trying to kill you."

His saying that made her love him all the more. And she did love him. From the moment they met, she had realized that her loving Dean Malloy was inevitable. But yielding to it had been impossible then, and it was impossible now. Other people had always stood between them. Jack, certainly. Now Liz.

She worked herself free of his embrace and said, "You should go now."

"I'm staying here tonight."

"Dean—"

"I'll sleep on the living room sofa." He held up his hands in surrender. "If you don't trust me to keep my hands off you, you can lock your bedroom door. But I'm not leaving you alone as long as there's a lunatic out there harboring a grudge against you."

"I can't imagine how he knew that Jack's death is on my conscience."

"And mine."

"What happened between you and me is certainly not public knowledge, and I've never discussed it with anyone."

"He probably did some research on you and surmised the cause of Jack's accident, just as Curtis did."

"Jack's accident could have been caused by any number of things," she argued.

"But only one would have busted up our friendship. It's not that much of a mind teaser, Paris. Valentino has got an ax to grind with unfaithful women. If he's concluded that you cheated on Jack with me, then you personify his nemesis. Even if it were a wrong assumption, Valentino has made it his reality and that's what he'll act on." He shook his head stubbornly. "I'm staying."

*　　*　　*

He napped on the sofa until dawn, when he silently let himself out of the house. He waved to the two officers sitting in the patrol car still parked at the curb, making certain they were aware of his departure.

He had hardly slept. He looked and felt as if he had been up most of the night. But this was an errand that couldn't wait. He didn't want to postpone it even for the time it would take to go home for a shower and a shave.

He rang the bell twice before he heard the dead bolt click on the other side of the door. Liz peered sleepily through the narrow crack allowed by the brass chain lock, then closed the door only long enough to unlatch it.

"It's unforgivable of me to show up at this time of morning," he said as he stepped inside.

"I forgive you." She wrapped her arms around his waist and snuggled against him. "In fact, this is a lovely surprise."

He hugged her. Beneath the silk robe, which was all she had on, her body felt warm, soft, and womanly. But he wasn't in the least aroused.

She eased back far enough to look up into his face, while keeping her lower body pressed intimately against his. "You look a little the worse for wear. Long night?"

"You could say so."

"Something new with Gavin?" she asked, her concern showing.

"No. He's not totally out of the woods yet, and until he is, I'll be apprehensive. But he's not the reason I'm here."

Her ability to read people had taken her far in her career and it didn't fail her now. After studying him for a moment longer, she said, "I was going to offer you some TLC in bed. But I think I should offer to make coffee instead."

"Don't bother. I can't stay long."

As though to shore up her pride, she dropped her arms to her sides, straightened her posture, and shook back her tousled hair. "Long enough to sit down at least?"

"Of course."

She led him to her living room sofa, where she claimed a corner, tucking her bare feet beneath her hips. Dean sat on the edge of the cushion and propped his elbows on his knees. On the drive over, he had rehearsed several ways to broach the subject, but had ultimately decided that there was no graceful way. He respected her too much to lie. He had decided to be forthright.

"For a long time now—months anyway—I've allowed you to believe that we would eventually get married. It's not going to happen, Liz. I'm sorry."

"I see." She took a deep breath and let it out slowly. "Do I at least get to know the reason?"

"At first I thought I had a classic case of cold feet. After being a bachelor for fifteen years, I thought the idea of marrying again was causing me to panic. So I didn't say anything, hoping that the misgivings would go away. I didn't want to quarrel about it or upset you unnecessarily."

"Well, I certainly appreciate your sensitivity to my feelings."

"Do I detect some sarcasm?"

"Definitely."

"I suppose I deserve it," he said. "I've just broken what amounted to an engagement. You don't have to be nice."

"I'm glad you think so, because I'm working my way up to a hissy fit."

"You're entitled to one."

She glared at him angrily, but then the hauteur returned. "On second thought, I'm not going to get into a fight with you. Histrionics would make it easier for you to storm out of here and never look back. Instead I'm going to put you on the spot. Because I believe I deserve a full explanation."

Actually he *had* hoped for a fight, during which they would swap invective and destroy any affection they'd ever felt for each other. A fight would have been swifter, cleaner, less painful for her, and easier for him. But Liz had slammed shut that cowardly escape hatch.

"I'm not sure I can explain." He spread his hands wide, indicating how futile it was to try. "It's not you. You're as smart and beautiful and desirable as the day I met you. More so."

"Please spare me the I'm-not-worthy-of-you speech."

"That's not what this is," he said testily. "I mean all of that sincerely. It's not about you. It's about *us*. It just isn't where I am, Liz."

"You don't have to tell me that. Lately you haven't been that involved whenever we've made love."

"Funny, I didn't hear you complaining."

"You're trying to pick a fight again," she said sternly. "-Don't. And don't be stung by the criticism. It's not your performance that's at issue. It's your emotional detachment."

"Which I acknowledge."

"Is it because of Gavin and his coming to live with you? The additional demands on your time?"

"Gavin provided me with a good excuse to pull back," he admitted. "I'm not proud of the fact that I used him."

"Nor should you be. But this isn't about him either, is it?"

"No."

"Someone else, then?"

He turned his head and looked at her directly. "Yes."

"You've been seeing someone else?"

"No. Nothing like that."

"Then what, Dean? What *is* it like?"

"I love someone else."

She was silenced by the simplicity of his statement. She stared at him for several moments, assimilating it. "Oh. You love someone else. Did you ever love me?"

"Yes. On many levels I still do. You've been an important and vital part of my life."

"Just not the grand passion of it."

"When we started seeing each other, I honestly thought . . . I hoped that . . . I tried . . ."

"You tried," she said around a bitter laugh. "Just what every woman wants to hear."

The sarcasm was back, but it was forced. She had picked up a throw pillow and was hugging it to her chest, literally and figuratively giving herself something to hold on to. He felt he should leave now before his brutal honesty wounded her pride more than it was already wounded.

But as he stood up to leave, she said softly, "The woman in the sunglasses. The one you were talking to at the police station. Paris?" Raising her head, she looked up at him. "Come now, Dean, don't look so shocked. If I were blind, I still would have known that you and she had been lovers."

"Years ago. Only once, but . . ."

"But you never quite recovered."

He matched her sad smile. "No. I never did."

"Just out of curiosity, when did you start seeing her again?"

"The day before yesterday."

Her lips parted in wordless surprise.

"That's right. This alienation of feelings, for lack of a better term, started long before she entered the picture. Seeing her just confirmed what I already knew."

"That you weren't going to marry me."

He nodded.

"Well, thank God you didn't." Tossing the throw pillow aside, she came to her feet. "I don't want to be anybody's second choice."

"And you shouldn't be." He reached for her hand and squeezed it. "I apologize for taking up two years of your biological clock."

"Oh, it's probably for the best," she said flippantly. "What would I do with a baby when I went on a business trip? Take it along in my briefcase?"

She was making light of it, but he knew she was deeply disappointed. Maybe even heartbroken. She was too proud to make a spectacle of herself by crying. And perhaps, just perhaps, she cared too much for him to lay a guilt trip on him.

"You've got a lot of grace, class, and style, Liz."

"Oh, yeah. Out the wazoo."

"What'll you do?"

"Today? I think I'll treat myself to a massage."

He smiled. "What about tomorrow?"

"I didn't sell my house in Houston when I relocated here."

"You didn't?"

"You assumed that I had, and I never set you straight. Maybe I felt intuitively that I would need a safety net. Anyway, as soon as I can arrange it, I'll move back."

"You're special, Liz."

"So are you," she replied gruffly.

He leaned forward and kissed her cheek, then headed for the door. When he reached it, he turned back. "Be well." And, saying that, he left.

chapter twenty-six

"Hello?"

"Is this Gavin?"

"Yes."

"It's Sergeant Curtis. Did I wake you up?"

"Sorta."

"Sorry to disturb you. I couldn't reach your dad on his cell. That's why I'm calling the house phone. May I speak with him, please?"

"He's not here. He stayed over at Paris's house last night." Gavin regretted it the instant the words were out. Being the suspicious person he was, Curtis would jump to the wrong conclusion.

"We had dinner at her place," he explained. "After her program, you know, because of Valentino's latest call, Dad thought she shouldn't be alone."

"Cops are guarding her house."

"I guess my dad didn't think that was enough."

"Obviously."

Gavin decided to quit while he was ahead, afraid he might say too much. Anyway, why was it Curtis's business where his dad spent the night?

"Okay then, I'll try and reach him there," the detective said. "I have her unlisted number."

"I could give him a message," Gavin offered.

"Thanks, but I need to speak to him personally."

He didn't like the sound of that. Did Curtis have to speak personally to his dad about something relating to him? "Any news on Janey?"

"I'm afraid not. I'll talk to you later, Gavin."

The detective clicked off before Gavin could even say good-bye. He got up and went to the bathroom, then looked through a window on the front of the house and saw that the police car was still parked at the curb.

Was he the only one who appreciated the irony of their protecting him from Valentino, while at the same time suspecting him of being Valentino?

It was too early to get up, so he went back to bed, but discovered he couldn't sleep. Until Janey was found, he was going to be quarantined at home. He might just as well resign himself to that. It could be worse, though. If not for his dad, they probably would have put him in jail.

Considering that his dad had caught him in several lies and discovered his membership in the Sex Club, he wasn't suffering overly much. Last night, with his dad and Paris, it hadn't been half bad.

He'd almost dreaded seeing her after so many years. What if she'd changed and now acted like an old person? He was afraid she'd have big, stiff hair and too much jewelry, that she'd be gushy and sappy, going on and on about how much he'd grown, make a big to-do over him like his mother's relatives always did at family get-togethers.

But Paris had been cool, just like he remembered her. She was friendly, but didn't overdo it like Liz did. She didn't talk down to him either. Even when he had known her before, she had talked to him like an equal, not like a kid.

Jack had always addressed him as Skipper, or Scout,

or Partner, something cute, and had talked to him bois-
terously, like he was a baby who had to be entertained.
Jack had been okay, but of the two, he had liked Paris
better.

He had liked Paris better than the girls his dad had
dated then, too. He remembered thinking that if Jack
wasn't in the picture, how cool it would be if his dad
liked Paris as a girlfriend.

His mom had thought that maybe he did.

She'd never talked to him about it, of course, but he
had overheard her say once to a friend that she thought
Dean had a "thing" for Paris Gibson, and that he only
dated other women because she belonged to Jack Donner.

At the time, he'd been too young to understand the
implications. Nor had he been particularly interested in
the relationships between grown-ups. But after having
seen how anxious his dad had been to get to her house
last evening, how he'd checked himself out in the
rearview mirror before they left the car, he thought his
mom might have been right. He'd never seen his dad consult a mirror before meeting Liz.

For as long as he could remember, his parents had
been divorced. As a kid, he had gradually begun to com-
prehend that his family wasn't like the ones in TV commercials where the mommy and daddy ate breakfast
together, and walked on the beach holding hands, and
rode in the same car, and even slept in the same bed. He
noticed that in other houses on his block, the daddy was
there all the time.

He asked questions of both parents, and after they
had explained the meaning of divorce, he had fervently
hoped that his parents would get back together and live
in the same house. But the older he got, the better he
came to understand and accept that a reconciliation was

an extremely dim possibility. Dumb kid that he was, he had continued to hope.

His dad had dated lots of women. Gavin forgot most of their names because none had lasted very long. He'd heard his mom talking to his grandmother about the "flavor of the month" and knew that she was referring to his dad's girlfriends.

His mom hadn't dated nearly as much, so it was surprising that she was the one to remarry. Her remarriage had dashed all hope that his parents would, somehow, miraculously reunite. That's when he'd gotten really mad at her and had determined to make her life with her new husband miserable.

Looking back, it had been a stupid, childish way to behave. He'd been a real jerk. His mom must have loved the guy or she wouldn't have married him. She didn't love his dad anymore. Gavin had heard her tell his grandmother that, too. "I'll always love Dean for giving me Gavin," she had said, "but we made the right decision early on to split up."

He figured his dad didn't love his mom either, and maybe never had. He tried to picture his parents as a couple, and it just didn't look right. Like two pieces from different puzzles, they didn't fit. It hadn't worked originally and it never would.

Live with it, Gavin, he thought.

His mom was happy now in her second marriage. His dad deserved to be happy, too. But Gavin didn't think Liz was the one who was going to make him happy.

He drifted off, thinking about it, but before he was completely asleep, the doorbell rang.

Jesus! Why was everybody up so frigging early this morning?

He made his way to the front door and unlocked it.

To his regret, he didn't check to see who had rung the bell before he opened the door. John Rondeau was standing on the porch.

Gavin's eyes darted past him to the squad car at the curb. He was comforted to see that it was still there. The cops inside were noshing on doughnuts. No doubt a gift from Rondeau.

"Don't worry, Gavin, your protectors are in place."

Rondeau's pleasant tone of voice didn't fool him. Not for a second. His cheekbone had finally stopped throbbing, but it was still sore and would remain discolored for days. Rondeau outweighed him by probably thirty pounds. He knew firsthand that the son of a bitch was capable of violence. But he'd be damned if he'd cower.

"I'm not worried about anything," he retorted. "Especially you. What do you want?"

"I wanted to add something to what I told you yesterday."

"If my dad finds out you're here, he'll whip your ass."

"That's why this is such a good time, because I know he's not at home." He was smiling, so to anyone looking, including the cops licking sugar glaze off their fingers, this would appear to be a chat between friends. "If you decide to tell anybody about my—"

"Crimes."

His smile only widened. "I was going to say extracurricular activities. If anybody hears about that from you, it won't be you I come after."

"I'm not afraid of you."

Ignoring that, Rondeau said, "I'll skip you and go straight for your old man."

"Is that supposed to be a joke? Because it's freaking funny." Gavin snorted derisively. "You're a computer geek."

"I'm working my way out of that unit and into the CIB."

"I don't care if they make you chief, you haven't got the balls to have a face-off with my dad."

"I wasn't talking about attacking him myself. That would be stupid because he would be watching for that. But what about some psycho jailbird he has to interview?

"Malloy goes into jail cells all the time, you know," he continued smoothly. "Talking to junkies and rapists and homicidal maniacs, trying to get information from them, manipulating them into confessing. What if one of them was tipped off that Dr. Malloy was coming on to his woman, making moves on her while he's in jail?"

"You're getting even funnier."

"Like the way he moved in on his best friend Jack Donner with Paris Gibson."

Gavin's next smart-alecky retort died on his lips. "Says who?"

"Curtis, for one. Says anyone with a grain of sense who can add two and two together. Your dad fucked his best friend's fiancée, which caused Jack Donner to try and commit suicide."

"You're making that up."

"If you don't believe me, ask him." Rondeau clicked his tongue against the roof of his mouth. "It's an ugly story, isn't it? But it fuels any rumor I might start among the jail population that Dr. Malloy, despite all his buddy-buddy tactics, is not to be trusted, especially with a lonely and susceptible female.

"You get my drift, Gavin? Cops get set up to die by other cops all the time. We're human, you know. We make enemies among ourselves. It happens," he said, shrugging. "He wouldn't see it coming, but he'd be just as dead and you'd be just as orphaned."

Fear struck Gavin's heart. "You get out of here," he said thickly.

In no apparent hurry, Rondeau pushed himself away from the doorjamb. "Okay, I'll leave you now. But I strongly urge you to think about what I said. You're nothing. You're dog shit on my shoe, not worth my time and effort. But if you rat me out," he said, poking Gavin's bare chest hard with the knuckle of his index finger, "Malloy goes down."

Paris's eyes came open slowly, but when she saw Dean sitting on the edge of her bed, she sat bolt upright. "What's happened?"

"Nothing new. I didn't mean to startle you."

She was relieved to know that there was no bad news, but her heart was still pumping hard from her initial fright and now from having Dean sitting on her bed. Not having quite regained her breath, she asked, "How was the sofa?"

"Short."

"Did you sleep at all?"

"Some. Not much. Mostly I worked, made some notes on Valentino's profile."

As tired as she'd been, it had taken her a long time to fall asleep, knowing that he was in the next room. It had hovered in her subconscious and had prevented her from getting a restful sleep. "I feel like coffee."

He nodded, but he didn't move and neither did she. The silence stretched out as they continued to gaze at each other across the narrow strip of bed separating them.

"Should have locked my bedroom door after all?" she asked in a voice barely above a whisper.

"Definitely. Because, as it turns out, I can't keep my hands off you."

He reached for her and she stretched toward him, but just before their lips met, she said, "Liz—"

"Not a factor."

"But—"

"Trust me, Paris."

She did, giving herself over to his kiss—his untempered, possessive, delicious kiss. Placing her hands on his stubble-covered cheeks, she tilted her head to change the angle of their lips and invited more intimacy. He pushed aside the blanket and sheet covering her and pressed her onto the pillows, following her down, lying close beside her.

He drew back in order to look at her, taking in her unglamorous tank top and boxers. "Fancy sleepwear."

"Designed to inflame."

"It's working," he growled.

She explored his face with her fingertips, smoothing his eyebrows, stroking the straight line of his nose, then tracing the shape of his lips and touching the shallow cleft at the bottom of his chin.

"Your hair is grayer," she remarked.

"You're wearing yours shorter."

"I guess we've both changed."

"Some things have." His eyes moved to her breasts and when he caressed her through the tank top, her nipple tightened. "Not that. That I remember."

He kissed her again, except with more urgency than before. Splaying his hand over her bottom, he lifted her onto the erection that strained against his trousers.

A rush of fluid heat spread through her lower body and into her thighs. It had been years since she had experienced that aching desire to be filled. She sighed with joy over feeling it again, and moaned with longing to have that desire assuaged.

"We've waited long enough," he said, rolling back only far enough to reach for his fly. "Too damn long."

But they would wait longer. Her telephone rang.

Both froze. They locked gazes, and each knew without having to say anything that she must answer the call. Too many things were at stake. Dean flopped onto his back and blistered the ceiling paint with his curses.

Paris pushed her tangled hair from her eyes and reached for the cordless phone on her nightstand. "Hello?" She mouthed to Dean that it was Curtis. "No . . . no, I was awake. Is there news?"

"Of a sort," the detective said brusquely. "None about Valentino or Janey directly. Brad Armstrong and Marvin Patterson are still at large. But actually I'm calling for Malloy. I understand he's there."

With more composure than she felt, she said, "Just a moment. I'll get him."

She covered the mouthpiece as she extended the telephone toward Dean. He looked at her inquisitively, but she raised her shoulders, saying, "He didn't say."

He took the telephone from her and said a curt good morning to the detective. Paris got up and went into the bathroom, closing the door behind her. She showered quickly and put on a robe before going back into the bedroom. Dean was no longer there and the telephone had been returned to the battery charger.

She followed sounds into the kitchen. Dean was scooping coffee grounds into the paper filter. Hearing her behind him, he glanced at her over his shoulder. "You smell good."

"What did Sergeant Curtis want?"

"Coffee will be ready in a few minutes."

"Dean?"

"Gavin told him I was here. He had called my house

because he couldn't reach me on my cell. When I went to see Liz this morning—"

"You went to see Liz this morning?"

"At dawn. I turned off my cell and forgot to turn it back on. As a courtesy to her, I didn't want a phone call to interrupt what I had to tell her."

Paris said nothing but felt the pressure of a dozen questions wanting to be asked. He calmly removed two coffee mugs from her pantry and only then turned to face her. "Which was that I wouldn't be seeing her again."

She swallowed hard. "Was she upset?"

"Mildly. But not shocked. She'd seen it coming."

"Oh."

He must have read her mind, because he said quietly, "Don't blame yourself for the breakup, Paris. It would have happened anyway."

"Are you . . . okay with it?"

"Relieved. I was unfair to her by letting it go on for so long."

The coffeemaker gurgled, signaling that the coffee was almost ready and giving her a graceful way to change the subject. She went to the fridge for a carton of half-and-half. "What did Curtis want?"

"Only to give me a status report."

"On the case?"

"No, on my employment with the APD. I've been placed on indefinite suspension."

chapter twenty-seven

"Hi, Mama, it's Lancy."

"Christ, what time is it?"

"Nearly nine."

"Where're you at?"

Last evening he had returned to the mobile-home park through a back gate and had parked two rows away from the lane on which his mother's home was situated. Risking barking dogs and skittish neighbors who would welcome a chance to shoot first and ask questions later, he'd sneaked between the narrow lots.

His reconnoitering seemed a bit melodramatic, but it was a precaution that proved to be warranted. He spotted the unmarked police car immediately. It was parked about thirty yards from his mother's patch of lawn. Anyone inside the no-frills sedan had an unrestricted view of her front door. It was a good thing he had gone to her trailer and dipped into his piggy bank when he had.

He had slinked back to his car and returned to Austin because he didn't know where else to go. He had called a neighbor, who was as trustworthy as anyone among Lancy's few acquaintances. He confirmed what Lancy suspected—the police had tossed his place. "I saw them carrying out boxes of stuff," the neighbor reported.

The tapes of Paris Gibson's shows would be in those boxes. *Shit!*

Now, disregarding his mother's question, he asked, "Have any cops come around?"

"Guy named Curtis. From Austin."

"What did you tell him?"

"Nothin'," she grumbled, "'cause I don't know nothin'."

"Did he search the trailer?"

"He poked around. Found your socks."

"Did he take them with him?"

"What would he want your dirty socks for?"

"Go to the window and look out toward the south end of the street."

"I'm in bed," she whined.

"Please, Mama. Do me this favor. See if there's a dark-colored car parked down the street."

She griped and cursed, but the telephone clattered when she obviously dropped it on her bedside table. She was gone an inordinate amount of time. When she finally returned, she was wheezing like a bagpipe. "It's there."

"Thanks, Mama. I'll talk to you later."

"I don't want none of your trouble rubbing off on me, Lancy Ray. You understand me, boy?"

He replaced the greasy receiver on the hook of the pay telephone. Thrusting his hands in his pockets and hunching his shoulders, he walked down the breezeway of the residence motel. Beneath the bill of his baseball cap, his eyes furtively watched for squad cars that he expected to appear at any moment with a squeal of brakes and shouts for him to freeze.

After learning that he couldn't hide in his mother's place, he had returned to his secret apartment to spend the night. He'd driven past it once. There'd been no police car at the IHOP across the street or anywhere else that he could see.

He got in without being detected, but it was hardly a comfortable refuge. It stank. It was dirty. It made him feel dirty.

He'd been up all night, and it had been a long one.

"You're screwed, blued, and tattooed this time, Lancy Ray," he muttered to himself as he unlocked the door and once again slipped back into the dank, dark lair of a wanted man.

Curtis's shiny cowboy boots were propped up on his desk, his ankles crossed. He was concentrating on the hand-tooled pointed toe of one of them when a yellow legal tablet landed on the desk an inch away from it. He turned to find Paris Gibson standing behind him. Even though she was wearing her sunglasses, he could tell by her body language that she was in a major snit.

"Good morning," he said.

"You're going to kowtow to that egomaniacal fool?"

He removed his feet from his desk and motioned her into a chair. She declined the offer and remained standing. He said, "That fool is a powerful county judge."

"Who has the police department in his pocket."

"It wasn't my decision to suspend Malloy. I couldn't even if I wanted to. He outranks me. I was just the messenger."

"Then let me rephrase," she said. "Judge Kemp has the *gutless* police department in his pocket."

Withstanding the insult, he addressed the issue. "The judge went straight to the top with his complaint. After he and Mrs. Kemp heard you talking about their daughter on the radio last night, he went into orbit. Or so I was told. He called the chief at home, got him out of bed, demanded that Malloy be fired for publicly maligning his daughter, dragging the family name through the dirt, and mishandling a delicate family situation, which should have been dealt with privately. He also cited conflict of interest since Gavin Malloy had been brought in for questioning."

"How did he know about that?"

"He's got moles within the department. Anyway, he threatened to sue everything and everybody if Malloy wasn't removed not only from the case, but from the APD. The chief wouldn't go that far, but he did agree that a temporary suspension was called for. Just until things cool down."

"Just to pacify the judge."

Curtis conceded with a shrug. "I got the edict from the chief before dawn this morning. He asked—make that *ordered*—me to notify Malloy since I was the one who'd brought him in to work the case. That was my punishment, I guess."

"I said nothing except flattering things about Janey last night," Paris argued. "In fact, I went out of my way not to allude to her bad reputation, the Internet club, any of that. We were trying to humanize her to Valentino, portray her as a helpless victim with friends and family who care about her."

"But the Kemps wanted to avoid all media, remember? Even a mention of Janey's disappearance. So your going on the radio, under the advice of the police department's staff psychologist, and talking about her, looked like defiance of their wishes."

"Dean told me that you were very keen on the idea."

"I admitted that to the chief."

"So why didn't the judge demand that you be fired, too?"

"Because he doesn't want to antagonize the whole department. He knows I've got a lot of friends on the force. Malloy hasn't been here long enough to cultivate that kind of loyalty.

"Besides, the judge wanted to get back at you, too. You and Malloy went to his house more or less as a team. He just didn't have the guts to criticize you publicly because of your popularity. It might be bad PR with voters to speak out against Paris Gibson."

"Leaving Dean the scapegoat," she concluded. "Has the media learned of his suspension?"

"I have no idea. If it gets out, you can bet Kemp will exploit it."

She sat down, but not because she was placated. He could tell that by her resolute expression as she leaned forward and spoke directly, to his face. "You go to your chief and tell him that I insist that he retract Dean's suspension. Immediately. Furthermore, if a story about it makes the news today, I'll be on the radio *tonight* talking about the self-serving political machine that drives this police department.

"I'll tell the public about the graft, officers receiving bribes in exchange for not making arrests when they're warranted, and about the department's blatant favoritism toward the wealthy and powerful.

"In four hours, I could do a lot of damage, more I think than even Judge Kemp could do. For all his chest thumping, I doubt if several hundred thousand people have even heard of him. But I have that many loyal listeners every night. Now, who do you think wields the most influence, Sergeant Curtis?"

"Your program isn't political. You've never used it as a soapbox."

"I would tonight."

"And tomorrow Wilkins Crenshaw would fire you."

"Which would win me even more public support and sympathy. It would become a media wildfire that I would fan for weeks. The Austin PD would have a tough time restoring John Q. Public's confidence."

Curtis couldn't see her eyes well behind the tinted lenses, but he could see them well enough. They weren't even blinking. She meant what she said.

"If the decision were up to me . . ." He raised his hands helplessly. "But the chief may not bend."

"If he refuses, I'll call a press conference. I'll be on television by noon. 'Paris Gibson goes public.' 'The first time seen on TV in seven years.' 'The face behind the voice revealed.' I can hear the promos now."

Curtis could hear them, too. "The story about Malloy may already have gotten out."

"Then your chief will issue a press release saying that it was a huge misunderstanding, overly eager reporting by someone misinformed, et cetera."

"Did Malloy send you to champion his cause?" She didn't even deign to answer and he didn't blame her. Malloy wouldn't stoop to that. Curtis had only taken the cheap shot because he didn't have any real ammunition against her arguments. "All right, I'll see what I can do."

"Take this with you," she said, pushing the legal pad toward him.

"What is it?"

"The work Dean was doing last night. He stayed up most of the night profiling Janey's kidnapper and rapist while the judge was plotting to have him discredited and fired.

"It should make for interesting reading. Your chief will realize what an asset he has in Dr. Malloy and what an egregious mistake it would be to take him off this case. Of course, Dean may tell you all to go to hell, and I wouldn't blame him. But you can try and persuade him to come back."

"You're pretty sure of our compliance."

"I'm sure only of how wise one becomes when it's a matter of covering one's own ass."

"I'll think about it and get back to you." Dean depressed the button on his cell phone, ending the call. "Meanwhile," he added under his breath, "go fuck yourself." Noticing Gavin's stunned reaction to his language, he chuckled. "Your generation didn't coin the phrase, you know."

They were having a late breakfast at a coffee shop when the chief of police himself called to nullify his suspension.

"Earlier this morning, he was ready to fire me," he told Gavin as he dug back into his omelet. "Now I'm an asset to the department. An excellent psychologist as well as a highly trained officer of the law. A cross between Sigmund Freud and Dick Tracy."

"He said that?"

"It was almost that ridiculous."

"If you're back on the case, won't Janey's dad be pissed?"

"I don't know how the department is going to deal with the judge, and I don't care."

"Do you want to keep working there?"

"Do you want me to?"

"*Me?*"

"Do you like it here, Gavin?"

"Does it matter?"

"Yes."

Gavin idly stirred his glass of milk with a plastic straw. "It's okay, I guess. I mean, it hasn't been too bad living here."

Dean knew that was probably as close to a yes vote as he was going to get. "I'd hate to leave this job before giving it a fair shake," he admitted. "I think I can do a lot of good here. Austin's a happening place. I like the city, the energy of it. Great music. Good food. Fine climate. But I also like having you living with me. I want you to continue to. So can we work out a deal?"

Gavin regarded him warily. "What kind of deal?"

"If I try out the job, will you try out the high school? I don't mean just attend it, Gavin. I mean really apply yourself, make friends, participate in school activities. You'll be required to put forth as much effort at school as I'll be putting into my job. Do we have a deal?"

"Can I have my computer back?"

"As long as I have access to it at any time. From now on, I'll monitor how much time you spend on it, and how you use it. That's a nonnegotiable point. Another condition is that you must take part in some school activity or sport. I don't care if you play croquet, so long as you don't spend all your free time locked inside your bedroom or just hanging out."

He gave Dean a fleeting glance across the table, then looked back down into his plate. "I was thinking about maybe going out for basketball."

Dean was pleased to hear it, but he didn't want to overreact and jinx it. "We've got the perfect driveway in back of the house for a basket. Want to see about putting one up so you can get in some shooting practice?"

"Sure. That'd be good."

"Okay, then. We understand each other. And just so you know, I broke it off with Liz."

Gavin's head came up. "You did?"

"Early this morning."

"That was kinda sudden, wasn't it?"

"Actually, I've been thinking about it for some time."

Gavin began playing with the straw again. "Was it not working out because of me? Because I live with you now?"

"It was because I didn't love her as much as I should have."

"You didn't want to make the same mistake twice."

It pained Dean for his son to think of his marriage to Pat as a mistake, although he was precisely right. "I suppose you could put it that way."

Gavin mulled it over for a moment. "Did Paris figure into it?"

"Hugely."

"Yeah, I thought so."

"Are you cool with that?"

"Sure, she's great." He took the plastic straw out of his glass and began bending and twisting it. "Did you sleep with her while she was engaged to Jack?"

"What?"

"You want me to repeat it?"

"That's a very personal question."

"That means yes."

"That means I'm not going to discuss it with you."

Gavin sat up straighter and looked at him with resentment. "But it's okay for you to pry into *my* sex life. I have to tell you what I did and who I did it with."

"I'm a parent and you're a minor."

"It's still not fair."

"Fair or not, you— Damn!" Dean said when his cell rang again.

He checked the caller ID, saw Curtis's number, and considered not answering. But Gavin had slumped into the corner of the booth and was staring sullenly out the window. It would probably be a one-sided conversation with him from here on anyway.

Dean answered on the fourth ring. "Malloy."

"You talk to the chief?" Curtis asked.

"Yes."

"You staying?"

Although he'd made his decision, he didn't see any reason to jump through hoops for them. "I'm considering it."

"Whether you do or not, I need you to come in."

"I'm having breakfast with Gavin."

"Bring him with you."

Dean's heart jumped. "What for? What's happened?"

"The sooner you can get here, the better. I just got some bad news."

Curtis didn't beat around the bush. "Your friend Valentino jumped his deadline. Janey Kemp's body was discovered half an hour ago in Lake Travis."

Reflexively Dean reached for Paris's hand and gripped it hard. He'd been surprised to see her waiting in Curtis's cubicle when he and Gavin got there. She told him she had been summoned just as he had, with no more explanation than he had received.

Curtis had arrived a few minutes behind them. He'd asked Gavin if he would wait for them with another detective in one of the interrogation rooms. As his son was led away, Dean had a strong sense of foreboding. Justifiably, as it turned out.

"Two fishermen found her nude body partially submerged beneath the root system of a cypress tree. I was called immediately and rushed out there. Although she hasn't been officially identified, it's her.

"The crime scene unit is combing the place. The ME is examining the body, even before he moves it. Hopes to get something. She looks pretty bad," he said with a heavy sigh. "Bruises on her face, neck, torso, and extremities. What appear to be bite marks . . ." He glanced at Paris. "Several places."

"How did she die?" Dean asked.

"We won't know until the autopsy. The ME estimated that she hadn't been in the water more than six or seven hours, though. Probably put there sometime last night."

"If you had to guess . . ."

"I'd guess strangulation, like Maddie Robinson. The bruises on Janey's neck match the ones she had. On the other hand, the two could be unrelated."

"Sexual assault?"

"The ME will also determine that. Again, if I had to guess, I'd say very likely."

They were silent for a time, then Paris asked softly, "Have the Kemps been notified?"

"That's why I was late getting here. I stopped at their house. The judge was still fuming over the chief's reversed decision and thought I had come to make amends. When I told them about the body, Mrs. Kemp collapsed, but she wouldn't allow him to console her.

"Each blamed the other. They shouted accusations. It was an ugly scene. When I left they were still going at it. I'm meeting them at the morgue in an hour to get a positive ID, and I don't look forward to it."

He stared into near space a moment, then said, "They wouldn't win a popularity contest with me, but I have to admit I felt sorry for them. Their only child has been brutalized and murdered. God knows what she endured before she died. I couldn't help but think about my own daughter, how I'd feel if somebody did that to her, then dumped her in a lake for fish to feed on."

Dean saw from the corner of his eye that Paris had pressed her fingers vertically against her lips as though to forcibly contain her emotion. "Why did you want to see Gavin?" he asked Curtis.

"Will he submit to a lie detector test?"

"Bad time for a joke, Sergeant."

"I'm not joking. We're no longer shooting in the dark. I've got a dead girl. I've got to tighten the screws."

"On my son?"

"He was one of the last people to see her alive."

"Except the person who kidnapped and killed her. Have you checked out Gavin's alibi?"

"His friends, you mean? Yes, we ran down several of them."

"And?"

"Unanimously they vouched for Gavin, said he was with them. But they were drunk and high, so their memories were fuzzy. None could nail down the time he joined them or the time he left."

"You're only subjecting Gavin to this because he's the one suspect who's available," Dean said angrily.

"Unfortunately, you're right," the detective admitted with chagrin. "So far there's been no sign of Lancy Ray Fisher even though we've staked out his apartment and his mother's place. One interesting thing turned up on his bank statement, though. There were several canceled checks made out to a Doreen Gilliam, who teaches high school drama and speech."

He looked at them meaningfully before adding, "Ms. Gilliam moonlights by giving private lessons out of her home. Lancy, aka Marvin, has been taking speech and diction lessons."

"*Speech* lessons?" Paris exclaimed. "He rarely spoke."

Curtis shrugged.

"To aid in disguising his voice, maybe?" Dean asked.

"That was my thought," Curtis said.

"He worked for the telephone company and would have the know-how to reroute calls," Dean mused out loud. "And he's fixated on Paris or else why the tapes?"

"One of the first things I'm going to ask him when

he's brought in," Curtis said. "Finding this body raises the bar considerably, so off come the kid gloves. With everybody. I hadn't heard back from Toni Armstrong, so I obtained a search warrant for their house. I made Rondeau personally responsible for cracking Brad Armstrong's computer. In my book, he's got a real good shot at being our man. His own wife testified that she caught him picking up a teenage girl.

"I've pulled in the sheriff's office, the Texas Rangers, and the Texas Highway Patrol. Every law-enforcement officer in the city and surrounding area is on the lookout for Armstrong as well as Lancy Ray Fisher. In any case, we're not putting the squeeze exclusively on Gavin."

"Is that supposed to make me feel better?" Dean asked. "My son being lumped in with a sex offender and a porn star? And since you can't find them, you're requiring Gavin to take a lie detector test."

"Not requiring, requesting."

Paris laid her hand on his arm. "Maybe you should agree to it, Dean. It will clear him."

He wanted to believe it would turn out like that. But Gavin was holding something back. It was only a gut instinct, but it was strong enough to make him afraid of the secret Gavin was keeping.

Curtis was frowning down at the folder on his desk that Dean guessed contained crime scene photos of Janey Kemp's body. "The evidence we have on Gavin is circumstantial. Nothing hard. You'd be within your rights to refuse the test." He looked up at Dean, and Dean recognized the detective's challenge for what it was.

"Fuck that. Gavin takes your damn test."

chapter twenty-eight

"Paris, it's Stan."

"Stan?"

"You sound surprised. You gave me your cell number months ago, remember?"

"But you've never called it."

"Only in case of an emergency, you said. I just heard about Janey Kemp on the news. I called to see if you're all right."

"I can't describe how awful I feel."

"Where are you?"

"At the downtown police station."

"I bet it's hopping. Did the body give up any clues to who did it?"

"I hate to disappoint you, Stan, but the only gruesome detail I know is that she's dead."

"Do you plan on doing your program tonight?"

"Why wouldn't I?"

"The GM notified Uncle Wilkins about the body. They discussed it and thought that, with everything that's happened, you might want to take the night off, replay a tape of an old show."

"I'll call the GM later and talk to him myself. But if anyone asks, tell them that I'll do the program live as always. Valentino is not going to scare me off."

"He's done what he said he was going to do, Paris. Do you think he'll call again?"

"I hope he does. The more he talks to me, the better chance we have of identifying him."

"Too bad you couldn't have caught him before he killed her." After a pause, he added, "Guess I shouldn't have reminded you of that, huh? I'm sure you already feel bad enough for being the one who set him off in the first place."

"I've got to go, Stan."

"Are you mad? You sound mad."

"I just don't want to talk about it anymore right now, okay? I'll see you tonight."

She clicked off. He wished he could have kept her talking longer because it tied up his phone line. If his uncle continued to get a busy signal, he might become discouraged and stop calling.

Ever since he'd learned that Janey Kemp's body had been discovered, Uncle Wilkins had been phoning periodically. He pretended to be concerned about the station's involvement, but Stan knew the reason for the frequent calls—Uncle Wilkins was checking up on him.

He should never have admitted to being attracted to Paris. You'd think that was all his uncle had heard during their meeting. He'd been referring to it ever since.

During their last telephone conversation, Wilkins had said in his most menacing voice, "If you've done anything perverse or inappropriate . . ."

"I've been an altar boy around her. I swear to God."

How could he have behaved otherwise with Paris? She wasn't rude, but she never acted particularly happy to see him. Sometimes, even when she was talking to him, she seemed preoccupied, as though she had something on her mind that was more important or interesting than him.

He was certain that if he'd ever made a move on her,

she would have cut him off at the knees. She'd never invited even the slightest flirtation. In fact, she often looked through him, as though he wasn't there. Much like his parents, she treated him with a casual disregard that was as hurtful as an outright rejection. He was always an afterthought.

His chance for a romance with Paris had always been remote. But it had been totally squelched when Dean Malloy entered the picture. Malloy was an arrogant son of a bitch, confident of himself and his appeal to the opposite sex. He would never need to coerce a secretary into raising her skirt or cajole a date into bed.

Fact of life: Things came easier to men like Malloy.

Another fact: Women like Paris were attracted to men like that.

People like Paris and Malloy had never known a day of rejection. It would never occur to them that love and affection didn't come as easily to others as it did to them. They shone like bright little planets, without an inkling of what it was like to be someone who could only orbit around them. They had no idea the lengths to which someone would go to attain the adoration they took for granted.

No idea.

Gavin's head was bowed so low, his chin was almost touching his chest. "In the lake?"

"Her body is being transported to the morgue, where it will undergo an autopsy to determine the cause of death."

Gavin raised his head. The news of Janey's death had caused him to go pale. He swallowed with difficulty, "Dad, I . . . You gotta believe me. I didn't do it."

"I believe that. But I also believe just as strongly that you're keeping something from me."

Gavin shook his head.

"Whatever it is, wouldn't you rather tell me than have it come out during a lie detector test? What don't you want me to know?"

"Nothing."

"You're lying, Gavin. I know you are."

The boy surged to his feet, fists clenched. "You have no right to accuse someone of lying. You're the biggest liar I know."

"What are you talking about? When have I lied to you?"

"My whole life!" Dean watched in dismay as tears sprang to his son's eyes. Angrily, Gavin swiped at them with his fists. "You. Mom. Always telling me you loved me. But I know better."

"What's makes you say that, Gavin? Why do you think we don't love you?"

"You didn't want me," he shouted. "You got her pregnant by accident, didn't you? And that's the only reason you got married. Why didn't you just get rid of me and save yourselves the trouble?"

He and Pat had never specifically discussed how much they would tell Gavin if he ever asked this question. Perhaps they should have. She wasn't here to consult, so Dean was left to answer his son's tortured questions alone. Despite the embarrassment it might cause Pat, and himself, he decided Gavin deserved the unmitigated truth.

"I'll tell you everything you want to know, but not until you sit down and stop looking at me like you're about to go for my throat."

Gavin battled with indecision for several moments, then plopped back into the chair. His expression remained belligerent.

"You're right. Your mother was pregnant when we

got married. You were conceived during a weekend fraternity party in New Orleans."

Gavin laughed bitterly. "Jeez. It's even worse than I thought. Were you college sweethearts at least?"

"We had dated a few times."

"But she wasn't someone you . . . not someone special."

"No," Dean admitted quietly.

"So I was a mistake."

"Gavin—"

"Why didn't you use something? Were you drunk or just stupid?"

"A little of both, I guess. Your mother wasn't on the pill. I should have acted more responsibly."

"Bet you shit when she told you."

"I'll admit that it came as a shock. For your mother as well as me. She was about to graduate and launch her career. I was beginning grad school. Her pregnancy was a hurdle neither of us had counted on at that time in our lives. But—and I want you to believe this, Gavin—abortion was never even considered."

He could tell by his son's expression that he wanted desperately to believe that, but was still finding it difficult to accept. Dean couldn't blame him. Perhaps he and Pat had been wrong to not discuss this with Gavin once he was old enough to understand how women became pregnant. If they had explained it to him, he wouldn't have developed insecurities about his self-worth, and harbored such resentment toward them.

"Nor was adoption discussed. From the start, Pat planned to have you and keep you. Thank God she paid me the courtesy of telling me that I had fathered a child. And when she did, I insisted that you have my name. I wanted to be in your life. Although neither of us wanted to marry the other, I wanted to make you legally mine. She finally agreed to go through with the ceremony.

"We didn't love each other, Gavin. I wish I could tell you otherwise, but it wouldn't be the truth, and that's what you've asked for and I think that's what you deserve to hear. We liked each other. We were companionable and respected each other. But we didn't love each other.

"We did, however, love you. When I held you for the first time, I was nothing short of awed and overjoyed. Your mother felt the same. She and I lived together until you were born.

"During that time, we tried to convince ourselves that love would eventually blossom and that we'd come to realize we wanted to be together for the rest of our lives. But it wasn't going to happen and both of us knew it.

"We cried on the day we finally agreed that staying together would only make for three unhappy people and postpone the inevitable. It was in your best interest that we split sooner, before you could even remember, rather than later. So when you were three months old, she filed for divorce."

He spread his hands wide. "That's it, Gavin. I think it would help if you also talked to your mother about this. Understandably, she didn't want you to know because she didn't want you to think badly of her. I don't want that either. She wasn't a party girl who slept with every guy on campus. That weekend was the last fraternity party we would ever attend because we were both about to graduate. We got wild and crazy and . . . it happened.

"Your mother sacrificed a lot in order to raise you as a single parent. I know you're upset with her for marrying now, but that's just too damn bad. Pat's not only your mother, she's a woman. And if you're entertaining some childish fear that her husband is going to replace you in her life, you're wrong. Believe me, he couldn't. No one could."

"I don't think that," he said, speaking to his lap. "I'm not an idiot. I know she needs love and all that."

"Then maybe you should stop sulking about it and tell her that you understand."

He gave a noncommittal shrug of his shoulders. "I just wish you'd told me, you know, before now. I knew anyway."

"Well, if you knew anyway, and it didn't make a significant difference in your life, then why are you using it as an excuse now?"

His head snapped up. "An excuse?"

"Lasting marriages don't necessarily make for happy homes, Gavin. Lots of kids who live with both parents have a far worse childhood than you've had, and, believe me, I know this.

"You're using your accidental conception as an excuse to behave like a jerk. That's a cowardly cop-out. Your mother and I are human. We were young and reckless and made a mistake. But isn't it time you stopped brooding over *our* mistake and started accepting responsibility for your own?"

Anger infused Gavin's face with color. He breathed heavily through his nose. But tears had once again collected in his eyes.

"I love you, Gavin. With all my heart. I'm grateful for the mistake your mother and I made that night. I'd willingly die for you. But I refuse to let you use the circumstances of your birth to distract me from what is more imperative and, right now, considerably more critical."

He moved his chair closer to the one in which Gavin sat and planted his hand firmly on his shoulder. "I've talked to you frankly, man to man. Now I want you to act like a man and tell me what you've been holding back."

"Nothing."

"Bullshit. There's something you're not telling me."

"No there's not."

"You're lying."

"Get off my back, Dad!"

"Not until you tell me."

His features reflected the turmoil within as he wrestled with his fear and possibly his conscience. Finally he blurted out, "Okay, you want to know? I was in Janey's car with her that night."

Paris checked her wristwatch. She'd been waiting outside the CIB for over an hour. Dean's attorney, whom she recognized from the day before, had arrived. He'd disappeared through the doorway and into the department. Beyond that, she knew nothing of what was going on. She didn't know if they'd begun Gavin's lie detector test or not.

Lack of sleep was beginning to catch up with her. She leaned her head against the wall behind the bench and closed her eyes, but still she couldn't rest. Haunting thoughts crowded her mind. Janey Kemp was dead. A sick, twisted individual had killed her, but Paris felt partially responsible.

As Stan had so tactlessly reminded her, Valentino had been motivated by the advice she'd given Janey. If only she hadn't aired Janey's call-in that night, Valentino wouldn't have heard it.

But tragically, he had. Once he'd issued his threat to punish Janey, what could she, Paris, have done differently? What could she have said to prevent him from taking the final step and killing her?

"Ms. Gibson?"

She opened her eyes. Before her stood a petite woman who was evidently in distress. Her face, though very pretty, was drawn. She was holding her handbag in a death grip. The skin was stretched so tightly across her knuckles, they looked like bare bone. Anguish had reduced her from dainty to frail. Although she was putting up a brave front, she looked about as stalwart as a dandelion puffball.

Paris immediately tried to ease the stranger's apprehension with a smile. "Yes, I'm Paris."

"I thought it was you. May I join you?"

"Of course." Paris made room for her on the bench and the woman sat down. "I'm sorry, I . . . Have we met?"

"My name is Toni Armstrong. Mrs. Bradley Armstrong."

Paris recognized the name, of course, and immediately understood why the woman was discomfited. "Then I know why you're here, Mrs. Armstrong," she said. "This must be awfully difficult for you. I wish we were meeting under pleasanter circumstances."

"Thank you." She was hanging on to her composure by a thread, but she did hold on, and that earned her Paris's respect. "When the police searched our house, they overlooked this." She removed a CD from her handbag. "Since they confiscated Brad's computer, I thought I should hand this over, too. It could have something important on it."

A confusing thought caused Paris to frown. "Mrs. Armstrong, how did you recognize me?"

Even with all the news coverage the story of Janey's disappearance had generated, Paris's picture had been kept out of it. Wilkins Crenshaw had personally intervened and put pressure on the local media to not use her photograph. Paris had no delusions: He wasn't concerned for her. He wanted to protect the reputation of the radio station. In any case, the local media had agreed to extend that professional courtesy. She wasn't sure how long their largess would last.

Toni Armstrong nervously wet her lips and ducked her head. "This CD from Brad's computer was only the excuse I gave myself for coming to see Sergeant Curtis. The real reason is that I didn't tell him everything yesterday."

Paris said nothing, her silence inviting Toni Armstrong to continue.

"Sergeant Curtis asked me if Brad ever listened to late-night radio. I said yes, sometimes. He went on to ask something else and never came back to that subject. Your name wasn't mentioned, so I didn't volunteer that we—Brad and I—had known you from Houston."

Her eyes were imploring, almost as though willing Paris to remember on her own so she wouldn't be required to recount the circumstances under which they'd become introduced.

"I apologize, Mrs. Armstrong. I don't remember ever meeting you."

"You and I never actually met. You were Dr. Louis Baker's patient."

Suddenly Paris's memory crystallized. How could she not have remembered his name? Of course, Armstrong was an ordinary name. Neither Curtis nor Dean had mentioned that their suspect Brad Armstrong was a dentist.

"Your husband's a dentist? *That* dentist?"

Toni Armstrong nodded.

Paris inhaled a swift breath. "I'm so sorry."

"You don't owe me an apology, Ms. Gibson. What happened wasn't your fault. I didn't blame you. You did what you had to do. Brad felt differently, of course. He said that you . . . that you had flirted with him, led him on." She smiled sadly. "He always says that. But I never thought for a moment that you had encouraged him to do what he did."

Paris had gone to Dr. Louis Baker for some dental work, but when she arrived at the clinic, she was informed that he'd been called away on a family emergency. Her choice was to reschedule or let one of his partners treat her. The appointment had been postponed twice, she was already there, so she opted to see the other dentist.

She remembered Brad Armstrong as a nice-looking man with an engaging manner. Since she was scheduled for several procedures, some of which might be uncomfortable, he'd suggested using nitrous oxide to help her relax.

She'd agreed, knowing that "laughing gas" had no lasting effect as soon as one stopped inhaling it and that it was safe when administered in a clinical environment. Besides, if a numbing shot was required, she would just as soon not know when it was coming.

Soon she was feeling completely relaxed and carefree, as though she was floating. At first she thought she had only imagined that her breasts were being touched. The caress had been featherlight. Surely it was only a false physical sensation brought on by her state of euphoria.

But when it happened a second time, the pressure was distinctly firmer and applied directly to her nipple. There could be no mistake. She opened her eyes and, shaking off her lethargy, removed the small mask from her nose. Brad Armstrong smiled down at her, and the leering quality of his grin convinced her that she had imagined nothing.

"What the hell do you think you're doing?"

"Don't pretend you didn't enjoy it," he'd whispered. "Your nipple is still hard."

Even reclined in the dental chair as she was, she came off it like a shot, knocking over a metal tray of implements and sending it crashing to the floor. An assistant, whom he had sent out on a trumped-up errand, came rushing back into the treatment room. "Ms. Gibson, what's wrong?"

"Have Dr. Baker call me at his earliest convenience," she told her before storming out.

The dentist had called her later that day, expressing his concern. She reported what had happened. When she finished her story, he said with chagrin, "I'm ashamed to say that I thought the other woman was lying."

"He's done it before?"

"I assure you, Ms. Gibson, this will be the last time. You have my utmost apologies. I'll take care of it immediately."

Dr. Armstrong had been dismissed. For several days afterward, Paris had shuddered in repulsion whenever she thought about the incident, but after a time it had faded from her memory. She hadn't thought any more about it until now.

"I assume your husband blamed me for getting him fired."

"Yes. Although he's been forced out of other practices for similar incidents since then, he's always held a grudge against you. While you were still in Houston, he turned off the television set anytime you appeared. He called you ugly names. And when your fiancé got hurt, he said you deserved it."

"He knew about Jack, the accident?"

"And Dr. Malloy. He theorized that it was a love triangle."

Paris exclaimed, a soft "Oh."

"When we moved here and Brad discovered you were on the radio, his resentment flared up again." Mrs. Armstrong lowered her head and twisted the straps of her handbag. "I should have told Sergeant Curtis about this yesterday, but I was so afraid they would think Brad was involved with this missing-girl case."

"She's no longer missing." When Paris told her that Janey Kemp's body had been discovered, Toni Armstrong finally lost her valiant battle against tears.

chapter twenty-nine

Anytime John Rondeau crossed paths with Dean Malloy, he went out of his way to be nothing but pleasant. But Malloy treated him with patent animosity. Curtis had noticed. Rondeau had overheard him asking Malloy what the problem was. Malloy had replied with a gruff, "Nothing," and Curtis hadn't pressed him.

As far as Rondeau was concerned, Malloy could glower at him until hell froze over. It was Curtis he wanted to butter up, not Malloy. The psychologist had the higher ranking, but it was Curtis who could recommend Rondeau for CIB.

As for Malloy's kid, he had him right where he wanted him, which was scared out of his skivvies. The results of the lie detector test had been in his favor and had basically cleared him of suspicion. So, one might wonder, why was he still so fidgety?

He was sitting in a chair near Curtis's desk, his shoulders hunched in a self-defensive posture. A bundle of nerves, he couldn't sit still. His eyes darted about fearfully. He looked like he would disintegrate if somebody said "Boo!"

Only Rondeau knew why the boy still looked so scared, and he wasn't telling. Neither was Gavin. Rondeau was confident of the kid's silence. He had frightened him sufficiently that he wasn't about to tattle on him. Brilliant to think of threatening his dad, not him. That had done the trick.

It was crowded inside Curtis's cubicle, where they'd all gathered for a brainstorming session. Curtis was there, of course. Malloy. Gavin. And Paris Gibson.

Rondeau welcomed any opportunity to share space with her, though it was hard for her to notice him with Malloy stamping around repeating ad nauseam that he feared she would be next on Valentino's to-do list.

Rondeau had stumbled on to this meeting when he came to report to Curtis what he'd found on the CD Mrs. Armstrong had hand-delivered to Paris. It wasn't all that earthshaking, but he grabbed any opportunity to impress Curtis and bump up his chances of getting into the CIB.

Paris—innocently, of course—had stolen his thunder before his arrival. What Toni Armstrong had withheld from him while he was searching her house, she had imparted to Paris—her husband had fondled Paris when she'd been his patient.

Had Mrs. Armstrong shared this with him and he'd been the one to bring it to Curtis's attention, it would have been a real feather in his cap. As it was, he'd have to earn that feather by some other means.

"I've got a bad feeling about this guy," Sergeant Curtis was saying of the dentist. "Has he contacted his wife today?" he asked Paris.

"She says no. All her attempts to reach him have been unsuccessful."

"If he called her from his cell, we could place him using satellite," Malloy remarked.

"I'm sure that's why he hasn't done it," said Rondeau, hoping he'd made Malloy sound like a fool. His neck was still sore from Malloy's squeeze yesterday. He and

Malloy were never going to be friends, but he didn't consider that any great loss.

"Have you checked out his phone records?" Malloy asked.

"Working on it," Curtis replied. "It'll look really bad for him if he's made repeated calls to the radio station." Turning back to Paris, he asked, "Mrs. Armstrong didn't recognize his voice on the tapes?"

"She's listening to them again, but I'm not sure how reliable her input will be. She's very upset. When I told her about Janey, she underwent an emotional meltdown that I think had been brewing for days."

"Would you recognize Brad Armstrong on sight?"

Paris frowned. "I don't think so. The incident happened a long time ago. I saw him only that one time, and I was high on nitrous oxide."

"Would a photograph be helpful?" Rondeau asked, nudging Malloy aside and wedging himself into the center of the enclosure.

"Possibly," Paris said.

He produced the CD that Toni Armstrong had brought from home and given to Paris. "Apparently Brad Armstrong scanned photos and burned them onto CDs. The ones we found during the search had porno shots taken out of magazines on them.

"But this last one has family photographs on it. I brought it back so it could be returned to Mrs. Armstrong, but it may be useful now. May jiggle your memory, Paris."

"Can't hurt to take a look," said Curtis. He booted up the computer on his desk, then stepped aside so Rondeau could sit down. He was aware of Paris moving in close behind him to get a better look at the monitor screen. He caught a whiff of a clean scent, like shampoo.

He executed the necessary keystrokes and within seconds a snapshot filled the screen. The family of five was posed in front of an attraction at a theme park. Parents and kids were wearing American clothing and American smiles, living the American Dream.

Rondeau turned toward Paris. "Look familiar?"

For several moments, she studied the man in the photograph. "Honestly, no. If I had spotted him in a crowd, I wouldn't have immediately recognized him as the man who fondled me. It was too long ago."

"You're sure you haven't seen him recently?" Malloy asked. "If he resented you as much as Mrs. Armstrong indicated, he might have been stalking you."

"If I have seen him, it didn't register."

Curtis, who was still studying the Armstrong family snapshot, said, "I wonder who took the picture."

"Probably he did," Rondeau said. "A guy who has a scanner and makes a CD photo album—"

"Would be into cameras," Curtis finished for him. He turned to Gavin. "Janey told you her new boyfriend took that picture of her, correct?"

The kid withered beneath the attention of everyone in the room. His left knee was doing a jackhammer number. "Yes, sir. When she gave me the picture, she said he'd taken that one and lots of others. She said he liked taking the pictures almost as much as the sex."

"I don't recall any camera equipment being found during the search of their house," Rondeau said. "But he's got to have a setup or he wouldn't have these family photographs. Some were taken with wide-angle or telephoto lenses."

"Has the lab turned up anything on that photo Janey gave Gavin?" Malloy asked.

Querulously Curtis shook his head. "The only prints on it belonged to Janey and Gavin."

"Sergeant Curtis?" Griggs poked his head in, interrupting.

"In a minute," the detective told him.

"What about the local outlets for photographic supplies?" Malloy asked.

"Still being investigated," Curtis said. "Running down their clients is a time-consuming process."

"You wouldn't think that many people had their own darkrooms," Malloy said.

"Mail-order customers. Faxed-in orders. People ordering on-line. It's a chore."

Griggs interrupted a second time. "Sergeant Curtis, this is important."

But Curtis's mind was moving down a single track. He addressed the detectives who had clustered just outside his cubicle. Some didn't work homicide cases, but he'd asked everyone in the unit for their cooperation and time if they could spare it.

"Somebody determine if there's a darkroom in Brad Armstrong's home. Garage, attic, toolshed, extra bathroom. I don't care how crude." One of the detectives peeled away from the group in a hurry.

"We need Brad Armstrong's telephone records ASAP. Find out what's taking so long." Another detective rushed away to carry out that assignment.

"Print out a picture of him—no family members, just him. Get it to all the TV stations in time for their first evening newscasts. He's wanted for questioning, got it? *Questioning*," he stressed to the detective who reached for the CD that Rondeau helpfully ejected from Curtis's computer.

"Also distribute it to the intelligence officers who're checking out those photo places," Curtis called out across the cubicles. "Have it faxed to all the other agencies that are helping us in the search."

That business dispatched, Rondeau said, "Sir, I apologize for not putting it together sooner."

"Never mind." Curtis, dismissing him in a way that stung, turned to Paris. "His wife will be our best source of information. Are you sure she'll cooperate?"

"Absolutely. Whether or not he's Valentino, she wants him to be found and has promised to cooperate in any way she can."

Curtis bobbed his head at a plainclothes policewoman. "Ask Mrs. Armstrong who takes their family photographs. Make it conversational."

While everyone was distracted, Rondeau looked over at Gavin Malloy and winked. The boy mouthed, *Get fucked*. Rondeau smiled.

"Sergeant?" Griggs was still making a nuisance of himself. "Excuse me?"

Finally Curtis turned to him and growled, "What is it, for christsake?"

"S . . . somebody to see you, sir," he stammered. "And . . . and Ms. Gibson."

"Somebody? Who?"

Griggs pointed across the tops of the cubicle walls. Curtis and Paris followed him through the maze of tiny offices to the double-door entrance where two uniformed patrolmen were holding a handcuffed man between them.

Paris exclaimed, "Marvin!"

Lancy Ray Fisher was seated at the table in one of the interrogation rooms. Paris sat across from him while Curtis stood at one end and Dean at the other. Even though they'd been focused on Dr. Brad Armstrong, the man she knew as Marvin Patterson remained a viable suspect.

He'd walked into police headquarters and introduced

himself to the officers at the lobby desk. Recognizing him instantly, they had put his hands in restraints for his elevator ride up to the third floor. He'd put up no resistance whatsoever. Each time Paris and he made eye contact, he looked away quickly, appearing to be guilty of something.

She was surprised by how nice looking he was without his baggy coveralls and the baseball cap he wore to work. She'd never seen his face in full light. Nor had he seen hers, she reminded herself. Maybe that's why his glances at her weren't only guilty, but also curious.

"Should I get a lawyer?" he asked Curtis.

"I don't know, should you?" the detective replied coolly. "You're the one who called this meeting and insisted on Paris being in on it. You tell me if you need a lawyer."

"I don't. Because I can tell you right off, and it's the God's truth, I had nothing to do with that girl's kidnapping and murder."

"We haven't accused you of having had anything to do with it."

"Then why'd those guys downstairs pounce on me and put me in these?" He thrust his cuffed hands toward Curtis.

Unfazed, Curtis replied, "I'd have thought you'd be used to them, Lancy. You've been in them often enough."

The young man slumped back in his chair, acknowledging the verity of that.

"Marvin," Paris said, getting his attention, "they found tapes of my shows, a large number of tapes, in your apartment. I'd like to know why you had them."

"My real name is Lancy."

"I'm sorry. Lancy. Why did you collect all those tapes?"

Dean said, "To us, it looks like you have an obsessive interest in her."

"I swear, it's not what you're thinking."

"What am I thinking?" Dean asked.

"That it's for some kinky reason. It's not. I . . . I've been studying her." He looked at their baffled faces. "I, uh, I want to be like her. Do what she does, I mean. I want to be on the radio."

If he'd said he wanted to pilot a nuclear submarine through the capitol rotunda, they couldn't have been more astonished.

Paris was the first to recover. "You want a career in radio broadcasting?"

"I guess you think that's crazy, considering my criminal record and all."

"I don't think it's crazy. I'm just surprised. When did you decide on this career path?"

"A couple years back. When I got out of Huntsville and started listening to you every night."

"Why Paris, specifically? Why not another deejay?"

"Because I liked the way she talked to people," he said to Dean. Then he turned back to her. "It seemed like you really cared about the people who called in, like you cared about their problems." Looking abashed, he added, "For a while there, I had it pretty rough. Getting back into life on the outside. You were like my only friend."

Curtis was staring at him with a skeptical scowl. Dean, too, was frowning. But Paris gave him a smile that encouraged him to continue.

"One night this guy called, told you he'd been laid off from his job and couldn't find another. You said it seemed to you that his confidence had suffered, and that's when you should aim the highest, reach the farthest.

"I took the advice you gave him. I stopped trying to get penny-ante jobs and applied at the telephone company. They hired me. I was making good money, enough to pay for voice lessons. Better clothes. A good car. But I got greedy, lifted some equipment I knew I could hock fast. They didn't file charges but they fired me."

He fell silent, as though castigating himself for such a bad judgment call. Paris looked over at Dean. He lifted his shoulders as though to say that Lancy could either be telling the truth or telling a whopper.

"After a few weeks of unemployment," he continued, "I couldn't believe my good fortune when I saw the ad in the paper about a job at the radio station. I didn't care that it was cleaning out the crapper . . . uh, toilets. I wanted to be in that environment any way I could get in. So I could observe you. See how you work. Maybe even pick up some of the technology.

"I rigged a recorder up to my radio at home and had it timed to tape every show. During the daytime, I'd replay the tapes and try to imitate the way you talked. I practiced, trying to get your diction and the rhythm of your speech down. I took more lessons to get rid of my accent."

He shot her a grin. "As you can hear, that's going to take a lot more work. And of course I know I'll never be as good as you no matter how hard I work at it. But I'm determined to give it my best shot. I wanted to . . . I *had* to, what do they call it?"

"Reinvent yourself?" she guessed.

His eyes lit up. "Yeah, that's it. That's why I was using an alias. My real name sounds too much like where I came from."

Curtis tossed a folder onto the table and when Lancy saw that it was his criminal record, he winced. "I know it looks bad, but I swear to God I've put that life behind me."

"It's a long list of wrongdoing, Lancy. Did you find Jesus in Huntsville, or what?"

"No, sir. I just didn't want to be trash for the rest of my life."

Curtis harrumphed, unconvinced.

Lancy glanced around and must have realized that they were still skeptical. He wet his lips and in a tone of desperation said, "I wouldn't do anything to hurt Paris. She's my idol. I haven't made any threatening phone calls. As for that girl who turned up dead, I don't know anything."

Curtis propped a hip on the corner of the table and addressed the younger man in a deceptively friendly way. "You like high school girls, Lancy Ray?"

"Sir?"

"You dropped out of school at sixteen."

"I got my GED while I was in prison."

"But you skipped all the fun of high school. Maybe you're making up for what you missed."

"Like the girls, you mean?"

"Yeah, that's what I mean."

He shook his head emphatically. "I don't pick up underage girls and have sex with them. I'm not perfect, but that's not my thing."

"Do you like women?"

"You mean, over men? Hell, yes."

"You've got a handsome face. Good build. It can get awfully lonely in prison."

Self-consciously Lancy cast a look at Paris, then lowered his head and muttered, "They left me alone. I stabbed one in the . . . in the testicles with a fork. I got a year tacked onto my sentence for it, but they didn't bother me after that."

She was embarrassed for him. She hoped Curtis

would let up, but she was afraid that if she interfered he would ask her to leave and she wanted to hear this.

Curtis said, "I met your mother yesterday."

Lancy raised his head and looked directly at the detective. "She's a cow."

"Whoa! Did you hear that, Dr. Malloy? Did that sound like latent hostility toward a female? A resentment—"

"I don't like my mother," Lancy said heatedly, "but that doesn't carry over into my sex life. If that was your mother, would you like her?"

Curtis persisted. "Do you have a girlfriend?"

"No."

"Want one?"

"Sometimes."

"Sometimes," Curtis repeated. "When you get a hankering for a girlfriend, what do you do?"

"What do you mean?"

"Come on, Lancy Ray." Curtis tapped the folder with a blunt index finger. "You were sent up for sexual assault."

"That was a bullshit rap."

"That's what all rapists say."

"This guy, this movie producer—"

"A pornographer."

"Right. We were making triple-X-rated skin flicks in his garage. He got upset when his girl started coming on to me. It was all right for us to . . . you know, while his camera was rolling. But not in private. So he and I got into it and—"

"And you cut him up pretty bad."

"It was self-defense."

"The jury didn't buy it, and neither do I," Curtis said. "When you finished with him, you started in on the girl."

"No, sir!"

He denied it so emphatically and indignantly that Paris had to believe he was telling the truth. "It was him. He worked her over good." He pointed to the folder. "All those things that were done to her, he did."

"They collected your DNA."

"Because she and I had been together earlier that day. He caught us. That's what started the fight."

"His testimony was corroborated under oath by two of the production crew and the girl herself."

"They were all junkies. He fed them dope. I didn't have anything to offer in exchange for them telling the truth."

Dean asked, "Why should we believe your version of this, Lancy?"

"Because I own up to all my other crimes. I did some awful things, but I never beat up a woman."

Paris leaned across the table toward him. "Why did you run away when the officers called to say they wanted to question you? Why didn't you tell them what you're telling us now?"

He sighed heavily and raised his cuffed hands to rub his forehead. "I freaked. I'm an ex-con. That automatically makes me a suspect. Then, I knew if they discovered that I'd been taping your shows, they'd for sure haul me in."

"Why did you leave the tapes behind?"

He smiled shyly. "Because I'm stupid. I panicked and got the hell out of there. Forgot them. Maybe I've lost my criminal instinct. I hope I have."

He had a safe-effacing manner that Paris liked. But Curtis didn't appear to be charmed by it.

"If you had admitted this to us the day before yesterday, we might have come closer to believing you."

Lancy looked at Paris and said earnestly, "I'm telling

the truth. I don't know anything about this Valentino character or those phone calls. I don't know anything about Janey Kemp except what I've heard on the news. The only thing I'm guilty of is wanting to learn to do what you do."

"You've been working at the station for months," she said softly, "but you've never even engaged me in conversation. Why didn't you come and talk to me about your ambition? Ask for advice? Guidance?"

"Are you kidding?" he exclaimed. "You're a star. I'm the guy who pushes around the mop bucket. I'd never have worked up my nerve to talk to you. And if I had, you would have laughed at me."

"I would never have done that."

He searched her eyes, behind her lenses. "No, maybe you wouldn't have. I see that now."

"Where've you been all this time?" Curtis asked. "You didn't return to your mom's place or your apartment."

"I keep a . . . I guess you'd call it a—"

"Hideout?" Curtis prompted.

Lancy looked abashed. "Yes, sir. I'll give you the address. You're welcome to search it."

"You can bet we will," Curtis said as he hooked his hand beneath Lancy's arm and hoisted him from the chair. "And while we're at it, you'll be residing with us here."

chapter thirty

*I*t was a great bar for trolling.

It was on the lakeshore, a cedar-shingle place well known to the locals. Fishermen might stumble upon it, but it wasn't a watering hole that would attract tourists or country club golfers. The clientele was comprised mostly of construction workers, cowboys, and biker types. A white-collar professional would feel out of his element, so it was highly unlikely that Brad Armstrong would be spotted here by anyone he knew.

Peanut shells crunched underfoot as he made his way across the dim barroom. It was lighted only by neon signs, nearly all boasting the Lone Star flag and a brand of beer. The shaded fixtures suspended over the billiards tables provided supplemental lighting, but it was obscured by tobacco smoke.

The bubbling Wurlitzer in the corner emanated a revolving rainbow of pastel colors, but there was nothing subtle about the music blaring from it. It was old country, the twangy, wailing, woebegone kind, pre Garth, McGraw, and the like.

Customers drank beer from the bottle, Jack Daniel's, or Jose Cuervo straight. Which was what the girl was shooting when Brad joined her at the bar. He recognized her immediately. That she was here today, now, was a cosmic sign that he was doing nothing wrong.

He glanced down at the two empty shot glasses in front of her and motioned for the bartender to serve up two more. "One for me and one for the lady with the nipple ring."

She turned to him. "How'd you—Oh, hi. Coupla nights ago, right?"

He grinned. "I'm glad you remember."

"You're the guy with all the porno."

His face registered a crestfallen expression. "I was hoping you'd remember me for my . . . other memorable quality."

She licked her upper lip and smiled. "That, too."

"I wouldn't expect to find you in a place like this," he said. "You outclass it."

"I hang out in here sometimes." She cracked a peanut shell between her teeth and daintily ate the nuts. "Before the Sex Club starts gathering." She dropped the shell onto the floor and dusted off her hands. "You don't exactly blend either."

"I think we were destined to see each other again."

"Cool," she said.

Makeup had been slathered on to make her look legally old enough to drink. Either the bartender was fooled or, more likely, didn't care that she was underage. He served the tequila shots that Brad had ordered.

"What shall we drink to?"

She rolled her large, dark eyes toward the ceiling as though the answer might be written in the chemically polluted layer of smoke that hovered there. "How about body piercing?"

Leaning forward, he whispered, "I get hard just thinking about it." He clinked his glass to hers and simultaneously they tossed back the fiery liquor.

This was so damn easy, he thought. Didn't mothers

warn their daughters against talking to strangers anymore? Didn't they tell them never, ever to go with a man they didn't know? What was the world coming to? It made him afraid for his daughters.

But thinking about his family killed the mood, so he tucked thoughts of them safely away and ordered another round of tequila shots.

After that one they agreed to leave. He smiled smugly as they passed the pool tables. He was the envy of tough guys with tattoos on their arms and knives attached to their thick leather belts. He'd been successful where apparently they had not. Maybe because his hair was clean.

"It's Melissa, right?" he asked as he held the car door open for her.

Her glossy red lips smiled over his remembering her name. "Where are we going?"

"I've got a room."

"Super."

Ridiculously easy.

Coming out this evening wasn't a wise thing to do, but he couldn't have stayed cooped up another minute or he would have gone crazy. He couldn't return home. Toni had been calling his cell phone at fifteen-minute intervals all day, begging him to come back. The police only wanted to talk to him, she said. *Right,* he thought. *They want to talk to me through iron bars.*

He hadn't answered his phone and he hadn't called her, knowing that the police had probably set up a system of tracking his cell by satellite. The discovery of Janey's body didn't bode well for him. News reports had said that an autopsy was being conducted. Hearing that had nearly sent him over the edge.

He'd fretted, stewed, paced, lambasted his wife for not

understanding him, and Janey for being a cock teaser he couldn't resist, even his mother, who'd punished him severely for masturbating when he was little.

Truthfully, he didn't remember such a time, but psychologists had asked him during therapy sessions if he'd been so punished and he'd said yes because that seemed to be the expected and accepted explanation for his sexual preoccupation.

As the news reports went from bad to worse, actually including his name in them, his anxiety increased. He had tried to distract himself by looking at his pornographic magazines, reading the letters and "true" experiences submitted by subscribers. But soon familiarity had made them boring. Besides, his craving wasn't going to be satisfied vicariously.

He was aroused and needed relief. With the pressure he'd been under recently, who could blame him? He resolved that if relief wasn't going to come looking for him, he would have to go looking for it.

Now he'd found it.

"This isn't the car you were in the other night," Melissa remarked as she punched through radio stations until she found one playing a thrumming rap song.

The police would've spotted his car, so he had called and ordered one from a rental place that delivered. Not a chain outfit that required all kinds of documentation, but one that, according to their yellow pages ad, would take cash. That signaled to Brad a business that was light on rules and regulations. The only amenity promised was a working air conditioner in all their cars.

While waiting for it to arrive, he'd showered and dressed, splashed on the Aramis, and put a supply of condoms in his pants pocket.

As anticipated, the man who delivered the car looked

as if his next stop might be a 7-Eleven store he could rob. Brad flashed him his driver's license and filled out a form with false information. He'd counted out the required deposit and added ten bucks for a tip. The man spoke only limited English and didn't seem to care one way or the other what day Brad promised to return the ten-year-old car to their lot.

"Had we met before?" Melissa asked him now. "Before the other night, I mean. You look familiar."

"I'm a famous movie star."

"That must be it," she said, giggling.

To distract her from that train of thought, he said, "Do you always look this sensational?"

"You think?"

Actually she looked like a whore. The dyed hair was spiked stiffer and higher than it had been the other night. Outside the dimness of the bar, her makeup looked even more garish. Her halter top was made of some flimsy fabric through which he could see her dangling silver nipple ring. Most table napkins were larger than her skirt.

In short, she was asking for it. She should thank him for saving her from being gang-banged by the rednecks in the bar.

He drew her eyes down to his lap. "See what you're doing to me."

She assessed the distention behind his trousers, then said, "Is that the best you can do?" and leaned back against the passenger door. She idly brushed her fingertips across the nipple with the ring piercing it.

The girl knew her stuff. His erection stretched. "I can't watch you and drive."

She gave the nipple ring a teasing yank.

He groaned. "You're killing me, you know that?"

"But you'll die happy."

He reached across the console and slid his hand beneath her skirt, felt the scratch of lace against his fingers, then worked his way past it.

"Hmm. Right there." Melissa closed her eyes. "Don't get stopped for speeding. At least not till after I come."

Gavin was waiting outside the CIB when Dean, Paris, and Sergeant Curtis emerged. His hope was riding on Lancy Ray Fisher. He shot to his feet, asking, "Was he the guy?"

"We don't know yet," his dad told him. "Sergeant Curtis is going to keep him here, ask him some more questions."

Paris glanced at her wristwatch. "If it's no trouble, I'd like to stop at my house before going to the station. I ran out in such a rush this morning."

"I'll drive you and drop Gavin at home on the way," Dean said. "We'll have our cell phones on, Curtis. If anything happens—"

"I'll call right away," he assured them. "I'm going to lean on Lancy Ray."

"With all due respect, I don't believe he's Valentino," Paris said.

The detective nodded. Gavin thought he looked very tired. A blond bristle had begun to sprout from his pink cheeks. "I'm still partial to Dr. Armstrong," he told them, "but I'm not ready to give up on Lancy Fisher just yet. I'll be in touch."

They were turning toward the elevators when Curtis spoke Gavin's name. His first thought was, *What now?* But he said, "Yes, sir?"

"I'm sorry I had to put you through that today. I know it wasn't any fun."

"It's okay," he said, not really meaning it. It hadn't been okay at all. He'd hated being made to feel guilty when he wasn't. "I hope you find out who did that to Janey. I should've told you from the beginning that she and I were in her car. But I was afraid you'd think, well, what you thought. I guess she met whoever killed her after she got rid of me."

"It appears that way. Are you absolutely certain she never mentioned who she was meeting afterward? A name? Occupation?"

"I'm positive."

"Well, thanks," Curtis said. "I appreciate your cooperation."

His dad nudged him toward the elevators and they left. Gavin sat in the backseat on the way home. Nobody said much, each seemed lost in his own thoughts. When they reached the house, a patrol car with two officers inside it was already parked out front. Inwardly Gavin groaned. He'd had his fill of policemen today. If he never saw one again—except his dad—it would be too soon.

"I don't need baby-sitters, Dad. Or am I still grounded?"

"You're grounded, but the cops are for your protection. They stay until Valentino is caught."

"He's not gonna—"

"I'm not taking any chances, Gavin. Besides, the guards are Curtis's mandate, not mine."

"You could call them off if you wanted to."

"I don't want to. All right?" When his dad was wearing that face, the argument was over. He nodded grudgingly. Then his dad reached over the seat and laid his hand on his shoulder. "I was proud of the way you conducted yourself today."

"At the risk of sounding patronizing, so was I, Gavin," Paris told him.

"Thanks."

"Call my cell immediately if anything happens. Promise me you will."

"I promise, Dad." He climbed out. "'Bye, Paris."

"'Bye. See you soon, okay?"

"Yeah, that'd be great."

He shuffled up the walkway. They didn't pull away until he had let himself in. Unlike his mom and dad, the two of them looked right together. He sorta hoped it would work out between them.

He waved at them from the front door before shutting and bolting it, effectively becoming his own jailer.

"Penny for them."

Paris looked across at Dean. "My thoughts? I was thinking about Toni Armstrong. I feel for her. I like her."

"So do I. Brave lady."

"I think she loves her husband. Deeply. Under the circumstances, that must be very conflicting." Curious, she asked, "From a clinical standpoint, when is a person considered a sex addict?"

"Tricky question."

"I'm sure you can address it, Dr. Malloy."

"All right. If a guy gets twelve hard-ons in a day, I'd congratulate him and probably urge him to try for thirteen. If he *acts* on twelve hard-ons in a day, I'd say that's a little excessive and we could have a problem."

"You're being facetious."

"Somewhat, but there's a basis of truth." His grin relaxed and he became serious. "Sex can become an addiction like anything else can. When the compulsion outweighs common sense and caution. When the activity begins to have a negative effect on one's work, family life, relationships. When it becomes the governing force and the exclusive means of personal gratification."

He glanced at her, and with a nod she prompted him to continue. "It's the same point at which a social drinker becomes an alcoholic. The individual loses control over the craving. Conversely, the craving gains control over the individual."

"Like making him willing to sacrifice a wife and family to get his thrills."

"That doesn't mean that Brad Armstrong doesn't love his wife," he said. "He probably does."

Reflecting on that, she stared through the front windshield. Even behind her sunglasses, she had to squint against the setting sun, which was doing a bang-up job of it. She wondered what Judge and Marian Kemp were doing just now. This spectacular sunset would go unnoticed by them.

"They have a funeral to arrange."

"I'm sorry?" Dean said.

"Thinking out loud. About the Kemps now."

"Yeah," he said with a sigh. "I can't imagine how devastating it would be to lose a child. I've counseled cops who did, but to my own ears, every word I said to them sounded like so much crap. If anything happened to Gavin . . ." He stopped, as though unable to articulate the dreadful thought. Then he said quietly, "I want to be a good parent to him, Paris."

"I know."

"Because of my own dad."

"I know that, too."

"How much did Jack tell you?"

"Enough."

He had told her that Dean's relationship with his

father had been volatile. Mr. Malloy had a fierce temper, and Dean usually caught the brunt of it. Sometimes his dad's rages had turned violent.

"Did your father beat you, Dean?" she asked.

"He could give me a hard time, yeah."

"Is that a gross understatement?"

He shrugged with an indifference she knew was phony. "I could take his shit," he said. "When he started in on my mom, that's what I couldn't take."

According to Jack, the defining incident had taken place when Dean's parents visited him for homecoming weekend his sophomore year at Texas Tech. During a party at the fraternity house, Dean's father had picked an argument with him. Dean tried to ignore it, but his father became increasingly vituperative and wouldn't be put off.

His mother, embarrassed for her son, tried to intervene. That's when Dean's father began disparaging her. His words were humiliating and cruel. Heedless of his friends and the other parents looking on, Dean took up the banner for his mother. His dad threw a punch. Before it was over, Dean was straddling Mr. Malloy's chest and, in Jack's words, "pounding the shit out of him."

After that night their relationship became even more antagonistic, and it remained so until his father died.

"I went a little crazy that time at Tech," he said now. "I'd never been like that before, and I haven't lost my temper like that since. If Jack and some of the other guys hadn't pulled me off him, I might have killed him. I wanted to kill him.

"I hated like hell that it happened, because of the embarrassment to my mom. But at least it made the old man think twice before he lit into her again, especially if I was around." He glanced at Paris; she'd never seen him look as vulnerable. "But it scared the hell out of me, Paris. I can't even describe it. A red rage? It consumed me, blotting out everything else.

"My dad launched into fits like that all the time. That night I learned that whatever caused him to be the way he was, it's inside me, too. It came out that once. I live in fear of it happening again."

Reaching across the console, she laid her hand on his arm. "He provoked you in the meanest way. You reacted. But that doesn't mean that you have this latent rage that can ignite in an instant. You're not like him, Dean," she said with emphasis. "You never were and never could be.

"As for Gavin, it's allowed to get angry with him. Kids anger and disappoint and make their folks crazy. That's what they do. It's inherent in being a kid. And it's all right for you to get mad at him when he does.

"In fact, Gavin might doubt that you love him if you didn't get mad at him. He needs to know you care enough to get angry. He's going to test you often, just to reassure himself that you still care." Then she laughed. "Listen to me. You're the psychologist and the parent. I'm neither."

"Everything you're saying is right, though, and I need to hear it."

She smiled at him gently. "As long as you praise him at least as much, if not more, than you punish him, you'll be fine."

He mulled it over for a moment, then winked at her. "Smart as well as beautiful. You're a dangerous woman, Paris."

"Oh yeah, that's me. A regular femme fatale."

"Maybe that's what attracted Lancy Ray Fisher. Your element of mystery appealed to his criminal instinct."

She rolled her eyes. "He wants my job."

"So he says."

"You think he's lying?"

"If he is, he's convincing. He's either sincere or a damn good con artist."

"That was my impression, too."

"What's it like to be someone's idol?"

She gave him a sad smile. "I don't recommend that anyone pattern his life after mine."

Just then his cell phone rang. He answered it with one hand. "Malloy . . . Huh, speak of the devil. No, Paris and I were just talking about him." He mouthed *Curtis* and she nodded.

"What about Lancy's home away from home?" He listened for a moment, then said, "Probably not a bad idea." Curtis had more to tell him, then Dean signed off with, "Okay, stay in touch."

After disconnecting, he updated Paris. "He 'drilled Lancy Ray good,' is the way Curtis put it. But Lancy is sticking to his story."

Officers sent to the apartment where he had been holed up reported that Lancy had been there, but it didn't appear that anyone else had.

"No sign of Janie being held captive there?" Paris asked.

"None. No amateur photo lab. Nothing naughtier than one issue of *Playboy*. So Curtis is hotter than ever for the dentist. He's about to have a heart-to-heart with Toni Armstrong."

"Hmm, what a dilemma for her. On the one hand, she wants her husband apprehended so he can get help, but on the other, she's incriminating him."

"He incriminated himself."

"I know that. I'm thinking as she will. She loves him

and wants him to be healed, but if he's beyond healing, how long can she be expected to stand by her man?"

"Good question, Paris."

Too late she realized that what she had said about Toni Armstrong could apply to herself.

Dean pulled his car to a stop at the curb in front of her house. Cutting the engine, he turned to face her, ready to speak, but she cut him off before he could.

"Jack needed me."

"*I* need you."

"Hardly in the same way."

"That's right. You were with him out of obligation. I want you to choose to be with me." He held her stare for several seconds, then pushed open his car door and got out.

As they went up the walkway, she stopped to collect her mail, which had been neglected for the last two days. Once they were inside the house, she tossed the bundle onto the entry table. "Lord knows when I'll get to that. My desk at work is even—"

That was all she had time to say before Dean pulled her into his arms and kissed her. While doing so, he removed her sunglasses and dropped them on the table. Then he embraced her tightly, drawing her up against him. Immediately responsive, her arms slid beneath his to encircle his torso. She dug her fingertips into the muscles of his back.

As his mouth fused with hers, he gathered up the fabric of her skirt until he could stroke her bare thigh. Her insides melted, but she pulled her mouth free of his kiss, gasping, "Dean, I've only got an hour."

"Then that'll be a record for us. So far our sexual encounters have lasted no longer than three minutes." He buried his face in her hair. "This time, I want to see you naked."

Laughing deep in her throat, she moved her head against his. "What if you don't like what you see?"

"Not a chance in hell."

He pushed his hands into her panties and gripped her ass. She made a low sound of pleasure but the voice of reason was louder. "What if Curtis calls?"

"I've learned to live with disappointment. But all the more reason for us to get busy."

Taking her by the hand, he walked purposefully toward the bedroom, dragging her along behind him. A girlish giggle bubbled up from Paris's chest. Her heart began to race. She felt terribly wicked and wonderfully, gloriously alive.

Dean was laughing, too, as he dealt with the stubborn fabric-covered buttons on her top. "Damn these things."

She was more deft. His shirt was soon open and she pressed a kiss against the warm skin just below his left nipple, feeling his heart beating against her lips.

Finally having succeeded with the buttons, he removed her top and unclasped the front fastener of her brassiere. Then his hands were on her, kneading her breasts with his strong fingers.

She watched his face as he looked down at her. His expression was at once passionate and tender as he saw her nipples responding to the glancing touches of his fingertips. His eyes met hers for barely a second before he dipped his head and took one into his mouth.

She unbuckled his belt and lowered his zipper, then worked her hand into the waistband of his underwear. He was velvety smooth, hard, throbbing with life. She rolled her thumb across his glans and he shuddered.

"Paris, stop," he said, stepping out of her reach. "If you . . . You can't do that. I'll come. And I want this to last."

She shrugged off her bra, then reached behind her to unfasten her skirt, pushed it past her hips, and stepped out of it. Feverishly, his eyes moved over her. In one swift motion, he removed his slacks and underwear. She gazed at him with frank appreciation, but when she reached for him again, he staved her off.

Then he dropped to his knees and kissed her through the silk bikini. His hands splayed over her bottom as he held her against his face. The heat and moisture of his breath filtering through the fabric made her weak. He kissed her again. And again. She closed her eyes and used his shoulders to brace herself.

Then the silk seemed to dissolve because the barrier was no longer there. His lips were hot and quick on her a heartbeat before she felt his tongue, separating and seeking and stroking. She gave herself over to the pleasure, and it was immense.

But she retained enough control to beg him to stop when it became critical. He came to his feet and enfolded her in his arms. They held one another tightly, her breasts crushed against his chest, his sex making a deep impression in the softness of her belly.

Finally, they lay down face-to-face on her bed, virgin until now. Her hand coasted over his torso, down past his navel, and into the dense hair surrounding his sex. She drew her finger up the length of his penis. He covered her hand with his and guided it up and down. "Jesus," he groaned.

"I can't quite believe this is happening."

"Me neither." He kissed her nipple, caressed it with his tongue. "I keep thinking that I'll wake up."

"If you do, please leave me in the dream."

He separated her legs and positioned himself between them, then entered her by degrees, giving her body time to accommodate him, pausing to test each new sensation before pressing deeper, until he was sheathed snugly and completely inside her.

Soaked in pleasure, they kept from moving as long as they could endure it, but it only got better when he withdrew, then thrust into her.

chapter thirty-one

Dean shook water from his ear as he raised his cell phone to it. "Malloy."

"Curtis."

"What's up?"

"What's that noise?"

"The shower," Dean replied, turning to wink at Paris, who was rinsing the shampoo from her hair. Head thrown back, soapy water streaming over her breasts and funneling between her legs. God, she was gorgeous.

"You're showering?"

"So I can look as fresh as you. What's up?" he repeated.

"One of the other detectives has been chatting with Lancy Ray. Remember when Paris asked him why all the subterfuge, why he hadn't just come to talk to her?"

"He was shy."

"That . . . and he didn't want to move in on another guy's territory."

"What guy?"

Paris looked at him with puzzlement as she stepped from the shower. He handed her a towel.

"Stan Crenshaw," Curtis said.

That was possibly the only statement that could have diverted his attention from Paris's naked form. "Pardon me?"

"That's right. Lancy Ray was operating under the misconception that Stan and Paris are lovers."

"Where'd he get that?"

"From Crenshaw."

Dean cupped the cell phone's mouthpiece and told Paris to hurry and get dressed. His urgency must have communicated itself to her, because she rushed back into the bedroom. "Tell me," he said to Curtis.

"Crenshaw told the janitor not to bug her. Made up some bullshit about it being company policy that he was the only one allowed access to her, told him she didn't like people staring at her because of her sunglasses, that she liked the darkness for reasons that were nobody's business.

"Lancy Ray wanted to keep his job, so he went along, kept his distance and rarely even spoke to her for fear of Crenshaw getting jealous and having him canned. He said the guy was jealous of anyone who went near her."

"Why didn't Lancy tell us this the first time we talked to him?" Dean asked as he struggled to dress himself with one hand.

"He took it for granted that everyone knew they were a couple."

"My ass. There's something about Crenshaw that isn't right. I knew it the night I met him. He took that proprietary stance with me, too, but I thought he was just a prick."

"Maybe he is just a prick."

"And maybe not. I want him turned inside out, Curtis. I want to know every fucking thing about him, and I don't care who his uncle is or how much money he has."

"I hear you. This time I'm skipping Uncle Wilkins. We're going straight to the Atlanta PD, the district attorney's office, the damn governor of Georgia if necessary.

One good thing, he's carrying on business as usual. He's at the radio station. Griggs and Carson are there and just called in."

"We'll be on our way momentarily. Tell those rookies to keep him there if he tries to leave. Have you checked his phone records?"

"Under way."

"Who's doing the digging into his background?"

"Rondeau volunteered."

"Rondeau." Dean made no effort to mask his displeasure.

"He's going to run a thorough computer check."

"He was supposed to have done that already."

"I told him to go deeper this time."

"Would've been nice if he'd dug deeper the first time."

"What's with you and him? I sense tension."

"He's cocky."

"That's it? You don't like his personality?"

"Something like that. Look, we gotta run."

"Maybe Paris shouldn't do her show tonight. Give us a chance to check out Crenshaw."

"Tell her that. She's determined. Besides, I'm not budging from her side. Later."

Before the detective could say more, Dean hung up and hustled Paris out of the house. Once in the car, she asked for details. "From what I could gather, his call was about Stan."

He filled her in on what Lancy Ray Fisher had divulged. She let out an incredulous laugh. "I can't believe it."

"It's not funny."

"No, it's hysterical."

"I don't think so."

"Dean," she said, giving him a fond smile, "in light of

recent, ahem, events, I can understand your male posturing. I'm flattered. I wish there were a dragon you could slay for me. But don't waste the machismo on Stan, for heaven's sake. He's not Valentino."

"We don't know that."

"*I* know. He's a prick, just as you said. And it upsets me that he misled Marvin—Lancy. And God knows who else. But he hasn't got the brains or the balls to be Valentino."

"We'll soon see," he said as he whipped his car into the station parking lot.

Griggs and Carson waved from the front seat of the squad car as she unlocked the door. As usual, the building was dark and the offices deserted. Harry, the evening deejay, gave her a thumbs-up through the window of the studio as they went past. Dean had learned the layout of the building and led the way through the dim hallways.

They reached her office, to find Stan seated at her desk, feet propped on the corner of it, desultorily sorting through her mail.

"Stan Crenshaw, just the person I wanted to see," Dean said as he strode in.

Stan lowered his feet from the desk, but they'd barely touched the floor before Dean took him by the front of his shirt and hauled him up from the chair.

"Hey!" Stan objected. "What the hell?"

"We need to have a little talk, Stan."

"Dean." Paris laid her cautionary hand on his arm. He released his grip on Stan's shirt.

"You've been telling lies about Paris."

Taking umbrage, Stan pulled himself up straighter and smoothed his hand over his rumpled shirt. But he might just as well have tried to defy a redwood, and he seemed to realize it. His gaze shifted to Paris. "What's your boyfriend talking about?"

"Lancy said that you told him—"

"Who the hell is Lancy?"

"Marvin Patterson."

"His name is Lancy?"

"You told him that you and Paris were sleeping together."

His head swiveled back to Dean. "No I didn't."

"Didn't you insinuate that you and she were more than coworkers? Didn't you warn him to back off, leave her alone, and not even talk to her?"

"Because I know how she is," Stan declared.

"Is that right?"

"Yeah, that's right. I know she's a private person. She doesn't like to be bothered by other people, especially while she's concentrating on work."

"So you told him to lay off in order to protect her privacy?"

"You could put it that way."

"I don't need you to screen the people I associate with, Stan," Paris said. "I didn't ask you to and I dislike the fact that you did."

"Well, gee, I'm sorry. I was trying to be a friend."

"Only a friend? I don't think so," Dean said. "I think you've been entertaining fantasies about Paris. You've deluded yourself into believing there's a romance between you two somewhere in your future. You're jealous of any other man who expresses an interest in her, even a platonic one."

"How do you know Marvin's interest is platonic?"

"He said it was."

"Oh, and he's to be believed over me? A janitor who's using an alias?" He made a scoffing snort. "You're the one who's delusional, *Doctor.*" He headed for the door, but Dean's next words halted him.

"That possessiveness could be a strong motivator."

Stan turned around quickly. "For what?"

"Let's see, creating an ugly situation for which Paris would be partially blamed. Placing her job at risk. Placing her life in jeopardy. Shall I go on?"

"Are you talking about that Valentino business?" Stan asked angrily. "Paris brought that on herself."

"I see. It's her fault that Valentino kidnapped and murdered a seventeen-year-old girl."

"A girl who went asking for trouble."

With deceptive calm, Dean sat down on a corner of her desk. "Then your opinion of women is basically low?"

"I didn't say that."

"No, you didn't come right out and say it, but I sense a large chunk of hostility against the fairer sex lodged deep inside your psyche, Stan. Like a seed caught between two molars. It bugs you like hell, but you can't get it out."

"Wooooo." Stan waggled his fingers an inch from Dean's face. "Don't try that psychological hocus-pocus voodoo on me. There's nothing wrong with me."

Dean's jaw bunched with anger, but his voice remained calm. "So I'm to believe that all your dealings with women have been perfectly normal and problem free?"

"Has any man's dealings with women been perfectly normal and problem free? Have yours, Malloy?" He cut his eyes to Paris. "I think not."

"You're not Dean," Paris said quietly. "He doesn't have your history."

His mocking smugness vanished. In the next heartbeat, he was seething. "Did you tell him about the harassment charge?"

Dean turned to her. "The *what?*"

"At his previous job, a female employee accused Stan of sexual harassment."

Dean gave her a look that said he couldn't believe she hadn't shared this information with him before now. She realized that she'd been wrong not to. Probably she also should have told him about Stan's promiscuous parents and his overbearing uncle's cruelty.

Dean turned back to him. "Obviously you do have issues with women, Stan."

"She was the office whore!" he exclaimed. "She had slept with every other guy who worked there. She gave head to the anchorman under the desk during a newscast. She kept coming on to me and when I responded, she turned into a vestal virgin."

"Why?"

"Because she was more greedy than horny. She saw a way to get her hands on some of my family's money. She cried foul and my uncle paid her to shut up and go away."

Dean assimilated that, then said, "Let's go back to when you 'responded' to her."

"Wait, how come I have to answer your questions?"

"Because I'm a cop."

"Or because you've been in Paris's pants yourself?"

Dean's eyes narrowed dangerously. "Because if you don't answer my questions I'm going to take you downtown and lock you up until you get talkative. That's my official, professional answer. Off the record, my personal answer is that if you say anything like that about Paris again, I'm going to take you outside and smear some of your pretty face on the parking lot."

"Are you threatening me?"

"You bet your skinny ass I am. Now stop dicking around and tell me what I want to know."

Despite what he'd said, Dean wasn't performing a hundred percent in an official capacity. He wasn't interrogating Stan in the calm, confidence-inspiring manner he usually used with suspects. But Stan probably wouldn't have responded to his usual approach. Taking a harder line with him seemed to be working.

Stan glared at Dean, fired drop-dead looks at Paris, but crossed his arms over his chest as though to protect himself. "I'm going to file charges of police brutality. My uncle will—"

"Your uncle will have more than me to worry about if it turns out you're Valentino."

"I'm not! Don't you listen?"

"When that woman said no to you, did you go ahead and complete the act?"

Stan's eyes darted between them. "No. I mean, yeah. Sort of."

"Well, which is it? Yes, no, or sort of?"

"I didn't force her, if that's what you're getting at."

"But you completed the act?"

"I told you she was the—"

"'Office whore.' So she was asking for it."

"Right."

"For you to rape her."

"You keep putting words in my mouth!" Stan cried.

"And you're going downtown with me. Right now."

Stan backed away from him. "You can't . . ." He looked frantically at Paris. "Do something. If you let this happen, my uncle will have your job."

She didn't even consider questioning Dean. Frankly, she was now afraid of Stan. Perhaps she had misjudged him. She had always thought of him as a worthless, mal-adjusted screwup, but basically harmless. Maybe he *was* capable of committing the crimes against Janey Kemp.

If he proved not to be Valentino, she would have to face Wilkins Crenshaw's wrath. Undoubtedly it *would* cost her her job. But she would rather lose her job than her life.

Dean took Stan by the arm and turned him toward the door. Stan began to struggle and Dean had his hands full trying to restrain him without handcuffs. When his cell phone rang, he tossed it to Paris so she could answer it for him.

"Hello?"

"Paris?"

She could barely hear over the crude invective Stan was screaming at Dean. "Gavin?"

"I've gotta talk to my dad, Paris. It's an emergency."

Gavin had been whiling away his time watching television, which was the only privilege his dad hadn't revoked. He'd put his favorite movie into the VCR, but the challenges confronting Mel Gibson seemed tame compared to what was happening in his own life.

He was worried about his dad and Paris.

He hadn't felt nearly as dismissive as he'd acted when his dad said that Valentino might come after them. This guy really could intend to harm them and didn't seem afraid to try. He shouldn't be underestimated. Who'd have thought he would murder Janey?

When the house phone rang, he welcomed the distraction. He rushed to answer and did so without even checking the caller ID. "Hello?"

"Why haven't you been answering your cell phone?"

"Who is this?"

"Melissa."

Melissa Hatcher? Oh, great. "I haven't had my cell on. It's been kinda hectic—"

"Gavin, you gotta help me."

Was she crying? "What's the matter?"

"I need to see you, but there's a cop car parked in front of your house, so I drove on past. You gotta meet me."

"I'm not supposed to leave."

"Gavin, this is no bullshit," she fairly shrieked.

"Just come over."

"With cops there? I don't think so."

"Why not? Are you high?"

She blubbered and sniffed, then said, "Can I sneak in through the back?"

He didn't want any part of her crisis, whatever it was. Having to take a lie detector test would clear up a guy's thinking and rearrange his priorities, but quick. He'd made a promise to himself that if he came out of this mess reasonably unscathed, he would cultivate a new circle of friends.

Another major infraction, and he could find himself on his way back to Houston. He didn't want to return to his mother's house. Now that things were square between him and his dad, he looked forward to staying with him, maybe until he graduated from high school.

It was definitely in his best interests to tell Melissa he was busy and hang up. But she sounded really strung out. "Okay," he said reluctantly. "Park on the street behind us and walk between the houses. There isn't a fence. I'll let you in through the patio door. How soon can you be here?"

"Two minutes."

He checked to make certain that both policemen were

in the squad car at the front curb, and that one wasn't making his hourly tour around the house, then went into the kitchen and watched for Melissa. When she emerged from the hedge of oleander bushes that separated the two properties, she looked like a trick-or-treater.

Tears had left tracks of black eye makeup down her cheeks. Her clothes looked more like a costume than anything a normal person would wear. It was a mystery to him how anyone could run in the platform sandals she was wearing, but she managed. She skirted the pool and clopped across the limestone terrace. He opened the sliding glass door and she flung herself against him.

He pulled her inside and closed the door. Supporting her against his side, he half-carried her into the den, where he lowered her into a chair. While she babbled incoherently, she continued to clutch at him.

"Melissa, calm down. I can't understand a thing you're saying. Tell me what's going on."

She pointed to the wet bar across the room. "I gotta have something to drink first."

When she tried to get up, Gavin pushed her back down. "Forget it. You can have some water."

He took a bottle from the mini-fridge, and while she drank from it, he remarked, "You're a freak show. What happened?"

"I was . . . was with him."

"Who?"

"The guy . . . the . . . the dentist. That Armstrong."

Gavin felt his jaw drop open. "What? Where?"

"Where? Uh . . ."

She looked around the room as though Brad Armstrong might be standing in a corner of it. Gavin wanted to slap her. How could anybody be so damned dense?

"*Where,* Melissa?"

"Don't holler at me." She rubbed her forehead as though trying to massage the answer out. "A motel. I think the sign out front had a cowboy, or a saddle, something like that on it."

A motel in Austin with a western theme. That narrowed it down to several hundred, he thought caustically. "If you met him there—"

"I didn't. He picked me up in a bar on the lake and drove me there. I was shit-faced. I'd been drowning my sorrow, you know, over Janey, with tequila shots. He showed up, bought me a drink."

"And you went to a motel with him?"

"It wasn't like I didn't know him. I was with him a few nights ago and we hit it off."

"Where was this?"

"That, uh, oh, you know the spot. Where we all go sometimes."

He anxiously motioned for her to continue.

"We did it in his car."

"What kind of car?"

"Today or then? They were different."

"Today."

"Red, I think. Or maybe blue. I wasn't paying much attention either time. He was nice to me. Really got off on my pierced nipple. It's new." She grinned at him and proudly raised her top.

"Nice."

Actually he thought she was grotesque. He'd never liked her much, had never been attracted to her, but just then, she repulsed him. He also began to question whether she was really hysterical or if this was all an act, a ploy to get inside his house, or more. She was jealous of Janey and could be trying to get some of the attention her murdered friend was receiving.

He pulled her top back into place. "Are you sure it was Brad Armstrong you were with, Melissa?"

"Don't you believe me? Would I go out looking like this on purpose?"

She had a point. "When did you learn that this was the guy the police are looking for?"

"We drove to this motel. Got in bed. He's humping away when I happen to glance across the room at the TV set. It was on, but the sound was muted. And his picture is on the screen. Big as Dallas. Everybody and his dog is out looking for him, and he's balling *me*."

"What did you do?"

"What do you think? I got him off me. I told him I had to leave, remembered I was late for an appointment. He put up an argument. Tried to talk me into staying. The more he talked, the crazier he got. First he called me a tease, then he said I was a cruel bitch, then he totally wigged out. Grabbed me and shook me and said I could go when he was good and finished with me."

She held out her arms to show Gavin the bruises beginning to appear on her biceps. "I'm telling you, Gavin, he went completely nuts. Slapped me, called me a cunt, said I was as much a cunt as Janey Kemp had been. That capped it for me. I started screaming bloody murder, and he let me go. I grabbed my clothes and hoofed it."

"How long ago?"

"Since I ran out? Maybe an hour. I flagged down a guy in a pickup truck and hitched a ride back to my car, then I drove straight here, saw the cop car. All this time I'm trying to reach you on your cell phone. Finally remembered your home number. You know the rest." She gave him an imploring look. "I'm in a bad way here, Gavin. Just one shot of something, please?"

"I said no." He squatted down in front of her. "Did you talk to him about Janey?"

"You think I'm stupid? I didn't want to wind up like her."

"Did you see any pictures of her around?"

"He had the newspapers."

"Any regular photographs?"

"No. But when I first got there, I wasn't looking, and later all I wanted to do was split."

"You said that when you met him earlier this week, he looked familiar. Had you ever seen him with Janey?"

"I'm not sure. Could be I've just seen him lurking in the crowd. He visits the Sex Club website and—"

"He said that?"

"Yeah. And the other night he had this huge stash of porn. He likes to party."

When Gavin reached for the cordless phone and began punching in numbers, she sprang from the chair. "Who're you calling?"

"My dad."

She grabbed the phone from him. "He's a cop. I don't want to get involved with the police. No thank you."

"Then why'd you come to me?"

"I needed a friend. I needed help. I thought I could get it from you. Of course, I didn't know you had dorked out since the last time I saw you. No booze, no—"

"There's a manhunt on for this guy." Angrily Gavin snatched the phone back. "If he's the one who killed Janey, he's gotta be caught."

Her facial features collapsed and she began to whimper and wring her hands. "Don't be mad at me, Gavin. I know they've gotta catch him, but jeez . . ."

He softened. "Melissa, the reason you came to me,

out of all your friends, is because you knew I would call my dad. Deep down, you wanted to do the right thing."

She pulled her lower lip through her teeth. "Okay. Maybe. But give me time to flush some stuff. On top of everything else, I don't need to get busted for possession. Where's the bathroom?" He pointed her toward the powder room in the hallway even as he redialed his dad's cell phone number. It rang four times before it was answered.

He could barely hear the hello above the yelling and what sounded like scuffling in the background.

"Paris?"

"Gavin?"

"I've gotta talk to my dad, Paris. It's an emergency."

chapter thirty-two

"This is Paris Gibson. I hope you're planning to spend the next four hours with me here on 101.3. I'll be playing classic love songs and taking your requests. The phone lines are open. Call me.

"Let's start off our time together with a hit from the Stylistics. It's what falling in love should be about, 'You Make Me Feel Brand New.'"

She shut off her mike. The phone lines were already lighting up. The first caller requested B. J. Thomas's "Hooked on a Feeling." "Since tonight's theme is how we feel when we fall in love."

"Thanks for calling, Angie. It'll be up next."

"'Bye, Paris."

She was going through her normal routine, although tonight wasn't at all normal or routine. It had been almost an hour since Dean had left in a rush to meet Gavin and Melissa Hatcher at the downtown police station.

Immediately after hanging up with Gavin, Dean had dialed Curtis and capsulized Melissa's story. Curtis milked him for information and immediately acted on it.

"It shouldn't be long till we have him in custody," Dean told Paris after concluding his conversation with Curtis. "We can start at the bar where he picked up Melissa. She has an approximate idea of how long it took Armstrong to drive from there to the motel, so that gives us a radius to search within. It's a wide area, but not as wide as before."

Paris had asked him if someone had told Toni Armstrong about this development.

He nodded somberly. "Curtis was with her when he took my call. Their attorney had joined her there." Then he hugged Paris tightly. "He'll soon be in custody, and you'll be safe. It'll be over."

"Except for the memory of what he did to Janey."

"Yeah." He sighed his regret, but his mind was clicking along at a mile a minute, in cop modality. "Curtis says the squad car remains outside until we've got Armstrong. Besides, Griggs practically considers himself your personal bodyguard." He looked over at Stan, who'd been momentarily forgotten. "I guess this lets you off the hook, Crenshaw."

"You're going to regret the way you treated me."

"I already do. I wish I'd kicked your ass while I had a good excuse." He kissed Paris swiftly on the mouth, then rushed out.

Stan followed him from her office, leaving in a huff. She let him go without saying anything. He would pout, but he would survive, and in the meantime she had a program to prepare for. Making amends with Stan could wait until she had more time and he was in a more receptive mood.

Now, at half past the hour, she engaged her mike. "I'll be back after the break with more music. If you have a request, or just something on your mind you'd like to share, call me."

She cut her mike and, sensing a presence, turned on her swivel stool. Stan was standing directly behind her. "I didn't hear you come in."

"I sneaked in."

"Why?"

"I figured as long as you and your boyfriend regard me as a creep, I should behave like one."

It was a typically childish, peevish, Stan-like thing to say. "I'm sorry your feelings were hurt by Dean's allegations, Stan. But admit it. For a while there, you looked like a plausible suspect."

"For rape and murder?"

"I said I was sorry."

"I thought you knew me better than that."

"I thought I knew you better, too," she exclaimed, losing patience with him. "If your behavior had been above reproach, no one would have suspected you. But aside from the sexual harassment charge in Florida, you've been lying about me, telling people we were lovers."

"Only Marvin, or whatever his name is. And not in so many words."

"Whatever you said, you managed to get your message across. Why would you lead anyone to believe that?"

"Why do you think?"

His voice cracked and he suddenly appeared to be on the verge of tears. The emotional display made her embarrassed for him. "I had no idea you felt that way about me, Stan."

"Well, you should have, shouldn't you?"

"I never looked at you as a . . . in a romantic context."

"Maybe those damn sunglasses keep you from seeing what should be obvious."

"Stan—"

"You only saw me as an incompetent whipping boy for my uncle, and a fag."

It was an uncomfortable truth that she couldn't deny, but she did apologize. "I'm sorry."

"For godsake, that makes three times you've said you're sorry. But you don't really mean it. If you wanted to change the way you feel about me, you could. But you don't want to. Especially now that you've got your boyfriend back. He slobbers over you, doesn't he? And you—who have always maintained a hands-off policy—you're suddenly in heat.

"I think you came here straight from bed, didn't you? When have you ever come to work with wet hair? Having fun, Paris? Isn't it nice there's no inconvenient fiancé to eliminate this time?"

"That's a tacky and extremely insensitive thing to say."

Leaning toward her, he smirked. "Did I prick your conscience?"

She had to curl her fingers into fists to keep from slapping him. "You don't know anything about that or about me. This conversation is over, Stan."

She turned back to the control board, checked the countdown clock, looked at the blinking telephone lines. She depressed one of them. "This is Paris."

"Hi, Paris. My name's Georgia."

"Hello, Georgia." She breathed slowly and silently through her mouth in an effort to calm her anger and focus on the business at hand.

"I've been having some doubts about my boyfriend," her caller said.

Paris listened while the young woman whined about her boyfriend's fear of commitment. During the monologue, Paris glanced over her shoulder. The studio was empty. As when Stan had come in, he'd left just as stealthily.

"We've got him!" Curtis shouted from his cubicle in the CIB. "They'll have him here in ten minutes."

Dean met the detective in the narrow passageway between offices. "Did he put up any resistance?"

"The arresting officers got the motel manager to open the door of his room. Armstrong was sitting on the bed, his head in his hands, crying like a baby. Kept saying over and over, 'What have I done?'"

Dean moved toward the exit. "I want to tell Gavin."

"Thank him for me. The lead he gave us narrowed the playing field considerably. And stick around, will ya? I'd like for you to be in on the interrogation."

"I plan to be. I'll be right back."

Gavin and Melissa Hatcher were seated on the same bench outside the CIB where he and Paris had been sitting . . . when was it? Only yesterday? God, so much had happened since then, with the case, with them.

As the double doors swung shut behind him, he gave Gavin and Melissa a thumbs-up. "He's just been arrested. They're bringing him in now. You did well, son." He placed his arm across Gavin's shoulders and gave him a brief hug. "I'm proud of you."

Gavin blushed modestly. "I'm just glad they caught him."

Turning to the girl, Dean said, "Thank you, too, Melissa. Coming forward took a lot of guts."

When Dean had arrived at the police station, Melissa and Gavin were already with Curtis. He and several other detectives were listening to her detailed account of the time she'd spent with Brad Armstrong.

Although she seemed to enjoy being the center of attention, she had looked a fright. Since then, she had washed the streaked makeup off her face and brushed her hair so that it no longer radiated from her head like spikes on a medieval mace. Someone, probably a policewoman, had located a cardigan sweater for her to put on over her sheer halter top, which had proved to be a distraction even to seasoned detectives.

Now she beamed at Dean's compliment, but then wet her lips nervously. "Do I have to see him?"

"We need you to officially identify him as the man who assaulted you."

"It wasn't exactly assault. I was wasted, but I knew what I was doing when I left the bar with him."

"You're a minor. He had sex with you. That's a crime. He also struck you and tried to hold you against your will. We can hold him on those charges while we're waiting for Janey's autopsy report from the medical examiner. I know it won't be easy for you to see him again, but your help is essential. Have your parents arrived?"

"Not yet. They freaked out when I called them, but they weren't as pissed as I would have thought, I guess since I coulda turned up dead, too. Is it okay if Gavin stays with me?"

"If you want him to. Gavin?"

He raised his shoulders in a shrug of consent. "Sure."

"Okay then, Dr. Malloy," Melissa said. "Bring on the pervert. I'll stay as long as you need me."

"This is Paris."

"It's me."

Merely the sound of Dean's voice caused her heart to flutter and brought on a silly smile. "Did you lose the hot-line number I gave you? Why are you calling on this line?"

"I thought I'd see what it was like to be an ordinary listener."

"You might be a listener, but you're certainly not ordinary."

"No? Glad to hear it." There was a smile behind his

voice, too, but it soon turned serious. "They've arrested Armstrong. He's due here any minute."

"Thank God." She was relieved, but her heart immediately went out to his wife. "Have you seen Toni?"

"Just a few minutes ago. She's distraught, but I think she's glad we got him before he could hurt anyone else."

"Or himself."

"The possibility of suicide had occurred to me, too. You're getting as good at my job as I am."

"Not even close. Oops, hang on a sec. I've got to do a station ID." She dispatched her business, then came back on the line. "Okay, I've got a few minutes."

"I won't keep you. I promised to call as soon as I knew something."

"And I appreciate it. My program will go a lot smoother now that I know he's been apprehended. I couldn't concentrate, and every time I answered a phone line, I held my breath, afraid it would be him."

"You don't have to worry about that now."

"Is Gavin still with you?"

"He's keeping Melissa company. What he did was great, huh?"

"I thought so."

"Me, too. Shows maturity and a sense of responsibility."

"And trust in you, Dean. That's the most significant breakthrough."

"After a few derailments, I think we're on the right track now."

"I'm sure of it."

"Speaking of misguided youths, Lancy Ray Fisher was released."

"I'm thinking of hiring him."

"I beg your pardon?"

She laughed at his shocked tone. "I've never worked with a producer, although management has offered me one. It would be a good way for Lancy to learn, get some experience."

"What would Stan think about it?"

"It's not his decision to make."

"Any backlash over what happened earlier?"

She hesitated, then said, "He's brooding, but he'll get over it."

Dean had enough on his mind without her telling him about her most recent altercation with Stan. It had made her uneasy. After everything that had been said, could they mend fences and resettle into a comfortable working relationship? Unlikely.

However, the prospect of dissidence in the workplace didn't upset her as it would have even a week ago. Then, her life had revolved around her job. Anything that affected it had a profound effect on her, because that's all she had. That had changed.

As though following her thoughts, Dean said, "I want to spend the night with you."

The declaration evoked memories of the abbreviated but precious time they'd spent in bed earlier this evening and sent a tingle through her all the way down to her toes. "I'm supposed to disconnect callers who say things like that."

He chuckled. "I want to, but unfortunately I don't know how long I'll be needed here."

"Do what you need to do. You know I understand."

"I know," he said, sighing. "But tomorrow night is a damn long time to wait."

She felt the same. With as much professionalism as she could muster, she said, "Caller, do you have a request?"

"In fact I do."

"I'm listening."

"Love me, Paris."

She closed her eyes and held her breath for a moment, then said softly but emphatically, "I do."

"I love you, too."

John Rondeau took the stairs rather than waiting for the elevator. His email exchanges with a counterpart in the Atlanta PD had yielded new information on Stan Crenshaw, which he was eager to share with Curtis. Rather than forwarding it by email or telephoning, Rondeau wanted to deliver it in person.

But when he reached the CIB, it was humming with activity. For the number of personnel bustling about, it could have been high noon rather than nearing midnight. As a policewoman barreled past him, he hooked his hand in her elbow, bringing her to an abrupt halt. "What's going on?"

"Where've you been?" she said, frowning at him as she extricated her arm. "We got Armstrong. They're about to bring him in."

Rondeau spotted Dean Malloy in conversation with Toni Armstrong and a gray-suited man who had "lawyer" stamped all over him. He found Curtis in his cubicle, hunched over his desk phone and rubbing his palm back and forth across his burred head.

He was saying, "No, Judge, he hasn't confessed, but there's a lot of circumstantial evidence pointing to him. We're hoping the autopsy will produce some DNA, although the body was washed—"

He stopped speaking, apparently having been interrupted. He rubbed his head a little more briskly. "Yes, I'm well aware of how long DNA testing takes, but maybe when Armstrong knows that we're submitting his for a possible match, he'll crack. I certainly will, Judge. By all means. As soon as I know more. My condolences again to Mrs. Kemp. Good night."

He hung up, stared at the receiver for several seconds, then looked up at Rondeau. "What?"

Rondeau raised the file folder he'd brought with him. "Stan Crenshaw. The guy has been a deviant since grade school. Raising girls' skirts. Indecent exposure. Interesting reading."

"I'm sure it is, but he's not Valentino."

"So what do I do with this? Ditch it?"

Standing, Curtis shot his monogrammed cuffs and smoothed down his necktie. "Leave it on my desk."

"Somebody should look at it," Rondeau insisted.

A sudden shift in the atmosphere indicated that something momentous was happening beyond the walls of Curtis's cubicle. Rondeau followed him out. They wended their way into the center of the CIB.

Rondeau recognized Dr. Brad Armstrong from the family snapshots taken off the CD. Flanking him were two uniformed policemen. Handcuffed, he stood with his head down, his aspect that of a defeated man. He was ushered into an interrogation room. Malloy, the attorney, and Toni Armstrong crowded in. Curtis was the last to enter the room. He closed the door behind him.

Rondeau, feeling rebuffed, tapped the folder against his open palm. If Curtis thought he had Valentino, then he should probably just let it drop and forget Stan Crenshaw.

But what if, after interrogating Armstrong, Curtis determined they had the wrong guy? What if the result of the autopsy cast doubt on or even refuted the circumstantial evidence against him? What if his DNA didn't match any samples they collected from Janey's remains, if they even could since her body had been chemically cleansed?

Reaching a decision, Rondeau left the CIB in a hurry. As he went through the double doors, he spotted Gavin Malloy and a girl seated together on a bench in the vestibule. He had missed seeing them when he came in. From the open staircase, he had turned right to enter the CIB. They were seated to the left of the stairs. At the sound of the doors closing, the girl turned her head toward him.

Oh, shit!

He didn't know her name, but he'd seen her plenty of times. If she recognized him, he'd be up shit creek.

John Rondeau made a dash for the stairs.

"Hey, Gavin, who's that guy?"

"Huh?"

The past few days had caught up with him. His head had been resting against the wall, and he'd been dozing.

Melissa nudged his elbow. "Hurry! Look!"

"Where?"

He raised his head, blinked open his gritty eyes, and looked in the direction of Melissa's pointing finger. Through the metal railing of the staircase, he caught a glimpse of John Rondeau's head just before he cleared the landing below and disappeared.

"His name is John Rondeau."

"Is he a cop?"

"Computer crimes," he muttered. "It was him who ratted out the Sex Club."

"Seriously? Because I've seen him somewhere. In fact, I think I might've balled him."

Terrific, Gavin thought. If she placed Rondeau as someone who hung out and partied with the high school crowd, then blabbed about it, Rondeau might think he was the one who'd fingered him.

"No way. He's got one of those faces that always remind you of somebody else." It wasn't a very good explanation, but it was all he could think of.

Melissa frowned thoughtfully. "Guess I'd have to see his cock to know for sure. But I could swear . . ."

Just then they heard a ping signaling the arrival of an elevator. They turned in time to see a nice-looking, well-dressed couple step around the corner and into their view.

Melissa stood up.

"Your folks?" Gavin asked, surprised by how presentable and respectable they appeared. He'd been expecting the Osbornes, not June and Ward Cleaver.

Awkwardly, Melissa wobbled toward them on her platform sandals, self-consciously tugging down her short skirt. "Hi, Mom. Hi, Dad."

Their arrival couldn't have been better timed. Gavin wanted nothing more to do with Rondeau, and that extended even to talking about him. He hated being the keeper of the cop's dirty little secret, but, remembering Rondeau's threat toward his dad, Gavin would carry that secret to his grave.

chapter thirty-three

"I'm sorry, Toni. I'm sorry. Will you ever be able to forgive me?"

Dr. Brad Armstrong seemed more concerned about his wife's opinion of him than he did about the serious allegations being made against him, which could potentially cost him his life. He appealed to her plaintively and somewhat pathetically.

"Let's get through this first, Brad. There'll be plenty of time later to talk about forgiveness."

She was stoic, her voice calm, which was amazing in light of the ordeal confronting her. She was probably being held together with the emotional equivalent of Scotch tape, but she remained intact. Dean gave her a "hang in there" nod as she left the interrogation room, leaving her husband alone with him, the attorney, and Curtis.

Curtis identified everyone present for the benefit of the tape recorder, then began by telling Bradley Armstrong everything they knew about him and why they considered him a suspect in the kidnapping and murder of Janey Kemp.

"I didn't kidnap that girl."

His earnest denial didn't impress Curtis. "We'll get to that. First let's talk about the time you molested Paris Gibson." Armstrong grimaced. "I see you remember the incident," Curtis remarked. "To this day you resent Ms. Gibson, don't you?"

"She got me fired from a lucrative practice."

"Do you deny touching her inappropriately?"

He lowered his head and shook it.

"Answer audibly for the recorder, please."

"No, I don't deny it."

"Have you called her radio show recently?"

"No."

"Ever?"

"I may have."

"If I were you, I wouldn't hedge on the easy stuff, Dr. Armstrong," Curtis advised. "Have you ever called her while she's on the air? Yes or no?"

The dentist raised his head and sighed. "Yes, I called her, said something rude, and hung up."

"When was this?"

"Long time ago. Shortly after we moved to Austin and I realized she had a radio program."

"Only that once?" Dean asked.

"I swear."

"Did you know that there was some involvement between Ms. Gibson, Dr. Malloy, and a man named Jack Donner?"

Dean looked at Curtis and was on the verge of asking him where the hell that question had come from, but Armstrong answered before he had a chance. "It was on the news down in Houston."

Then Dean realized the validity of the detective's question. Valentino had said Jack's death was on their consciences, indicating that he was acquainted with their history.

"When you called her, where did you call from?"

"My house. My cell phone. I don't remember, but I certainly never called her about Janey Kemp."

Curtis had learned that Armstrong's cell and home phone records didn't list any calls to the radio station, but he'd only requested records going back several months. Armstrong could be telling the truth, or he could have used a public telephone to make the Valentino calls, or he could have an untraceable cell.

Curtis asked if he had disguised his voice when he called.

"No need. She would never have recognized my voice. We only met that . . . that once."

"Did you identify yourself to her?" Curtis asked.

"No. I just said, 'Screw you,' or something to that effect, then hung up."

"Where'd you get Valentino?"

He glanced at his lawyer, then at Dean, as though seeking an explanation.

"What?"

"Valentino," Curtis repeated.

The news stories had cited Paris Gibson's telephone warnings as a key element in the case, but the caller's name had been withheld to prevent chronic confessors from gumming up the investigation with false leads.

"You pick that name up from the silent movie actor?" Curtis asked. "And why seventy-two hours? Did you pluck that deadline from thin air? Why not forty-eight, which is closer to what it turned out to be, isn't it?"

Armstrong turned to his attorney. "What's he talking about?"

"Never mind. We'll come back to that," Curtis said. "Tell us about Janey Kemp. Where did you meet her?"

With his attorney closely monitoring every word, Armstrong admitted that he'd frequented the Sex Club website and had eventually begun joining its members at the specified meeting places. "I invented reasons to leave the house."

"You lied to your wife."

"That's not a crime," the attorney said.

"But engaging in sexual activity with minors is," Curtis fired back. "When did you first meet Janey, Dr. Armstrong?"

"I don't remember the exact date. A couple months ago."

"What were the circumstances?"

"I already knew who she was. I'd noticed her, asked around, and learned that her user name for the website was pussinboots. I'd been reading the messages she left on the boards, knew she was . . ." He stammered over his next word, then rephrased. "I knew she was sexually active and willing to do just about anything."

"In other words, she was prey to predators like you."

The lawyer ordered him not to respond.

Curtis waved a semi-apologetic dismissal of the statement. "The night you met Janey, did you have sex with her?"

"Yes."

"Janey Kemp was seventeen," the attorney stipulated.

"Barely," Curtis said.

In an anguished voice, Armstrong said, "You've got to understand, that's what these girls were there for. They came looking for it. I never had to coerce a single one of them into having sex with me. In fact, one—not Janey, another one—charged me a hundred dollars for five minutes of her time, then went right on to her next customer. She said she was working toward a Vuitton handbag."

"You have proof of this?"

"Oh, sure, she gave me a receipt," Armstrong replied sarcastically.

Curtis failed to see the humor in this and remained stone-faced. Dean believed the dentist was telling the truth about the prostitution because it coincided with what Gavin had told him.

Curtis continued the questioning. "On the night you met Janey, you had sex with her where?"

"In a motel."

"Where you were found tonight?"

He nodded. "I keep an efficiency apartment there."

"Which you rent for that purpose?"

"Don't answer," the attorney instructed.

"Did you take pictures of Janey?" Curtis asked.

"Pictures?"

"Photographs. Different in subject matter from the kind you take of your family vacations," the detective added dryly.

"Maybe. I don't remember."

Curtis narrowed his gaze on him. "Your den of iniquity is being searched even as we speak. Why don't you tell us what we might find and save us all some time here."

"I have some porno magazines. Videos. I've taken pictures of . . . of women on occasion, so maybe, yeah, there might be some pictures of Janey."

"You develop these pictures there in your makeshift darkroom?"

He looked genuinely mystified. "I don't know how to develop film."

"Then where'd you have your pictures of 'women' developed?"

"I send the film to a lab out of town."

"What lab?"

"It doesn't have a name. Just a post office box. I can give you that."

"Let me guess. This is a film-developing outfit that caters to specialized customers like you?"

Shamefaced, he nodded. "I don't use it often, but I have."

Armstrong's answers to this line of questioning were inconsistent with what Janey had told Gavin about her new boyfriend's passion for photography. Either he was telling the truth or he knew how to lie convincingly.

Curtis must have thought so, too, because for the time being he let the subject drop and asked about the last time Armstrong had seen Janey.

"It was three nights ago. I guess it was the night she disappeared."

"Where'd you see her?"

"At a spot on the shore of Lake Travis."

"You went there for the specific purpose of meeting her?"

Armstrong answered, "Yes," before his attorney could caution him not to. Too late Armstrong saw his lawyer's raised hand. "It's not a crime to make and keep a date," he said to him.

The lawyer addressed Curtis. "I'm only agreeing to let my client go into detail here because he adamantly denies anything beyond having congress with the victim, who was a consenting adult. This isn't to be considered a confession to any allegation of kidnapping or murder."

Curtis nodded and motioned for Armstrong to continue.

"Janey was waiting for me in her car."

"What time was that?" Dean asked, remembering that Gavin had said that he, too, had been in Janey's car and that she had seemed to be waiting for someone else to join her.

"I can't remember exactly," Armstrong said. "Around ten, maybe."

Curtis asked, "What did you do in her car?"

"We had sex."

"Intercourse?"

"Fellatio."

"Did you use a condom?"

"Yes."

"Then what happened?"

"I . . . I wanted to stay with her for a while longer, but she said there was something she had to do. I think she was waiting to see someone else."

"Like who?"

"Another man. She insisted I go on my way, but she promised to see me the following night, same place, same time. When I left, she was in her car, listening to the CD player. I went the next night. She wasn't there. I didn't know about her disappearance until I read about it and saw her picture in the newspaper."

"Why didn't you come forward then?" Curtis asked.

"I was scared. Wouldn't you be?"

"I don't know. Tell me. Would I?"

"I'd violated the terms of my probation. A girl I'd had sex with several times had gone missing." He raised his shoulders in a gesture of helplessness. "You do the math."

Curtis snickered. "I've done it, Dr. Armstrong. My tally says you wanted more of Janey than she was willing to give you that night. Things got rough. You tend to get rough when a woman doesn't give you what you want when you want it, isn't that right?"

"Sometimes I get angry, but I'm working through it."

"Not fast enough. In the meantime, your anger got the best of you, and before you knew it, you were choking Janey. Maybe she died right then, maybe she just became unconscious and died later.

"In any case, you panicked. You took her to that swell

room you've got in that lousy motel and tried to figure out what to do with her, but in the end you rolled her body into the lake and then crawled into your hidey-hole and hoped to God you'd get away with killing her."

"No! I swear I didn't force her into doing anything, and I sure as hell didn't murder her."

The attorney was massaging his eye sockets as though wondering how in the hell he was going to construct a defense out of his client's frantic denials. Curtis looked as stern and unyielding as a cigar store Indian.

"I don't think you did it intentionally," Dean said quietly.

Armstrong turned to him with the desperate expression of a drowning man in search of a lifeline.

The role of good cop fell to him because he played it well. Let Curtis be the hard-ass. For the next several minutes, Dean would be Brad Armstrong's best friend and only source of hope. He folded his arms on the table and leaned into it.

"Did you like Janey, Brad? I assume it's okay if I call you Brad."

"Sure."

"Did you like her? As a person, I mean."

"Truthfully, not much. Don't get me wrong, she was something else." Suddenly cautious, he glanced at his attorney.

"Sexy and willing?" Dean prompted. "The kind of girl we all wanted to date in high school?"

"She was just like that. But I didn't particularly like her personality."

"Why not?"

"Like most girls with her looks, she was conceited and self-absorbed. She treated people like dirt. You either played her way or she didn't play at all."

"Did she ever turn you down?"

"Only once."

"For another guy?"

He shook his head. "She said she was PMSing and not in the mood."

Pal to pal, Dean smiled at him. "We've all been there."

Then he sat back and folded his arms across his chest, his smile reversing into a frown. "The problem is, Brad, that most guys would blow it off. Oh, there'd be some frustration and maybe some hard cussing, but eventually your average guy would go have a beer or two, watch a ball game, maybe even find a more accommodating girl. But you take rejection hard. You can't tolerate it. Which causes you to lash out, doesn't it?"

He swallowed hard and mumbled, "Sometimes."

"Like you did tonight with Melissa Hatcher."

"I haven't had time to confer with my client about Melissa Hatcher," the lawyer said. "So I can't allow him to talk about her."

"He doesn't have to say a word," Dean said. "I'm going to talk to him." Then, without waiting for the attorney's permission, he continued. "This girl advertises the merchandise. She's advertised it to me, to Sergeant Curtis here, and all the detectives in this unit. Any man would take the way she dresses as a 'come and get it.'"

"So who could blame me for—"

"Do not say a word," Brad's lawyer snapped.

Ignoring the lawyer, Dean kept his attention riveted on Armstrong. "Unfortunately for you, Brad, the state of Texas blames you. If you penetrate the sexual organ, mouth, or anus of a child, it's called 'aggravated sexual assault.' Correct?" he asked, turning to the attorney, who nodded curtly.

"How old is Melissa?" Brad asked.

"Sixteen until next February," Dean told him. "She claims you had sexual contact and intercourse."

"What if . . . what if . . . it was consensual?" Armstrong asked, seeming not to hear the admonitions of his attorney instructing him not to say anything.

"Doesn't matter," Curtis answered. "You're a convicted sex offender. Under Chapter Sixty-two that makes what you did indefensible."

Armstrong buried his head in his hands.

Dean said, "Your previous conviction for indecency with a minor was a third-degree felony. This is the big time, Brad. It's a first-degree felony."

"Not to mention capital murder," Curtis chimed in.

Without acknowledging Curtis's statement, Dean proceeded. "You've paid dearly for your inappropriate and illegal behavior. You've lost jobs, the respect of your colleagues. You're in danger of losing your family."

The man's shoulders rose and fell in a harsh sob.

"Yet in spite of the costly consequences of your unacceptable behavior, you haven't stopped it."

"I've tried," he exclaimed. "God knows, I've tried. Ask Toni. She'll tell you. I love her. I love my kids. But . . . but I can't help myself."

Dean leaned forward again. "That's precisely my point. You can't help yourself. Melissa got you so hot tonight that when she said no, you flipped out. You grabbed her, shook her, slapped her around. You didn't want to, but you couldn't control the impulse, even knowing how much you were going to regret your actions later.

"Your desire to sexually dominate this girl shot your conscience and common sense all to hell. You had to have her, simple as that. Nothing else mattered. Not the punishment you would face when caught. Not even your love for Toni and your children could stop you. It's a compulsion you haven't learned to contain. It caused you to do what you did to Melissa tonight, and what you did to Janey."

"Do not respond," the lawyer said.

Dean lowered his voice another degree and spoke to Armstrong as though they were the only two people in the room. "I have a clear picture of what happened three nights ago, Brad. Here's this sexy, desirable girl who you thought was as enamored of you as you were of her. She'd been seeing you regularly, and you thought exclusively.

"That night, she goes down on you. And it's great, but you know she's insincere. You know she's a liar and a merciless tease. You know that she's waiting for her new interest to come along and replace you.

"When you confront her about it, she tells you to get lost. You've become jealous and possessive, and she can't stand your whining any longer. Did you honestly believe that she would give up other men for *you?* she asks. You poor, delusional slob.

"You get furious. You ask yourself, where does she get off treating me like this? Calling up Paris Gibson and talking about me on the radio? Who does she think she is?"

Dean's gaze held the suspect mesmerized. "When you got into Janey's car that night, I don't think you had already plotted her kidnapping and murder. I think you'd planned only to confront her, have it out with her, clear the air.

"And maybe if she hadn't mocked you, that's the way it would have ended. But Janey laughed in your face. She emasculated you with her ridicule, insulted you in a way you couldn't tolerate. You lost it. You wanted to punish her. And that's what you did. You devised a punishment of sexual abuse, befitting what she'd done to you. You hurt her until you decided you'd had your vengeance, to hell with the deadline you gave Paris, and then you choked her to death."

Armstrong stared at Dean in stunned horror. He looked over at Curtis, whose visage remained unmoved and unchanged. Then, folding his arms on the table, he laid his head on them. In a tormented, cracking voice, he groaned, "Oh, God. Oh, *God.*"

Curtis and Dean honored the attorney's demand to have a few minutes alone with his client and left the room. Curtis was smiling and rubbing his hands together, relishing the coup de grace.

"He hasn't signed a confession yet," Dean reminded him.

"It's a matter of pen and paper. By the way, you're good."

"Thanks," Dean said absently. This had been round one of what would probably be a lengthy and exhausting interrogation, but several things about it were nagging him. "I didn't ask him specifically if he'd heard Janey on the radio talking about the jealous lover she was about to dump."

"But you alluded to it and he didn't deny it."

"He denied calling Paris about Janey."

"Before we even asked, which says 'guilty' to me," the detective argued.

"He knew about Paris's connection because it was in the news. His phone records refute the allegation that he called her."

"There are several ways he could have placed those calls without it showing up on records."

"Making weird phone calls hasn't been part of Armstrong's MO before. Why now?"

"Maybe he needed a new thrill. The Valentino phone calls spiced things up for him, and at the same time wreaked havoc on Paris. He wanted to get his kicks and get revenge. The calls accomplished both."

That made sense, but only after you massaged it into place. "Valentino's calls have a meanness to them that I just don't see in Armstrong. He's sick, but I don't think he's evil."

Curtis frowned at him irritably. "Forget motivation for a moment and consider some facts."

"Such as?"

"His occupation. He's a dentist."

"The chemical scouring," Dean said, musing out loud. The medical examiner had been able to confirm that, like Maddie Robinson, Janey's body had been astringently washed.

"Right. It's the kind of thing a medical man would do."

"It's the kind of thing a meticulous psychopath would do, too. Someone with a compulsion for scrubbing away his guilt."

"Armstrong straddles both categories."

Dean glanced over his shoulder at the closed door of the interrogation room. "Janey was restrained. She was tortured. She had bite marks, for godsake."

"We'll get impressions of his bite for comparison."

"My point is, none of Armstrong's priors involved violence or even hinted at a propensity for it. He was a creep, but he wasn't a violent creep."

"What is this, Malloy?" Curtis asked crossly. "His own *wife* told us that his violent tendencies had been escalating. *You* said that was a natural progression for his particular psychosis. Are you second-guessing your-self?"

"I know what I said, and I was right."

"Okay then. He knocked Melissa Hatcher around tonight."

"There's a wide gulf between knocking a woman around and torturing one before squeezing the breath out of her."

"Not in my book. And probably not in the book of the woman being knocked around."

"Don't be obtuse, Curtis," Dean said angrily. "I'm not excusing either. I'm just saying—"

"Ah, shit, I know what you're saying," Curtis grumbled, then expelled his frustration on a gust of breath. After a short pause that allowed tempers to cool, he asked, "Any more misgivings?"

"The photography."

"Armstrong admitted that he might have taken some pictures of Janey."

"'Some.' 'Might have.' He talked about the photography as though it was no big deal. Janey indicated otherwise. Before we start on Armstrong again, do you mind if I get Gavin in here and ask him more about this?"

Curtis shrugged. "I'm for whatever will help nail this guy."

Dean stepped into the corridor and motioned for Gavin. He got up, leaving Melissa sitting with a couple Dean assumed were her parents.

"What's up, Dad?" he asked. "Has he confessed?"

"Not yet. In the meantime, I'd like you to talk Sergeant Curtis and me through everything Janey told you about Valentino. Any detail you can remember. All right?"

"I already have, a dozen times."

"One more time. Please."

They found Curtis pouring himself a cup of coffee. He offered them one, but they declined. Curtis took a sip from his Styrofoam cup, then said, "At the risk of beating a dead horse, even an off-handed remark Janey might have made could be important, Gavin."

"I wish I could remember something else, sir. She told me the guy was older. Older than us, I mean. That he was cool, knew how a woman liked to be treated."

"We're mainly interested in the photography," Dean told him.

"She said he was a camera freak," Gavin said. "Lights, lenses, an elaborate setup. He posed her himself. Moved her around, you know, her arms and legs. Head. Everything."

"Could she have been exaggerating to impress you? Make you think of her as a model, like in *Penthouse?*"

"It's possible," he replied. "But if she was exaggerating, she sure did her homework, because she knew a lot about it. She mentioned shutter speeds, stuff like that. Said he tinkered with gadgets to get each picture just right, and would get mad if she didn't cooperate."

"He didn't just fire off a few naughty snapshots," Dean said to Curtis. "If you study the picture that Janey gave Gavin, you can tell it was taken by an amateur trying to be artistic."

"And you don't think Armstrong is capable of that?"

"Capable," Dean said. "But if you're out cheating on your wife, who is more than likely waiting up for you, do you take that much time with photography?"

While Curtis was still mulling that over, he happened to glance beyond Dean's shoulder. "What are you doing here?"

Dean turned to see who had caused Curtis's distraction and saw Officer Griggs coming toward them. The rookie's grin dissolved under Curtis's frown and tone of stern disapproval.

"I . . . I was given the all clear, sir. Told it was okay to leave. But I was anxious to know if Armstrong had confessed, so instead—"

"You left Paris out there alone?" Dean asked.

"Well, sir, not—"

"Who told you to leave?"

"John Rondeau."

From the corner of his eye, Dean noticed Gavin's reaction to the mention of Rondeau's name. He reacted not with the expected dislike, but with alarm.

"Gavin? What is it?" His son stared back at him, whey-faced. *"Gavin?"*

"Dad . . ." The boy had to swallow hard before he could continue. "There's something I've gotta tell you."

chapter thirty-four

Through the glass-block walls, the blue-white fluorescent lighting of the radio station's lobby relieved the surrounding darkness, but only marginally. Downtown city lights were obliterated by hills. The moon was too slender to shed significant light. At this time of night, only an occasional car sped past on the narrow state highway. The nearest commercial building was a convenience store a half mile away, and it had closed at ten.

From the vantage point of the FM 101.3 building, nothing was visible except hills dotted with cedar trees, limestone boulders, and an occasional herd of beef cattle. It was an ideal spot for the transmission tower that intermittently blinked its red lights as a warning to low-flying private aircraft.

Rondeau dawdled beside his car until the taillights of Griggs's patrol car disappeared behind a hill. He frowned with contempt for the officers driving away. Sure, he had wanted them to leave. But shouldn't they have verified the order, which he told them had come straight from Curtis, rather than taking his word for it? That kind of carelessness was unacceptable. Tomorrow he would report them. It wouldn't win him their regard, but one didn't advance one's career by making friends.

He started toward the entrance, carrying with him the folder of information on Stan Crenshaw. It painted a disturbing portrait of a man whose dysfunctional family and personal insecurities had led to sexual malfeasances dating back to childhood, which were credible harbingers of Valentino's aberrations.

What offended Rondeau most, however, was the injustice it signified. Crenshaw had gotten away with his misconduct. His uncle had bought him out of every scrape. By doing so, Wilkins Crenshaw had slowly created a monster capable of kidnapping, raping, torturing, and murdering a lovely young woman.

Because of his myopic focus on Brad Armstrong, Sergeant Curtis had dismissed the juicy contents of this folder. Initially Rondeau had taken offense at the snub, but it had actually worked to his advantage. Unwittingly, Curtis had handed him a golden opportunity to become everyone's hero.

Rather than press the buzzer, he knocked on the glass door.

He didn't have to wait long before getting his first look at the singularly unimpressive and unimposing Stan Crenshaw. He appeared out of a shadowed hallway off the lobby and approached the door warily, peering through the glass that, with the darkness beyond it, Rondeau knew would be reflecting like a mirror. Crenshaw did all but cup his hands around his eyes in order to see who had knocked.

He assessed Rondeau with the condescension of the born rich, then looked beyond him toward the parking lot, where the squad car was conspicuously missing. "Where're the policemen?"

Rondeau, already tasting success, held up his badge.

"That, of course, was Johnny Mathis with his classic, 'Misty.' Definitely music to nuzzle by. I hope you have someone near you tonight as you listen to 101.3, classic love songs. This is Paris Gibson bringing you up to midnight with Melissa Manchester's 'I Don't Know How to Love Him.' The phone lines are open. Call me."

When the song began, she disengaged her mike. Two of her phone lines were blinking. She pressed one of the buttons, but got a dial tone. Mentally she apologized to the caller who obviously had given up on being answered.

She pressed the second blinking light. "This is Paris."

"Hello, Paris."

Her heart actually stopped before a burst of adrenaline restarted it with the hard, fast pounding of a sprinter coming off the blocks. "Who is this?"

"You know who it is." His laugh was even more frightening than his whispery voice. "Your faithful fan Valentino."

Frantically she looked over her shoulder, hoping that perhaps Stan had silently rejoined her in the studio. She would have welcomed his sneaking up on her now. But she was alone in the room. "How—"

"I know, I know, your boyfriend thinks he's nabbed his culprit. His egotistical bungling would be comical if it weren't so pathetic." He laughed again, and it caused goose bumps to break out on her arms. "I've been a bad boy, haven't I, Paris?"

Her mouth had gone dry. Her heart continued to thump against her ribs and her pulse vibrated loudly against her eardrums. She ordered herself to calm down and *think*. She must alert Dean, Sergeant Curtis, Griggs outside, someone, that they had the wrong man in custody and that Valentino was still at large. But how?

What was she thinking? She had a microphone at her

fingertips! Hundreds of thousands of people were tuned in.

But even as she reached for the mike switch, she reconsidered. Should she blurt out over the airwaves that the Austin PD had blundered? What if this call turned out to be a hoax, someone playing a cruel trick on her? What if she started a public panic?

Better to keep him talking until she could figure out what to do. "On top of everything else, you're a liar, Valentino. You moved up the deadline."

"That's true. I have no honor."

"You killed Janey before giving me a chance to rescue her."

"Unfair, wasn't it? But I never claimed to be honorable, Paris."

"Then why did you call me in the first place? If you intended to kill her all along, why set up this elaborate telephone campaign?"

"To rock your world. And it worked, didn't it? You feel positively rotten over your inability to save that slut's life."

Paris refused to buy into his baiting. She'd been down that path, and Janey had died anyway. The only way she could redeem herself would be to identify this son of a bitch and see him brought to justice, and that couldn't be done by arguing with him.

She could dial Dean on her cell phone, but—damn!— it was in her office, in her handbag. Could she create a technical problem that would alert Stan? Soon the Manchester song would end. It was the last in a series. Dead air would bring Stan into the studio to see what the problem was.

While she brainstormed, Valentino rambled. "She had to die, you see, for fucking me over. She was a heartless bitch. I enjoyed watching her die slowly. I could tell when she realized that she would never get away from me. She knew she wasn't going to survive."

"That must have been a real head trip for you."

"Oh, absolutely. Although it was actually heart-rending the way her eyes silently pleaded with me to spare her life."

That statement made Paris forget her recent resolve not to be riled by anything he said. "You sick bastard."

"You think I'm sick?" he asked pleasantly. "I find that strange, Paris. I tortured and killed Janey, yes, but you tortured and killed your fiancé, didn't you? Wasn't it torture for him to learn about your unfaithfulness with his best friend? Do you think of yourself as sick?"

"I didn't drive Jack's car into a bridge abutment, he did. The accident was his fault. He determined his fate, not me."

"That sounds like a rationalization," he said in the reproving tone of a priest in the confessional. "I don't see the difference between your sin and mine, except that your fiancé's torture lasted much longer and he died much more slowly. Which makes you much crueler than me, doesn't it? And that's why you must be punished.

"Would it be just to let you go on your merry way and live happily ever after with Malloy? I don't think so," he said in a nasty singsong. "That is not going to happen. You will never be together because you, Paris, are going to die. Tonight."

The line went dead. Instantly she reached for her hot-line phone. No dial tone. Nothing. Silence. In quick succession, she tried all the phone lines, but to no avail. They were dead.

Realization crept over her like an encroaching shadow. Either he had the access and ability to disable computerized telephone equipment from off the premises or—and this is what she feared—he had simply interrupted telephone service from inside the building.

She shot from her stool. Yanking open the heavily padded door, she shouted down the dark corridor, "Stan!"

The Manchester song was winding down. Racing back to the control board, she punched her mike button. "Hello, this is Paris Gibson." Her voice sounded thin and high, not at all like her normal contralto. "This is not a—"

The sound of a high-pitched alarm interrupted her.

She swung her gaze toward the source. The sound was coming from the scanner, which recorded everything that went out over the air. You never knew it was there, really. The alarm only alerted you to an interruption in transmission.

Terror seizing her, she punched her mike button repeatedly, but, like all the others on the board, it refused to light up.

Again she lunged for the door. "Stan!" The echo of her scream seemed to chase her as she ran toward her office. Her handbag was where she'd left it on her desk, but it had been toppled onto its side. The contents had been spilled onto her desk. With shaking hands, she riffled through cosmetics, tissues, loose change, hoping to find her cell phone, but knowing it wouldn't be there.

It wasn't.

And something else was missing—her keys.

Frantically she searched through the mail scattered across her desk and even dropped to her knees and looked beneath it, but she knew that both her key ring and her phone had been taken by the same individual who had cut the phone lines and shut down transmission. All lines of communication had been severed by the man who had killed Janey and had promised to kill her.

Valentino.

Her breathing was so harsh, she couldn't hear anything else. She held it for several moments in order to listen. She crept to the open door of her office but hesitated at the threshold. The hallway, as always, was dim. Tonight the familiar darkness gave her no sense of security and comfort. It had a sinister quality, maybe because the building was as silent as a tomb.

Where was Stan? Hadn't he noticed that they weren't broadcasting? If he had checked the studio and discovered she wasn't there, why wasn't he going through the building calling for her, checking to see what had happened?

But even before her mind could completely form that question, it had arrived at the answer: Stan was unable to come and check on her.

Valentino had dispatched him, possibly even before he had called her. He could have been in the building for quite some time before she'd know of it, sealed as she'd been inside the soundproof room.

How had Valentino gotten past Griggs and Carson? Once he had, how had he opened the door to the building? A key was needed to unlock the dead bolt from either side. Had he persuaded Stan to open the door? How?

Questions for which she had no answers.

She was tempted to slam her office door, lock herself inside, and wait for help to arrive. Already, listeners all over the hill country would be wondering what had caused the station to go off the air. Dean might even know. Sergeant Curtis. Soon somebody would be rushing to her rescue.

But in the meantime, she couldn't hide herself in here. Griggs and Carson could be hurt. And Stan.

She stepped out into the hallway. Putting her back to the wall so she could see in both directions, she inched along it, toward the front of the building. As she moved along the corridor, she turned off every light switch she passed. One distinct advantage she had over Valentino was knowing the layout of the building. She was accustomed to navigating it in semidarkness.

Moving quickly, but as silently and cautiously as possible, she made her way toward the entrance. She approached each intersection of hallways with the fear of what awaited her around the corner, but when she turned the last one, the stretch of hall between her and the well-lighted lobby was clear. She raced down it and across the lobby, intent on launching herself against the door and pounding on the glass in order to get the attention of the policemen guarding her.

But the squad car wasn't there and the front door was bolted.

With a soft cry, she backed away from the door until she came up against the receptionist's desk. She rested against it to catch her breath and decide what to do.

Suddenly her ankle was grabbed. She screamed.

She looked down to see a man's hand reaching from beneath the desk. But before she could even try to work herself free of his grasp, the fingers relaxed and the hand fell lifelessly to the grimy carpet.

Stumbling over her own feet, she rounded the desk but drew up short when she saw the form lying face-down on the floor. She dropped to her knees and took the man by the shoulder, turning him over.

John Rondeau groaned. His eyelids were fluttering but remained closed. He was bleeding profusely from a wound on his head.

Gladness surged through her as she gasped his name.

"John. Please, wake up. Please!" She slapped his cheek smartly, but he only groaned again, his head lolling to one side. He was unconscious.

Just beyond the reach of his outstretched hand lay an official-looking file folder. She read the name typed on the identifying tab: *Stanley Crenshaw*.

Her stomach dropped. "Oh my God."

Stan? It had been Stan all along?

But why not? she reasoned. His ineptitude could be an excellent guise. He had the time and opportunity to commit the crimes. His days were free and so were his nights before and after her program. He had just enough technical knowledge to reroute telephone calls. He was an electronics and gadget junky. Surely among all his toys was camera equipment he could easily afford. He was attractive enough to lure a thrill-seeking teenager.

And he had a lifetime's worth of anger and resentment pent up, more than sufficient motivation to kill a woman who had spurned him. And with chilling clarity, Paris realized that just tonight she, too, had rejected him.

"Help will be here soon," she whispered to Rondeau. He didn't respond. He'd slipped deeper into unconsciousness. The policeman was out of commission and she was on her own.

But she wasn't going to wait for Valentino to find her. She was going to find him.

Quickly, she patted down Rondeau's clothing. She didn't know if computer cops were armed or not, but she hoped so. She didn't like guns, was revolted by the whole idea of guns, but she would use one if she had to in order to save her life.

She exhaled her relief when she felt a bulge beneath his jacket. She flipped it back only to discover that the holster clipped to his belt was empty.

Stan must have had the same idea. He was armed.

After murmuring another assurance to Rondeau that he would be all right—which she hoped was true—she cautiously abandoned the false security of hiding behind the desk.

As she left the lobby, she switched off the fluorescent lighting, although it occurred to her that Stan knew the building as well as she, so the darkness was no longer her exclusive advantage.

Actually, she wasn't going to hide any longer. She and Stan were in the building alone together, as they had been hundreds of nights before. She wasn't going to play a childish cat-and-mouse game with him. If she went on the offensive and confronted him, she was confident she could talk to him long enough for rescue to arrive.

The engineering room was empty, so was the men's rest room and the snack room. All the offices, including her own, were deserted. Gradually she made her way to the very back of the building, where there was a large storeroom. The door to it was closed.

The metal knob felt cold in her hand when she grasped it and pushed the door open. She was met by the dank smell of disuse and oldness. The room was cavernous, darker even than the rest of the building. The open doorway cast a wedge of light across the concrete floor, but it was so faint as to be negligible.

Paris hesitated on the threshold until her eyes could adjust to this deeper darkness. When they did she noticed the walk-in closet where Lancy/Marvin's custodial equipment and supplies were stored. The door to it was ajar. Listening intently, she was certain she heard the sound of breathing coming from inside it.

"Stan, this is silly. Come on out. Stop this craziness before anyone else is hurt, including yourself."

Gathering all her courage, she entered the storeroom. "I know you've got a gun now, but I don't believe you'll shoot me. If you had wanted to kill me, you could have on any given night."

Had the breathing inside the closet become more agitated? Or was she imagining it? Or was it an echo of her own breathing she was hearing?

"I know you're angry with me for spurning your affections, but until tonight, I didn't even know you felt that way about me. Let's talk about it."

As she tiptoed across the concrete floor, toward the closet, her ears strained to listen for the merest sound beyond the walls, indicating the arrival of help. Even now, were marksmen taking up positions? Were special tactical officers scaling the exterior walls to get onto the roof? Or had she seen too many action movies?

When she was still a few feet from the partially open closet door, she paused. "Stan?" Reaching far out in front of her, she pushed the door open all the way.

No gunshots shattered the stillness. She reminded herself of what he had done to Janey. Now that he knew he was caught, he would be desperate, conscienceless, capable of anything. The situation required training she didn't have. Dean did.

Dean. In fear and longing, her heart silently cried his name as she took the final step that placed her in the open doorway.

At the sight of Stan, she stared in bafflement.

He was breathing heavily through his nostrils because his mouth was sealed closed with duct tape that had also been used to bind his ankles and wrists. His legs were bent so that his knees were up under his chin, and he had literally been stuffed into the industrial-size stainless-steel sink.

"Stan! What . . ." She was reaching out to tear the tape off his mouth when his eyes, already wide with terror, looked beyond her and stretched even wider.

She spun around.

"Surprise!" John Rondeau said.

But it was Valentino's voice.

chapter thirty-five

"*F*uck it, fuck it," Dean repeated as he punched the rubberized digits on his cell phone.

He was steering his car with one hand and using his cell phone with the other. Several times he had redialed the hot-line number Paris had given him. She didn't answer. He dialed the radio station call-in number repeatedly, but kept getting the standard recording saying that Paris would be with him as soon as possible. He called her cell number, but got her voice mail.

"Why didn't you tell me about Rondeau?" Curtis, who was riding shotgun, was also on his cell phone. He had been put on hold, awaiting more information on John Rondeau.

"You heard it when I did."

The detective had been standing right beside him when Gavin revealed what he knew about Rondeau. It would be difficult to say who had moved first. Dean remembered shoving Curtis out of his way as he ran for the exit.

He had gained a little ground when Curtis shouted over his shoulder for units to be dispatched to the radio station. "SWAT, too! Now, now, move it!"

Dean wasn't going to hang around and see that the sergeant's orders were carried out, and apparently Curtis shared his urgency. They burst through the double doors and clambered down the staircase, taking two or three stairs at a time until they reached the garage level. Dean's car was parked the closest. The way he was pushing it now, they would beat the squad cars to the radio station.

"You failed to tell me Rondeau had accosted your kid in the bathroom."

"It was personal. I thought he was just an asshole."

"An asshole with—" Curtis broke off and listened. "Yeah, yeah," he said into the phone, "what've you got?"

While Curtis was getting the scoop on John Rondeau, Dean dialed Paris's numbers again. When he got the same result, he cursed lavishly and pressed his foot harder against the accelerator.

In what seemed like a direct correlation to his stamping on the gas pedal, the car radio went silent. Since his ears had been attuned to listen for Paris's voice, the sudden static hiss was as jarring as a blood-curdling scream.

The implication splintered his control. Viciously he punched the buttons on his radio dial. All other stations came through loud and clear. The radio wasn't malfunctioning; 101.3 had stopped transmitting.

"The station just went off the air."

Curtis, who'd been absorbed in his conversation, turned his head. "Huh?"

"She's off the air. She's stopped broadcasting."

"Jesus." Then into his cell phone Curtis said, "That'll do for now." He clicked off.

"What? Talk to me," Dean said as he took a corner practically on two wheels.

"No father in the Rondeau household. Ever. They're checking now to see if he died during John's infancy, or if there ever was a Mr. Rondeau. No significant male role model, like an uncle, scoutmaster—"

"I got it, go on."

"Mother worked to support John and his sister, older by one year."

"What have they got to say about him?"

"Nothing. Both are deceased."

Dean whipped his head toward Curtis. "He referred to them in the present tense."

"They were murdered in their home when John was fourteen. He discovered the bodies. Sister had been drowned in the bathtub. Mother had an ice pick shoved straight through her medulla while she was napping."

"Who did it?"

"Unknown. It's a cold case."

"Not anymore." Dean's fingers tensed around the steering wheel.

"We don't know that," Curtis said, reading Dean's thought. "He was interrogated, but never really considered a suspect. Mom and kids were devoted to each other. Mother worked hard to support them. Brother and sister were latch-key kids. Reliant on each other. Very close."

"I'll bet," Dean said tightly. "Real close."

"You're thinking incest?"

"Valentino's behavior is symptomatic. Why wasn't all this in Rondeau's record?"

"The facts are. APD carefully screens every applicant."

"But no one looked beyond the tragedy of his losing his whole family. Nobody was looking for incest. What happened to young John after the double murder?"

"Foster care. Lived with the same couple until he was old enough to go it alone."

"Other children in that home?"

"No."

"Luckily. Did he get along with the foster dad?"

"No record of any problems. They doted on him."

"Especially the wife."

"Don't know," Curtis said. "But they gave him a glowing review. Said he was an ideal child. Respectful. Well behaved."

"A lot of psychopaths are."

"He had an excellent academic record," Curtis continued. "No problems at school. Went to two years of college before he applied to the police academy. Wanted to become a cop—"

"Let me guess. To prevent other women from dying the way his mother and sister had."

"More or less." Curtis glanced at him. "One tiny detail . . ."

"Yeah?"

"When she died, the sister was five months pregnant." Dean risked giving him a questioning look.

"No," Curtis said. "They checked. It wasn't Rondeau's baby."

"I could have told you it wasn't," Dean said grimly. "That's why he killed her."

Curtis's cell phone rang. "Yeah," he snapped.

Dean could see the lights on the broadcast tower. What were they, a mile away? Two? He was tailgating the SWAT van. It had caught up with them several miles back and Dean had let it pass them.

The van was speeding, but Dean willed the driver to move it even faster. They were the two lead vehicles in a motorcade that included several police units. Bringing up the rear was an ambulance. He tried not to think about that.

Curtis ended his call. "They went into Rondeau's apartment. Wasn't much of a place, but he had some fancy photographic equipment. Albums chockfull of dirty pictures. Lots of Janey. Long blond hairs visible on the bedding. He's our guy."

Dean stared straight ahead, clenching his teeth so hard it made his jaw ache.

Curtis checked the pistol he carried in a belt holster, and a second one in an ankle holster. "You got a piece?"

Dean gave him a brusque nod. "I started carrying when he started threatening Paris."

"Well enough, but listen to me. When we get there, you're gonna keep out of the way and let those guys up there do their job." He nodded toward the SWAT van. "You got it?"

"I got it. Sergeant."

The reminder of their respective ranks wasn't lost on Curtis, but he didn't back down. "You go in there half cocked, you'll do something that would fuck up our arrest and he'd walk on some legal bullshit technicality."

"I said I got it," Dean said testily.

"So you're cool?"

"I'm cool."

Curtis slipped the pistol back into his ankle holster, muttering, "Like hell you are."

Dean said, "Right. If he's hurt Paris, I'm going to kill him."

She gaped at John Rondeau's grinning face, but her astonishment was only momentary. Then she reacted swiftly. With all her strength she pushed against his chest, but he shoved her against the metal shelving in the closet even as he fired his pistol at Stan.

The report deafened her. Or maybe it was her own scream.

Rondeau slapped her. "Shut up!" Grabbing her by the hair, he dragged her from the closet and kicked it closed with his foot. Then he pushed her with such impetus that she pitched forward onto the concrete floor.

"Hello, Paris," he said in the chilling voice she now knew well.

"Did you kill him?"

"Crenshaw? I hope so. That was the point of firing a bullet straight into his heart. What a loser. But stronger than he looks. He actually gave me this," he said, indicating the bleeding scalp wound. "He was obliging at first. Showed me how to stop transmission. At gunpoint, of course. Then he made this ridiculous but very valorous attempt to protect you by hitting me with a bottle of Snapple." He was still speaking in Valentino's voice.

"The voice . . . that's quite a trick."

"Isn't it? On the outside chance that any of my cop buddies were also Paris Gibson fans, I didn't want them to identify my voice when I called in."

"You were Valentino from the start." Her mouth was so dry, her tongue was sticking to the roof of her mouth on each word.

"Yes. That takes us back to . . . Let's see." He scratched his cheek with the barrel of his pistol. "Sometime before Maddie Robinson came along."

"So that makes two women you've killed."

He smiled indulgently. "Actually no, Paris."

"More than that?"

"Un-huh."

Keep him talking. The longer he talks, the longer you'll live. "Why did you kill them?"

Resuming his normal voice, he said, "Because they didn't deserve to live."

"They cheated on you like Janey did."

"Janey, Maddie, my sister."

"You murdered your sister?"

"It wasn't *murder*. I meted out justice."

"I see. What happened? What did your sister do to you?"

He laughed pleasantly. "Everything. We did everything to each other. I slept between them, you see. Between her and my mother. Get the picture?" He bobbed his eyebrows up and down.

He'd wanted to shock her and he had, but she tried to keep her expression impassive. She wouldn't give him the satisfaction of seeing her revulsion.

"We kept it all in the family. Our little secret," he said in a stage whisper. "'Don't tell,' Mommy warned us. 'Because if you tell, they'll take you away and lock you up where they keep bad little boys and girls who play with each other's pee pees. Promise? Good. Now suck Mommy's titties and she'll do something extra-special nice to you.'"

Nausea rose in Paris's throat.

He continued in his blasé manner. "But then we begin to grow up. Sis gets an after-school job at a record store. She's there every afternoon instead of at home with me doing what we loved doing best. She starts staying later at the store so she can be with one of the guys who works there. She doesn't have time for me anymore.

"She's never in the mood. She says she's too tired, but it's really because she's fucking him all the time. And Mommy thinks it's grand, the way Sis has fallen in love. 'Isn't it romantic and aren't you happy for her, Johnny?'"

He lapsed into a brooding silence, then his chest heaved as though he were about to cry. "I loved them."

Taking advantage of his preoccupation, Paris glanced toward the door, gauging the distance.

His laughter brought her eyes back up to him.

"Don't even think about it, Paris. This little stroll down memory lane hasn't distracted me from what I came to do."

"If you kill me . . ."

"Oh, I am going to kill you, but it'll be blamed on Stan Crenshaw."

"He's dead."

"As a doornail. I had to kill him. See, when I got here, I found you already dead, choked to death by Crenshaw, who'd been a twisted, sick fucker from the time he was a kid. It's all there in his file, the recipe for a sexually deviant psychopath.

"Anyhow, I sized up the situation and tried to apprehend him. During the ensuing struggle, he managed to get in one good one on my noggin, which, by the way, inspired that little trick I played on you. Clever, wasn't it? You were completely taken in, weren't you?"

"Yes," she admitted.

"Sorry, but I couldn't resist. Especially the bit with your ankle," he said, chuckling. "Where was I? Oh, yes, the way I'll tell it is that I was finally able to subdue Crenshaw and was binding his ankles and hands with duct tape I found in the closet when he attempted to escape. Sadly, I had no choice but to shoot him."

"Very tidy," she said. "But not perfect. The crime scene experts will find discrepancies."

"I've got answers for any questions that could arise."

"Are you sure you've thought of everything, John?"

"I've done my research. I'm a good cop."

"Who preys on women."

"I never 'preyed' on them. My mother and sister were hardly victims. They were my coaches. Every woman I've been with since has benefited from what they taught me, and all were willing partners. I wasn't even particularly attracted to Maddie at first. But she kept after me. Then she was the one who wanted to break if off. Go figure." He shook his head with disbelief.

"And if you're referring to the girls in the Sex Club as prey, you haven't been paying attention. They're whores looking for adventure. I have no inhibitions. They love me," he whispered, waggling his tongue at her.

Again, she swallowed her nausea. "Apparently Janey didn't love you."

"Janey didn't love anybody except Janey. But she loved what I did to her. She was a heartless little bitch who used people's emotions for target practice. And you sympathized with her, Paris. You put her on the radio to complain about me. Do you know why? Because you're exactly like her.

"You play with people's emotions, too. You think you're hot shit. You've got Malloy, even Curtis, panting after you, begging for any crumb of attention you might toss them."

Suddenly he checked his wristwatch. "Speaking of Malloy, I'd better get down to business. You've been off the air for five minutes."

Five minutes? It seemed like an eternity.

"Folks are going to start noticing, and I'm sure your psychologist friend will come charging in here like the cavalry and—"

From the front of the building came what sounded like an explosion of breaking glass, followed by shouting voices and running footsteps.

Paris kicked Rondeau in the kneecap as hard as she could.

His leg buckled beneath him and he screamed in pain.

Paris scrambled to her feet and made a dash for the door.

She didn't hear the gunshot until after she felt the impact of it.

It was more forceful than she could ever have imagined. The searing pain that followed stole her breath and almost caused her to black out instantly, but adrenaline kept her running, through the door, out of his line of sight, where she collapsed.

She tried to cry out and alert the police to her location, but she was unable to utter more than a faint moan. Blackness closed in around her, until the dim corridor elongated and narrowed, like the tunnel of a nightmare.

Dean would be leading the charge. Even Rondeau had said so. She must warn him. She tried to pull herself up, but her limbs had turned to jelly and she wanted badly to throw up. She opened her mouth to call out, but her well-trained, carefully cultivated voice failed her completely.

Rondeau was coming nearer the door. She could hear his groans of pain as he hopped across the cement floor of the storeroom. Soon he would reach the hallway. He would have the advantage over anyone coming around the blind corner at the end of it.

"Dean," she croaked. Once more she tried to stand. She made it as far as her knees, but she swayed unsteadily, then collapsed against the wall, hard. The resultant pain was like a branding iron burning through flesh, all the way to the bone. She left a blood trail on the wall as she sank to the floor.

Though her ears were ringing, she could tell that the shouting voices were coming closer. Flashlight beams crazily crisscrossed on the walls at the end of the hallway.

But hearing another sound, she turned just as Rondeau appeared in the storeroom doorway. He grunted with pain as he braced himself against the doorjamb. She took satisfaction from the odd angle at which his right leg was bent. His face was bathed in sweat and twisted into an ugly mask of rage as he glared down at her.

"You're just like them," he said. "I've got to kill you."

"Freeze!" The shout ricocheted off the walls like the beams of the flashlights.

But Rondeau didn't heed the warning. He raised his pistol and aimed it directly at her.

The barrage of gunfire was deafening and filled the corridor with smoke.

As she fell forward, Paris wondered vaguely if she was just losing consciousness, or dying.

chapter thirty-six

"Who actually brought him down?"

"Call it a group effort. Rondeau gave us no choice. Several of us hit him."

Paris leaned back against the hospital bed pillow, relieved by Curtis's answer to her question. She wouldn't have wanted Dean to carry the burden of taking John Rondeau's life. She learned later that he'd been the first one into the hallway, as she had known he would be. But Curtis and several SWAT officers were there, too. Any of the bullets fired at Rondeau could have been the fatal one.

This morning Curtis was looking even spiffier than usual, as though he had dressed up to pay her this visit. He was wearing a gray western-cut suit. His boots had an extra sheen. She could smell cologne. He had brought her a box of Godiva chocolates.

Yet his demeanor was all business. "Rondeau was computer savvy enough to learn how to reroute calls," he told her. "Our guys finally traced that last call to a cell phone. But he had planned on that, too. The phone was unregistered. A throwaway. That part of it was easy for him."

"He could change his voice at will, too. It was eerie."

Sometimes minutes would pass without her thinking of Rondeau and that agonizing period of time with him in the storeroom. Then, without warning, a recollection would thrust itself into her consciousness and she would be forced to relive the terrifying moments.

When she described this phenomenon to Dean, he assured her that each day the recollections would become less frequent and her memory would dim a bit more. Although she would never entirely forget the experience, it would sink into her subconscious. His counsel had a footnote: He would see to it that she lived in the present, and for the future, not linger in the past.

"Rondeau wanted to move to CIB," Curtis was saying. "He had already approached me about it. Said he wanted to work in the child abuse unit."

"Where he would have unlimited access to child pornography."

Curtis nodded, his disgust plain. "He went to the radio station that night to fulfill his personal agenda, and at the same time distinguish himself as a police officer by delivering Valentino.

"With you and Crenshaw dead, he might have pulled it off. Janey's body rendered none of the perp's DNA. Apparently he'd learned about an agent that served that purpose in a homicide case in Dallas." He shook his head with chagrin. "His police work taught him well."

"About Stan, have you received any updates on his condition?" she asked.

"Elevated to fair."

Miraculously Stan had survived the gunshot to his chest and the delicate surgery that had removed the bullet. He'd had a collapsed lung and extensive tissue damage, but he would survive. When he was stable enough to be moved, Wilkins Crenshaw had flown him by private jet to Atlanta.

"I asked his uncle to call me as soon as Stan is able to

talk on the phone," she said. "I want to apologize."

"I'm sure he won't hold a grudge against you. He'll be too grateful to be alive."

"Rondeau told me he had shot Stan straight through the heart."

"If that's where he was aiming, he should've spent more time at the practice range," Curtis said with a grim smile. "Lucky for you he didn't."

She'd been told that her blood loss was significant because the bullet had entered her back just below her shoulder socket and had gone straight through. She would bear an ugly scar and her scorching tennis serve was a thing of the past, but she was alive.

If the bullet had cut a path a few inches lower, her life would have been over. Dean had advised her not to dwell on that either, although it was the common reaction of a survivor.

"Don't examine the reasons for your life being spared, Paris. To do so is futile. You could never arrive at an answer. Just be grateful you're here. I am," he'd said, his voice made husky by emotion.

Curtis brought her back to their conversation by saying that the incestuous relationships of Rondeau's boyhood had left him angry. "I don't think even he knew how angry he was," he said. "He'd learned to hide it well, but he harbored a deep-seated rage against women because of what an abusive mother had done to him."

"Dean explained it to me."

"I'm paraphrasing him," Curtis admitted. After a beat, he asked if she'd seen that morning's newspaper. "Judge Kemp is using Janey's murder as part of his campaign platform."

"That goes beyond tasteless."

"Some people," the detective snuffled with contempt.

"What's going to happen to Brad Armstrong?" she asked. "Will he go to prison?"

"He has to face the aggravated-sexual-assault charge, which carries a stiff sentence if he's convicted. But Melissa Hatcher admitted that she went with him willingly and engaged in numerous acts before she called a halt. He might plead to a lesser charge in exchange for a lighter sentence, but I predict that he'll serve time. Hopefully he'll use that time to get himself straightened out."

"I wonder if his wife will stay with him." Her eyes strayed to the floral arrangement Toni Armstrong had sent.

"Remains to be seen," Curtis said. "But if I was a gambling man, I'd say yes." They were quiet for a moment, then he slapped his thighs and, with a sigh, stood. "I should shove off and let you rest."

She laughed. "I've rested until I'm blue in the face. I can't wait to be released."

"Anxious to get back to work?"

"By next week I hope."

"Your fans will be happy. So will the hospital staff. They said every flower within a hundred-mile radius is in the main lobby downstairs."

"Dean wheeled me down there yesterday to see them. People have been exceptionally kind."

"Speaking for myself, I've missed listening to you." His entire scalp flushed a bright pink as he added, "You're a class act, Paris."

"Thank you. So are you, Sergeant Curtis."

A bit awkwardly, he reached for her right hand and gave it only one swift shake before releasing it. "I'm sure I'll be seeing you around. I mean, now that you and Malloy . . ." He let the sentence trail off.

She smiled. "Yes, I'm sure I'll be seeing you around."

*   *   *

Dean arrived just as she was adding the finishing touches to her makeup.

"Paris?"

"In here," she called from the small bathroom. He moved in behind her and their eyes met in the mirror above the basin. "How do I look?"

"Luscious."

She frowned dubiously at her reflection. "Hair styling isn't easy to accomplish one-handed. At least it's my left one that's out of commission."

He reached for her right hand, the back of which was bruised from the IV port that had been removed only the day before. He kissed the discolored spot. "To me you look fantastic."

"Your opinion definitely counts." She turned to face him, but when he only pecked her lips, she looked up at him with disappointment.

"I don't want to hurt you," he explained, indicating her bandaged arm and sling.

"I won't break."

With her right hand, she pulled his head down and gave him a real kiss, which he responded to in kind. They kissed with sexual passion, as well as with the desperation of knowing that they'd almost lost each other for the second time.

When they pulled apart, she said, "I received a get-well card from Liz Douglas. Very gracious of her under the circumstances."

"She's a lady. There was only one thing wrong with her. She wasn't you."

They kissed again, then, leaving his lips against hers, he whispered, "When we get home . . ."

"Um-huh?"

"Can we go straight to bed?"

"Will you do—"

"Everything. We're gonna do everything." He gave her a hard, quick kiss, then said, "Let's get out of here."

They gathered the last of her personal things and placed them in a tote bag. She put on her sunglasses. He ordered her into the hospital-mandated wheelchair and pushed her to the elevator.

As they were riding down to the ground floor, she said, "I expected Gavin to be with you."

"He sends his regards, but he left for Houston this morning to spend the weekend with Pat. He hopes to patch things up with her. Maybe even offer an olive branch to her husband."

"Good for him."

"He didn't fool me."

"You don't believe he's sincere?"

"Oh, he's sincere about setting things right with them. But he chose to go this particular weekend so we'd have time alone." As the elevator doors slid open, he leaned down and whispered directly into her ear, "I owe him."

Returning his grin, she said, "So do I."

"You are going to marry me, aren't you?"

Feigning affront, she said, "I wouldn't consent to a honeymoon otherwise."

"Gavin will be glad. He wants to make friends at his new school, and he told me what an advantage it would be to have a stepmom who was famous and also a total fox."

"He thinks I'm a fox?"

"Cool, too. You've got his unqualified approval."

"It's nice to be wanted."

Humor aside, Dean stepped around to the front of her chair and leaned down until his face was level with hers. "I want you."

They had an audience comprised of hospital staff and visitors in the lobby. Unmindful of them, he reached for her hand again and this time pressed her palm to his lips. They exchanged a look rife with meaning and implication, then he let go of her hand and said, "Ready?"

"Ready."

"Be forewarned, Paris. You'll be running a gauntlet. There are cameras galore outside that door. Every news outlet from Dallas to Houston to El Paso has a reporter and a photographer here to cover your hospital release. You're big news."

"I know."

"And that's okay?"

"It's okay. In fact"—she removed her sunglasses and smiled up at him—"it's time I came out into the light."

Grinning, he pushed the wheelchair toward the automatic doors. They slid open and camera strobes began to flash.

Paris didn't flinch.

acknowledgments

I really hate having to ask people for help and information. An autographed copy of the book and an acknowledgment in the back of it seem insufficient thanks for all the trouble these professionals went to on my behalf.

Public Information Specialist C, Laura Albrecht of the Austin Police Department never lost patience with me, even when I continued calling her with just "one more question." She opened doors that would ordinarily have been closed. Thanks also to the detectives of the Centralized Investigative Bureau, who all too frequently go unrewarded and unrecognized for the difficult job they perform. They were cordial and informative even after I explained to them that there was a rotten cop in my story.

In my next life, I want to be a drive-time deejay like Bill Kinder of KSCS-FM. Unlike me, he gets to talk to his fans every weekday. They call in by the hundreds. What a kick! He made it look easy to do a dozen tasks at once. He never broke stride, not even to answer my questions. If I got the radio technology all wrong, it's no fault of his.

A few unfortunates work with me on a daily basis. My agent, Maria Carvainis, deserves more gratitude than I'll ever be able to express. Amie Gray's middle name should be Britannica for her diligent fact checking and her gleaning of information on the most outlandish topics. I also wish to thank Sharon Hubler for the years that she streamlined my life. Without her I would often have been at the wrong place at the wrong time, doing the wrong thing. I wish her much happiness in her new life.

And to the dear man who lives with me: Michael, my thanks and my love, always.

Sandra Brown
1 April 2003

SIMON AND SCHUSTER

PROUDLY PRESENTS

white hot

SANDRA BROWN

Coming in hardcover from Simon and Schuster
on August 17

Turn the page for a preview of
WHITE HOT

The highway was barely recognizable. Countless times, Sayre Lynch had driven this stretch of road between New Orleans International Airport and Destiny. But traveling it today was like doing so for the first time.

In the name of progress, landmarks that had made the area distinct had been obscured or obliterated. Rural Louisiana's charm had been sacrificed to gaudy commercialism. Little that was quaint or picturesque had survived the onslaught. She could have been in Anywhere, USA.

Fast food franchises now occupied the spots where once had been mom and pop cafes. Homemade meat pies and muffaletta sandwiches had been replaced with buckets of wings and Extra Value Meals. Hand-painted signs had given way to neon. Menus scribbled daily on chalkboards had been supplanted by disembodied voices at drive-through windows.

During the ten years she had been away, trees draped with Spanish moss had been bulldozed to allow for additional highway construction. This expansion had diminished the vastness and mystery of the swamps that flanked the road. The dense marshes were now ribboned with entrance and exit ramps jammed with semis and minivans.

Until now Sayre hadn't realized the depth of her home-sickness. But these substantial changes in the landscape made her nostalgic for the way things had been. She longed for the mingled aromas of cayenne and file'. She would like to hear again the patois of the people who served up Cajun dishes that took more than three minutes to prepare.

While superhighways made for faster travel, she wished for the roadways she had known, the ones lined with trees that grew so close to it the branches over-lapped to cover it like a canopy and cast lacy patterns of shadow on the asphalt.

She longed for the times she could drive with the win-dows down and rather than choking on motor exhaust, inhale in the soft air that was perfumed with honeysuck-le and magnolia, and the seminal scent of the swamp.

The changes that had come about in the past decade were jarring to her senses and an affront to her memories of the place in which she'd grown up. But then, she sup-posed that the changes in herself were equally as drastic, although perhaps not as apparent.

The last time she'd driven this road, she'd been travel-ing in the opposite direction, away from Destiny. That day, the farther she got from home, the lighter she felt, as though she were molting layers of negativity along the way. Today she was returning, and her dread was as heavy as chain mail.

Homesickness for the area, no matter how acute, would never have brought her back. Only her brother Danny's death could have compelled her to return. Apparently he had withstood Huff and Chris for as long as he could, and had escaped them in the only manner he'd felt was open to him.

Fittingly, as she approached the outskirts of Destiny, she saw the smokestacks first. They jutted belligerently above the town, large and black and ugly. Smoke billowed from them today as on every other day of the year. It would have been too costly and inefficient to have shutdown the furnaces, even in observance of Danny's demise. Knowing Huff, it probably hadn't even occurred to him to make this concession to his youngest child.

The billboard marking the city limit read Welcome to Destiny, Home of Hoyle Enterprises. *As though that's something to boast*, she thought. Quite the contrary. Iron pipe casting had made Huff rich, but it was a blood-stained wealth.

She navigated the streets of town which she had first explored on bicycle. Later she'd learned to drive on them. Then as a teen she had cruised them with her friends, looking for action, boys, and whatever amusements they could scare up.

While still a block away from the First United Methodist Church, she heard the organ music. The pipe organ had been a gift to the church from her mother, Laurel Lynch Hoyle. It bore a brass plaque in her memory. It was the small congregation's pride and joy, being the only pipe organ in Destiny. None of the Catholic churches had one, and Destiny was predominantly Catholic. Her mother's gift had been generous and sincere, but it was yet another symbol of how the Hoyles lorded over their town and everyone in it and refused to be outdone.

How heartbreaking that the organ was playing a dirge for one of Laurel Hoyle's children who had died fifty years too soon, and by his own hand.

Sayre had received the news Sunday afternoon upon returning to her office from a meeting with a client. Ordinarily she wouldn't have worked on a Sunday, but that was the only day this particular client was free for an appointment. Julia Miller had recently celebrated her fifth year as Sayre's assistant. She wouldn't let Sayre work on a weekend without working herself. While Sayre was with the client, Julia had been catching up on paperwork.

When Sayre returned, Julia passed her a pink memo slip. "This gentleman has called three times, Ms. Lynch. I wouldn't give him your cell number, although he demanded it."

Sayre had glanced at the area code, then wadded up the memo and tossed it into the wastepaper basket. "I don't wish to speak to anyone in my family."

"He's not family. He says he works for the family. It's imperative that he reach you as soon as possible."

"I won't talk to anybody who works for my family either. Any other messages? By any chance has Mr. Taylor called? He promised those valances by tomorrow."

"It's your brother," Julia had blurted out. "He's dead."

Sayre stopped short of her private office. For a long moment she stared through the wall of windows toward the Golden Gate bridge. Only the very tops of the orange supports were visible above a solid blanket of fog. The water in the bay looked gray, cold, and angry. Foreboding.

Without turning around, she asked, "Which one?"

"Which—"

"Brother."

"Danny."

Danny who had called her twice in the last several days. Danny's, whose calls she had refused to take.

Sayre turned to face her assistant, who was regarding her sympathetically. She said gently, "Your brother Danny died earlier today, Sayre. I thought you should be told in person, not over a cell phone."

Sayre had released a long breath through her mouth. "How?"

"I think you should speak with this Mr. Merchant."

"Julia, please. How did Danny die?"

Gently she said, "It appears he killed himself. I'm sorry." Then after a moment, she added, "That's all the information Mr. Merchant would give me."

Sayre had then retreated to her private office and closed the door. She heard the phone in the anteroom ring several times, but Julia didn't put the calls through, realizing that she needed time alone to assimilate the news.

Had Danny been calling to tell her goodbye? If so, how would she live with the guilt of refusing to speak to him?

After about an hour, Julia knocked tentatively on the door. "Come in." When Julia stepped inside, Sayre said, "There's no point in your staying, Julia. Go home. I'll be fine."

The assistant laid a sheet of paper on her desk. "I've still got work to do. Buzz me if you need me. Can I bring you anything?"

Sayre shook her head no. Julia withdrew and closed the door. On the sheet of paper she'd brought in she'd written down the time and place of the funeral. Tuesday morning, eleven o'clock.

Sayre hadn't been surprised that it was scheduled so soon. Huff always acted with dispatch. He and Chris would be impatient to put this behind them, to bury Danny and get on with their lives as soon as possible.

However, the timeliness of the funeral had probably worked to her advantage, too. She hadn't had time for a lengthy internal debate on whether or not to attend. She couldn't languish in indecision, but had been forced to make up her mind quickly.

Yesterday morning she'd caught a flight to New Orleans via Dallas/Fort Worth and had arrived in the late afternoon. She'd taken a walk through the French Quarter, eaten dinner at a gumbo shop, then spent the night at the Windsor Court.

For all the comfort the luxury hotel afforded, she'd had a virtually sleepless night. She did not want to go back to Destiny. She *did not*. Silly as it was, she feared walking into some kind of snare that would trap her there, keep her in Huff's clutches forever.

Daybreak hadn't lessened her dread. She'd gotten up, dressed for the funeral, and set out for Destiny, planning to arrive just in time for the service and to leave immediately thereafter.

The church parking lot was already overflowing into the surrounding neighborhood streets. She had to park several blocks away from the picture book church with the stained glass windows and its tall white steeple. Just as she stepped onto the columned porch, the bell chimed the hour of eleven.

The vestibule was cool compared to outdoors, but Sayre noticed that many in the sanctuary were waving paper fans to supplement the inadequate air conditioning. As she slipped into the back row, the choir finished singing the opening hymn and the pastor stepped up to the pulpit.

While everyone else bowed their heads for prayer, Sayre looked at the casket in front of the chancel rail. It was simple, silver, and sealed. She was glad of that. She didn't think she could bear her last image of Danny to be his lying like a wax doll in a satin lined coffin. To prevent thoughts of that, she concentrated on the elegant purity of the arrangement of white calla lilies on top of the casket.

She couldn't see either Huff or Chris for the crowd, but she supposed they were seated in the front row pew, looking appropriately bereaved. The hypocrisy of it all made her nauseous.

She was named among the surviving family members. "A sister, Sayre Hoyle of San Francisco," the minister intoned.

She wanted to stand up and shout that Hoyle was no longer her name. After her second divorce, she had begun using her middle name, which had been her mother's maiden name. She'd had her name legally changed to Lynch. That was the name on her college degree, her business stationery, her California driver's licence, and her passport.

She wasn't a Hoyle any longer, but she had no doubt that whoever had supplied the minister with the information had intentionally given him the incorrect name.

The homily was straight out of a how-to clerical textbook, delivered by a shiny-faced minister who looked too young to vote. His remarks were directed toward mankind in general. There was very little mention of

Danny as an individual, nothing poignant or personal, which seemed particularly sad since his own sister had refused his telephone call.

As the service concluded with the singing of "Amazing Grace," there were sniffles among the congregation. The pall bearers were Chris, a fair-haired man she didn't know, and four others whom she recognized as executives of Hoyle Enterprises. They carried the casket up the center aisle of the church.

It was slow-going, giving her time to study her brother. He was as trim and handsome as ever, with the suavity of a 1930s matinee idol. The only thing missing was a thin mustache. His hair was still as black as a raven's wing, but he was wearing it shorter than he used to. It was spiked up in front with gel, a rather hip look for a man in his late thirties, but nonetheless the style suited Chris. His eyes were disconcerting because the pupils were indistinguishable from the dark irises.

Huff followed the casket. Even on this occasion he carried himself with an air of superiority. His shoulders were back, his head high. Each footstep was firmly planted, as though he was a conqueror with the sovereign right to claim the ground beneath him.

His lips were set in the hard, thin, resolute line that she remembered well. His eyes glittered like the black bead eyes of a stuffed toy. They were dry and clear; he hadn't cried for Danny. Since she'd last seen him, his hair had turned from salt-and-pepper to solid white, but he still wore it in a flat-top of military preciseness. He had put on a few pounds around his mid-section but appeared as robust as she remembered.

Fortunately neither Chris nor Huff saw her.

To avoid the crowd and risk being recognized, she slipped out a side door of the sanctuary. Her car was last in the procession to the cemetery. She parked quite a distance from the tent that had been set up over the newly dug grave.

In somber groups and singly, people made their way up the slight rise for the grave site service. For the most part, they were dressed in their Sunday best, although armholes had sweat rings and hatbands were stained with perspiration. They walked in shoes that were too tight from infrequent wear.

Sayre recognized and remembered many of these people by name. They were townsfolk who had lived in Destiny all their lives. Some owned small businesses, but most worked for the Hoyles in one capacity or another.

She spotted several faculty members from the public school system. Her mother's fondest desire had been to send her children to the most exclusive private schools in the South, but Huff had been adamant. He wanted them to grow up tough and under his tutelage.

Whenever the argument recurred, he would say, "A sissy prep school isn't the place to learn about life and how to muscle your way through it." Like all their arguments, her mother had conceded with a relinquishing sigh.

Sayre remained in her car with the motor idling. The service was mercifully brief. As soon as it concluded, the crowd dispersed and returned to their cars, making an effort to conceal their haste.

Huff and Chris were the last to leave the tent after shaking hands with the minister. Sayre watched them make their way to the waiting limousine provided by

Weir's Funeral Home. Amazingly the ancient Mr. Weir was still plying his trade when he was way past due going to his own reward.

He opened the limo door for Chris and Huff, then stood at a discreet distance while they conducted a short conversation with the blond-haired pall bearer. When the conversation concluded, they climbed into the limo, the man waved them off, Mr. Weir got behind the wheel and chauffeured them away. Sayre was glad to see them go.

She waited another ten minutes, until the last of the mourners had left. Only then did she kill her engine and get out of her car.

"I've been asked by your family to escort you to the house for the wake."

Startled, she spun around so quickly that her shoes sent up a shower of dusty gravel.

He was leaning against the rear bumper of her car. He'd taken off his suit jacket and folded it over his arm. His necktie was askew, and the collar button of his shirt was undone, shirt sleeves rolled up to his elbows. He'd put on a pair of dark sunglasses.

"I'm Beck Merchant."

"I guessed."

She had only seen his name in print and had wondered if he used the French pronunciation. He didn't. It was the standard pronunciation, and his appearance was as American as apple pie, from his dark blond hair, to his easy smile and straight teeth, to the Ralph Lauren cut of his trousers.

Giving no heed to her ungracious tone, he said, "Pleased to meet you, Ms. Hoyle."

"Lynch."

"I stand corrected." He spoke with utmost courtesy, but his smile mocked her.

"Does delivering messages fall into your job description? I thought you were their lawyer," she said.

"Lawyer, errand boy—"

"Henchman."

He laid his hand over his heart and flashed an even wider grin. "You give me far too much credit."

"I doubt it." She slammed shut her car door. "You've extended their invitation. Tell them I decline. Now, I would appreciate some time alone to say goodbye to Danny." She turned and headed up the rise.

"Take your time. I'll wait for you."

She came back around. "I'm not going to their damn wake. As soon as I'm done here, I'm returning to New Orleans and catching a flight back to San Francisco."

"You could do that. Or you could do the decent thing and attend your brother's wake. Then later this evening, Hoyle Enterprises's corporate jet could whisk you back to San Francisco without all the hassle of commercial flight."

"I can charter my own jet."

"Even better."

She'd walked right into that one and hated herself for it. She had been back in Destiny barely an hour, and already she was reverting to old habits. But she had learned how to recognize the traps and avoid them.

"No thank you. Goodbye, Mr. Merchant." Once again started up the rise toward the grave.

"Do you believe Danny killed himself?"

Of all the things he could have said, she didn't expect that. She turned to face him again. He was no longer leaning indolently against the car fender, but had taken a few steps toward her as though not only to hear her answer but to gauge her reaction to his surprising question.

"Don't you?" she asked.

"Doesn't matter what I believe," he said. "It's the sheriff's office that's questioning the suicide."

Visit
❖ **Pocket Books** ❖
online at

....

www.SimonSays.com

....

Keep up on the latest new
releases from your favorite
authors, as well as author
appearances, news, chats,
special offers and more.

SIMON & SCHUSTER
A VIACOM COMPANY
www.SimonSays.com

Pocket
Books

Praise for the novels of
Karen Harper

"Harper…has a fantastic flair for creating and
sustaining suspense.… [The] deft knitting of fact and
fiction enables Harper to describe everything from
wilderness survival to supernatural lore with the kind
of detail that convinces readers anything is possible."
—*Publishers Weekly* on *The Falls*

"Her deft juxtaposition of the cast of creepy
characters and a small-town setting…
makes for a haunting read."
—*Publishers Weekly* on *The Stone Forest*

"A glimpse into the lives of the modern-day Amish…
Harper's choice of setting and lifestyle for her
heartwarming characters adds a fresh twist."
—*Publishers Weekly* on *Down to the Bone*

"While the story moves quickly, the mystery builds
slowly and hooks readers, as Harper gradually
introduces one clue or suspicion after another.
The characters are well drawn; readers suspect
nearly everyone."
—*School Library Journal* on *Down to the Bone*

"Mystery, intrigue, love—it's all here.
Don't miss this fascinating and exciting story."
—*Rendezvous* on *Shaker Run*

"With a wonderful feel of suspense and a
well-plotted story, Ms. Harper delivers a
fabulously frightening late night read."
—*Romantic Times* on *The Stone Forest*

"There are enough crimes and suspects in this
action-filled romance to satisfy everyone."
—*Ohioana Quarterly* on *Down to the Bone*

"Exciting, dramatic and spine-tingling."
—*Rendezvous* on *The Baby Farm*

Also by KAREN HARPER

THE FALLS
THE STONE FOREST
DOWN TO THE BONE
THE BABY FARM
DARK ROAD HOME

Watch for the newest novel of romantic suspense from
KAREN HARPER

DARK HARVEST

Coming June 2004

KAREN
HARPER
SHAKER RUN

MIRA®

ISBN 0-7783-2117-7

SHAKER RUN

Copyright © 2001 by Karen Harper.

All rights reserved. Except for use in any review, the reproduction or utilization of this work in whole or in part in any form by any electronic, mechanical or other means, now known or hereafter invented, including xerography, photocopying and recording, or in any information storage or retrieval system, is forbidden without the written permission of the publisher, MIRA Books, 225 Duncan Mill Road, Don Mills, Ontario, Canada M3B 3K9.

All characters in this book have no existence outside the imagination of the author and have no relation whatsoever to anyone bearing the same name or names. They are not even distantly inspired by any individual known or unknown to the author, and all incidents are pure invention.

MIRA and the Star Colophon are trademarks used under license and registered in Australia, New Zealand, Philippines, United States Patent and Trademark Office and in other countries.

www.MIRABooks.com

Printed in U.S.A.

This book is dedicated to all the hardworking volunteers, docents and guides who keep America's many historical villages alive.

Especially to Ellen Maurer, administrator of the Milan, Ohio, Historical Museum, as well as to Lois Wolf and the staff there.

1

O Rose, thou art sick.
The invisible worm
That flies in the night,
In the howling storm,

Has found out thy bed
Of crimson Joy,
And his dark secret love
Does thy life destroy.

—William Blake
"The Sick Rose"

Toledo, Ohio
Saturday, September 25, 1999

The mansion and grounds of Groveland were awash
with lights, roses and people, most of them in appropriate attire of tuxedos and evening gowns, though
Sarah had seen some of the younger set in outrageous
jeweled jeans. But then, from a generation that
thought tattoos, branding and body piercing were perfectly *de rigueur*, what was one to expect? At least
they had all come with generous donations for the
Shelter for Abused Women, which would profit from
this charity event.

People seemed to be everywhere, even about the
house, though that was a risk the seventy-five-year-

old Sarah Denbigh was willing to take to help a good cause. Her husband Palmer might be turning over in his grave, but she really couldn't abide police officers or security people lurking about—though an off-duty officer did control the traffic out on River Road. At least it was a great help to have Kate about, not only to keep the massive rose beds in late bloom, but to help tonight. Sarah had given up asking her own two children to set foot here, since they were furious she insisted on supporting so many charities with "their" money. The "Denbigh heritage," as Palmer, Jr. so snidely put it.

"Oh, Kate, there you are!" Sarah called to her rosarian, who had become her dear friend, too. A tall, willowy blond with a darling page-boy haircut that softened a classic face of wide-set, smoky blue eyes, elegant nose, and full mouth, Kate was the very best "refugee" Sarah had ever taken in. Imagine her being held responsible for something her husband had done. He'd absconded with a fortune and had left Kate to shoulder the blame. It had shaken Kate deeply but hadn't broken her, Sarah thought with deep pride and affection.

The thirty-six-year-old woman looked stunning in the only dressy gown she hadn't sold to consignment shops, one in simple black satin with a deep square neckline and long sleeves, though she refused to wear the pearls Sarah had offered to lend her tonight. Despite Kate's dire financial straits, Sarah knew her friend detested anything that smacked of charity. A modest person, perhaps Kate would never grasp the priceless gift of companionship she had given an old woman deeply disappointed in her own daughter.

"The silent auction for the bouquets and rosebushes

seems to be going well,'' Kate reported, out of breath as if she'd just taken a run through the acres of gardens.

Until two years ago, Katherine Browne Marburn and her husband, Mike, had been very much on the social scene here in Toledo—flashy, new fish in the small, old pond, in which the Denbighs and others had swum circumspectly for years. Michael Marburn, with his business acumen and Irish good looks, had been a prominent broker and investor of other people's money. A widower with one daughter, Mike had brought his second wife, Kate, into his burgeoning business as a sort of silent partner, mostly because she was hardly silent. Kate had many prominent contacts from her small business designing flower gardens.

Kate and Mike's companies merged like a David and Goliath into the now-infamous Marburn Securities, though Kate, who knew next to nothing about brokerage or investments, spent most of her time mothering her stepdaughter, Erin, breeding roses and entertaining for Mike. Until everything exploded in her face.

Before Mike could be arrested for illegally selling millions of dollars in promissory notes to investors, he was evidently tipped off. About to be charged with fraud, by federal prosecutors and the Securities and Exchange Commission, for what amounted to swindling, he disappeared with millions of dollars, leaving his wife to take the brunt of public outrage. He'd also left a suicide note, but a body was never found, and Kate had testified she could not believe Mike would kill himself. After a year, she'd divorced him *in absentia* for desertion.

"I'd love for Erin to see the way we've decorated tonight," Kate was saying. Erin was a freshman at Ohio University in the southern part of the state; she'd only been gone a little over a month, and both Kate and Sarah missed her greatly. "You realize," Kate continued, "not only the rose swags and arrangements, but the Shaker rocker and set of oval boxes are drawing fabulous bids."

"Mmm, well, you know what authentic Shaker furniture and memorabilia are going for these days," Sarah said, patting Kate's arm. "Fortunately, Palmer and I got into collecting before prices went sky-high. We started about the same time the Rockefellers collected Shaker, but long before several other wealthy Americans began buying up a lot of it, cornering the market so items are getting to be like rare gems— Oh, dear, what's going on over there?"

Kate spun around to glance in the same direction. "It looks as if someone's fallen or jumped in the fountain with the floating petals," she observed. Her eyes were much sharper than Sarah's, even with these new glasses.

"Probably someone," Kate went on, "with so much champagne in him he thought he could walk on water. I'll see to it and call Security if I need to."

"That's all right, dear. I know you don't like to get in the midst of brouhahas anymore, or rely on the police, so—"

"No, Sarah, it's all right," Kate insisted, and hurried toward the melee, rolling up her long sleeves as she went, as if she were going to spray some sort of garden pest.

Kate had become what Sarah's own daughter Varina refused to be. Varina as ringleader with her younger brother Palmer in tow thought the Denbigh fortune should be their due before they'd done one thing to earn it, or before Sarah was cold in the grave. And that is why she'd changed her will to make Kate an heir, along with the charities close to Sarah's heart—not that she'd cut her own children off.

Sarah shook her head as she recalled a painful, unfortunate accident last month, but it had taught her a lesson, too. She'd been clipping long-stemmed tea roses for one of her bouquets and trying to talk to her daughter on the cell phone at the same time. Juggling things, she'd pressed the phone between her neck and shoulder.

"Varina, I know you and Brad lead busy lives," Sarah had said, "but I would so like for you to come meet these people at dinner here tomorrow. And since you asked, yes, I suppose a lot of the conversation will be about Shaker antiques but—ah-ah!"

Sarah dropped her armful of roses and stared aghast at the deep slice she'd made on her own left index finger. It didn't look bad at first, but as the pain increased, crimson blood filled, then spilled from, the long cut.

"Mother? What now?" Varina had asked over the phone Sarah still had propped to her ear. With her uncut hand, Sarah grabbed the receiver.

"I—I've cut myself with the rose shears. Deeply."

"Ugh, I hate blood. For heaven's sake, tell the staff to call your doctor or maybe 911. Or have that assistant of yours, Saint Kate of the Catastrophe, get help. I can't believe you cut yourself after years of doing that, especially after you fell and hit your head a while back. You've got to be careful—with yourself—and others," she scolded ominously, though Sarah was no longer listening to a word she said.

Kate must have seen what happened from across the gardens, for she came running. She gasped at the blood and immediately wrapped Sarah's finger in her own shirttail.

"Getting an ER squad can take a while out here, and they'd only make you go in for stitches," Kate said. Her eyes filled with tears but her voice was steady. With one hand she put pressure on the base of the cut finger and elevated Sarah's arm until it yanked the shirt up. "I can drive you right to the hospital, Sarah. Let me cut off this part of my shirt. Or is someone on the line bringing help already?" she added as she pried the phone from Sarah's grip.

"No," Sarah had said calmly, despite her growing pain and panic at the throbbing, slippery finger. "No one who wants to help."

"Let me know if you feel faint or dizzy," Kate said, cutting the bottom of her shirt away with the offending shears, then hustling Sarah off, even as her maid and the gardener came running to see what was wrong.

"I'm fine. Just fine with Kate here," Sarah called to them in a quavering voice.

It was only later that Sarah realized Varina had heard all that over the phone. Blood may be thicker than water, but a friend can be better than a daughter, Sarah had told herself then. Kate's just being here was hands-on healing. And Sarah knew she'd done the same for Kate when she had been cut to the core by Mike's desertion and betrayal, and everyone's baying for her blood.

Sarah shook her head to snap her attention back to

the party. Kate had the contretemps at the fountain under control, but Sarah noted that the lights were on in her bedroom suite overlooking this patio and the sweep of gardens at the back of the house. That shouldn't be. People going upstairs to the powder room might think they could go in the bedroom, too. Or maybe someone had wandered in already. Besides, she had to visit the powder room herself, so she'd just pop up and be sure her private suite remained just that.

Chatting with a few others, shaking several hands along the way, Sarah slipped out of the crowd, went in the kitchen door and then up the servants' back stairs. Along the second-story hall, hung with her husband's old English hunt lithographs, Sarah hurried toward her rooms. Her eyes caught her full-length reflection in the long mirror at the end of the corridor.

It always shocked her to see that she had aged so much. How foolish to still expect that lithe, blond debutante she'd been when Palmer first came calling, instead of this delicate, silver-haired doyenne with a beginning widow's hump her doctor insisted on calling osteoporosis. These days that woman in the mirror was truly happier in the company of her heirloom flowers and antique Shaker furniture than with parties and people, just like dear Kate.

The door to her room was closed, so perhaps she'd been wrong about someone being up here. Or else they'd gone and had closed it on their way out.

Before Sarah entered her sitting room, she pictured it abloom with flowered wallpaper to echo the bounteous bouquets of fragrance and extravagant color. Two of her larger pieces of vintage Shaker furniture sat there, a double work desk and a sturdy pine-andfruitwood blanket box she used as an end table next to the sofa. Also, before the large windows, sat two rockers. Kate loved the simple sturdiness of the Shaker style—something Varina always called primitive and plain.

Traversing the soft hall carpet, Sarah swept open the door to her sitting room and gasped. Two strangers, dressed in baggy dark coveralls and with baseball caps pulled low, were busy packing into wooden wine crates two of her smallest but most unique Shaker pieces: a child's rocker and a washstand. No, maybe they were unpacking them.

For one stunning moment, they all froze and stared agape at one another.

Muted orchestra music wafted in, merging with the distant buzz of people's voices. "Whatever do you think you're doing?" Sarah got out.

"Grab her," one barked.

A woman?

Sarah tried to run. Flicking the light switch off to plunge them into darkness, she got as far as the hall, when one of them grabbed her arm and yanked her back. Her glasses flew off and she spun into the dark sitting room. She fell and hit her head hard on something. She touched her hand to her head and felt warm, thick wetness—her blood?

No...no, she must have simply cut her finger on the rose shears again or taken another tumble on the flagstones of the garden walk. That was it, because the sun came back out now. That music must be from Kate's favorite classical radio station she listened to as she tended the roses, the wet under her head a puddle from the early morning sprinklers. Kate was calling something to her about her roses.... Kate was saying she would take care of her cut finger, her head. Sarah could hear the bees buzzing again and smell the petals of every single, stunning bloom....

But as Kate tried to help her up, a cloud cloaked the sun, and everything went oh so dark and cold.

As soon as Kate got the fountain fiasco under control, she slipped away behind the fragrant boxwood hedges into the first tier of antique roses. Her huge cuttings for this party and the early chilly temperatures were bringing the roses to an end for this year. These Apothecaries and Gallicas were far beyond their brilliant, once-a-year June bloom, but the spills and sprays of their graceful, leggy stems pleased her as no fountain ever could. Even the new strain of Blood Thorn she'd bred from Bourbons and Chinas in the next tier of bushes couldn't hold a candle to these heirlooms with their iron constitutions—just like Sarah's, she mused.

Kate glanced back at the house and watched the lights in Sarah's suite go off, then back on again. Sarah must have gone upstairs after they'd spoken, though it was nearly time for the announcement of the silent auction winners. Sarah had promised to read the names and would no doubt give a little speech about each Shaker item.

Kate hoped Sarah kept her promise not to call on her to present the rose prizes. She preferred to stay behind the scenes right now. She'd been badly burned at center stage, though she'd be damned if she was going to skulk around as if she were guilty of anything. If it weren't for Erin—and if she knew where to look—Kate would have found and forced Mike to return, not to her but to stand trial. That, at least, would be worth.the glare of the limelight again.

With another glance through the gardens, Kate skirted the party and headed toward the mansion. Sarah had insisted Kate and Erin live in the guesthouse by the pool after Kate had declared bankruptcy. They'd had to move and auction off most of their goods to cover their lawyer Mason James's fees, but his help had been worth it.

He had established in court that however much Kate *should* have known about Mike's fraud and embezzlement, she hadn't. Of course, Mason had to make her look like the town idiot to keep her from having to assume all Mike's massive debts or serve prison time—but then she *had* been the town idiot. She had totally trusted and loved Mike Marburn and had.paid a huge price in reputation, sanity and circumstances. But never again...with a man. Never.

Kate went into the house, quiet by contrast with the noise outside, and climbed the central, curving staircase. It rose from the marble-tiled floor, but the wonder of the Denbigh mansion was its tall glass windows, which seemed to suck in sun or stars. Versailles on the Maumee, Sarah jokingly called the place, built in the 1930s with the Denbigh fortune made from industrial glass in the city once called the Glass Capital of the World.

But Kate didn't see Sarah in the hall or on the stairs. She'd better go look for her outside. Sometimes the unpretentious woman used the back servants' stairs. Strangely, the house now felt deserted, however alive it had seemed before. Kate peered down the main upstairs hallway. The door to Sarah's suite was closed.

"Sarah?"

For some odd reason, she sensed her friend was up here. Sarah had become somewhat accident-prone lately. She'd cut herself not long ago, and had fallen last month on the stone walk in the farthest garden, bruised both arms, and seemed a bit unsteady on her feet at times. What if she'd fallen again?

"Sarah?"

Kate turned the big brass doorknob to the sitting room where she and her hostess had spent some "grand" hours, as Sarah put it. Sarah had been her angel sent from God when things looked the blackest. After she'd hired Kate and Kate and Erin had moved into the pool house, Sarah had invited the younger women to tea, and the three of them had picnicked on the grounds. And then there were the times she'd invited them to candlelit, dress-up dinners in the mansion.

Erin had rolled her eyes and sulked at first, saying it was all so out-of-it to do those things at her age, but eventually she'd come to love the old woman, too. Somehow Sarah's fussing had helped Kate pull Erin from the depression that lingered after her father had left. These last weeks Erin had been at college and Kate had missed her so, with the result that Kate and Sarah had become even closer.

Kate clicked on the light. All was in order, and the scent of the late roses curled around her in their usual welcoming way. But some strange, acrid scent hung heavily in the air, too.

She went in, glanced around, and saw something spilled on the carpet near the Shaker blanket box. But the crystal vase on it was not tipped or broken. She put her hand in the water on the coral-colored rug and saw that it was blood. Horrified, she wiped her hand on her gown.

"Sarah!"

Kate ran into the adjoining bedroom, which looked undisturbed, each piece of furniture, each bouquet untouched. Then she noted the bathroom door was closed. Sarah was in there and just hadn't heard her calling, that's all. But the blood...

She knocked on the door. "Sarah, are you in there? Are you all right?"

No reply. Slowly, as Kate opened the door, she saw the room was black. Its soft mauve and ecrus muted to grays in the dim echo of light from the bedroom. Her shadow leaped across the tiled floor and darted up the wall; her hand trembled as she reached to flick on the light switch.

Sarah was sprawled facedown on the floor by the commode, her white head in a halo of crimson blood.

"Sarah! Sarah, it's Kate!" She fell to her knees beside her friend and fumbled for a neck pulse.

Nothing. Had she slipped and hit her head while coming to use the toilet? Or had she fallen in the other room, then come to wash the blood away but fainted here?

"Oh, God, oh, God, please help Sarah!" she cried as she ran for the phone in the bedroom and dialed 911. It was a frenzied call that would be played repeatedly on newscasts and reported word for word in the papers.

2

The fairest things have fleetest end,
Their scent survives their close;
But the rose's scent is bitterness
To him that loved the rose.

—Francis Thompson
"Daisy"

"**Y**ou just went out in the gardens by yourself,"
the detective repeated patiently, "and then took the
long way around back into the house through the side
door which you seldom use?"

Weren't there at least three questions in that question? Kate agonized. Exhausted and drained—
stunned—she sat in the Denbigh library in a fog of
grief. She knew she should call her lawyer, but she
wasn't accused of anything, and most certainly was
not guilty of harming the most generous, wonderful
woman she had ever known.

The most wonderful, that is, since her mother had
died so early Kate could barely recall her. Sometimes
she wasn't sure if she was really remembering or just
calling to mind the few photos of her.

Right now the forensic team was taking photographs of every inch of this house. It was the return
of a nightmare she had thought she'd escaped, only

worse. Mike's body had never been found, and she and Erin had first grieved, then harbored hope, then bitter resentment, that he might yet be alive. But she could still hear Erin's inconsolable wails, feel her shaking body as Kate tried to comfort her on the girl's bed, after the police had confiscated the suicide note and most of Mike's things.

"They can't take his goodbye note, too—like his computer and his other stuff," Erin had choked out, gasping for breath, racked with hysteria, her red-blond hair matted to her face with tears. When Kate tried to hug her, the girl held to her pillow instead, so Kate rubbed her trembling back.

"Erin, sweetheart, I can't believe he'd—he'd hurt himself."

"They took his things, but they can't take him away!" she screamed. "Mom, he can't be dead!" She tried to shrug off Kate's persistent touch, but Kate had held her tighter, frantic with her own fear at the enormity of it all, until Erin's sobbing stopped and she clung to Kate, too.

But now there was no one to hold on to, and Sarah's body lay upstairs. Worse, it had been there for hours until the so-called rescue squad finally took it to the morgue in a dark green, zippered plastic bag.

Police and a forensic team in white coats still swarmed the house. Crime-scene tape wrapped the grounds, though Detective Rudzinski and his older, brusque partner, Lieutenant Tina Martin, both told Kate that no one was being charged with anything. Seeing a bloodstain on her gown, they'd asked her to hand it over, and she now wore one of the maid's extra dresses. The forensic team had taken scrapings from under her fingernails because she'd touched the blood on the floor. But then the detectives also took fingerprints and the names and phone numbers of all two hundred guests, before releasing them in the wee hours. The silent auction remained silent, though the memory of Erin's voice kept screaming in Kate's head to rival Stan Rudzinski's questions.

"Go ahead," Lieutenant Martin prompted Kate with a decisive nod of her head. "You saw the blood by the end table..."

Tina Martin seldom spoke, and seemed to be overseeing everything as well as questioning Kate. The prematurely silver-haired, no-nonsense woman popped in and out, either to observe Kate or to advise the apparently wet-behind-the-ears Rudzinski. He was a few years younger than Kate, blond with a buzz cut and a military bearing. But Tina Martin's taut, leathery skin—too much summer sun or a tanning booth—made her look old enough to be the man's mother. Besides, Lieutenant Martin was built like Ms. Universe, and by contrast Rudzinski seemed the ninety-pound weakling.

"It's an authentic Shaker blanket chest," Kate corrected him automatically, but she couldn't focus and her voice didn't sound like her own. She felt dazed, as she often had after hours of questioning by the federal prosecutors over Mike's financial scam.

"Right, but you said there was much more blood where you found the body in the bathroom, is that right, Ms. Marburn?"

"You saw her there, too, so what do you think? That's what I said when you asked me that the last two times, Detective. Look, I want to be a good eyewitness, but I'm exhausted. Can't we go over this again tomorrow?"

"The guest house is being searched right now, too," he admitted, as Lieutenant Martin left the room again.

"Without a warrant?" she challenged, sitting up straighter.

"It's being searched as part of the estate, not as your domicile, Ms. Marburn, so just sit tight and you can go soon. Once they case the place, you can sleep there tonight, though the heirs are so distressed I think you'd better figure on finding another place soon."

"Oh, yes, they'll come swooping in now," Kate muttered, "but they've hardly been speaking to her for months."

"Is that right? Bad blood—pardon the wording—between them?"

Blessedly, a police officer poked his head in from the hall. "Guest house is clear, Zink—Detective," he said and closed the door behind him.

"I was a patrolman until recently," the young man said, almost to himself. "You heard him, Ms. Marburn—let me walk you over, as you were always free to go. Your guest house is ready."

The way he said that reminded Kate of the O.J. Simpson case, in which that hanger-on, Kato Kaylin, had been in residence in a guest house on the grounds during a double murder. But these detectives hadn't said Sarah had been murdered. And Kate was no hanger-on.

"I insisted Sarah deduct rent from my salary," she told Rudzinski, as they went out across the back patio and started through the rose gardens. "I'm an employee, even if I'm living in the guest house."

"And a friend, as you said. You know, I understand the deceased's daughter didn't put it so—so nicely or objectively.''

Kate's stomach lurched. Something was being said just under the surface that threatened her. She'd gravely misjudged Mike and paid the price, but surely no one would ever suspect her of harming Sarah. But if Varina was turning really vicious...yes, she could imagine that. Kate would have been furious with anyone who alienated *her* mother's affections. But then, Varina had done that on her own. Kate jerked when the detective spoke again.

''There'll be officers on the grounds tonight, ma'am. And when they've released the site tomorrow, I'd like to take you back to the scene to have you tell me if anything looks amiss. That all right?''

''I'd do anything to help, of course,'' she said, as he hesitated at the door of the guest house. She shuddered to think of that group of white-coated forensic people going through her personal effects. It was just like the time their very lives were violated when the police had searched for proof that Mike—and his wife—were in collusion in the Marburn Securities scandal.

''Ma'am—Ms. Marburn, I know all this is double hard on you, considering what you went through before and all.''

Kate could only nod. She felt she was swimming in a sea of exhaustion and disbelief. And she was beginning to be swept under by the familiar, cold riptide of terror.

The phone's shrill ring pulled Kate from the dark depths. Why was she on the sofa instead of in bed? She fought her way up from sodden sleep. Often she had insomnia, so at least she'd been sleeping soundly for once, but—

The slant of morning light blinded her. Then she remembered.

Sarah was dead. Kate had lost Sarah—and the disaster of her marriage made her doubly fearful of being implicated and blamed.

But she was not going to be a victim here. Never again.

The phone continued to ring. If this call was from someone wanting a statement, she'd slam the receiver down and take the phone off the hook. But she had to call her lawyer—maybe he'd heard and was phoning her. She swung her feet to the floor, astounded at the instant slam of a headache behind her left eye. She picked the receiver up gingerly, as if it would bite.

"Hello."

"It's Erin."

Kate squeezed her eyes tight shut as her stepdaughter's face flashed into her mind. Huge green eyes with pale lashes she mascaraed dark blue, freckles she tried to cover, a pert-nosed face framed by shoulder-length pale strawberry-blond hair that she insisted on calling "Irish red" because that had pleased her dad.

"But it's—oh, it's eight on a Sunday morning, sweetheart," Kate managed with a glance at the clock. "Is anything wrong?"

"Why didn't you call me last night? A newspaper reporter did and asked all kinds of questions about us and Mrs. Denbigh. He said she's dead and you found her."

Kate hunched over her knees, her forehead resting on her free hand. For one moment she thought she would be violently ill. She'd only had about two hours sleep, though for her that was a normal stretch.

"Kate, are you still there?"

"Yes, sweetheart, I'm here. I'm sorry—so sorry if you've been pulled into—another tragedy."

Now nearly nineteen and a freshman in college, Erin had been eight when her own mother died. That loss had been one of the things that had initially made them close, for Kate and Erin had each survived the same loss early in life. As Erin's stepmother since the girl was nine, Kate had worked hard at building their relationship. So hard, she realized in retrospect, that she had overdone time with Erin, trying to make up for Mike who was obsessed with his investment firm. When Mike disappeared, he'd left a love letter to them, though it was part suicide note. Unfortunately, his departure and its aftermath had not kept her and Erin as close as Kate had hoped. Just the opposite.

"Now I'm *really* an orphan!" Erin had wailed when they had first found the note from Mike. They had just walked into the house from shopping for things for Erin when they found the note that had begun the nightmare. That day, Erin had actually locked herself in her bedroom and had refused to be comforted or counseled. And more often than not these past two years without her father, Erin had called her "Kate" instead of "Mom."

"They aren't going to blame you, are they?" Erin was asking now. "I mean, some of this reporter's questions sounded really kind of, well, suspicious."

"Of course they're not going to blame me, but since I'm the one who found her..."

"I'll bet that witch Varina had a hissy fit because you were with Sarah at the end."

"Erin, you're not to speak disparagingly of Sarah's children."

"Meaning adults can do no wrong? But Dad left and you didn't know what was going on or how to help or keep him..."

Erin began to cry. There was no sound, but Kate knew. Her stomach cramped at the accusation, both spoken and implied.

"Sweetheart, listen, don't mix this up with what happened to us. Everything will be all right. But just to be sure we're not bothered by reporters anymore, I'm going to call Mason James to—"

"Not a lawyer again. Not all that."

"You're upset, Erin, and I understand. I am, too, believe me. Sarah was more than a friend, maybe like the mother or grandmother we never knew."

"A fairy godmother," Erin whispered, and sniffed hard.

"The point is, I don't want you to worry about things here. I'll be down to see you as soon as I can get away. I might have to change my phone number again, move too, but I'll let you know. Is everything all right there? You're not homesick?"

"My roommate Amy is, but by comparison I got over that years ago after—"

"After your mother died, I know. I *do* know."

Audible sobbing now. Kate's eyes burned with tears, and she gripped the receiver to try to seize control. She had hoped and prayed that when Erin went away to college they could both start over, looking forward to their reunions and maybe living together again someday.

"Sweetheart, if you can, concentrate on things there. I'll call you every day—and see you soon.

Maybe you can help Amy feel better, take her somewhere or have a good talk with her. Don't let her be
alone.''

''Yeah, I hear you.'' Another big sniff. ''Reach out
and touch someone and that will help you, too. It used
to be your motto. Then you do the same, okay? Promise.''

''Yes, I promise.''

''But if we—you—have to move out of Groveland,
where's our home now, Mom?''

Above all else, that last word so swamped the remnants of Kate's control that she couldn't even answer.

The gong of the doorbell only made Jack bury his
head deeper in the covers. Then he squinted…what
time was it? Dawn had not yet lit the eastern sky, he
noted as he glared at the digital bedside clock. Six-
twenty a.m. Now who in hell needed an antique furniture builder at this time of the morning? And on a
Sunday—not that he wasn't going to put in a full
day's work.

He stumbled to his feet on the cold, bare wood
floor and didn't even bother looking for his shoes or
socks. He liked to live a spartan existence—deserved
to. Still groggy, he lurched out of his bedroom and
across the hall into the front room he used as his
office. It looked out over the old turnpike road that
ran toward the Shaker village about half a mile away.
He lived alone in this place, but once so many had
lived here together.

He remembered he still had his screens in the windows. He hadn't taken the time to put in the storms
yet or even to clean out his frost-blasted garden. He

hated to do household things. He unlocked and heaved up the sill.

"What is it?" he called out into the gray autumn mist.

"It's Josh Harvey and my dad, Mr. Kilcourse," a young boy's voice called up. "I'm just helping him 'cause it's Sunday and this is a real special 'livery letter. We got it for you here, and you got to sign for it."

Jack leaned closer to the screen to see the squat, white mail van pulled up close to the house. It annoyed him that Frank Harvey often let his kid do his work, official government work. It annoyed him how the boy hung on to his father's every word, adored him. Damn, maybe it was his own harsh, bitter self that annoyed him.

"Be right down," he called.

He pulled on jeans and a sweatshirt. Downstairs, he snapped on the porch light before he unlocked one of the two front doors. The boy did not hold the letter or the clipboard, but stood there all bright-faced and important-looking when Frank handed them over. The pain of that simple scene sliced Jack so deeply that he could have shoved them both off the porch.

He scribbled his name and managed to make some sort of small talk.

"See you later, Mr. Kilcourse! Have a nice day of rest—that's what my Mom calls it. She said we should've waited 'til it got light!" the kid called back as they started away. Mild-mannered Frank just patted the kid's head and smiled, either sheepishly or proudly, and turned away, too. The boy practically skipped along next to his dad before they got into the little truck, beeped the horn and drove away. Its headlights slashed across Jack's face and startled him. Then the western darkness swallowed them. He stood staring blankly down the road, until he realized he was shaking from the predawn chill.

He went in, slammed the front door, clicked on the hall light and ripped open the registered letter. It was from the Toledo, Ohio police department. He was used to getting orders and requests from all over— but the police? He skimmed it for the signature: a homicide detective named Stanley Rudzinski. Never heard of him.

*Since you are the closest expert in assessing the authenticity of Shaker furniture, and we have an emergency where we need your help...*the letter began.

Jack sat down on the lowest step and let the letter drop to the floor between his knees. That's about all he was an expert in. *We have an emergency.* Yeah, that was a good one. But anything to fill his hours, to have different, solid things to do to keep his own emergency away.

3

Money, which represents the prose of life, and which is hardly spoken of in parlors without an apology, is, in its effects and laws, as beautiful as roses.

—Ralph Waldo Emerson
Nominalist and Realist

"Since you discovered the deceased in the bathroom, can you suggest any way she could have fallen to get blood here?" Rudzinski asked Kate, pointing at the missing square of carpet labeled "4." "Then," he went on when she didn't answer immediately, "there's nothing but tiny drops until she made it into the bathroom, where she bled significantly again."

Kate glanced at where he pointed. In daylight, she could see a line of speckles—numbers "5" through "12" laid out on the carpet in Sarah's suite. "I didn't see those last night," she said, trying not to sound defensive.

"You were in a hurry. So what if you didn't see a few drops?"

Though he seemed to be on her side, Kate's wariness level skyrocketed. He kept watching her face for a reaction to each thing he said. She wished Mason

James would get here, even though she had absolutely nothing to hide.

"For one thing," she replied, "those other drops might have led me to find her faster, to get help sooner."

Detective Rudzinski—Zink, Kate kept hearing the officers call him—seemed much more nervous as he took her back to the place of Sarah's death late the next afternoon. He looked like some retro preppie college kid with loafers and a V-neck sleeveless sweater over his button-down shirt. A college kid...damn, she had to get her mind off Erin. And though she was still slogging through exhaustion, she had to concentrate on everything this man was saying.

In Sarah's suite they stood on a plastic runner that was there to keep everyone's feet off the carpet. The plastic ran from the hall door to the blanket chest, then into the bedroom and to the distant bathroom door. The piece of coral carpet with the bloodstain had been completely cut out, and the floor was flagged with little signs in a scrawl Kate could not read from this distance, though the numbers on each paper stood out.

Her insides lurched. She supposed this had to be treated as a crime scene. But surely no one would have murdered Sarah.

"You said last night that you 'sensed' she was up here, though you heard and saw nothing out of order except the light going off and then back on," Rudzinski pursued. "You often have these feelings? Is it ESP or something like that?"

Suddenly everything he said sounded accusatory, though Kate told herself she was just overly sensitive after all she'd been through. She noted Rudzinski had a habit of never taking notes, unlike the government and financial investigators she'd spent hours with over Mike's case. She was tempted to ask him if he had a photographic memory, but she said only, "You know what they say about women's intuition. And I've called my lawyer. He'll be back in town tomorrow and said not to answer any untoward questions."

"Untoward, that's me," Rudzinski said, stretching to his full five feet six inches. She noticed his slacks and shirt looked wrinkled, as if he'd slept in them or been up all night. Yes, that was what he'd worn yesterday, at least she thought so. Adrenaline coursed through her, but she still couldn't clear her head. "Look, Ms. Marburn, I'm just trying to find out how the woman you call your mentor, and say you cared deeply for, died, because it's real hard for me—and others—to figure how it could've been an accident."

Her heart began to beat faster, harder. "I'm surprised, too, but she did take a tumble last month."

"So the maid and her doctor told us, and the coroner mentioned previous external bruising on her arms. It's lucky you were there to find her then, too. So maybe she just tumbled into the chest there," he said, turning and pointing again, "then managed to stop the bleeding on her head except for a few drops, long enough to stagger into the bathroom where she fell again." As he spoke, he paced the walkway to the bathroom, then came back. "But we found her with nothing that could have stanched her blood, and the amount on your gown was negligible."

"I said I don't know, Detective. I only know you asked me up here to tell you if I thought anything was removed from her private suite, and I'm telling you I don't think so, all right?"

"If I showed you the contents of her jewelry box, would you know if anything was taken from that? In addition to things in her wall safe, she kept a jewelry box out in her bedroom on an antique chest of drawers—"

Kate fought for control and calm. He was right in her face now, despite his deceptively calm demeanor. "The only time I've seen her jewelry box open was when she tried to loan me a strand of pearls for last night, and I declined."

"For last night? And you declined because…"

"Because she'd already done so much for me, and I didn't want to take a chance on their being broken or lost. I've had things snag in stems and thorns more than once when I've bent over to work with my roses."

"I see," he said with a lift of his blond brows.

"I hope that's it, because I'm starting to feel I'm on trial here, so if you'll excuse me," she insisted more stridently than she'd intended.

"I didn't mean to stress you even more, Ms. Marburn," Rudzinski said, shifting so he stood between her and the hall door. He was short enough that she looked down at him slightly, but he suddenly seemed as formidable as a pit bull.

"Before you go," he went on, "how about answering my ESP question? You good at sensing things, maybe at psyching people out?"

"Not really, or I wouldn't have come up here without a lawyer today, Detective Rudzinski. And I would have known that my husband was a shyster who would stop at nothing to ruin our clients and friends, not to mention his daughter and wife. Excuse me, please."

She pushed past him into the hall—and bumped into Varina Wellesley. The woman's chunky gold jewelry clattered as they made contact, then stepped apart. Large-boned, the striking Varina usually wore her raven hair swept back in a twist that made her look older than Kate, although they were the same age. Against her severely cut pantsuit, and without her usual cosmetics, her complexion looked ghostly pale. Varina resembled her mother only in the bone structure of the face, not in size or style—and never in heart. A cold wave of loss rolled through Kate again.

"Once they're finished with you," Varina cried, pointing at Kate, "I don't want you back in here again." Kate saw her eyes were bloodshot. At least Varina seemed to be suffering, too. "And that includes moving out of the guest house."

"Hey, Mrs. Wellesley, please," Rudzinski cut in, stepping between them. "Of necessity, Ms. Marburn will be moving out, but the deceased would hardly want her thrown out before she finds someplace else."

"Unfortunately, my mother isn't here anymore, and Palmer and I are her heirs," Varina insisted, running a lacquered index fingernail under each eye to smear tears.

"Which makes you feel *how* about losing her, ma'am?"

Varina glared at him. "Deeply bereft. And ready to assume any duties to preserve all she and my late father worked for."

Kate forced herself to walk away. At least it appeared that the police were suspicious of everyone. If this did turn out to be a murder investigation, she supposed, Varina and Palmer could be suspects.

"Hey, Ms. Marburn, for your own best interests, hold up until I get an officer to walk you out," Rudzinski called after her. Kate wondered where his previously omnipresent partner was. She heard him order Varina in a softer voice, "Stand right there and don't go in yet, Mrs. Wellesley."

"Look, Detective," Kate heard Varina say, "all I know about Mother's antique furniture is that she was switching it around all the time—lending, selling, donating."

Waiting at the top of the stairs, Kate glanced out the bank of tall windows at the Maumee River glinting beyond the back gardens.

"Besides," Varina went on, "I thought you were going to get an expertiser in from that new Shaker village that's holding a lot of her furniture. Palmer and I want to get that back as soon as possible to reassemble her entire collection of the stuff."

Though Varina probably couldn't care less, Kate knew the Shakers had once been prominent in many areas. In gardening, design, and the liberation and elevation of women and blacks, the Shakers had left their mark. And Varina dared to call her mother's precious treasury of the Shaker heritage "stuff"!

Sarah's elderly lawyer cleared his throat and began to read. "'I, Sarah Clayton Denbigh, residing in Lucas County, Ohio, do make, publish, and declare this to be my Last Will and Testament, hereby revoking all Wills by me heretofore made.'"

Four days after Sarah's death, Kate sat with her silver-haired and steely-faced lawyer, Mason James, across a long, polished cherry conference table from Varina Wellesley and her husband, Brad, the nervous Palmer, and their lawyer Pete Scofield. They were assembled for the reading of Sarah Denbigh's will by her lawyer, the portly but imposing Seth Myerman. As soon as Sarah's will had been probated, beneficiaries and the next of kin had been summoned by certified mail for this reading. Kate had been touched and surprised to be included; Varina was seething.

Kate was more apprehensive than pleased, though, for this haste, though entirely legal, seemed indecent. Sarah wouldn't even be laid to rest for two days, partly because the coroner had just released the body to the family and partly because the funeral had been set back a bit for out-of-town guests.

Through half-glasses, the lawyer peered down at the multipaged document, his jowls shaking as he talked. His voice was sonorous and impressive, as if it should belong to an evangelist or network news anchor.

"'I give, devise and bequeath the following items to the below named individuals as follows…'"

The Groveland mansion and grounds were deeded to the City of Toledo Metro Parks, with an endowment for upkeep of the house and gardens, the latter to be overseen by Katherine Marburn. Ms. Marburn was to receive a yearly salary from the estate of fifty thousand dollars with a three-percent per-year increase for inflation for as many years as she chose to remain in the position. If she wished, considering that the grounds and gardens would be open to the public, Ms. Marburn could continue to live in the guest house.

Varina's loud sniff—whether of grief or of contempt, Kate wasn't sure—punctuated Myerman's pause. Sarah's great gift and the admiration and love behind it moved Kate deeply. Sarah had mentioned her property becoming a park someday, but she'd never hinted at the rest to her. Perhaps Sarah's heirs had known, though, and accepted it because current death and property taxes could be ruinous.

Stone-faced, Varina shifted in her chair, though the balding, tanned Palmer glowered. "The bulk of the estate's still to come," Kate heard Varina mutter to her brother as she patted his arm.

There followed a long list of pieces of art or furniture—none of it Shaker antiques—to Varina and Palmer. Between the padded arms of their chairs, they grasped each other's hands, as Seth Myerman read off the growing list of endowments and bequests to various charities. Then came what they were evidently awaiting; both leaned forward.

"'Item nineteen. One-half million dollars to each of my two children, Varina Clarissa Denbigh Wellesley and Palmer Jones Denbigh.'"

That figure boggled Kate's mind, for her math teacher–father had never thought women proficient at handling money and had left her but ten thousand dollars when he died. But Varina and Palmer looked surprised and dismayed.

"Go on," Varina prompted, her voice shaking, when the lawyer paused. "How has she parceled out the rest to us? In stocks or bonds or the Shaker collection?"

"Not that I see," he said, flipping and scanning the last three pages. "There are two more bequests to Katherine Marburn," he said with a glance at Kate. He adjusted his bifocals and read, "'Item twenty. My collection of Shaker furniture, including those items in my home and those loaned to various museums (see list attached) as well as my core collection currently displayed at the new Shaker Run Village in southeastern Ohio, to my dear friend, Katherine Marburn, who admires the Shakers as I did.'''

"That's insanity," Varina spat out, smacking an open palm on the table. "Some of that furniture belonged to both my parents—and Mother's made decisions for everyone. And do you know what some of those pieces go for? Just the other day there was an online auction house sale for one work counter from the Sabbath Lake Shakers—a *work counter*. It went for $220,000, and some side chairs worth $20,000 apiece. So that can't be—be quite right."

"So you've already been checking on prices for your sale of what you call 'her stuff'?" Kate spoke up, unable to hold in her frustration any longer. "Perhaps your mother *knew* you'd unload the whole lot of her treasures the moment she died."

"And you won't?" Varina demanded.

"Never."

"Ha!" was all Palmer managed. The blood had drained from his face, and he still gripped his sister's hand.

The two of them began to whisper. All Kate could discern was Palmer's "Rina, can you believe that? How could she do that?" as Myerman plunged on.

"'And my antique rosebushes, from among the many others which shall stay in Groveland gardens, I bequest to Katherine Marburn should she ever leave this area.

"'In witness whereof, I have hereunto set my hand on the margin of the preceding twelve pages and at the end of this my last Will and Testament, at Toledo, Ohio, this fourth day of August 1999.'"

"Wait, there has to be more," Palmer cried.

"Oh, there is," Varina insisted, yanking her hand free of his grip. "August 1999—this year? Mother just changed her will last month? And leaves a fortune in furniture and a longtime sinecure for gardening to a new friend who suddenly finds my—*our*—mother dead?"

"After," Palmer added, "her head hit one of the pieces of furniture which now go to Ms. Marburn?" Varina and Palmer both spoke in low voices, but their frustration and fury seethed under that control.

"I know all this is a shock," their lawyer interrupted, "but in due time we can file—"

"You let Mother be taken in like this and didn't stop her," Varina accused Sarah's lawyer, who looked like an angry Buddha. "Why didn't you at least tell us she'd suddenly shifted the bulk of our heritage to a new employee? I cannot believe Mother changed her will so suddenly, so close to her sudden, strange death."

"Now see here," Mason James countered. "Mrs. Wellesley, I'll not have you slandering Mrs. Marburn, even indirectly. That's a legal document and—"

"Which can and will be contested!" Varina cried, half rising and leaning straight-armed on the table with both hands. "Isn't that true, Pete?" she asked their lawyer, who nodded, just as Palmer kept doing.

"Quite true," Pete Scofield said, steepling his fingers before his mouth and nose. "The state of Ohio provides a four-month window for a will to be contested for fraud, duress, undue influence or incompetence—"

"Incompetence of our poor mother perhaps, for I must admit that Kate Marburn obviously has been skilled here—and not just at growing roses. I always said your resume must have read that you were clever at defrauding people and getting off scot-free yourself," Varina hissed. "But how daring of you to try it again after wriggling out of that embezzlement caper."

"Varina, that's enough," Scofield cried, and reached for her wrist. She shook him off. "It isn't," she insisted. "All that has to happen to freeze this will and take Kate Marburn out of it for life—*for life*—is for her to be charged and convicted of…certainly more than duress or undue influence!"

Kate's insides had been in free fall, but she wasn't just going to run. Mike had done that, and she hated him for it. She stood, scraping back her chair, and Mason did the same, evidently thinking they were walking out. But Kate simply wanted to face this woman eye to eye.

"Varina," Kate said, her voice steady despite her distress, "I can grasp how hard this is for you, but you'd better be careful before pointing fingers so publicly. Since you and Palmer obviously believed your mother's previous will was in effect, one which evidently made you her favorite charities, if I were Detective Rudzinski and his partner, I'd think that you two would have motives galore for—"

"Don't try to shift the blame," Palmer put in.

"By the way," Kate said, sitting back down again because her legs were shaking so hard, "Sarah never told me a thing about these bequests, though I knew she wanted me to care for the roses in the future."

Before Varina could reply, Kate went on, "All of

these generous gifts are a shock to me, although, in part, a pleasant one. However, I deeply grieve the loss of a great woman whom I shall always remember for her warmth and accomplishments—not for her stocks, bonds or fortune—as her own children evidently define her memory.''

She rose again now, slowly, to stand by Mason. ''At least someone who cares about her value,'' Kate said, ''and not what she was worth, will be able to oversee the two great loves of her later life—the furniture and the roses.''

For one moment, Kate regretted she'd come down so hard on them, but she had sworn to herself she would never again be left holding the bag for something she didn't do. At least, for once, even three lawyers were speechless.

But by the next morning someone had leaked details of the new will and Kate's defiance to the newspaper and TV stations.

Jack Kilcourse had never been a slave to money, but this job examining the authenticity and value of some great Shaker furniture—he was properly called an expertiser—was too lucrative and fascinating to pass up. Although he'd had to leave his own workshop where he produced authentic replicas of Shaker pieces—even though the CEO of a wealthy hi-tech Tokyo firm was waiting for his new dining room suite—he'd dropped everything to drive to Toledo. Besides, he figured he was doing it for a fine old lady who had loaned the struggling new Shaker village a big part of her collection to help draw visitors. The great Shaker heritage was worthy of honor and preservation, however strange some of the original Believers must have been.

Now Jack had set up bright lights to be able to closely examine the pieces. He had opened his kit of tools: magnifying glass, screwdriver, needles, plastic gloves and envelopes, and specimen bags. He felt something like the forensic guys who had finally cleared out just ahead of him with the tools of their trade. He'd eyeballed all the furniture in the suite, picked the piece that looked most likely, and hauled it under the lights for its examination.

"Hey, how's it going?" the young detective, Stan Rudzinski, asked as he came back in. He had a folded copy of the *Toledo Blade* in his hand. "Can I bring you back some chow when I return? Got to run downtown on this case." Rudzinski pointed to the headline, which read What Does Kate Marburn Know—Again? It was followed by a smaller headline that said something about a new will.

None of that meant a thing to Jack, nor did it interest him. He detested and avoided newspapers and newscasts unless they presented a business item or world news. He couldn't stomach the local domestic tragedies the media fed on, so he pretty much kept his nose to the grindstone, or, rather, to the wood. But he had to admit, as he looked at Kate Marburn's photograph that even appearing frenzied and with a fold right through her face, she was one good-looking woman.

"I'll pass on the food," Jack told Rudzinski. "I'll take a break at noon and grab some fast food around here somewhere. So much of this is detail work that I give my old back and forty-four-year-old eyes a break now and then."

"Sure, no problem. Officer Cook will be right out here if you need anything. You know," the detective said, hitching up his pants as if that would give him a few more inches facing the six-foot-three antique furniture expert, "you're kind of a detective, too. See, I figure if there's some kind of funny goings-on with any of this furniture—like maybe some of it's fake— I got myself another motive to play with. Not that the cast of characters surrounding a rich, old lady won't keep me busy enough."

"Technically," Jack told him, rapping his knuckles on the desk, "I've found no fakes—but maybe one fraud so far."

"What do you mean?" Rudzinski asked, snapping to attention. "And what's the diff?"

"A fake is phony from the get-go—a complete fabrication," Jack explained, pulling a drawer out of the desk-bookshelf combination. "But a fraud is an antique that's been altered, disguised or misrepresented. Frauds are easier to pass off and, therefore, usually more lucrative to unload."

"This here?" Rudzinski asked, suddenly eyeing the cherry-and-butternut piece with suspicion.

"I'd bet on it, though I haven't done enough tests."

"Like what? It looks old to me."

"It's easy to dent, bruise or gouge such a piece to make it pass for old. It's called 'distressing.'"

"Good name. I feel that way half the time in this job."

Jack bit back a grin. "I'll have some lab samples done, but it looks to me as if someone's put random ink stains on this desktop and smoked the shelf wood to brown and dry it. Then they get rid of the burn smell with a saltwater soak."

"No kidding," Rudzinski observed with a shake of his head.

"Here's another telltale sign that they were thorough but not thorough enough," Jack told him, taking a darning needle from his kit. He easily ran the needle down several tiny holes on the side of the bookcase. "Worm holes, which are natural and expected with fine antiques, twist and turn. These worm holes were made by power drills."

"Frauds must be worth big bucks."

"Shaker grain sacks are going for a couple hundred dollars, and seed labels for at least that much. Compared to that, 'there's gold in them thar Shaker furniture.'"

"Got you," Rudzinski said. "And the rest of the pieces in here?"

"It'll take time, like I said. This one just stood out."

"What's so special about Shaker furniture?" the detective asked, crossing his arms over his chest so Kate Marburn's newsprint eyes stared at Jack. "Before this case, I didn't know that style, let alone the people, existed."

"That they did. There were once nearly twenty utopian Shaker communities scattered across the East and Midwest. They thrived as outposts of a unique group of people known for their wild style of dance in their worship services, but now more for their celibacy. They had a dark side, too, but don't we all?"

"In this job—tell me about it."

"But what's so special about the Shakers is their uniqueness, which shines through in all their products."

"Unique how?" Rudzinski pursued.

Jack didn't have much use for nosy people, but this guy was at least honest about what he didn't know. "Let me just put it this way since you're leaving and I've got a lot to do before giving you a decent report," Jack said, putting the needle away and going back to examining the dovetailing on the side of the desk drawer. "The Shakers were perfectionists in their work, but practical, too. Their female founder once said, 'Work as though you have one thousand years to live but might die tomorrow.'"

Jack wished he'd put it another way when he saw Rudzinski glance around the room as if Sarah Denbigh's ghost had lingered. "Or to raise it to another level, which they always did," Jack went on, "some Shaker furniture designers actually believed that their patterns came from heaven and were transmitted to them by angels."

"In short, they made practical things but lived in some sort of weird world of their own making. You know, Mr. Kilcourse—"

"Jack."

"Jack. I'd have to call that kind of people at least a little dangerous," the detective said, shaking his head and starting for the door. "I'll check in with you after I get back. And, like I said, I'm hoping your brand of detective work's gonna somehow jump-start mine."

4

You may break, you may shatter
The vase if you will,
But the scent of the roses
Will hang round it still.

—Thomas More
"Farewell! But Whatever"

Kate tried to calm herself and prepare for Sarah's funeral tomorrow by working with her roses. It was so great to be out in the open air instead of closed up in a lawyer's office or in a room with Rudzinski and his prickly partner—though it seemed Tina Martin spent more time with Varina and Palmer, while "Zink" had been assigned to her.

Kate kept pruning bush after bush and wheelbarrowing the cut canes to an enclosed trash pile, where Jeff, Groveland's handyman, would compost them. But she wielded her clippers with a vengeance, furious that Pete Scofield—Varina and Palmer's lawyer—had leaked word of Sarah's new will to the papers and put the worst possible spin on it.

The same article had quoted Rudzinski repeating that "Sarah Denbigh's death is still under investigation, though it appears to be an accident." But the man's tenacity was actually starting to make Kate fear otherwise. And if anyone had somehow deliberately hurt Sarah, Kate vowed, she'd make the Toledo homicide squad look like rank amateurs in an attempt to find out who was guilty.

Kate knew full well that she had filled a great gap in Sarah's life, but Sarah had been her salvation, too. "I can't think of a job I'd rather have than working with your antique roses while living on this beautiful estate," she'd told Sarah the day the elderly woman had offered her a future when she was still facing a possible trial for Mike's misdeeds. "But my stepdaughter needs some stability in her life right now," Kate had admitted, "so I'd hate for her to have to change high schools if we move into your neighborhood. Not to mention that the hours I could give you would be erratic at best for a while because of all the time I'm still spending with my lawyer and government investigators."

Sarah had nodded understandingly. When she took a step closer and put a thin hand on Kate's shoulder, the scent of flowers had emanated from her. It wasn't like that staggering smell of powder or perfume when certain woman sat too near in church or at a concert. Sarah Denbigh smelled fresh and real, which stunned Kate with a memory that came back with a bang.

Her mother. Her young, laughing mother she could barely recall had smelled like that. Of freshly turned loam and summer sun and clear sky. Of crisp breeze and mingled flowers. Her mother had loved to garden, and little Kate had toddled at her side to help her pick flowers...long before she had been swept away on the winds of time....

"Kate, are you quite all right?" Sarah's concerned voice had interrupted her thoughts. "You know, there's not a day goes by that either my maid or my yard man doesn't go on an errand into town, and when you are tied up somewhere, they could even bring your Erin back and forth from school. Or we have several cars, and she could borrow one to drive herself. She is a senior, you said, so she surely drives, and I'm sure we could get permission for her to remain at her same school.''

''I—yes,'' Kate had managed, blinking back tears that matted her eyelashes. At this point in her life, she'd given up crying over common cruelties, but moments of quiet kindness moved her deeply. ''I'll talk to her about your generous offer, Mrs. Denbigh. And I can't thank you enough.''

And now she'd never be able to thank Sarah enough, Kate thought as she kept working. For good or ill, gardening was always her best thinking time, and it made her miss Sarah, and her mother, fiercely.

She forced her mind to the tasks at hand. Besides using mulch to hill up the roots, she decided, she'd cover the beds with fir branches, too. A harsh winter was predicted, and the winds off Lake Erie could shake the roots loose if all of these were not properly pruned. Trying to calm herself, Kate cut and tossed and cut again, ignoring thorns and snags.

In the distance the buzz of Jeff's hedge trimmers stopped. He was not actually trimming, but was cleaning and oiling his various pieces of equipment. She'd rather liked the white noise of his machines. Today, her favorite classical music on her transistor made her think and grieve too much; it was as if even recorded music conspired against her.

She worked with a will, making sharp cuts on a slight slant to open the center of each bush to sun and air next spring. Bending to turn her radio off again when Jeff restarted his electric trimmers, she moved from the Chinas to the *Belle de Crecy* bush that would produce the most exquisite mix of cerise, violet and lilac-gray hues Sarah loved—had loved—so dearly.

Even through her earphones she heard Jeff come closer. Was he trimming, too, she wondered as she straightened and turned with her arms full of thorny canes. She gasped to see Varina hacking with the electric trimmer through the precious heirloom bushes at the other end of this long bed.

"Varina! Stop it!" Kate shouted. "Those are—were—your mother's roses, too!"

Varina merely glanced up, then plunged on. The fierce whine of the long trimmers with its moving blades drowned her out.

Yanking off her headphones with one hand, Kate ran toward Varina and, suddenly wary of getting too close to the woman when she had that determined, almost demented look on her face, threw an armful of cut canes at the trimmers.

Varina swung around with the electric tool, arced it once in the air toward Kate as if to hold her off, then bent to rip through the next Bourbon bush.

"Stop it, Varina!" Kate repeated, hoping the woman could hear her at closer range. "They were her roses, too!"

Again, Varina swung the heavy trimmers. Kate jumped back, and the tool thudded to the ground. Thank God, its blades stopped when Varina lost control. The moment Varina lunged to retrieve it, Kate tried to yank the cord, but there was too much slack to kill the electricity. It restarted in Varina's hands.

"I saw you trimming!" Varina shrieked. "I'm

helping! I'm showing I care about her roses, too, damn you!''

When Kate tried to dart behind her, Varina swept the trimmers at her again. The end snagged Kate's garden glove and ripped it off to shred the thick material. Crimson anger flooded her. She wanted to run for help, but refused to leave the plants to this—this butcher.

Kate strode to the main sprinkler control and yanked it on. Why didn't someone come out here and stop this woman? Who knows what Varina would do to these bushes. Could she get a restraining order on Varina to protect roses?

The extensive sprinkler system came on full force, spraying both women, as Kate charged back. She picked up her rake and shoved the metal tines in the blades of the trimmer. It jammed and jerked from Varina's hands. Too late, Kate realized the mix of water and electricity could have electrocuted them both.

Soaked, flailing, sobbing, Varina threw herself at Kate. Varina's weight took them to the ground. Kate rolled, heaved her off, and squirmed away. Varina lunged again, pinning Kate down until the woman's weight suddenly lifted away. A tall, dark-haired man Kate did not know held Varina upright with her arms pinned to her sides and her feet off the ground. Pushing her to her knees on the wet grass, he grabbed the long extension cord, yanked it to get slack, and firmly wrapped it three times around the struggling woman. Before he could help Kate up, she scrambled to her feet and ran to turn off the water and pull the plug.

Shoving her shirttails back into her soaked jeans, Kate headed toward him and his sputtering prisoner.

She knew she looked a mess; she pulled leaves and mulch from her hair and wiped mud off her face. What made matters worse was how good the man looked, even with water dripping off his nose, chin and earlobes.

His sodden shirt stuck to his broad shoulders and chest; stretched against strong thighs, his jeans bore big water blotches. At least he wore beat-up running shoes. Though she was tall at five foot eight, he towered a good six inches over her. His black hair, which was probably quite thick ordinarily, lay plastered on his brown forehead until a big hand shoved it back. Cocked at a devilish angle, thick eyebrows slashed above deep-set, dark blue eyes. His face seemed all planes and angles, and white crow's feet perched at the corners of his eyes, indicating he didn't wear sunglasses.

"I'm sorry that happened, but glad you came along," Kate told him, awkwardly wiping her palms on the hips of her jeans. He was looking her over with the same intensity that she had him. Their gazes, both nervous, snagged and held. She felt the impact of that down to the pit of her stomach.

"I glanced out the master suite windows and saw her go nuts with the trimmer," he explained. His voice had a rough timbre to it that fitted his rugged, square-jawed face.

"The master suite?" Kate said. "Oh, you're in forensics, working with detectives Rudzinski and Martin?"

"I'm Jack Kilcourse, an antique furniture expertiser specializing in Shaker. There was supposed to be a cop right outside my door, but I guess he took a break, or I would have sent him. You want this woman arrested for assault and battery?''

Kate was shocked that this stranger had almost made her forget Varina. ''No, though if you'd back me up on how she acted, I'll probably try to get her barred from these gardens. Pity, too, as her mother loved them so much, and she's just defaced about a quarter of them,'' she said, addressing Varina now instead of Jack Kilcourse. ''Pruning or trimming's one thing, but a chainsaw massacre's another.''

Jack unwrapped Varina and tried to help her stand, but she shook him off and scrambled up on her own. ''I don't care what it takes,'' Varina muttered, glaring at Kate. ''I'll get the things she meant to leave to me. And don't you show your face at my mother's funeral tomorrow!'' she cried as she backed away a few steps, her eyes darting once to Jack before she turned to hurry off.

''You sure you're okay?'' Jack asked Kate. ''You look—dizzy.''

''I probably look worse than that,'' she admitted, bending to pull the rake from between the hedge trimmer's teeth. She shoved her wet hair back from her eyes. ''I'm Kate Marburn, Mrs. Denbigh's rosarian,'' she told him as she straightened.

''Oh, right,'' he said, as if he either finally recognized her name or face. But with a hint of a smile, he extended his hand. Clean compared to hers, it was huge, callused, and so warm despite the quickening chill breeze that she clung a moment too long.

''Actually, Mrs. Denbigh left her Shaker collection to me, but the will is—obviously—being contested,'' Kate explained. ''I love her Shaker furniture,'' she added. She glanced toward the house, then riveted her eyes back on his piercing blue ones. ''Shaker furniture is so lean yet strong and handsome...''

Her voice trailed off. She looked away from him and felt herself begin to blush. Of all the stupid, adolescent things. Why, when she knew better than to trust any man, was she confiding so much to this one?

''Again, I'm grateful for your help with—against Varina,'' she said as she started back for the guest house where she'd begun packing earlier today. Right now, she just couldn't face this man's scrutiny, nor the ruined roses. But as dangerously as Varina was acting, Kate was still going to Sarah's funeral tomorrow.

After the funeral in the church, people stared at Kate Marburn from the moment she got out of her car at Woodlawn Cemetery. Head high and shoulders back, she looked straight past the bereaved family, friends, television people and watchful police.

The western sky glared gun-barrel gray in contrast to the overhead sun that shot through the vibrant leaves of the gnarled beech guarding the burial site. But even larger loomed the gaping hole in the earth that would soon swallow Sarah Denbigh's coffin. The family plot where Sarah would be buried next to her husband lay in the shadow of the historic Denbigh mausoleum, which stood over the site like a massive tombstone. Beyond the grave, the sweep of lawns set with regularly spaced statues, pyramids and urns made the cemetery seem one giant chessboard.

Again, as so often, Kate's love for Sarah and her sense of loss over the older woman's death summoned a memory of her mother. Kate was holding her daddy's hand, standing at an open hole in the

ground that looked so large. And they were putting
Mommy in it in a pretty box and placing flowers all
around the hole, not planting them but leaving them
to die in the sun—and Kate didn't like that. She
wanted to save each one, to put each in water the way
she and Mommy had. And now she had lost Sarah,
too....

"'Let not your heart be troubled,'" the minister
began.

Heads turned toward the coffin again. Despite herself, Kate quickly scanned the crowd for the tall, dark-
haired Jack Kilcourse. But then, why should he come
to this?

"'In my Father's house are many mansions...'"

Kate frowned at the green plastic turf that stretched
to the brink of the grave. That shiny rug, the hump
of pink carnations and the ornate metal casket were
all wrong. Sarah would have wanted a simple spray
of her favorite antique roses on a plain, wooden coffin, lovingly handcrafted like a piece of fine Shaker
furniture.

The stiff, gilt banner flared over the carnations
pompously proclaimed, OUR BELOVED AND
CHERISHED MOTHER. FROM YOUR VARINA
AND PALMER. The ribbon tail with their names
kept rapping against the top of the casket, as if Sarah
were knocking to get out.

A shudder racked Kate. She couldn't bear for Sarah
to be placed in a concrete vault in the deep grave.
Sarah had loved to be outdoors under the vast sweep
of sky.

"'If it were not so, I would have told you...'"

The two crimson Damask roses nearly vibrating in
her grasp, Kate strode closer through the crowd. Sarah

had filled the aching void in her life, just the way Kate had tried to fill poor, angry Erin's. And Mike's desertion of his daughter had brought back the fury Erin harbored over what—to a young child—looked like a mother's desertion.

"'I go to prepare a place for you...'"

Except for leaving her stepdaughter alone, Kate would gladly have died for Sarah, but no one evidently believed or understood that. Not when Sarah had been the uncrowned patron saint of the city and Kate the most notorious woman in it.

"'...that where I am, there you may be also.'"

Varina's stare stabbed at Kate from across the bowed heads, as the pastor began a prayer. Kate closed her eyes to shut out that fierce face and, next to it, that of the younger Palmer. Kate was so angry at both of them that she'd like to plant them in that hole in the ground. Yet Varina had known loss, too. And grief, no doubt, took different guises.

"'And now to Him who is able to keep you from falling, and to present you faultless...'"

Kate caught sight of Stan Rudzinski, hunched in a black trench coat against a large tree trunk, looking her way, too. Did he lift his eyebrows as if to ask another question, or was she imagining that, imagining all sorts of things again?

"'...now and forever.' Amen."

When people began to bid farewell to the Denbigh family, Kate moved around the back of the casket under the green canvas canopy. Despite the fact that she saw Palmer striding her way, she thrust the two fragrant Damask blooms, the last roses of summer, atop the heap of cloying carnations.

"In other words," Palmer said, "you want to make

a public statement we should have bought her roses?
You know, somehow, that just doesn't set real well
with Varina right now."

Kate turned slowly to face him. "And who cares
what Sarah's wishes would have been about it—about
anything, right?" she challenged before she could
take the words back. "You were welcome to every
single rose in her vast gardens, Palmer. But as you
must know she hated the smell of carnations."

He flushed right through his tan and could not meet
her eyes.

"You're not making decisions for her anymore,"
he muttered, fingering the loose ribbon on the casket.

"And never was. You surely knew Sarah Denbigh
too well to believe that."

Yet, as if he were ten years old instead of thirty,
he plucked her two flowers from the casket and
dropped them back among the other arrangements
clustered around. She felt some satisfaction when she
saw he'd stuck his fingers with the prominent thorns.

"Is there a problem here?" Detective Rudzinski
said, stepping up to them. Kate had learned he'd recently been promoted to Homicide and was aching to
make good, especially with this high-profile case. She
felt adept at psyching out investigators, and this one
scared her. He was out to make his own name, not
save hers.

"I can't believe you'd show your face here after I
told you to stay away," Varina accused under her
breath as she emerged from the crowd. She wedged
herself in to shut out the men and face Kate on her
own.

"I came to honor a woman I deeply admired, who
opened her life and home to me," Kate said, keeping

her voice in check, as others looked their way and shuffled closer. "She was unique and wonderful. There is none—*none* like her," she said directly to Varina, then moved quickly away.

The buzz began again as Kate strode from the graveside. She heard the whir of the TV cameras even before Mandy Ross, one of the city's all-too-familiar top reporters, stuck a mike in her face and asked, "How are you answering the Denbigh family's charges, Mrs. Marburn? How—"

"The same way I answered the other false ones you people continue to resurrect and revel in. No comment."

Kate shouldered past the woman and picked up her pace. The reporter wore high heels, which bogged her down in the thick turf. She also had to drag her mike and cameraman with her. Kate had reached her car when a well-attired couple stepped swiftly forward, as if they'd been waiting for her. Some of Sarah's friends? She didn't recognize them.

"Mrs. Marburn, one moment please," the silver-haired man, older than the woman, called to her as they stayed politely a short distance away.

"I'm sorry. As you can see, I'm in a hurry."

"We're Dane and Adrienne Thompson, Board of Trustee members from Shaker Run. Mrs. Denbigh loaned us so much of her fine furniture," the man explained hastily.

Despite the way the television people were closing on her—another reporter from a competing network had appeared with a big mike on a handheld boom—Kate opened her car door but did not get in. "Shaker Run meant a lot to Sarah. How kind of you to come clear up from southern Ohio. I visited your village with her last winter.'' She remembered these people now; Sarah had spoken with them about where particular pieces of her loaned furniture might be placed in various buildings.

''We'd like to call on you, if that's all right,'' Adrienne said. ''A bit of business, yes?'' She was sleek and svelte-looking with a faint French accent; she sounded and looked completely out of place here, let alone how she'd look in a simple Shaker village, tourist attraction or not.

''I'm leaving the guest house at Groveland,'' Kate explained hastily as she got in, slammed the door, but cracked the window open. Just then, Mandy Ross appeared and thrust the microphone in, while her cameraman shot Kate through the glass. The other station's boom mike swooped before the front windshield like a bat. She'd be damned if she was going to give her new address only to have it recorded for the six-o'clock news, Kate thought.

''I'll just phone you at the village later,'' she promised the Thompsons. She rolled her window up, turned the ignition key and hit the gas pedal. The boom mike bumped away. Too late, Kate realized she'd caught Mandy's microphone in her window. In the rearview mirror, she gasped to see the cord snag the reporter's lapel mike from her suit, ripping her jacket open to reveal a white flash of bra and flesh.

Though Kate's life was in public ruins for the second time in two years, she laughed until the tears ran down her face, then dissolved in sobs so wrenching she had to pull over to the curb on a side street outside the cemetery. Finally, when she could calm herself, she heaved the mike out the passenger window into the gutter.

As she wiped her eyes and cheeks, she smelled on her hands the clinging scent of the Damasks she'd brought for the grave. And somehow she felt stronger and surer than she had since she'd found Sarah lying last week in that blooming pool of crimson blood.

"The new place is a cute little apartment with no view like this, but I got almost everything in it," Kate assured Erin over the phone, trying to sound perky.

"But you hate little places," Erin protested.

The day after Sarah's funeral, Kate had worked all morning to repair the rosebushes Varina had damaged; then she'd called her stepdaughter. Though Kate was ready to leave the guest house with her last carload of belongings, she had wanted to talk to Erin once more from this shelter where they'd tried to reconstruct their lives. Kate gave Erin their new home phone number and the address of the upstairs apartment in the big, old house she was renting from Sarah's maid's sister.

"No, really, this is fine," she told the girl. "I only needed to lease a small storage space for my bigger garden tools, not to mention those boxes of my rose books and my old client files, in case I ever try to get back into business."

There was a moment's silence between them. *But not in Toledo,* both of them thought but didn't say.

"With all the stuff we sold at the auction, I should hope you'd get most of it in," Erin said, picking up the conversation with a slight scolding tone, as if she were the parent now. "But even if Mrs. Denbigh left you that job, roses and furniture, do you really want to stay around Toledo, waiting for her will to clear?

Especially if Varina and Palmer are contesting it and trying to blame you?''

"If I go somewhere else, it may look like I'm running—and I can't stand that.''

"Can't stand what he did or just plain can't stand him anymore?'' Erin demanded, as if Kate had mentioned Mike.

She was shocked at the quick switch to Erin's strident tone.

"Never mind,'' the girl went on, calmer now. "Don't answer that. But the thing is, it's pretty neat to be away—to just be yourself and be free.''

To be yourself and be free, Kate thought. Yes, she'd always wanted that, and now it was being threatened again. She wasn't going to let that happen.

"Sweetheart, as much as I'd like to go away to college in a pretty, small town on the edge of the Appalachians,'' Kate said, describing Athens, where Ohio University nestled in the southern Ohio hills, "unlike you, I don't have anywhere to go. But as I said, I'll be down to see you as soon as I get resettled.''

After they said goodbye, Kate picked up her last packed box and glanced around at the guest house living area for the last time. But the phone rang again. Erin calling back? Her lawyer with more advice? Or Stan Rudzinski wanting another interview?

Putting the box back down, she glared at the phone, then snatched it up. "Kate Marburn.''

"Mrs. Marburn, it's Dane Thompson.''

The man from the Shaker village who had tried to talk to her yesterday at the funeral, Kate thought. She could hear the woman's lighter tones in the background, as if prompting him what to say. Behind all that was some sort of echoing buzz, maybe voices in a big room.

"You see," Dane went on, speaking quickly as if she'd hang up, "we're still in town and just took a chance you might not have left this number yet. We called Mrs. Denbigh's old number, and her maid gave us yours."

"I'm just on my way out the door—permanently, I'm afraid," Kate explained patiently. She could hear the muted, lilting, foreign voice of Adrienne again, as if Dane had partly covered the receiver with his hand. Then his voice came through clear and strong again.

"Frankly, Ms. Marburn, we have what we believe is a very attractive offer for you, one that we are certain you cannot afford to refuse."

That old threatening line from *The Godfather,* Kate thought, but she could not help being curious.

Despite her reluctance to talk to anyone about any business dealings, Kate decided to meet them. She hoped the Thompsons hadn't just read in the paper that she was to inherit the furniture currently on loan to Shaker Run and wanted to try to buy it. As she had vowed to Varina, she wasn't selling.

She agreed to talk about their offer at the Toledo Museum of Art cafeteria at four that afternoon. They knew the museum was a fine one, Dane explained, and, before heading back to southern Ohio, they'd decided to stay overnight to catch the Louis XIV touring display of *objects d'arts* from Versailles.

As Kate packed her final load in the car, she thought of Sarah again, and glanced at the Groveland mansion through the vibrant autumn trees. "Versailles on the Maumee," she whispered. She gazed at the tall, shining windows of Sarah's suite and wondered if Jack Kilcourse was still examining its fine furnishings.

Strangely, unbelievably, for she considered herself quite realistic and unromantic now, her stomach cartwheeled at the mere memory of the man. Shaking her head, Kate got in her car and drove away.

5

Rose leaves, when the rose is dead,
Are heaped for the beloved's bed;
And so thy thoughts, when thou are gone,
Love itself shall slumber on.

> —Percy Bysshe Shelley
> "Music When Soft Voices Die"

Within the hour, Kate had changed clothes, and had driven to the marble, pillared, three-block museum. The graceful, Greek-style building had been donated to the city long ago by Edward Drummond Libbey, one of the glass barons who had made a turn-of-the-last-century fortune in Toledo. As she went in the back entrance, the interior felt cool. Her footsteps echoed even through the hum of distant voices.

Kate shook hands with the Thompsons as they indicated a table in the corner. While the women commiserated over Sarah's death, Dane left momentarily to get coffee and carrot cake for everyone.

When he returned, he quickly steered their conversation to business. "Since you've visited Shaker Run Village before and understand we are in the process of building it up to become not only a tourist attraction but an authentic piece of living history, let me get right to the point," Dane said. "Shaker Run is expanding its meager staff, and we need a rosarian to design, plant and maintain our flower beds and extensive future rose gardens—with the two, old-time roses the Shakers allowed, of course.''

That piqued Kate's interest immediately. A job away from here with a garden, antique roses...

"The two Shaker breeds would be the *Rosa Gallica Officinalis,* sometimes called 'Apothecary rose,' and a summer Damask,'' Kate said, recalling what she'd learned at the village during her visit. She gripped her coffee cup harder. "Each rose has one big annual flowering, but the bounty of dried petals is a treasure that lasts all year long.''

"Precisely,'' Dane agreed with a nod, while Adrienne leaned toward him, apparently hanging on his every word. "We would hope you could distill that famous Shaker rose water for the village to sell. That is, if you would consider accepting the position.''

It was a dream job, but Kate felt honor-bound to stay here to care for Sarah's roses—if she got the chance. Varina and Palmer's contesting the will could delay its bestowments to her or cancel them entirely. Besides, Sarah had wanted both Shaker Run and Groveland to prosper.

"And,'' Adrienne added, "we'd like you to work closely with the part-time herbalist we have hired, yes?''

Not to mention the fact, Kate thought excitedly, that the Ohio University campus and Erin were just twenty miles from Shaker Run, instead of the nearly two hundred from Toledo! Kate bit her lower lip to keep from blurting out that she'd kill for such a job—though she dare not put it that way.

"We can discuss salary, of course, if you'd be willing to drive down to meet the others on the Board and the staff,'' Dane explained, shifting his feet under their small table where Kate had curled her toes so hard in excitement they almost cramped. "We'd like to share our vision with you about the future of Shaker Run—a vision…'' he repeated, gazing toward the ceiling. "Now that's a good way to put it, as the Shakers were so attuned to their visions from angels and those who had gone on to their rewards."

His last words snagged in Kate's mind. She knew the Shakers were unusual, but obviously needed to know more. Imagine a life and place where people put stock in visions, angels and visits from the dead. And if they believed in angels, did they believe in demons, too?

"*Mon amour,* the apartment…'' Adrienne prompted her husband in the slight lull that followed.

"Oh, yes,'' he said, his voice steady again. "Our offer to you would include spacious living quarters above the Trustees' Office, at least until you find some other place if you'd like. I'm sure it isn't quite up to Mrs. Denbigh's guest house and grounds, but it's—forgive me for putting it this way—but we believe it's a fertile opportunity for a woman with your interests and talents.''

"Your offer sounds wonderful,'' Kate admitted, still agonizing over whether to leave what Sarah had entrusted to her here. "If I accept—and I repeat *if*— I could transplant my own bushes. The village wouldn't even have to purchase starts as most of mine are much more mature, and I could propagate others this winter.''

"How splendid,'' Adrienne said, beaming with apparent relief. "Dane, isn't that splendid that she will consider it? I'm sure Mrs. Denbigh would approve, my dear,'' she said, addressing Kate directly at last, ''for she obviously favored our cause.''

''If you can assemble the board and staff, I'll come down this week,'' Kate promised, smiling at the thought of a new career she would love—and one near Erin.

''Didn't your mother ever tell you that if an offer seems too good to be true, it probably is?'' Detective Rudzinski demanded, when she explained the job offer to him the next day. They were sitting in the small living area of Kate's newly rented apartment. Kate hadn't wanted Rudzinski here, but neither had she wanted to, as he put it, ''make it a formal foursome with Tina Martin and her lawyer in his office.''

''Look, Detective, I lost my mother when I was young and hardly remember a thing she said,'' Kate blurted, though she hadn't meant to share that with him. She knew her voice was too strident again, but he was really beginning to annoy her. ''I know,'' she went on, trying to keep calm, ''you didn't mean anything by the remark, but you can't understand how her loss still haunts me.''

''Actually, I can. Someone shot my dad dead when he went out for a bottle of milk for us kids when I was five, and I can't recall one damn thing about him but his dedication to his job.''

He looked away before going on. ''He was away a lot on his job as a street cop who walked a beat for years.'' He heaved a huge sigh. ''Then a stray bullet hits him 'cause a dairy store's getting robbed for a few bucks the week before Christmas.''

''I'm sorry,'' she faltered, leaning slightly forward.

"I see." She really did see. That explained a lot about this man's doggedness.

"And here I thought you were dedicated to Mrs. Denbigh's gardens," he went on, obviously as eager as she to change the subject.

"I haven't decided to take the offer," she repeated. "I'm just exploring possibilities."

"You sound pretty excited about it to me."

"If the new will wasn't as frozen as the ground soon will be," Kate told him, gripping her hands in her lap, "I might wait it out here, hoping to get to care for Sarah's—hers and my—roses. But, as is, it might be years before I see that job her will leaves me."

"I'd stick around if I were you," he observed, throwing one arm along the back of the short sofa as if they had all the time in the world. "Why risk the windfall of a lifetime by taking off where you can't keep an eye on Varina—who, I think, ought to be darn grateful you didn't hit her with assault with a deadly weapon for her attack on you in the rose garden."

"The thing is," Kate admitted, not wanting to re-open their mutual wound of losing a parent, "I like to think that she is grieving her mother's loss and has just...well..."

"Lost it?" he put in. "You know, you and Varina seem like night and day, Kate, but maybe you're a woman who likes taking risks, too."

She noted he'd used her first name. If he thought he was going to pretend to get friendly with her, he could forget that ploy.

"You stand to be a rich woman if a judge rules this new will is valid," he pursued.

"Rich only if I'd sell the Shaker heritage, which I won't."

"Maybe these people at Shaker Run think you will—sell to them—or better yet, donate the furniture."

"It's not mine to donate, and I can't live my life in limbo, Detective, waiting for some judge's ruling or Varina's next lawsuit. My stepdaughter goes to college near Shaker Run, and, frankly, I could use the change of scenery. And I think—I pray—Sarah would understand. You aren't going to tell me I'm not free to go, are you, even to the interview?" she challenged.

"Why would you think that?" he parried, drumming his fingers on the back of the sofa. "Though, if you really do move down there, I just might have to learn a bit more about the Shakers with a visit or two."

Kate just stared at him. Surely he wasn't implying a personal visit. "Looks like cause of death will be ruled accidental," he went on, "though I don't know if that satisfies me. Does it you?"

"I think we've both said enough today," she countered. "Why don't you just continue this little conversation with my lawyer? I thought you had something to tell me, not that you wanted me to tell you all sorts of things again."

"You know, if I did visit you there, though," he went on as if he hadn't heard her, "I'd also drop in on that furniture expertiser we hired who lives near there. The guy even makes Shaker reproductions."

"Jack Kilcourse?"

"He said you'd met. Gave me a blow-by-blow of your encounter with Sarah's daughter."

Kate nodded grimly, then said, "You evidently had gone AWOL, and Mr. Kilcourse was kind enough to help me hold off Valkyrie Varina."

Rudzinski laughed. "She is hell on wheels and makes no bones about her feelings, which is why I just can't believe she's really a possible perp in her mother's demise. Can you?" he asked, suddenly leaning forward, his chin propped in his hands and his elbows on his knees.

"You never give up, do you, Detective? You're implying Varina would be more subtle if she were guilty?"

"Don't you agree? She's a hothead but not an idiot. She'd back off a bit from seeming to want control of the Shaker furniture and the fortune behind it. She wouldn't publicly assault someone near the site of her mother's death, however much she blames that person *for* her mother's death."

Again Kate's hackles rose; she stared Rudzinski down. He was right, but he was also much more devious than she'd given him credit for. And he obviously still considered her a—or *the*—prime suspect in Sarah's death. She sat up even straighter. If Sarah had been murdered, Kate might need this man's help to be sure the killer was brought to justice, but she trusted "Zink" less than she did other men—and that was not at all.

"I believe I've proved by now that I don't run from something—even the mere appearance of something—I am not guilty of," Kate said coolly as she stood. "But I do believe in running toward something good, and that's why I am going to seriously consider this job. Now if you'll excuse me..."

She marched across the room to open the door for

him. He went jauntily down the stairs, but he dared to call back over his shoulder, "Guess I'll have to tell you about the blood splatter evidence later. Best of luck with the interview for the great escape."

Though Kate supposed it seemed a crazy thing to do, she planned to talk to Sarah—that is, to visit her grave to say the solemn farewell she had not been able to say at the funeral. Before even going for the interview at Shaker Run, she was considering taking the job.

Kate decided to go to the cemetery in the early morning when no one else would be around. The last thing in the world she needed was to face Varina or Palmer at their mother's grave. But she'd miscalculated the opening time, and only the walk-through gate was open; the large, front Central Avenue gate accessible to cars was locked. She parked her car just outside, and went in the small entrance that evidently served the caretaker's nearby house. The gate's iron hinges screeched in protest.

Kate had brought two more roses with her, mere buds caught in the plunging temperatures she'd picked before she'd left Groveland. Perhaps they wouldn't even open, but Sarah would understand. New possibilities, ready to bloom but still a bit unknown.

Woodlawn was the grand old cemetery of the city. Kate had always admired the beauty of its mature trees and overall landscaping. Yet it seemed a heavy place, burdened with the weight of massive monuments to great Toledo families such as the Libbeys, DeVilbisses, Talmadges, Berdans and, of course, the Denbighs.

Though she hadn't seen it on the streets, a morning mist still hung here and the grass was damp with dew. She stuck to the main, curving entry road that passed the section on the right belonging to the Romany community of local gypsies. Several of the monuments were benches, for they often visited and communed with their dead, even picnicking there in celebration of their free-spirited, wandering lives. Right now, that struck Kate as appropriate and moving.

She took a turn to the left and walked over the bridge that spanned the narrow lake, for the Denbigh plot wasn't much farther in. The old crematorium sat near here. Kate shuddered in the morning chill as she cut up across the silvered grass, walking between stones and crypts under the thickening canopy of autumn beeches. The deeper she went, the thicker the drifting patches of faint fog.

Without people pressing in around it under the canvas canopy, Sarah's grave looked different. It was barren but for decaying carnations heaped, wilting and dying, on the replanted turf over her resting place. Kate closed her eyes to envision it abloom with heirloom Chinas, Gallicas and Bourbons. She would think of it that way—that Sarah simply slept under a beautiful blanket of roses and in the memory of those who truly loved her.

"Sarah," she whispered, placing the rosebuds atop the pile, "I've had a wonderful job offer. I'd have to leave the gardens at Groveland, but I'd be tending Apothecaries and Damasks I'd take with me to Shaker Run."

She felt foolish speaking out loud, and she glanced nervously around. The sounds of traffic were but a dull buzz. If it were warmer, she would have sat right here with her thoughts for a while. And then she saw that the door to the Denbigh private family mausoleum stood wide open.

It hadn't been open the day of the funeral, she was sure of it. And even if the family had been in there, or the caretaker, surely it would not have been open overnight. The cemetery hadn't had vandals that she'd heard of, but in this day and age, you never knew.

Thinking she would slam the door shut, Kate started around the grave for the mausoleum. She gasped to see a trail of rose heads, leading toward the stained and moss-covered stone building. It stood twice as tall as she and, like other monuments here, was built in a classical style. As she approached, a musty smell exhaled from its dark, gaping mouth.

She reached out with both hands to close the iron door. The lock had been broken, or at least neatly cut off. Then it must be vandals. She hoped things weren't defaced inside, but either way she should report it to the caretaker.

Instead of closing the door, she peered around it. No way she was stepping into the small interior to be sure everything looked all right. From here, the crypts in the wall looked undisturbed, though she saw someone had scattered rose petals on the floor. Varina or Palmer? But roses? And why break the lock?

Kate frowned as she studied the crimson rose petals in the wan light. No, not petals or full flowers but entire buds, just like the ones behind her. Quickly, she counted those inside the mausoleum and out. Twelve. Someone had evidently bought a dozen flower-shop roses, decapitated them, and thrown only their heads both on Sarah's grave and in here.

Kate was moving to close the door, when she heard

a muted slam. She jumped back, thinking it was a sound from inside. But it must have just echoed here against the building.

She spun around to see an old, black car had pulled up near the crematorium on the lane. A man had gotten out and evidently had slammed the car door. Wearing an unbelted, dark trench coat, his head and face covered by an old-fashioned fedora, he stood, bushes and monuments between them, just staring at her. Hunching his shoulders, he reached a gloved hand to tug the brim lower over his face.

She knew instantly it was not the caretaker. Was there something vaguely familiar about him? She wasn't sure—perhaps the set of the head or the way he raised his hand.

At least the gates must be open now, and others would be coming in. Squinting to see better at this distance, she began to walk toward him, around tombstones and trees.

For one moment she thought it might be Palmer. She couldn't imagine him in a hat like that, but then, who did wear those anymore?

"Hello," she called to him. "Is there a problem? Are you looking for a particular grave?" When he didn't answer, she added, "I was just going to get the caretaker." She hesitated, then stopped when he did not respond or move. "Who are you?" she demanded.

In reply, he opened his car door and got in. Kate wasn't certain, but she thought someone might be in the front passenger seat. She couldn't see inside because the car's window reflected sky and trees. She heard the engine rev. As the vehicle pulled away, she ran, hoping to catch a glimpse inside or at least get the license plate, but she saw now the windows were all tinted and there was no plate.

"People are so damn weird!" she muttered, and stopped running. After glancing back at the now distant Denbigh plot, she set a good pace toward the caretaker's cottage. Someone was going to have to fix that lock, and she was not going to phone Varina to tell her it needed repair. She even considered just leaving and calling the caretaker anonymously. She cut down the narrow, gravel lane off the main paved one, because it led more directly to her car. Walking briskly, she was soon perspiring and out of breath.

And then she heard a car behind her. She spun to squint into the rising sun. Crunching stones under its tires, the same antique, black vehicle—from the 30s or 40s?—was creeping much slower than the posted speed limit signs suggested. Kate glanced back over her shoulder, then moved to the berm and glared at it. For one instant she was certain two people were in the car, but the dark windshield obscured forms and faces.

It kept coming, edging over to this side of the lane, right at her. The front of it was studded with fancy metal grillwork, which seemed stuck in a toothy grin. Kate froze in disbelief and shock. The car windows were one giant mirror; she could see her own slightly distorted reflection in the dark glass.

Just before the car got to her, Kate cut up among the tombstones again. As though it could chase her through them, the vehicle sped up and barreled by on the lane, coming to a screeching halt a ways past. Was someone demented playing games with her? Down the lane, she saw the car slowly turn around in a crossroad and creep back.

Cutting deeper into the cemetery section, Kate broke into a run. She saw she'd have to skirt the far edge of the lake. At least she was nearly to the iron fence that ran along Central Avenue, and it was full of morning rush traffic. But she saw the black car along this outer loop of road, waiting, hulking down as if ready to spring when she crossed to the gate or caretaker's house.

She tore back up into the stones, darting around tall urns and crypts, then crouched to see what the car would do next. If it would just go by, she'd dash across the road.

"You'll be all right," she encouraged herself aloud, panting. "It's just some jerk harassing a woman he doesn't even know."

The car edged along the outer road, keeping pace with her, so easily, so smoothly, as if trying to wear her down. She ducked behind an angel monument and peeked out. The car stopped, its engine humming. She'd turn to go the other way. Even if it backed up, it would never get to her if she ran hard.

Huddled under the white marble angel, Kate sucked in two deep breaths. But when she stood and turned to run, the angel came to life before her, around her, all fanned white wings and shimmering robe, lifting, whirling, flapping. Something screeched at her and hit her, bringing pain and night.

6

When I am dead, my dearest,
Sing no sad songs for me;
Plant thou no roses at my head,
Nor shady cypress tree.
Be the green grass above me
With showers, and dewdrops wet;
And if thou wilt, remember
And if thou wilt, forget.

> —Christina Georgina Rossetti
> "Song"

"Hey, lady, you okay?" a man's voice asked. "You musta fell and hit your head."

Kate eyes flew open. She saw a burly, bearded man in jeans and a green sweatshirt squatting beside her. Despite her pounding headache, she was relieved he did not wear a black raincoat and fedora. Or had she dreamed the man and that black car after she hit her head?

Staring upward, Kate saw a stone angel, and beyond that the branches of an evergreen or cypress. The angel, at least, just hovered, unmoving now. She was in the cemetery, and this man must be a worker.

"I guess I fell and hit my head," she whispered. Had she said that a moment ago? *Sarah*. Sarah had fallen and hit her head. And died. Things were going in circles, and she was so dizzy.

"You're not supposed to be in here yet," the man said, as she struggled to sit up, then leaned back against the base of the angel. "The gates are just op'ning now."

"Then who was in that black car?" she asked, tentatively fingering her painful head bruise.

"Didn't see no black car. Nobody'd get in with the front gates locked, 'less they drove in the service entrance way at the back, and hardly nobody knows about that. The caretaker who lives on the grounds there—" he said with a nod in that direction, "drives a red van."

"It was a black car with tinted windows!"

"Can't help you, lady, but I can go get a car to take you to a hospital if you want that head bump looked at. It's gonna be a big one. Gotta watch out for concussions and all that."

Kate's mind darted after answers and kept hitting dead ends. She had seen a man in a car, and he had followed her and even tried to hit her. And then she'd hidden behind this angel monument and turned to run—

"Didn't you hear a screech of brakes a while ago? I'm not sure when but..." Her voice trailed off as the vision of that avenging angel swooping down replayed itself in her mind.

"The only screech I heard was that last white peacock we got on the grounds. You get near, she'll fan that tail and shriek like a banshee. Might even fly right at you. Rich folks in Europe used them for watchdogs on their estates," he explained importantly. "We had two of 'em 'fore one got kilt. But its mate was a coupla monuments away when I seen you. Let me just help you down to the caretaker's place—but he's not gonna be too pleased you trespassed on the grounds 'fore opening time.''

Big deal, Kate thought. That couldn't hold a candle to the other accusations she'd faced. "All right," she said, getting to her feet with his hand on her elbow. "I have to report a broken lock on the Denbigh mausoleum, anyway."

"Denbigh? I knew I recognized you!" the man cried.

His faced crushed in a frown, he folded his arms over his chest as if she'd insulted him. It was the same old story, and Kate was sick of it. She refused to let anyone drag her down as Mike had. Nor would she be cowed by the fact that she had, at least temporarily, lost the right to oversee the Denbigh gardens, or was probably under suspicion for Sarah's death.

At that moment, staring back at the angel she had hallucinated had come to life to attack her, Kate decided she would take that dream job at Shaker Run.

Two days later, on a crisp, sunny afternoon, Kate got out of her car in front of the Trustees' Office at Shaker Run Village and looked around at the panorama. She was so excited and on edge that she hadn't had to fight exhaustion while driving. Her insomnia had been in full bloom these past few years, and she'd often had to roll down her windows, sing and shout on long drives, to avoid falling asleep at the wheel. And ever since her visit to Sarah's grave she'd been glancing over her shoulder and in the rearview mirror to be certain she wasn't being followed. But not today.

She sucked in a fresh, free breath of air. The lawns and fields of this plateau stretched to the forests and foothills of the Appalachians. As it cut through the village, the stream that gave the place its name sparkled in the sun. No wonder some people had sought refuge here as the nineteenth century approached. It felt safe even on the edge of the new millennium.

Kate surveyed the neat wood frame and sturdy stone buildings of the 1820s-era dwellings, workshops and outbuildings. The village had once encompassed more than two thousand acres and had supported more than four hundred of The United Society of Believers in Christ's Second Appearing. That second appearing, they believed, had been the birth and ministry of their illiterate, immigrant founder, Ann Lee.

The Shakers, as they were more commonly called for their wild, trembling dances of worship, renounced sex and marriage. In their striving to create a celibate heaven on earth, they had increased their numbers only through converts. Under the philosophy set forth by "Mother" Ann, they farmed and traded with the outside world. A booming business in garden seeds, brooms, furniture and rose water helped the Shakers flourish but after the Civil War, Believers began to drift off and villages closed.

Finally, four years ago, the Thompsons had convinced some wealthy investors to finance the restoration of Shaker Run. It had only opened to tourists last spring and still had a long way to go. And, Kate thought determinedly, she and her roses could be part of that.

"I saw you drive in," Dane Thompson called to her as he stepped out through what was no doubt the men's entrance of the double doors of the Trustees' Building. "Just looking around?"

"Exactly," she said, shaking his hand. "I'm seeing it through new eyes now."

"You will grow to love it dearly if you join us, I promise," he said fervently. "The outside world will never look quite the same."

"Exactly where is the perimeter of the village?" she asked.

He walked her away from the building and, despite the fact he wore no coat in the brisk breeze, began to point and explain.

"To the west, the way you came in on this Old Turnpike Road, which runs parallel to the modern highway, was the West Family Dwelling House and what used to be the school for what was called The Gathering Order."

"Where novices and new converts were prepared until they were ready to commit to the covenant," she put in.

"You have been reading up on us," he said, smiling. "We'd eventually like to buy those two buildings and their land—which are about a half-mile away— but they are owned by a very independent Shaker furniture designer who lives in the dwelling and uses the schoolhouse for his shop. Other than that holdout, all else you can see on this plateau is ours."

"What's his name—that independent builder?" she asked.

"Jack Kilcourse. Keeps to himself and has declined to join us in our efforts, though I must admit he makes some of the best, and most expensive, authentic Shaker reproductions in the world. Ah, you looked interested. Do you know the man?"

"I met him recently," she said, disappointed that

Jack was not a part of things here, "when he was expertising the Denbigh furniture collection in Toledo. So you were saying all these other buildings we can see belong to the village?"

"Indeed they do, though we're still in the process of restoring some. But the garden shops are ready for you and the herbalist. They're behind the Meeting House across that side lane, back toward the old burying ground and the holy ground where the Shakers sometimes worshipped outside. Why don't we go inside to meet everyone who's assembled, and I'll have someone show you those later."

Kate walked back toward the Trustees' Building with him, admiring the neat look of the structure in which the Thompsons had promised her temporary living quarters. No one else lived here at night, so Jack would be her nearest neighbor; she found that both reassuring and alarming. But she had always wanted to live in the country, and this might be as close as she'd ever get. The Thompsons themselves lived twenty minutes away, and they'd told her that everyone else drove in from homes near Athens or up in the hills. Dane opened both doors and indicated she should enter through the one on the left.

"Here comes our newest convert," he called to the staff assembled at a long table in the front room. Everyone looked up from their meeting. "And we hope and pray she'll agree to sign on the dotted line, just like in the old do-or-die covenants!"

Despite the way he'd put that, Kate felt right at home.

In addition to the Thompsons, there were four others at the table—the working staff for the place, as Dane put it. He introduced Kate to each in turn.

"This is Clint Barstow," Dane began, as a strapping man stood and leaned down the table to shake her hand with his beefy one. He pressed the flesh just a bit too hard, but she didn't wince. "Clint oversees a staff of four carpenters who do building maintenance and repairs but are also getting big-time into the Shaker reproductions we are going to start selling here when we reopen," Dane explained.

"So you have no relationship with Jack Kilcourse's work," Kate observed.

"He's a black sheep," Barstow muttered, "close to us only in the proximity of his workshop. 'Course, I guess he did put Dane and Adrienne onto you."

"Ah, yes," Dane said, glaring at Barstow as if he'd said too much. "Kilcourse isn't hostile to us, but usually isn't so helpful either. He mentioned Mrs. Denbigh had an antique rose grower who might be looking for a job."

That surprised Kate. Had Jack Kilcourse figured out all that while he was saving her from Varina, or had he wormed some information out of Rudzinski? At any rate, she owed her guardian angel two favors now.

But what really caught her notice was that Dane had lied to her, or at least misled her. Earlier he'd asked if she knew Jack, when clearly he was aware they'd met. She noted there was a slight lull before Dane said, "Of course, you realize that Adrienne and I serve as the movers and shakers here—"

Everyone laughed at his pun, though Kate sensed he'd said it before. "I act as curator, and chair the board," he went on. "And Adrienne buys for and oversees our gift shop in the Meeting House down the way. And this lovely, authentic couple are Ben and Louise Willis, volunteers—priceless ones."

"I like to think," Ben said with a little sniff, "that all true Shakers were volunteers."

It was only then, since the Willises were hatless, that Kate noted they were garbed in Shaker clothing. His big-brimmed hat sat next to his notes on the table. He wore a white, long-sleeved collarless shirt, and Louise was in a plum-hued long gown with the traditional kerchief crossed over her breasts. Her hat, a deep, tightly woven straw bonnet, hung by ribbons on her chair back. The couple were both brown-haired and nondescript-looking, somewhere in their fifties, Kate guessed. In a way, they looked as if they could be brother and sister, and not just Shaker ones.

"True," Dane was saying, though Kate had nearly forgotten what Ben Willis had said. "Anyhow, I was going to explain that the Willises are heading up a new effort to oversee some volunteer presenters."

"That is, Kate—if I might call you Kate—" Ben put in, "workers on the grounds will *become* Shakers, as it were, answer questions as the real Believers might have as they go about their daily duties, etcetera. That's done other places, such as at Jamestown and on the Mayflower, and it adds authenticity."

"As a matter of fact," Louise put in, her brown eyes flashing with purpose, "Ben and I were just going to introduce the suggestion that it would be marvelous if each of the presenters—all of us included—actually read some of the Shaker diaries—they were wonderful record keepers—and picked a person to become."

"It's a good idea," said the only woman who had

not yet been introduced, an attractive, young African American. "But no way any of us would want to do some of the things they did. It's kind of creepy, too, like becoming a dead person speaking from the grave."

"Well," Louise said, sitting up even straighter, "I certainly wouldn't look at it like that. Why do you always have to jump on other people's ideas, Tanya?"

"All right," Dane said, holding up both hands, "we'll get back to all that later. I was saving Tanya for last since she's our talented herbalist, and you'd be working most closely with her," he explained to Kate. "Tanya Dodridge, herbalist extraordinaire, meet Kate Marburn, rosarian extraordinaire."

"Come on now. Just let me show you the places that *really* count around here," her guide said.

After an hour's discussion with the Shaker Run staff—which had culminated in Adrienne's showing Kate the charming, top floor, four-room apartment and Dane again offering Kate the job—Tanya Dodridge took her outside to see the garden workshops they would share if Kate accepted. And Kate fully intended to do just that, if the financial offer Dane said they'd discuss before she left was even reasonable.

"That will be my main herb garden," Tanya explained, pointing out a bare, neatly tilled square of ground beside the Meeting House. It had obviously been planted in neat rows and sections during this past growing season. "You'll be free to put in one on the other side of the house to balance this garden and make whole hedges of rosebushes pretty much wherever you want in the village. As far as I can tell from my studies, they had them all over, even lining the lanes. I've seen a rambling remnant of them here and there on the grounds, though you'll have to pretty much keep them in lines—Shaker idea, you know.''

"So I see. It will be like an archeological excavation, finding where they used to put the bushes.''

"Speaking of that, wait until you see the dig the university's going to do here," Tanya said, her expression and gestures even more animated as she pointed toward the other side of the village. "They're going to dig out an old well, and they predict they'll uncover all kinds of Shaker artifacts.''

"I can't wait to look around and get going."

"I *thought* you'd take the job," Tanya said, looking not only pleased but smug. She had a habit of dramatically emphasizing certain words.

The young woman smiled often, displaying perfect teeth that made her entire face light up and lifted her sharply defined cheekbones nearly to the outer tips of her bright eyes and sleek eyebrows. Her hair was cut close to her head. She wore a floor-length denim skirt and jacket over western boots, a compromise between the Shakers and her own style, Kate surmised.

"These four buildings are the ones we'll share," Tanya explained. "I'm pretty sure they were for flower and herb work even then, though on the old maps of the village, they're labeled simply Sisters' Shops. That'll be us," she said with a raucous laugh, "two Shaker *soul* sisters, just *workin'* away."

Tanya's enthusiasm was infectious. Kate wished Tanya lived on the grounds, too, but she'd told Kate she kept the same apartment in Athens she'd lived in for her grad work. As Tanya gestured at the different garden shops, Kate noted her long, white-lacquered fingernails, an impractical luxury for any gardener. She shoved her own short fingernails into her palms, as Tanya walked her toward the cluster of buildings, still talking.

"That's the garden shop, then the herb shop, the extraction shop and the finishing shed," she recited. "The garden shop amounts to a tool and work area. Extraction is where you can distill rose water, and I plan to turn herbs to medicines—"

"Not for sale the way the Shakers used to?" Kate asked. "I know modern people are getting back into herbal cures and preventatives, but..."

"No, especially not some of the things I plan to grow, reproductions of what they *really* planted back then," Tanya admitted, her voice more clipped now. "In those days of desperate diseases, they used desperate cures—what they used to call 'heroic medicine.' Foxglove, aconite and belladonna, for example—but I'll grow the more common things, too."

"Foxglove is a curative but too much could be poison," Kate put in.

"But they knew what they were doing, and so do I. I'm even going to grow lettuce starts in these hotboxes this winter."

Kate had no idea how lettuce was used as an herb, especially a strong, "heroic" one, but she decided to ask later, since Tanya was demonstrating her composting hotbeds with their glass sashes made from small windowpanes. Authentic but antique Shaker again, Kate noted, even though other modern materials might have been better.

Kate studied the vibrant, young woman and hoped they would soon be friends. Tanya Dodridge's moods changed as swiftly as the expressions on her striking face. She was her own hotbed of emotions, ideas and opinions, Kate thought.

"As I said, straight rows, neat gardens, no weeds, no litter," Tanya explained, flinging gestures again as they walked toward the herb shop. "They had a lot of far-reaching ideas. They thought plants were nourished by what they called 'invisible forces in the air.'"

"Which shows they were way ahead of their time in realizing the importance of good aeration?" Kate asked.

"Not exactly," Tanya said, shaking her head. "I think they were referring to otherworldly beings that watched over everything. But, yeah—or *yea,* as they always said for *yes*—they were practical, too. They grew plants to be useful, not ornamental. You know, like when they picked a rose, they *never* cut the stem or leaves with it, so it could be used only for herbal cures or their precious rose water and not for worldly adornment."

Kate stopped walking at the single-doored entrance to the herb shop. The roses around Sarah's grave and on the floor of the Denbigh mausoleum had been beheaded like that—

"Do you agree with it?" Tanya demanded, turning toward Kate in the doorway.

"Not with that part of their philosophy."

"No, I mean, I thought you were staring at the sign I put up. See—?" she said, pointing a pearly fingernail.

Under drying clusters of pungent herbs hanging by little nooses was a sign lettered in old-fashioned, fancy script: *If you would have a lovely garden, you should live a lovely life.*

"Mother Ann," Tanya said, her voice almost proud. "I swear, that woman had more amazing things to say than my own mother. Come on and let me show you what else is inside, and then you'd better hustle back to tell Dane you'll take the job before he has a fit. He's like that, you know, way up and way down," she said with a roll of her eyes.

Kate wanted to ask her what she meant, but Tanya was already explaining something else.

7

In Victorian dining rooms, a rose motif on the ceilings recalled that to the Romans roses were a symbol of secrecy. To speak sub-rosa implies this since Venus dedicated her flower, the rose, to Harpocrates, the God of Silence, to conceal her sweet thefts.

—Peter Coats
Flowers in History

"Hello!" Kate called. "Anybody here?"

On her way to Athens, which was a mere twenty miles away, to see Erin, Kate had stopped at Jack Kilcourse's place. His large, vintage home and the building that had once been the Shaker schoolhouse had fieldstone foundations and timbered walls. Two of the smaller wooden buildings on the grounds looked as if they were used as a garage—the one to the far side of his house—and maybe a storehouse, since that one was closed up and even padlocked. The trim buildings sat neatly among gardens that, in contrast, were not neat. They had all gone to leggy riot, past their prime. Kate wondered if the insides of the tidy-looking house, shop, garage and storehouse were in the same chaotic state.

"Hello!" she called again, then leaned back into

the car to honk the horn. She heard the hum of a saw and realized it came from his furniture workshop. That door was wide open, so she walked to it.

As she took a step in, she smelled sawdust and felt a slight vibration on the wooden floor. She sneezed, but Jack didn't hear her, even at this close range. His back to her, he was bent over a band saw. She knocked on the open wooden door, then realized she'd have to wait until he was done to avoid startling him. His wide shoulders hunched, his head down, the tension of concentration—and intensity of the man— struck her again like a physical force. She tore her gaze away from him to survey the surroundings.

The interior of the large, one-room edifice was full of stunning wooden furniture, everything from a trestle table to a corner cupboard to slat-back rocking chairs with woven seats. Yet unlike his gardens, it all seemed ordered and aligned. Jack appeared to not be working on any of the massive pieces now; his hands held something small.

She glanced around and saw, just inside the door, a steaming tub of water with thin strips of wood inside. The haze of setting sun through the western windows and the sawdust aureole seemed to gild his dark silhouette—black hair, black jeans and a navy flannel shirt shoved up to show muscled, hair-flecked forearms.

Slowly, as if he'd sensed her presence, he turned her way. The saw slowly began to run down, then stopped. Wearing big work goggles that obscured his eyes like smoked glass, Jack seemed some sort of alien. He pushed his goggles up on his broad, brown forehead and pulled plugs out of both ears.

"I didn't hear you or expect you," he said. She

almost felt she'd trespassed. His expression was hard, his eyes narrowed.

"I've just accepted the job of rosarian at Shaker Run and hear I partly have you to thank—for that and lassoing Varina Wellesley the other day. I just wanted to say I appreciate it."

"Don't thank me too much," he said, putting the thin piece of wood he'd been cutting on his workbench. "That is, there are challenges with each new endeavor, including that Shaker Eden over there. They told you this is my place?"

"That's right. Beautiful furniture—but what are you doing now?"

"Shaker oval storage boxes," he said, and reached onto his massive workbench to select a large one from which he produced two other smaller ones, to show her a stack of variegated sizes. "They used them to store lots of things. You know the Shakers. A place for everything and everything in its place."

"They're little works of art and so delicate looking," she said, reaching out to stroke the gentle curve of one, then drawing her hand back.

"Actually, they're sturdy as heck," he said, pulling his goggles over his head, which mussed his hair even more. "Curves are stronger than corners, so you can stand on the bigger ones and they won't split. Want to try?" he asked with the first hint of a smile she'd seen from him.

She knew she must have looked surprised. "I believe you. Are you soaking the wood so you can bend it?" she asked, indicating the hot-water bath by the door.

He nodded. "You mold them around a form while they're wet and nail them in place—" He gestured slightly as he talked, and she found herself staring at his hands. Rough but graceful, strong but obviously capable of great gentleness. She shivered slightly, annoyed the man's hands, voice—all of him—affected her so elementally.

"I only do them," he was saying, "when I need a break from the big projects. Things were piling up, and I just needed a little downtime," he added awkwardly, as if reluctant to share even that much of a personal admission with her.

A man, Kate thought, who took a break from building big things by building small things. A man who worked himself too hard. To substitute for not having what? She recognized the symptoms, but was still looking for her own cure.

"So, you'll be working with Tanya Dodridge," he observed. "I hope you don't mind if I nail down these dovetails before this wood splits or warps the wrong way."

"No, go right ahead. Yes, with Tanya. Do you know her and the Shaker staff very well?"

"Not really, though I totally sympathize with their cause. But yeah, Tanya and I are friends."

"It sounds as if Clint Barstow and his boys, as he calls them, will be competition for you soon," she observed, realizing he'd said all he intended to about Tanya. She'd do better asking the talkative herbalist herself.

"No," he corrected her. "Barstow's shop does Shaker reproductions, but they won't be competition. I already have as much work as I can do building and trying to protect the integrity of my craft."

"Like quality control—quality assurance," she

said. "I suppose the Shaker builders were hoping you'd join them."

"I've made it clear I don't get invol—I work alone," he said, still hammering tiny copper tacks into holes he'd already drilled in the curved side and in the overlapping dovetails. "I know Tanya better than the others because her great-aunt is one of the foremost private collectors of Shaker furniture in the country, so she's especially interested in what I do, that's all."

"I see," she said, though that explanation didn't really satisfy Kate's curiosity about him and Tanya. She wondered if Sarah had known Tanya's aunt or vice versa. "Her great-aunt isn't Oprah Winfrey, is she?" she went on. "Mrs. Denbigh said Oprah's got a fabulous Shaker collection."

"Her great-aunt is the gospel singer Samantha Sams. Quite a few well-to-do African Americans collect Shaker because they admire the way the Believers treated blacks back when. Namely," he went on, as he tapped in the last tack, "even before the Civil War, they bought and freed slaves, then allowed them to rise as high as the whites in the Shaker hierarchy. Never heard of a Shaker with a prejudiced bone in his body. However strange they were sometimes, they were admirable, too."

Kate listened intently to him, but still kept her eyes riveted on his big, skillful hands. She was almost afraid that if she stared at his face, he'd look at her and she'd give away how insanely attracted she was to him. But she took a step closer as he fitted a lid on the box. It was perfect.

"Let me show you what I'm making for Tanya," he said, moving across the room. "But I told her delivery might take a while because my bigger orders have to go out first.''

He moved a tall, unfinished corner cupboard aside, and pulled out from the shadows what appeared to be a half-finished desk with many small compartments stacked above its work surface. Even in the dimmer light against the back wall, the unfinished wood seemed to glow with warmth.

''An herb cupboard made from butternut,'' he told her. ''These will all be separate drawers she can label.''

''It's great. Your own home must be absolutely full of unique, lovely things.''

She wondered if she'd said something wrong. Jack seemed to freeze, and a frown flashed across his rugged face.

Jack's heart had been thudding right in rhythm with his hammer. He'd actually been thinking of Kate Marburn when she'd appeared in his doorway, as if he'd conjured her up. He'd been trying to decide if he wanted to get involved in using her like—like another tool. Could he keep her at arm's length while he did? If he used her, she'd take some watching. Unfortunately, he was also attracted to her, and that sort of complication was the last thing in the world he needed. But, as if it were a sign, she'd come looking for *him*.

Jack knew where she was going with the comments about his house. He could scent an intrigued woman a mile away. He supposed he had to get all the chitchat over without letting her know what he was really thinking. He stiffened his spine as she went on.

''I mean, your family is so fortunate,'' she was

saying. "They probably never have to see the inside of a furniture store."

"I'm not married," he said, wishing that didn't sound so blunt, "except maybe to my job. And these pieces I create are as close as I get to having kids."

"And, of course, you keep busy with the expertising, too," she noted as if trying to help him through this. He gave her points for not pursuing the family thing.

"I usually expertise only in my spare time," he said. "But your Toledo detective friend is very persuasive."

"If you mean Stan Rudzinski, he's not my friend. So did you find any of Sarah's—Mrs. Denbigh's—furniture was phony?"

"I'm not at liberty to say," he admitted, pushing the herb desk back in place. "But don't think I'm in league with him. It's just that I was asked to keep it confidential until all the evidence is assembled."

She nodded, looking suddenly forlorn. He had the nearly overwhelming urge to touch her, to comfort her. Kate Marburn was just the sort of graceful, sensitive—yeah, blond and leggy—woman he used to be intrigued by before all hell broke loose in his life.

So why was he taking this risk with a woman he could really grow to want, and maybe couldn't resist after all these years of living like a monk?

"Well," she said, breaking their awkward silence as they walked back toward his workbench, "I've got to get going. I'm going to see my stepdaughter at Ohio U., take her out to dinner, then head home tomorrow. I've got a lot to do to get ready to transplant roses and myself here. They may go dormant, but *I* can't afford to."

Her words blurred by as that old wound tore open. Kate Marburn had a child to go to—to love and watch grow. Andy would have been fourteen next week, into studies and sports in junior high school....

"Sure," he said, picking up the smallest size of oval box. "Let me walk you out."

At her car, he opened the door for her. Then when she got in and rolled her window down, he handed her the box. "A good-luck gift for your new job here." Damn, she looked like she'd cry.

"Oh, I can't accept that after all you've done for me. But tell you what—I'd like to make you a deal for it."

Better and better, he thought, entirely fascinated. Maybe she'd make this deceit easy for him. "Shoot," he said, when she hesitated, nervously licking her lower lip. He leaned closer, his elbows on her car as he leaned toward her open window.

"I see you've been too busy to prepare your beds—flower beds—for winter. I'll clean them out and do your autumn and spring yard work if you'll just let me put about a dozen of my antique rose-bushes out back. They're beautiful bloomers, but they're not the breed historically planted on Shaker land."

"Great. I like antiques, even living ones." He looked deep into her smoky blue eyes. "Deal," he added, and thrust his hand in to shake with her.

"What do you mean she's not here?" Kate asked Amy Baldwin, Erin's roommate. Kate had just knocked on their door in Jefferson Hall, only to have Amy answer it. "Not here or not on campus? She knew I was coming late this afternoon."

"I mean, yeah, she will be back, and she did know you were coming, and she's not off campus," Amy replied, crossing her arms over her loose flannel shirt. "She's just gone out for a bit. Come on in, Mrs. Marburn. She'll be here in a sec."

Realizing she'd overreacted, Kate sat on Erin's bed rather than pulling out the chair from a cluttered desk. The girls had pretty much split the room in half to decorate it. Amy's bulletin board and sliding closet doors were adorned with a lot of family and friend pics, while Erin's side was conspicuously lacking in those. Instead, a poster of actor George Clooney and another of Leonardo DiCaprio with Kate Winslet on the *Titanic* covered Erin's closet doors.

"She didn't go to pick up a pizza or something?" Kate asked Amy, who offered her a fruit drink from their minifridge. "I told her I'd take her out to eat uptown."

"Oh, you know," Amy said with a shrug that bounced her straight, blond hair, "just the usual for a Sunday afternoon."

Kate didn't want to pry, but Amy was really nervous. Kate's stomach twisted tighter. "Nothing's wrong, is it, Amy?"

"Oh, no, no way. She's just dating someone and went out for a little while with him."

"I didn't know that. She probably meant to surprise me today. Is she bringing him back with her?"

"I don't think so. That's not what she said."

"Do you know him?"

"Ah—he's from home. Some guy she went with in Toledo, so you probably know him," she said, flopping on her bed but not meeting Kate's gaze.

"Mark Winslow? Mark drives down here to see her—on Sundays?"

When Amy nodded, Kate bounced up and started pacing, though there was little room for that. However minuscule this room, it was unbelievable that college kids lived so poshly today compared to when Kate had been in school. There was not only a minifridge, but a TV, a CD player, two PCs, printers and an answering machine for the phone on the desk. Kate and her roommate had shared an electric typewriter, and there had been one hall phone for the entire floor, when she was at Toledo University in the good old days.

Kate pulled the curtains open farther to look out. The girls' room faced the Education building across the road at the bottom of a steep hill. Kate scanned the sidewalk and street, studying each walking or standing couple. Then she gasped and leaned so close to the window that she bumped her head on it. A black car with tinted windows was parallel-parked with others along the curb.

"If she comes in, tell her to stay put, and I'll be right back," Kate cried, and ran from the room. She hurried down the hall and burst out into the second-floor reception area, where she ran right into Erin.

"Oh, Mo—Kate."

"Wait here," she ordered, half hugging Erin, then quickly setting her back. "I have to see something outside."

"No, wait!" Erin cried, and ran down the staircase after her and out onto the street. "What is it? Come back!"

The car was still there: pastel Florida license plates with the Spaceshuttle *Challenger* on them. But she saw now that the vehicle—a Pontiac—was not the car from the cemetery. This was a newer, different model.

"What is it?" Erin demanded. "What did you see?"

"I thought this car belonged to someone I knew," Kate said, flushed with her exertion and embarrassment, as an elderly couple came along to get in it after hugging a girl who was apparently their granddaughter.

"And where have you been, young lady?" Kate asked, trying to force a smile and keep from looking like an idiot, as they started back inside. "What's this about Mark Winslow?"

"Amy had to tell you, huh?"

"Why didn't *you* tell me? And don't blame Amy," she added, when she saw the color drain from Erin's already pale face, "because I wormed it out of her."

"I—yeah, he just left a while ago. Since I've been away, I guess he's missed me."

"He's been coming down on Sundays? And then here I come to horn in on your time with him, huh?" Kate said, as they crossed the lobby.

"Don't say it like that. I'm glad to see you."

"Good, because you're going to see more of me. I've taken the job at Shaker Run."

"So it's 'Goodbye, Toledo.' Congrats and all that!" Erin cried, and they hugged hard in the hall before they walked back to her room.

"Surprises all around," Kate said. "You and Mark, me and—"

She was horrified that she'd almost said "Jack Kilcourse," but she caught herself. "—Shaker Run. Come on, I'm starved, so let me take you to dinner."

* * *

"Let's eat at the 7 Sauces again," Kate suggested. "You said it was your favorite place, and I'll bet you haven't been in there since the day I moved you into the dorm."

"Well—all right," Erin agreed, and Kate was certain it was reluctantly.

It was six o'clock as they walked up the steep hill into town. Kate loved the look of the campus, mostly redbrick, Georgian architecture with a central green where the chimes could be heard ringing out on the hour. The campus gate's inscription said the university was founded in 1804. That was at the beginning of the Ohio Shaker era, Kate thought, but there was probably no connection between early university students and the more isolated Shakers living about twenty miles away.

As they ate at the homey restaurant on North Court Street, Erin more or less just pushed her delicious *primavera* pasta around on her dish.

"You ate earlier with Mark, didn't you?" Kate asked. "You should have told me and just ordered a salad or something, or I could have just grabbed some fast food."

"Yeah, I did eat, but that's okay. You never really were the fast-food type, Kate."

Kate's insides felt hollow, despite how much she'd eaten. An invisible wall—what was that Tanya had said about the Shaker belief in invisible forces in the air?—seemed to stretch between her and Erin. And the girl was still calling her "Kate" instead of "Mom."

Kate recalled how devastated she'd felt when Erin had started that, as if her stepdaughter wanted distance from Kate after her father left—as if she blamed Kate, not him.

"You know, I don't disapprove of Mark's visits," Kate said, putting down her fork and gripping her hands in her lap, "but I do want you to have plenty of time to study. And it's hard to be on a campus when you're going with someone who's not there— local social life and all, you know what I mean."

Erin leaned back in the booth with a sigh. "I think I'm still trying to adjust to everything around here."

"Of course you are, so maybe that makes you want to hang on to Mark, a little bit of home, though I thought you'd been saying you're fed up with Toledo. It's been almost two years since your dad left and you broke up with Mark, and I was just a little surprised to hear he's back in your life," Kate said, and reached across the table to cover Erin's hand with her own. Erin's skin felt cold, and she didn't budge to return the touch. "You know, sweetheart, since you kind of cut him off—and since his uncle—"

"Stop it! I know, I know," Erin cried, snatching her hand back and throwing her napkin beside her plate. "His uncle, like half the population of Toledo, was taken in by Dad's scheming. Is that what you were going to say? Is that what you want me to admit?"

"Erin, I didn't mean—" Kate began, starting to slide out of the booth, as Erin stood.

"I'll be right back," the girl said, shaking her head as if to warn Kate off. "Got to hit the little girls' room, that's all."

Kate wilted back in her seat and stared at her nearly empty plate. She had prayed that her news of moving closer would bring *them* closer. Her head jerked up when their server, a tall young man named Stone, returned to their table.

"I think I'll take the check," Kate told him. "My daughter's a little under the weather."

"Or she's just had too much to eat," he said with a knowing smile as he took Erin's nearly untouched plate. "I saw her here earlier today. With that red hair, I remember her."

"And—not alone," Kate prompted.

"With a man. Can't recall him. Like I said, that red hair just draws attention to her. I'll have your check in just a moment," Stone said, and moved away just as Erin came back to sit down.

Rather than confronting Erin with what she'd just learned, Kate decided there was a bright side to all this. After all, Erin hadn't wanted to hurt her feelings by saying she'd already been to this place with Mark today; she'd come back in so Kate wouldn't be disappointed at this so-called celebration for her new job. Only now, Kate realized, she'd have to work as hard at rebuilding a relationship with Erin as she would at building new ones at Shaker Run.

Until Christmas and the millennial New Year, life was a blur for Kate. She transplanted her Apothecary roses to the village and her other, non-Shaker antique breeds to Jack's newly cleaned-out flower beds. More often than not, he was gone, overseeing the delivery of pieces people had bought for Christmas, even making a three-week trip to Japan at Christmastime, when most people wanted to be home near their families.

Despite spending more time with Erin, Kate took her own crash course in Shakerdom, concentrating on Shaker Run and its rosewater industry. She was part of much planning, especially with Tanya, for the all-important May first opening of the village.

Meanwhile, carload by carload, Kate settled her household goods in the spacious third floor of the Trustees' Building, overlooking the distant cemetery and holy ground. What she had stored of her and Erin's furniture in a rental space in Toledo, she had transferred to Rent-a-Room Storage just outside Athens. Most of her apartment was furnished in authentic Shaker items, and she felt as if she'd stepped back into the past. Despite the presence of her phone and PC, she didn't even unpack her TV, VCR or CD player. Had the entirety of modern life, Kate wondered, been reduced to abbreviations and anagrams? She couldn't wait to relax and really enjoy life again in this safe, simple setting.

During the last week of Erin's Christmas vacation, the two of them drove to Pensacola, Florida, and hit the beach. But for some reason Erin hadn't wanted to go, and had turned as prickly as a Rambler rose again. Kate could only pray this new millennium would mean a new beginning for both of them.

Unfortunately, Kate continued to deal with Toledo lawyers and Stan Rudzinski over the mess Sarah's will had made. If it weren't for wanting to honor her dear friend's wishes, Kate might have told them to chuck the whole thing, not that that would have prevented Zink from sticking like superglue. Sarah's officially "accidental death" still haunted Kate. She'd overheard Zink tell Tina Martin, "Something's fishy, and I'll never let this turn to a cold case—never."

Kate was cold now as she got into her car in late January, in bitterly subzero Toledo after her latest conference on Varina and Palmer's lawsuit. It had been a contentious meeting, with them and their lawyer present.

Before starting the drive back to Shaker Run, Kate leaned her forehead on her steering wheel, completely drained. She wasn't sure if she was racked by emotions or drained of them. No, she thought, knowing Jack had proved she wasn't drained of them. As austere and conflicted as he seemed sometimes, the man really got to her. She smiled as she recalled a recent discussion with Tanya over him.

"Don't you go giving *me* that all-knowing look, Kate Marburn," Tanya had scolded, when Kate finally asked her how well she really knew Jack Kilcourse. "You thinking there's something going on between him and little, old, celibate-Shaker me?" Tanya had rolled her eyes as she'd confided in Kate that her love life was nil right now. "We're not much more'n friends with a few interests in common, not partners in passion. And you been *dying* to know that, haven't you? Why didn't you just ask, girl?"

"Well—I didn't want to pry or maybe offend you."

Tanya laughed. "I just think you need another dose of Tanya's *terrific* herbal tonics, that's what I think."

"Right," Kate had countered, standing and stretching from bending over her rose starts. "All I need is a big dose of one of those good news–bad news herbs you're working with. The wonder drugs that may help you out with a little ache but may also kill you in the process," she teased.

"I could put a pinch of autumn crocus in that good valerian herb tea I mixed for your insomnia," Tanya had told her.

"Autumn crocus? For what?"

"You know, I often wondered if the Shaker herbalists slipped it in some of the brethren or sisters' food. For what?" Tanya had said dramatically and lowered her voice. "It lowers sexual excitement. But too much of it—just like sexual excitement—can be *deadly*."

Tanya had gotten a good laugh out of that, and Kate had decided her new friend's sense of humor was pretty weird. But today as she began the four-and-a-half hour drive back to Shaker Run, she wished she had some sort of herbal cure for her exhaustion. If only she could be an insomniac when she drove and be this tired at night. If only—

Kate jolted awake as her car swerved into the other lane. Her heart pounded and she broke out in a sweat as she shook herself awake. Thank God this was a four-lane highway, and no other car was close.

She glanced in her rearview mirror. The nearest car was way back on this stretch through rural, flat land between Findlay and Columbus. Her heart still thudding, she slapped her face, then rolled down her window and let the icy air hit her full force. She could just envision the headlines now: Suspected Embezzler, Suspected Murderer Suspected Of Falling Asleep At Wheel And—

"Damn you, Mike Marburn!" she snapped as she rolled her window back up.

She never used to have trouble sleeping before Mike had deceived and deserted her. It had been months since Kate had felt so angry at her former husband, but at least now, she realized with relief, she no longer loved him. And maybe her anger would help to keep her awake. The psychiatrist who'd counseled her through everything after Mike left would be proud of her. She felt completely cured of him and of the terrible habit of thinking people were stalking her that had developed after he left. That unsettling incident with the black car in Woodlawn Cemetery would have made her absolutely paranoid before, but now she knew it was pure mischance that someone with a warped sense of humor had stumbled on her there.

She was a new person, her own person now, Kate told herself as she hit the power button of her car radio and turned up to full blast the first FM station that came on. Despite Erin's problems with it, Kate knew she'd done the right thing to divorce Mike rather than have him declared legally dead. The bastard was probably living on the French Riviera with a woman as young as Erin and the hunk of money he'd embezzled, suicide note or not.

At least she felt completely safe living at isolated Shaker Run, even if she was the only one on the grounds at night. Surely she'd start sleeping better soon, and be done with her past and with making this grueling drive alone.

As she glanced once more in her rearview mirror, Kate began to sing along with the music on the radio. She'd just consider it a good sign, for it was that bouncy, cheerful song "Everything's Coming Up Roses."

"Did you see her almost weave off the road?" the woman said to the driver. "She probably reached for something and looked away. At least we know where she's going, so keep this car back."

"Yeah, and she's staying put more and more," he muttered. "Right where we want her, thinking she's home free. Having her out in the sticks, we can watch her better.''

"If she doesn't cooperate, we'll have to do more than hope and wait.''

"I know,'' he said with a deep sigh, taking off his hat and tossing it into the back seat. "We made a mistake with Sarah Denbigh but—''

"But this time, no mistakes.''

8

The dreary wilderness must blossom like the
rose.

—Mother Ann Lee

"Now, doesn't that gown make you feel a part of
the Shakers, more than all that studying and work
you've been doing?" Louise Willis asked, as Kate
came downstairs from her apartment in the Trustees'
Building.

For one moment, Kate stopped and stared at the
others. It was like stepping back in time, to a darker,
stranger world, to see Shakers looking up at her, assessing her, watching her. Kate wondered if everyone
had driven in already costumed. Although Tanya
lived twenty miles away on the edge of Athens, the
others owned rural homes a bit farther out. Like the
rest, Kate had donned her new Shaker costume for a
group photograph.

"It's amazingly comfortable for walking and standing," Kate admitted, coming down the last few steps,
"but I don't know about doing my gardening in it all
spring and summer." When she saw she'd hurt Louise's feelings, for the woman had overseen the sewing
of the costumes, she added, "But the gown's lovely

and makes me able to get more inside their skin as well.''

''Of course, it does,'' Louise insisted as she adjusted her own small, white cape that the Shakers called the shoulder handkerchief. It crossed the bodice and, like the long, narrow apron and ankle-length skirt, obscured a woman's body to stem temptation among the brothers in the Shakers' celibate world.

If the weather was cold, as it was today when an early spring storm was lurking outside, the women also wore long, hooded capes, some in stunning colors. Their gowns, however, were muted hues. Kate's was a soft blue, while Louise's was plum-colored, and Tanya's and Adrienne's were brown and gray.

Kate carried her deep, woven sunbonnet with her rather than putting it on over the net cap the women wore, and she hadn't pinned her hair back the exacting way Louise always wore hers. And no way, Kate thought, looking over Louise's bent head as the woman straightened her apron, was Tanya ever going to like wearing one of these. Across the room, Tanya rolled her eyes. When Louise was on one of her we-must-do-everything-exactly-right missions, there was no stopping her.

''After all, it *is* April Fool's Day,'' Tanya mouthed to Kate with a little smirk.

''All right, everyone, please stand between the table and stove for one of the photos for the new brochure,'' Dane announced, as the professional photographer hustled in from outside with a gust of chill wind. ''Then, storm coming or not, we'll be going out to have more taken with the men and women standing by the separate brethren's and sisters' doors.''

"You know the Shakers," Tanya said, speaking up so all could hear this time. "Two sexes with no sex. Twin staircases, twin doors, two sets of workshops—the original 'separate but equal.'"

Dane just shot her a dark look and began arranging everyone before the photographer could. Like the other men on the staff, Dane was dressed in full old-fashioned attire of striped trousers, white, collarless shirt, vest and dark-hued frock coat. Plans for the Shaker Run staff to be presenters who dressed and spoke as if they were the original brethren had come to fruition during the past winter months of hard work.

Dane and Adrienne were taking the roles of elders, and the Willises the parts of deacons, or overseers of all that went on. Clint Barstow and his furniture makers would portray brethren, while Kate and Tanya were the sisters, although Louise and Ben had managed also to arrange for a rotating list of costumed docents to volunteer their time when Shaker Run officially opened a month from today. Though overworked, everyone was excited as they prepared for that momentous event. And Kate, though she shuddered in the chill and felt goose bumps suddenly sliding over her skin, was very pleased with the way her own life had been going since the new year. She told herself that again and again.

For one thing, she was sleeping better than she had in years, thanks to Tanya's valerian herbal tea, which she drank every night. "In just the right dose, a calmative," Tanya had explained as she showed Kate how to measure it out, "but more than a teaspoon, it'll keep you up, to say the least."

Kate had also been seeing more of Erin, who didn't seem to blame Kate quite as much as before for divorcing her father. And she and Jack Kilcourse had become friends, though an unspoken sexual undercurrent always arced between them. She was learning to almost trust him. Still, she admitted, she hardly knew the real man, and so little of their talk had been personal. Barriers seemed built between them as thorny as her roses and as solid as his furniture.

"Kate, I said, please line your bonnet up here with the other hats on the table for this picture," Louise was evidently repeating herself. Kate realized she'd been daydreaming again. "At least we have a lot of photos of the Shakers, so we can replicate how they looked and acted," Louise announced to everyone. "They surely weren't like the Amish who shunned the camera. Actually, I don't think they were so much reclusive as quite bold."

Kate had come to see Louise that way, too. However much of a nitpicker and complainer she was, the woman was dedicated to making the time warp that was Shaker Run absolutely authentic. Although retired from an insurance business they'd run together in Columbus, the Willises still kept an office and apartment there, where Louise's elderly mother also lived. They went back and forth a great deal, as well as putting in long hours for this dream of theirs. Kate wondered when they found time to sleep. For the Willises, just as for Dane and Adrienne, Shaker Run was a labor of love.

As she stood patiently for several photos, Kate realized she did feel *somewhat* Shaker. That is, she'd come here to join a group with a common cause, and they had become a bit like a family. She and Tanya were fast friends, if not quite sisters, with their very different backgrounds. As it had been for many Shakers, Kate tried to tell herself, this place where she could make her roses bloom was a safe, little Eden, hacked out from the wilderness of her past. But sometimes, as the only one on the grounds at night, with Jack a half-mile away—when he was home—the nights stretched out so silent, deep and dark.

"Looks like we're in for a bad, late winter storm," Dane observed, squinting out the front windows. The staff, still in their Shaker garb after an hour of posing for publicity photos, were finally sitting down for their meeting. "I'll make this brief so you can be on your way if you need to—Tanya especially." Tanya was driving to Kentucky for her great-aunt's—soul singer Samantha Sam's—ninetieth birthday celebration held by her Baptist Church. "If you weren't going to be gone for a long weekend, Tanya, we'd have put all this off, but we've got to get this brochure to the printer. Which is why I need to bring up this next item of business—the main theme for the brochure."

"Don't forget to mention about the well," Adrienne put in, tapping her pencil on a notepad she always had with her.

"Oh, yes, that too," he said. It amazed Kate that Adrienne's interruptions to give advice or orders never seemed to faze Dane. If Kate had blurted things out to Mike when he was holding court, his Irish temper would have flared.

"Now that the weather should take a turn for the better," Dane said, with another rueful glance at the encroaching clouds outside, "the archeological team will be excavating the old well. I, for one, can't wait to hear and see what they discover in those depths. It's definitely a heyday-of-the-Shakers era well."

"And the other benefits," Adrienne prompted.

"The village is sharing in their grant money for the dig," Dane went on, "and we can bank on some good publicity from it, too. And that, at least until we get fully established, will be the name of the game around here. We are still operating on a shoestring, to use a phrase the old brothers and sisters might have known.

"Now," he continued, talking even faster, "to the reason I called this meeting. Since we've just come into a new millennium, Adrienne and I believe we should emphasize that the Shakers were also planning what they called a new millennium—in their case, not the turn of the century but a new age of unity and strength."

"But according to my reading," Kate observed when he paused, evidently to get their reactions, "the Shaker concept of a millennial age was a time to become stricter and more inward, more separated from the world—when we here at Shaker Run need to be opening our doors to it."

"Right," Tanya said. "All those millennial laws they had were rules and regs against just about *everything* in the world. Orders about the way people talked, how to eat at meals, mandates for rising and retiring, and, of course, what they called orders concerning *intercourse* between the sexes—"

"The old-fashioned meaning for that," Louise put in, glaring at Clint Barstow, who had dared to laugh. "The term meant just daily dealings such as simple communications to work together."

"True," Tanya admitted, "but it went so far as to include things like making the opposing sexes—"

"I think you mean 'opposite' sexes," Adrienne suggested.

"Well, if I was talking about men and women today, maybe I'd mean a little of both," Tanya insisted. "Anyway, their old rules say they can't so much as pass each other on the stairs, shake hands, whisper or *blink,* for heaven's sake. Their little, line-up-in-their-chairs chats at night were even strictly controlled. And I just read one millennial law the other day that said nobody can keep secrets from the elders. Is that where this is going, Dane?" she concluded with a teasing grin and overt batting of her eyes that was hardly Shaker. "No secrets from the elders?"

Everyone laughed, though Dane actually looked guilty of something.

"Yeah," Clint Barstow, who said so little in these meetings Kate felt she hardly knew him, added with a sly grin. "And that's why they have those little peepholes up high in the Meeting House. It's so the elders, or watchers, as they called them, could spy on the others meeting there or doing the sacred dancing."

Gooseflesh swept Kate again. She heard the wind pick up, whining around the building. No matter how much they bantered here or kept to business, she began to feel uneasy. Maybe, she scolded herself, it was just the barometric change from the approaching storm. She often got headaches and felt nervous when bad weather lumbered in.

"That is *not* why," Louise declared indignantly. "At Shaker Hill in Kentucky the elders had two watchtowers on roofs so they could be certain members weren't behaving out of union, as they used to say—but not here, not according to my extensive research. The holes in our Meeting House were built so that the deacons or elders could be sure the dancing did not get out of hand, especially when Believers had spirit visitations.''

''Oh, right,'' Clint said, his voice openly mocking now. ''Visits from dead folks could get things out of hand. That'd just be par for the course around here. There's always more to the Shakers than meets the eye.''

''I wish,'' Ben Willis interrupted, ''we could all practice not using these modern slang sayings such as 'par for the course,' since we've been working on being authentic, nineteenth-century presenters when our doors open to the world. Maybe we should all practice their favorite phrases so—''

''Don't change the subject,'' Clint argued. ''And don't think I haven't read about those crazy doings out on that so-called back forty where they had their holy ground. But I'm just sticking to my furniture, especially if you try to get some of us to do dance demonstrations, Louise.''

''I heard you all loud and clear on that before,'' she said with a sniff. ''I'm bringing in some dance majors from the university, though Adrienne and I intend to instruct them and probably rehearse them in the Meeting House. Yes, Clint, you just stick to your precious furniture!''

''Speaking of which, Kate,'' Adrienne put in, ''can we assume all is well with Mrs. Denbigh's furniture loans to us staying here? I don't suppose there's been any change in the litigation over it.''

Kate was relieved to be able to swing things to a different subject, even that one. ''The last word,'' she explained to everyone, ''was that my lawyer has hopes Mrs. Denbigh's wishes to give the furniture into my care will stand, though her heirs are still contesting that.''

In the moment's silence, she heard only the ticking of the clock and howling of the wind. She shifted nervously in her seat.

"Well," Tanya spoke up, "we're all on your side, Kate—in *everything.*"

Kate was surprised. She'd told them about the furniture and the will, but not about the fact that the heirs, and maybe the police—though, thank God, Rudzinski had not yet been here—might suspect she'd harmed Sarah. But no one asked what Tanya meant, so maybe the Thompsons, who'd surely seen the Toledo papers, had told everyone all that. Did they know about the earlier financial scandal, too? If so, as far as she knew, they had accepted her here without a look or whisper over it.

Sadly, Kate realized again, that she still couldn't trust anyone. It was mere illusion that this staff was pulling together as some sort of family. It made the storm, glaring at her through the tall windows, seem to blow right into her heart.

An alternately whining and howling snowstorm gripped Shaker Run to bring an early darkness. With everyone gone, the solitude oppressed Kate. And then, for the first time in the three months she'd lived here, the electricity went off.

It really annoyed her that she couldn't find where she'd put her flashlight when she'd moved in. Surely, she'd put it right here in this drawer by her bed.

She felt her way to the phone, but the lines were evidently down. There was no dial tone, no static—nothing. But that was not surprising in a wind like this. Kate never used her cell phone around here, and its batteries had run down. She hoped more than the village was affected, so phone and electrical repairs would be made soon. At least, living in Toledo all her life with its lake-effect snow and winter winds, she was quite used to this.

She fumbled for her stash of candles and matches in the top drawer of the corner cupboard of her kitchenette. Although they used kerosene lanterns in the village for appearance's sake, she still wasn't comfortable with them. All she needed was to burn down this valuable building when so much money was going into restoring others.

The candle flared to life, and she lit three more, one a fat, sturdy one. In the wan, flickering light, her rooms seemed suddenly unfamiliar. Shaker walls were uncluttered, all whitewashed with their traditional, head-high, dark blue pegged rail, on which they used to hang garments and even chairs to avoid clutter when they cleaned. *There is no dirt in heaven,* Mother Ann used to say. But now Kate's rooms were filled with shifting shadows thrown on the stark, white walls by the furniture, much of it Sarah's. It was as if her dear friend's spirit flitted from her furniture to be with her. "Spirit visitations, indeed," Kate whispered as she put her candles on a table and stared out the back windows from her bedroom. "You're starting to think like loony Louise."

The frosted panes partly obscured her view. Though the trees were creaking with cold as their limbs thrashed from the wind, now and then she could catch glimpses of her and Tanya's workshops, and beyond, the old cemetery and the plot called holy ground, now lying pristine in a cloak of snow.

Snow was not falling now, but suddenly she thought she saw something sweep across the lane. Was that a cloaked figure, darting from the graves toward holy ground?

"No way," she whispered. "Just something blowing."

The bare branches of trees had whipped across her sight, and that had made her think something was moving out there, she told herself. Other branches knocked against the windowpanes as if someone wanted in. Still, if she squinted toward the holy ground where the Shakers used to hold special rituals, she could almost imagine a dark figure standing there against the snow. No, that was that young pine tree, whipped by the wind.

Shaking her head at her foolishness, she moved her candles back into the kitchenette. Then, since her eyes had adjusted to the darkness, she went to each window on all four sides of her apartment and peered out, just as the wind seemed to exhale its last breath.

In the sudden silence, the moon darted from behind the clouds, casting a pale light reflected by newly swept snow. And then she saw footsteps, clearly etched beneath her front windows. They must be fresh or the wind would have swept them away. They came almost to the front door of this building, then went on. Had she not heard a knock on the front door below? Could someone lost have been seeking help or looking in? If the candlelight was too dim to be seen, could the person have run around behind the building, thinking no one was here?

"Someone walking in here at night—ridiculous," she said aloud, pressing her face to the front window again. She held her breath this time so she didn't steam it up. This village road was a dead end, and someone coming off the distant highway looking for help would have to traverse too many fields and the ravine.

And then she saw that dark form again—or maybe another. It was by the furniture shop where Clint and his team worked in the large building that had once been the Center Family Dwelling House, across the lane from her and Tanya's realm. Half of it held his workrooms and the other half the infirmary and sample Shaker living areas.

Kate dropped to her knees and watched as the figure stopped, seemed to huddle there, then went in the right side—the men's—front door. She breathed a sigh of relief, which clouded the windowpane again. It must just be Clint or one of his men, but why now, and where was his car? Maybe he'd just gotten stuck on the narrow lane and left it, not wanting to bother her. But he didn't have any blankets over there, and could probably use a lantern. Heat and light were both minimal even when the electricity was working.

Blowing out her candles, Kate bundled up, took two blankets and an unlit lantern, and went out into the snow. It wasn't half as deep as it looked from the house because the wind had scoured much of it off this plateau. And it was amazingly light out here compared to in the house. She always preferred the outdoors to being cooped up. That was why she'd refused to "go to ground," as her psychiatrist had suggested when she'd been obsessed with being followed after Mike left. Even if someone could be watching her, she'd choose being out under God's open skies over being trapped in a building anytime.

Crunching the stiff grass, she followed the tracks

across the lane. Large footsteps, big feet—no doubt Clint. Maybe he'd have some idea about how to get the lights back on.

But she hesitated outside the square stone-and-frame building. Its double doors glared at her like dark eyes in a vacant face. What if it wasn't Clint, and she went barging in on a stranger, especially one who was breaking in?

Feeling strange at being the watcher, Kate walked around the right-hand side of the building. She knew two places she could peer in, either the back steps or the slanted, wooden root cellar that leaned here to match the one on the other side.

The cellar looked too slippery, so she decided on the steps. Someone already had a light inside, a moving beam, maybe from a flashlight. And she could see that the intruder was playing it along various pieces of tall, standing furniture.

She thought of Rudzinski's theory, which she'd finally figured out on her own, that someone had been selling Sarah fake furniture. The fact a Shaker antique expertiser had been called in by the police and not by the appraisers for Sarah's will meant that it was somehow tied to her death. If Sarah had found out she was being swindled, Kate had surmised, and was going to accuse someone, maybe that person had paid to have Sarah killed. It was a wild idea, but so was the concept that her own husband could bilk hundreds of people out of millions of dollars and get away with it.

If only her phone were working right now, she'd call the local police, or at least phone Jack, she thought, peering in the back window. And then, when she saw the man inside set his light on a tabletop and bend to examine something nearby, she gasped.

The intruder *was* Jack.

9

Change in a trice
The lilies and languors of virtue
For the raptures and roses of vice.
                    —Algernon Charles Swinburne
                                    "Dolores"

Kate nearly knocked on the window, then hesitated. How did Jack get a key? Surely, he hadn't broken in. And why was he coming here at night during a storm? He could probably finagle an entry in here with his fellow furniture makers, or ask her if she could get him in to look around. She had a master key.

Her curiosity to know what he was doing got the best of her, and she tried her key carefully, quietly in the back sister's door—force of habit from Louise always preaching they should follow tradition on that. One of the first things the village would purchase from early entrance fees this year, Dane had said, was an electronic security system for the buildings, despite the fit Louise had had over lack of authenticity.

Now the door creaked briefly, but then so did old houses and furniture in the cold, so she didn't worry Jack would hear her. Putting the lantern down outside, but holding the blankets to her chest, she slid in the half-opened door and closed it quietly behind her.

At least Jack was making enough noise in there to cover her sounds. She heard a tapping, cupboard doors opening and closing, and drawers sliding in and out. What could he be looking for, and why now?

Kate shuffled through what had been the pantry but which currently held tools. Slowly, she peered into a vast, dark room, once the big kitchen, its old counters now converted to workbenches. She saw the light across the room, and stepped in.

Suddenly, hard arms clamped around her. Her breath whoofed out as she hit the floor, a big body on top of hers.

His hand over her mouth bumped her nose. Furious, she bit his fingers.

"Damn!" he cried, and yanked his hand away.

"I'll scream!" she choked out instinctively.

"Who's going to hear? I didn't know it was you and didn't want the intruder to scare you by screaming in a supposedly deserted village."

"Oh, how thoughtful. But you're the intruder here!"

"I'm assuming you knew it was me before you walked in, because this would have been an even more stupid move on your part, otherwise."

"You're the one into stupid moves tonight! Get off!"

He only stopped shaking his hurt hand. "Why were you sneaking in, if you saw who it was?" he demanded, frowning.

"You still have no right to be in here. I wanted to see what you were doing."

They glared at each other at breath-tingling range in the dim, reflected gleam of his distant flashlight. As crazy as it seemed, she realized they had never argued before, hardly said anything emotionally charged to each other, though she felt that way around him all the time. Somehow, for her, his presence was always overwhelming. But they had never been this close.

Kate still held the blankets, but shoved them away to try to get up. "You brought bedding?" he asked as his eyebrows lifted to widen his dark gaze.

Her heart began to beat even harder. "So, what are you doing here and in the dark?" she demanded.

He shifted his weight and sprawled next to her, one arm around her waist, one foot still over her ankles. "I'm more or less holding you, which is something I've been wanting to do for a while, but I wasn't ready for the complications."

"Give me a break and don't be ridiculous. Or change the subject," she said, but her voice quavered. "And you've got complications of another kind now. Who gave you the key to get in here?"

He sighed, rose and helped her up. It was only then she realized that, as startled as she'd been, she had believed he would not harm her. But she didn't need to be trusting any man—getting into complications, as he put it. Especially not this one, with his quiet charisma that both built up walls but somehow invited her to try to scale them.

Though a long bench and several rocking chairs were nearby, Jack blocked her between the backs of two tall cupboards set sideways against the wall. Of necessity, they stood close together in the small space. The warmth of his breath caressed her face in the chill air.

"Let me explain," he said. "I want to trust you."

"Isn't the line that you want *me* to trust *you?*

You're the one on thin ice. I came over here because I thought Clint or one of his workers had a car that had acted up in the storm and he'd need these supplies. You aren't here trying to see what your competition's building, are you?''

"I told you they are not my competition. But all right," he said and cleared his throat, "I'm checking whether some of this furniture matches some fine museum and collectors' pieces and so could be switched with those authentic antiques. It would be a great place to make and hide fakes and frauds.''

"So would your workshop," she accused, feeling defensive about the village staff. "But—run that by me again. And why are you here in the dark during a storm?''

"I thought blowing snow would help cover my tracks, and knew no one would be out now.''

"Is the electricity off at your place?''

"Not that I know of, and I wasn't planning on using it here. Then, too, I just recently came into possession of a key. I'm not desperate enough for breaking and entering—yet.''

"And then the wind quit blowing, and I followed your tracks," she told him. "But where did you get the key? And who are you suspecting of furniture forgeries? You aren't still working for Stan Rudzinski, are you? Does he think there's some theft ring at Shaker Run that could tie in to Mrs. Denbigh's death?''

"Whoa. Slow down," he murmured, lifting both hands as if to hold her off in the small space, but the gesture made him nearly touch her breasts. "I'm working for myself, Kate. I had some furniture stolen last year, not from here but hijacked from an airport warehouse while still in shipping cases. Later, they were substituted for authentic pieces that were stolen from a couple of Shaker villages.''

"But not here? Not Mrs. Denbigh's things?"

"Not unless she'd donated pieces to villages on the East Coast. No one would have noticed the switch for years if I hadn't become suspicious and gone looking," he explained. "I never do exact replicas, but I do what I call 'inspired pieces.'"

"Inspired? Now that sounds really Shaker."

"Yeah, but I'm not making fake identical pieces to allow thefts of the originals. Kate, the reason I've been gone so much this fall is that I've been in England as well as Japan. A British museum curator who discovered he had a well-made replica and not the original Shaker desk they'd purchased years ago traced the replica to me. Hell, that wasn't hard. I'd signed the piece as I do all of mine—that was one thing that helped exonerate me. Anyhow, international customs authorities were going to arrest me until I convinced them I was clean. I don't know," he added with another shrug, "they probably still suspect me."

Kate didn't say so, but her heart went out to him. She suddenly understood perfectly what he was going through. If only she could help and comfort him, however much little warning signals about trusting him went off in her head.

"Go on," she urged.

"Customs is working on it from their end and told me to stay out of it, but I figured I'd try to cover some bases here to see if I could turn up something."

"But Shaker furniture stolen from England?" she marveled.

"It's admired all over the world," he insisted, his voice tinged with pride. "And one of the best European collections of Shaker is in the American Museum in Claverton Manor near Bath."

"So," she said, "you're thinking Clint Barstow might be behind a worldwide, lucrative, switch-and-steal scheme?"

"Or someone pulling his strings is."

"Jack, no one pulls Barstow's strings. If you ask me, he's not the brightest guy in the world to mastermind anything, but he's fiercely independent and doesn't like taking orders from anyone."

"Yeah, but you don't really know what someone is like until a crisis hits," he argued, shifting his weight so he leaned on his forearm close to the side of her head, still blocking her into their small space. "Or until you deal with them up close and personal."

She nodded as if she were drugged by his closeness and the raspy timbre of his voice. The faintest halo from the flashlight illumined his tousled head, though he hardly seemed angelic. With his craggy features and big shoulders, he seemed a darker spirit, a compelling, luring demon.

But she managed to merely nod. *Until a crisis hits, you don't know someone…* It sounded as if he were describing her marriage, but she wondered if he was thinking of his own. The only personal revelation he'd made to her before tonight was that he also was divorced, but he'd volunteered nothing else.

"So," she said, pressing back against the solid wood, "even though you have to take risks, you're determined to discover who is behind all this. And you're working alone and undercover."

"In a nutshell, that's it."

"Alone—not with or for Rudzinski or some other law agency?"

"Kate, this is not *Mission Impossible*. Besides, I always work alone."

"But now you've been found out," she said, "and confessed to an outsider. Perfect place for it, since the Shakers used to confess all their sins."

"You gave me no choice. The only other thing I can do is silence you."

His words and piercing gaze made her tense up even more, but only because she was certain he was going to kiss her. He shifted his shoulders, and his mouth hovered close. But she was wrong.

"You could have lied," she insisted, clearing her throat, "and are still lying, for all I know."

"You *are* a tough cookie," he said, his voice getting even huskier. "I wouldn't risk lying because I want you to cover for me—or, at least, to not tell anyone you found me in here tonight."

"So I'd really be abetting your actions, then. Which, Jack Kilcourse, returns me to my oft-asked but not answered question—how did you get in here if you didn't break and enter?"

He shocked her by leaning even closer across their small space, tipping his head and covering her mouth with his.

Though it was a careful kiss, Kate felt it down to her lower belly. She knew she needed to hold him off instead of pulling him to her, but she wanted him. Still, both palms flat on his leather jacket, feeling amazingly out of breath, she set him slightly back.

"I just wanted to get that in at least once," he whispered, "in case you won't accept my next confession."

"Which is?" she whispered.

"Being a builder of old-fashioned furniture, I used the old-fashioned way of copying a key," he admitted, bending his arms so he leaned closer against her, barely touching, not pressing her back into the wood. He shrugged so slightly that she felt, rather than saw, the movement. "I made a wax impression of a master key and had a copy made."

"From Tanya's?"

"From yours. Last week, when you were out back checking on your rosebushes and left your stuff on my porch."

She shoved him hard. Sliding out from their nook, she picked up the blankets from the floor and started for the front door before she realized she needed to get him out of here, demand his key and relock both doors. One hand on the cold brass knob, she turned back to face him. He stood in the middle of the open work space, hands thrust under his armpits, his face etched in the meager light, all unreadable angles and lines.

"The bottom line for all these—these 'complications,' is that you've been using me," she accused.

"No more than you've been using me."

"I haven't lied to you and stolen your property."

"I don't know about the lying, but your roses are on my property."

"Hostages for my silence, I suppose?"

"Kate, you do understand why I'm trying to get to the bottom of this grand-scale furniture scam, don't you?"

"Yes. I really do. And if I help you, it's because I believe Stan Rudzinski thinks that if Sarah Denbigh was murdered, it could be linked to such a scheme.

Sarah was very dear to me, almost a second mother. It's like Tanya says, I guess, that you have to take some bad to get to the good sometimes.''

"Tanya's talking about herbal medicines. Besides, that can backfire,'' he said, his voice bitter now. Kate was amazed to see his eyes tear up; they glinted not in the flashlight glow but in reflected moonlight off the glaze of snow outside. She realized he must be seeing a sort of mental vision, remembering something else.

"Look, Kate,'' he said as he sucked in a deep breath, "I don't know if what I'm trying to discover could lead to information about whether someone harmed Sarah Denbigh, but some of her furniture was fraudulent. She was too savvy a collector to buy a fake in the first place, so I'm thinking, like the other examples, hers were substituted *after* she purchased them.''

"So—someone might have broken in, or just walked in that night, with all those people at the party, to examine or switch some of her furniture,'' Kate reasoned aloud. "Maybe Rudzinski believes that now, too, and that's why he hasn't been down here grilling me as he hinted he would. Or else he's got someone spying on me here.''

"It's not me,'' Jack declared, slowly coming closer. "And city police don't hire spies or do long-distance stakeouts, especially in a place like Shaker Run. Don't get paranoid about this.''

Relieved Jack didn't know she used to be exactly that, believing she was being watched, she insisted, "You don't know Rudzinski. He's like a leech—masquerading, of course, as a friendly, helpful leech.''

He gave her a tight smile. "But then, as you said,''

she added, "you never really know people, even the ones closest to you, until you get in a crunch."

"I'm in a crunch now, Kate, and asking for your help. Give me an hour or so to look over this furniture. I won't harm anything, and Barstow and company will never know I was here."

"If I don't tell, it's because you—or we—might turn up something that would help me, too, not because of your forged kiss, thinking you could soften me up. Talk about trying to use someone to—"

"That kiss," he interrupted, his voice adamant, "was entirely authentic. But I should have done a much more thorough, inspired job of it. Are you any good with a darning needle?"

"What?"

"You can save me some time by lighting that lantern you left outside—"

"So you did see me coming. You said before that—"

"And start checking wormholes in this wood. I'll show you how."

Damn, Kate thought, as she put the blankets down and stomped out to get the lantern. Even if he was taking her in, she was willing, right now, to go along for the ride.

"Come in," Kate called, when someone knocked on the door as she tended her Apothecary rose seedlings two days later. She'd been working hard all winter to propagate them under growing lights in this so-called garden shop. "The door's open," she prompted, when no one entered. Her stomach was still in free fall at the thought it might be Jack.

"It's not really open, but unlocked," Louise observed as she came in, scraping mud off her feet onto the mat.

"Hello, Louise," Kate said, trying to sound cheerful. "You look different in modern dress—well, not really a dress but slacks and a slicker."

"*Touché*," Louise said with a hint of a smile. "I hope you don't mind my popping in."

"Not at all. I can use some company, with Tanya still gone."

Tanya's great-aunt had become ill so she wasn't back yet. And Kate should have known it wasn't Jack—he'd gotten what he wanted for now here at Shaker Run.

He'd found two large cupboards of Clint Barstow's furniture he was quite sure were being painstakingly, fraudulently aged. But he admitted that wasn't illegal, and it didn't mean a thing until he could prove the pieces were going somewhere to be switched with the real, priceless articles. And that would take some time. Besides, who knew that Barstow wasn't just trying to make authentic, antique reproductions? Kate, like a fool, had said she'd try to find out.

"What can I do for you, Louise?" Kate inquired, when the woman just looked around at first, her high forehead crumpled in a frown.

"I wanted to be certain that you plan to have all this modern equipment out of here before we open in less than a month. Visitors will pretty much have the run of the place, you know, and we can't have a rosarian in Shaker garb using phosphorescent tube lights, fertilizer, etcetera."

"If I could have done old-fashioned air or soil layering instead of this in the middle of winter, I would have," Kate explained patiently. "But since *Rose*

Gallica Officinalis is the only authentic Shaker rose allowed on the grounds..."

"I thought I read that Damasks and Apothecaries were used for their rose water, too."

"A little learning is a dangerous thing," Kate said, amazed anew that Louise knew as much as she did about so many aspects of Shaker life. "Both of those are old-fashioned names for this very breed. And as I was saying, if I didn't give them a jump start, even the twenty mature bushes I have, and these I've got started, wouldn't give us much of a show this year."

"The Shakers were most certainly not interested in show," Louise said with a noticeable shiver.

"I know that, but modern-day tourists just may be. Besides, transplanting bushes can really stress them, and I want to have enough blooms to distill some Shaker rose water this June. And you, Sister Louise, will be presented with the first bottle."

She cocked her head suspiciously. "Why me?"

"Because I think things matter more to you than anyone else here. More even than to Dane and Adrienne. And I appreciate that."

Louise looked relieved. "Then I'd like to walk you out back to holy ground. I take everyone there sooner or later, when I think they're ready. You see, I can't bear for anyone to think that the Shakers were evil or one bit mad, when they were only different—strange in a good way. I want you to understand them."

"All right," Kate agreed. She clapped soil from her hands and quickly watered the rest of the peat pots containing her precious seedlings, which she'd plant outside as soon as the last threat of frost was gone. "But I've already read a lot about holy ground," she assured Louise. "I know it used to be enclosed behind a taller fence and adorned with fir trees. The so-called holy procession was once a year, with the Believers accompanied by the spirits of departed village members and an angelic host. Spiritual gifts were given out, and it was a day of soul-searching and awesome judgment, I believe I read.''

''So, you have done your homework. The yearly official visit to holy ground and the Midnight Cry were their two happiest, holiest, if wildest events.''

''The Midnight Cry?'' Kate asked, her head snapping up. ''I don't recall reading about that.''

''I shall save that for another time,'' Louise promised. ''Let's just enjoy Shaker Run in all its silent beauty before we're inundated with those well-diggers tomorrow, not to mention the volunteer workers and dancers.''

They walked together down the gravel lane and stood between the cemetery and the perfectly square piece of well-tended spring grass called holy ground. Both were set off by fences of piled, flat stones. Kate had more than once explored the old cemetery, its brothers and sisters buried in separate sections, just the way—but for some tasks, such as relegated social time and worship—they had kept separate in life. Here, only their first names were carved in limestone, slowly being washed away by the elements. One day Adrienne had even pointed out the headstone of long-time rosarian Sister Jerusha, whose diary Louise had wanted her to read but could not find.

''Believers used to sing two particular songs when they processed out here to holy ground for their special day,'' Louise said, her eyes narrowed, her voice almost a whisper as she gazed at the other section across the way. ''One was 'Brethren, We Have Come to Worship' and the other was 'Ye Watchers and Ye Holy Ones.' Both songs mention angels, as they believed this holy ground was guarded by an avenging angel with a flaming sword, just as the entrance to Eden was, once Adam and Eve were thrown out. And angels were the ones who sent the Shakers their dances, their furniture designs and their visions.''

Turning their backs on the cemetery, they approached the nearby holy ground. Kate nodded at Louise's lesson, but her thoughts skipped back to the statue of the angel in the cemetery in Toledo. She shivered and wrapped her jacket closer. ''So the Shakers thought they had to rebuild that lost heaven-on-earth here to get into the eternal one,'' Kate mused. ''I can't say it wasn't a lovely idea, but impossible since they were dealing with people. I'm afraid Mother Ann had some very misleading visions at times.''

''Don't let me hear you telling any visitors that. A sister would have been cast out of union and condemned by the whole village for such talk back then,'' Louise insisted.

''I know you love the past, Louise, but I'm rather glad we're living now,'' Kate said, unwilling to back off.

''Then, just recognize that this is the spot where they sincerely believed that their dear departed, including Mother Ann, came back to dance with them and impart visions,'' Louise said, her voice almost pleading. ''I sometimes wonder if it wasn't why the founders of Shaker Run built their holy ground so close to the cemetery.'' She glanced toward one and then the other. ''The holy ground in most Shaker villages is more remote. You know, Kate, you are probably the only person in the world to have a box seat, as it were, to watch the goings-on here.''

''You don't mean to imply that you believe there are actually ghosts—''

''I only mean,'' Louise interrupted, turning toward her, ''that I am going to ask Dane if we might not have a sort of festival once a year, among our other annual events, where the dancers I'm training will come out to holy ground and reenact some of the visions and spirit visitations. I'd very much value your support when I bring it up in a staff meeting. By the way,'' she said, starting back toward the village so Kate had to hurry to keep up, ''has Tanya phoned? With our grand opening barely a month off, she's sorely needed here.''

''No, but I hope her great-aunt's all right—even if she has lived a good, long life.''

''A good and long life, yes, indeed, that's something to be hoped for,'' Louise said as she quickened her steps.

''How is your mother doing?'' Kate asked, trying not to slip in the mud as they cut off the lane toward the garden shops and Trustees' Building. ''I know both you and Ben go to see her quite a bit. I lost my mother early and think you're so fortunate to have yours for so long.''

''I'm sorry to hear about your mother, and it is kind of you to inquire. Mother's up and down. With her,'' Louise explained, as they paused by the garden shop, ''it's that her spirit is willing but her flesh is weak. Rather sounds like something Mother Ann would say, doesn't it?—and my mother's name is Ann, by the way. Now you just drop by the dancing some late afternoon, Kate, and see how everyone's doing,'' she repeated as she disappeared around the corner as if she'd simply vanished.

Kate realized she should have thanked Louise—or should she? When Louise opened the door to Shaker Run's past, it was intriguing, but also downright disturbing.

10

Sweet is the rose but grows upon a briar;
Sweet is the juniper but sharp his bough;
Sweet is the eglantine but pricketh near;
Sweet is the nut but bitter is his pill;
And sweet is moly but his root is ill.
So every sweet with sour is tempered still...

—Edmund Spencer
Sonnet 26
"The Amoretti"

The next morning, Kate took only a moment to watch the team of archeologists from the university excavating the old well near the Center Family Dwelling House that was now Barstow's furniture shop. They had erected some sort of drilling apparatus to widen it and had suspended a metal-and-canvas cradle to lower things, or perhaps themselves, into its depths. Fascinating, but she had no time for that today.

Kate felt a sense of urgency she hadn't had since arriving here in the village. Tanya had called to say her great-aunt was still ill and had asked Kate to tend her herbs and run a few errands. At least one of the favors Tanya asked had fit in perfectly with Kate's desires to get some information out of Clint Barstow.

And despite feeling like a liar and a spy, she was on her way to do it.

"Hi, Clint," she called as she stopped in the open front door of the busy furniture shop. Though he was standing by the window apparently just looking out at the well excavations, she could see three of his workers bent over various tasks.

She had to raise her voice to be heard above the sound of hammering and high-pitched whine of an electrical circular saw. The Shakers had always adapted current technology, whether it be water, steam, wind power or electricity, but Kate wondered if Louise scolded these guys for not sticking with hand tools of the early 1800s era of the village. And had Louise dared to tell Clint he'd have to get rid of his "unauthentic" tattoos Kate could see wrapped around both strong forearms below his un-Shaker-like T-shirt sleeves?

"Hey, what's up?" Clint asked as he ambled toward her. "Just been watching the treasure-hunt guys. Told me they'd be using tiny brushes and dental picks, but looks like they're going at it big-time so far."

"I noticed. Clint, Tanya's great-aunt is still ill so she asked me to bring you this lemon balm oil," she told him, putting the large bottle of it in his callused, dirty hands.

"Yeah, great. We're almost out. We mix it with beeswax to give us a real close polish to what they used to use."

"So you really are striving for replicating the original pieces," Kate observed. She nodded, hoping to show him she approved. "It amazes me how antique some of your furniture looks when the pieces are obviously brand-new.''

"Bigger demand for reality," he explained, looking pleased. "Still, it does take some getting used to when I take a chain or hammer to new wood to make it look old," Clint said, bouncing the bottle of lemon balm hand to hand as if it were too hot to handle. "It's the main difference between us and Kilcourse's workshop. He uses old techniques but doesn't go out of his way to age the stuff like we do—not that we get a lot more profit per piece than he does. But we will, once we get our reputation built up, once this village really thrives and visitors see what we got to offer.''

Kate tried to remember everything Clint had so freely told her. But the fact he'd been so forthcoming meant he wasn't trying to hide anything, didn't it? Keeping an eye on Barstow and his boys, as Jack called them, could be a dead end. Either that or she wasn't much of an investigator, because she'd believed from the first that Clint Barstow wasn't capable of enough cleverness to switch furniture, let alone lie about it.

Kate headed back to work at a good clip, then stopped in her tracks and gasped. Getting out of a black, unmarked car parked in front of the Trustees' Building was Stan Rudzinski.

"I can't really say it's great to see you, Detective," Kate said as she walked Rudzinski out to the garden shop. She had no intention of anyone overhearing whatever this man had to say to her.

"Now, don't go making snap judgments, Ms. Marburn. Maybe I'm here with some real good news." It annoyed her that the man actually looked glad to see her.

"If so, I'd love to hear it," she prompted, as he stared up at Tanya's quote, *If you would have a lovely garden, you should live a lovely life.*

"Interesting people, the Shakers," he observed as he came in and stood at the end of her potting worktable, only to drum his fingers on it nervously. "I've been reading up on them."

She decided not to bite on that lure. "So *are* you here with good news for me, Detective?"

"I don't suppose you'd want to call me Zink."

"I don't suppose so."

"Look," he said, and smacked his palms down hard enough to make her clay pots rattle, "I don't like being treated like some sort of pariah. And here I read that Shakers always showed great hospitality to visitors."

She sighed and turned to face him down the length of the cluttered worktable. "I don't want you to think I have some sort of guilty conscience," she insisted, "because I don't. But it's hard to feel real chummy toward someone who pretends to be a friend but could well be waiting to fry me."

"Fry you? Sounds like you're having visions of electric chairs, Kate. Surely you want answers—the truth—about what happened to Sarah Denbigh."

"Of course, I do. But I can see in your eyes that you are out to blame m—"

"I'm not! Look," he said, thrusting out both open hands in supplication, "I admire your backbone, but I think because of what you've been through before, you're overreacting."

"No, I think I'm reacting to a homicide detective's

driving way down here to see me over what's evidently a hot case to him. You still think she was murdered, don't you?''

"You ever get a gut feeling about something?" he challenged, hitting his chest with his fist.

She sensed she had him on the defensive for once. "Of course, I do. I told you I had that feeling when Sarah was up in her suite the night of the party, even before I found her there."

"So I recall," he said, nodding. "It's one of the things, along with the fact that you called for help the minute you found her there, that makes me believe you're innocent. You're a bright woman, and with what you went through before with the investment scandal, you're a cautious woman. No way you'd do anything to land yourself in the negative limelight again. So if you'd harmed Sarah, you'd never arrange to be the one to find her and call for help. Unless..."

"I've been waiting for the other shoe to drop, Detective."

"Unless you got her blood on your gown and figured you couldn't explain it any other way."

"You never change, do you? I'm going to have to ask you to leave and take your next little field trip to see Mason James, my lawyer." She walked over and yanked open the door. He didn't budge.

"Kate, the point is, having thought all that out, I believe your story," he plunged on, speaking even faster. He made no pretense of calm nonchalance now. "There's only one thing I'd like you to tell me, so I can close all this in my own mind. I hear you went to a shrink after your husband left—which sounds really reasonable to me."

"Detective Rudzinski, we are finished talking. It

may be public record I sought counseling, but it's none of your business for what reason I went. Are you going to try the approach that I'm mentally off and didn't even recall I hurt Sarah, or that I'm some sort of pathological liar? I don't know where you get your information, but—''

''You'll kill me when I tell you, but I'm going to level with you, anyway,'' he said, still holding his ground, though he was now fidgeting and shifting from foot to foot. ''After you first went to live at Groveland, Varina evidently pried out of her mother that you were at a shrink's.''

''Varina again!'' is all she managed to say.

''And I wanted to warn you that she also let slip that her lawyer found some precedent for the last will being overturned, since you were living on her mother's property at the time and had, as they're claiming, alienated the woman's affections from Palmer and Varina.''

''And you came here claiming to have good news?'' she cried, flinging out both hands.

''Now hear me out. In addition to Mrs. Denbigh's death being officially deemed accidental, I also have good news for Jack Kilcourse—I finally brought the check the city owes him,'' he said. ''But as for the case, yeah, the blood splatter evidence is inconclusive. Mrs. Denbigh could either have fallen hard or been thrown into that blanket chest. She could as easily have removed her glasses, and placed them at arm's length, as lost them if she were shoved.''

''Then that's it, right?'' Kate queried, with a shudder at the visions of Sarah's death his words evoked. ''Case either closed or at least shelved?''

"Kate, is it true you used to have hallucinations and that's why you went to that shrink?"

"You know, Detective," she said, completely exasperated, "I almost fell for your helpful routine that time. But if you don't get out of here, there's going to be blood splatter when I smash a clay pot over your head. Now *that* will give you an open-and-shut case!"

He forced a tight smile and shook his raised index finger. "If you did that you'd ruin my main theory that, unlike Varina, you don't have a volatile temper. And then I'd have to start following you around again until you made a slip," he said, and finally stepped outside with a half wave over his shoulder. "And I'm sure I'd never blend in with the roses here, or—" he glanced at the little cemetery out back "—with the tombstones."

Kate stared wide-eyed at him. Was he hinting that he'd been the one following her in the Toledo cemetery? That black car he drove today was not the one, but she had been certain there had been a woman with that driver, and it could have been his partner. Kate had observed that he always drove when he and Detective Martin were together.

To be sure he left, Kate followed him around the Trustees' Building. He strolled back to his car as if he hadn't a care in the world, got in and drove away. She watched until he turned into Jack's distant driveway, then, distraught at all he'd told her—or had he intentionally, helpfully warned her?—hurried inside to call Mason James.

Late that afternoon, Kate checked on Tanya's herbs, which were drying in the distilling shed where

Kate would also make rose water this summer. With her own rose starts taking up a lot of room in their main garden shop, Tanya's work had spilled over from the herb house to this small building, too. Usually working with plants in any of this cluster of sister's shops calmed Kate, but not today.

On top of everything else, Rudzinski's visit had set her on edge. Standing here in this silent, fragrant shed, she pictured tourists she didn't know wandering in to watch her making the double-distillation rose water, which early Americans used not so much for fragrance but for a common cooking flavoring, much the way people today use vanilla. But even those warm thoughts couldn't take away the chill of picturing strangers staring at her as she worked. "Ye Watchers and Ye Holy Ones," began one of the sacred songs for the holy ground Louise had mentioned.

And now Rudzinski had reminded her of her stalking obsession and suggested he, too, had watched her for wrong moves.

"Tanya," Kate said aloud, "wish you were here to buck me up."

"Talking to yourself already, or communing with the old Shaker spirits?" a man's voice behind her asked. Startled, Kate spun to face a smiling Dane Thompson.

"Just wishing Tanya were back," she explained, as he stepped into the small space. "But even with all the work here, I'd never want her to be called away from comforting her aunt. I know how much I wish I'd had time with Sarah Denbigh before she died, to thank her again and tell her how much she'd meant to me."

"The great bounty she left you in her will shows

she knew you cared," he said, his voice comforting. Dane always did sound half professor, half preacher.

"I'll always treasure that," Kate admitted, "even though I had a visitor today who told me things may have taken a turn for the worse in the heirs' challenge. Evidently, Sarah's daughter's lawyer has found some loophole to overturn the last will. I swear, I'd like to be rid of that woman."

"That's terrible news," he commiserated with a frown furrowing his high brow. "You're in Adrienne's and my thoughts all the time in this difficult situation."

"I appreciate that. But what can I do for you?"

"Tanya said that she had a couple of things for the display on old-time Shaker herbal drugs over at the brethren shop we're using for the infirmary this year. I hope you can be more accommodating than Clint. He just had a fit when I reminded him we needed an adult-size invalid cradle for the display. You know, those things actually look like modern-day coffins, but Shaker nurses found rocking adult patients as good as rocking babies to comfort them."

"Never underestimate Shaker ingenuity," she said, reaching for her flashlight. She'd restocked it with fresh batteries so she'd be prepared next time the lights went out. It was quite dim back in some of Tanya's herb bins. "Let me see if I can help," she offered. "What's needed?"

"Belladonna, for one."

With a shake of her head, Kate surveyed the way Tanya had taken over this shed with stacks of drying racks for her herbs. Kate was going to have to get them out of here soon, or the distillations would put humidity into them, not dry them. While Dane waited,

Kate shone the light on canvas rack after rack, and scrabbled through the drying layers of leaves and roots looking for what was labeled *belladonna*.

"Too much can be toxic, she says here," Dane explained, evidently reading from Tanya's notes. Kate heard a piece of paper crinkle. "She says that the Shakers used and sold it as a relaxant and narcotic. Hmm," he went on, "I guess they were ahead of their time on that, too. Today it's used for digestive tract relaxants, like Donnatal. But it says here that Southern belles used to use drops of it to dilate the pupils of their eyes when that was in style, even though mere daylight then gave them piercing headaches. You believe that?"

"I'm continually amazed at the arcane things Tanya knows, but not at the lengths to which people can go," Kate admitted.

Kate finally found the belladonna and took out a large piece of dried leaves and root. "It's probably one of Tanya's pet herbs," she told him as she wrapped it in a piece of paper towel. "Too much is poison but a little can help. What else?"

She dug out henbane, which smelled terrible and was used to produce a deep sleep in patients. "It kills insects like crazy," Dane explained, "an early pesticide."

"Maybe I could use that to protect my roses," Kate observed. "What's next?"

"Hmm, this is a good one. Angel's Trumpet. Perfect name for the Shakers with their angel visitations and all. Says here it used to be a form of opium to relieve pain."

"A pretty name, but it smells about as weird as henbane," Kate said as she located it and took a handful. "It doesn't say any of this is a contact poison, does it?"

"No, all ingested, I think," he said with a little laugh.

"Thanks a lot."

Kate couldn't find lettuce seeds until she'd gone through several small tin cans on what served as Tanya's desk.

"Here it is," she told Dane, who hovered over her so close Kate wished he'd give her a little breathing room. "Tell me what these were for, because I was wondering when she showed me the lettuce starts in her hotboxes."

"Ah, says here they allay coughing and are a good sedative for hypochondria, nervous complaints and—get this one—nymphomania," he said, and chuckled. "Let's not let Louise in on that. Can't imagine they'd need a cure for that in a celibate Shaker village. But it says here they used to collect a milky substance from incisions in the lettuce stalk with a piece of cotton, then make an extract of it to produce a false kind of opium, too."

"I'd be the last one to criticize Tanya's fascination with harmful herbs that can also be helpful," she admitted. "I've often planted white lobelia between roses for the visual impact, and lobelia can cause death if overingested. And I've read the Shakers planted rue among their roses as a natural insecticide, and that can cause everything from rashes to abortions. People just have to be careful with all this."

As they spoke, she carefully wrapped the tiny seeds in paper amidst Tanya's array of corks, funnels, scales and an herb press. "She's even going to write a book on it someday," Kate added.

"Someday?" Dane said with a little snort of surprise. "Last time I asked, she was halfway through it. Thanks, Kate. I know her being away has put an extra burden on you. I think having the opening so close is making us all a little crazy."

He patted her shoulder on the way out. So her friend Tanya, who had already begun her book, had lied to her, just the way Jack had the other night. But then, not everyone could be as painfully accurate and as truthful as Louise and Clint Barstow.

"So, do you have a favorite place to eat in Athens?" Jack asked Kate as he drove them into town for dinner the next night.

"Not really, though I know the 7 Sauces has great pasta."

"Sounds good to me, though it seems we should be eating Greek food in a place called Athens. So Clint sounded like he had nothing to hide, huh?" he circled back to their earlier conversation.

"A few years ago I would have staked my life on the fact he was telling the truth, but I realize I'm not such a good judge of people anymore," she admitted.

"Since me, you mean?"

"Do I hear a guilty conscience speaking? No," she said, shifting slightly sideways to see him better, "I mean since my husband ran out on me and Erin."

"Sorry I brought it up. I'd like to meet Erin, though."

"I thought maybe you didn't like kids, or at least teenagers. You've never asked about her before."

"It's not that I don't like them, but just that I don't know any," he said. "You know—have any in my life."

A long pause followed where his silence seemed to scream at her. Why didn't he even try to follow up on what she'd said about her husband deserting her—unless he somehow already knew all about that? Or did he think such a conversation would mean *he'd* have to make confessions, too.

"Did Rudzinski tell you he'd been to see me first?" Kate asked.

"He did. I think he admires you and wants to help."

"Oh, right. Now that makes me think you're not such a good judge of character, either," she insisted.

A tight grin twisted his lips. "The guy's fascinated by the Shakers, so I showed him a lot of furniture and explained how they lived and thought."

"Did you confide in him about your furniture thefts—I mean, the thefts of your furniture?"

"No, I let him confide in me that he's still working on that angle in Mrs. Denbigh's death." Kate sat up straighter and leaned toward him. "He asked me quite a bit about my furniture again, and what was being made in Shaker Run."

"I *knew* he hadn't given up on her death!"

"Kate, if she met with some sort of foul play, thank God for someone like Zink, however plodding or annoying he is. Besides, I've been an insomniac for years, and he killed some of the dark hours, as I've come to think of them. We had breakfast at four a.m. before he headed back to Toledo. I really think you may have misjudged the guy."

"Maybe, but I have something better to make you sleep than staying up with Zink Rudzinski all night. I've had trouble sleeping for years, too."

He gave her an intense look before returning his

attention to the road, then put a hand to the seat back behind her head, slightly snagging his big fingers in her hair. Vibrations feathered down her nape to her spine. Too late, she realized he thought she was coming on to him. And had she meant it that way? She was very attracted to him, though that was the last thing she needed in her life right now. Or maybe it was exactly what she needed.

"I'd like to hear about any cure you have," he said with a grin that lifted his thick eyebrows. He kept glancing from her to the road—full face to aquiline profile. She was so close that, though he was clean-shaven, she could see the outline of where his beard would be. He emanated the slight tang of pine as if he'd been out among fresh fir trees all day.

"Don't get any ideas," she said, laughing but hitting his shoulder with her fist. "Tanya's valerian herbal mix tea is the antidote for insomnia. I know others have used melatonin pills or popped sedatives—"

"I don't take anything like that," he interrupted, and put both hands back on the wheel. His teasing, open expression had slammed shut; his voice had gone sharp-edged, his face stony. She was amazed at how swiftly he could change moods and close the invisible door on his thoughts and emotions.

"Not even vitamins?" she pursued.

"You got it. By the way, I meant to tell you," he went on hurriedly, "I found out more about why the lights went out at Shaker Run during the storm."

For once she was relieved when he changed the subject instead of stonewalling her. "You said earlier that the wind had snapped a pole in front of your place that carried both electric and phone lines to the village," she reminded him.

"Not exactly," he admitted, shrugging his big shoulders. "I ran into one of the guys from the repair crew at the gas station in town. He says the wind didn't topple the pole—a car snapped it."

"Snapped a telephone pole—then just backed away and disappeared in that storm?"

"This guy saw definitive tire tracks in the mud where the wind had scoured the snow away. He said it was really strange that there was no scattering of plastic from broken headlights, which is always expected from low-slung cars today. The vehicle's fender hit the pole higher than most cars would, too, so he figured it might have been a truck or four-wheel drive, until he saw that the tire tread imprints were from a car."

Kate's stomach cartwheeled. If it wasn't a modern car and wasn't a truck, maybe the vehicle that hit that pole, plunging her into the dark, was the one she'd seen. "Are those tire tracks still there?" she asked, trying to keep her voice calm and sound merely curious.

"No. I looked. The warmer weather's turned it all to mush again. A minimystery, Ms. Marburn, but we've got to keep our minds on fake Shaker furniture—and dinner. I'm starved."

With his right hand, he reached over to squeeze hers clenched on her lap. Staring straight ahead, Kate saw not the sleek, silver hood of his car. In her mind's eye, she saw that antique, black car from the cemetery ramming the pole as it had meant to ram her.

Kate remembered the waiter she and Erin had had a few months ago, more by his unusual name than his face. "Hi, Stone. The redhead's mother—remember me?" she asked when she and Jack were seated in a back booth.

His open face showed surprise, but he smiled, looking slightly embarrassed. "Oh, yeah, sure. She's been back in on Sundays as regular as can be. Is her name Angel?"

Kate laughed and was relieved to see Jack smile. He'd been really uptight since they'd arrived, and she'd almost started to regret this formal date she'd accepted with him. She needed a break from tensions at the village, not a roller-coaster plunge into even more.

"No, you misheard—unless he's nicknamed her that," Kate said. "It's Erin."

"Oh, that suits her, the Isle of Erin and all that," Stone said as he gave them their menus. "And the guy's name is an *M* word, uh—"

"Mark."

"Oh, yeah. Glad to see you again, Erin's mom."

Jack buried his nose in the menu. "Jack, I was really looking forward to this but do you think we're making a mistake?" Kate asked.

He put his menu down and leaned toward her. "I have made a lot of those in my life, but if you're a mistake for me, I don't ever want to know it."

"That's hardly one of the nicest compliments I've ever had. We can just call this quits now and—"

"Kate, Zink is not the only one who admires you and hasn't let you know about it because he—I'm just not good at...feelings anymore."

Stunned at the admission, she nodded. He had just told her so much. "Then it's not just insomnia we have in common,'' she assured him. ''There's nothing like the blind leading the blind, but I'm willing to pursue a relationship—friends, at least, if you are.''

Kate was aching to ask him, *You're just not good at feelings since when? Since what happened?* But instead, her gaze riveted on his, she nodded in a silent pact.

Stone returned to find them shaking hands across the table.

11

Persian legends maintain that the rose's red complexion came about because a nightingale loved the white rose too much and grasped it tightly to its breast. The thorns pierced it and the blood turned the white rose red.

—Peter Coats
Flowers in History

Kate had returned to the village late, since she and Jack had eaten a leisurely meal and driven back to sit in front of his fireplace with snifters of brandy. And yet, she realized when he returned her to the Trustees' House in the village, as much as they had discussed family—his retired parents lived in Florida—current events, careers and plans, he had avoided his personal history again.

Kate wondered if it could be because he didn't want to make her feel that she must discuss her own painful past. She loved being valued for herself for once, with no questions asked. Or was Jack's avoidance of such revelations simply to protect himself? And could she really know and trust a man who was certain where he was going, but who wouldn't say where he'd been?

Now, this mutual good-night kiss in his car was

enough to make her push all that aside. It could not just be her imagination that his kisses were as dark as they were delicious, and therefore as mysteriously luring as Jack himself.

She feathered her fingertips through the slightly silvered, dark hair at his temples, then cupped her hand around the back of his neck as if to hold the kiss. As dizzy as she felt, he made her want to soar. Though he had restrained himself when they'd sat before the fire, it seemed now that something had snapped in him. He trailed frenzied kisses down her chin to her throat, his hands pulling her across the seat toward him until the gearshift stopped them.

"Darned new cars," he murmured, his breath warm against the hollow of her throat. He kept kissing her there, his hair tickling her chin. Slowly, he lifted his head. "Right now, I'd much rather be driving one of my dad's old-fashioned ones with one big front seat." He reached back to click his seat belt free, then leaned over her, as if he were embracing her, to undo hers.

"What's that line from an old movie?" she said, her voice husky. "'Fasten your seat belts, everyone. It's going to be a bumpy ride.'"

"Or was that 'It's going to be a bumpy night?'" he whispered, cradling her closer and kissing her hard again.

"I, for one, intend to sleep tonight," she said when their lips parted. "No bumps if I take some of my herbal tea, though maybe that brandy will be enough. Are you sure you don't want some of that tea to take with you?"

"No medicinal tea, nothing like that," he insisted, and set her away from him.

"You aren't a Mormon or Christian Scientist, are you?" she blurted.

"Kate, I'm not a health nut. Used to be but no more. I'm—was a Methodist, before..."

He paused and looked past her in the darkness.

"Before what?" she prompted.

"Before I had to rebuild myself. Like you said, it's late, and I'd better get going."

She had a hundred questions now, but he opened his door and got out, slamming it after him. Cold night slapped her back to reality. Was it worth it, she wondered, to become intrigued by this Jekyll-and-Hyde? She should forget it right now, but she couldn't. At least she knew what she was up against. Mike, the once beloved betrayer, had always seemed so open and up-front, but he and Jack were like night and day—thank heavens for that, she thought, as he opened her car door.

He walked her up to the Trustees' House and watched while she used her key. He had given her back the master he'd had made, though that didn't mean, she knew, that he hadn't made a second one. And she was just too tired to demand to know that tonight.

When she'd turned the lights on, he left and drove away. Silence settled like a cloak on the village, as Kate made her way up to the third floor of the large building, turning lights on, then off, behind her, as she went. This sturdy dwelling creaked like an old person's bones at night, and sometimes it seemed to breathe with muted memories and voices of the past. Maybe, she thought, that's what they meant by Shaker spirits. They had put so much into this village that they never quite left it, even in death.

The moment she went into her apartment, she heard the beeper on her answering machine, telling her she has a message. Not even taking her coat off, praying Erin did not have some emergency, Kate hurried over and pushed the play button.

"Kate, it's Tanya, still in Covington. Aunt Samantha died late this afternoon." Her voice snagged. *"It was a* blessing *since she was suffering. Please tell everyone I'm* sorry *but there's no way I'll be back till at least Sunday evening, as the calling hours and funeral are noon Saturday at her big Baptist church here. Thanks for doing whatever you can to cover for me—you know, take care of the herbs and all. Uh, let me give you my phone and address here in case you need it…"*

Kate played the message back twice and copied the information carefully. If it weren't so late, she'd call the Thompsons and Willises right now to let them know.

As harried as things were here, she wanted to go to the funeral. She knew how Tanya felt, and she wanted to be there to support her.

Erin heard the phone ringing as she came into her dorm room. She'd just taken a shower down the hall; Amy had already snatched up the phone.

"Oh, hi, Mark. Yes, she's coming in right now. Just a sec."

Erin's pulse started to pound. She put her plastic bucket with her soap and shampoo down and took the receiver from Amy. She closed her eyes to picture him.

"M-Mark?"

"Hi, baby. Just wanted to be sure we're on for Sunday."

"Oh, yes, sure. Is everything okay? I mean, you don't usually call this late."

"So why are you just coming in, then?"

"I haven't been out, just taking a shower. This is not the plush life, you know, and I have to go clear down the hall."

"Life's tough, huh? I just wanted to tell you I might not be able to call you on Saturday to set up our Sunday, because I've got to take a little business trip. But same time, same place, okay?"

"Sure. It seems like everyone's heading somewhere this weekend. Kate's going on a trip, too, to a funeral at some Baptist church in Covington, Kentucky, for some once-famous gospel singer."

"Is that right? Well, love you, angel. Gotta go."

Before Erin could say more, the line went dead. She put the phone down slowly and just stood there.

"Not problems?" Amy asked as she scooted down in her bed where she'd evidently been studying. The covers were wrinkled, and an open book was half buried.

"No. No problems."

"Why don't you ever bring him up to the room?" Amy asked, stifling a yawn. "We'd all like to meet him, your 'phantom lover.'"

"He's not my lover."

"Well, if he was, I wouldn't tell your mother."

That jolted Erin back to the here and now. She put her things away and yanked her covers down on her bed.

"Or you could at least ask him to the spring dance, or get him to stay for a whole weekend," Amy went on.

"He has a long drive to get here, and he's got a— a job as well as classes there. We decided Sunday is our day, and that's that."

"Okay, okay. Does he still look like his picture?"

Erin glanced at the old picture of Mark she'd taped on her closet door over the poster of Leonardo Di- Caprio and Kate Winslet windblown on the prow of the *Titanic*.

"Yeah, he hasn't changed much. Just like all of us, a little older."

"He always sounds that way. Nothing like an older man. Don't forget to set your alarm, or you'll over- sleep again." Amy's voice became muffled as she hunched into the covers again, her book over her crossed knees.

Yes, *Mother,* Erin almost said, angry at Amy's bossiness, but she bit her lip. Lately, she'd been un- able to sleep at night, as if insomnia were suddenly in her genes, her *Y* ones, at least. She didn't think her father had ever lost one wink of sleep over anything, not even when his world fell in. But her mom used to be a real mess.

Erin shut her eyes and pictured her stepmother dart- ing around their living room like a trapped animal in a cage that night Erin had tiptoed downstairs. It had been a few weeks after the embezzlement scandal broke and her dad had disappeared. As usual, Erin had cried herself to sleep, then woken up suddenly panicked and sweating, only to find Kate's—her par- ents'—bed empty.

Like a crazy woman, Kate was rushing from one living room window to another, peering out into the darkness. As Erin stared aghast from the staircase, Kate also darted from one piece of furniture to another, looking under things peering, up into lampshades, rummaging through drawers she yanked open. She was pawing through her houseplants in the front bay window by the time she noticed her stepdaughter on the stairs.

"Oh!" Kate had shrieked, jamming her fists against her lips, knocking a plant onto the hardwood floor. The ceramic pot cracked, spilling soil and an African violet at Kate's bare feet.

"What's the matter?" Erin had cried, gripping the banister. "What is it?"

Kate's eyes had looked sunken, haunted. Though she'd always been slender, lately she looked gaunt, especially bare-legged in one of Dad's big T-shirts. She crossed her arms and clasped her elbows as if to hold herself up.

Sucking in a breath, she lied, "It's nothing, honey. Can't you sleep, either?"

"I just wanted something to eat—crackers or a cookie. But—*what* are you doing?" she demanded, slowly going down the last few steps.

"I...I just wanted to be sure no one was outside— you know, a reporter or someone upset about what happened."

"At midnight? And what are you looking for in here?"

"You just never know if they've put in a hidden camera or bugged this place, since they follow me everywh—"

Kate had stopped talking, evidently realizing how nuts she sounded. And then, sobbing into her hands, she'd collapsed beside the broken pot. Scared of maybe losing Kate, too, Erin had held her and rocked her like a baby. And she'd made Kate call a doctor to get help the very next day.

Now, Erin jumped as her roommate slapped her textbook closed and clicked off her light. Erin sighed, set her clock and turned her lamp off, too. She'd better get her head together, because her grades were starting to suffer. She snuggled deep under her comforter. Maybe she could pray herself to sleep, because, despite increasing stomachaches and restless nights, she had a lot to be thankful for lately.

Waiting in the long line to greet the large number of bereaved family members at the Covington New Hope Baptist Church, Kate listened intently to the recordings of Samantha Sams, in her prime, singing gospel songs. Kate tried to let the swells of "Swing Low, Sweet Chariot" calm her.

I looked over Jordan, and what did I see,
Coming for to carry me home.
A band of angels coming after me,
Coming for to carry me home...

Although no one in the throng recognized Kate, she saw some reporters and TV people. This whole situation was starting to remind her of losing Sarah, and her heart flowed out to Tanya again. The family had even brought in several pieces of the deceased's Shaker furniture and placed some of the huge floral displays on them, up by the altar. Sarah would have loved that, but, of course, Varina and Palmer couldn't have cared less. Still, the flowers and the furniture were not making Kate feel at home here.

"Thanks so much for coming!" Tanya greeted her, when Kate got to the front of the line. They hugged hard, something they had never before done, but death always brought the living closer. "It means a *lot* to me."

"To me, too" was all Kate managed at first, tears blurring her vision. Despite being gone such a short time, Tanya looked thinner. Her beautiful chocolate-hued skin was tinged with gray, her eyes were blood-shot. She wore not the black worn by most of her large family, but a striking jade wool suit with a long skirt.

"I couldn't *not* come," Kate told her. "I wanted to honor your aunt, even if I didn't know her, and just be here with you."

"You came alone?"

Kate nodded. "Jack wanted to come, but he has clients in from the East Coast. Some guy he says always knows exactly what he wants him to make." Everyone at Shaker Run had asked her to make excuses, but she didn't want to launch into all that, and she knew Tanya understood.

"I promise," Tanya went on, blotting under her eyes, "that the service will be a blessing to you. I'll see you in the church Fellowship Hall for the meal after the interment, okay?"

"Yes, I'll be there."

After Kate shook hands and introduced herself to a few of the many family members clustered around the closed casket, she moved on, examining the various flower arrangements. One, mostly roses which she wished could be her own flowers, read, The Staff and Your Friends at Shaker Run Village. She shook her head. The Shakers would probably have sent beheaded blooms so that they could not be used for ornamental display. She remembered the flower heads thrown on the Denbigh graves.

Kate edged toward the back of the crowded sanctuary, looking at the photographs. Stretching back decades, events in Samantha Sams's life included singing everywhere from churches to the *Ed Sullivan Show,* the Grand Ole Opry, and the White House during Kennedy's presidency. Kate heard someone say that Samantha had "helped break down the color lines in this country—just one step behind Marian Anderson, singing at the White House..." It was an impressive and moving display.

But however Kate tried to distract herself, she kept feeling she was being watched. She glanced at Tanya to see if she was looking her way, but her friend was still greeting people. It was probably just the fact that local media were covering this, that set her on edge, Kate thought. But she made her way toward the back of the sanctuary, from where she could survey the room better. She sank gratefully onto the end of a pew.

Two elderly African-American women were sitting two pews ahead of her, both fanning themselves with the memorial programs, though it wasn't that warm in this high-ceilinged room.

"Can't believe it came on her so fast," the heavier of the two finely dressed matrons confided to the other, though she talked loudly as if she were hard-of-hearing. "I mean, I knew she was getting up there, but I always thought she had a cast-iron stomach."

"You live that long, somethin's gonna get you, too, Bessie, don't tell me it won't. I'm just wondering who's gonna get all her collections of things. Why, they could make a paying museum out of all that woman had, signatures and gifts, photos of famous people, not to mention all that Shakes furniture.''

''*Shaker* furniture,'' Bessie corrected her friend. ''Shakes is those rough-cut kind of shingles like to blow off roofs in a storm. Well, the storms of life are over for our Sammy Sams. And the good Lord's gonna be glad to see her coming to join her voice to those angel choruses. Just wish her homegoing could have been a bit more peaceful, I do. Pains and convulsions from complications of food poisoning's no way for one of the Lord's earthly saints to go, not if you ask me.''

Food poisoning, Kate thought. Tanya hadn't mentioned that.

As moving as the funeral was, it seemed to blur by for Kate. She wondered if Tanya had tried to help her aunt with her healing herbs in the end. Although Tanya hadn't mentioned food poisoning, why should she? With a person as old and frail as Samantha Sams looked in the latest photos, any complications could be fatal ones.

The entire congregation sang Samantha's favorite hymn, ''Amazing Grace.'' The pastor and several other speakers paid their tributes to ''the amazing Samantha.'' The large choir raised their voices in a rocking rendition of Samantha's beloved gospel songs. Often people broke into rhythmic clapping and occasionally shouted, ''Amen! Praise the Lord!'' It was a far different service from those Kate knew, but wonderfully exuberant and spontaneous—so real. Maybe, she mused, this was more like the Shakers, who used to let their emotions run their worship. Kate sensed she knew now what Louise meant when she kept after her dancers to "start out in control, then just let it run away with you."

Everyone rose while the casket was carried from the church and put in the hearse at the front of the long procession. Cars with purple-and-white funeral flags snaked twice around the old church and disappeared down a side street. Kate's car was about halfway back in the outer line.

Like everyone else, she got in and sat with her engine idling. There were so many family members of the deceased that they got in the limo, several cars behind it, and scattered into others throughout the first part of the long line. Kate lost sight of where Tanya was riding, but it was somewhere up ahead.

Finally, the hearse and the family limo pulled out, and then the cars in the inner line began to move, passing her. She sat mesmerized by the faces, yet seeing Sarah's and remembering the large turnout at that funeral.

An idea hit Kate so hard that she jerked her hands on the steering wheel and hit the horn. When the people ahead of her, who couldn't possibly move yet, turned to glare she tried to signal them that it was an accident. But was it an accident that Kate had lost Sarah and now Tanya had lost Samantha? Kate wondered if Tanya would inherit her great-aunt's Shaker furniture and bring it to Shaker Run. If Dane and Adrienne were trying to orchestrate that, they wouldn't even have to recruit Tanya the way they had Kate. Worse, had someone tried to take some of Samantha's valuable pieces of furniture but decided to get rid of the old woman when she became suspicious or caught them at it?

"You're nuts," Kate told herself aloud. "You're getting absolutely paranoid again. There is no pattern here, and no one is following you."

And then, as the unwinding coil of cars snaked by, her worst nightmare sprang to life.

"We're going to go right by her car," the man said. "These dark windows better hide us."

"You know they darken in full daylight. Duck down if you have to."

"Do we need to do this to keep her in line?"

"Not in line, but off balance. She's begun to question others, when we want her to just question—doubt—herself."

The woman slouched in her seat, but the man only tugged his fedora lower as they drove by.

"It's them!" Kate cried. "It wasn't in my head!"

The old-fashioned black car with tinted windows looked so proper—so perfect—in this procession for the elderly Samantha Sams. Though Kate's insides tensed, she did not physically react at once. After all, the black hearse and black limo also had tinted windows. But this one—

They were two cars past her now, and she was still stuck without enough clearance front or back to get out of line. The cars behind the black one kept her from seeing its license, from even seeing it anymore. It was as if she'd imagined it.

Kate unhooked her seat belt and jumped out. Leaving her car idling, she darted between it and the one ahead. The people she had honked at were still looking askance at her. Ignoring them, she darted between the moving and stationary lines of cars.

She could see the old black car again. It was four or five ahead, and the entire entourage was accelerating now. Kate ran faster, trying to catch up, to see. Surely this could not be a coincidence: that someone in Samantha's community of elderly friends had a car like that. If so, it would have a license plate. When she caught up and knocked on its door or window, they would stop or roll it down, and she could see their faces—their normal, real faces.

Her blood roared in her ears. She was out of breath and maybe out of her mind. Far ahead, as the line of cars turned right onto the main street, she could see the police motorcycle escort had stopped traffic. The officer was saluting as the cars came out and rolled by. But he got back on his vehicle and sped away, just as Kate reached the street.

She began to run along the sidewalk. Her high heels were tripping her, killing her, but she pressed on, darting around occasional pedestrians. She could see the top and side of the black car now, but not its plate. When she realized she wouldn't be able to catch up, she darted into the parking lot of a strip mall, trying to find a better angle from which to read the plate.

Unlike before, there was a license plate this time, white, but she could not read it from here. With a stitch in her side, she turned and ran back toward the church. She'd get back in her car—catch up with them that way.

At the church, the procession had moved away to leave her car first in line, but the cars behind her were so closely parked, they couldn't budge.

"I'm sorry—sorry," she called to the driver behind her, and got in, trying to ignore the glares. Thank God her keys were still here. She hit the accelerator and sped up to the car that had been ahead of her.

Should she keep her place and try to find the car and its inhabitants at the cemetery? Or if they had spotted her running after them—she always thought of the occupants as them, a man driving and a woman in the passenger seat—would they leave before she could get there? This was taking forever, and she had no idea how far the cemetery was. But city traffic was heavy even though the procession was moving through red lights with the motorcycle escort. Should she try to tell the policeman that a black car like that had followed her before in another cemetery?

No, she told herself. *He'd think you're crazy—and maybe you are.*

But it all seemed so unreal—just like when she had been sure someone was following her everywhere after Mike had screwed half of Toledo out of their savings. She could easily understand why someone would have been after her then, but now...? Unless it was someone Varina hired, someone paid to harass a rose grower from a rural southern Ohio Shaker village.

It seemed an eternity before the procession turned into the cemetery. As they wound their way around the various plotted sections—the vintage of the place reminded her of Toledo's Woodlawn—she decided not to get trapped in this long line again. She had to park where she could get out easily, and in a place from which she could see that car.

She turned out of the procession, pulled over under a tree near a hand pump, and got out, locking her car. Sprinting down the gravel lane, she stood back to spot where the car must be in the procession. Unless it had gotten out of order, it wasn't there.

More frustrated than fearful now, she strode toward the cars. Again, her eyes skimmed over to where she was certain it should have been. Even during the short graveside service, she stalked up and down the entire lineup of parked cars. Finally, out of breath and with her heart pounding, she leaned on a tall tombstone and tried to stop her legs—her whole life—from collapsing.

Kate hoped she wasn't making even more of a fool of herself than she already had. During the buffet dinner back at the church in the basement of Fellowship Hall, and after she had spent some time with Tanya, she forced herself to go from table to table, asking people, "Did you see an old, black car with dark-tinted windows in the funeral procession today? Friends of mine have a rare car like that, and I thought it might have been them, though I couldn't find them later."

Finally, a thin, well-dressed young man with a wife and four cute kids said, "You're the lady who honked at us, and then got out and ran."

"Yes, I'm sorry. I hit the horn by mistake when I was so surprised to see my friends drive by."

"But you didn't see them at church during the calling hours or at the graveside?" he asked disbelievingly. He stopped eating chicken to stare up at her.

"Uh, no," she admitted, feeling sheepish as well as silly.

"And they're not here now?" he pursued. "What's their names?"

"Sorry to have bothered you," Kate said, realizing

she'd have to go about this some other way. Maybe she should tell Stan Rudzinski what had happened in both Toledo and here today. Maybe he could check it out somehow, and it would help convince him that someone hostile was out there. But since she couldn't even give him a license plate number...

"Didn't say I didn't see them," the young man said, as she started away. Kate turned back. She could have hugged him.

"So you did see them?"

"Saw the car, if not the folks in it. Not many old Packard sedans still around. This one's prob'ly vintage late '40s. My grandpappy had one like it once, when everybody else in the 'hood was buying Caddies."

"Oh, thank you. Did you notice anything else about it—a license plate?"

He squinted as if trying to envision it again. "Maybe an Ohio plate—white with that funny, peachy-colored blur on the bottom of it—but sure don't know none of what it said. In it though, think it was two people. Yeah," he said, stroking his chin in thought, as if he had a beard. "And a man with a real bad, old kind of hat was driving."

Kate thanked him profusely and even got his name and address in case she needed corroboration later. Though she still hadn't eaten, she went to the back of the hall and skimmed every name in the guest book. Nothing hit her as familiar or unusual.

But *Ohio* plates! And the car *had* really been here—surely the same one that had followed her before.

But why? *Why?* If it was the last thing she ever did, she was going to find out.

12

All things uncomely and broken,
All things worn out and old...
Are wronging your image that blossoms
A rose in the deeps of my heart.
                        —William Butler Yeats
          "The Lover Tells of the Rose in His Heart"

As she left the church to head home, Kate knew she had to get hold of herself. But driving through busy Covington, then the Cincinnati traffic across the Ohio River, she kept glancing in her rearview mirrors for that damn black car. The traffic was too thick, and vans and trucks obscured her view. Once she almost rear-ended the vehicle in front of her. Though she forced herself to concentrate on traffic, she missed a turnoff and had to circle back.

"That's what I've got to do—circle back in my mind," she said aloud as the revelation struck her. "And not panic."

She took the next exit off I-75 when she saw the signs for several chain restaurants. It was still mid-afternoon, not dark for hours yet, thank God. She needed to take a break and try to discover who could be harassing her with that black car. It could not be mere coincidence. And she meant to figure out why.

Kate drove into a Wendy's Restaurant, locked her car, and went back to *check* that it was locked. Looking all around to be sure the other car hadn't come into the lot, she hurried inside. With a coffee and chicken sandwich in hand, she chose a corner table and sat with her back to the wall so she could see both building entrances, her car, and the field beyond the parking lot. Still, it bothered her that it was a dark day and brightly lit inside. She felt as if she were sitting in a fishbowl, if anyone wanted to watch her.

To force herself to focus, she flipped her paper place mat over and wrote on it, *Suspects 1—Varina & Palmer.*

They would benefit the most, Kate thought, from making her crack up, either in her car or in her head. "Or," she muttered, "they meant to hit me in the cemetery and are looking for another chance to finish the job." Running her out of Toledo wouldn't be enough for the Denbigh heirs, because she could still inherit Sarah's furniture. Varina, especially, was so vitriolic that she'd love to see Kate as dead as Sarah.

But that could not be all of it, she scolded herself silently. They obviously weren't simply out to kill her. Then why would they have appeared in a crowded funeral procession? No, they were sending her a message. She sat up straighter as a new possibility hit her. The fact they—she still felt there was a couple in that car—harassed her at cemeteries or funerals was a threat in itself. They enjoyed tormenting her, scaring her…perhaps before they did more.

Kate shuddered and drank more coffee. She'd had very little food back at the church, so she forced herself to eat some of her sandwich. For what she had in mind, she was going to need her strength.

> *Evidence—Varina told Zink I went to psychia-*
> *trist & she could know why—could want to make*
> *me feel watched, followed to set me off again.*
> *Then my death could look like an accident. Jeal-*
> *ous of Sarah's feeling for me, wants to make me*
> *suffer first—or thinks I'll break under pressure*
> *& she & Palmer will get Sarah's goods.*
> *Evidence—never seen any of them, but Sarah*
> *said Palmer collects vintage cars—1940s Pack-*
> *ard sedan?*

She underlined *vintage cars* repeatedly until her pen point slashed through the paper.

Kate knew she could call Rudzinski and tell him all this, ask him to find out if Palmer Denbigh had such a car in his collection. It was one of the things Sarah had said her son valued. "My children have, at least, inherited the urge to collect," Sarah had told Kate. "Palmer loves his classic cars—and beautiful but brainless women, whom he trades in as often as he does the autos. Varina has her jewelry and horses. I don't fault them for that or for their disdain of my 'old furniture and flowers,' but they ought to at least understand my passion for my collections…"

Kate shook her head to clear it. Sometimes Sarah's voice came back so sure and strong, unlike the broken and worn-out memories of her mother that she still clung to. Yes, that old car had to lead her to whomever was behind the dark windshield and windows. And if she could prove it was Palmer and Varina, then she'd call in Stan Rudzinski.

"But there could be others," she whispered as she craned her neck once more to scan the parking lot and street outside. There could be other candidates who wanted to observe, scare or harm her. She scribbled haphazard lines through all she'd written about Varina and Palmer, then wrote at the bottom where her spiderweb of lines didn't reach, *Zink*.

Zink might want to watch her, to pressure her until she was willing to confess something or other to him, but she couldn't believe he'd do it in an old car. And he must have had her under extensive surveillance to find her that early morning in Woodlawn Cemetery and then at a Kentucky funeral, for heaven's sake. Although he'd suddenly appeared at Shaker Run recently, the man couldn't spend that much time away from his job, unless to stalk her *was* part of his job. That's why she couldn't—wouldn't—go to him for help on this, at least not yet.

The Mike connection, she wrote next. She supposed there could be someone from among her ex-husband's defrauded clients who was wealthy, weird and vindictive enough to harass or hurt her. And then, she thought with a chill that racked her so hard she slopped coffee on the table, there was the missing Michael Marburn himself.

Rubbing her arms to stem the gooseflesh that swept her, she realized she had no doubt that he was out there somewhere on the run, probably blaming and hating her for testifying against him, and then divorcing him. Mike liked classic cars, and they'd been to an outdoor show or two to see them, but he'd neither owned one nor said he'd wanted to—at least, while she and he had been together. Yet Mike could have found out she'd been traumatized by all he'd done to her and Erin, and could be hoping to take advantage of that. Would Mike stage something as elaborate as a phantom car gliding in and out of settings related to death?

Kate sucked in such a loud breath that the couple at the next table turned to stare at her. She hastily gathered her things. She'd had a sudden memory—a vision—of that shadowy form that had glided from the Shaker cemetery toward holy ground during the snowstorm the night a big car had rammed the light pole. *Was* all this a message? A threat? Why? Even if it was, she wasn't running away from it but toward it. She was determined to find out what was going on.

Kate hit the rest room, then stood in line to get more coffee to take with her. She had a long drive ahead. Despite the fact they were expecting her back tonight, she'd call Dane and Adrienne and let them know she'd return tomorrow instead. Whatever it took, she was going to get some answers about her prime suspects.

Kate strode out of the restaurant with new purpose. But as she approached her car, she saw something splattered on her front windshield. She gripped her coffee cup so tightly, the plastic cap exploded off. Nearly scalded, Kate dropped the coffee, jumped back, and stared aghast. In the short time she had not been watching her car—rest room break or standing in line—someone had evidently been watching her. And he or she—they—had broken a wicker basket of flowers against the front windshield. One windshield wiper caught a tattered ribbon, which fluttered forlornly in the breeze.

Kate glanced between adjacent cars to be sure no one lurked there, then kneeled to look under hers.

Carefully, she edged closer to the front of her car, which faced an open field.

The smashed basket still held some stems and wilting rose leaves, but the blooms had been cut off and evidently thrown elsewhere. Perhaps they were strewn on Samantha Sams's grave, just as others had been thrown near Sarah's. Then Kate realized this was the basket of flowers that had been sent to the funeral from Tanya's Shaker Run friends—including herself.

Her hands pressed to her mouth to keep her from being sick, her legs shaking, Kate leaned back against her car and again scanned the weedy field, parking lot and busy street beyond.

Nothing amiss.

Nothing but more beheaded roses stolen from a fresh grave as another warning.

However fearful Kate was, she was furious, too, and she was not turning back. She'd start by driving by Palmer Denbigh's place. Though she knew where Palmer lived in Sylvania—a northwestern, affluent suburb of Toledo—she'd only driven by his house once before. The maze of streets in his neighborhood confused her at first. Finally, about six o'clock that evening, she found his home, a sprawling, gray stone house sitting on a good-size, treed lot. She was not surprised to see that his landscaping consisted of clipped taxus and yew bushes, without one hint of the crocus and daffodils that adorned the other early spring lawns.

But it was his deep, three-door garage that interested her now—and one of the doors was open. She was hoping, as well as fearing, she'd find an old Packard sedan in there, with its motor still warm from its drive back from southern Ohio and northern Kentucky. Maybe a car with a dent in its big front fender from knocking down a telephone pole. Maybe one with remnants of butchered funeral flowers on the seats or the floor.

Kate coasted by the house twice, then parked on the cul-de-sac one street over. It had looked as if no one was home, but that didn't mean anything, and she was not about to do a frontal assault. Though it pained her, she was going to use the same stealth and spying tactics that Palmer and Varina were probably using on her. Of course, the Denbigh heirs had enough money that they might have hired someone to do their dirty work. Even so, the car would be the link.

Since Kate had changed into comfortable clothes at a gas station when she'd filled up the car, it was easy enough to look like a neighborhood jogger. She tied a silk scarf over her head, knotting it under her hair at the nape of her neck. It was at least a minimal disguise, in case Palmer looked out a window. Glancing around again, she stuck the keys to her car in the pocket of her sweatshirt jacket and started to walk back toward Palmer's.

Though the weather was fairly mild for early April in northern Ohio, Kate felt flushed even before she picked up her pace. Her keys jangled, and her heart beat much harder than her exertion warranted. At least, she thought as she approached the house again, one of the three huge garage doors was still up. She wouldn't dare to break in, but she was planning on entering. She grimaced at the thought that she was acting just as deviously as Jack had that night he got into the Shaker Run furniture workshop.

She ran back around the block and located the

house directly behind Palmer's. She jogged up their driveway as if she belonged there. She was going to sneak in through the adjoining backyards with her eyes peeled for Palmer, so she could become a watcher, a phantom gliding in and out. Turnabout was fair play.

She hoped it was a good sign that she'd chosen a house with an as yet bare rose garden surrounding a fountain, one that had not been turned on yet this year. And as she had seen from the street, there was no back fence separating this house from Palmer's.

Kate slowed as she looked for a good spot to get through Palmer's hedges. Still, she scraped her legs and snagged her nylon running pants. Making no pretense of jogging now, she kept close to the side bushes and headed for the garage. Despite its lack of flower beds, the yard had several bulky stone statues, modernistic ones that suggested the human form.

Suddenly, this place reminded her of the cemetery with its monuments. All it needed was a strutting peacock guarding the grounds, instead of the crows cawing at her to get away as they pecked something from the spring grass.

Keeping on the far side of the attached garage, which fortunately could not be seen from the house, Kate scanned the front street and yard, then peeked in. The garage was so big that it had places for six cars. One of the two parking spots next to this open door was empty, the other held a low-slung red sports car, an old Corvette. That was certainly not what she was searching for. The next two garage doors were closed, but a large auto—maybe a vintage Cadillac— was parked behind the middle door, and next to it, what she would call a Model-T. Farther down behind the third door, and closest to the house, she saw what looked like another empty space and then a covered car. But in the dim depths, she wasn't sure.

Yes, she thought as she stood on tiptoe, the one parked back against the inner wall was covered with some sort of tarp. It had a hulking shape that could be the car she sought. Hearing nothing, seeing no one, she darted farther in and, keeping to the back wall, headed for the covered car—

She nearly jumped through the roof when she heard an engine start. No, not start, but come closer from outside. Headlights shone on the back wall. A car coasted into the parking spot, the open garage door began to descend behind it and ceiling lights sprang on.

Kate scurried deeper into the garage. Crouched behind the Cadillac, she peeked over its hood to see Palmer with a blonde. Their vehicle was one of those squat, camouflaged Jeeps from the Gulf War called Hum-Vees. Quickly, with the noise of the descending garage door to cover her, Kate darted farther away, around the Model-T's far side, and opened the driver's door. She dove inside and crouched on her hands and knees on the floor. The garage door's descent and the woman's voice covered the click of the latch behind her.

"Now, that's a fast, fun ride," the woman was saying. "I'll just pretend you're some sheik who abducted me during the 'mother of all battles' and swept me off to his desert tent."

Palmer boomed out a laugh. "Then step inside, my darling, though I hadn't planned on a battle."

"Mmm," the blonde murmured, as sounds in the lighted garage told Kate they were getting out of the

Hum-Vee and coming closer, toward the house, "maybe just the battle of the sexes."

At least Kate had a lot of floor room in this uncluttered, boxy, old car. She held her breath, praying they'd just go by and into the house. She wanted to peek under the tarp on that car, then get out of here. All she needed was for Palmer to find her on—in—his property.

She heard keys clink but the house door did not open. Where were they? Why didn't they talk again so she could get a fix on their position?

A throaty feminine laugh suggested the woman and Palmer might be kissing. The Model-T bounced a bit. Damn, but they must be pressed against it. It was a rhythmic rocking, making her feel sick to her stomach. Surely they weren't...wouldn't...

Kate recalled a scene in the movie *Titanic,* which she and Erin had seen together here in town last year. Erin had been so swept away by the tale of fated love that she'd seen it several times, but Kate had gone only once. While the villains searched for the young lovers, they were hiding and making love in a vintage car below decks in the belly of the big ship, the very night the *Titanic* went down. Kate envisioned that poster from the movie in Erin's dorm room. And she desperately wished Jack—that had been the hero's name in the movie, too, the one who drowned—her Jack—were here.

"Let's take it inside, my lord and master," the woman murmured. "That hood ornament's branding my bottom."

"Don't want to do that—not with a hood ornament," Palmer murmured.

Kate rolled her eyes as she heard the keys again,

then the door opening. The couple went inside, and closed it behind them.

Kate forced herself to stay put for a minute, then sneaked a look. The coast was clear but the timed ceiling light went out and, with all the garage doors shut, it was suddenly pitch-black. She would need to get out of this place but she wasn't sure where to find the garage door opener, or the light switch.

Carefully, quietly, she got out of the car, which bounced each time she shifted her weight. She didn't quite close the door behind her, afraid the latch would make a sound, however distracted Palmer and his friend might be inside.

Kate felt carefully along the garage wall for a switch, but wasn't sure if the one she found would trigger the door or the light. So she felt her way past the draped car, past the Model-T and, holding her breath, opened the door of the next automobile, the big Cadillac. As she had hoped, a light popped on inside.

Though the bulb was distant and dim, with her eyes now accustomed to the dark Kate managed to see well enough to get around. She tiptoed back to the covered car and tried to lift the tarp. It didn't budge. Tied at the bottom?

Feeling more hurried now, she yanked at the heavy material. It came free over the front bumper where she stood. She lifted the canvas to bare the hood. A dark color! Hard to tell which color, though, in this wretched light.

She freed more of it. A four-door. It could be *the* car, but she'd always seen it before at a distance. This close, in the dark, it was so hard to tell.

She pulled the canvas away from the hood ornament, hoping to find the name of the car somewhere. Where would it say Packard? She'd never noted the car's make. She was just trusting what some strange man had told her.

She felt and rubbed the hood ornament but could not tell what it represented. A flying bird? A woman's flowing garments? The make of the car was not written here. She dashed toward the back and skimmed her hands over the cold, metallic skin of the trunk. Yes, a word was here, a fairly long name. She touched the raised metal script as if she were reading Braille. It seemed longer than the name *Packard,* and she was sure the first letter was an *O*. Oldsmobile?

Hoping Palmer was too deep into other things to hear her, Kate went back to the switch on the wall by the entrance to the house. Sometimes garage doors opened of their own accord, she thought, especially if someone with a similar switch nearby hit their opener. If she got out of here quickly and no one saw her, maybe Palmer would never know—except for the mess she'd made of the car cover, but some kid could have done that.

She hit the switch. The garage door she'd come in through lifted with a steady, loud *hum*. Every light in the long garage sprang on. She still made herself stop to read the make of the sedan—Oldsmobile—and to see that the color was maroon. Then, without even taking the time to replace the tarp, she ran out the door. She tore around the side of the house toward the backyard, this time pushing through the prickly hedge into the next-door neighbor's yard before hurrying to the other street.

She was scratched and frenzied; she was also furious with herself at first for her failure to find proof.

But, she thought, gasping for breath as she started her own engine, this didn't mean Palmer didn't have another car that wasn't here right now. There was a spot for one, and Sarah had said he was always trading them. "Or," Kate said aloud, "it could mean I'm still looking for someone else."

"Jack, is Kate here?" Tanya called up to him, when he opened up a second-floor window at his house that evening.

"Tanya?" he called down. "You're back already? No, she's not here? You mean she's not in the village? She should be."

He shoved the window closed and hurried down the stairs to open one of his two front doors.

"I was *sure* she'd be back by now," she told him, out of breath. She was still dressed formally in a green suit, but she looked as if she'd been through the mill.

"I mean, I saw her at the funeral, and she got a good head start back but she seemed really nervous. I've got *tons* of stuff to do and needed to get out of there, anyway—family overload," she told him, and rolled her eyes.

He nodded, understanding full well what she meant. Despite having lost his immediate family, his parents' continual consolation had worn him ragged before he'd finally moved here to find some peace and quiet. But he'd found neither.

"You surely took the same route Kate did?" he observed, shoving his fingers through his hair. "You didn't see any road accidents or—"

"No," she said, almost scoldingly. "Don't worry. She's a big girl, but I guess you've noticed that. Who knows—maybe she stopped in some garden store or whatever.''

''Or a restaurant. She's probably with her daughter at O.U. Listen, Tanya, I'm sorry I had clients scheduled here and couldn't come to the funeral.''

She patted his arm, then grasped it a moment. ''The card and flowers were *really* nice. The village staff sent a big basket of roses, too. I didn't expect you or them to attend, since you didn't know her, so it was special that Kate was there. Well, got a lot of work, like I said. You guarding my writer's workshop?''

''Sure. Even if the village rents that building, I keep an eye on your things. Dane comes and goes fairly often, usually at odd hours, getting or stashing something, but I'm sure he doesn't disturb your work.''

''You know the village would like to rent or even buy your entire spread here,'' she reminded him with a glance around the grounds.

''Too bad, because it's perfect for me. You want to check on your stuff while you're here?''

''Might as well,'' she said with a huge sigh. ''With the village opening up soon, I have *no* idea when I'll get back to that book of mine. Got some other experiments to complete before I write more, too.''

He walked her toward the back building, beyond the one he used for his garage, on the other side of the house from his furniture workshop. When Dane Thompson had rented it, they'd agreed Jack would have a key, too.

''A Shakerabilia treasure trove,'' Tanya said, as Jack unlocked the padlock and shoved the old door open on its rollers.

''I think of it as the biggest Shaker storage box

I've ever seen,'' he said with a grin. "That reminds me, I'm hoping to have your herb desk ready for the opening of the village, but I just can't promise.''

"No," she said, playfully punching his arm. "Whatever the real reason you're supporting my writing project, Mr. Jack Kilcourse, I know you're not one to be making admissions *or* promises.''

Not one to be making promises. The words echoed in Jack's mind. Since he'd lost Andy—and then Leslie, too, damn her—he'd been unwilling to get close to any woman, and he'd certainly steered clear of commitments. But now with Kate, the temporarily missing and somehow always elusive Kate...

"Would you *look* at this *mess.*" Tanya's voice cut into his agonizing. The setting sun illuminated the stacks and piles of Shaker goods that were not currently being displayed or stored in the village. Some of it was furniture too damaged to be used until Barstow's men got around to fixing it. Two small crates of new things that Dane must have brought over sat here, too, Jack noted. Maybe he'd just have a peek in those when he got a chance, since they were the sort of crates that furniture was best shipped in, despite their diminutive size.

Tanya's makeshift writing desk sat beneath the single window. She used an extra light, and in the cold months Jack would bring out a space heater when she came here to write in private. He didn't want to discuss with Tanya why he was really helping with her project; she was writing, but he was underwriting it.

At first, he'd been staggered to hear her book would focus on how overdoses of medicine and drugs could harm and kill. *Cures Can Be Killers* she was calling it, though it had some longer subtitle, too. At least she never pried about his passion to see her book in print. He'd tell her someday and ask her to help him expose a murder—the tragedy that had devastated his life.

Within this storage area also sat stacks of old wicker, extra bricks, and a large, plastic, airtight box of Shaker memorabilia that Louise Willis and Adrienne had yet to sort through. And, of course, the classic antique touring car that had belonged to the last Shakers about the time they closed Shaker Run.

13

Roses have thorns, and silver fountains mud;
Clouds and eclipses stain both moon and sun,
And loathsome canker lives in sweetest bud.
All men make faults.

—Shakespeare
"Sonnet 35"

Shock drained the color from Erin's face as she saw who stood at the door of her dorm. "Mo—Kate," she gasped. "Is everything all right? You look like—I don't know, you've seen a ghost or something. Uh, come on in."

Kate had forced herself to get some sleep in a motel last night, then she had headed straight to Athens. She needed to see Erin, to be with her, and to get her to quit calling her "Kate" instead of "Mom."

"Honey, I know this is your day with Mark. I thought he might be here already, but I just couldn't wait any longer to have a real good talk with you. And it's about time Mark realizes I approve of him, if that's been worrying you. So I thought I could take you both out for dinner, after you and I have a talk…"

Kate realized she was rambling and flinging gestures. Conflicting emotions flitted across Erin's face:

annoyance, surprise, confusion, maybe even fear. "But," she told Erin, hauling her into her embrace for a long, hard hug, "if that doesn't suit you, how about if I come for you tomorrow after your last class? I'd love to take you over to Shaker Run to see the dancing rehearsals I've been telling you about."

Blessedly, Erin hugged her back. She'd been losing weight; Kate could feel the girl's ribs and backbone.

"Sure. Why not?" Erin whispered, before tugging loose and stepping back into her room to indicate Kate should follow.

Kate was relieved Amy wasn't in the dorm room for once.

"Actually," Erin said, "the reason I was kind of upset when you arrived was that Mark can't make it today, anyway. He's a little under the weather."

"Oh, then this is perfect," Kate cried. "Let's get out of here for a while, see the Shaker dancing, then just hang out and talk without everyone around."

"It was that funeral you went to, wasn't it," Erin asked as she grabbed her jacket and threw some other things into her backpack. Kate was amazed at how hurried Erin seemed to be to leave. "The funeral?" Kate repeated, puzzled.

"Tanya's great-aunt you told me about. When you lose someone, it makes you think about all the things you regret, like mistakes. I thought maybe that triggered your just showing up like this."

"Loving and needing you is what triggered my just showing up like this," Kate said, but she realized Erin had read her well. Not that it was the funeral itself, so much as her fear and her failure to pin down the person who was after her. She had to be certain they weren't after Erin. She was sure, at least, that she hadn't been followed to Toledo or here. She'd nearly sprained her back rubbernecking, and almost ran off the road staring in her rearview mirror. Of course, if the people following her knew where she'd be, that was another problem, she agonized, glancing nervously out Erin's windows.

Kate waited as Erin glanced at her watch, scribbled Amy a note, then hustled Kate out the door. "Let's go down the side stairs—it's closer," Erin said, leading her to the exit at the end of the building.

"You don't even know where I'm parked. And don't you have to sign out?"

"Not just for the day, and Amy won't worry now."

Erin hurried Kate along, leading her downstairs and out the side entrance. Still, even as they got in the car and Kate headed out of town, she saw and sensed Erin was looking around as anxiously as she was. It made her want to shelter Erin at Shaker Run, to feed her, and to distract her from the strange mood the girl was in. Kate wanted to pull a roof over both their heads to keep them safe and sane.

"I make you kindly welcome, for the Believers used to allow 'the world's people' in to see their worship," Louise Willis told Erin, as she and Kate sat on the sisters' bench to observe the rehearsal later that day. Louise and all her performers were in full Shaker attire. "All right now, brethren, sisters," she called to the dancers and her husband, who made the third man in the troupe despite his slight limp, "let us begin at the beginning, if you kindly please."

Everyone had been trying to "speak Shaker" in preparation for being presenters at the village opening, and Louise was still the guardian of the frontier for all things authentic. But Kate was coming to admire greatly both the Willises. Shaker Run was their dream, and they were giving it their all, including hosting a working dinner for the staff at their home tomorrow evening.

As the Believers used to do, Louise and Ben had cleared all furniture from the polished wooden floor, pushing the benches to the sides of the room. Their dancing, of course, was all individual—nothing with partners in this celibate world. Louise and Ben seemed such rigid personalities that Kate found herself wondering if they even went so far as to abstain from what the Shakers used to call "marital relations."

She recalled the peepholes high on the walls, accessed by narrow, hidden stairways where the elders used to observe what went on here. As she tipped her head back, she glanced up, and in the sun filtering through from outside she could almost imagine someone staring down right now. But she didn't *feel* she was being watched, not as she had at the church before the funeral. Besides, Dane and Adrienne were at their home today and the Willises were in plain sight, she thought smugly, so who could be up there spying?

Kate was grateful that Erin seemed interested, even excited to be here. Erin knew one of the female dance majors from among the eight women and two men from campus. Or maybe it was just the fact that Kate had fixed the two of them their old comfort food of macaroni and cheese with a side salad. Kate had coaxed every bit of what was on Erin's plate into her, and Erin seemed a bit calmer now. Actually, it was also the first time in days that Kate had felt like eating.

She and Erin had spent a little time with Tanya. Kate had been so pleased to hear Erin express condolences to her bereaved friend, whom she herself hadn't had the time to talk to privately since the funeral.

But having time to get through to Erin about taking better care of herself was more important. The girl had admitted that she was still having adjustment problems, and that her grades were slipping. But Kate knew they had much more to cover than that today. Just a little while here, and then she'd get Erin off alone again.

Beginning the dancing slowly, in an intricately patterned wheel, the women and men sang as they moved and swayed,

> *Awake, my soul, arise and shake,*
> *No time to even ponder,*
> *Keep awake, keep awake*
> *Lest ye be rent asunder...*

"That's a good one," Erin whispered to Kate. "I've been keeping awake too much lately. I think," she said, leaning even closer to be heard over the shuffling steps and singing, "I've caught your insomnia."

Kate put her arm around Erin's shoulders. "Too much worrying about grades," Kate whispered. "Maybe you're actually working too hard. You're not falling behind because Mark's taking up one of your good study days every week, are you? Are things all right between the two of you?"

"Kindly hush, Sister Jerusha!" Louise hissed as if they were speaking too loudly in a library. "You should know better and set an example. All right now, everyone, let's go right into the 'Angels Watching' pattern.'' Louise conducted the singing as if she were a choir director, swaying along with the dancers. Kate had noticed that Louise often joined in.

"Step livelier, keep it moving, moving," Louise called to her dancers. "It's not called an 'endless chain' for nothing. Keep weaving, weaving."

"Let's step outside," Kate suggested with a nod at the open double doors.

"Just a sec," Erin whispered. "I've got to see this when it gets crazy."

Kate had described to Erin how the movements became wilder as the dancers broke away from the slow, set pattern to mimic receiving heavenly gifts with outstretched hands. Some of them were already making the motions of sweeping the devil from the room. Even now that the slower dancing called "laboring" was ending, individuals began the jumping steps that symbolized flying up to heaven, and the trembling movements that indicated visions of angels. It was all choreographed by Louise, of course, whom Kate suspected of seeing some Shaker visions of her own.

But what surprised her the most was Ben Willis, whom Kate considered quiet and circumspect. Not only did his weak leg not stop him, but also he had a beautiful baritone voice that soared with the Shaker songs. And he looked almost...dazed.

The regular singing—they had just finished the best-known Shaker song "Tis a Gift to Be Simple"— was breaking down into shrieks and shouts. Faster, jerkier, the dancers spun off into the spontaneous displays of whirling, leaping and shaking that had given the Shakers their name. The more dramatic of the young women seemed frenzied, as if seeing things that obviously were not there.

Evidently awed yet embarrassed, Erin indicated they should step outside. They skirted the edge of the large, echoing room, and went out the sisters' door into the brisk wind and gentle sun. Though muted now, the noise chased them outside through the doors set ajar.

"The Shakers were pretty weird," Erin said, tossing her red hair. Kate had always thought her stepdaughter's pale beauty a cross between that of an Irish princess and one of those pale classical nymphs emerging from the sea in a painting by Boticelli. But, thinner and wanner now, the girl seemed more like a wraith or woodland sprite who could dart off in the wink of an eye.

"That dancing," Erin went on, "was starting to remind me of that Arthur Miller play the high school did when I was a junior. You know, *The Crucible*, with all those Puritan girls flipping out because they thought witches were everywhere around them, or were pretending they saw them just to pull the wool over people's eyes. But back in the Meeting House, it seemed almost like they were *on* something."

"Not around Sister Straight-and-Strict, they weren't," Kate protested with a little laugh, but she realized Erin had been quite observant. Kate sometimes thought the so-called angel visions the Shakers claimed could have been something far more scary. It always amazed her that the peace-loving, quiet and celibate Believers could suddenly turn loud and passionate.

"That's part of the mystery about the Shakers," Kate told Erin. "They careen between light and darkness, simplicity and depths. And speaking of the depths, wait till you see this old well the university is excavating over here,'' she added, glad to shift subjects as they strolled across the lane.

Though the progress made in the old well near the Central Dwelling showed Kate that the crew had worked long hours since she'd been away, no one was here on Sunday afternoon. Carefully, standing outside the rim of flimsy wooden fencing they'd put up to protect the site, Erin and Kate peered at the digging equipment and the slightly widened hole.

''Any money or treasure?'' Erin asked with a nervous laugh.

''Things like combs, buttons and bottles so far, I guess, but that doesn't mean something significant won't turn up.''

''Yeah, like the body of somebody who croaked dancing that way. Or of someone who fell in forbidden love here in this 'do ask and do tell place.'''

''You've been doing a lot of deep thinking about all kinds of things lately,'' Kate observed, looping her arm around the girl's waist. ''Being away at school, even this short time, seems to have changed you, matured you.''

''But that's good, right?'' Erin demanded. She shrugged away, and they walked through the village to the fence that ran beside the frothing stream called Shaker Run. It was still full of spring rain from the surrounding hills, churning more wildly than Kate had ever seen it. Erin perched on the stone fence, so Kate did, too, though the stones hurt her rear. The strange songs and cries from the ''Shaker high'' going on inside the Meeting House drifted to their ears on the wind.

"You seem very upset," Kate began, choosing her words carefully. "Tell me if there's anything I can do to help." She wanted to hug Erin again, to reach out to touch her hand or knee at least—but she didn't.

"It was too late for that once Dad left. You know, all that water over the dam," the girl said with an awkward little laugh as she pointed to the swollen stream.

Kate was shocked that Erin had instantly referred to her dad's desertion. She'd expected to hear about grades and school. "Erin, I know I'll never fill the void your dad left, but I'm here for you," Kate said simply.

"You should have been there for *him.*"

"Do you still think I turned on him? Honey, don't you think he turned on us first?"

"He was trapped by circumstances," she insisted, frowning at her fists on her knees. "Would you like to face spending the rest of your life—years of it, at least," she added, looking up, "in prison, when it wasn't really your fault that all the investments fell in like a house of cards?"

Kate's jaw dropped, but she quickly recovered. Mike's guilt had been proven and widely published. Kate thought Erin had come to accept it. But *like a house of cards* was exactly the way Mike had described the financial mess he'd "fallen into," which "had collapsed on him through no fault of his own." That's the way he'd always talked and precisely what he'd written in his farewell letter to them.

"Erin," Kate said, "I know it's so hard to accept that someone you love and need—"

"You used to love and need him, too. You said you did."

"—could be deceitful or betray you. But he ran, Erin, and left other people, including me, holding the bag—a bag he made sure was empty when he took off."

Erin jumped down from the fence as if it had turned hot. "He had to keep from starving if he was driven away," she shouted at Kate, hands on hips. "And it's hard to accept that a person fighting for his financial life—his very life, considering some of the threats he got—could just be dumped, jettisoned by his wife, who was supposed to stand by him for richer, for poorer, and all that."

Kate slid down from the fence. She felt it had just fallen on her. She could not believe this explosion of emotion. She'd thought Erin had moved on from their family catastrophe, as Kate was trying to do. But Erin had failed to do that—and she'd failed Erin. Yet above all else, one thing the girl had said snagged in Kate's thoughts.

"'Threats' he got?" Kate repeated Erin's words. "'Fighting for his very life'? No one ever suggested to me that someone threatened or endangered your father's life. Is that what you mean, Erin? Did you somehow hear about that, but didn't tell me? I've got to know."

"Don't!" Erin shrieked, turning away and flinging up her hands as if to hold Kate off. "Don't try to tear him down any more. He's not here to defend himself, and I just can't talk about it. It's your problem, your fault, Kate, and I've got enough on my mind with getting my grades up and—"

Kate tried to pull Erin close, to stem the rising hysteria. To Kate's surprise, Erin let Kate wrap her arms around her, but the girl stood stiff and cold in her embrace. Then Erin pulled away and strode back to stand in the door of the Meeting House, as if fascinated by the wild dancing.

"You *look* like I *feel*," Tanya told Kate, when Kate dragged herself into the garden shop early that evening. It wasn't dark yet.

Kate had taken Erin back to school, stunned and sick at heart that the girl was barely speaking to her. She'd decided to give her a little cooling-off period, then insist they see a family counselor together if things were still so bad between them. Somehow, she needed to convince Erin to explain the threats made against Mike. That could be the link to whomever was after Kate. On top of everything else, this emotional crisis with Erin was all she needed.

Tanya gave Kate the warm hug that Kate wished she'd had from Erin. "I'll bet you're exhausted, too," Kate told her as she took the rake she'd come in for. She almost told Tanya about the flowers from her aunt's funeral being thrown at Kate's car, but that would lead to a full confession of all that was wrong, and Kate didn't want to upset her friend even more. "Why don't you get a good night's sleep and start over tomorrow?" she suggested.

"No can do 'cause too much to do," Tanya said with a shake of her head. "And I don't just mean around here. I'm supposed to be back in Covington late next week so the family can divvy up Auntie's Shaker furniture with the church."

Kate leaned on the rake. She ached all over, but that comment grabbed her attention. She'd been agonizing about whether to discuss a possible pattern between her loss of Sarah and Tanya's loss of her great-aunt—and the fortune in furniture involved. And now Tanya had given her the perfect opening.

"Her collection will be divided up?" Kate asked, trying to keep her voice calm. "So evidently there will be no surprises like the kind I had with Sarah's," she mused aloud, hoping Tanya would add more information.

"Since she had no kids of her own, the church will get the bulk of her estate," Tanya explained, continuing to sort herbs. "But my mother says all her nieces, nephews—great-nieces and great-nephews, too—will be getting some Shaker heirlooms. She also said Auntie left me some special pieces since she was so *proud* of my efforts here."

Kate nodded as her mind raced. She decided to try to lead Tanya into the other topic she wanted to discuss. "Then it was a special blessing you were there to help her in the end. Tanya, I overheard she died of food poisoning," Kate blurted, "and..."

She hesitated, when Tanya knocked over a small sack of dried leaves, then hurriedly brushed them up. "And," Kate went on, "I was thinking that was ironic. You know, with your work and all, the curing herbs and the book you're going to write," she prompted lamely.

She'd done it now, Kate thought, gripping the rake handle so hard that her hands went numb. By setting a trap for her best friend, she'd sunk lower than she had when spying on Palmer Denbigh. But Dane had said Tanya had half her book written when she'd told Kate something quite different. And though Kate hated herself for so much as suspecting Tanya, she was dying to know if her friend had tried to dose her great-aunt back to health.

Kate watched now as Tanya continued to scrape crushed leaves into her hand, then dumped them back in the sack. A bitter scent drifted between them.

"When someone's as old as Auntie Sams," Tanya said as she kept busy with her back to Kate, "you think they're *indestructible*. But when they're that old, even something as small as indigestion or food poisoning—which the doctor put on the death certificate—can be a big thing. And yeah," she said, turning to look Kate full in the face, "can you believe I tried to dose her with peppermint tea? Too little, too late, I guess."

"I'm sorry," Kate said. "But she had a long, rich life."

"And right when she died," Tanya went on, her gaze going past Kate to fix on the wall as if she saw a scene there, "her eyes opened real wide, though she'd earlier had them scrunched shut in pain. And when I leaned over her, I heard her say, 'There are angels here, and they are the prettiest ones I've ever seen.' It seemed so—so *Shaker*."

Kate reached out to touch Tanya's hand, and her friend grasped it hard. "Her happiness—acceptance—at the end must be a great comfort," Kate said as goose bumps skimmed her skin. She decided then that she had been wrong to mistrust Tanya. So what if her friend hadn't told her the truth about her book. Or perhaps it was Dane who hadn't told the truth.

"I'll let you get back to work," Kate told her as she edged out the door, holding it ajar. "I'm going to rake mulch off those transplanted roses. Time to uncover their canes so the spring sun and air can do their thing." Still feeling guilty that she had sprung so much on her bereaved friend for her own purposes,

Kate added, "Let me know if I can do anything to help."

"Oh," Tanya said, following her to the door and leaning through as Kate started away, "I meant to ask you if you ever found that car you were asking everyone about at the funeral—some old sedan. Why didn't you ask me?"

Kate just stared at her for a moment. Tanya suddenly seemed angry. "I thought," she said simply, "you had enough on your mind."

"So who would have been at Auntie's funeral that were friends of yours?" she pursued.

Again Kate almost spilled everything to Tanya, but something held her back. She needed to reason things out just a bit more, maybe see what Tanya inherited from her aunt before she told her everything. Besides, what did she really have to share but some suspicions with no proof, no clear motives?

"I thought it might be some people I met in Toledo," Kate said, tipping the rake handle back and forth. "I knew it was crazy to think it could be them, but the car was so distinctive."

"Probably just one of Auntie's elderly friends still driving their old junker," Tanya said. "I don't recall seeing it, not that I was looking. And if it just disappeared," she added with a sharp shrug and sharper laugh, "maybe you've just been hanging out with Louise too long—and you're seeing things."

Though Jack Kilcourse had permission to enter the Shaker storage shed on his property and had done it before, he felt a little guilty this time. But he couldn't afford to pass up this opportunity right under his nose. He had to look in those two, small boxed crates, just the sort, if not the size, in which he used to ship furniture. These looked more like wine crates.

He sneezed at the dust as he entered and slid the door shut behind him. Light flooded in from the window above Tanya's writing desk. The odd thing was that the other items stored here were tattered, broken or generally unused—including, he now noted, the car Dane used and had evidently dented. But these crates were pristine.

Then it hit him. Dane must have been out in that car in the snow and slid into that light pole, and he was too ashamed to tell anyone. That would reassure Kate, but it might get Dane in trouble if anyone else found out. He wondered if the electrical repair crew would charge the driver for the repair costs.

He edged around the old Shaker vehicle that Dane kept in good shape but refused to put on display. "The vision of Shakers we want for the village is circa 1840s, not 1940s," he'd told Jack one day when he'd driven it back after a fill-up or tune-up. "Louise says someday we'll do an End of the Shaker Era display, and then we'll haul it out."

Jack quickly put his small crowbar to work on the first crate. He'd opened and sealed hundreds of these. It would be a joke if they actually held wine that Dane just didn't have room to store at home for that French wife of his—the one who loved the good life but didn't really have it right now. That, Jack thought, made the Thompsons worth watching on this furniture fraud thing. Kate had mentioned that though Barstow and his guys were doing the construction, Dane Thompson was overseeing the marketing.

With a groan and a creak from the protesting wood frame of the crate, Jack pried his way into the first box. Expensive wooden shavings rather than foam or newspapers were packed around whatever sat inside—maybe wine bottles, indeed. If so, he'd seal this up without a mark on it and get back to work.

Jack lifted out handfuls of the shavings until the carved finial of a chair back appeared, and then another. It was Shaker for sure, but so small. A child's? And was it the traditional Shaker rocker?

He uncovered the rest of the rocker, then thrust it quickly back into its protective nest. He'd never made one for a child, wouldn't want to, even though they were rare and that made them expensive. His appraisal of originals would be sky-high.

Quickly, he restuffed the packing and hammered the crate closed, then cursed himself that he hadn't checked the chair for authenticity. He turned his attention to the other, same-size crate. It was identically sealed and packed.

Another child's rocker? No, he bared a flat wooden cherry surface the moment he pulled out a handful of wood shavings. He had to lift this piece out a ways to see what it was.

A small washstand, obviously a child's height. Could these be stored here close to his house because it had once been the so-called gathering order, where they took in children to make new converts? he wondered. Were Shaker Run's modern-day leaders collecting furniture they'd use if they ever got this property from him? Dane did seem awfully secretive about things sometimes.

He checked the dovetailing, the wormholes, the finish on the washstand's single drawer. The underside was haphazardly stained where someone had cleaned a brush against the wood—waste and carelessness of which the Shakers would never be guilty. And the finish had not weathered darker where it had been exposed to the air. Fairly new wood, then—a replica, but one that would pass a layman's examination.

He repacked the washstand, puzzled and angry. He could hardly go storming after Dane and demand to know what was going on, because he'd give himself away. Should he tell Kate what he'd found and ask her to keep her ears and eyes open even more? She'd said she was going to a staff party tonight at the Willises' house.

And then he realized why he had to tell Kate about the furniture, even if he didn't betray Dane's dent in the car. He'd seen the authentic matches for these two Shaker fakes before—in Sarah Denbigh's suite at Groveland.

14

If neglected or in hardship, a rose refuses to flower until it is severely cut back and weeded.
—Sister Jerusha Lockhart
Shaker Run Diaries

"Oh, Jack," Kate said, surprised. She was in her silk bathrobe when she opened her apartment door. "I thought you'd be Tanya. She's due here to pick me up for the staff party."

"This will only take a minute. I thought I'd stop by rather than calling, since I was out walking—thinking. I came over the back way past the cemetery," he said in a rush.

He had been taking a long walk, trying to decide whether to trust Kate enough to get her more deeply involved. But in more ways than one, he guessed, she already was.

"Come in," she said, and closed the door behind him.

Her silk print robe, tied tightly to her slender form, accentuated her curves. He tried not to stare.

"What is it?" she asked, her voice agitated. She might as well be, he thought, because *he* was. The woman really got to him. She obviously was partly dressed under the robe, but she was barefoot. Her hair was damp and disheveled as if she'd just taken a shower, and she had on only some of her makeup, which conveyed a certain intimacy. She appeared sleepy, kind of tousled, and...

"Kate, I've stumbled over something that makes me think it's possible that Sarah Denbigh's furniture was being tampered with or, let's say, was about to be tampered with. I've discovered that identical fake pieces to two of hers exist."

"In Barstow's workshop? But you gave me back the key to it."

He shook his head. "In another storage area that belongs to the village. I'd rather not say where right now, because I don't want you insisting that you or the police go through it yet. I'm hoping you'll trust me on this."

"Is it at Rent-a-Room Storage where they keep other things?" she demanded. "I know where that is. I have my extra furniture and other things there."

He looked surprised. "The village rents storage rooms in town?"

She nodded. That, he thought, opened another whole Pandora's box. What if Barstow, or even Dane, were keeping furniture there until they could switch it with authentic pieces? Maybe the children's pieces were the overflow or en route to the Athens storage.

"I didn't realize that," he admitted, crossing his arms over his chest so he wouldn't reach for her as he so badly wanted to do. "Look, I know you're heading for the staff dinner, so I'm just hoping—without giving yourself or me away—that you can keep an eye out, maybe even steer a conversation to children's furniture pieces. I'd better get going before I really get in your way."

"But I need to know more. Which pieces? Why children's?"

"A small rocking chair and child's washstand— you know, what some collectors call a commode. The washstand is cherry, the rocker butternut-and-ash with a dark blue-and-beige woven tape seat. Can you recall if those were the colors of Mrs. Denbigh's taped child rocker?"

"Yes," she said, nodding. "I know the exact pieces you mean. She said that children's furniture is difficult to find. I guess they were harder on the furniture than adults were."

"That's why they'd be especially valuable as fakes. But the forgers don't dare flood the market with such rare pieces."

"But, Jack," she said, and reached to touch his arm, "what do you mean by perhaps they were 'about' to be substituted for Sarah's furniture? Do you mean that very night she died?"

"I don't know. But it would explain intruders."

"Whom she stumbled on. But to kill her over substituting pieces of furniture? And the thing is, they *didn't* substitute them. But maybe because she caught them at it, and they panicked..." she reasoned aloud.

Her words were half conjecture and half question, but they seemed to shake her. When Kate gripped her arms as if to hug herself, Jack took a huge step forward to finish the job.

He crushed her to him, but she held him tight, too, her face pressed into his shoulder. Her body seemed to fit so perfectly against his. She was soft and supple where he was solid or angular. When she clung closer, he cradled her with the top of her head nestled in the hollow of his throat. And then she lifted her head, offered her lips, and he was lost.

Jack held her close and hard. His mouth slanted over hers crazily and hungrily, but she held to him, both taking and giving. His hands moved over her supple back and soft bottom; his heart pounded against her breasts. He lost the sense he was a separate being as he shifted his stance to bring her closer, never breaking the kiss. They breathed together, belonged together.

It had been forever since he had felt so open and needy. Kate seemed to feel the same, stoking the wild, devouring emotions he had exiled to some dark place. It shook him to his core knowing how strong he felt, and yet so weak.

He heard the doorbell ring—darn Tanya. No, it was a telephone to shatter both reality and the dream.

"Better get it," he managed, out of breath, his lips buried in her hair. She smelled like roses, but he set her back, desperate to rebuild the barriers he tried to keep between them. "Tanya could be late, the party canceled. Don't I wish."

At first she didn't move away, but held to him. He wanted to smash the phone and lift her in his arms. When it kept ringing, she pulled back and knotted her sash tightly. The moment she stepped away, he tried to tell himself he was fine now, self-controlled and contained again. That it had only been his body reacting, not his mind or heart.

Kate stepped over to her desk and picked up the phone. "Kate Marburn here," she said, her voice uncharacteristically throaty. "Oh, hello, Mason. How's the world of big, bad law in Toledo? Any new word on Sarah's death?...I know you're not the police, but

I said it's more important that I know about any developments on Sarah's death than details about the legal ramifications of Palmer and Varina's claims.... What? Tomorrow?''

Her voice sounded exasperated now. ''But I'm buried with work here. With everyone there? Palmer and Varina, too? Yes, I understand. One o'clock tomorrow at your office it is, then. You know, I'd do anything for this to be over—except give in to them against Sarah's last wishes. Yes, I'll try not to worry,'' she said, shaking her head and rolling her eyes at Jack. ''See you.''

''Not good news,'' he observed, as she hung up and leaned a moment on the old Shaker desk she used.

''Probably not,'' she admitted, still frowning. ''A joint meeting of all parties involved in the dispute over Sarah's will. Though the Denbigh children are about the last people in the world I'd like to see, it will be a chance for me to tell them to keep out of my life. And I have other things to discuss with Mason.''

He sensed she wanted to say more, but didn't. ''Do me a favor,'' he said in the awkward silence, ''and don't tell him about the lead we have. I'm not making accusations yet.''

''Yes,'' she said, nodding slightly as their gazes met and held again. ''I understand.''

They both jumped at a rapid knocking on the door. ''Kate, we're gonna be late,'' Tanya called. ''And Louise will probably refuse to feed us if we're not there on Shaker time!''

''Go ahead,'' he said, and nodded toward her bedroom. "I'll talk to her until you're ready. Sorry I slowed you down."

"I'm not," Kate said with a pert smile that made him feel he'd ridden a roller coaster down a drop-off. If Tanya hadn't been rapping on the door again, he might have tried to get Kate to go along for the ride.

"Now everyone is to 'Shaker your plates,' and that means eating every bit of food here!" Louise announced as she put the finishing touches on the buffet table. Ben had summoned them all into the Willises' living room.

Despite her worries, Kate had been enjoying herself. The support of the village staff always bucked her up. Everyone had been solicitous when she'd been asked to update them about the state of Sarah's will and she had mentioned the meeting tomorrow.

"Give 'em hell!" Clint Barstow had said, best summarizing everyone's feelings.

But now they were *ooh*ing and *aah*ing over the lovely, unique spread of food Louise had prepared— authentic Shaker, of course. They'd been drinking fruit shrubs, a delicious mix of pureed strawberries and made-from-scratch lemonade, while Dane conducted a rather informal meeting during which each person had explained what he or she had yet to do to prepare for opening day—a scant three weeks away. Now steaming cups of ginger tea awaited them with the other offerings. It was quite a spread, both in selections and quantity. But then, with Clint Barstow and six others to feed, the bounty was necessary.

"The corned beef and cabbage was one of their old standbys," Louise was explaining as she pointed out the dishes and uncovered the hot ones. "This is blue flower omelette made with early chive blooms to lend color and flavor. Buttermilk herbed biscuits with apple paring jelly here..."

Smiling, Ben put in, "They used every bit of their apples, especially during hard times."

"These are watermelon pickles they actually sold from time to time," Louise continued. "And the salad, which they called sallet, is lamb's lettuce they kept covered in hotbeds all winter. It's flavored with basil and other herbs."

"Have you helped her with this?" Kate mouthed to Tanya.

Her friend shook her head. "Louise was the village's herbalist before they hired me," she whispered, "but I don't think she knew much about it."

"Evidently she knows enough. She's amazing," Kate replied, shaking her head, "just amazing."

"And last but most certainly not least, we have Mother Ann's Cake for dessert," Louise was saying. "The Believers celebrated her birthday with this cake—probably scores of them—on March first every year, so we've missed that special day, but this will have to do."

"You'll never be able to place the gentle, fabulous flavor of it," Ben noted, pointing to the pale peach-colored, iced layer cake. "The master chef said I could give her secret away. It's flavored with rose water, which we hope Kate will provide fresh for us next year so we won't have to buy it at an import shop. But the key is in the beating.

"You beat the batter with peach twigs," Ben explained, "which are cut and bruised so the flavor imparts itself very subtly."

Across the room, Kate saw Adrienne whisper

something to Dane. She was stunning but overdressed for this gathering in a long, print silk skirt and blouse.

"I think," Dane said, "we all owe the Willises a round of applause."

Everyone clapped, while Louise and Ben beamed. "And we don't insist you eat silently, despite how the Believers did it," Louise put in. "Sometimes rules, like those peach twigs, are meant to be broken."

After dinner, while the men huddled downstairs, Louise proudly showed her three female guests around their home. Although Kate would term the decor Early American, it wasn't strictly Colonial; several fine Shaker pieces of furniture were in evidence.

"Beautiful furniture, Louise," Kate observed. "Did Clint and his workers make it or are—"

"We have a few authentic pieces. Several, no doubt, came from this area, as we found them years ago in estate or yard sales before things got so pricey."

"You know," Kate pursued, "since the Shakers took in so many orphans and entire families to swell their celibate numbers, why don't we find more Shaker furniture for children?"

"Well, for one thing," Adrienne said rather huffily, "around our Shaker village, at least, the children's order buildings and property were sold off early and never came back to us. And your friend Jack Kilcourse apparently isn't about to sell. But as Dane says, we have a lot more important things to worry about before we can find the time or money to deal with that."

Kate frowned. Adrienne had put that final remark

in a threatening tone she'd never before heard from her. The lilting, charming French accent had never sounded less captivating. Kate filed that away to tell Jack.

"I imagine," Louise put in as if it were her hostess duty to smooth things over, "children's furniture would fetch a pretty penny, as they used to say. We really should suggest to Clint that his men make some of it."

"Good idea," Kate said, "if they haven't already. I'd like to ask him."

"But, my," Adrienne said, "what you've inherited, Kate, and Tanya, too, evidently, is a real treasure. Why, if I had just a few real, rare Shaker pieces today, children's or adults', I'd be able to afford my dream home, my *pied-à-terre* in the south of France. Provençal, that's my favorite style in everything, yes."

"I had *no idea* you two would want to move to France," Tanya said.

"We 'two' don't, but I'll manage it someday," Adrienne insisted, looking quite smug. "Dane loves France, too, you see, as he was attaché at the French embassy—a vice-consul—there when we met."

"Vice-consul," Louise repeated. "It almost sounds as if he were in charge of something illegal, doesn't it?"

Adrienne shot her a quick glare before going on. "My point is, you know men in love and lust will promise the moon, but he vowed we'd have a getaway home someday, and I shall pick the place, you just wait and see."

"Getaway, you say." Louise kept at it, looking appalled. "But I thought Shaker Run was in your blood, too."

Kate's mind drifted as the two women sniped at each other. *Love and lust*, Adrienne had said. Though it revealed a lot about her and Dane, did the woman have to put it that way? Weren't the French supposed to be more romantic and subtle? Kate had always thought Adrienne so smooth, but tonight she had actually said more than she realized.

The tour ended in the large, country kitchen still strewn with the remnants of Louise's preparations for the meal. "Let's all us sisters just pitch in and Shaker this place up," Tanya suggested. Soon, over Louise's protests, Tanya had her hands in dishwater, while Adrienne cheerfully dried dishes. Kate put them away, while Louise covered and stored leftovers.

Their conversation was freewheeling, and Kate managed to work in another question that she thought might help Jack. "I have some things stored at the Rent-a-Room in Athens. Does anyone know if that's a good, safe place?" she asked of no one in particular.

"Oh, dear," Adrienne answered, "you'll have to ask Dane, but I know the village has at least one cubicle rented there, maybe more. But I'm sure they're reputable, don't you think, Louise?"

"With our large cellar and attic here, I really wouldn't know, but isn't that the place they had some vandalism? You know, so many doors there and some terrible young people with no respect for things spray painted graffiti all over?"

"Yeah, I heard that," Tanya said. "The college newspaper covered it—the news, not the doors," she said with a little laugh. "It was a year or so ago, but they never caught the guys, I think."

"Maybe it wasn't guys," Clint Barstow put in as he entered the kitchen. Kate wondered how long he'd been listening in on them. "You got a few toothpicks, Louise?"

"What do you mean, maybe it wasn't guys?" Tanya asked as she hauled another clean serving dish out of soapy water. "Who else would do it, extraterrestrials?"

"I mean," Clint said, starting to pick his teeth, "it takes a bunch of women to want to blame men for things. Maybe girls did it."

As he went back out with the box of toothpicks, Adrienne just shook her head. *"Liberté, egalité, fraternité,"* she muttered. "If Clint and his 'guys' had the chance, they'd be the first of the unwashed rebels over the barricades around here, yes."

Tanya and Kate gave each other looks that said simply, *Huh?*

As Kate placed dishes on shelves in the pantry near the back door, she glanced out the single window to see a lighted room that extended toward the backyard. She could see office shelves, and a glowing computer screen with a moving screen saver that looked like flying birds with huge, beating wings. The room must be connected to the dining room, but the common door was closed. Other than the attic and basement, Kate had thought Louise had shown them about everything.

"I see you keep a large home office here," Kate observed, as Louise popped into the pantry to place a chafing dish on a high shelf.

"Ben's never really gotten completely out of the business—insurance," she added hastily. "He may seem an authentic Shaker antique, but he's good at planning for the future, too.''

Fascinating, good-hearted, real people, all of them, Kate thought. If she could only handle the mess her own family life was in, maybe she could appreciate this group a little more.

Again she fingered the card in her pocket lettered in old-fashioned script. Louise had placed one at each person's place at the table. Kate's quote was by Jerusha Lockhart, whose diary Louise said she had misplaced, evidently after she'd copied several passages, including this.

If neglected or in hardship, a rose refuses to flower until it is severely cut back and weeded, it read. After the quote, since the rose grower was the persona Kate would be assuming as a presenter, was lettered, *Kate Marburn is Sister Jerusha Lockhart.*

''Thank heavens that's over, and we're still standing,'' Kate told her lawyer as they left the meeting in Toledo the next day.

''Since they believe, erroneously, they have won, they are in their gloat mode instead of goad mode,'' Mason whispered, and she had to laugh.

Kate and Mason had not even mentioned that she intended to contest their latest claim of ''undue influence and intentional alienation of affection under duress.'' Mason had assured Kate that Sarah's longtime maid Marie—from whom Kate had rented her short-term apartment after Sarah's death—was willing to testify that Kate was guilty of none of that. And Dane had told Kate last night that the Shaker Run staff would assist her with legal funding to fight Sarah's heirs if she would agree to keep Sarah's furniture where it was for at least the next five years, should Kate win the case. Though Kate was a bit annoyed that Dane had dealt directly with her lawyer and not with her on that, perhaps it was just so she would not be embarrassed, she thought.

That term *alienation of affection* kept haunting Kate. Yes, she'd seen Sarah turn to her almost as to a daughter, but then Sarah had been like a second mother to Kate. It was Varina and Palmer who had alienated their mother's affection, not her.

At that thought, Kate's mind turned to Erin, her own daughter. What had happened to turn Erin more and more against her?

Mason and Kate huddled together in the cul-de-sac in front of the Denbigh lawyers' building. It was set in a new office park out on Secor Road, and Kate intended to get directly on the nearby outer-belt to head back home. Strange how Shaker Run was home now, she thought.

"So you'll call me as soon as you've deposed Marie?" Kate said, with a glance down the street at Varina and Palmer. They, too, were standing in the cul-de-sac with their lawyer, Pete Scofield, in the sweet spring sun, talking, not yet getting in their cars parked down the way. Palmer had driven his red sports car today. Kate could see Varina gesturing dramatically toward them, as if they were plotting more dire things against her. This was not over yet, Kate vowed, as she turned her back on them.

"I'm also going to try to find some other character witnesses, since it's come to this," Mason said, pulling out a small leather notebook and flipping it open.

"That's a good one, isn't it," Kate said with a rueful little laugh and shake of her head. "Character witnesses for the hated scapegoat of the Marburn Securities scandal. Can't eat lunch in this town no more.''

''What?'' he asked, frowning up at her into the sunlight.

''Nothing. Just a book I read once, something like that title.''

''Anyone else besides Marie you can think of who observed you with Sarah on a day-to-day basis?'' Mason pursued.

''I wish I could use the staff of my current employment,'' she admitted with a sigh, ''as I feel so valued and appreciated there. But yes, I'm sure the Groveland gardener, Jeff Petersen, would testify for me and against Varina, as she's the one I'd like to jettison the most...''

Her voice faded. Erin's angry words about *jettisoning* Mike when she should *have stuck by him for better or worse* danced through her mind again. Damn, she had to get back to Erin and work on a solution to their problems. If only there were a healing herb for that—

As Mason droned on, Kate heard a distant squeal of brakes. An engine revving made her turn to look at what Mason had already seen down the court over her shoulder.

Kate gasped. The car—an old black car—was coming straight at them.

15

Prick not your finger as you pluck if off,
Lest, bleeding, you do paint the white rose red,
And fall on my side so, against your will.
—Shakespeare
King Henry IV

Kate screamed. The car leaped from her worst nightmare, growing, blocking out the sun.

At first it seemed to hurtle toward her, then veered toward Palmer and Varina. Kate watched in frozen horror as—it seemed in slow motion now—Varina, Palmer and their lawyer shouted, then scattered. But it plowed into them. Kate screamed again as Varina flew over the hood and Palmer disappeared. Only their lawyer was able to scramble through parked cars onto the sidewalk.

Mason shoved Kate away in the split second the car careered closer. It brushed by so close she could feel its breath, but she was sure it tried to miss, not hit her. It screeched into a U-turn around the curved end of the court. Kate rolled once on the sidewalk, got unsteadily to her knees, then to her feet.

She gaped as it swerved to miss another car, turned the distant corner onto Secor Road, and disappeared. Tears blurred her vision. Everything had begun and ended so fast. The entire, seemingly-eternal horror must have happened in less than a minute.

"Are you all right?" Mason demanded, taking her arm. "I'm going inside to call a medical vehicle. See if you can help them—no, you go call. We don't need you bending over your fallen enemies."

Kate nodded. Varina and Palmer were down, with Pete Scofield leaning over them. She had been so certain Palmer owned that car, or at least had hired someone to torment her. She shuddered with a new possibility, more dreadful than what she'd believed before.

Whoever was in that death car had meant not to hurt or hit her, but help her.

The receptionist in the lawyer's office had heard the accident, run outside, and had already called 911. But Kate demanded the phone and dialed it again.

"I can read your telephone number on my monitor," the woman who answered said in a monotone. "If you are calling from the same number about the same accident—"

"It wasn't an accident. It was a deliberate hit-and-run, attempted murder," she insisted, her strident voice rising. "I want you to call Homicide Detective Stan Rudzinski and get him over here. Tell him Mrs. Marburn is waiting for him and needs his help. And the car that hit them is a black one with tinted windows, probably a 1940s Packard. It turned left onto Secor Road. The police have got to find it!"

Without hearing what else the 911 operator would say, Kate handed the receiver back to the astounded receptionist and ran outside. A crowd had gathered; a man she didn't recognize was trying to hold them back. Both lawyers knelt by the victims. On trembling legs, Kate ran toward them.

Palmer had been thrown onto a strip of grass and wasn't moving. Unconscious or dead? Varina was lying sprawled in the street on her back, still but apparently alert, her face and arms covered with blood.

Kate ripped off her suit jacket and bent to cover Varina with it. Both lawyers gaped up at her but let her do it.

You, Varina mouthed when she saw Kate. She didn't look in pain; maybe she was beyond pain. "My mother..." she said, but her voice drifted off in a rasping sound. She sucked a slow, shallow breath. "My moth—"

"Your mother loved you very much," Kate told her, her voice breaking. "She told me so more than once. She just wanted to spend more time with you and Palmer."

Varina gave a barely perceptible nod. Her eyes closed tight, then her entire face relaxed. She opened her eyes and stared blankly straight up at the sky, as still as a statue.

"Get back," Mason warned Kate, pushing her away as she tried to kneel by Varina. "I hear sirens. Let's just all stay back."

He stood and pulled Kate away, his arms around her. Scofield moved from Varina to bend over Palmer. He felt for the pulse at the side of his neck. "He's alive—I think," he called to them.

Screeching sirens, a medic and a fire engine raced into the court, then a second medic and a police car. Though Kate was certain Varina was dead, they took her in the first medical vehicle. Palmer had a concussion or was in a coma—Kate wasn't sure what she heard—and they took him in the second ambulance.

Two more police cars arrived. Officers taped off the scene and drew crude chalk lines around where the bodies had been. One ran a long-handled tape wheel along the skid marks to measure their length. Kate knew the car had only put on the brakes to make the turn to escape the court, not to avoid hitting anyone. An officer began to take statements from eyewitnesses. Then from a fourth car, a plain black one that had just pulled in, Stan Rudzinski and his partner, Tina Martin, emerged.

"Is this *déjà vu* all over again?" Kate heard Tina Martin ask Rudzinski out of the corner of her mouth.

But when Kate cried, "Zink, I'm glad you're here. I have so much to tell you!" Rudzinski threw an arm around her and led her—with Mason James in quick pursuit—back into the building.

"You should have told me you'd seen that car twice," Zink said a half hour later. Kate and Mason faced both police detectives across a conference table Zink had commandeered from Varina's lawyer.

"I am telling you," Kate insisted.

"Should have told me *before*."

"Get off it, Detective," Mason cut in, holding up both hands. "or we're out of here right n—"

"It's all right, Mason," Kate said, turning to him. "I want to get this thrashed out. I'll answer their questions because I want them to find that car and whoever's in it."

"I didn't tell you about the car before today," she explained, looking straight at Zink, "because it—they—hadn't done anything illegal. And I was trying to figure out who it was before I told anyone. I didn't tell Mason, either. And I'm not going to crumble to some—some stalking terrorist.''

"You're not some damn detective!" Zink shouted so loud that his partner jumped. "You want to get yourself killed next?"

"No, and I wouldn't want to be some *damn* detective!" Kate shouted back before Mason could protest again, though he threw up both hands and turned away slightly. She stared down Zink, and he glared back as some strange feeling leaped between them. Mutual anger? Attraction, on his part? Kate had to admit they were starting to sound like bickering mates.

She rested her chin back on her hands, elbows on the conference table again. "Sorry, I'm just shook and starting to imagine all kinds of crazy things."

"Of course, you are," Detective Martin put in. "But we've got to go back over all this again before we let you go."

Kate nodded as Zink resumed, in a calm tone. "Despite the fact you and Mr. James say the car seemed to intentionally swerve away from you, we can't be sure of that. It still could have meant to hit you instead of them. Police investigators outside and the witnesses say that old car had up a pretty good head of steam for a dead-end street. It may have been out of control in more ways than one."

Kate nodded again. It didn't make sense that it would have been terrorizing her but then hit Palmer and Varina—unless it had simply careened out of control and not accomplished its intent to kill her—yet.

"So, is there anything else you haven't told us,

besides that you've seen that car before?'' Zink prompted, his voice on edge again. ''Tina and I want to help, Kate. And I still say we need to run you in to the ER or a doctor to get checked out.''

''No, I'm all right, physically,'' she insisted, though she'd been shivering, even wrapped in Mason's suit coat.

''Okay, like Tina said, let's rerun some of this,'' Zink repeated. ''In Woodlawn Cemetery, the driver actually got out of the car, but you only sensed there was a woman beside him and never saw him otherwise, so there's no way you could pick him, or either of them, out of a lineup.''

''That's right. It was distant, and he pulled down that old-fashioned fedora-type hat. I don't know, maybe it goes with the car.''

''You're sensing things again,'' he said matter-of-factly. ''Like you *sensed* that Sarah Denbigh was up in her suite that night you found her dead.''

Though she ached all over, Kate sat up straighter. She had almost been lulled into trusting Rudzinski because she had needed him to help her figure all this out, maybe even to protect her. But if he was going to put her on the defensive about Sarah's death again, she'd just go on the offensive.

''I can't believe the police couldn't find that car,'' she said, glaring at both Zink and Tina. ''It had to stick out, and I gave them the direction it was going.''

''Look, Ms. Marburn,'' Tina said, as Mason started to protest again, then just slumped back in his chair. ''The perp's vehicle could have turned into any nearby garage. Maybe the driver knows Toledo well. If this is as calculated as it sounds, the escape must have been planned, too, so we may have to go at it another way besides the old cops-chase-robbers. For starters, we can try to trace those dark-tinted windows every eyewitness has mentioned. That kind of dark glass is illegal in Ohio and most other northern states.''

''Illegal?'' Kate repeated.

''Yeah,'' Zink said. ''Officers of the law really don't need to be approaching a stopped car when they can't see what and who is on the other side of the dark glass. Limited light tinting is okay, but not that black one-way mirror glass.''

Words her grandmother used to say spun through Kate's brain: *Now we see through a glass darkly but then face-to-face.* She had to figure out whose face was behind that black mirror glass, watching her, stalking her. And that meant she had to know why. So, on her own, without telling these people or anyone, she had to become what she'd just taunted them about: a damn detective.

''But it's legal and common in other states, mostly down South,'' Tina was explaining. ''Zink, we can hardly canvas every shop that darkens windows in this country to see if they did an old Packard. We'd be better off just going back through the list of the investors her husband swindled.''

''My thought exactly,'' Mason agreed.

Kate knew she should follow his lead, but she added, ''That's too long a list.'' She was intrigued that the detectives seemed to be taking her into their confidence—or was that some sort of ruse to get her to trust them even more? Zink had been wanting that for so long. Today she'd finally caved by calling him for help. She felt he'd always liked her, but she couldn't afford to start liking him.

"It's a mile-long list," Zink agreed. "I've already looked at it, thinking someone might have wanted to frame you for Sarah Denbigh's death—but nothing jumped out at me."

Kate knew she could help narrow that list if she could get Erin to give her the name of, or details about, the person she'd evidently heard had threatened Mike. But she didn't want to tell Zink that yet. The last thing Erin needed was to be grilled by the police. Kate was just going to have to get it out of her.

"Then, too," Zink said, downing the last of his coffee, "we can start at the other end of the suspicion spectrum, so to speak, and go looking for a party of one—not that the law hasn't already tried that."

"Yeah," Tina agreed, leaning back in her plush leather chair, "but that's like looking for a needle in a haystack, too, unless someone can give us a hint about what part of the haystack to start in."

"What do you mean?" Kate asked, staring at Zink, daring him not to tell her.

"We mean," he said, standing and stretching, "you're on record as saying you didn't think your husband would really kill himself. But maybe he'd kill someone else."

"But Varina?" she demanded. "Surely, you don't mean Sarah, too."

"It would make you look guilty," Tina said, "or, on the other hand, help you get the Denbigh furniture inheritance. Maybe Mike Marburn thinks he could blackmail or coerce it out of you once the contesting heirs were eliminated."

"I'm afraid," Zink went on, leaning toward her on stiff arms across the table, "your husband—"

"Ex-husband!"

"—would know your habits well. He could be watching or following you."

"Unfortunately, that's highly possible," Mason added.

None of this was news to Kate, but she was not going to let on that the possibility terrified her more than any car bearing down on her. Her insides lurched as a dreadful thought uncoiled itself in her brain. Not just that Mike could be involved, but that he could have secretly contacted Erin and turned her against her stepmother. Who but Erin could tell Mike where to find her at each place she'd gone? Kate had told Erin about this meeting with the hostile heirs, though she'd told the entire Shaker Run staff, and Jack, too, for that matter.

"I—I don't know—" Kate floundered. "Mike would be crazy to hang around me, even covertly. I swear to you he hasn't contacted me, and I'd never take him back. That can't be."

"Weirder things have hap—" Tina began, just as Pete Scofield rapped on the door and opened it.

"We've just heard from Flower Hospital," the lawyer told them, his face ashen. "Varina Wellesley was DOA. Palmer's critical but he may make it. Thought you'd want to know, Detectives. And, Mrs. Marburn, considering that I'm sure you would have liked her out of your life, that was nice what you said to Varina there at the end, whether it was true or not."

Tina Martin shook her head, and Zink hung his, though he watched Kate out of the corner of his eye. Mason blew his nose. But Kate cried, especially since Sarah was not here to mourn for her children.

* * *

"Varina dead and her brother hurt badly?" A wide-eyed Erin repeated Kate's words. They sat together the next morning in a corner of the Jefferson Hall lounge on campus. "By some old black car that's—been following you around?"

"A car that's known where to find me from time to time, at least," Kate said. "Oh, I don't mean the car itself as if it's some demonic being, but whatever idiot is driving it. And that's what I have to find out."

They were sitting knee to knee on a sofa, but Erin had not hugged her, so Kate didn't push her luck touching her stepdaughter, either. Kate was just grateful Erin had agreed to come with her to talk. But she could tell, once the girl had heard what her news was, that she was not eager to stay.

"And you came here," Erin said, seeming to grope for words, "to tell me this in person to make up for not coming to see me about Sarah's death before the reporters called?" She looked pale and her hands trembled, though she had gripped them in her lap.

"I came straight to you from Toledo because I thought maybe you could help me figure out who would want to terrorize me like that. And then either try to kill me in a hit-and-run, or kill Sarah's children."

"Me help? How can I help you figure it out?" Erin demanded in a shrill voice before getting hold of herself. She glanced over at the main desk to see if they'd been heard—they had—and back to Kate again.

"Because it could have something to do with someone's sick vendetta," Kate said. When Erin's high brow crushed in a frown, Kate thought for a moment she didn't know what *vendetta* meant. "Revenge, Erin, over what your father did."

"What *he* did?" she repeated, and wrapped her arms around herself. "Oh—you mean someone thinks you were in on everything no matter what you claimed in court, and they want to scare or—or hurt you."

"That's one of the theories the police are working on. But there is another, isn't there."

The girl stared at her mutely, but Kate read fear in her eyes. Surely not just a reflection of her own, even though she knew kids could sense a parent's emotions without being told.

"Erin, I desperately need your help." Kate took a deep breath and decided to just spit it out. "Your father hasn't contacted you, has he?"

Erin gasped as if she couldn't get her breath. "You're going to try to blame it on him?" she cried, her voice rising again. "Hasn't he gone through enough? You think he's driving around in some old, black car trying to run you down?"

"Or just scare me and run down my enemies so I get the fortune in Sarah's furniture. Either way, it could be him, and you haven't answered my quest—"

"Of course, he hasn't contacted me. Thanks to you, he's on the run somewhere, just—"

Kate seized both Erin's wrists as the girl started to stand. She could see and smell fright in her eyes, her body. "Honey, think. Don't just feel for a minute—think! I'm not the one who worked covertly for years to set up those dummy investments, I'm not the one who took off when it looked like there was no choice but to take responsibility. Just listen to me a moment so—''

Erin wrenched free, flinging Kate back in her chair. ''No! It's stuff like this that drags my grades down, drags me down. I've got to go to class, or I'll flunk out and waste your hard-earned money to keep me here. Just leave me alone if all you ever want to do is upset me!''

Kate started after her across the large room as Erin hurried away, banging the door to her hallway behind her. The two student receptionists at the desk were staring. Kate glared back and stalked out. But she was not leaving any of this alone, however much it upset anyone, or everyone.

Kate began to work her Shaker Run rose beds with a vengeance, but her mind was miles away. She'd always done her best thinking like this. As she agonized over everything, it was now the terror of Mike's returning and turning Erin against her that scared her the most.

''Oh, so glad to see our Sister Jerusha back at her roses.'' Louise's voice floated to Kate. ''But I do hope, when our visitors start coming, you'll use the village's antique rose cutters and not those shiny, new ones of yours.''

Kate nodded, waved and went on working, hoping Louise would leave her alone. Thank God the woman went on about her business. On her knees, Kate pruned deadwood and weeded even harder. But she did stop work when two big boots and jeans-encased, long legs appeared on the other side of the rows of bushes. She looked up to see Jack.

''What are you doing here?'' she asked bluntly,

shading her eyes to see him better. As if to help her out, he shifted slightly so she was sitting in his shadow. It wasn't the way she'd meant to begin with him, but it was too late to take back the brusque tone. She just wasn't ready to face him—or the way she was coming to feel about him. Sensing he wanted to help her up, she quickly got to her feet.

"Thanks for coming by or calling to let me know you're back safe and sound from that meeting in Toledo with Sarah's heirs," he said, his voice edged with annoyance.

She wanted to tell him about the car hitting Varina and Palmer, but no words came. She'd completely lose control out here, so she'd just have to tell him later.

"I should have called you or stopped by," she admitted, "but it was a—dreadful, draining experience. I meant to come see you—to tell you about it."

"All right. I just thought you should know the police came." He sounded calmer now, but she could tell his emotions were still pent up. His big body was rigid but for his fists, which he kept flexing at his sides. She had the urge to hurl herself into his arms, but trusting a man too much was dangerous.

"They took a paint scraping off that broken pole across from my house," he went on. "When I walked over to talk to them, one said you were the one who had tipped them off about a car taking down the pole. You didn't happen to tell them I was in Clint's workshop that night, did you?"

"Of course not. But it was the Toledo police? Was Zink with them?"

"Now why should he come all that way for a piece of paint? Besides, I thought you went up there for a legal meeting with Sarah's heirs, not to see Zink. What's the deal?''

''You're starting to sound just like him with your parade of questions,'' she cried, throwing down her pruners and ripping off both garden gloves. *''Is that your* final *answer, Kate Marburn?''* she mimicked. She knew she was overreacting, but she felt pressured and panicked by too many things, including her own emotions everytime Jack Kilcourse so much as looked at her.

''Kate, I am not the enemy,'' he said, holding up both hands as if to ward off an attack. ''I thought we were working together on probing this furniture scam and Sarah's death. And it was the Athens police,'' he went on, ''though, of course, they admitted the Toledo jurisdiction requested the search. You know, sweetheart, I think you've got a lot to tell me, and you've suddenly decided not to.''

''It's just that I have some serious, personal problems with Erin right now,'' she insisted, nervously wiping her palms on her jeans. ''I realize, since you don't have kids, you might not appreciate or understand but—''

''Sure, I get it,'' he threw back, his voice even harder. He clasped his arms over his chest. ''What would I know about raising or protecting a kid, right? My own, let alone anyone else's.''

''What?'' Her hands shot to her hips. ''You're the one who's chock-full of secrets about your past, no matter how much you pretend to tell me what's going on in the present.''

''Don't tell me anything else, then,'' he said over his shoulder as he started away. ''Because I'd want to help and then I'd get involved, and that's the last damn thing I need!''

Kate was appalled this had gotten so bad so fast between them. She gaped after him as he strode away. For such a private, controlled man, that was a tirade. But one that, finally, had given her a glimpse into his explosive emotions. The trigger had been the mere mention of a child and the hint he was being shut out, even though that was exactly the way he operated. Worse, she feared she could not help him when she was so volatile and needed so much help herself.

Kate burst into tears and hurried in the other direction, to the garden shed. Sucking in great sobs, she tore in and slammed the door. But she was not alone; to her surprise, Tanya was bending over the worktable, crushing herbs in an old-fashioned mortar and pestle.

''Hey,'' her friend said, then caught Kate's expression. ''What happened?'' she asked, dropping the heavy marble pestle.

Although Kate had not cried on anyone's shoulder since Mike left, she soaked Tanya's, spilling out to her about Varina and Palmer, the black car's most recent, deadly appearance, her sudden blowup with Jack, and her fear that Mike was back and using Erin.

''You told anybody else here about Ms. Denbigh's daughter being dead?'' Tanya asked, when Kate got control of herself again.

''I'm going to tell them all, of course, but Dane and Adrienne aren't around, and I've only seen Louise—and Jack—just now. And no, I didn't tell him—yet.''

''Or go crying on *his* shoulder.''

"Of course not," she said, sniffing back tears. "Do you know if he ever had a child?"

"He had a stupid wife who left him, but if there was a child, he never said, and I never quite asked. Why?"

"Just a feeling. I can't believe how badly I'm screwing things up with people I really care about."

"You *do* know that Varina's loss," Tanya went on, "might make things easier for you in getting Sarah's goods? I don't mean to say it's a break for you, but…"

"Don't even breathe something like that!" Kate protested as she blew her nose. "I'd never want things to end this way. But I think my ex might be behind Varina's death. It's a wild idea, except that someone's turned Erin against me. It's possible Mike could think he would profit from my inheritance. As for Jack, I'll try to explain to him, but there are two things I have to do first."

"Which are?" Tanya prompted as Kate dabbed at her eyes.

"I've got to try to keep up with my responsibilities here, but start spying on Erin. I've been stupid not to put two and two together about her before now."

"Like what?"

"Like the fact she supposedly spends Sundays with an ex-boyfriend I've never seen—at least, not since she broke up with him two years ago."

"You don't have me convinced yet, girl."

"She's swung back to believing her father did no wrong and that I have. She adored her father, used to worship him, mostly because he wasn't there much for her, like some distant god from Olympus who swooped in from time to time, smiled and bestowed his bounty on her. You know," Kate mused, "he even used to call her angel——"

Kate slammed her fist on the worktable, making the mortar and pestle thump.

"What? *What?*" Tanya demanded.

"The guy who's a server in a restaurant where Erin meets her boyfriend, Mark, told me that Mark calls her 'angel.' And I'm the one who said his name was Mark, when the server looked like he was going to say something else. But he might just have accepted a name from me that sounded like Mike..."

"But Erin wouldn't call her daddy 'Mike,' would she?"

"I don't know. But she calls me Kate, and maybe he told her not to call him 'Dad' in public. Tanya, if you can cover for me here, I'd be grateful because I've got to go back to campus and do some—well, some undercover work."

"Now, you listen," Tanya scolded, wagging a finger in her face. "I'll cover for you here, sure, just like you did for me when I was away, on *one condition.*" She gripped Kate's upper arms hard; they stared face-to-face.

"Tell me," Kate said, not willing to commit to anything but finding out about Erin.

"You discover it's your ex, you call the police or you get me—maybe Jack—but you don't go facing that man alone."

"All right. Unless it means Erin's safety somehow, I'll get help. But not until I know I'm right. Not until I turn over a few rocks to see if he's hiding under them."

"Yeah, well you just watch out," Tanya warned, frowning, "'cause cornered snakes can bite, and some of them are *poison.*"

16

The roses fearfully on thorns did stand,
One blushing shame, the other white despair...
But, for his theft, in pride of all his growth
A vengeful canker eat him up to death.
                                        —Shakespeare
                                        "Sonnet 99"

"Is Mark Winslow there, please?" Kate asked the young girl who answered the telephone. It was early afternoon, but Kate figured she'd just talk to his mother if he wasn't in. She was calling long-distance from Shaker Run to Mark's home in Toledo because she needed answers now.

Though the child evidently walked away from the phone, Kate could hear her yell, "Mom, it's not for you! It's another girl for Mark!"

Another girl? Kate thought. In addition to Erin? Someone he was dating in Toledo?

"Hi. This is Mark."

"Mark, this is Erin's mom, Kate Marburn. Listen, if it's okay with you, I thought we'd throw her a little surprise party at the 7 Sauces this Sunday when you come on your regular day."

"Ah—okay. But it's not her birthday, is it?"

"No, you're right about that," she said, fighting to

keep her voice in check. She wound the phone cord so tightly around her index finger, it turned red, then white. Mark merely sounded cautious, not shocked or caught off guard, so he must be the one visiting Erin on Sundays. Could Kate be completely crazy?

"It would just be to kind of cheer her up," Kate went on to get past the awkward pause, "to get her mind off the pressure on her right now. What time do you usually arrive?"

"Oh, it depends." He sounded more than cautious—wary now.

"I've got to tell you I was really surprised you two were back together, but pleased about it, really. I'd love to stop by and see your parents when I'm in town next, so do you mind if I talk to your mother about it for a moment?"

"She's not here."

"Oh, I thought I heard your sister say she was."

"No. Maybe she thought she was."

"Let me ask you one more thing. Do you think Susan's a good roommate for Erin? I guess I just wanted someone to reassure me. I know you've met her." Out on a limb here, Kate thought. If he'd been visiting Erin, he'd surely know her roommate was Amy, so he'd correct her.

"Yeah, I think she's fine. They get along and all. Are you sure you want to surprise Erin, though? Maybe she'd look forward to it if you'd tell her ahead, do it on her birthday."

Was Mark lying for—with—Erin? Kate agonized. If she had to guess, she'd say he was, but there was still no positive proof, and she didn't want him tipping Erin off that her stepmother might be swooping

in for a surprise this Sunday. No, she wanted to head
that off for sure.

"You know, Mark, I think you're probably right
about not trying this out of the blue. I think I will just
wait for her birthday to do it. Besides, I'm *so* busy at
work here in southern Ohio," she added, trying to
sound light and spontaneous. "But don't tell her, because I will do the party later, maybe invite her dorm
friends as well as you. But it's great to talk to you,
anyway, and thanks for being such a support to her."

"Oh, glad to. I—so you won't be calling my
mother back or anything?"

"I think I'll just let you pass on my good wishes
since she's not there right now," she said, shaking
her head at how she'd gotten into, then out of this
conversation.

As they said goodbye and hung up, she thought
Mark sounded more than nervous. Yes, scared. But
not as scared as she was starting to feel.

Kate dressed in jeans, T-shirt and denim jacket to
blend in with the campus crowd, but it made her feel
even more conspicuous instead. She did, at least, have
Erin's schedule for this semester, shared when they
had been getting along better. Keeping her distance,
she followed Erin up the hill to her eleven o'clock
class, then decided not to wait the whole time until it
ended. She'd go uptown to see if she could talk to
Stone at the 7 Sauces. Soon, she thought perversely,
she'd have every young man who'd ever known Erin
thinking her mother was nuts.

The restaurant manager told Kate that Stone would
not be in until the dinner shift, but suggested she
might find him at the Beta house. She thanked him

and went back out onto Court Street. But fraternity houses were not on her campus map. She asked a student on the street for directions, and shortly afterward located the white-facaded, pillared house with its statue of a dragonlike creature peering down from the roof.

Within five minutes of her asking for him, Stone came down the staircase, stooping first to look at whoever was waiting for him in the first-floor foyer.

"'The redhead's mother,' the guys said," he greeted her with a nervous grin. "Now you've got them thinking I'm in trouble with some girl's mother."

"I couldn't think of any other way to let you know who I was. I don't mean to invade your privacy, but I would really appreciate your help," she told Stone, as he congenially shook her hand. Tall and thin with an open, pleasant face framed by coal-black hair, Stone looked as much at ease here as he had in the restaurant. She could use some of that calm demeanor right now.

"My name's Kate Marburn," she explained, still unsure about how to go at this. Yet Stone had always been accommodating, so she decided to risk honesty. "You see," she said, "I'm afraid my ex-husband has been visiting Erin when he—well, he isn't supposed to. I recall you said the man Erin eats with on Sundays calls her 'angel.' I told you his name was Mark—but could it have been Mike?"

"Tell you the truth, Ms. Marburn," he said, cocking his head as if in deep thought, "Mike's what I thought it was, but I'm not sure. The guy looks older than someone she'd date, though he's in great shape,

good-looking and all. But I never overheard her—
Erin, that is—call him 'Dad' or anything like that.''

Kate almost told him that Mike was on the run and
might have told Erin never to call him that in public,
but she wasn't up to sharing that. ''He's not a redhead, too, is he?'' she asked, gripping her purse strap.

''Naw, if that settles your mind. He's got hair almost as dark as mine, but he's got a mustache, and
his skin's pretty pale for the hair. He always has a
big roll of bills, leaves great tips. Well, actually,'' he
added, shoving his hand through his hair, ''it's in a
neat gold money clip, kind of old-fashioned.''

Kate felt as if the floor had given way. Mike loved
his money clips and had a big collection that he'd
taken with him.

Kate shadowed—actually, she admitted to herself—stalked Erin to her midafternoon class, then
waited and walked behind her in the crowd from
Scripps Hall, following her across the green and down
the hill to her dorm. She saw nothing unusual, but
then why should she? If Mike was coming to see Erin,
it must be on those sacrosanct Sunday afternoons.

That's why Erin had been so nervous when Kate
had shown up last Sunday, Kate reasoned. The girl
had been disappointed, probably because her stepmother was there to wreck her weekly reunion with
her father. Then she'd lied about Mark's not coming
that day when, in fact, he probably never came,
though Erin must have had Mark covering for her.
Erin had hustled Kate out of the dorm, practically
running down the back steps. The girl had been a
nervous wreck as they drove away. And then she'd
exploded at Kate about forcing Mike away.

But now Kate was torn about lurking around the campus. She couldn't ignore the fact that things had to be ready for Shaker Run's big opening in just over two weeks. What if Amy saw her and told Erin? Kate decided not to confront Erin's roommate because she might tip off Erin, who would then tell Mike. Sunday was the key: she'd be back then...to see if Erin's caller was Mark or Mike.

"You realize you're keeping to the same schedule the Shakers went by?" Tanya asked, as they crossed paths en route to their separate gardens the next morning.

They were running themselves ragged, trying to prepare for the village opening. Frenetically, Kate tended her bushes as the new reddish shoots popped with buds. She'd been up at four-thirty; she couldn't sleep, anyway. By lantern, since the staff was trying to become adept at using those, she'd done duties in the garden shops until dawn, then headed outside.

"Maybe you *are* Sister Jerusha, like Louise says," Tanya teased, though Kate wasn't in the mood for it. "The diary I've been reading says *my* Sister Faith had prayed, washed up, aired the sheets, swept the floor and wiped the woodwork for both the men and women's retiring rooms *before* breakfast, which they fixed before seven-thirty. I think that makes them kinda hardworking but kinda crazy," she concluded in her best rendition of Louise's starchy Shaker voice. But Kate just couldn't laugh, however relieved she was that Tanya was up-tempo when Kate herself was down in the dumps.

"There's supposed to be a diary by a brother who used to be an herbalist," Tanya went on, "but it's missing just like that one of your Jerusha, so I'm stuck reading about dirty sheets..." Tanya's voice trailed off.

Kate shook her head. Let Louise look for the lost diaries. But Kate managed to give Tanya a grateful smile and a quick hug, before Tanya trudged back to her workshop.

She knew Tanya was almost as frenzied as she was. For the division of her great-aunt's furniture, she was heading to Kentucky tomorrow—Friday, two days before Kate would return to campus to watch for Mike.

How Kate wished she'd had time to ask Tanya for one of her soothing herbs. The efficacy of the herbal tea she drank every night seemed to be wearing off, and she wasn't sleeping well. As a result, despite how revved up she felt, she nearly nodded off while working. Sometimes her brain just seemed to slow down.

Startled from her stupor, Kate jerked as a thorn pierced her hand right through her glove. Someone behind her had spoken. She stood and straightened. It was Dane, his arms full of new color brochures, and Adrienne, hers with hand-wrapped packets of Tanya's herbal teas for the gift shop.

"You've been making up for lost time," Dane observed with a nod at the rows of rosebushes.

Lost time, Kate thought. So much lost time with Erin, maybe with Jack, too—time she could never make up, never get back. Adrienne stepped forward and squeezed Kate's arm. "We heard about the tragedy in Toledo—the latest one, yes."

"You should have told us everything the moment you got back, even phoned us from there," Dane commanded, his voice suddenly hard and accusing. Kate marveled that, for someone who had been in the diplomatic corps, he could at times be so blunt and harsh. When Tanya had once said he was either up or down, she must have meant his moods.

"I fully intended to when I returned, but I've had other concerns and didn't realize you were back," Kate explained. "I don't know if the tragedy will make any difference in my inheriting the furniture, if that's what you're wondering. I'm praying that Palmer will recover, and I certainly know better than to try to go to Varina's funeral Saturday. Again, I'm grateful for your offer to help pay my lawyer's fees if this drags on, but your continued understanding and support is even more valuable to me."

Kate felt as if she'd made a political speech, but Dane's expression seemed distant, as if he were thinking about something or someone else.

"We knew we were right to hire Kate, weren't we, Dane," Adrienne prompted, elbowing him.

He started, then nodded. "Absolutely. Despite the fact Jack Kilcourse first mentioned you, it was my decision and a good one."

"I love it here and hope to help build things—or should I say, grow them?—over time," Kate assured them.

"You see, we weren't primarily concerned about the furniture, but about you," Dane said. "It must have been dreadful for you to have to go through seeing that hit-and-run after losing Sarah Denbigh, too."

However stilted this conversation seemed to Kate—as if it had been staged somehow by the Thompsons—she was relieved they seemed to understand. "Did someone call you about the car accident in Toledo," she asked, "or—?"

"Dane read it online in the *Toledo Blade*," Adrienne explained with another little squeeze of Kate's arm as she stepped back next to her husband. They started to walk away. "If there's anything we can do, just anything," Adrienne threw back over her shoulder, "let us know. And please keep us informed."

That evening as the sun sank, Kate ate a peanut butter and jelly sandwich—downed some breath mints—then showered, picked a small bouquet of white violets and bloodroot from the edge of the forest beyond holy ground, and set out toward Jack's. The way they'd parted had been eating away at her.

Although it was for its pale, pretty flowers that Kate had picked the herb bloodroot, she had a real affection for it, too. When Erin was little, it had grown in their backyard. She and her friends had cut it to make "Indian paint" on their faces, for the stalks, when sliced open, bled a bright red-orange liquid.

When Kate had mentioned that memory once, Tanya had said that American Indians had used it not only to dye their skin but to treat breast cancer. But, she'd warned, like so many things in nature, too much of a good thing could be harmful.

"You mean it's poison?" Kate had yelped. "And I let Erin play with it as a kid?"

"Don't worry," Tanya had assured her. "You'd need *toxic* doses of it, lots and lots ingested. You go ahead and keep your happy memories of it. Just be sure your grandkids don't make a salad of it someday."

"What would happen if they did?" Kate had asked.

"Oh, intense thirst, burning in the stomach, vertigo, collapse and paralysis—the *usual*," Tanya had said with such a smug look that Kate hadn't been sure whether she was kidding or not.

But knowing Tanya, she was not.

Jack saw Kate coming up his drive with measured steps, carrying a nosegay in front of her with both hands the way a bridesmaid might. He'd had an ache in his gut since their argument, but it infuriated him—actually, scared him—how she turned him upside down emotionally. She made him want to resurrect and share all sorts of things he thought he'd buried for good.

As he opened the front door, she thrust out the little bouquet of pale flowers.

"Truce?" she said, and smiled. It lit her face, which helped because she looked so pale and drawn—so defenseless, though he knew better.

"Come on in."

"Let's just sit here in the rockers for a few minutes. And don't drink the water you put this bloodroot in. It's one of Tanya's pets, if you know what I mean."

He laughed. "I don't think a woman's ever given me flowers before, so I'm desperate enough I'll even take poison ones. Thanks, Kate, for coming over."

Though he wanted to pull her onto his lap in one of the rockers, he went in the house and came back out with a pint jar filled with water for the flowers. The water turned pink.

"Now tell me about where you've been and what happened," he said, and pulled the second rocker close to hers. "And how Erin's doing at O.U."

"She's got problems, maybe some piled as high

and deep as her stepmother's," she told him. "I want to explain all that to you sometime, but as you've never told me much about your—your family past— I feel funny unloading about mine."

He flinched but forced himself to return her riveting stare. "I'm bitter about my divorce," he said.

"Thanks for trusting me enough to share that," she said, but her voice was not sarcastic or bitter as he'd expected. "Jack, divorce is a bad thing and means someone or something failed, but it happens. It happened to me. And my marriage and divorce was public knowledge, whereas at least yours was private."

"We lost our son," he stumbled on, still scared to say more when he hadn't told a soul here even that much. "After that, things fell apart, and Leslie—left me. That's it. End of story."

Unfortunately, she waited, poised on the edge of her chair for the rest of it. He could tell she wanted to ask what happened and why. He thought about lying, saying crib death or a fall down the stairs. He knew people had different ways of running from their grief, and, sitting stone still, he knew he was still running.

"Jack, thank you for telling me. I didn't come to put you through all that, really. But any time you want to talk about it, please tell me. The loss of your child—that's got to be devastating. I'm so sorry and I would love to hear about your child. Was it a boy or a girl?"

"Andy. He would have been just a little younger than Erin."

She took his hands, and he held hers hard. They rested their wrists on their touching, trembling knees.

He wanted not only to haul her into his lap, but to sob on her shoulder.

"Tell me why you came," he insisted. "I'm not just changing the subject. I want to know."

"I think my timing's terrible, but that seems to be the way things are lately. I came to tell you something before Zink shows up on your doorstep again to fill you in on the latest Denbigh death."

"More evidence on Sarah's?" he asked, rocking toward her, grateful for a new topic, a different death to dissect. When she shook her head, and her eyes teared up, he asked, "What? You don't mean something happened to her crazy daughter?"

Kate jerked erect. "Did you...know—or just guess because of what we've been saying?"

"I didn't know," he insisted, reaching out a hand to stroke her damp cheeks gently with his callused fingers. "It's just that the one time I met Varina up close and personal, she seemed wacked out to me. Come on, Kate, give. Now you tell me what happened."

It both helped and hurt Kate to share the nightmare with him. It was like living it all again, but at least he knew now. And he seemed to listen intently, to really empathize. She described Varina's death, her two previous encounters with the Packard, and her latest interview with Zink. But she did not tell him her suspicions about Erin and Mike. Besides, she kept praying she was wrong about Mike being back and Erin siding with him.

"You're not thinking of going to Varina's funeral," Jack said, his voice adamant.

"No, though I'd go for Sarah if I could."

"It's horrible that someone would do that so deliberately," he said with a sharp sniff. "Life is precious, then here comes some accident. You're sure they didn't mean to hit you instead of her and Palmer?"

"Why do you say *they* hit them? I didn't say there was more than one in that car."

"Just a figure of speech, a sexless way to refer to the driver since you don't have a clue who it is. You don't, do you?"

"I'm working on it, but—"

"It sounds similar to the old, black Shaker car Dane keeps here, but he said he never takes it farther than the shop or gas station in town—and it's not a Packard."

She stopped rocking and jumped to her feet.

"Dane keeps a black classic car? That the Shakers had? I've never seen it. Is it at his house?"

He reached up to pull her back into the chair, but she didn't budge. "Kate, it can't be the same car. Not only is it a different make, but it doesn't have black-tinted windows. When the village closed in the '40s, the Shakers sold it. I heard it was pretty much kept in mothballs until someone donated it to the village a year or so ago."

"Where is it?" she demanded. "Or if you don't know, I'm going to see Dane right now. Okay, it's not the same one, but maybe if I could see it I'd learn something about the other. Jack, I'm getting desperate."

"It's here, in storage," he said, standing and cupping her shoulders in his big hands.

"Here, where?"

"If I tell you—even show you—you cannot let Dane know. I happen to have a key to the place, but

I'm not supposed to let anyone in there, though Tanya uses the shed to write in sometimes. I don't need him or anybody else knowing I keep an eye on the furniture they store in there, and that I'm in and out as much as I am.''

''Shaker furniture? Children's Shaker furniture?''

''Yeah, that's where I saw the copies of Sarah's pieces. Do I have your word? I'll help you get to the bottom of this, but I can't have you blowing the new way I have of keeping track of Shaker Run furniture.''

''I promise,'' she vowed, craning her neck to stare in the direction he'd first glanced when he'd mentioned the shed. ''You mean that old shed out there— the one that you said was too full when I wanted to keep my tiller there?''

With a sharp nod, he went into the house and came out with a single key on a large ring.

''Tanya writes her book out here?'' she asked as she followed him through the graying dusk toward the shadowed shed. The red sunset silhouetted it.

''So if you tell her what you know,'' Jack went on, ''I'm in as much trouble with her as I'll be with Dane. I'd make you wait until after dark, but a light in here at night might be seen more easily from the road or village.''

''How often is Dane in and out of here?'' she asked, sticking close to him as he turned the key in the padlock. *Dane.* Could Dane somehow be related to the death car? It didn't make any sense.

''I actually don't know,'' he admitted as he shoved the big door on tracks to the side. ''And I'll show you why else I'm not sure.''

Kate stared into the dim, crowded shed. It was hard

to see at first. When Jack stepped in, she stayed right behind him.

"I'm trusting you here," he said as he rolled the door closed behind them. "Though I'm at odds with village staff sometimes, I've forged ties to Tanya and even Dane."

"So have I, and I don't want to endanger that, either," she said as they stood close to each other. Slowly, her eyes adjusted to the dim interior. It would have been very dark in here if the sunset through the single window had not bathed the place in a pinkish glow.

Though anxious to see the car, she was suddenly afraid. Not of Jack, but of what might happen between them because she felt so needy and vulnerable. She had not had someone to lean on since she lost Mike, and he'd turned out to be as damaged and deceptive as his business.

They stared at each other in the warm glow of sunset. Even when something scurried away on tiny feet in the back of the shed, they didn't move.

"Trust me," he said.

Kate knew better, but she wanted to, desperately. She leaned toward him, and he toward her. She wanted to yield, to let him take over, but that had been her fatal mistake with Mike.

"When you really trust me, too," she blurted. Taking a step back to look in his eyes, she saw rage surge in him, but he mastered it.

"I could just toss you out of here right now," he said, "but I have a feeling you'd find a way back in. Come on, Kate Marburn, but you owe me."

He led her past a makeshift, messy desk that must have been Tanya's. Books about herbs, yellow legal pads of notes, a mechanical typewriter. The stacked, typed pages lay open to one labeled Angel Trumpet, Also Known As Jimsonweed And Devil's Trumpet. Her friend had indeed lied about not having started her book, but Kate had other things to worry about now.

They walked around boxes and a knee-high, very un-Shaker-like clear plastic bin with a snap-on top, filled with what appeared to be paper and books. They passed furniture, most of it broken, draped piles of something or other, and a few stacked crates.

"It's gone," Jack said, and stopped so abruptly she bumped into him.

"The car?"

"Hell, yes, the car. Do you see one here?"

She peered around him into the space at the back of the shed. "When he does take it out," he said, calmer now, "he goes out the back sliding door, which he has the lock to. This used to be a hay shed, so they once drove wagons and tractors straight through. Sometimes he even drives out around the old cinder lane to the road, instead of using my driveway."

But none of that mattered to her.

"And it is black?"

"Yeah, I said black. A lot of the early ones were."

"And you're positive it isn't a Packard?"

"Give me some credit," he said, as they both stared at the oil spot on the packed dirt floor. "It was a Buick from the end of World War II when they started making cars again. Listen, if you don't over-react, I'll ask Dane where it is and let you know what he says. Maybe he just took it to get the dent pounded out of the front grill."

Dent, Kate thought. From a telephone pole or from Varina? She pressed her palms to her temples. For one moment she thought her head would explode: dented grill and black paint, but no dark windows and the wrong make. Yet right now, tracking down all the old black cars in the universe was not going to distract her from finding out who Erin was seeing on Sundays. Her worst fear now was that Mike would drive up to Erin's dorm in a vintage black Packard. Which would mean not only that he could have been driving the death car, but that Erin could have been the one on the seat beside him.

"We should come back another time, maybe tomorrow night," she told the man. "They say these darkened windows don't obscure the view looking out, but at twilight or dawn you don't have really clear vision if you don't turn the headlights on."

"I'm hardly turning them on here. Who's to say they won't glance over this way."

"With us hidden in this thicket? But why do you suppose they went into that shed? They even closed the door behind them."

"Meaning hanky-panky?" he said with a little snort.

He started the engine again but still didn't turn on any lights. At least these old classics didn't have headlights on day and night like new models, he thought.

It annoyed him that she was giggling. "Hanky-panky?" she repeated. "*Hanky-panky?* That's a good one."

"Cut it out. But I agree we back off now. I want her alone to shake her up or shut her up. We've got to do more watching to find out how much she really knows. This isn't going quite like we planned so we might have to improvise.''

"I'll get out of her what she knows one way or the other.''

"I'll drop you off, then stow this car. Who knows, maybe cops all over the state are looking for it, even though I switched plates again and got the dent pounded out. If I wasn't so attached to her—this car, not our dear Kate—I'd deep-six this big baby for good.''

He pulled out slowly and didn't turn the headlights on until they were almost to the main road. He loved the dark satin night, so slick you could slide right into it and disappear.

17

As soon
Seek roses in December, ice in June;
Hope constancy in wind, or corn in chaff;
Believe a woman or an epitaph,
Or any other thing that's false...
> —George Gordon, Lord Bryon
> "English Bards and Scotch Reviewers"

In the dead of night, Kate sat straight up in bed. The red glow of the digital clock read 3:04 a.m. Something had awakened her, but now she heard nothing but the whine of wind and the normal creaking sounds of the old building.

She threw the covers off and stood, feeling she moved in slow motion, not nauseated or dizzy but slightly disoriented. She was just groggy from sleep, that was all, she assured herself. Wracking her brain for what she'd eaten at dinner, something that could have upset her, she recalled nothing suspicious.

Then she remembered the dream she'd just had. Erin had been throwing calendars at her as if they were Frisbees, but not ones with the usual pictures of animals, landscapes or flowers. Each page of each month had displayed a big, black car with gleaming front grills like metal teeth.

"It can't be Mike," Kate muttered as she clicked on a light. She shoved her feet into slippers and pulled on her terry-cloth robe. "And it can't be Erin—never, ever."

But she forced herself to do what she'd been dreading. Digging Erin's class schedule out of her purse, she went into the other room and sat at her desk. From the top drawer of the Shaker antique, she looked for her current calendar—the one with new breeds of roses for each month. Where was it? Why wasn't it where it should be?

Finally she found it in the right drawer, but it had been neatly placed under a stack of envelopes and another of paid bills. She couldn't remember straightening the drawer, but then, she'd been so distracted lately....

She flipped back to the small calendar for last year, then figured out the three dates she had seen the black car. Why was she having such trouble remembering? She had to get more sleep. Finally, she wrote down the date the car might have hit the pole near Jack's knocking out electricity to the village.

She scribbled the dates in order, then stared at them on the page because the letters seemed to swim into each other. She squinted and tried to concentrate. The car had first appeared in the Toledo cemetery near Sarah's grave on Tuesday, October 5, 1999. The other two dates she'd actually seen the car were this year: at Tanya's aunt's funeral on Saturday, April 8, and the day it killed Varina on April 11, a Tuesday. If it had struck the pole down the road, it would have been during the storm of April 1, a Saturday.

"Its visits are getting closer together," she whispered.

She shook her head. The car was not a living, demonic entity in itself, but a machine driven by someone perverted and evil. At least one pattern emerged. The dire events had all occurred on a Tuesday or a Saturday. With trembling hands she smoothed open Erin's current class schedule, then rummaged through her desk until she found the girl's first-quarter schedule.

It annoyed her how small they were printing something as important as a class schedule now. The words seemed to waver on the page, too, but that must be because she was so tired.

Yes, as she had thought. Erin had no classes on Saturdays; she had Tuesdays off her first quarter, back in October, so technically she could have been in Toledo at Woodlawn Cemetery that first day Kate saw the car.

But Erin surely, would not betray her like that even if Mike had come back into her life.

As for Erin being off that second Tuesday—just a few days ago when the car hit Varina—it could not be. Erin had an English class at one on Tuesdays, Thursdays and Fridays. Her bad grades couldn't be the result of skipping class to go wheeling around with her father looking for revenge, could they?

"Oh, Lord, please don't let Erin be involved, even if Mike is," Kate muttered, lacing her fingers tightly together. "She's all I have left. Don't let him pois— hurt her that way."

But, she thought as she stood and snapped off the light, right after the staff meeting this morning she was driving back into Athens to talk to Erin's English professor. She prayed he kept attendance; she had to know if Erin was in class the day that car killed Varina.

Kate was suddenly so chilled that she went to lie back down under the covers in her robe and slippers, curled in a fetal position. But she soon heard a strange sound again. Was that what had awakened her or was it the nightmare of Erin throwing calendars—her own subconscious telling her Erin could be involved in this horror?

Lying still and stiff, Kate strained to listen. Singing. Outside. She had one window slightly ajar to suck in the sweet spring breeze.

She lifted herself on one elbow, though that made her a bit dizzy. If it was a melody, it was a dissonant one, like some of those Shaker laboring songs that accompanied the dancing. But perhaps it was her imagination, or her exhausted, overworked brain playing tricks on her. Now she heard not only the music, but her name.

She jerked alert and listened again. A man's voice that time? Could Jack be outside, calling to her?

Wrapping her robe tighter, she hurried from window to window, stooping or kneeling to peer out. She heard no one now, saw no one. It was her imagination that was betraying her. Just the way it had when Mike had deserted her and Erin, when she had thought someone was stalking her everywhere and she'd lost control to—

"No, you're all right," she told herself fiercely. "You are not going to lose control again."

But she was certain she'd heard music. As she peered out the back window of her bedroom, she saw someone dashing—or dancing—from the cemetery toward holy ground, lit only by the glimmer of the cold half-moon.

"Oh, Mark, I'm go glad you called," Erin whispered into the phone, cupping her hand around it. She'd had to scramble out of bed to get it before Amy woke up.

"Who is it?" Amy mumbled from the darkness of the dorm room.

"I've got it. Go back to sleep. I'll take it out in the hall." They sometimes found more privacy for personal calls by threading the phone cord under the door and closing it on roommates or visitors.

"Just a sec," Erin whispered into the mouthpiece, then yanked her quilt off her bed to wrap around her. No way was she turning on a light to find her robe.

"But who is it?" her roommate repeated.

"It's just Mark. Go to sleep," Erin said, and finally got situated, sitting on the floor in the hall with her back to the wall.

"You surprised to hear from me this late?" he asked.

"I'm just so glad you called! You should have given me your number so you don't always have to phone me."

"Not a good idea. I don't need this phone number recorded anywhere it could be traced."

"Oh, right. But the thing is, I think Mom—Kate's on to us."

She heard his sharp intake of breath. "Tell me."

"She came here and asked me flat out. Actually, accused me."

She waited until two girls, obviously up late studying, passed in the hall.

"Then let's do our little car trip early."

Kate was as furious as she was fearful. She had definitely heard singing and had seen a human figure out there. Perhaps that person had called her name. Who was doing this to her? And damn Dane Thompson for not installing flood lights and a modern security system here, no matter how unauthentic they would be. As soon as Shaker Run had its opening, she was going to look for someplace to live in town, even if Erin didn't want her so close.

She huddled at the windowsill, peeking over it, squinting out into the moonlit scene. Perhaps that snow-cloaked figure she'd thought she'd imagined two weeks ago had been real.

Refusing to be terrified, she stripped off her nightclothes and yanked on jeans and a sweatshirt. She donned her parka, hoping its downy filling would stop her trembling, though it was not really cold out. Maybe the fresh night air would clear her head.

Taking a flashlight and a hammer, she went downstairs and let herself out the back. She had almost phoned Jack first, but then decided she'd just stay in the shadows and look around. The last thing she needed was for him to think she was wacko.

She stood quietly in the moonshade of the evergreen near the back door, peering through its branches. It was never as dark outside as it seemed inside. And now she'd turned the tables on whoever was out here; she was watching for them—him.

Then she heard the singing again, louder, clearer. It *was* a Shaker song. When the breeze shifted, it seemed to emanate directly from the cemetery or holy ground out back.

Then she recognized the song and smiled in relief. It was that "Awake My Soul" song that Louise had taught the dancers. It might even be Louise's voice.

Carefully, looking all around and not using her flashlight so as not to call attention to herself, Kate edged out from the Trustees' Building and headed toward the Meeting House. The moment she passed Tanya's herb garden, she could see the downstairs windows were dimly lit.

Louise should have told her she was practicing late. Everyone was harried trying to get things ready for the opening, but this was above and beyond the call of duty, even for someone as obsessed with perfection as Louise and Ben were. Perhaps that had been Ben she saw darting toward the Meeting House. Could he even have called her name, thinking she could critique or participate in the dancing?

Feeling like a felon, she stood on tiptoe to peek in the window of the large, lighted room. But it was Adrienne who danced and darted about the floor to what must be a tape recording of Louise's voice. And the French woman was not attired in Shaker dress or her own usual striking garments.

Adrienne Thompson was stark naked.

"Pick you up Friday—hey, that's today already— instead of our usual Sunday," he told Erin, his voice at first authoritative, then, when she hesitated to agree, wheedling. "Hey, it's not good for us to get into a set schedule, anyway. Pack some things. If she can't find you, she can't blame you, and your temporary disappearance will give you more leverage to deal with her."

"What about school? I don't want to flunk out."

"You won't flunk out. You may only be gone for the weekend, and if not I'll clear it with your profs."

"Mark—Mike—this isn't high school anymore, where dads just write an excuse for days missed, you know."

"I told you not to say things like that. Not unless we're really alone. And we will be soon. The usual place, one o'clock, okay?"

"Okay," she agreed with a sigh, "but I'll be cutting English for it. I'll tell Amy I'm going to see friends for the weekend and leave it vague. But I don't really want to do any more than we already have to hurt her."

"Trust me. See you tomorrow, with no bells on. In short, just be sure no one hears about this. And don't worry about Kate. I'll take care of everything, angel."

Smacking her hand over her mouth in surprise, Kate ducked, as Adrienne cavorted nude past the window. She was whirling, leaping and singing off key, along with a recording of Louise's song. Could the usually elegant and self-contained woman be drunk? Kate shook her head and smothered a laugh.

And then Kate realized how she'd heard the song and music, however distant and walled-off she'd been. This window was slightly ajar, perhaps forgotten earlier when the university dancers had been practicing under Louise's eagle eye.

Kate knew she should tiptoe away. How embarrassing if Adrienne or Dane knew she'd seen this. And where was Dane? If it weren't for Adrienne's outrageous display, Kate would love to corner him right now about his old Buick. Perhaps that had been him running around out back. Maybe he was even getting an erotic kick—Kate giggled as she saw Adrienne kick her way past the window—out of watching this from outside. But if so, he might spot Kate spying.

Kate had just headed back to the Trustee's House when the shrill voice stopped her. "You naughty peeping Tom!"

Thinking Adrienne had spotted her through the window, Kate whirled back, only to hear Dane's voice boom out from somewhere. "A peeping Dane, you mean." His words echoed. "I kind of like it up here. It's a great place to watch from."

Totally intrigued, Kate tiptoed back to the window. Now draped in her black slip as a sort of Isadora Duncan scarf, Adrienne was waving up at the ceiling. Scooting down, Kate saw Dane peering through one of the high observation slits overlooking the meeting room.

"I'm coming down for an up-close-and-personal look, my love," he called out, and dared to wave his fingers through a slit.

Kate quickly headed back toward her apartment. Maybe she could hold it over Dane's head to get better security and lighting, or to make him tell everything he knew about the black Buick. But if *he* was in the tiny upstairs room spying on his wife's display, who was that man out back?

Kate was downstairs early the next morning. The staff meeting was to start at nine, and she had much to do first. She let herself in the small, unlocked office at the back of the building and turned on the PC and printer there. A fax machine hummed away in the corner as something came in. None of this was off-limits, and most of the staff had used it from time to time. Louise had been on a campaign to have it all removed, but Dane had stubbornly refused. Why she hadn't done this before, Kate didn't know, but she hadn't thinking clearly lately. But then, why hadn't Zink thought of it if he was so hell-bent on solving this case? Maybe he thought it best not to tell her everything. After all, she'd held things back from him, especially to protect Erin. And she hadn't told him about the old Buick the Shakers had owned because she didn't need him questioning or accusing the village staff when she had no proof anyone was involved in anything.

Kate heaved a huge sigh as she did an Internet search for PACKARD. When she'd pulled up a lot of useless information on the modern company Hewlett-Packard, she went back and tried PACKARD CARS. The screen filled with car clubs and personal sites. It didn't take her long to find, on a page labeled 1947 Packard Automobile Page, the picture of the car.

"'Packard Clipper,'" she read aloud, her voice solemn. She printed the page off. It was somehow like finally having a wanted poster or police drawing of a criminal. She faxed it to Zink with a scribbled cover page of explanation, then sat back down again.

In the search box, she typed in BUICK CARS. It took a lot longer, but she found and printed a picture of a 1947 Buick. She stared aghast at it: it looked amazingly like the other car in shape, and it also had heavy front grillwork. Still, the Packard's grill was a bit broader, more wraparound. However frenzied she'd been each time she'd seen the car, it had been the Packard and not the Buick—hadn't it?

"What's happening?" the man's voice behind her asked.

She spun in the wheeled chair to face Dane. Although Jack had said he'd broach the subject of the Buick with him, she might be caught now, anyway. She quickly shuffled the Buick picture under the one of the Packard, though she knew the Buick ink wasn't quite dry.

"I wondered if I could locate online a picture of that car that hit Varina Palmer," she explained hastily. "I did, and faxed it to the Toledo police to be sure they are looking for the right vehicle, since I never was really sure of its year or make."

"Good move. Kind of like looking through mug shots, huh?" He came in to hang his coat on the wall peg. Kate wondered if Adrienne was sleeping in for obvious reasons. In addition to her wild display last night, like everyone else, Adrienne Thompson had been burning the candle at both ends.

"Actually," Kate said, "I was going to show it to you because someone said the last Shakers here had an old black car that you're carefully preserving—so I thought you might know something about old cars— in general." She hoped playing dumb would get her some information from him, though a few moments ago she'd decided not to give that old black Buick a second thought.

"The one we—the village, that is—owns is a '47 Buick Eight, a beautiful thing," he said, leaning in the doorway as she hurriedly rose and gathered her material from the desk.

At least she knew now he wasn't going to explode at her. And if he was guilty of anything, which was as wild an idea as Mike and Erin in the death car, he was hiding it well. She remembered to bend down to click the Buick site off the screen, not sure if he'd noted it.

"I'll show you the car sometime," he went on, still blocking the door. "We'll even put it on display, I imagine. And, Kate," he added, his voice almost sonorous as she edged closer to the door, "Louise has several old pictures of it filed somewhere. If you want to see it before I bring it back from getting its yearly overhaul, just ask her."

Before she could react, he reached toward her and pulled the smeared picture of the Buick out from under the one of the Packard she'd showed him. "If we can't be up-front with each other, this place doesn't have a snowball's chance in hell," he told her, his voice hard-edged now, "and our days will be numbered."

He pushed past her and sat down at the PC as if she'd been keeping him from doing something essential on it. She felt fortunate that he hadn't demanded to know who had told her about the old Buick. Neither, evidently, had he wanted to confront her on why she'd printed and hidden the Buick picture when she'd implied to him she hadn't seen it.

And since it wasn't the same car, why was she in a sudden sweat over the Buick? Just because it had been stored nearby? Yet Dane's last words to her had sounded like a veiled threat. She was getting so paranoid, she didn't believe anyone.

"I'd like to formally introduce all of you to Dr. Myron Scott, though I know most of you have already spoken to him, as he led the archeological dig of our old Shaker well," Dane announced to the staff later that morning in the meeting room of the Trustees' Building. "I've asked him to give us an initial report about some of the exciting things they've turned up in its depths."

Though Kate was interested in the findings, she was so shaken and exhausted that she had to force herself to concentrate. And she had the wildest impulse to giggle when she saw Adrienne sitting at the head of the table, so serious and—so dressed.

"It has indeed been a fascinating excavation," Dr. Scott said. He had spread before him on a card table several artifacts, some covered with a white cloth. "Not that we're finished. But we have turned up some real surprises so far that I want to share with you Shakers."

A small ripple of laughter, but a stern nod from Louise, who was sitting right in Kate's line of sight.

"Some of this we could have predicted," the man went on. He hardly looked the part of a stereotypical professor, Kate thought, with his golf shirt and a single earring barely showing under his straight, longish hair. But his hands looked like those of an archeologist: large and rough, even a little dirty.

"However," he went on, "let me start with the surprises we found by looking closer than ever at the commonplace and the familiar. For example, let's peruse the bottles we found down the well, something I guessed we'd discover. But I hardly would have predicted what sort and what the final conclusion might be."

Kate saw Dane frown and sit farther forward in his seat. Clint Barstow looked fascinated. Tanya was totally on edge, fiddling with her car keys in her lap; she was leaving for Kentucky as soon as the meeting was over. Kate leaned in a bit to see past everyone else, as she sat at the foot of the table, hoping no one would notice how bad she looked in this bright window light.

"Here we have the well of a group of strict people who have renounced what they think of as 'the world,'" Professor Scott went on, "but what kind of bottles do we get? I present to you this brown one clearly marked in the glass, World's Hair Restorer. I'll pass it around. I don't have to tell you to handle it carefully."

"But it doesn't have to be a product used by a Shaker," Dane protested. "Anyone could have thrown it down there."

"That's why we are very careful with the dated layering of artifacts, Dane," the professor explained. "I can show you bottles from the later periods after the Shakers had departed, but the things I'm sharing with you today are definitely Shaker and definitely eye-opening. There were even several early-era bottles that once held perfume."

"I don't believe it," Louise snapped. "I'm afraid you're so-called layering work has been a bit shoddy."

"Now, Louise," Ben put in, as Dane shot her a glare. But nothing seemed to faze Myron Scott as he displayed his artifacts.

"Here's my other favorite," he went on, passing a cobalt-blue bottle around. "Note on the back of that one the raised words PAIN KING. Order pain out the door."

"Amen to that," Tanya put in, "though I'd like to think that our belief the Shakers used traditional—

that is herbal—cures was the true story. Do you have any other bottles of cure-alls?''

''Only,'' he said as he pulled a cloth off what he'd kept covered, ''if you count these, which once held wine, beer and whiskey. Obviously, it's not an accident that these were all down the well. I'd say the early, supposedly disciplined, Shakers were as rebellious and secretive as most of us are today.''

That seemed to be the general signal for chaos. Louise kept tut-tutting, while everyone else put in their opinion all at once. Dane looked furious that he'd ever allowed the dig. Clint Barstow laughed; Adrienne was arguing with Ben; and Kate slipped away when Tanya went out to get in her car.

As Kate watched Tanya head for Kentucky to meet with her family, she decided she couldn't wait one more moment to check up on Erin. It might be two days early, but she had the strangest feeling Erin needed her.

In her casual collegiate clothes, Kate waited outside Erin's dorm, figuring the girl would soon be heading to her one-o'clock English class after her lunch in the dorm cafeteria. Kate hoped she hadn't missed her. If so, she'd head directly to the class and pick Erin up there.

But at a quarter to one, out came Erin, her red hair gleaming in the spring sun to give her away among the clusters of other blondes and brunettes. Kate had dropped back and followed her up the hill to the main green before she realized that the girl was pulling her wheeled overnighter carry-on suitcase.

Kate's stomach lurched. Going where? Away for the weekend? Going directly from her last class?

Kate turned around abruptly when she saw Erin glance back. She'd looked back before, but Kate had been mingling with the other kids and hadn't worried Erin would spot her. On the green many students walked its cross paths, and she felt more visible. She cut over to another walk that ran at an angle to the direction Erin was walking, but saw the girl look back again.

Her heart went out to her beloved stepdaughter. Kate knew how it felt to be watched, pursued. Poor Erin, like her, wasn't sleeping well, and that took a terrible toll.

To Kate's surprise, Erin stopped at the small, single-spired and pillared chapel wedged between two large buildings, Ellis Hall and the hulking Memorial Auditorium. Was Erin so distraught that she was going to go in to pray or meditate—or just to ditch someone she sensed was after her? She watched as Erin went in and the chapel doors swung shut behind her.

Ignoring the web of brick paths, Kate cut straight across the green toward the chapel. She opened one of the double doors a crack and peered in one direction, then the other. The interior was bathed with light pouring in windows onto the emerald carpet. She did not see Erin, at least in this small foyer that lay outside the small nave itself, which she could partially see through double doors. The appearance of the place almost calmed her foreboding.

Kate darted inside and held her hand against the door until it closed quietly. A plaque on the wall told about this chapel being donated by a man named Galbreath, who had met his now deceased first wife on the same spot. A paper sign by the open doors announced a poetry reading. Could Erin be having her English class here today? But it seemed so silent, deserted.

And then Kate heard a strange humming inside. It reminded her of last night, of hearing music but not being able to place it. To peer in without entering, Kate moved behind a door that stood ajar between the foyer and the nave. Perhaps Erin was sitting in a side or back pew and had begun to sing a hymn.

Looking through the crack where the door was hinged, Kate tried to get hold of herself. Perhaps it was time this charade ended. It could even be a sign that Erin had come to a church, looking for help and security. Kate loved her and wanted, above all, to help her. Enough of this lurking. She was going in to find out exactly what was going on.

But Kate jumped back when she heard a distant door close, maybe one at the front of the nave somewhere near the ornate pipe organ. A man's voice echoed, but she still saw no one. Gooseflesh gilded her arms. Dark-haired with a mustache, he stepped into her view, his arms held wide before the small silver cross on the altar, as if he were the welcoming minister or a living tableau of Jesus Christ himself.

"Angel," he called, as Kate saw Erin rush down the aisle to him. "There's my girl."

18

Marriage is like life in this—that it is a field of
battle, not a bed of roses.

> —Robert Louis Stevenson
> *"Virginibus Puerisque"*

It was Mike! Disguised, her ex-husband had finally
appeared. Kate gasped in shock, then she was sure
they had heard her. But they were already intent on
each other.

"No phone calls from Kate, no problems?" Mike
asked Erin.

He looked heavier. His dark hair and mustache did
a lot to change his appearance, too. As she stared at
him through the crack between the open door and the
doorway, he jammed a baseball cap on his head. He
also wore a bright green-and-white O.U. athletic
jacket, probably so he'd fit in with the students and
not be spotted. But Kate thought it made him stand
out like a parrot among sparrows.

"No problems," Erin said, "except I'm still scared
to do this. What if she thinks I'm kidnapped and calls
the police?"

"You just let me worry about that. Besides, the
weekend may be all we need to settle things."

"How? What are we going to do?"

"Erin, let's get out of here and talk on the way, okay? I'm parked illegally behind the Alumni Center across the street and don't need to be towed. Get your stuff, and we'll go out the other door."

Kate let Erin walk toward the back of the nave to get her suitcase, then turn toward Mike, pulling it. When the girl was several steps down the aisle, Kate darted out and grabbed Erin's arm, thrusting herself between the two of them.

Erin shrieked and froze; Mike, instead of running as Kate had hoped, moved forward to block the aisle. They stood about twelve feet apart.

"Long time, no see," Kate said, "though you've been watching me, haven't you."

"That I have. You've been a busy little bee."

"Dad, I didn't know she was here."

"It's all right, angel."

"Oh, of course, it is," Kate said, amazed her voice sounded strong when she was shaking so hard. "Everything's just absolutely peachy. No sweat about embezzlement, financial disaster for people who knew and trusted us. What's theft, or desertion of a wife and child? So no problem with running from the law or illegally taking Erin off somewhere when I'm the one who has custody—not to mention menacing and maybe even hitting—"

"Just shut up," he interrupted, slashing the air with a flat hand. "You've done enough damage to Erin and me."

"I cannot believe your arrogance." She stood her ground, her hand still hard on Erin's arm. "And once again, I see you're going to run, this time with Erin, so you can disrupt and ruin her life even more."

"I'm her father, Kate. You're just the ex-wife and ex-stepmother, and you're the one who chose that."

"The one who chose not to desert her."

"Hurry up," he ordered Erin, yanking the brim of his baseball hat down harder.

Kate gaped at him. The tilt of his head or the way he'd lifted his hand—was Mike Marburn the man driving the old car in the Toledo cemetery? If his cap were a fedora and the bright jacket a dark trench coat, she could be certain it was Mike.

"Erin," Kate said slowly, trying to stare Mike down, "go back to your dorm and your life. You are right to question going away with your father. He's a man on the run who could get dangerously desperate if—when—he's caught."

"'Dangerously desperate,'" he mocked. "That's good, Kate, very dramatic. You want a demonstration of that? Move, Erin!"

"No!" Kate cried, but Erin yanked away and Mike stepped between them. When he backed up, following Erin to keep an eye on Kate, she advanced.

"Let's sit down and talk about this," Kate said, trying to sound calm and rational.

"Oh, sure," he said. "I'd love for all of us to put ourselves on public display."

"No, we can stay in here. Don't involve her anymore, Mike. Last time you left her, you broke—"

The moment Erin was out the door behind the altar—Kate could hear it close—and before she could scream or run, Mike lunged at her, one hand clamped hard over her mouth. He dragged her toward the door where Erin had gone out, but then veered off into the small room behind the pipe organ and altar.

He must have been here before, Kate thought. He'd

cased this place, probably been everywhere she'd been, too, waiting to retaliate. He'd admitted he'd been watching her.

She struggled and kicked as he shoved a handkerchief in her mouth. Instantly, she began to gag.

"Quit fighting, damn you!" he muttered. "I'm just going to tie you up."

Shoving and holding her, her face against a small pillar, he somehow unbuckled and yanked off his belt. He pulled her hands down at her sides, belting her to the post. Gagging, she could hardly breathe.

"You'll wiggle out of that as fast as you do everything else. Listen to me, 'cause I gotta go." He stepped around the post to seize her face so hard her mouth puckered, even with the gag. "We'll call you, so stick by the phone at the village. I'm willing to take you up on that little talk—just the three of us, though. I swear, you bring your cop or village friends, and you'll never see her again."

Though she couldn't talk, Kate shouted through her gag at him. About those threats. About what he'd done to Erin and her. Frustration and fury poured from her, even as he turned and hurried away.

She scrambled to twist and writhe out of the belt, scraping her skin. Stumbling, she ripped out her gag as she ran, though she knew she'd be too late to stop them. She pictured them pulling away in a big, black Packard.

But as she raced out the back of the chapel and looked frantically up and down the street, she saw only a gold compact car turn the distant corner.

The phone call came just two hours later: Erin's voice. It was obvious from the background noise that she was calling from a public phone. Kate stood, leaning against her desk, hoping it would hold her up because her legs were trembling so hard.

"He wants to talk to you, Kate."

"Honey, are you all right? Are you sure this is what you want?"

"To be with him? He's sorry for being too busy for me before and wants to make it up to me. And none of this is his fault so—"

Her voice stopped abruptly, as if Mike had covered the phone. She came back on.

"See, these are the kinds of things we can hash out if you meet us," Erin said, obviously repeating what he'd just told her.

"I don't trust him enough to meet him someplace alone, and I won't—"

"No, this is a public place, a peaceful place," Erin insisted, sounding on the verge of tears. Kate's love for Erin roared through her. The child might not have been born from her body, but she was always hers in her heart.

"Where are you?" Kate asked calmly, raking her free hand through her hair.

"Kate, it's me." Mike's voice. "Let's make plans."

"Please, please, take her back to school."

"Not until I have that talk with you, make a deal about how we can share her—without you turning me in."

"You said you've been following me. You mentioned the police and my friends at the village."

"You still psychotic about being followed, Ms. Marburn? Kept your name—that *disgraced* name—didn't you, even when you cut me loose."

"How could you just run and leave us to face all—"

"Save the questions. Here's the deal, take it or leave it—and take Erin or leave her. We're in a busy public park on government land, so that sounds safe enough, doesn't it? Lots of campers, hikers, even park rangers. Old Man's Cave at Hocking Hills State Park, not more than a half hour away. Meet us here at four today or I'll take Erin to get her schooling, life and a new mother somewhere else."

"Mike, I won't just—"

"Be here or just wish us *bon voyage*. And no cops, Kate, or else."

The phone went dead in her hand.

Kate had less than an hour to get to a place she'd never been and didn't know. If Zink weren't hours away, she would have called him, no matter what Mike said. But it would take too long to phone the Athens police and explain it all. Besides, then it would be in their hands, and she couldn't take that chance.

She had to save Erin from Mike, make the girl realize that he was the one who'd stalked Kate and killed Varina. She should have told Erin all about seeing that black car in the cemetery and at Tanya's great-aunt's funeral. Maybe she could get Mike to admit it. With his arrogance, it was worth a try. But even then, would Erin realize he wasn't some betrayed hero? Or worse, did Erin know about the appearances of that black car because she'd been right with him all the way?

Kate grabbed her keys, purse and Ohio map, and ran for the stairs. If Tanya had been here, Kate would have taken her, had her stay in the background, perhaps, to blend in with the other hikers.

She was terrified to go alone.

Downstairs, she flew past Louise and Adrienne, who were huddled in conversation.

"I thought you said you didn't feel well, yes?" Adrienne asked. Kate hated to lie, but she had just wanted them to stay away while she waited for Mike's call.

"Got to go to the doctor's," Kate cried, and ran for her car. "I'll be happy to go with you!" Louise called, following her to the door of the Trustees' House.

Pretending she didn't hear her, Kate started her car and pulled away. Whether they were still watching her didn't matter. Down the road, she turned a sharp right into Jack's driveway, honked twice and got out.

He came to the doorway of his workshop, a table leg in hand. One look at her, and he threw it down and came running.

"What is it?" he yelled. "Something at the village? That car again?"

"My ex-husband has taken Erin to the Hocking Hills State Park and demands I come talk to them. I'm afraid he's dangerous and I've got a deadline and orders to come without the police. Do you know where it is?"

He pushed her back in her car, on the passenger side, and ran around to the driver's door. "I've been there more than once," he said, putting his hand on the back of the seat behind her and craning his neck to back out. "Tell me everything while we drive."

Jack drove just slightly over the speed limit on the highway. Kate kept looking in the rearview mirror.

Not one car—especially a black one or a pale gold compact—was anywhere behind them. But what if this was a trap to see if she left the village with anyone? Erin and Mike could have lied about being at the park to test her.

Kate fought back tears of fear for Erin, tears of gratitude for Jack. "You can't come with me at the park," she told him. "Mike may have spied on me, and I can't risk it. He may know what you look like if he's been spying on me."

"The mystery man in the deadly black car. Then he could be doubly dangerous, but I'll go in way behind you and keep back. Now it's time you listen to me," he insisted. "Try to picture everything I'm describing."

They turned south off Route 33 onto 668 when they saw signs for Old Man's Cave, but she closed her eyes to try to concentrate on his words.

"We'll leave the car in the main parking lot, and you'll follow signs northwest to where the trail starts over a stone bridge," Jack told her. "You're going to descend into a fairly rugged gorge, a hiking area with waterfalls and caves. Old Man's Cave is beyond the bridge. Hang right—the trail is well marked—and cross a creek, then climb up to it. You can't miss the cave because it's huge."

Her eyes flew open. "What if I can't find them? No, I guess they'll find me. I think they're good at that."

"At the cave, try to stay out of its depths. It goes back in about—I don't know—over a hundred feet."

Kate pictured the depths of the dark Shaker well, yielding up its surprises.

"Is it dark inside?"

"Way back in, but it has a large mouth, and even if the gorge is all in shadows by then, the sun won't be down. Don't go back into the cave and don't stay in the park after dark, or I swear I'll come after you."

"You'll be hiding somewhere nearby, hanging back?"

"I'll try to locate a park ranger. We may need him if anything goes wrong. And the footing can be dangerous in there," he warned, seizing her wrist as he stopped in the parking lot.

"I'll be careful," she insisted as she reached for her door handle.

"Kate," he said, holding on to her a moment as she started to get out. "Stay on the path, in sight of people—and not just because of Mike and Erin. Hikers have fallen to their deaths in there."

America's Discovery Trail one sign read, as Kate hurried across the parking lot in the direction Jack had indicated. She looked back only once. He was out of the car and already striding after her, though taking a roundabout way and keeping his distance. She skirted the check-in station and found the trail, marked by blue blazes. No one seemed to be going in at this late afternoon hour, but the parking lot suggested a few visitors must still be inside.

Ahead stretched the stone bridge Jack had mentioned, and beyond and beneath that, a gorge hewn from bone and buff sandstone. Waterfalls thundered from cliff to cliff beneath the bridge. It took her breath away, but she started across. Sharp shadows crept into the crevices and lurked in jagged rock faces. Cold and dampness seemed to seep from the rock walls.

On the other side of the bridge, she stopped momentarily at a signpost with arrows that listed park attractions: Old Man's Cave, the Devil's Bathtub, Cedar Falls, Ash Cave. All she cared about was Old Man's Cave, so she moved on.

She was relieved to see sporadic groups of hikers, though most were on their way out. Another sign about Old Man's Cave explained how the elderly hermit who came here years ago in search of game was buried beneath the ledge of the cave. Kate shuddered and hurried on, trying to watch her steps on the slick rock. The wind whined through hemlocks huddled along the trail.

A ways beyond the bridge, she turned right as Jack had said, though the path was clearly marked. Bluffs and cliffs towered over her as she descended toward a rock-strewn stream. Fortunately, someone had lashed three heavy logs across it, or she would have had to ford the thigh-deep water. Though she knew it was rude, she rushed to the makeshift bridge and crossed it before the campers who were closer could reach it.

"Sorry," she said, and hurried down the trail, not stopping to read the entire sign about violent flooding wiping out other bridges.

The rocky surface here was even slicker with spray, and she slipped, going to her hands and knees. Quickly, she got up and hurried on. When she looked up to see Old Man's Cave stretching above her, plunging back into the sandstone cliff face, she hesitated.

What if Mike was amusing himself by sending her

on a wild-goose chase? Or what if he'd laid some trap for her here?

She glanced at her watch: ten minutes before four. She'd made such good time. Surely, if he was waiting for her here, he'd never suspect she'd brought someone with her.

Jack's thoughts roared like the nearby waterfalls as he crossed over the stone bridge and took the blue-blazed trail about five minutes behind Kate. He felt cold without his jacket, and these smooth-soled western boots slowed him down. He hadn't even gone back into the house when he'd seen how distraught Kate had been.

It scared him how much he'd come to care for her in a short time. More than that, he was panicked that her stepdaughter, whom he'd never met and used to avoid in conversation, was in danger. The last thing in the universe *he* had wanted was to hurt his own child; evidently, the same could not be said for Mike Marburn.

As he hurried down the trail toward the stream, he cursed himself for not stopping at the check-in cabin to locate a park ranger. He thought he'd find one out here—but, even if he did, should he risk having Mike Marburn see one? At least there were still hikers in the area, and a few were heading into the gorge—like the guy not far behind him. Jack had already checked him out and he didn't look a bit like Kate had described Marburn.

Jack picked up his pace but got really annoyed when the man bumped him just before he crossed the stream on the lashed-log bridge.

"Hey, watch it," Jack told him, swinging around to make sure the man stayed back.

But the burly blond with a backpack stepped even closer. Jack's muscles tensed; the back of his neck prickled. He had to locate Marburn, so he couldn't see bothering with this guy.

But suddenly, he *could* see bothering with the snub-nosed gun the man pointed right at his chest.

The roof of Old Man's Cave—actually, a deep, eroded recess in the cliff face—loomed above Kate. As she climbed to its floor level, it opened before her, vast and dim. Daylight still grayed its mouth, but its throat was dark. She stayed put, not going deeper in, looking all around. Where were they? Could she have beat them here?

She strained to listen. Someone's shout echoed down in the gorge, but this place seemed so empty. She heard a scuff of stones from someone on the path she'd just climbed, though she'd seen no one behind her. Could Jack be this close and, seeing no one else, was he coming up?

She backed onto the cave floor. When she saw who it was, her heart thudded and she wanted to flee, but she stood her ground. Besides, as far as she could tell, there was only one way up here, and Mike had emerged on the trail, cutting it off from her.

"You screwed up again," he accused without preamble as he stopped about ten feet from her. He was no longer dressed like a student but as a camper in jeans, flannel shirt, down vest and hiking boots. "You think I wasn't watching? I saw, in the parking lot, you brought a damn posse."

Her pulse pounded even harder. "That's just a

friend of mine who knew how to get here when I didn't,'' she tried to explain. ''There are no cops involved. Your phone call and deadline panicked me. I was too upset to drive when I had no idea where this was—where's Erin?''

His clenched features relaxed; perhaps he believed her. ''Later for that, but I will tell you where your friend is.'' He looked smug now, folding his arms over his chest but not coming closer. ''Back a ways off the trail with a friend of mine.''

''What do you mean?''

''I mean, I hired a guy—one with a very convincing gun—to be sure you and I got this chance to chat alone.''

''A gun? Are you crazy?'' she cried, smacking her hands to her sides, then gesturing wildly. ''He'd better not hurt him.''

''Maybe a real close friend of yours, huh?''

''The point is, you don't need any more trouble.''

''Not with you back in my life, I don't. And Erin's here. You'll see her on our way out—all of us, together—unless you want to keep fighting me. But let's get down to business. Exactly how much is that furniture worth you killed Mrs. Denbigh for?''

''You bastard!'' She could have launched herself against him, but she lowered her voice. Besides, maybe he had a gun, too. She wouldn't put anything past him now. ''I didn't kill her,'' she said, fighting to keep her voice steady, ''and I want to see Erin right now.''

''You seem to think you're in charge here. I'm a wanted felon, but you could be, too, and for murder. Seems I recall from before I left,'' he said, dramatically stroking his chin, ''you told me all about a plan to get in tight with the old lady, worm your way into her affections and her will, then knock her off. I'd hate to testify to that the way you did against me.''

Kate realized she hated this man. She'd never really known him. ''Oh, come on,'' she said. ''I hardly knew her when you left, and everyone knows you're a liar, except your poor daughter. But you're even more despicable than I imagined. My hurting Sarah Denbigh is as obvious a lie as the ones you told about loving me or Erin. It's all about you, isn't it?''

''Or, tell you what—rather than us going on the run together,'' he went on maddeningly as if she hadn't even spoken, ''Plan B is I'll take Erin for 'insurance,' and you can start supporting both of us in the manner to which *you* used to be accustomed. With Mrs. Denbigh's heirs disappearing, you can sue for that furniture, then start to sell it off and send the funds our way—to Erin and me. When you've paid me enough for what you put me through by testifying against me and divorcing me, I'll tell you where to find Erin so that—''

''So that I can try to pick up the pieces of her life again? You're demented. I want to see her right now or none of this is going to happen—ever. And I want to know if she's been with you in that car.''

''Sure she has.''

''The old, black car? Where did you get it?''

''What old, black car? I meant here, today.''

He was so skilled at lying and shifting subjects. Surely, he had been the one in the old Packard, though that didn't mean Erin had been with him. He just didn't want to have anyone know he'd done the hit-and-run that killed Varina, that was all.

''Okay, okay,'' he said, holding up both hands, ''I

told Erin to get way back in the cave and wait for us. Come on, and we'll all talk things over." He stepped past her toward the cave and motioned her into its depths.

"I'm not going in there with you," she said, not budging. "I don't need to get yanked around any more. Get her out here."

"You're not calling the shots here, Kate, never were," he said, advancing on her for the first time. "When are you going to get that through your stupid, stubborn head?"

"I've been stupid, all right. To ever have loved you. To not have realized you were making another attempt to ruin Erin's life by horning back in on her after she'd gone to make a fresh start at the university."

"She wants me back in her life!" he roared, and rushed her.

Though Kate had tried to stay on guard, the sudden attack after all this talk surprised her. She ducked, circled him and scrambled for the trail down. Erin probably wasn't even here. Or, what if both she and Jack were being held by his friend with the gun?

"Not up toward the cave," the blond ordered Jack and jerked the barrel of the gun downstream. "Family reunions need to be private. This way."

Scanning the deserted area, waiting for a chance to get rid of the gun and the guy, Jack had no choice but to do as he was told. The waterfall roared so loud in his brain that he knew he'd never even hear that gun if it went off, echoing up and down the cold rock walls.

But he figured it was now or never. If Mike Marburn had run down Varina Wellesley and her brother in cold blood, he probably didn't choose or hire accomplices who were nice guys.

Jack pretended to slip on the slick rocks along the stream. He cried out as if in pain and rolled directly at his captor. When the guy jumped away from Jack, he slipped, too, and Jack lunged at him.

Jack had been wrong, because he did hear the crack of the gun. For one minute he expected to feel the agony of a bullet, but the man had missed. However furious he was, what came back to him was his high school football coach's patient voice: "No, Kilcourse. Tackle him low, take out his feet and you get the whole guy."

But he could not be patient and deliberate. His boy Andy would never get a chance to play football, never have a girl to love or a child of his own. Jack slugged the gunman, again, again before he could even hit back. The man lay gasping.

Panting, exhausted, Jack heaved the gun in the stream and hit the man in his gut one more time. He didn't even take the time to tie him, but stumbled to his feet and tore in the direction from which he had come, praying he was not too late.

19

Oh, no man knows
Through what wild centuries
Roves back the rose.

> —Walter de la Mare
> "All That's Past"

The path down was impossible for Kate to handle at a run. Mike caught up, grabbed her arm, swung her back around to him on the narrow path. For one moment, she was sure he'd slam her into the rock face or try to throw her over. But Erin stood on the next turn down.

"Let her go!" Erin shouted. "She could fall."

"He'd like that," Kate cried, trying to keep her balance and shove him away, "except he'd lose his future meal ticket. Have you already spent all the money you took off with?" she demanded from Mike as she tried to yank free. "Finally bought an antique car you used to just look at, right? Have you seen his classic black car, Erin?"

"What? Stop it," Erin screamed, "both of you."

Mike cocked his head. "Now you've done it. Someone's coming—running."

One hand in a fierce grip on her wrist, he yanked Kate down the path, forcing Erin to retreat ahead of them. Kate went willingly, glad to be coming down off the cliff, trying to pick a level spot to get free from him. But she was not going to leave Erin with him again. And someone *was* running somewhere in the gorge.

"Help! Help *meeeee...*" Kate screamed, before Mike slapped her across the face so hard her ears rang.

"Dad, don't! Let her go!"

Though her jaw stung, Kate wasn't going to let him shut her up. She had to make Erin see her father for what he was. But Mike bent her arm behind her back to make her walk with him deeper into the gorge.

"Dad, don't, don't," the girl cried, jerking his arm. "I heard some of what you said up there. You're acting wild. I'll go with you if you just leave her alone."

"Shut up!" Mike hissed at Erin, but it was Kate's arm he wrenched. She almost blacked out as the shaft of pain pierced her, but she staggered on her tiptoes. The path was uneven, and dark devoured the bottom of the gorge. The sound of roaring water became louder again. Why was he taking them deeper into the park?

"He's been hurting you, too, Erin—whether or not you know it," Kate muttered from between gritted teeth.

Her eyes darted wildly to take in her surroundings. At least they were still on the blue-blaze trail, so if she had a chance to grab Erin and run, she'd know where to go. A blur of a sign went by with large letters, The Devil's Bathtub. Under a small bridge, Kate saw a gaping hole in the rock, a sandstone pothole with white water frothing so furiously it looked like a boiling cauldron.

"You're either with me—us—or not, Kate," Mike said, gasping for breath between words. "Plan A or B, like I said before. Which is it going to be?"

"I said stop it!" Erin cried, and jerked Mike's arm until he partly loosed Kate's.

It wasn't until he freed her that Kate realized Erin had hit him with a small rock. Kate heard it bounce away, over the edge. Leaning against Kate, he went down on both knees, holding his head, then grabbed for her legs when she tried to shove him away. She kicked but slipped. Sitting down hard, she bounced against him. Mike seized her again. They rolled and landed sprawled on the edge of the rock basin, with Erin screaming, "Stop it, stop it!"

When Mike tried to push Kate over, Erin grabbed Kate's legs to hold her back. This time when Mike rolled, he took Erin down. She slid even closer to the edge than they had.

"Er—in!" Kate screamed. She fought like a wild woman to free herself from Mike. Didn't he see Erin could go over? Kate butted him with her head where Erin had already turned his forehead bloody.

A man's boot stepped on Mike's neck, and a big hand grabbed him by his hair. She looked up. *Jack!*

"Get Erin!" Kate screamed. "Erin!"

"Where?"

Oh, dear God, she'd gone over. She was gone.

"Here!" the girl screamed from someplace close.

"Hang on!" Jack yelled, then ripped Mike's weight away from Kate.

When Mike swung a fist, Jack hit him twice, a left to the gut, then a right to the jaw. Mike flopped back, hitting the bridge stones and blacking out. Jack was already on his stomach, reaching over the ledge for Erin. Kate scrambled to her hands and knees, gasping for breath, peering over. It was so dark in that hole, but she could see Erin clinging above the rocks and churning water, her upper torso on the lip of a narrow ledge, her hips on the edge, her legs dangling. Beneath her was a twenty-foot fall into the Devil's Bathtub.

"Kate, go back on the trail for help," Jack ordered, ripping his shirt off and knotting one sleeve around his wrist. "If I can't reach her, we're going to need help. Can you walk?"

"I can run," she vowed.

"Come on, Erin," Kate heard him say in a calm, coaxing tone, when she herself wanted to scream the cliffs down. "Reach up and try to grab this sleeve. I can't get to you otherwise. Come on...come on."

"I'll be right back, Erin!" Kate cried, and loped away, shouting for help. She couldn't bear to leave, but she saw instantly that Jack had the best plan. It had been years since she'd trusted a man, but she had to now.

Jack knew his hands were slick with sweat and blood, and Erin's were probably wet with spray. But if his flannel shirt didn't rip, she could hold on to it. He'd knotted it around his wrist and grasped it tightly. He had to pray that Mike didn't come to and shove them both over.

"No, don't look up at me because that tips you back," he told Erin. "Keep your head down, your weight forward on the ledge."

"I'm slipping."

"Just let your legs hang there. Stop trying to get back up. I've got a shirtsleeve dangling almost by your right hand. Just lift that hand from the elbow, not the whole arm. Okay, great. Open your hand— I'll put the sleeve right in, and then you grab it."

She did. The shirt went taut, yanking his arm down. He wished he wore a belt. He tried to find a solid, comfortable position on the rock above her, but there wasn't one.

"Can't you pull me up?" she cried, her words muffled as she kept her face down on the ledge. The constant hiss and rumble of the water in the big pothole below also muted her voice.

"It might tear. But I'm going to hold you right where you are until your mom brings help. All you have to do is keep as much of your upper body on that ledge as you can. If you start to slip, I can pull you back onto it." He had no idea if that were true, but it was all he had. "The shirt won't lift you up here," he tried to explain, keeping his voice calm, "but it will hold you there, okay?"

"Okay. Please talk to me. Please don't let go."

"I won't. I swear it. Just like your mother never wants to let you go."

"She's my stepmother, you know."

"I can tell she loves you more than most mothers love their kids."

"Is she okay—Kate?"

"She's been through one hell of a lot, Erin. Was your dad the one in the black car that's been stalking her?"

"What? I don't know. He's been hiding—he wouldn't."

"Wouldn't try to shove your mother over a cliff and delay helping you, either, would he?"

Only a sucking, sobbing sound.

"Just hang on, Erin. I'm right here with you, and I'll never let go. I've got strong arms, honest. I work with wood all day, making furniture. I'll get Kate to bring you over to see it. Will you come visit me?"

"Okay. By the way, I can swim," she said, her voice even weaker.

"Great. How about rock climbing?"

"Anything to get out of here. Whatever happens, thanks."

"What's going to happen is that you're going back to school and get your grades up. I had a terrible time my first year at college. The sudden freedom kind of makes you drunk, you know, turns into all kinds of strange rebellions."

He felt her slip; he thought he heard—felt—the flannel rip somewhere.

"Erin," he said when the shirt pulled even tauter, "I don't mean to be preaching about what I did when I was a kid. I hate to be preached at myself. The point, believe it or not, is that adults like your mom and I can understand some of your problems. She wants to be here helping you right now, but you got me for just a little longer—as long as you need..."

He choked back a sob, not of terror but for the memory he had of hanging on to his son. He'd held his little hand in that coffin and had not wanted to walk away, even at the funeral, until they'd all insisted it was time for him to just let go.

* * *

"Erin! Erin!" Kate cried, leaning over the edge next to Jack. The park rangers pulled Kate away and soon flooded the scene with portable lights.

"I'm okay...okay now" came the faint voice down the ledge.

The park rangers looped ropes between Erin's legs and another around her waist just in time, Kate thought, for she saw how much her stepdaughter had slipped.

Erin kept quiet as they pulled her up, but it was Jack who was talking. "I was scared that with no leverage I wouldn't be able to keep her from going over," he told the rangers. "Thank God you're here."

Kate saw he stood back in the glare of portable lights, watching as one ranger cuffed and arrested a groggy Mike, while the others pulled Erin up. Summoned by park rangers, two medics soon appeared with a stretcher.

"I can walk," Erin insisted, even as she hugged Kate. "How's—how is he?" Erin asked the ranger who pulled Mike to his feet.

"Fine, for someone who's dumb enough to try assault and kidnapping on State Park land," the ranger muttered, and pulled Mike away. Erin took two steps after him, then stopped. His face bruised and swollen, Mike looked back at her.

"Blame her," he muttered through a split lip as he glared at Kate. "I sure as hell do."

They marched him away, while another ranger wrapped Erin in a blanket. "Thanks, but I'm not cold," she told the officer, shrugging out of it. "Actually, I'm still sweating bullets."

"Luckily not bullets," the ranger said. "We've got the accomplice under arrest. He had bullets on him."

"I meant to tell you about that guy," Jack spoke up. "Sorry, but I threw his gun in the stream. So much for evidence."

Kate wondered if Mike would admit he'd been the one watching and stalking her. Since he'd no doubt go to prison for years, anyway, would he confess that he'd killed Varina and tried to kill Palmer that same day? He'd said enough to her to indicate he was guilty, including mentioning that the Denbigh heirs were "disappearing" to allow her to inherit that furniture he intended to benefit from. Despite this dire predicament tonight, Kate concluded, it had been worth it to be free of being harassed and threatened by Mike Marburn.

"You still need to see a doctor, Erin, even if you can walk out of here," Kate said. "I'll go with you. I can't thank all of you enough," she said to everyone. "I'm so grateful, to Jack, especially."

He nodded. She wasn't sure, but it looked as if he'd been crying. His eyes glinted in the artificial glow of the rescue lights. Despite not wanting to let Erin go, Kate walked over to Jack and straight into his arms.

He held her hard. Despite the pain in her arm from Mike's wrenching of it, nothing mattered now but that Erin and she—and Jack—were safe. She held him tight, too, her arms linked around his waist.

"How can I ever thank you?" she whispered, her words muffled against his shoulder.

"Helping her—saving her—meant a lot to me," he choked out. "But besides that," he added, clearing his throat, "we'll think of something."

As if in celebration, Kate's antique Apothecary roses began to burst with blooms in the bright spring sun over the next few days. The flowers so far were few but stunning with their flat, full ruby petals and stark yellow stamens. Their sweet fragrance assaulted the senses, though it was nothing compared to the overwhelming scent that would fill the air later when more buds opened. These were the harbingers of all that was to come, for the non-Shaker breeds in Jack's backyard would bloom much later.

The early display of the once wild roses took Kate unaware, because the spring had been early and mild, and they were much farther south in the shelter of the Appalachian foothills than on the shores of Lake Erie. Most of the bushes had been transplanted, and they seemed ready to rejoice in her freedom from fear. Besides, who knew what heirloom strains like these would do? What defiant, deviant tendencies were hidden in them that could suddenly explode, just like in people?

Mike had been handed over to the federal prosecutors, with additional charges of assault, battery and attempted kidnapping. Charges of murder and attempted murder were still pending, and Kate was hoping Stan Rudzinski could prove Mike had killed Varina. Zink was to be able to interview him about that as soon as he got permission from the feds. But in her heart she knew that Mike was guilty.

"I gotta hand it to you for flushing him out," Zink had told her on the phone earlier this morning. "It's going to save me a lot of time, because I'd actually begun calling and visiting shops that do all kinds of window tinting, hoping to track the driver of the car that way. It's not illegal *per se* to darken passenger windows in Ohio vehicles, because commercial ones like limos or trucks can have it. And cars are allowed up to five inches of fifty-percent tinting on a front windshield, but none of it is as extensive or dark as you and other eyewitnesses have described on that Packard that hit Varina.''

''Sounds as if you've become an expert on this.''

''If that's a compliment, I'll take it. I'm on another case—have been for weeks—but I can't let the Sarah–Varina one go. My gut still tells me they were both murdered.''

Kate had slumped over the phone at her desk. Surely, Mike would not have killed Sarah, too, or contracted to have it done, even though he'd shown himself capable of hiring help. At least they could question his accomplice, too. The thing that scared her now was that he'd threatened to accuse Kate of planning to kill Sarah.

''I have to tell you something,'' she told Zink.

''Shoot.''

She bit her lip at his wording. ''In addition to the hints Mike gave me that he was the one driving the Packard, he also swore he'd testify I set Sarah up and then—got rid of her.''

Silence.

''Zink, none of it's true. I should never have told you that without telling Mason James first, but I'm trying to level with you. I want this nightmare over— all of it, for Sarah and, yes, for Palmer, so Erin and I can pick up our lives again.''

''A life with Jack, too, maybe? He called to give me his read on your ex, so I know how deeply he's gotten involved.''

''What else did he say?''

''Ask him. He's the boy next door, isn't he? But if Mike Marburn accuses you of anything, I'll consider the source. And if he's behind the Denbigh deaths, Palmer's coma and your troubles, I'll get it out of him. And thanks for the heads-up on the pic of the Packard and now all this. We'd make a hell of a detective team. Now run by me again everything Mike said that made you believe he was the one driving the Packard. It'll give me ammo when I do get to question him.''

She closed her eyes, then opened them to stare out the side window at her roses. "For one thing, the moment I asked if he'd been watching me, he said, 'That I have.'''

"What else?"

"I tried to pin him down on the fact he slipped up when he asked if I brought my cop or village friends.''

"He knew about me?"

"I guess he could have gleaned all that from the newspaper or Erin, but she says he spent his time talking against me, not inquiring what I was doing now. I just feel he's the one who's been watching me.''

"Anything else?"

"He asked if I was still psychotic about being followed.''

"You realize you just told me what you refused to share before," Zink said, his voice soft now. "Why you went to a shrink.''

"Maybe I'm trusting that you're trying to help me now, not do me in.''

"Praise the Lord and pass the ammunition.''

"Zink, the only reason I don't want it to be him in that black car is that he might have coerced Erin to go with him. I'm just hoping and praying you'll be able to come up with some other woman who was with him in all this—through fingerprints or hair samples—if you can trace that car.''

''The paint sample the Athens police sent us from the phone pole across from Jack's isn't paint but chrome alloy, and most cars of that era had the same stuff on their grills and fenders. Our sample won't differentiate makes or models, so we'll have to go at it another way.''

''You *are* going at it another way. You'll get it out of Mike Marburn, I know you will.''

''Don't overdo thanking the local hero for helping save your daughter,'' he'd said, his voice suddenly sounding almost bitter. ''Meanwhile,'' he'd added, ''I'll try to clear her mother once and for all. Talk to you or see you soon.''

Now, encouraged by Zink's help, Kate continued to examine her roses, looking for pests or problems on their buds, but her mind still drifted. Despite Zink's continually teasing her about Jack, Kate felt her relationship with ''the boy next door'' had gone to a deeper—or was that a higher?—level. Best of all, a sadder but wiser Erin had agreed to counseling and was back in school this Monday. She would soon be answering a lot of questions from investigators, but they'd agreed to go to Athens to talk to her. Erin and Kate hadn't reconciled, but the girl was seeing chinks in her father's armor. It was the most she could hope for now, Kate thought, because noses seemed out of joint here at Shaker Run.

''I cannot believe you just ran out without telling us the truth,'' Louise had sputtered, when Kate had explained everything to the staff. ''And here I offered to go with you! You had to go to the doctor's, indeed,'' she'd concluded with a sniff.

"Kate," Dane had remonstrated, "you should have come to me for help. We've got to be able to trust each other. I knew where that park was, so you hardly had to go running to Jack Kilcourse. I stress again that we are a family here and can trust each other."

"It wasn't that I didn't trust you or anyone here," Kate had countered. "I was just in a hurry to get to Erin. You've all been great to me, but..."

"But Jack Kilcourse has been greater," Dane had concluded, and went on to other business while Adrienne glared at her. Kate hoped Tanya would come back soon, because she might be the only one who understood.

Now, as Kate noted the first signs of aphids on her baby blooms, Dane and Ben Willis walked toward her. It looked as if Ben, who was two steps behind the bigger man, was actually propelling him. Ben usually lagged, walking not quite with a limp but with hesitation in one leg. Kate always thought of Ben stepping hesitantly through life with Louise pushing him, so this was a big change.

"They're looking great," Dane said, folding his arms over his chest, staring at the roses instead of at her.

Kate nodded and waited for what was coming next. Surely, they weren't going to fire her, not with the opening of the village just thirteen days away.

"Aren't they?" she finally said. "I'm thrilled at their early progress, though I see a few signs of aphids. I'll probably be able to make some rose water next month, but I must admit I'm going to hate the Shaker practice of picking roses without their stems."

"A little sacrifice for authenticity," Ben put in. For

one moment, with Dane looming and blocking out the thinner man, Kate had almost forgotten he was here.

"Kate," Dane said, looking quite uncomfortable, "I don't want you to think I, or we, are not supportive of you through your troubles. I thought I should tell you something I've just admitted to Ben and Louise."

Waiting, holding her breath, Kate stared at him. *Admitted* implied some sort of guilt.

"It was me driving the antique Shaker car when it slid into a light pole and knocked the lights out in that snowstorm. I was so annoyed and embarrassed, I just kept going and didn't tell anyone about it. I've paid to have the dent on the grill hammered out myself, and it will soon be good as new. It's in a shop in Columbus, but if you want to see it sooner, Louise and Ben have some photos of it."

"I'd love to see them, but I realize I overreacted about the car. Although I've learned that a '40s Buick and a '40s Packard can look a lot alike, I hear your car doesn't have dark-tinted windows like the one I was looking for."

"Tinted windows?" Ben piped up, his voice incredulous. "Back in the '40s?"

Dane cleared his throat and shifted from one foot to the other, glaring at Ben instead of her. He obviously had something else to say. "I don't appreciate your even thinking that our village car could have been involved in something dire, but I realize your past makes you—shaken and suspicious," he said.

"I think the nightmare's over now," she said, trying to assure herself as much as him.

"Maybe not—the publicity fallout, I mean."

When he hesitated, Ben added, "The thing is, we covet publicity for Shaker Run's opening—but the right kind. The capture of your husband is kicking over the beehive in the papers and other media.''

Dane held up a hand and took up the explanation. ''We've gotten numerous calls in the office about reporters wanting to come here to interview you about your husband—''

''Ex-husband.''

''Well, yes. I've told those reporters to stay away, but the press and TV people are not known for following protocol or propriety. I'm just warning you they might try sneaking in or following you if you leave the premises.''

''That's the last thing I need!'' she admitted before she got hold of herself. ''I know they're good at that, but I don't want to see them, and I'm grateful if you've turned some away. If we only had more security here at night when everyone's gone but me, it would help. I mean, I realize someone on the staff might come back for dancing or singing practice late, but...''

Dane's eyes narrowed. She could tell he wasn't sure if she was implying she'd seen him and Adrienne.

''You tell Louise it's going to come to that, Ben,'' Dane muttered huffily. ''Security lights and alarms, however un-Shaker-like. Meanwhile, I've got enough problems around here.''

He glared at Kate before relaxing his expression again, but in that unguarded moment he'd looked absolutely malevolent.

20

Rose, shut your heart against the bee.
Why should you heed his minstrelry?
Refuse your urgent lover, rose.
He does but drink the heart and goes.
                                                    —Humbert Wolfe

"I hope you're proud of me, Louise," Kate told her as she gently washed aphid scales with soap and water from the tips of her budded Apothecary rosebuds. Louise, in full Shaker garb to meet with the volunteer presenters, had come out to see what she was doing. After Kate's earlier visitors, Dane and Ben, she was almost glad to see Louise for once.

"I'm being straight Shaker here in fighting these aphids," Kate explained. "Otherwise, I'd be using a modern nicotine sulphate product. The soap-and-water cure was in one of those old diaries I read, but since you keep insisting I'm Sister Jerusha Lockhart, I wish you'd relocate hers for me."

Kate almost inquired if it could be with the loose, stored papers over in Jack's shed, but she dared not give away that she'd been in there. Again, she thought of Jack and how much she owed him.

"I've been searching everywhere for that journal," Louise said, sounding either disgusted with herself or

Kate. "But I came out to ask if you'll be here to kindly lend a hand when I give the volunteers a tour of the village. Sister Jerusha, are you listening?"

"Sorry. I'm still so exhausted from everything. Did you ever get so tired that you have little dizzy spells or just nod off?"

"Not since I pulled all-nighters when I was in college," she said, but she came closer and looked in Kate's eyes. Their bonnet brims bumped. Louise had been right about one thing. The Shaker sisters might not have used or permitted sunglasses, but these bonnets were cool and shady. Lately, Kate had worn hers quite often; Louise almost never took hers off, at least around here.

"You'd best ask someone to go with you if you need to drive to see your daughter," Louise added, suddenly quite motherly herself as she patted Kate's arm. "She's a lovely girl, and she was quite interested in the dancing. I'd like you to have her back sometime so I can show her around more."

Kate almost retorted, *She doesn't need your tour of the graveyard and holy ground,* but she said only, "Even if she decides to go to summer school, I'm hoping she'll be here much more, maybe even help me with the flowers or assist Adrienne in the gift shop, if it works out."

"I'd like that. We would all like that very much. I hope she appreciates the Denbigh Shaker furniture heritage as you do."

Kate nodded, thinking how fortunate she was that Erin thought the furniture was "way cool," unlike Varina, who had thought so little of what had been Sarah's pride. Kate hoped that she didn't have to continue to fight for what Sarah had wanted to share with her, and that somehow she and Jack could find out who was switching and stealing precious pieces of it.

"Instead of helping with my tours, you'd best go in and drink some of Tanya's herbal tea and take a nap," Louise ordered, squinting as if Kate were some specimen under a microscope.

"I just might. Both Sister Jerusha and Kate Marburn are dead on their feet, even though they're relieved to have a lot of problems solved and questions answered."

Louise patted her arm again and headed back to her duties. She was probably right, Kate thought, about not driving until she got some more sleep. She could just walk over to Jack's and check on her rosebushes there, though since they'd bloom much later than these, they would hardly need pest poison yet. But she needed to thank Jack again.

She stowed her anti-aphid ammunition of pail, old toothbrushes, and rags in the garden shop. It seemed quiet and lonely without Tanya here, and Kate hoped again that her friend would be back soon. Besides, she needed some other kind of herbal bedtime tea, though she fully expected to sleep better now that her stalker, and Varina's murderer, was locked up. It would just take a little while to unwind.

She changed to a fresh blouse and long skirt, her and Tanya's compromise with Shaker style when they weren't in costume. She changed her bonnet for sunglasses and walked down the road toward Jack's. It was such a stunning spring day that she seemed to be drifting, flying. No wonder those eccentric Shakers thought they were having angel visions, she thought as she whirled once around, flinging out her arms, then, dizzy, stopping to steady herself.

Jack came out of the furniture shop to meet her; he must have seen her coming. "Is everything all right?" he asked. "Have you talked to Erin today?"

The man had done a one-hundred-eighty degree turn about Erin. Whereas he used to avoid so much as mentioning her, now he'd made Erin's safety and happiness his cause. Wasn't there some Indian legend, Kate tried to recall, that when you saved someone's life you felt responsible for them the rest of yours?

"I talked to her before breakfast," Kate assured him. "She was looking forward to hard work and getting her grades up. And she said, yes, she'd love to see your furniture shop this weekend."

"Good," he said, his rugged face lighting. "Then she can chaperon us at dinner here Saturday evening. We can pick up something in town when we go in to get her. And how's her mother today? Kate, you haven't been drinking, have you?" he asked, cupping a palm on one shoulder and tipping her chin up in his other hand. "You look a little tipsy."

"I'm fine—just exhausted. I haven't been better in weeks, though go ahead if you feel you must give me a Breathalyzer test," she said with a smug, little smile.

"You mean the mouth-to-mouth type, I hope, because that's what I was planning."

He stepped closer and bent to kiss her. His lips were masterful and strong, but it seemed a mere taste of him before he pulled slightly back.

"Hmm," he said. "Inconclusive. I'm going to have to try again."

"I, of course," she went on, linking her arms around his neck and swaying them slightly as if they

would dance, "only came here to see how my rosebushes out back are doing."

"Yeah," he said. "Let's get out of this front yard
with the village view. They might need binoculars to
see us down here, but you never know. Sometimes I
think the old Shaker ghosts still have eyes."

Despite the disconcerting way he'd put that, no
way she wanted to be spied on, ever again. They half
walked, half waltzed behind his house, and strolled
back among the clusters of her Damasks and Bourbons. She wished they could burst into full bloom this
very moment, just the way she felt she was doing.
But she had no desire, for once, to look at or touch
them. She only wanted Jack, as they came together
in a vibrant kiss.

The entire garden, maybe the whole world, tilted
and spun. Kate couldn't breathe apart from this man
and didn't want to. His strength both stoked and
sapped hers until she leaned into him and held to him.

It was good that he held her up, for his hands were
urgent on her back and waist, making her more dizzy
yet. Her brain buzzed, or was that the early summer
bees back here? But all such random thoughts stopped
as she kneaded his powerful back muscles and
propped her trembling legs against his thighs. His lips
slanted over hers, both devouring and feeding her.
Tipped back in his arms, she tilted her head to bring
him even closer. Finally, they broke the kiss and simply stared, inches apart, into each other's eyes.

"At first I didn't want this," he whispered.

"Do we now?"

"I want you, yes. Let's go in. If I make a phone
call right now, then take the phone off the hook, I

can stop a client from coming, and we can have some time together.''

They went in the back door, holding hands. As he made the call, she heard him say, ''Yeah, sorry. You're my favorite client, Mick, because you always know precisely what you want, but I'm just gonna have to reschedule. I'll call you tomorrow, okay?''

He crossed the kitchen to reach for her again. She raked her hands through his hair. ''Mmm,'' he murmured, nuzzling the hollow of her throat, ''you smell like roses.''

''They've started to bloom at the village.''

''I saw them, even in the dark.''

She pulled slightly away, looking up at him.

''You came over in the dark?''

''Kate, I've walked Shaker Run for years at night when I can't sleep. And I wanted to be closer to you after everything that's happened.''

''I'm very sure that Mike was my problem—and that's over now, thanks partly to you.''

''Since you haven't had a thing to drink, let me get some wine,'' he whispered in her ear, warming her, though it also gave her gooseflesh. ''We can go in the other room.'' He banged around in a cupboard, then closed it. ''I've got some glasses in here somewhere.''

She watched him open sparsely filled cupboards, slamming them shut as if he were in a stranger's kitchen. He finally produced two glasses, then opened a nearly bare refrigerator and pulled out a bottle of white wine. He began a rattling search through a utensil drawer, evidently looking for a corkscrew. Kate felt so finely wired she could have pulled the cork out with her teeth.

"I'll take the glasses," she volunteered, realizing he was so nervous he might break them, though she wasn't sure she wouldn't. She walked ahead down the center hall of the big, old Shaker building and saw both front doors stood ajar, though there were screen doors, too. How wonderful to live out here in the country now, she thought, without a shred of fear.

But she jumped when someone peered in the left-hand door. It was Tanya, shading her eyes as she looked through the old sisters' entrance.

"Oh, sorry, guys," she said. "I yelled for Jack in the shop and turned up the music 'cause I was so excited to tell you both what I've got."

"Tanya, hey," Jack said as he came up behind Kate, but his voice carried his disappointment that she'd shown up now.

As they all stood there, Kate could hear the music she'd mentioned, a gospel song with Tanya's great-aunt's clarion voice singing about *leaning on the everlasting arms.* It was pouring from Tanya's car, behind which she was hauling a large, bright orange U-Haul trailer.

"*Wait* till you see the *great* furniture I got," Tanya cried, as Jack opened the screen door and they went out. "I'm hoping you can store some of it here, and I'll offer a few pieces for the infirmary for the opening, and maybe use that Rent-a-Room storage, since no way I can handle all this in my apartment."

Kate saw Jack's body stiffen as if he scented something on the wind. She wondered if Tanya had any pieces that were fake, because surely that's what he was thinking.

"I'll get another glass," Kate said, "and we'll drink to Tanya's inheritance."

"Oh, no," their friend cried dramatically, smacking her forehead with her hand. "You guys and a bottle of wine, and here I come crashing in. Sorry, but I was just so thrilled—"

"And so are we," Jack assured her, giving Kate a silent sigh and slight shake of his head behind Tanya's back. "Let's see what you brought."

Tanya went out to the U-Haul with Jack. Kate stomped back into the kitchen to get a third glass. She was not angry with Tanya but with herself for resenting her friend's arrival, when until now she'd been eagerly awaiting Tanya's return. And worse, Kate had once suspected Tanya might have had something to do with the death of her elderly great-aunt. Mike might have killed Varina and maybe even Sarah, but surely Aunt Samantha Sams had just died of old age. And with those larger questions settled in Kate's mind, she could focus on helping Jack solve the furniture fraud—maybe now with Tanya's help.

But as Tanya drove the U-Haul behind Jack's shop where they could examine her bounty in privacy, Jack told Kate, "I don't necessarily want her to know everything about the forgeries. I'm going to look closely at these pieces, and if some of them are fake I'll try to explain to her."

Tanya got out of her car with a big grin. "All right," she said, "take a look. Auntie donated about half to her church. All family members got a few pieces, but she had written a note that I was to have more because of my work with the black Shaker heritage. What do you think? It all means so much to me because *she* meant so much."

Kate put an arm around Tanya and squeezed her

shoulders, as Jack let down the makeshift ramp, then strode up. "That's why I'm fighting for Sarah Denbigh's pieces," Kate explained. "It's like still having part of her—her beauty, love, talents…"

"Tanya, you've got a real treasure here," Jack said excitedly, peering into the depths of the U-Haul. "If I lift one end of these pieces, think you ladies can help handle the other end so we can take a better look at all this?"

Into the sweet spring sun and breeze, they unloaded six large pieces of furniture and four rocking chairs, which Tanya had carefully packed in the trailer with towels and blankets to keep them from bumping or rubbing the fine patina of wood.

"Look, this one's a bigger herbal cupboard than the one you're making for me, Jack, though I'm not going to part with either of them," Tanya said. "But I think I'm going to make the Thompsons and the Willises nearly as happy as I am, because I want *this* and—" she darted over to a work counter "—*this* to go in the Shaker Run infirmary for the opening. All they have in there so far is a table, corner cupboard and that adult invalid cradle that looks like a coffin."

"This piece is cherry, ash and walnut," Jack observed of the work counter. As his big hands stroked it, Kate held her breath, for she could still feel those hands on her. She saw him slide open the top drawer and bend to size up the dovetail molding and probably check the wood for weathering. "It looks great," he added, to her relief.

Kate's favorite piece was a tall food cupboard with twenty-four elaborately pierced tin squares set in a wood frame on the front and sides of it. The metal had provided ventilation within during the days of pre-refrigeration.

"And look," Tanya said, leaning closer to it. "I didn't notice this before, but the designs punched in the tin look like stylized *angels* blowing horns! It almost makes it look Christmasy."

"I've seen another piece similar to this," Kate said, frowning. When she was this tired, it actually made thinking difficult at times. "I think it's in Sarah's collection, but it's been on loan in the East for years, in some museum. I've never seen it in person, but it's on the inventory list of other pieces I inherited, with a photograph of it."

"Maybe there was once a matched pair that somehow got separated," Tanya surmised. "You know the Shakers—two of lots of things, one for the brethren and one for the sisters."

Kate's eyes met Jack's over Tanya's head. Evidently he wasn't going to tell Tanya about identical fake pieces; he must think hers were all authentic.

"Or else," Kate put in, "more than one Shaker furniture designer or builder was inspired by the same angelic vision."

"More like a hallucination," Tanya muttered.

When they both looked at her, she said, "One theory I've been working on—and *don't* you two go telling the so-called elders or deacons of Shaker Run— is that, at least at this Shaker village, some pretty strong and strange herbs were used to keep people in line. Or," she added, "to get them *out* of line with hallucinogens—so they'd see visions."

"That's why you've been focusing on curatives that could become injurious," Kate said.

Tanya nodded firmly but her voice was tentative.

"That's one reason, anyway. It's kind of been a theory that's an offshoot of my other studies, and I'm trusting you two to keep my secret till I can get to the bottom of this. I trust you guys, and maybe you can help me think it through."

Jack's gaze snagged Kate's again; he raised his eyebrows as if to say *Why not?* Realizing he'd finally decided to take Tanya into his confidence about the possibility of the furniture scam being tied to Shaker Run, Kate nodded.

"Tanya," he said, his face and voice solemn, "I— we—have something we want to tell you. Let's sit down in these rockers, and just listen a minute, okay?"

To Jack's surprise, Tanya was furious when he explained his theory and asked for her help in return. He saw her emotions crash from exhilaration over her furniture to outrage over his and Kate's theory about the thefts.

"Then—this wonderful gift from my great-aunt," Tanya stammered, "could all be worth—nothing."

"Tanya," he said, "the few pieces I've looked over so far seem authentic. I'm not saying your great-aunt knew any of it was fake. I don't know if it is fake, so it wouldn't change the intent of her gift."

"But *she* believed in it, so someone's ripping off her memory, let alone my heritage from her. Jack, please, can you expertise these pieces here right now?" she asked, leaping up again. "Even if you think they look real, be sure, okay?"

"Not and do a decent job," he admitted. "But maybe the two of you can help narrow it down if I tell you what to look for. Then I can focus in on a suspicious piece. It's worth a try. There are telltale signs, definite clues, however subtle.''

He knew Kate was still exhausted, but she seemed energized by Tanya's anger. Though he'd been upset when Tanya had shown up when she did, this was better. He shouldn't have been plying Kate with wine when she was already so tired, though the idea of time alone with her, even in the middle of the day, made his pulse pound.

''Where are you going?'' Tanya's tense voice demanded when he walked away.

''To get my doctor's diagnosis kit,'' he threw over his shoulder, then turned back. ''Hey, girl,'' he told her, ''you've got to calm down.''

''The whole thing's insulting,'' she said. ''And I'm mad as hell at the two of you for not telling me before. I could have found out something for you—at least, whether Clint Barstow or other village staff are in on this.''

''I've been careful because it's an undercover operation that's needed here,'' he tried to explain, ''not some seek-and-destroy mission. Don't make me—us—sorry we told you.''

But he was sorry when, during his perusal of the furniture, he discovered that the unique piece Kate loved most, the tin-and-wood food pantry with angels, was a modern fake.

''And that means the similar one Sarah owned could be, too,'' Kate whispered, half to herself.

''Or it could mean,'' he said, ''that this one was originally made to be substituted for that one, but then the fakers saw a chance to sell this to an elderly woman as an original. The possibilities boggle the mind.''

"They don't boggle mine," Tanya declared, hands on hips. "There's three of us working on this now, and you two just better keep me informed."

That afternoon, Jack drove Kate to see Erin, and the three of them had dinner, but not at the 7 Sauces, though Erin said she'd been in to thank Stone for his help and explain a bit more about what had happened. He'd asked her out for coffee, but she'd said she'd take a rain check.

"So don't worry," she'd assured Kate. "I'm not going to have any time for men right now, any of them, because I'm hitting the books."

"Not even time for the one who's asked both you ladies to a Saturday-night tour of a furniture shop and take-out Chinese?" Jack had asked.

Erin still had not warmed up to her again, and the girl playfully hit Jack's shoulder with her fist. Time, Kate thought. I just have to give her time and love.

And, she decided now as she finally stretched out on her own bed at night, she had to give herself some sleep. Why couldn't she just unwind, let go and relax? Jack would surely get to the bottom of the furniture fraud. Her harasser had been Mike. It made perfect sense. Her ex-husband had betrayed her before, and she'd learned to live with that. Her tough times were finally over. She had a wonderful man in her life, Tanya was back and the village would open soon.

Kate lifted herself on one elbow and took a final swig of tepid tea—she had added slightly more than a teaspoonful, figuring she was getting resistant to the stuff—and lay back on her bed. But when she closed her eyes, the room seemed to spin. It was as if she whirled in Jack's arms again or—she was a Shaker sister, dancing, dancing.

Yes, she was better with her eyes open. She glanced at the few early roses on her bedside table. She had not been able to resist cutting them, stems and all. They, too, seemed to move, to shake.

Her phone shrieked once, then again and again. She got up slowly and walked barefoot into the other room, wishing she'd had a phone jack put in by her bed. She fumbled for the receiver, not turning on a light.

"Kate Marburn."

"Kate, Tanya. I'm on my cell phone, just leaving the storage place in Athens. Call Jack and tell him I'll meet you both at Barstow's workshop. I've found the tin angels! And it all may tie into their horns and Angel's Trumpet!"

"You're losing me. You mean we're going to get into Clint Barstow's workshop? Jack told you that we already did that—"

"I've got the master key to the building and the master key to this mess," she insisted. "I'll explain everything in ten minutes!"

As soon as Tanya hung up, Kate dialed Jack. Though it was nearly eleven o'clock, his phone rang and rang, then his answering machine came on. He was either working late in his shop, making a racket, or hadn't heard the phone, because she knew he didn't sleep soundly at night. Maybe he was on another after-dark walk. Perhaps he'd come over to the village again.

"Jack, this is Kate at 10:56 p.m.," she said, leaving a message. "Tanya needs to see us pronto, at the village wood shop. I'm going over now to find out what's going on. See you there, or we'll fill you in tomorrow.''

Kate stripped off her nightgown, and pulled on slacks and a sweatshirt. Her stack of clothes on the shelf in her closet looked more neatly piled than she remembered. Louise or Adrienne must have had that local girl who cleaned downstairs pick things up here, too, so she'd have to remember to tell them she'd do it herself and try not to sound as if she wasn't grateful. Kate had said the girl could sweep and dust up here, but she must have gone beyond that. Louise had just been preaching last week about how the Shaker sisters always pitched in to help each other like one big family—but privacy still mattered to *this* Shaker sister.

Kate took her flashlight and keys and started carefully down the women's side of the stairs. Tanya had said she had a master key. Given to her by Dane or ''borrowed''? Kate wondered. And Tanya had been to the storage place in Athens, so maybe she had the master key to the village's Rent-a-Room there. That could be the missing link, Kate thought, a place for someone in the village to store the duplicate pieces of fake or authentic furniture. How Shaker, she thought: perfect pairs of furniture. But since they were ones used to deceive and defraud others, it was a scheme of which Mike Marburn himself would be proud.

Though still exhausted and dizzy, Kate went out into the blowing spring night to meet Tanya.

21

Then glut thy sorrow on a morning rose.
—John Keats
"Ode on Melancholy"

"Tanya. Tanya?" Kate cried as she crossed the road toward Clint's wood shop.

She turned back when she heard the motor of a distant car. Either she'd beaten Tanya here, or Jack had received her message and was driving over. She hoped it wasn't Dane and Adrienne in the village again tonight, because she was starting to think they were prime candidates for masterminding the furniture scheme.

But where was the car she heard? Maybe Tanya was driving in with her lights out for some reason. Surely, a car on the highway would not sound so loud at night.

Kate stepped into the narrow road, glancing up and down, then realized that the car she heard wasn't coming into the village, but going out. It must be behind her.

She turned. A car came at her, dark as the night. So close. Just like when Varina was killed. Kate screamed.

Its headlights came on, slashing into her. Like a

deer in the double shafts of blinding brightness, she stood, staring blankly. The headlights, big, wide-set, round. Not modern.

The car! *That car here!*

She turned to flee, and it seemed an eternity—but so fast, too. Her scream echoed, echoed. She thought she heard another scream. The vehicle roared three feet past her, evidently with the windows down, because someone threw something at her. She put her hands up as it pelted across her face, scratching her arms.

Too late she thought to click on her flashlight, but it would have done no good. Like two red animal eyes, the taillights peered at her as she gaped after the car. Had it meant to hit her, or was it only trying to escape the village and she had been in the way?

Kate crumpled to her knees. She had been so certain that it had been Mike watching her, trying to terrorize her. She had felt so safe since he'd been caught.

She blinked back tears and squinted into the night to make sure the car left the grounds. It kept going, over the bridge that spanned Shaker Run, past Jack's house, where it either turned its lights off again or disappeared. Had it gone straight or turned? Could it have been the old Buick Dane drove? As black as it was out here, with the car's side windows rolled down, she wasn't sure if it was a car with dark-tinted windows.

Expecting Tanya to come running out from behind the wood shop to demand what had happened, Kate got to her feet. Feeling dizzy again, she walked a few steps and sank onto the front stoop between the double doors. As she propped her head in her hands, she realized she had indeed been scratched by something.

She fingered slightly raised marks on her forearms and felt a trickle of blood. Looking all around, straining to listen, she walked back to the edge of the road to see what had been thrown from the car. Her flashlight illuminated about a dozen of her full-budded Apothecary roses, the thorny stems cut off separate from the beheaded crimson blooms.

"Zink Rudzinski here." He finally answered the phone.

Kate's call hadn't been picked up at the home number he'd given her, or at his office. At last the dispatcher had patched her call through to his cell phone. She was grateful Zink had left word she was to be put through, day or night.

"It's Kate," she told him, stretching her desk phone cord to enable her to look out her front windows over the now deserted street. "I've just seen the antique black car again, here in the village, but it's gone now."

"Damn! You all right?"

"Physically."

"That sure beefs up Marburn's alibi for not being implicated in Varina's death," he muttered. "You call the Athens police?"

"Zink, what can they do now?"

"Get somebody there to help, look around, guard you. You should go to Jack's or something. No, sit tight. I'll call the police and get them there."

She thought she could hear Tina Martin in the background, whispering something to him, but he evidently ignored her.

"I thought for sure it was Mike," she admitted.

"I was willing to believe you until I got a chance to talk to him, which the feds haven't let me do yet."

"The people in the car whizzed past me—shades of when Varina was hit." She thought about explaining that there was an old car kept nearby, but she didn't want to implicate Dane—yet. Besides, he had said the Buick was in a shop in Columbus and that she could see photos of it or the car itself. No, however much she didn't want to admit it, that must have been the Packard.

"They threw some of my roses at me, out the passenger window," she went on, "so I'm certain someone was sitting on that side. And it means someone's been watching me closely and recently, because they've just begun to bloom." She closed her eyes and swayed against the window frame. It could mean the village staff was involved, and that thought sickened her. Shaker Run had become her home and haven, until tonight.

"Kate, you there?" Zink's voice brought her back to reality.

"I'm okay. I only hope their little visit this time was not to hit me but strictly to harass me more, this time by beheading some of my roses."

"Like you found at the Denbigh crypt, and the ones ripped off from that gospel singer's grave," he said with a huge sigh. "Sit tight, and I'll get the local cops there fast."

"But where are you?" she demanded, before he could hang up. She couldn't bear to be alone again, and Jack hadn't called.

"On an all-night stakeout. I'll get you some help,

then call you back in a little while, since I don't know what's coming down where I am now.''

With a click, he was gone.

Kneeling in her second-floor roadside window to wait for the police, Kate shoved up the sash to listen for their sirens. That might bring Jack. As she stuck her head out, for once she was grateful screens were not authentic Shaker. They hadn't put them in here, another of many reasons she had to move into Athens when the warm weather came with its flies and mosquitoes. She wished that were her only worry. It would upset the Thompsons and Willises if she moved, but it had to be done. She could not stay here alone anymore. Unless the police would stake this place out, she was not staying one more night.

But as she strained to listen, she was sure she heard a voice calling her name—a woman's voice. Oh, no, she thought, she wasn't going for that again, whether it was a naked Adrienne cavorting through the grounds or just her imagination. But it sounded like Tanya, and her friend had to be out there somewhere. The police would surely be here soon. But what if the car had hit Tanya and she was lying out there calling for help?

Resolutely, Kate went down and out the sisters' front door again, looking both ways on the deserted Shaker street. Tanya had lied about not writing that poison herb book. But she'd seen so much of herself in Tanya, especially with her friend's joy then outrage over the inheritance of her Shaker furniture. And they had been friends working together almost as Shaker sisters, however different their pasts and personalities.

Kate walked around the Center Family Dwelling

with its furniture workshop occupying the right of the building and the smaller infirmary on the left side. As she turned around the back of the large edifice, she gasped. Tanya's car was parked there, hidden from the street.

Kate hurried to it and shone her light inside, though the window glass reflected most of its wan beam back at her. No one inside, nothing odd looking or apparently out of place. The car was unlocked, so she opened the door and reached in to pop the trunk lid. No one and nothing—not even Tanya's purse—was in the car or trunk. Tanya had come here to meet her but had parked where her car wouldn't be seen, then had gotten out and gone…where?

Peering around the other back corner of the building toward the excavation site, Kate saw nothing amiss. Picking up her pace toward the well, she played her light before her. She gasped to see the wooden barrier that guarded the well was broken, the jagged wood shoved inward.

She opened her mouth to call Tanya's name, but as in a nightmare, nothing came out. Earlier when she had tried to flee the car, she'd felt her feet were lead and she couldn't run. This whole thing was a dreadful dream she wanted to wake from.

"Tanya?" she whispered, then called her name loudly. *"Tanya!"*

She walked inside the broken barrier. It was slippery footing because the archeologists had lined the well with layers of sheet plastic in case of rain. Holding on to the metal arm they used to swing themselves into the depths, Kate leaned closer to the widened well to shine her beam down.

At the bottom, partly swathed in clear plastic as if

she were under ice, Tanya lay crumpled in the hole, not moving. Kate heard sirens coming close—or else it was her own screams.

Gesturing frantically, Kate met the cruiser the moment it roared into the village. The officers called the medics.

Jack showed up just behind the police. After the paramedics worked on Tanya at the scene, Kate and Jack followed in his car as the ambulance rushed Tanya into Athens Memorial.

"I tried to call you," she told him. "I couldn't believe you didn't answer."

"I must have been in the shower. Thank heavens I checked my messages before I went to bed."

"I know I heard Tanya calling me, but then she was unconscious when I found her," Kate explained, as he drove even faster. "I guess she could have slipped into the well, but she knew where it was. And why would she crash through the wooden barrier?"

"Tell me again what she said on the phone," he insisted.

"That she was just leaving the storage place in Athens. She has to mean that Rent-a-Room where some village things are kept. I rent a small space there, too."

"We've got to get in the one the village owns. What else?"

"That she found the tin angels—something about Angel's Trumpets."

"Maybe she found a third food cupboard with those angel designs," he suggested.

"I think it's time to stop trusting the entire village

staff. Oh, yeah, Tanya also said she had the master key to everything.''

''So she must be able to link what she found in Shaker Run's storage unit to a particular person. If she doesn't regain consciousness soon to tell us what she knows, we'll have to retrace her steps.''

''Not until I know if she's all right.''

''They're doing what they can,'' Jack assured her. ''I heard one paramedic say they were trying to stabilize her.''

Kate closed her eyes to picture Tanya immobilized, her head and neck restrained in case she had a neck injury. Her skin had looked gray.

''She wasn't hit by a car, was she?'' she had asked the medics.

One, an auburn-haired, freckled woman, frowned at her. ''And the car threw her into the bottom of a well?'' she asked incredulously.

Kate knew she sounded crazy. She had come to think of the car itself as some demonic entity. Everything was falling apart again. At least she had Jack to trust—and Zink, who'd called the cops.

''I know you said you hate hospitals,'' Kate told Jack as they parked and headed in together. ''But thanks for bringing me. I never could have made it on my own.''

''I keep seeing Erin hanging over that ledge,'' he said with a shudder. ''And this night-run into a hospital—I've done that before. I mean, not here, but years ago...''

It took this tragedy, Kate thought, for Jack to even mention his own.

Kate and Jack waited all night in a room for families and friends of those in surgery. They had called

Tanya's parents, who were now on their way from Kentucky. The doctors were putting pins in Tanya's shoulder and doing a spinal fusion to stabilize her back. She'd received a compression fracture and a concussion, but they were grateful since it could have been so much worse. Not, Kate thought, that what happened to Tanya wasn't attempted murder.

"It's like she's some piece of furniture who can be patched," Kate told Jack, shuddering at the idea of metal pins and spine fusions holding her friend together. She was so strung out, she didn't even know if she was making sense. "Thank God her injuries aren't life-threatening."

"I just hope her head's okay when she comes to," Jack said, handing her another styrofoam cup of coffee as he sat back down beside her on the well-worn couch. At least this stuff was clearing her head, Kate thought, sipping it despite its bitterness. "The doctor said," Jack went on, "that the concussion could develop into brain swelling, and then there's the general anesthetic that might keep her from recalling what happened right away. Sometimes after a traumatic event like an accident the memory never comes back."

"I only hope she'll tell us she slipped on that plastic sheeting and fell down there herself," Kate said. "I can't bear it if the idiots in that car hurt her and then roared past me to escape. Maybe they drove back in to cut some flowers, and she was already there waiting for me, then she accosted them and they— did that to her."

"Don't beat yourself up by imagining things," he said so forcefully that she swung around to face him.

That was exactly what her psychiatrist had said so many times.

"I'm not," she insisted. "I must have heard Tanya shouting for me before she blacked out, so I'm not imagining things."

At least he didn't argue about her instincts the way Zink usually did. Jack sighed, slumped to lean his head back against the couch and rubbed his eyes with thumb and index finger.

"The thing is," he said, "it doesn't help to want things to be different. It doesn't help to keep playing things over in your mind a million different ways, blaming yourself, hating yourself..." His voice trailed off.

He sat up suddenly, hunched over his knees. She reached out to rub his back between his shoulder blades, but his tense muscles did not relax.

"I really did kill my son, you see," he said, so quietly she was certain at first that she hadn't heard him correctly.

Leaning closer so their shoulders touched, Kate forced herself just to listen. "My son was only four and wanted to be like his daddy," he whispered. "I was on a real health kick then, jogging, weights, power boosters. Anyway, he found my vitamins, got them off the bathroom counter. Just vitamins...good for you, right?" he asked, his voice cracking.

He turned to look at her, his eyes glazed with unshed tears. "You know the iron in vitamins can kill a kid?" he demanded. He flung one hand out helplessly. "When he was dying of systemic poisoning with all his organs shutting down, he said, 'Daddy, I knew if I took more than you do, I can get big and strong like you.'"

She stared at him. All she had been through was nothing compared to that. Everything about him made sense now. Even why he let Tanya do her writing, on her strange topic, secretly in the shed.

"But it wasn't—" Kate began.

"Just cut the phony, psychobabble, feel-good lines!" he exploded, getting up to pace. "Sure, it wasn't my fault. I didn't tell that little boy to take an entire bottle of my pills. It was just an accident," he mocked.

"And she—your wife—blamed you and left you," she said.

She thought he would be angry at that, but he simply nodded and crunched his cup before flinging it in the trash can.

"Case closed," he said. "No one at fault. If I'd been a judge I would have put me in prison for life."

"And that's exactly what you've tried to do to yourself," she insisted. He didn't look at her for a moment, then nodded jerkily. He rubbed his jaw. "No," he said slowly, "not exactly prison. More like I tried to bury myself alive before a few things dug me out."

As she began to rise, he walked quickly to her, pushing her back in the seat. He sank down beside her again, his hands clasping hers. She wanted to hold him, shelter him.

"One," he said, "I found a cause in fighting some brilliant, nameless bastard who's screwing with my life work through fakes and frauds. Two, I found a woman I care for deeply when I really thought I never wanted that again."

He hesitated and cleared his throat, squeezing her hands even harder than she squeezed his in return, as if by her sheer strength and love alone, she could hold him up. He was crying openly now, but so was she. Tears blurred her vision, making two Jacks leaning closer to her.

"And three?" she whispered, her heart pounding.

"She's nothing like my Andy," he said, and winced as if it pained him to say his son's name, "but I helped save Erin."

He pulled Kate into his arms, and they embraced a long time in that waiting room, holding each other hard.

"Let's lay out our plans to prove who's behind all this," Jack said, as they sat at his kitchen table in midafternoon. They'd just returned from the hospital and were eating what amounted to breakfast, though Kate was picking at her food. Neither of them had slept, having kept a vigil until Tanya's parents had arrived.

The surgeon had told them Tanya might regain consciousness today, and Tanya's mother had promised to phone them if she did. Kate had called Dane and Adrienne this morning; Dane had said they would go over to sit with Tanya's parents as soon as they could.

"First of all, I think you ought to move in here," Jack told Kate as he reached across the corner of the table to take her hand. "Or, at least, stay here at night now. As much as I'd like that to be some sort of come-on, it isn't. Shaker Run's obviously not the great escape you thought it would be."

"I know," she said, lacing her fingers through his. "And as much as I wish we had time for us, this is deadly serious. Do you know if the Buick's back in the shed yet?''

He sat up straighter at her sudden shift of topic. "It wasn't yesterday—but that seems ages ago. You want to check the tires for mud, match tracks, or what? We could get Zink down here to do fingerprints.''

Kate pictured her tormentor, the driver of the Packard, swathed in a trench coat and hat, as she'd seen him that first day in the cemetery. And he'd worn gloves. She'd tried to question him but he'd said nothing. Now, somehow, she had to make him reveal himself.

"I think this person—persons—is clever enough that he would leave no prints, and the rest is police work," she said. "Actually, if the Buick's there, I'd like to search it for Shaker Apothecary rose petals. think it was the Packard last night—but maybe not.''

Nodding, he got the shed key and they hurried out to unlock it. Even as they passed Tanya's messy writing desk and the large plastic container of Shakerabilia, they could see the Buick was back. They rushed to it and quickly checked all four doors. The car was completely locked.

"Can you open this back door of the shed he drives in and out of?" Kate asked, trying to peer into the front seat, then the back. "It's too dim to see inside the car.''

"Dane's the only one who has the key to that..." Jack's voice trailed off as they looked at each other.

"And Tanya said she'd found the master *key*. Certainly she meant not to a car but to whomever might link the car to the fake furniture.''

"In other words, Dane? Yeah, I've thought of him.

I never did believe Barstow had the brains to orchestrate an international furniture scam, but he could be working with someone else.''

''I've got to start suspecting all of them, but Dane's in first place right now,'' Kate said. ''After he and Adrienne made me the offer to come here, maybe they thought they'd better scare me out of Toledo to make sure I took the job. So they followed me until I gave them the perfect spot—the cemetery near Sarah Denbigh's grave.''

''But why appear at Tanya's great-aunt's funeral in Kentucky?''

''Just another warning associated with a death of a Shaker furniture collector? I don't know!'' she cried. ''Sorry,'' she added, and hugged him. His arms crushed her to him, but the luxury of that moment couldn't last. ''What if,'' she reasoned aloud, her face pressed in the hollow of his throat, ''Dane and Adrienne wanted me here because of Sarah's furniture and not my roses. That could be why they tried to eliminate Varina and even Palmer—to make sure I inherited the furniture they want here.''

''Or which they want to substitute with fakes. Then they could sell the originals to buy Adrienne's dream house in France that you mentioned. Granted, they've left Palmer Denbigh alive, but he has no heirs, and who knows when he'll regain consciousness.''

''Tanya and Palmer both—there is a sick pattern here. And as important as Tanya is to the village, they figured she had to go when she learned too much.''

''Or they figured now that her Shaker furniture was here, they could keep it here if she died.''

''Or they were here last night to harass and hurt me and simply stumbled on her,'' she said with a shudder. She stepped reluctantly back from his embrace.

"The thing is, we can't just wait for the other shoe to drop," he said.

"Exactly. Can you go get a flashlight, maybe a couple of them? We can at least look into this car, though I'm tempted to break in. But I am going to look at what's stored in this plastic bin. If you can open their few furniture crates here, I can open that."

Though he looked surprised, he nodded. He started out, then turned back. "And somehow, we're going to look in that Shaker Run storage space at Rent-a-Room," he vowed. "That has to be where Tanya found furniture, the Packard, something. I don't believe Dane when he says that a car can't fit in that storage space. Look what's crammed in here."

"If Tanya somehow got or made a master key to their storehouse," Kate said, "it might be with her things at the hospital."

"Which has probably been given to her parents as part of her personal property. The hospital and her parents wouldn't know what keys were what. But Dane and Adrienne might, if they get there before I do."

Jack tore into the house for a big flashlight and handed it to her. As she shone the beam into the car, he searched his pockets for his own car keys. She could not see one rose petal on the seats or the floor. But some might be obscured by that trench coat thrown across the front seat.

"A trench coat, Jack!" she cried excitedly, as he produced his car keys. "The driver of the other car wore a trench coat."

"What does that prove?" Jack challenged. "Zink wears one, and I've got one, too."

She was suddenly so frustrated she wanted to throw herself across the hood and windshield of the Buick and literally punch its lights out.

Not Zink, she thought. Not her protector, even if from afar. She knew he liked her, and wanted to be trusted and called on for help. And he was obsessed with solving his cases, and must be a mastermind when it came to stalking and stakeouts. But surely, he could not have some fatal attraction to her. She was going right over the edge with all this agonizing, that was all.

"Go on to the hospital," she urged Jack, when he hesitated, watching her closely. "Besides getting Tanya's keys, maybe you can ask for a police guard for her. What if someone tries to sneak in to finish what they evidently started when they threw her down the well? I'm going to look through this plastic bin of Shaker papers, and we'll check that storage unit as soon as you get back."

"All right. I'll keep my cell phone with me, so call if you figure out anything here or need me."

Or need me. Despite his hurry, he kissed her good-bye. For one moment, she felt afraid to have him leave. But he'd be back soon, and this was best. Even if they went down separate paths for a while, they were working as a real team now.

As she heard him drive out, she unsealed the bin and pulled out the books and letters on top. If anyone caught her going through this stuff, Kate thought, she could always say she was looking for Sister Jerusha Lockhart's lost diary.

She put the pile of things on Tanya's desk. Yes,

some early records of the village—typed letters signed by Dane, dated just a few years ago, apparently all about rebuilding and redecorating. But these books looked older.

She opened one and smelled its age before she noted the yellowed pages and spidery scrawl of old-fashioned handwriting. It appeared to be a business record about plants and flowers, not by Sister Jerusha, but by some Shaker brother named Benjamin Owens who must have been an early herb gardener. Surely Tanya could use this for her research.

With a silent prayer for her friend's recovery, Kate touched the papers on Tanya's desk as if she could reach out to touch her. Then Kate took in what she had glimpsed before, what was staring her in the face now in Tanya's bold handwriting:

Jimsonweed, Nightshade, Mad Apple, Devil's Trumpet. But the Shakers called it Angel's Trumpet.

And farther down the page in script:

In small quantities Angel's Trumpet is medicinal to control pain. Large doses bring wild hallucinations and death.

22

Footfalls echo in the memory
Down the passage which we did not take
Towards the door we never opened
Into the rose garden.

—T.S. Eliot
Four Quartets

"Angel's Horns—Angel's Trumpets," Kate muttered to herself. "That's what Tanya said was the key. But to what, exactly?"

Puzzled and awed, she read more of Tanya's notes about the Angel's Trumpet herb. Some of the early signs of ingestion were rapid pulse and breathing, restlessness, depression, dilated pupils and insomnia. "Also, polydipsia," she read slowly, sounding out the strange word, but at least Tanya had annotated it as "extreme thirst."

Angel's Trumpet, alias Jimsonweed, Kate read on, had originally been dubbed the "Jamestown Weed" because eating it in a salad had caused British soldiers at Jamestown to "take leave of their senses." Some cavorted naked, most danced and whirled about, and all were in a "frantic condition" until they were confined. Because their doses had evidently been minimal, they did not die, but after eleven days of hallucinations "returned to themselves again, not remembering anything that had passed."

Kate pictured Adrienne dancing naked in the Meeting House four days ago. What if someone took the drug willingly for the dangerous high it gave? Or worse, what if someone was secretly dosed with it?

She covered her mouth with both hands. Mother Ann's work, as the Shakers used to call it, led to riotous dance sessions, some out on holy ground, where the brethren and sisters claimed they'd seen visions of angels and other departed friends and famous people. Could it be because they intentionally took or were covertly dosed with something like Angel's Trumpet? And maybe it was kept inside a special herbal cupboard decorated with angels. Could *that* have been the missing link Tanya referred to on the phone—a link in her own theory—rather than the car being linked to a murderer?

Kate scooped up Tanya's notes, the old herbal diary, and as many of the other loose papers from the plastic bin as she thought she could carry. Stuffing them in a large canvas bag that must be Tanya's, she went out and clicked the padlock closed. Hefting her pack like a Shaker peddlar, she walked as fast as she could toward the village.

"Dane, how long have you and Adrienne been here?" Jack asked, coming to a halt as he hurried into the hospital waiting room.

They stood like sentinels, as if guarding access to Tanya's parents. Jack realized he hadn't seen Adrienne for a while. She looked really wiped out from all the pressure of getting ready to open the village, or maybe she'd been sick or was upset over Tanya.

He saw Louise Willis was also here, dressed in modern clothes, sitting off in the corner.

Great, just great, he thought. He'd get everybody upset and probably tip Dane off when he suggested to Tanya's folks that a cop should guard her room. He'd never get any privacy here to talk them into it. And how was he going to get Tanya's keys now?

"It was good of you and Kate to stay here last night," Dane said, shaking his hand. "As soon as we could after she called, Adrienne and I rushed over to comfort the Dodridges."

Jack lifted a hand to Ted and Yvonne Dodridge, whom Kate had met briefly before at their family funeral. Mr. Dodridge, a grizzle-haired man, slumped next to his weary wife, who wore a wrinkled turquoise pantsuit.

"Is Kate all right?" Dane enquired. "Where is she?"

"Resting," Jack said. "Excuse me a moment. I'd like a private word with the Dodridges."

That kept Dane where he was, but who knew for how long. Jack's next problem came from a quick hand on his sleeve.

"Hello, Mrs. Willis," he said, looking down at Louise. She plucked at his sleeve as they talked, making him even more nervous. "Who's watching the village?"

"Ben's running errands, so I guess Clint Barstow, though that's a sobering thought. I suppose we must install modern security to keep outsiders away," she told him huffily.

"I get the message."

"Oh, not you—that is, if you'd just join forces with us. Clint's best work cannot rival yours, and you know that West Family Dwelling House you own should be returned to the village.''

"I'd love to debate all this, Mrs. Willis, but—"

"Kindly call me Louise or Sister Louise.''

He stared down into her steady gaze. Sometimes she sounded slightly off, but she always looked rock steady. Kate thought she was smarter and more talented than most people realized. "Excuse me," he said as a sudden inspiration hit him, "but I need to offer my place to Tanya's parents in case they don't want a hotel or if Tanya's recovery gets drawn out.''

"They will surely want to stay closer to her, watch her," Louise called after him. "But at least you're taking folks in as the Believers used to in that Gathering Order House you have."

"Mr. and Mrs. Dodridge," Jack said, speaking fast and trying to block out the others. Hoping his voice didn't carry, he squatted next to the short couch they shared, holding hands. The Dodridges looked close to tears. Damn, he hated places like this where parents waited to hear if their kid would make it, clinging to each other, yet ready to be torn apart. But at least it was a place that tried to help; he could accept that now.

"I'd like to get your permission," he went on, "to ask the local police to put a guard on Tanya's door, since the circumstances of her being hurt—"

"I heard," her father interrupted. He let go of his wife's hand and took his glasses off to wipe them on a handkerchief. "The flimsy barricade around the excavated well was caved in, as if there'd been a struggle. But I also heard there's some question about who was on the grounds. Besides Kate Marburn, that is. If the police pursue an investigation, that will surely implicate her. Dane Thompson didn't say exactly what, but isn't there something in her past about being suspected of foul play?''

Kate hid the sack with Tanya's notes and the Shaker records under the worktable in the distilling shed, then pulled on her work gloves. She was not going to so much as touch these special herbs of Tanya's anymore—at least, not the ones in here.

Kate realized now that however much Tanya worked with standard herbs in the sisters' shop or in her main garden outside, this was her research lab for potentially poisonous ones. Kate just hoped that didn't entail actual experimentation. Surely Tanya had not tried to prove her theories by dosing Adrienne or even Kate herself. Some of the symptoms caused by ingesting powerful herbs hit home, especially the insomnia—but Kate admitted she'd been sleepless in Toledo long before she knew Tanya. Besides, her friend had always warned her to take exact doses of valerian tea because too much could be a problem.

Kate took a small paper sack and began to clear out the supply of dried Angel's Trumpet. But she froze in midmotion. In the small, narrow bin next to it was valerian. What if some of this deadlier herb had accidentally gotten mixed in with the valerian when Tanya mixed her tea? It must be that, for surely her friend would never intentionally harm her.

Kate cleaned out the valerian, too, dumping the dried herbs in separate sacks. Then, just to be sure no one could get at any of these curative poisons while Tanya was away—she recalled how fascinated Dane had been with them when he had stood right here—

she emptied the other herb bins and drawers into the paper bags.

Using a wooden planting flat, she lugged all the bags up to her room, then hurried back down to get the big canvas bag of Shakerabilia she'd hidden. Upstairs in her kitchen again, she got out her tin of loose valerian tea and dumped it out on a dinner plate. On a second plate, she spread out the valerian from the bin in the garden shed.

She closely compared the samples. They looked and smelled different, she reasoned, though maybe just a pinch of Angel's Trumpet couldn't be spotted in her insomniac's cure.

No more herbal tea, she vowed silently. *Ever.*

Jack tried to recover from his surprise at Mr. Dodridge's suspicions—and at his annoyance that Dane must have let something slip. Surely, Tanya's parents wouldn't expect the police to bring charges against Kate. Because she'd discovered Sarah Denbigh's body, did the local police suspect her of hurting Tanya?

His heart began to thud even harder. Now he had something else to do here besides try to get Tanya a door guard and get her keys.

"Kate Marburn was Tanya's friend, Mr. Dodridge. I can vouch for that," he insisted, keeping his voice low. "I don't have time to explain everything about the police guard on Tanya's door, but I think it's important and I hope you will request it. I certainly didn't mean to imply that Kate could have hurt Tanya."

"But Kate admitted our girl had phoned her to meet her, so Kate obviously knew Tanya was coming,'' he argued quietly, as his wife, leaning closer, nodded.

''Kate saved Tanya's life,'' Jack retorted, then realized he was talking too loud.

The couple exchanged glances. ''Tanya thinks a lot of her,'' Mrs. Dodridge said, ''and Kate did come to Aunt Samantha's funeral, Ted, the only one from here. Tanya spoke highly of you, too, and that herbal cabinet you were making her, Jack.''

''Mrs. Dodridge, I'm asking you to trust me, trust Kate,'' Jack said, speaking low and fast again. ''Tanya probably had in her possession, maybe in her purse, if you have that, some sets of keys. I need those keys so Kate and I can find out if and why someone pushed your daughter—and I swear it wasn't Kate.''

''Keys to…?'' Mr. Dodridge prompted, putting his glasses back on and narrowing his eyes.

Jack heard Dane's voice getting louder. He must be approaching. If he overheard this, he'd ask for the keys and probably get them.

''That's what I need to know. If you'd just—'' Jack got out before Dane spoke, standing behind and above him.

''Jack, I'm going to suggest to Tanya's folks that they take a little break, you know, go down to the cafeteria, while Adrienne and I drive back to the village to check on things.''

Louise spoke up, her voice so loud Jack knew she was standing as close as Dane. Sometimes the woman seemed to glide silently rather than walk. ''And I'm just going to stay right here for a while in case Tanya's condition changes,'' Louise said, ''so I can let you all know. I'll call Ben to come pick me up later.''

When the Dodridges rose in obvious compliance to walk out with the Thompsons, Jack knew he'd failed. They would probably have the keys before he got the couple alone again.

But partway out the door, walking between Adrienne and her husband, Mrs. Dodridge turned back and motioned him over. "Tell Kate again we are grateful for her getting the emergency squad and then calling us last night. Please give her this little note of thanks I've written...."

Blocking out the village staff, Yvonne Dodridge dug into her big purse, which Jack saw had a smaller purse within it. She pressed into his hand not a piece of paper but a ring of four keys. Squeezing them tight to keep them from clinking, he pocketed them immediately.

The mother was as sharp as Tanya, he thought. She hadn't let anyone else, even her husband, see what she'd done.

Kate called Jack's house and left a message telling him she was in her apartment. In case he was with Tanya's parents, she didn't want to interrupt him by using his cell phone number. She continued to pore over both old and new correspondence from the sealed plastic bin, some of it fascinating glimpses into the past of Shaker Run, some of it boring daily records. She read so much her eyes began to ache, so she took some of it outside.

Her roses were blooming even more today, despite the assault on them last night.

Their fragrance was starting to invade the air, and it comforted her, because she was thinking more clearly than she had for days. Kate just knew she could get to the bottom of this. But she still could not stay in this village another night. She would take Jack up on his offer to stay at his place.

She walked around the back, past the sisters' shops toward the graveyard. Not going in, she leaned on the stone fence and stared at Sister Jerusha's headstone. Though there were no dates on it, Louise had recalled that Jerusha had lived into the 1940s, the era when the last of the sisters departed—though evidently Jerusha had died here before that.

On a whim, Kate whispered, "Did you know anything about all this, Jerusha Lockhart?"

She wondered if Louise didn't lose Jerusha's diary on purpose because it revealed that the Shakers were on a special kind of Shaker high—a drugged one. Jerusha had been the rosarian, but she might have had something to do with herbs, or else she had worked closely with the Believer who was the herbalist.

Kate shook her head. She was getting as strange as Louise, hanging about this place, communing with the departed. This village as well as the entire Shaker culture was like a drug in itself, with glimpses into scenes one could only imagine.

Grateful to be alone in the village in full daylight, however low the sun was sinking, Kate forced herself to skim the papers she'd brought out. Another bunch of bills, she thought, stuffing them down under the letters. But she saw one modern bill for remodeling, attached with an old-fashioned hairpin to a handwritten bill under it for the same thing. Darn. It wasn't for an antique car; it wasn't for herbs, or Shaker furniture. Who cared?

But it snagged her gaze. It was for observation slits in the Trustees' House, each floor. Not for the Meet-

ing House, where everyone knew observation holes
existed and were even pointed out to visitors. This
was for the Trustees' House, where Kate lived. The
older bill had "each floor" crossed out and "each
ceiling" neatly lettered in.

Kate strode back into the Trustees' Building and
climbed on a chair in the staff meeting room. She
skimmed the ceiling but saw nothing like the peepholes in the Meeting House. She climbed up onto the
long trestle table.

There, over at the very edge, in the corner by the
staircase where the ceiling met the wall, was a narrow
slit. She supposed someone could have looked or listened through it in the old days. But there had been
a recent bill for the repair of it, too, as if it had once
been boarded over and only recently uncovered—here
she dug out the top bill again—last year...just last
autumn.

Kate got down and went out into the broad hall
with its twin staircases. She saw no observation point
on the wall beside the staircase that adjoined the
meeting room. Besides, someone would have to balance on a chair on the stairs. She must be misreading
the bills or just overreacting.

But the bills had said *each floor, each ceiling.* Kate
ran upstairs so fast she began to feel dizzy again. That
panicked her, but she was obviously just paranoid
about poisons right now. She felt fine, she tried to
convince herself: fine and furious.

In the spot above where the possible slit in the
ceiling was located downstairs, she craned her neck
to look up at her own ceiling. Yes. A crack or a slit,
one she'd discounted as just a sign of an old house.
But what if someone—Dane and Adrienne—had

urged her to take this apartment to keep an eye on her? But why? Why? It reminded her of those one-way mirrors she'd seen on police TV dramas where detectives peered at the guilty as they were interrogated.

But that was a crazy thought, too. These were obviously historic Shaker observation slits that Dane had uncovered to show tourists; then she'd ended up living here and no one had mentioned them. If she asked, they'd say they were never used, of course. But her skin still crawled at the thought of being watched. Someone looking through the slit at this apartment level, she thought, scanning angles and distances, could probably see half of her living room and into the kitchen. At least the bedroom and bath could not be viewed from here. She scanned the rest of her rooms for slits but found no others.

But that dreadful scene of herself searching her house for hidden cameras or bugs after Mike deserted her flashed through her mind. It had been the breaking point for her. Erin had come downstairs late at night to find Kate hysterically ransacking the house for evidence to prove someone was watching, watching.... And that had sent her over the edge, sent her to the psychiatrist because she felt her sanity was slipping....

Kate pressed both hands to the sides of her head. She would not let that happen again. She would not!

She rushed out into the hall that divided the former men's and women's sides for what they called their retiring chambers. Again, she could find no entrance to a place for a watcher to stand. And the slits did not come through to this hall. Yet the words to one of the Shaker hymns, "Ye Watchers and Ye Holy Ones," taunted her.

What was keeping Jack so long? she fumed. He'd know about construction, and how things might have been built, and he could help her with this.

Kate went back downstairs to be certain she'd locked the sets of outside doors, front and back, then went up the two sets of sisters' stairs toward the attic level. There was only one narrow staircase here, as if for once the brethren and sisters could be trusted to use the same treads.

Kate climbed them cautiously and surveyed the large, bare attic. The light was good enough outside that it slanted in sharply through narrow dormer windows. She wondered why the staff didn't store things up here instead of paying for a place in town, but perhaps it was because this was a long climb and the roof banked so steeply. She'd stuck her head up here when Adrienne had originally showed her around, but she'd never returned. Still, someone else could have.

Walking the floor, Kate tried to figure out exactly what part of this ceiling was over those slits on each level below. She sneezed from the dust. Mother Ann had preached that there must be no dirt, so Louise had better send her local cleaning girls up here once in a while. She sneezed again, then saw a square trapdoor in the floor, nearly hidden because the wood grains were matched so well. It must have been built by a skilled woodworker. Its metal ring was recessed flush with the floor. Yes, this was approximately above where the slits should be.

Closer perusal showed that someone had recently dusted the door off, the only clean area of floor; it looked as if a person had sat down next to it, perhaps to scoot into the hole.

"Good," she whispered, trying to buck herself up. "At least it isn't Shaker ghosts."

Holding her breath, recalling Tanya down that dark well, Kate tugged the recessed metal ring and heaved the door up to look inside.

The orange, corrugated metal doors of Rent-a-Room Storage on the outskirts of Athens all looked the same to Jack. Aside from their location, they were only differentiated by the spray-painted numbers above each one and the random graffiti that had been crudely painted over. He had finally gotten out of the manager here, with the help of a twenty-dollar bill, that Shaker Run Village had rented E-11.

Jack knew Kate would be upset that he was checking this without her, but he was dying to know if fake Shaker furniture was stored here. Had that been the key Tanya mentioned, or was it possible Dane Thompson had more than one old car he drove? Jack had been to the Thompson house once and had just driven by again on the way here. They had a two-car garage. The sporty model Adrienne usually drove was out, and their minivan had been in the extra spot, so Dane wasn't keeping any old cars there. Besides, Zink had assured Jack that the state police were looking for the Packard, so Dane would be nuts to keep it at home.

Leaving the motor running in case he had to get away fast—afraid the manager might phone someone at the village—Jack got out and glanced up and down the maze of sheds. This entire back area was for the large units with wider doors than those out in front.

You'd think they'd put the smaller compartments back here so U-Hauls and other trucks didn't have so far to drive with heavy loads. The other poor thing about the layout was that many of these alleys, including this one, were dead ends.

In the large padlock on E-11, Jack tried each of the four keys Tanya's mother had slipped him. The fourth one opened it. His heart pounding, he bent and lifted the door. It grated up to reveal a concrete slab floor and a jammed collection of Shaker furniture with a single, narrow path down the middle.

"Bingo!" he exulted with a grin. "Expertiser's heaven."

He didn't have to check any of it, he thought. It must be wall-to-wall fakes and frauds. Dane must be the mastermind behind what was becoming an international theft and contraband scheme. Fake pieces were being produced that were clones of the authentic ones, which were then stolen and replaced with the phonies. But he couldn't resist a quick look at what pieces were here before jumping back in the car to call Kate on his cell phone.

And then he saw what Tanya meant by saying she'd found the Angel's Trumpet. A food cupboard with the tinwork metal squares stood at the back of the narrow center aisle. He hurried toward it, noting that someone had pried one of the squares loose. If Tanya had taken it, why hadn't they found it in her car or with her things?

"Because whoever threw her down the well took it." He muttered the answer to his own question, just as the door to the storage space closed with a shuddering rumble, plunging him into total darkness.

23

King Henry II had a mistress named The Fair
Rosamond. Queen Eleanor poisoned her husband's mistress, disguising the deadly poison
with the oil of the apothecary's rose.

—Peter Coats
Flowers in History

Kate was furious after her trip down, then up, the
modern metal ladder into the narrow shaft, which
measured about a yardstick square. But amazingly,
she was not filthy. After getting a flashlight so she
could see between floors, she had assumed the tiny
space into which she'd descended would be all spi-
derwebs and dust, but it had been as clean as a Shaker
wall. Someone who liked things clean had used it
often, and recently. And no doubt to spy on her. It
had taken care, cunning and a certain fastidious nature. Clint Barlow was off her list of suspects, for
sure: the one watching her must have been either
Adrienne or Louise.

Kate's mind raced over the numerous times she'd
had private conversations with Zink or her lawyer—
or Jack—from the phone here. She recalled the day
Jack had come to tell her he'd found children's furniture in his storage shed and could link it to Sarah's

collection. Kate had told him she'd give anything to have her struggle with Varina and Palmer over. They'd kissed and embraced, perhaps while being watched. And if someone had been spying on her then, what he or she heard that day could have endangered not only the Denbigh heirs, but Jack, too. Jack could be in just as much danger as she was. She had to reach him.

Kate closed the heavy trapdoor and headed downstairs. She supposed it was a long shot, but he could still be at the hospital. She also wanted to check up on Tanya. And then she would have to pack some things and get out of this so-called Trustees' House before it got even darker. If Jack wasn't back, she couldn't just camp out at his place, either. The car had been on that road last night. And without him, his house was just as deserted as this place.

The Shakers, she fumed, must have been crazy to live communally with the knowledge they were being watched. And Dane and Adrienne must have been crazy to think they could conveniently forget to tell her about this ladder and slits in the walls, and expect her to trust them.

Adrenaline and anger rampaged through her. For the first time in days, she was suddenly hungry. Stopping at her desk, she couldn't get Jack at either his home or cell phone number. Realizing she'd have to look up the hospital's number and that the phone book was in the kitchen, she rushed out there. She grabbed a bottle of water from the fridge and an unopened bag of taco chips from the counter as she skimmed the fine print for the hospital number, then punched it in.

"This is Kate Marburn, calling for a patient's

mother, a Mrs. Yvonne Dodridge,'' Kate told the receptionist. ''I was told I could call to see how her daughter, Tanya Dodridge, was doing. The patient is in ICU after surgery, but I really need to talk to her mother.''

The phone rang and rang. Frustrated, Kate ripped open the sack and ate a few chips; then, with the phone wedged between her neck and shoulder, bent to ransack the refrigerator. She yanked out bread and jelly to make a peanut butter sandwich, then a half-used jar of spicy salsa. After the receptionist came back on and said she'd try the ICU line again, Kate jammed the chips in the salsa and crunched them down.

''Needless to say,'' the receptionist explained, coming back on yet again, ''if there's an emergency in ICU, answering the phone's the last thing that gets done.''

Kate had just started to worry that an emergency could mean Tanya was worse, when her mother came on the line. Swallowing, Kate forced herself to inquire first about her friend's condition.

''They tell me that both the good news and the bad news is that her condition is unchanged,'' Yvonne Dodridge explained. ''They're still watching for brain swelling, and I overheard a nurse say they're hoping she doesn't get an epidural hematoma, so they'd have to relieve the pressure somehow.''

Relieve the pressure somehow, the woman's words echoed in Kate's brain. ''Is Jack still there?'' she asked.

''Oh, my no, long gone. And,'' she added, whispering now, ''I gave him Tanya's keys. He said the two of you had to check on something, and I trusted

him. I've always had good instincts about who to
trust, you know."

Kate promised to check back soon and closed the
conversation, not certain of what she'd said at the end.
She had once been so certain she had good instincts
about people. But her former mistaken faith in Mike
jabbed at her when she wanted so to trust Jack. He
must have gotten Tanya's key to the Athens storage
sheds and had gone there on the way back.

She tried his home phone once again; then, when
the answering machine picked up, she slammed down
her receiver. While she spread peanut butter on a
piece of bread, one-handed, she grabbed the phone
again and punched in Jack's cell phone number.
Maybe he was back in his car now.

"Hey!" Jack shouted, feeling his way out in the
pitch black on the narrow path between the stacks of
furniture in the storage unit. "Someone's in here!
Open the door!"

Silence, as if the door had closed itself.

He should have turned on the interior light before
he stepped in, but in the rays of the setting sun he
hadn't thought of it. He didn't even know where the
light switch was. He couldn't get near the walls, anyway, unless he climbed up and over these massive
pieces of furniture or shifted a few of them around
single-handed. He shouldn't have come here without
Kate, but he was relieved he had. It was bad enough
that he was trapped, without her having to go through
more anxiety.

Making his way back to the metal door, he banged
on it. It had been lifted just a crack. He got on his
knees, then sprawled on his belly to look out. Because

his body lay in the aisle at a right angle to the door, he had to twist his neck.

He saw shoes, a man's, old-fashioned dressy brown ones. They lifted one at a time as the wearer got into Jack's still-idling car. Hell, in the middle of all this he was getting his car stolen, and he'd been so stupid he deserved it.

In the waning daylight, Jack watched the tires turn to take it away, slowly, strangely toward the back of this dead-end alley, not in the direction out. He fumbled for his cell phone in his jacket pocket and realized that was in his car, too. He cursed, then strained to listen. Distant footsteps. Then someone bringing his car back—a short joyride—or else pulling up in another vehicle.

It was another car, coming from the open end of the alley, a car with huge whitewall tires, polished hubcaps and a high-slung chassis, one too far off the ground for a modern car. The grillwork, like five bright silver pipes wrapping around the side to the front wheels, wasn't anything he recognized.

Jack sucked in a sharp breath as he realized the worst. Getting to his feet, he began to beat his fists on the metal door.

Kate was afraid Jack was not going to answer his cell phone. As when she called the hospital, it seemed to ring forever. She had felt energized a few moments ago, but now her stomach cramped with foreboding. Her pulse pounded, harder, harder.

Finally, he clicked on the phone.

"Jack," she cried, "it's Kate. I'm back at my apartment. Where are you?"

He didn't answer, but she could tell he was there, listening, breathing. At least, someone was.

"Jack, are you all right? Are you somewhere you can't talk?"

She was certain she heard the purr of a car engine in the background and some kind of metal pounding, as if the engine were knocking. Or could there be interference in the call somehow, and he could hear her but she couldn't hear him? Perhaps he was driving past power lines or something like that.

"Jack," she shouted, "it's Kate!"

Her voice didn't sound like her own, as if it were somehow coming from outside her body. To keep from tilting to the floor, she gripped the edge of her kitchen counter, pulling the spiral phone cord straight to reach this far from her desk. As it uncoiled, it looked like a snake—a snake in the rose garden.

She shook her head, trying to clear it. That was a stupid thought, wasn't it? Snakes weren't white, and this was thin and twisty.

But what if the snake were poisonous?

Kate pressed the phone harder to her ear, trying to hear Jack so she could know where he was. She still felt dizzy, the way she'd been before, though she'd felt better lately, hadn't she? She didn't want to be in the hospital the way Tanya was. But she was pretty sure Tanya hadn't been poisoned.

Then she heard whoever was on Jack's cell phone whisper something. It was a hiss like a snake.

Kate screamed and threw the phone down. Thank God, it slithered away from her as the snake coiled itself again.

Then, though her thoughts kept coiling up just like

that, she did know one thing for sure. She had to find out what had made that snake poisonous.

Kate dropped the bag of chips in her scramble for the herbs in the canvas sack she'd put under her sink. In the dried, molted snakeskin of their wrinkled sacks, they looked undisturbed.

"But I'm disturbed," she said aloud. She talked louder so the person on the phone could still hear. "I'm disturbed. But why?" She grabbed the jar of jelly and tipped it upside down until it all fell out. Red. Strawberries as bright as roses. She dumped the jar of salsa on the counter, bending close to examine the crimson spill. Chopped green peppers in it, onions, chilis. She was chilly, cold, then hot. But what about these pieces of dried leaves in this salsa? Parsley? Oregano, like in pizza? Pieces of pizza, pieces of furniture, pieces of herself.

Kate fought to keep her thoughts from drifting, from flying. What were those early symptoms of Angel's Trumpet? She had to call the hospital to be sure she wasn't poisoned, but what if it was in her head? She had finally come to realize her stalker was all in her head after Jack left—no, that was after Mike left. She wanted to call the hospital for help, but a long, coiled poisonous snake was still on the kitchen floor, biting the phone, and she didn't want to touch it.

"Dear God in heaven, help me," Jack whispered as he watched the same feet emerge from the black vehicle that had just pulled up, even closer to the metal door than his car had been. He'd given up pounding when he heard the engine.

He craned his neck and shoved his cheek flatter to the gritty cement, trying to catch a higher glimpse, but his angle was bad and it was getting dark in the narrow alley between the two rows of storage units. The man walked out of his line of sight; Jack couldn't see around these big pieces of furniture that formed the front of the narrow aisle. But he heard the man doing something at the corner of the storage room door.

Fortunately, he saw the feet get back into the car, so at least the man was leaving. It panicked and enraged him that the guy had probably wedged something in the door to keep him from opening it. Worse, it must be the driver who had tormented Kate. The bastard probably thought he was getting Jack out of the way so he could go after Kate again without interference.

But there was something familiar about those feet and that walk. He knew that man, didn't he? But he couldn't quite place him.

Jack heard him rev the big, old engine, but the vehicle didn't move. He didn't smell anything, but he heard it, rasping, like through a hose.

Now he knew what it was, what the man intended. He was getting him out of the way, all right. On his knees, Jack went back to shouting and beating on the metal door with all his might.

Kate was tired from so much Shaker dancing and she was pretty sure she'd lost track of time. Instead of whirling barefoot like this in such a little place— let's see, it was a kitchen—she should go outside. She could dance on holy ground, take her clothes off just like that other Shaker sister did.

But when she danced over to look out the front

window to see if it was dark out there yet, she saw a car's headlights slash the front street and then go out.

She knelt quickly by the window. ''The lights died,'' she whispered. ''Why did Sarah die? Varina, too, maybe Tanya—all dead.''

Kate scrambled on her knees to turn off the lights in this place, because she knew she should be using lanterns. But she didn't want to burn things down. Leaning toward the half-opened front window, she looked out again.

A man's voice, then a woman's. She wanted it to be Jack. She wanted Jack. But it was those people who were in charge. That's right, it was Dane with Adrienne.

Kate wasn't exactly sure why, but that scared her and made her mad, very mad. For some reason, she didn't want them to come upstairs and find her. It might be because Dane would fire her for wanting roses to be beautiful, not just useful. She didn't want to cut their heads off.

Kate heard the people come in downstairs. Had she unlocked the door or had they? So much she was sure she should remember…things just out of reach. But, after all, it was their office downstairs. Then—she wasn't sure why, maybe since that white snake that held the phone hissed it to her—she knew she could just watch them and they would not see her. She knew where to peek in a window just like this open one that she'd thought about flying out of earlier.

Taking her Angel's Trumpet with her, which was really a flashlight she'd left by the door, and glad she was not really sick in the head with a swollen brain like Tanya, Kate darted out into the hall. She could hear whoever was downstairs coming up now, two people. Maybe it was Erin and Mike, because Kate was so exhausted she knew it must be time to go to bed.

Kate tiptoed partway up the stairs to the attic, then realized she was a Shaker sister on the brethren's stairs. No, there was only one set of stairs here. She heard the woman tell the man, "He said she was resting but I'm worried about her. Are you sure we have to do this now?"

"Yes, right now," he said. "If she hasn't figured it out, she's going to."

Peering around from the last steps to the attic, Kate watched them knock on her apartment door in the hall below. Dane called her name, so Kate almost went down to meet them. But when he jingled keys in his hand and opened the apartment door, she knew he shouldn't do that. What else shouldn't that man do?

Kate hurried up to the attic and lifted the door in the floor. Going down into a deep well, just like Tanya, she thought. It would be a good place to hide. She jammed her small flashlight in her cleavage, inside her bra, and descended. If she went too fast, the ladder made noise, so she slowed down. What was it that these people had done that was bad? And how had she gotten so funny-headed again?

She remembered Alice in Wonderland, falling down the rabbit's hole, falling, falling. Kate held on tighter, hugging the ladder, wishing it were Jack. Alice had eaten things that made her grow large, then small—a mushroom. Maybe, Kate tried to reason, she had eaten some kind of mushrooms, too. But there had been no mushrooms in the peanut butter, jelly, or bread or chips. But what about that spicy salsa?

"This place is a mess" Kate heard the woman say

as she stopped her descent at the top level of slits to look out. The flashlight pointing up under Kate's chin made her blink, so she held on with one hand to turn it off.

"Just look at this," the woman went on. "The phone receiver's dropped on the floor as if she'd got shocking news and just took off. Plates of dried leaves. It looks like some of Tanya's herbs, yes. Spilled chips, strawberry jelly and salsa, and a pile of papers—look, Dane, she's been going through old Shaker records, and some of your paperwork we never filed away but probably should have."

Kate squinted to watch the man—Dane—stoop to read the papers the kneeling woman handed up to him. But he tossed them back to the floor where the kitchen met the living room.

"Harmless stuff," she heard him say. "I just hope she didn't hear Tanya's taken a bad turn and go there. Maybe we'd better call the hospital. I'll just leave these photos here and talk to her about everything later, see how much she's figured out so we know exactly what to do."

Wide-eyed, Kate watched as the man pulled two pieces of paper from his shirt pocket and put them on the wooden chest in the living room. Then he picked them up and wrote something on the backs.

"Come on," he said, "we've got to find her. Let's check for her car—Tanya hid hers the other night. Maybe she's somewhere else in the village or at Kilcourse's house."

Kate started to climb back up to the attic as soon as she saw them go out and heard them close the apartment door. She was breathing much harder than she thought the climb should make her. And she was so thirsty. But she really felt like a Shaker now, keeping an eye on everyone. That woman Sister Louise would be very proud of Sister Jerusha.

Kate tiptoed back toward her apartment door and turned the knob. *Locked.* And her keys were inside. But she knew if she thought hard, very hard, she could find a way to unlock it.

Jack could only smell the tailpipe exhaust fumes—but carbon monoxide was odorless, and he knew it was flooding this nearly airtight storage unit. Since it was coming in at floor level, he could probably buy some time by climbing on top of the furniture and yelling for help from there. But how many people would be driving through a Rent-a-Room dead-end alley after dark on a Monday night?

The moment he got off the floor where the door was slightly ajar, he realized his dilemma. The only source of fresh air was the crack on the floor, so would climbing buy him more time? To avoid wearing himself out, and sucking in more fumes by shouting, Jack made himself calm down and think.

Quickly, he felt his way back to the Angel Trumpet food storage cupboard and kicked at the side of it where Tanya had evidently pulled a metal sheet loose. The one next to her hole came free in his hands, though the tin was so sharp he sliced his palm open. Ignoring that, he stuck the piece down the back of his shirt, tucking it in his belt. Its corners scraped his skin right through his shirt and T-shirt.

He felt his way back to the front of the garage and, wedging himself in the small clearance between the metal door and the outer edge of an upturned trestle table, he managed to get the table rotated so it filled the aisle. Edging along, he shoved the next piece of furniture, a corner cupboard, if he remembered correctly. Yes, his first touch confirmed that. With difficulty, he scooted it along into the space where the table had been.

He was getting so nervous and exhausted, even his palms were sweating—or was that his blood? No matter; he had no choice but to forge ahead, to fight how weak and muddled he was feeling. Concentrate. *Concentrate*.

He was now very close to the corner of the storage unit. His would-be killer had probably not reckoned on him getting to the hose to shove it out, cut it or block it with a piece of sharp metal.

If he didn't pass out first.

Kate sat at the bottom of the attic stairs for a while—she wasn't sure how long—feeling depressed and lethargic.

She had a good notion to get up and whirl and dance again, but she was exhausted. She knew she was supposed to be figuring something out, but it eluded her. The hall was dim, because the Shakers who had been here had only left a light on downstairs. Kate didn't care. Lights were starting to hurt her eyes, anyway, and she felt she could see in the dark.

Then she remembered she had a key, hidden in case she did lock herself out. Humming, twirling, then going to her tiptoes, she felt along the top of the single hall windowsill. There it was. Kate opened the door and went in to see two photos on the table. That's right. She'd seen that man leave them, and he'd written on them, too. She was better now, thinking clearly about something, like where to find keys.

She turned on a light, then shaded her eyes from it. The top photo was a yellowed black-and-white of a humped, dark car.

She knew that car! She flipped it over and read, *Shaker Run Village Buick Eight, circa 1947.*

"I've seen that before," she said, wishing her head would clear of the thick fog. "It's at Jack's sometimes."

She read the back of the next photo before she looked at the picture: *Rare photo—just found. Both are Shaker cars, brethren's Buick, sisters' Packard.*

"Two of everything!" Kate cried. "Two doors, two stairs, two cars."

She flipped to the photo side. It was a more distant shot than the other, but it had two cars in it. The car with three Shaker men standing near it was the Buick from Jack's storage shed. The other vehicle was a car she was so afraid of that it hurt her head to think about it. It was a dark car, too, with five bonneted Shaker sisters gathered around it. Each woman's name was on the photo in blue ink, with an arrow pointing to her.

Four of the names didn't mean a thing, but Kate thought she'd heard of the one named Jerusha Lockhart.

24

Ash on an old man's sleeve
Is all the ash the burnt roses leave.
Dust in the air suspended
Marks the place where the story ended.

—T.S. Eliot
Four Quartets

"Jack, are you there? I called before, but couldn't hear you. I think I'm sick. I need to go to the hospital, just like Tanya. Where are you? Can you come get me?" Kate cried into the phone.

Finally, she'd summoned the courage to pick it up from her floor. She had been afraid because part of it still looked like the snake that had gotten into her Shaker rose garden. But she'd dialed his cell phone number again. Jack didn't answer his phone, not at first.

But then he said, in a whispering, shivery voice, "I'm coming for you."

"Can't you talk?" she asked. "My head's dizzy but my voice is all right."

"Stay there," Jack whispered. "I'll be there soon."

"Talk louder. Is someone there? How's Tanya?"

It sounded as if he said, "Soon, soon." She threw

the phone with its coiled tail back on the floor. Jack better get here fast, she thought, pressing her fingertips to the sides of her head. She should be feeling better but she was feeling worse.

Jack had a roaring headache, and his legs were shaking. Worse, he was so sleepy, maybe dreaming. He knelt near the hose, he could hear the hissing now. He reached for the metal piece he'd jammed down the back of his jeans. Maybe he could shove the hose out with it, cut off its tip to make it vent outside, or jam it shut.

He tried to hold his breath but the air was bad. He thought of Kate. If he died here, she'd be alone against the man in the car, against *them.* Jack wanted to start over with Kate, with Erin, too, a new family. He hadn't let himself plan that far, and now it might be too late. Wedged in the narrow space between the furniture and metal door, he sank lower to the floor.

As he tried to block the end of the hose with the metal square, he saw Andy's face. Not Andy dying but Andy smiling...and he had wanted...to have that memory...for a very long...lost time.

"Dad, I wanted to be as strong as you," Andy said, and reached for Jack's hand to tug him toward the door to freedom and light.

Jack wished he could have been stronger, too.

When Kate heard another car outside, she turned out the light and ran to the window.

It must be Jack. She didn't see a car, but she recalled one roaring out of the darkness at her, just missing her. That car threw Tanya down a deep shaft with no ladder. It was a car filled with Shaker sisters who didn't trust men. Never ride with a man, do not use the same door or stairs. Dance in the same circles but keep away from them. Especially if the man's name is Mike or Dane.

Kate stuck her head out the window and sucked in a breath of fresh, cool air. The darkness suited her. She had looked at herself in the bathroom mirror and seen how big her eyes were—her pupils black and big like a cat's. With just her head stuck through the open window, she looked outside.

Leaning this far out, she saw the car from the photograph parked way down the street. Yes, the sisters' car, huddled, a dark shape in the nightmare. And walking away from it, coming toward the Trustees' House, was someone she recognized by his size and walk.

It was Zink, his trench coat flapping in the breeze.

"Zink!" she called out, waving wildly to him. "I need to go to the hospital. I'm dizzy and sick, and Jack's not here."

He looked up at her and came closer, faster. "I'm here for you, Kate. And I know Jack's not here. What's the matter with you? Can you come down and open the door for me, or shall I break in?"

"I'll try to come down."

"I got your call about Tanya being hurt and figured I'd better come for you," he called, directly under the window now.

Kate pulled her head back in. She could not recall phoning Zink about Tanya. What about Tanya? Then a glimmer of memory teased her. Her friend was in the hospital where Kate wanted to go, where Zink would take her now.

Leaning heavily against the wall, she started slowly

downstairs to let him in. The single ceiling light at the bottom of the stairs was on. Kate recalled Louise saying that despite its antique fittings, it ruined the whole building. Use lanterns, lanterns. Use old-fashioned rose cutters, not modern ones. Kate was relieved she was remembering some things, at least.

But when she was halfway down, Zink came in. He'd used the sisters' door, but as a worldly man he didn't know any better. "Someone must have left it unlocked," he told her.

He sprinted up the stairs and put his arms around her. She leaned on him.

"Kate, that car's out there. Whose is it? I've got to call it in, but I wanted to be sure you were all right. What happened?"

"What happened?" she repeated, trying to focus on him. "I think I maybe poisoned myself with food, but someone helped. But you can work on that car if you want, since Jack's coming here. Soon, soon," she tried to assure him, nodding repeatedly.

"We're not waiting for Jack," he insisted, setting her back down on the step. "Let me just get my car and drive it up to the door to get you. You wait right here."

"But that other car—"

"I'll get its license on my way to my vehicle, then call it in while I rush you to the hospital. Stay put. I'll be right back. Whoever drives that car, we've got them now, so just relax. Trust me and don't worry."

He wrapped her fingers around the banister rungs to help her hang on. But the moment he thudded down the stairs and rushed outside, she dropped her hold on it and put her head in her hands. Her thoughts dragged, but she knew she couldn't go to sleep, couldn't just pass out. There was something about Zink she was trying to remember, something about his trench coat, something about his doing a stakeout, and then just showing up like this.

But where was he now? It was as if that black car out there devoured people. He had been gone awhile, missing for as long as Jack, hadn't he?

"Midnight Cry! Midnight Cry!" someone screamed.

Kate awoke with a start. She was sprawled on the stairs just above the doors of the Trustees' House. Below her, at the threshold, with brooms sweeping madly back and forth in a ritual dance step, were a Shaker sister and a brother. Her big bonnet and his flat hat obscured their faces.

"Up, Sister Jerusha. Up, kindly up!" the woman cried in a singsong voice that was so familiar. "Tonight all sins must be examined and judgments given! The worldly men you have trespassed with have been locked away."

Kate's heart pounded, and she shook uncontrollably. Where was Zink? Did this woman mean she'd locked him away? Jack, too?

Kate half rose, half dragged herself to her feet and tried to get up the stairs. She feared they would pull her back, and was shocked when the woman came to help her. Now carrying a lantern, the man thudded up the matching brethren's staircase.

In the hall, they took her elbows to hurry her into her dark apartment. They half pulled, half shoved her into a rocking chair. As the man set the lantern down on the table, light leaped to his face, though the woman's was still hidden in the cavern of her bonnet.

Kate expected it to be Dane and Adrienne come back for her. But she knew now who it was before she saw his face.

Ben Willis.

"I should have known—it was you, but too late, too—dizzy. Louise, what are you doing here so late that—"

"*Sister* Louise. And I'm afraid you haven't had enough of a Shaker high yet," she said, her voice sharper than ever.

"You said," Ben whined to his wife, "she'd had the stuff building up for so long in that tea you doctored that she wouldn't know which end was up by now. Wouldn't know us, even if we got close this time."

"I thought she acted really out of it when I watched her just an hour ago," Louise snapped at him. "Sister Jerusha," she went on, leaning over to pull Kate's arm so hard the rocking chair tilted forward, "listen to me. Did you eat the pickle relish, mustard, the salsa or tomato juice from your refrigerator? Did you drink more of your tea?"

Kate stared into the dark depths of the woman's bonnet. Two eyes glinted. When Kate didn't answer, Louise thrust her away so Kate's head hit the back of the rocker and made it move again. Even that motion made her head spin faster, wilder.

"I put that herb in about everything in that kitchen!" Louise cried, this time to Ben instead of to Kate. "But I need to know how much of it she took."

Ben snatched the lantern and went into the kitchen. Painfully rolling her eyes to watch him, Kate recalled that he dragged his left leg slightly, though he'd certainly learned to hide that as he must have hidden so much else.

"The salsa, I'd say," he called to Louise. "It's out and spilled."

"I put a lot in there," Louise said, "but who knows how much she ate if it's spilled. It was spicy enough to hide the flavor of it."

"Valerian or Angel's Trumpet?" Kate asked. She realized too late she should not have spoken, but she felt raging fury. It was clearing her head, wasn't it?

"Too sharp, as usual—you, not the salsa spices," Louise retorted. As Ben returned with the lantern, Kate saw she looked pleased instead of angry now.

"Perhaps," Louise went on, "you'd better bring Sister Jerusha a little more un-Shaker salsa, Brother Benjamin. I wasn't the herbalist before Sister Tanya interfered, nor have I been keeping a good eye on both of you for nothing, you know," she added smugly.

Kate fought for every thought. If they forced more of that down her they must mean to kill her, unless they planned for her to remember nothing later. Yes, that's what had happened to those men at Jamestown after days of being high. But she had to make the Willises believe she was deeper into the drug than she really was. Maybe her adrenaline was an antidote, but she'd have to outsmart them. Her body felt even more lethargic than her brain, and she'd never fight them off or outrun them.

Trying to keep her head clear, Kate began to hum a Shaker song, *Keep awake, keep awake, lest ye be rent asunder.* She lifted her arms in the gathering-blessings motion Louise had taught her dancers. As Ben came in, not with the jar of salsa but the can of tomato juice, Kate managed to get to her feet and walk toward him, swaying to her own tune. She took the tomato juice can from the surprised man and held it close to her as if she would drink it of her own accord.

It was then she saw that he had a handgun of some sort stuck in the waist of his Shaker trousers. It looked like the one Zink always wore in the holster. It sometimes showed along his ribs when he stretched or when his suit coat flew open.

"Rose water, all bright and red, and I am cutting off each head," Kate sang.

She slowly, unsteadily pirouetted, letting the remains of the tomato juice dribble on the floor around her in a circle and splattered Ben's trousers and Louise's Shaker skirts like drops of blood.

"Stop her before she makes more of a mess of things, Brother Benjamin. If you can't control her, I will at last! And be sure you have the rest of the crushed herb with you. The moment she doesn't do exactly as her deaconess bids, we will see that she is thoroughly dosed again. Of course," she said, pushing Kate against the wall with her broom handle, shoving hard across her chest, "she did take the first dose willingly to be part of Mother Ann's work."

"She did, indeed, Sister Louise," Ben agreed.

The man never did have a backbone, Kate thought. But perhaps he was more dangerous following Louise's orders, especially with a gun. Although Kate had admired Louise's energy and talents, she had completely underestimated her.

"Hold her here while I fetch her proper garb," Louise commanded. "She's shockingly attired for the Midnight Cry ritual."

Louise took the lantern and went into Kate's bedroom. Kate wished she had more strength, for now was the time to shove Ben and run. Yet he held the broom harder against her than Louise had.

But the pain helped her head to clear. The old car outside... They must have been the faces behind the black glass, maybe the ones running the furniture scam. Had they murdered Sarah because she caught them stealing her furniture? They had killed Varina, too. They'd hurt Palmer and Tanya. Jack and Zink were missing. And what did she face now?

Looking quite pleased with herself, Louise emerged from the bedroom with Kate's Shaker gown, apron, breast scarf, bonnet—and a pair of panty hose.

"Brother Benjamin, turn your back, while Sister Jerusha properly clothes herself. Hurry up," she goaded, poking Kate with the broom handle when she fumbled, but then threw it down to help her don the Shaker garments.

Kate had felt momentarily better, but her whirling dance had worked against her. She felt she still spun around. Trembling at the touch of this horrid woman's hands, she managed to sway slightly as Louise tied the bonnet on for her as the finishing touch. At least, her face was hidden from them now, but Louise must have thought of that, too, because she yanked the bonnet back, nearly choking Kate before the bow came loose.

"I must tell you what happened to poor Sister Jerusha when she tried to ruin everything for the village," Louise said. She motioned Ben to bring the lantern closer. He shone it directly in Kate's dilated eyes. Even that hurt, but Kate hoped it would convince them she was deeply drugged.

"Sister Jerusha? Me?" Kate asked. At least, she didn't have to fake her fear.

"Yes, you," Louise said, studying her at such close range that her bonnet brim kept bumping Kate's brow. "She was a traitor to the cause, to the village. It was utter betrayal that a sister, whom the elders and deacons had taken in and favored, was going to go to worldly authorities with claims of drugs being forced on folks in this village."

Tanya had been right, Kate thought. But had the Willises thrown her down the well for that? Or had Tanya discovered they ran the furniture scam?

"Sister Jerusha loves roses," Kate said, hoping that sounded off-track. She had to find out about Jack and Zink, then escape to help them. If she could only grab that gun from Ben. "I do, too—love roses," Kate stammered. "Shaker roses and my Shaker furniture —Sarah's."

"You *are* Sister Jerusha," Louise insisted, so Kate nodded. "You see, the Shakers took her in and let her follow the dream of her heart to grow their roses. She became friends with Brother Benjamin when that was absolutely forbidden. He was the village herbalist."

"And my grandfather," Ben put in. "I was named for him—first name, anyway. His last name was Owens, Benjamin Owens."

The man who had written the herbal diary she'd read earlier today, Kate thought.

"After Sister Jerusha told the police the Shakers were being drugged, he had to leave this heaven on earth—they all did," Ben explained, his voice rising with anger. "Later he wed and had a family."

"Never mind all that," Louise snapped, though Kate wanted them to keep talking.

"So the Believers found out about their forbidden friendship—Brother Benjamin and Sister Jerusha's?" Kate prompted. "And made them leave before it caused a scandal?"

"Hardly. Worse than that," Ben said, his voice bitter now. "Sister Jerusha betrayed not only the entire village but Brother Benjamin, who was supposedly her friend. She told the local police that he was the one overseeing drugs for use in the village, the same ones the Shakers sold for curatives to worldly people, only, of course, in different dosages. But that got everyone in danger—deacons—"

"Deacons like we are now in Shaker Run," Louise said. "After we took you in, hoping you'd bring us your roses and Mrs. Denbigh's furniture, you put us in danger."

"Sister Jerusha ruined everything for the elders, too," Ben said. "Elders like Dane and Adrienne, who don't know a thing about our dedication and plans for the future of this village."

Then that cleared Dane and Adrienne of the furniture scam, and, Kate hoped, of everything else.

"Enough of all this," Louise interrupted. "Sister Jerusha betrayed the village. The police went to the Believers and told them they must close down or be publicly exposed—closed down in shame and sent to prison. Can you imagine, celibate brothers and sisters in prison? After being sheltered here in this paradise they had built, Sister Jerusha ruined everything. But the tables turned on her and she received justice, meted out from Mother Ann during a Midnight Cry ceremony. And you, Sister Jerusha, follow in her steps, for you, too, have brought in worldly men and tried to ruin everything. You would not accept your dark visions, but tonight you will, at last.''

Praying they would believe she didn't get the full impact of what they'd said, Kate started to hum a Shaker tune again. Her heart was thudding so hard she almost couldn't hear herself. She had to get away now, because if they wanted her to follow in Sister Jerusha's steps, that meant death.

Glancing at the photos of the two old cars Dane had left on the table, Kate was suddenly sure she knew how Jerusha Lockhart had died. The Shaker Run Believers might have used separate cars for the celibate sexes, but she'd bet her life that one of the vehicles had struck and killed Jerusha. Whether or not the original Benjamin was at the wheel, Kate could picture *this* Benjamin driving the Packard with Louise at his side, urging him on, ordering him to scare and harm—to murder—people who defied them or got in their way. Whether they were insane or criminally ingenious, Kate had to run.

She jerked free of their grasp and lunged for the gun. Yanking it from Ben's waistband, she held it with both hands, whirling to face them, pointing it, dizzy as she was.

But Louise shrieked and swung her broom to crack Kate's hands, just as the gun went off. The broom or the blast threw Kate back. Ben shoved her to the floor where she hit her head again. He pried the gun from her. Had she shot Louise?

''Praise Mother, this place is a ghost town at night,'' Louise muttered, her voice seeming to come from a great distance now. ''She's shot the wall right through a peephole, but that noise could wake our precious dead. Let's finish this. We've been watching her long enough to know how clever she is. Fetch a glass of water and give me some of those crushed leaves you're carrying.''

Before Kate could react, Louise pressed the broomstick across her, this time at her throat. Kate tried to kick and scratch. But Ben now held the broom, while Louise swished a crushed handful of leaves into the water. To avoid choking, Kate swallowed the gagging gush of water that went partly up her nose. She hacked and gasped when they sat her up; that damn woman dared to pat her on the back.

She was still sputtering as they jerked her to her feet. She tried to reason out how long it had been before she'd felt the effects of the drug in the salsa, but she only knew it had been soon, too soon.

As she gasped for breath, they bound her hands behind her back with the panty hose. They pushed her out the door, carefully locking her apartment behind them.

The only good thing, Kate thought as she stumbled down the sisters' stairs, was that she soon wouldn't even be aware of what was going to happen next. Had they given her enough of a dose to ruin reality again or to ruin her?

''What happened?''

He heard someone ask the question from far away—voices wandering down a long, gray corridor. He tried to remember where he was—remember *who* he was.

''Is he still unconscious?'' a woman asked. He wondered if it was Kate.

"His skin looks really weird—kind of bluish. Did he have a heart attack, or what?"

"I guess he got trapped in this storage shed and ran out of air. Or maybe paint thinner or something was stored in here with all this old furniture, and the fumes got him. I don't smell anything, though."

"Did you get the manager to call 911?"

"Taken care of," someone, out-of-breath, said. "How'd you see him in the first place, Andy?"

"A hand holding a piece of metal sticking out from under the door."

A boy's voice. *Andy?* Andy was here. Then he must have died and gone to heaven. He had the strangest feeling Kate should be here, too.

25

Cease your efforts to find where the last rose lingers.

—Horace
Odes

"Stop dragging your feet," Louise ordered, as they forced Kate downstairs and out into the night. "It will take a few more minutes for that Angel's Trumpet to work, so don't try anything."

"Then let's cut the lies and Shaker stuff you've been putting over on everyone," Kate dared. "You two are the fakes behind the other fakes—the antique furniture, aren't you. I'll bet you've got a fortune squirreled away from switching replicas with the real antiques, then selling or using the originals. But that's not what I really want to know."

Louise swung her around so hard Kate smacked into the front of the building between the double front doors. "You've assured your departure from here now," Louise insisted, while Ben nervously fingered the gun he still held. "Sister Jerusha's fate can well be yours. If you got out of holy order—it was my hope that you would not—that was my plan all along."

"We can't just run over her, too," Ben blurted. As

he stepped closer to his wife, Kate noted again that he had trouble with his left leg. If she could just knock Louise down and get a start on him before he could pull out his gun...

"The furniture is not to support us but to guarantee the future of this precious place," Louise said archly. "One of our goals is to have building after building here, including Jack's property, filled with authentic furniture to honor the Shaker past and future."

"I wouldn't doubt that Dane and Adrienne are on your hit list, too," Kate accused. "That way you can run everything here. But people are on to you, even foreign authorities whom Jack has already tipped off about your massive furniture scam."

Instead of the sobering effect she'd hoped for, Kate saw that Louise looked even more agitated. "On to us, hardly. It's your paramour Jack Kilcourse who's been scamming you. He's running that furniture bait-and-switch theft ring he's so zealously pretending to pursue. It's like your former husband revisited," she taunted from the depths of the bonnet. "You're wretched at picking men, aren't you? Once again, one's taken you in."

But Kate did not doubt Jack, as she would have any man a short time ago. Though she could feel the drug taking control of her again, she did not flinch or waver.

"That's not true," she insisted, as much to herself as to Louise. "I think it's Clint Barstow who's done your dirty work."

"That simpleton," Louise exploded, smacking her hands into her skirt, "is good for nothing more than taking orders."

"Exactly the way you treat Ben," Kate declared,

then nearly panicked. What, exactly had they been arguing about? Oh, yes, she remembered.

"Where's Jack?" she demanded.

"I really wouldn't know, would you, Brother Benjamin, where he is this very moment?" Louise asked, turning to frown at him.

"No—'course not," Ben said, shuffling his feet.

"And as for your suggestion that we can't just run Kate down with the sisters' Packard because that's been done before," Louise went on to him, "I'm afraid you'll have to bring that worldly pistol along so the policeman we have tied and locked in the trunk can shoot Sister Jerusha and then himself. He was arresting her at last, you see, for Sarah Denbigh's murder, and she tried to escape."

Kate wanted to argue that, but no words came. She wanted to scream at them that they couldn't keep harming people and getting away with it. But they had so far.

"Tell me what happened with Sarah Denbigh," Kate said, trying to form her words carefully so they would not think she was so affected by the drug yet. It was just the opposite of what she'd been trying earlier, because she was sinking fast. "How could you hurt her when she donated so much great furniture to this village?"

"That," Louise said, as she bent closer to study Kate, "was pure accident and sadly regrettable. But it wasn't our fault, was it, Brother Benjamin? She just came in on us, and one thing, sadly, led to another."

"We never wanted to harm her, never, nor any of the others," Ben insisted. "It's you who caused their situations. We only meant to watch you to be sure you were settling in well here and were worthy of replacing the original, defiled Sister Jerusha.''

"But," Louise interrupted him, "we saw you were keeping Sarah's death in your heart, and now we know you won't let go of Tanya's unfortunate demise."

"Though she's not dead yet," Ben added. "If she comes out of it as Varina's brother never has, we'll have to see to her." He sighed heavily, and Louise nodded. Kate's eyes widened as she took in the enormity of all they were admitting—and the fact that their confession meant they intended her to die, too.

"Here, we attended Tanya's aunt's funeral—" Louise went on, becoming more impassioned, "just as we paid respects to Sarah Denbigh—and then Tanya betrays us, too. She found the furniture we had stored in town and, thinking the Thompsons were behind it, jumped to the conclusion that she could trust us to work with her, you and Jack."

"Because you were so dedicated to the Shaker cause," Kate whispered, fighting to form her thoughts. "She believed you'd never do anything—to harm it or her. But you're out to help—only yourselves."

"Don't shift the blame," Louise said so solemnly it sounded as if she were pronouncing final judgment. "After we killed Varina Wellesley for you and took her weak brother out of commission, you betrayed us again and again, much worse than Sister Tanya. At least, with both of you gone, there will be one other young convert we hope to trust—one especially," she said smugly, "who is about to inherit vast amounts of Sarah Denbigh's precious furniture."

Kate's skin began to crawl, and not because she

felt the drug working—herself slipping, slipping again—but from what Louise had said last.

"Whadya mean?" Kate asked, suddenly sounding drunk to herself.

"Why, I mean someone young and pliable who is fascinated by the holy dancing and will be dedicated to this village because her mother worked here. Someone who lives nearby and will surely be willing to live at the village this summer in honor of her dear, departed stepmother, someone—"

No! Kate thought she screamed, but she must have only thought it. Though she felt she was spiraling down into a black well, Kate knew she had to make her move—and soon.

The men lifted him into a coffin on wheels and tried to close the lid. No, they were lifting him into an ambulance and kept trying to put a mask over his face.

"Breathe, breathe," one of them said. "Somehow you got carbon monoxide poisoning, so this is pure oxygen. I know you're disoriented, but just breathe, buddy. It's a miracle you're alive."

Though his limbs were weak as water, Jack tried to push the mask away.

"Feet—small feet," Jack whispered so low the other man leaned over him to try to listen. "Not Dane. A limp."

"He's worried about his extremities," that man told the other. "He probably can't feel his feet. He said 'nothing' and thinks he'll end up walking with a limp."

They pushed the mask back over his face and slid a strap behind his head to keep it in place.

Jack was so sleepy—everything was heavy in his head, his heart. Andy and Kate and Erin and that black car and the man with the small feet and the slight hitch when he walked.

"Ben. It's Ben," he said into the mask.

"Can you read his lips?" the first man asked.

"He said, 'It's been...' but he didn't finish the thought."

"It's been one hell of a night, and it's only midnight right now," a voice said, as Jack surrendered again to the dark.

"Let's forget this Midnight Cry cleansing ritual," Ben said. "We can just put her in the car and take them out on some road. You drive the Packard this time, and I'll drive the detective's car. We can't do it here."

"I'd like to do it right between the cemetery and holy ground, but she owes us a Midnight Cry first. Then she'll pay for her sins and Sister Jerusha's. I'll go get those brooms."

Though Kate's brain had started to merge with her body—light and spinning—she saw her chance when Louise walked back through the darkened door of the Trustees' House. Ben held Kate's arm, firmly but not harshly, evidently certain the drug was taking her strength again. And—it—was.

But she bumped into him to set him back, then tripped him. No chance to get his gun with her hands tied behind her back, but she'd risk his not using it. He didn't go down, but she ran toward the dark dwelling house across the street, stumbling, fighting to keep on her feet.

"Louise! Louise!" Ben cried.

Fearful of the sound of the pistol, the agony of the bullet, Kate did not look back. Her head spun, but she ran, her Shaker skirts grabbing her legs. Darkness flew at her as she danced, danced at Shaker Run.

Kate avoided the side of the house with the well and tore around the other way, past the half of the building laid out now as the infirmary. Beyond was the brethren's realm, their shops and fields. If she could just keep herself from falling, just keep the night sky from tilting...

She passed a window sash halfway up. The acrid smell of varnish or paint was strong here, like ammonia under the nose.

"Here—she went this way!" she heard Ben shout behind her.

Kate banged her knee into the corner of the root cellar. The sharp pain jolted her alert. Her mind cleared enough that she realized she should hide, not try to outrun them.

Slipping, sliding back, she mounted the slanted wooden door of the root cellar to the open windowsill. Both sitting on it and ducking her head to miss the raised sash, she rolled into the room and sprawled facedown on the floor, scraping her nose and chin.

Her eyes were already adjusted to the dark, or else they were dilating again with that drug. The corner cupboard loomed over her: if only it held a cure. Kate could imagine the Shaker sisters here, nursing those who were ill, maybe too ill from this drug that made them dance and see visions of the dead.

But Kate saw the dead in here now, too: Varina chasing her with hedge trimmers and Sarah saying, *She hates my roses, but you love them, Kate. Hide in the garden here, hide in this bed of roses.*

Kate shook her head to fight the slick slide of her thoughts. Someone was after her, and she had to hide.

"This window's open," a man's voice said, very close.

"But her hands are still tied, aren't they?" a woman asked. "That stupid Clint probably just left it open to air things out. Damn, I wish we would have tried to bribe Kilcourse into making the furniture for us, instead of that dolt. Well, go on up on that root cellar. We've got to at least look in. No, you climb in, while I look through the other outbuildings on this side of the street. Give me that lantern and be careful with that gun."

Kate saw the coffin just ahead of her, long and dark. They'd buried Sarah in one that should have been strewn with roses. She would stay here, working in this garden, until she tended the very last rose, the one that lingered after all the others were gone....

Her hands still tied behind her back, Kate got into the deep invalid's cradle and hoped it would quit rocking before everyone at the funeral saw it. Not only did it smell, but it was sticky and felt as if it could keep her glued inside forever. Back, forth—it made her even more light-headed.

The man chasing her thumped into the room, then walked slowly through it, close to her hiding place, *thud, thud.* Lying on her hands and arms, Kate held her breath. Why was she tied like this? No one tied dead people in their coffins.

"Well, is she in there?" a woman's voice called as the room became more light. "Here, take this lantern!"

"How the hell do I know, when you've got the only light?"

"She's not in the outbuildings," the woman said. "They were all locked with closed windows. Well, go let me in the front door. Never mind. Just take this lantern, and I'll climb in. I really think she's in here."

Kate lay still, very still in the dark, curled depths of the lovely last rose.

And then the sun came out blindingly bright and someone shouted her name and pulled her out.

"Is she still tied?"

"Yes. Let's get this over with, Louise! Strangers are bad enough, but Tanya and Kate, Shaker sisters—"

"They betrayed everyone just as Jerusha did. Kate Marburn *is* Jerusha Lockhart. And she owes us a Midnight Cry confession and will receive her judgment now!"

Jack woke the moment they stuck the needle in his arm. They'd done that to Andy, and he had wished he could take all the pain for his child. Though his head hurt so bad he could hardly see or talk, he said, "Get help for Kate. My house near Shaker Run. Help Kate."

"'Help Kate'? Do you know anything about this?" the doctor asked the nurse. "But he didn't get this carbon monoxide poisoning at his house, did he?"

"I know where Shaker Run is, and his address is on his driver's license."

"It's probably just the carbon monoxide talking, but have somebody check it out. After all, that village is where the police found that girl down the well."

"All right," she said. "I'll take care of it, but you're going to have to hold him down and keep that mask on him. He's got to behave or else."

* * *

They half marched, half dragged Kate toward the squat, black car. She hated it but wasn't sure why. She could hear its heartbeat; because there was a knocking, knocking from the inside of it, maybe the back part. It was almost like the knocking she'd heard on the phone when she'd called someone earlier. Had that been Erin at her door? There was something she had to remember about saving Erin.

"You will do what we say or else, Sister Jerusha," the woman told her, and yanked her to a halt before they got to the car.

They stood by her thickest, longest display of rosebushes. Kate inhaled deeply. This was much better than that terrible smell in the coffin.

"I thought you wanted to take her out to holy ground," the man argued.

"This is her holy ground, and I want her to obey me on it!" It was very dark out here, Kate thought, but darker yet inside that woman's bonnet and inside her brain.

"Untie her hands, but knock her out with that broomstick if she tries to disobey again," the Shaker woman said. "Unfortunately, we can't shoot her here."

The Shaker brother—with his hat missing—did as the woman said. When her hands were free, Kate rubbed her sore wrists, wishing she could hide herself in these roses. She recognized them, no matter how bad she felt. They were Apothecary roses, meant for curing in the old days, and she could use that now.

"Take these old shears and cut them off—one dozen," the woman said. "And I'm putting my hands on top of yours, so kindly don't try anything cute with these. No, no, we are cutting the stems off and then the rose heads separately. At least, since you brought the furniture to us here, you deserve the same roses near your grave as Sarah Denbigh and Samantha Sams had. Not on the grave, so they can be traced, but near. We regret all you have made us do. All must confess and be cleansed at the Midnight Cry.''

Kate didn't want to cut the roses this way—it hurt her, but she did it, guided by this woman's hands.

''Brother Benjamin, put the roses in your hat,'' the sister said.

''I—I lost it chasing her.''

''No wonder Mother Ann could not abide men!'' the woman said, and pulled off her own bonnet. Under it, her hair was fastened up with old-fashioned pins.

Kate knew the face and didn't like it anymore.

''Here, in here,'' she ordered, taking the clippers back.

Dutifully, Kate and the Shaker brother dropped in the rose heads.

''You carry the stems—I don't want any more of those thorns!'' the woman insisted loudly to Kate, as if she were deaf.

They marched her the rest of the way toward the black hulk of the car. Kate pulled back. ''No,'' she said. ''No, I can't get near that, can't get in it.''

The muffled knocking from the depths of the car began again. ''Kate! Kate, is that you?''

She knew that voice. But before she could think of the man's name, the Shaker sister pulled open the big back door and shoved her in. It was everything she hated, everything she feared: the dark well, the huge cave, Sarah's and her own mother's caskets.

''And tie her hands again, this time to the metal

handle on the back of the front seat,'' the woman ordered.

The man produced the panty hose again and tied her hands, in front of her this time, to the door handle. He put the woman's bonnet with the rose heads in it on the floor of the car and left the thorny rose stems lying across Kate's lap.

She could feel as well as hear a man's knocking and voice now, coming from the trunk. "Who is it?" she cried. "I can't let you out!"

The Shaker woman stuck her head in the back and acted as if she didn't even hear the man, though Kate was pretty sure now that he was a policeman.

"Get in his car and follow me in case this thing balks," the woman told the Shaker man. "I think I can handle this old monster for once."

She made certain Kate was tied, slammed the door, then went around to get in the driver's seat. As the muffled roar of the engine began and the car jerked forward, Kate flew back in the seat. The ties around her wrists tensed but stretched away from the metal handle. At least, now she sat farther back from that woman behind the wheel.

The man in the trunk was still shouting something, but this engine was so loud she hardly heard him. She wished he'd stop because her head hurt so bad. Kate wanted to cry and scream. She wanted to claw her way out.

The woman turned the headlights on, and Kate could see ahead now. They bumped over the Shaker Run bridge and started toward that other house.

Jack's. It was Jack's, but it was all dark, so dark in here. And she was afraid of this car but not of this woman or the man. If this car could, it would kill her roses, cut them all off, all of their heads, right off. Her dear roses, which were like a daughter to her, all shining bright, red-haired and loving just like Erin.

Erin! These people wanted to hurt Erin and she wouldn't let them, wouldn't let them cut and kill more roses. If she could just get a little more length in this piece she was tied with, she could reach this woman's neck and cut off her head, too.

Kate scraped her arms on the thorny stems in her lap. Despite the pain, she gathered them and, yanking her wrist ties as tight as they would go, lifted the long stems over the woman's head, then scraped them down her face and across her neck.

The woman screamed and jerked the wheel. Kate saw headlights coming at them, topped by shining, blinking light-bars of red and blue and whirling white.

Their car turned, spun as if in some crazy Shaker dance, screaming like a woman. It rolled, rolled. Kate flew and bumped around inside, but her hands came free. She heard glass shattering and closed her eyes. Finally, the car—everything—lay still.

Yes, she was free now. The female driver looked broken and bloodied. As bright lights glared from every direction and men's voices came closer, on her hands and knees, Kate climbed out the side window, even though she cut herself on broken glass.

She squinted into the lights. The car following them had hit a tree, and this car was partly crushed, lying on its top. She heard shouts again, heard her name, ''Kate? Kate?'' They might be after her—angry, angry that Mike had taken their money and their dreams away.

Kate staggered into a nearby big building full of Shaker furniture and crumpled between some to hide.

Only the pulsing lights from the vehicles outside lit the hulking pieces, pieces of her life.

She knew where she was now, she thought, sitting up to press her painful back against the side of a cupboard. She was in Sarah's sitting room at Groveland in Toledo, waiting for her friend, who was like a mother, to come in and bring Erin, too. Or was she at Shaker Run where she'd fallen in love with Jack?

But she couldn't just stay here, hidden away. She had to face it all and not be afraid anymore, ever.

Though it took the last shred of strength and sanity she had, Kate Marburn stood as the door filled with policemen with lights and guns.

"We have to help the others," she said, holding an arm up to shade her eyes.

"They're—gone," one man said. "We'll call the medic for you."

She was pretty sure they meant they would get it for Tanya, but she nodded. And then she saw a man she knew, but he looked as banged up as she felt.

"Kate, thank God you're safe," he cried, tears in his eyes as he hurried toward her. He was all cut and bruised. "These officers say Jack and Tanya are going to make it, too."

"Make it here in time for the dancing?" she asked. She sounded silly to herself. Something was very wrong.

The floor and furniture rose up to meet her, and she was afraid Sarah would hit her head. Though she only wanted one man in the entire world to touch her, several caught her as she fell.

Kate climbed up, up from sodden sleep, fighting her way to daylight. When she opened her eyes a slit, the first thing she saw was Erin's dear face, solemn, so pale.

"How—long?" Kate whispered.

"Four days," Erin said, leaning closer to her. Kate realized the girl held her hand. "You're really bruised, but they think the fact you were drugged kept you relaxed so you didn't break any bones."

Kate tried to smile at that. She hadn't felt relaxed for years.

"But you were out of your head," Erin went on, "so they just tried to make you comfortable. You sure talked a lot—about everything. Some of it was kind of crazy, but—some of it—I understand you more now."

Kate nodded. Her throat was so dry. She tried to smile again from the sheer joy of seeing Erin safe, but her face felt so stiff she thought her skin might crack.

"They've been feeding you intravenously," Erin went on, "but I can get you ice chips. Oh, Mom, I'm so sorry," she blurted, and burst into tears. "I was so scared I would lose you, too. You are really my only parent, the one who didn't ever desert me, and I promise I'm going to take good care of you from now on!"

Erin hugged her, and Kate managed to cling, tubes and wires and all. And over Erin's shoulder, looking around the edge of the curtain by her bed, Jack's face appeared. It was the most wonderful vision she'd ever seen.

"I hope two of us can get in on that," he said, coming closer. "The taking care of you, I mean."

"Is that all?" Kate whispered as her view of them

blurred through her tears. "Don't you want to get in on the parent part, too?"

Jack leaned over the bed, embracing Kate and half hugging Erin, who was caught between them. "I'd be honored to be Erin's stepfather," he admitted, his voice cracking with emotion, "but I think I'll start making children's Shaker furniture, too."

Epilogue

Live now, believe me,
Wait not till tomorrow;
Gather the roses of life today.

—Pierre Ronsard
Sonnets pour Helen

Shaker Run Village opened the first Saturday in June, only a month later than they had planned. Dane had thought that once the bad publicity was no longer headline news the crowds would go down, but the fields that served as parking lots were packed and Kate demonstrated to group after group of visitors how she distilled the fragrant rose water.

"And the first batch was to be for Louise," she whispered to Erin, as, both dressed as Shaker sisters, they carted pecks of petals from the vibrant Apothecary bushes to the distilling shed. With each trip they made, Tanya would look across the herb garden and wave. At least, Kate thought, her bandaged skull didn't show under that deep, woven bonnet. The doctors had tried to make her promise to work half a day, but they didn't know Tanya.

But best was when Kate glanced toward the old dwelling house across the lane that housed the infirmary and woodworking shop.

Strangely, she thought of the fanatical Louise and Ben again, and of the night she had hidden from them there.

Though the Willises had told her that the authentic Shaker furniture they switched for fakes was meant for building up this village, an investigation was revealing they had sold much of it to amass a fortune for themselves. Searches of the basement and attic of their renovated farmhouse and their Rent-a-Room storage in Athens provided links to other treasure troves of real and replicated pieces waiting to be sold or switched through their extensive furniture scam. Though they had started small and locally, they had begun to branch out internationally. Kate was amazed that the Willises could function with one foot in the real world and one in their own warped minds that justified not only theft but murder.

But because both Louise and Ben had been killed in the double-car wreck just outside the village, Clint was the only one who had been arrested. Jack was overseeing things here—just for this opening week, he'd said.

"I know who you want to see," Erin whispered with a giggle, and gave Kate an elbow nudge. "Go on over and see how he's doing. I can pluck and sort these petals myself, and I'll let you salt them when I get back. I'll just answer the questions like you've been doing. Mom," she said in an exasperated voice, hands on her hips, when Kate hesitated, "I'm not a freshman in anything anymore. Go!"

"All right, but I'll be back to relieve you before Stone arrives," she said, and went tripping across the lovely scene, wishing Sarah could be here today with the other special guests who had cut the ribbon, including Governor Taft. Now, *that* was the kind of good publicity they all needed.

But halfway across the lane, a man called her name. She turned to see Zink pushing Palmer Denbigh in a wheelchair. For one moment, she froze, furious with Zink for doing this to her today and without warning. Palmer was a paraplegic since emerging from his coma, though the doctors weren't yet certain it was permanent. Kate walked toward them and extended her hand to Zink, who put a long-stemmed flower-shop rose in it. The thornless stem was stuck in a plastic water vial. Kate sniffed at the flower's aroma, but like most overbred nursery roses, it had no scent, just the lovely bloom itself.

"That rose," Zink said, "is from the big city, so you don't forget that we exist. Besides, you're too much of a modern woman to deal just with antique roses. Know what this new hybrid tea is called?" he asked, indicating his gift to her.

"My, my, Detective," she said, impressed. "You've not only become an expert of Shakerabilia but of roses. I'd say it's Honors."

"Wrong. All-American Bride," he said smugly, folding his arms across his chest. "See, Jack Kilcourse doesn't know how to keep a secret," he added, alluding to the fact Jack had asked Kate to marry him.

Jack and Zink used to do nothing *but* keep secrets, Kate thought, but she couldn't sustain this banter in front of Palmer. He was staring up at her so solemnly that she braced herself for a tirade.

"Palmer, it was good of you to come," she said, thinking his next words would be that he had come to see *his* furniture. "I was wishing Sarah could be here today, and she would be honored you came in her place.''

"Zink asked me, and I said, sure, why not.'' He shrugged his powerful shoulders, which showed that at least his upper torso was in good shape. She wondered if his partial paralysis would affect his collection of women, as well as of cars.

"I'm getting a couple of custom-built cars made so I can drive again,'' he told her, as if to answer one of her silent questions. "I'm really anxious to take delivery now, since the new government model Zink's been issued, after those Shaker psychos crashed his other one, is not my idea of an exciting set of wheels.''

Zink laughed, but Kate was still tense as she said, "I'm very sorry about Vari—''

"I want to ask you someth—'' he got out, before they both realized they were talking at the same time and stopped.

"Varina wasn't a happy person,'' he said, and cleared his throat. "I—I actually think she was born that way. But our lawyer told me what you said to her when she was dying—and that you covered her up with your jacket. Anyhow, I just wanted to say that I'd appreciate it if you'd let me pick out a piece or two of my mother's Shaker furniture I've decided to sign off on. Maybe you can choose something she really liked, and the rest should be here—be yours.''

Kate clasped her hands. She could have hugged him, but biting her lower lip as her eyes filled with tears, she blurted, "She was like a mother to me, too. I know that's hard for you to hear, and Varina didn't believe me but—''

"I believe you. I believe you now,'' he repeated

so deliberately that it was if he spoke for all those from their hometown who had once blamed her.

"Yes, of course, the furniture," she stammered. "I'll pick several of her very best, favorite pieces for you."

Palmer just nodded as if he'd said enough for one day. Zink gave Kate a hug and pushed Palmer's chair away, leaving her standing in the middle of the lane that separated the brothers' side of the street from the sisters'. Hearing Jack's strong voice the moment she crossed the lane, she hurried into the woodworking shop through the left door.

"So please feel free to look around." Jack was evidently concluding an explanation. "And don't hesitate to ask any questions," he added hastily when he saw her come in.

But he beat a path straight for her through the small crowd, leaving one of Clint's staff to demonstrate the making of Shaker boxes and two others showing the sanding and fitting. He took her elbow and moved her out the door she'd come in and around the back by the well, now returned to its historic appearance.

"But I have a question, Brother Jack," she said, trying to keep a straight face for this. Her heart was so full today, she wanted to both laugh and cry.

"Let's hear it," he said as he walked her past the well where several tourists were pitching coins into its depths. "We can't steal too much time away, not with this crowd."

"I want to know if your offer of a formal engagement of marriage is still on the table."

He almost tripped over his own feet. "It is, but a strict Shaker village hardly seems the place to talk of that forbidden state. Spiritual union, yes, but physical? I am just shocked," he said, grinning. "But since you've asked so kindly, yes, Sister Jeru—"

"Sister Kate," she corrected. "Dane didn't have time to change my name tag or the brochures, but I am Sister Kate—at least, in front of all these folks. In front of you later—we'll see."

"We will, indeed," he said, still hustling her on, away from the main crowds. "And my offer is still very much on the table, one of my handmade Shaker ones. You said you needed to talk to Erin to tell her what you were going to do. Did you?"

"Yes. I told her I'm going to marry you. She clapped and cheered and made some cornball joke about crossbreeding roses."

Jack shouted such a loud laugh that several visitors looked their way. Ignoring them—and what the long line of celibate Shakers who had once lived and toiled here would have preached—Jack pulled Kate into the small storage shed behind the furniture shop and banged the door shut behind them.

Author Note

Although the village of Shaker Run is fictional, some historically preserved Shaker settlements may still be visited today. My favorite is Pleasant Hill near Lexington, Kentucky, where visitors may spend the night in the original, beautifully restored dwelling houses and eat delicious Shaker meals.

I have completely fictionalized the idea that the Shakers used herbal hallucinogens to achieve their Shaker highs, but most of the information about this fascinating religious sect is authentic. Their furniture surely goes for such prices today that my furniture fakery ring could be valid and very lucrative. Even the archeological finds in the Shaker well are based on a *National Geographic* excavation of a well at Canterbury Shaker Village in New Hampshire. "No one wants to attack the Shakers," the author of the August 1999 article writes, "but the reality is that they were often part of mainstream America." And yet, I believe, their fascination lies in the fact that they were so very different from most Americans of their day.

Jack and Tanya's concerns with overdoses of herbal and medicinal remedies being deadly is a real, current problem. As I conclude this book in the spring of 2000, I see a recent newspaper article (in this case, from the *San Francisco Examiner*) titled "California cautions of use of herbal remedies."

Ohio University in Athens, Ohio (not to be confused with Ohio State University in Columbus, from which I also hold a degree), is my undergraduate college, and I hope I have described the lovely campus well. Thanks to Tatum Vittengl for her help and to Dean Julia Zimmerman.

Also I appreciate the expertise of the following people—if I have made mistakes in my rendering of information, the errors are mine:

Cathy Senalik and Don Love for help with legal questions;

Dick Springer for information on foreign embassies;

Craig Tiano for help in describing a Packard sedan. (If you'd like to see an online photo of this story's Packard, at the time I searched this book it was at www.voicenet.com/ctiano/packard/1947.htm);

Nancy Armstrong and Laurie Miller, RNs, for help with medical concerns;

Elizabeth Baldwin for her advice on freshman college life; my mother, expert on Toledo, and my best PR rep there; and especially our family friend, Gus Pappas, who showed me how he makes his beautiful oval Shaker boxes.

As ever to my wonderful support team, Don Harper and Meg Ruley.

Karen Harper

Turn the page to read an excerpt of
Karen Harper's
upcoming novel of romantic suspense

DARK HARVEST

*Available from MIRA Books
June 2004*

Monday morning Luke left his windmill shop and farm chores and drove his buggy into town to talk to the sheriff. He tied his horse behind the hardware store and went in the back door of the new civic building, feeling as if he were undercover himself. He didn't want word around the English community that he was going to the sheriff. It had been his people's custom since they were persecuted and martyred by the authorities in Europe years ago to have no truck with worldly law enforcement. If he'd have thought of it, he would have sent word the sheriff should meet him somewhere on neutral ground, but too late for that. Still, he and all the Plain People must learn to keep secrets now.

Walking down the back hall, Luke saw Sheriff Martin sitting in his office. Not only was the door open, but the top half of the walls were glass. Luke glanced through to see three women in the large, front room: an elderly one sat at the reception desk, a pregnant one stared at a computer screen and a blonde with a trim bottom bent over the shoulder of the pregnant one.

He rapped his knuckles quietly on the sheriff's door.

"Hey, Mr. Brand, come on in," Sheriff Martin said, rising and shaking his hand. "Sorry to say I don't have anything yet to report about arrests or even a clue who trespassed and assaulted your young people on Friday. I hear your boy may lose an eye—the sight of it, I mean—and that your niece is still comatose.''

The man closed the door to the hall as he spoke. The three looked their way. The white-haired receptionist and the pregnant woman showed surprise to see an Amish man here, but the blonde just studied him, her face alert with interest. Her wide-set eyes under arched brows, a pert nose and full mouth made her pretty in a natural way, especially since she wore little makeup. Her sky-blue gaze locked with his before he looked away.

"I ran into a dead end," the sheriff was saying, "trying to see if the Boosters Club—that's the parents' group which supports athletics at the high school—had any of their halftime fireworks missing, but they said no. What can I do for you?"

He sat in the chair next to Luke rather than retreating behind his desk. The sheriff was obviously trying to be accommodating, and he listened intently as Luke explained his idea to get some outside help. But Luke was distracted by the blond woman outside the glassed office, right in his line of vision behind the sheriff's head. She wasn't looking in anymore but kept nodding and talking in a lively way to the pregnant one. The blonde was trim, but shapely, too. Though she had no covering on her head, she wore her shoulder-length hair in a simple way.

"I wish I had someone to spare for that, Luke, but I'm really short-handed here. We're underfunded from government cutbacks and facing the demands of a growing community, one which—obviously—has some real problems lately. I wish like heck I could afford someone to loan you for a few weeks to work undercover, but I'm stretched to the limit lately.''

Luke's hopes fell. Perhaps this wasn't God's plan. Did that mean he had to find a way to do the detecting himself? With the harvest season, the shop and his family, he'd never spread himself that thin.

Perhaps the sheriff has noticed he'd been watching the woman on his staff, because he turned in her direction. ''I really want to help your people any way I can, Luke,'' he said, now looking back at him again. ''I know some folks around here have various beefs with the Amish, but I consider your people to be fine, upstanding citizens. You're always willing to help your neighbors, whether it's a barn raising, charity sale or just plain obeying the law.''

Feeling deflated, Luke started to rise.

''Now, I'm not saying no,'' the sheriff said, holding up both hands as if to keep him in his seat. ''Look, if I could wing it on my end, is there any way you could make a woman cop look Amish instead of a man?''

''What?'' Kat cried when the sheriff brought her into his office to explain a possible assignment. That tall, striking Amish man had disappeared, but he must have been the one who'd made this outrageous request. She lowered her voice. ''Undercover among the Amish? But I hardly know my way around here, and certainly don't know the Amish.''

''That's the point, Kat. Hardly anyone knows you, either, and you'd be coming in with an objective mind. That's what it's going to take, that and the investigative skills you've learned. The story is that you'll be a visiting Amish cousin from Pennsylvania. The Amish will take you in—ah, train you, help you. And you, in turn, will try to get me some leads to follow up on theses hate crimes. I'm not asking you to arrest anyone yourself, but it's pretty obvious if I go sniffing around, I'm gonna hit nothing but brick walls.''

''I'd be in touch with you? Take a cell phone in or—''

''No cell phone, in case we're dealing with someone who could monitor calls. The Amish have access to phones, though usually not on their property. No, I think you should go in without the usual gear. We'll make plans to meet at night on a regular basis, somewhere near the Brand farm.''

''The Brand farm?''

''That was Luke Brand in here, the bishop's son. He's become a sort of Amish community leader since his dad has bouts with stomach flu or something lately. Him and his brother Dan have built some bridges between the two different cultures around here, made it possible for Amish to work the worldly shops, opened small but thriving businesses since only about half the Amish can make a living off the farms anymore.''

''Luke Brand.''

''Right. You'd pass as his cousin or something like that.''

''Sheriff, I really want to help but I came here to be your dispatcher, and, with her baby coming, Patty's eager to leave her post.''

''I'll finagle it so she can stay an extra week or two, or I'll get our night dispatcher to take extra hours. Believe me, both of them will be grateful for the extra income, and of course you'll be on payroll. I don't know who else I could possibly use, and you're a new face around here, but the thing is, I think you'll suit this assignment to a T. The Amish are asking for our help, and they usually don't, see? But since their kids got hurt, even Luke's son—''

Kat's insides cartwheeled. ''It was Luke Brand's boy who was hurt?''

''Right, and his young niece, too, still in a coma. And I'd count it a personal favor to me and this town if…''

But Kat hardly heard him now. The dispatcher had told her about the two nine-year-olds who'd been hurt when they'd panicked and run from the fireworks, the boy who might lose his sight and the half-Amish girl who was on life support at Children's Hospital in Columbus. From her days on the force, Kat knew the hospitals there only too well.

''Kat?'' the sheriff interrupted her thoughts. ''Look, if you need some time to think it over, I'll tell Luke I'll let him know later and send him on his way now.''

''No—I…I'd like to talk to him.''

''The deputies are all out, so why don't you two use the locker room. He's waiting there. I'll come along and see if we can strike a bargain then. And, Kat, I can't think of a better way for you to start to put down roots around here.''

''Roots just aren't my thing, Sheriff, but trying to help people, kids…'' Her voice broke. ''I might give it a try,'' she said, ''at least for a little while, just to give you something to go on.''

''I'm real grateful and know the Amish will be, too, even though it's not their way to throw a bunch of *pleases* and *thank-yous*, since that's considered prideful talk.''

What had she gotten herself into, Kat asked herself. The truth was, she'd hoped to find peace and quiet here, not a new challenge. And not an Amish man to deal with whose eyes seemed to assess her as if she were standing at roll call again with the toughest sergeant she'd ever seen ready to ream her out.

As Sheriff Martin introduced them, the impact of Luke Brand stunned Kat anew. He was tall, deep-voiced, and amazingly well-spoken, although the unique cadence of his speech and his clothing made her feel she'd stepped back into another century. She asked immediately about how his son was doing.

"We won't really know if he'll lose the sight in that eye until its lacerations heal some," Luke explained. "He's in pain but not letting on, so we can't tell how to dose him with the medicine."

"I'm glad you were able to get him immediate care," she added, grateful she wasn't dealing with a religious group which could let a boy die of appendicitis when getting him to a doctor would help. No, obviously the Amish had compromised with necessities like phones and modern medicine. She felt better about this already. "Is he in the hospital like the injured girl?" she asked.

"He's home and insisting on doing his share of chores. His grandmother—she and my sister Emma help tend him and my girl, Sarah, since their mother's passed on—always says he's nine going on sixteen.''

Kat's eyes flittered from Luke's firm mouth to his eyes as she spoke. Their color was almost indigo, the deep hue enhanced by his light blue shirt under his black denim jacket. Somehow this very different man's mere presence bombarded her senses; her nostrils flared in the clean scent of pine soap and—was it mingled with cloves?—that emanated from him.

He had removed his black, broad-brimmed hat and held it in his hands as he explained the situation to her. Thick chestnut hair, covering his ears and touching his collar, gleamed gold when he turned a certain way in the window light. His beard was barely etched with silver. His face was square-jawed, rugged, and sun-browned with white crow's-feet at the edges of his heavily lashed eyes. His hands were tanned, too, but hands with clean, blunt fingers.

Luke Brand was a very muscular man, but what did she expect of an Amish farmer who must still work mostly by hand? His broad shoulders tapered to a narrow waist and hips above the thrust of his thighs against his black denim broadfall trousers.

His voice bore a rough-edged burr, and she thought erratically that he could be an announcer on TV or do voice-overs for ads.

"We were expecting a man," he was saying, "but a woman will be even less suspected by whoever is doing these thing to my people."

The three of them sat over coffee and glazed doughnuts that only Sheriff Martin seemed to partake of. Kat cradled the hot mug against her palms, while Luke, too, let his coffee get cold.

"I must admit I've been away from police work for a year because of injuries," she told him, forcing herself to stare down into her black coffee instead of continually at him. "And I'm used to working city streets, not a rural area. Which remind me," she added, looking up again, "I hear your niece is in Children's Hospital in Columbus. I know it well, if you'd like me to drive you or your family in to see her."

"That's a kind offer. I'll talk to some others about it. As for making you *look* Amish," he told her, and she saw a hint of a smile crimp those taut lips, "that won't be too hard. The challenge will be your acting Amish and blending in. I'll bring my niece, Leah Kurtz, with me to meet you. She can get you some proper clothes and explain a few things you'll need to know before you arrive in our midst. She's the teacher of our school, and it might make sense you say you've come to help her for a while, keep you close to the *kinder*—the kids."

"Yes, that's a good idea," she said, though it brought back the raw memory of visiting the elementary school where she'd met little John Seyjack. She had to admit that hearing kids were hurt is what made her agree to this wild proposal. Surely, that was the only thing.

"I'll need to change my name, right?" she asked. "Something German? My last name, Lindley, is Swedish." He nodded, started to speak, then evidently thought better of it.

"I did take two years of German in high school," she told him in the sudden silence. "I wasn't a very good student, but maybe some of it will come back to me." The truth was, she had signed up for the class because the young male teacher was cute and supposedly graded easily. Back then, she couldn't have cared less about school and teaching, though she wished she'd paid more attention now.

"Our young people and adults can speak English

with you," Luke assured her. "And the kids are partly in school to learn English, so you'll be a big help there, too."

He took a gulp of his coffee and rose. "I'd best be going now, to clear some things up at home and prepare a background for you."

"In other words, a cover story," she said as she stood, too. Their eyes met and held again.

"You ever worked undercover, Kat?" Sheriff Martin asked. Kat jumped, slopping her coffee on her wrist. She'd forgotten he was there.

"Nothing like this," she said only, because damned if she was going to tell Luke Brand that she'd posed twice as a hooker in stings to snag pimps and johns. In a way, she thought, she was venturing into another world now, one with aliens. She might as well be setting out on a *Star Trek* spaceship where no female cop had ever gone before.

MIRABooks.com

We've got the lowdown on your favorite author!

 Read an excerpt of your favorite author's newest book

 Check out her bio

 Talk to her in our Discussion Forums

 Read interviews, diaries, and more

 Find her current bestseller, and even her backlist titles

All this and more available at

www.MiraBooks.com

KAREN HARPER

66909	THE STONE FOREST	___ $6.50 U.S.	___ $7.99 CAN.
2117	SHAKER RUN	___ $4.99 U.S.	___ $5.99 CAN.
66695	THE FALLS	___ $6.50 U.S.	___ $7.99 CAN.
2115	DOWN TO THE BONE	___ $4.99 U.S.	___ $5.99 CAN.
2116	THE BABY FARM	___ $4.99 U.S.	___ $5.99 CAN.
66433	LIBERTY'S LADY	___ $5.50 U.S.	___ $6.50 CAN.
66278	DAWN'S EARLY LIGHT	___ $5.50 U.S.	___ $6.50 CAN.
2043	DARK ROAD HOME	___ $4.99 U.S.	___ $5.99 CAN.

(limited quantities available)

TOTAL AMOUNT $_____
POSTAGE & HANDLING $_____
($1.00 for one book; 50¢ for each additional)
APPLICABLE TAXES* $_____
<u>TOTAL PAYABLE</u> $_____
(check or money order—please do not send cash)

To order, complete this form and send it, along with a check
or money order for the total above, payable to MIRA Books,
to: **In the U.S.:** 3010 Walden Avenue, P.O. Box 9077, Buffalo,
NY 14269-9077; **In Canada:** P.O. Box 636, Fort Erie, Ontario,
L2A 5X3.

Name:_____
Address:_____ City:_____
State/Prov.:_____ Zip/Postal Code:_____
Account Number (if applicable):_____
075 CSAS

   *New York residents remit applicable sales taxes.
    Canadian residents remit applicable GST
    and provincial taxes.

MIRA®